SACRAMENTO PUBLIC LIBRARY
828 "I" Street
Sacramento, CA 95814
11/15

PENGUIN BOOKS

THE DARK CHRONICLES

Jeremy Duns grew up in Africa and Asia, and his journalism has been published by *The Daily Telegraph*, *The Guardian*, and *The Sunday Times*. He lives in Stockholm, Sweden.

D0721508

The Dark Chronicles: A Spy Trilogy

FREE AGENT

SONG OF TREASON

THE MOSCOW OPTION

Jeremy Duns

PENGUIN BOOKS

PENGUIN BOOKS
Published by the Penguin Group
Penguin Group (USA) Inc., 375 Hudson Street, New York, New York 10014, U.S.A.
Penguin Group (Canada), 90 Eglinton Avenue East, Suite 700, Toronto,
Ontario, Canada M4P 2Y3 (a division of Pearson Penguin Canada Inc.)
Penguin Books Ltd, 80 Strand, London WC2R 0RL, England
Penguin Ireland, 25 St Stephen's Green, Dublin 2, Ireland (a division of Penguin Books Ltd)
Penguin Group (Australia), 250 Camberwell Road, Camberwell,
Victoria 3124, Australia (a division of Pearson Australia Group Pty Ltd)
Penguin Books India Pvt Ltd, 11 Community Centre, Panchsheel Park, New Delhi – 110 017, India
Penguin Group (NZ), 67 Apollo Drive, Rosedale, Auckland 0632,
New Zealand (a division of Pearson New Zealand Ltd)
Penguin Books (South Africa) (Pty) Ltd, 24 Sturdee Avenue,
Rosebank, Johannesburg 2196, South Africa

Penguin Books Ltd, Registered Offices: 80 Strand, London WC2R 0RL, England

Free Agent: First published in Great Britain by Simon & Schuster UK Ltd 2009
First published in the United States of America by Viking Penguin,
a member of Penguin Group (USA) Inc. 2009
Published in Penguin Books 2010

Song of Treason: First published in Great Britain as *Free Country* by Simon & Schuster UK Ltd 2010

The Moscow Option: First published in Great Britain by Simon & Schuster UK Ltd 2012

This omnibus edition published in Penguin Books 2012

10 9 8 7 6 5 4 3 2 1

Free Agent: Copyright © JJD Productions, 2009
All rights reserved

Song of Treason: Copyright © JJD Productions, 2010
All rights reserved

The Moscow Option: Copyright © JJD Productions, 2012
All rights reserved

PUBLISHER'S NOTE
This is a work of fiction. Names, characters, places, and incidents are either the product
of the author's imagination or are used fictitiously, and any resemblance to actual persons,
living or dead, business establishments, events, or locales is entirely coincidental.

LIBRARY OF CONGRESS CATALOGING-IN-PUBLICATION DATA
Duns, Jeremy, 1973–
    The Dark chronicles : a spy trilogy : Free agent, Song of treason, The Moscow option / Jeremy Duns.
—Omnibus ed.
        p. cm—(A Penguin mystery)
    ISBN 978-0-14-312069-8
    1. Intelligence officers—Fiction. I. Title.
    PR6104.U565D37 2012
    823'.92—dc23   201200372

Printed in the United States of America

Except in the United States of America, this book is sold subject to the condition that it shall not,
by way of trade or otherwise, be lent, resold, hired out, or otherwise circulated without the publisher's
prior consent in any form of binding or cover other than that in which it is published and without
a similar condition including this condition being imposed on the subsequent purchaser.

The scanning, uploading, and distribution of this book via the Internet or via any other means
without the permission of the publisher is illegal and punishable by law. Please purchase only
authorized electronic editions, and do not participate in or encourage electronic piracy
of copyrighted materials. Your support of the author's rights is appreciated.

Contents

FREE AGENT

For Johanna, Rebecca and Astrid

'Man is not the creature of circumstances; circumstances are the creatures of men. We are free agents, and man is more powerful than matter.'

From *Vivian Grey* by Benjamin Disraeli

I

Sunday, 23 March 1969, Hampshire

As I edged the car onto the gravel, the front door of the house swung open and Chief's steely grey eyes stared down at me. 'What the hell took you so long?' he hissed as I made my way up the steps. But before I could answer, he had turned on his heels.

I followed the sound of his slippers gently slapping against the floorboards, down the dark oak-lined corridor. I knew from years of working for him that the best thing to do when he was in this sort of mood was not to react – his gruff tone usually gave way quite quickly, and more often than not he ended our sessions treating me like the son he'd never had. So I resisted the temptation to tell him I had driven up in record time, and instead hung my coat on one of the hooks in the hallway. Then I walked into the living room and seated myself in the nearest armchair.

It had been a while since I'd last visited Chief out here, but little had changed. There were a couple of porcelain birds I didn't remember, and a new *bois clair* bookcase that looked similar to the one he had in his office. But the framed photographs on the piano, the portrait of his father above the mantelpiece and the golf bag propped against the fireplace were all still in place. A selection of books and papers were spread across a garish Turkish carpet at the foot of one of the armchairs, and a sideboard within easy reach was home to a telephone, an inkwell and what looked like a half-eaten egg sandwich. He still hadn't learned to cook since Joan's death, it seemed.

I imagined him nibbling the sandwich as he had barked down the telephone at me less than two hours earlier. He had refused to give any hints as to what he wanted to discuss, and I was naturally intrigued. What could be so urgent that it couldn't wait for tomorrow's nine o'clock meeting? One possibility that had nagged at me all the way from London was that he had somehow found out I was seeing Vanessa and was so furious he wanted to dismiss me on the spot.

I thought back over the day. Had I been careless somewhere? We had visited a small art gallery in Hampstead in the morning but there hadn't been another soul in the place apart from the owner, and after that we had spent the entire afternoon at her flat, pushing the sheets to the bottom of the bed. Then I'd headed to mine for a quick shave and change of clothes. We had arranged to meet at Ronnie Scott's at midnight: there was a hot young group from the States she wanted to see. But then the call had come through, with the request to come and see him at my 'earliest convenience'.

It wasn't convenient at all, of course. Vanessa and I rarely had a whole weekend together, and it had taken careful planning — perhaps not careful enough, though.

'Something to drink?' Chief called over his shoulder from the sideboard. 'I have some Becherovka, which I remember you used to enjoy.'

What *was* going on? A few moments ago he had been furious; now he was buttering me up. When he'd been Head of Station in Czechoslovakia in '62, we had often shared a few glasses of this local liqueur in his office.

'Good times,' I said. 'Have you kept some back since then? I can't imagine anyone stocks it in the village shop.'

He poured a few glugs of the stuff into a tumbler and passed it over. 'Barnes finds it for me,' he said.

Barnes was a Mau Mau veteran he had reluctantly taken on as a minder when he had been appointed Chief. He had resisted all entreaties for Barnes to be allowed to move into the house, claiming that the place had been his weekend retreat for years and he wasn't about to have it invaded by a stranger. So Barnes rented a cottage in the neighbouring village, and popped his head in as regularly as he could without annoying the old bugger too much. Apparently, he also made sure he never ran out of booze.

Chief settled back into his armchair and raised his glass solemnly towards me, seemingly in a toast. As I lifted mine in return, I was surprised to catch the scent of Vanessa's sex still on my fingertips. I breathed it in, and its rawness overcame me for a moment.

'One never quite gets used to it,' he said softly, 'does one?'

I looked at him blankly. 'I'm sorry, sir?'

He pointed at his glass. 'My Prague poison, Joan used to call it. Do you remember?'

He gave a short uncharacteristic laugh, which I did my best to imitate.

'Yes,' I said. 'I do remember.'

I was relieved, but also, I realized, a little disappointed that he apparently wasn't about to sack me, after all. I'd become so bloody soft I had actually been looking forward to a bit of drama.

Chief was leaning down, running his hand through the papers at his feet. Then he gave a triumphant snort and edged a manila folder out from beneath a copy of *The Sunday Telegraph*. He fished it up and placed it on his knees. It was a file from the office – a new one, by the look of it.

'Bad news, I'm afraid,' he said, handing it to me. 'Traitor country.'

*

The folder had been sent by diplomatic bag from our station in Nigeria and concerned one Vladimir Mikhailovich Slavin, a cultural attaché at the Soviet Embassy in Lagos. He had turned up at our High Commission there on Friday evening and announced that he wanted to defect.

It was a slim folder: as well as a transcript of the interview with Slavin in Russian and an English translation of the same, it contained a page of notes by the Chief of Station, Manning, and two grainy, passport-sized photographs that had been taken at some point in the previous two years as part of the station's routine surveillance of foreign diplomatic staff. It had a very restricted distribution: just Chief and Heads of Section.

It took me a good ten minutes to get through it. I found that I desperately wanted a cigarette, but as there was nothing more certain to get Chief's dander up than that, I made do with drumming my hands on the arms of the chair.

'High stakes,' he muttered, tapping his glass with his fingers.

That was an understatement. Slavin claimed to be a colonel in the KGB and was asking to be smuggled out of Nigeria to a new home in England. In return, he was promising to reveal information about a British agent who had been recruited by Moscow in 1945.

Since Burgess and Maclean had fled to Moscow in '51, several Soviet agents had been uncovered in the Service, Five and elsewhere. Philby had been the biggest blow – he had been tipped by many for the top. In the six years since his disappearance, the Service had become almost paralysed by the fear that other traitors remained undetected. I'd lost count of the number of officers whose pasts had been put under the microscope; I had even faced questioning myself.

'Has Henry seen this yet, sir?' I asked. Henry Pritchard headed up Africa Section; as Slavin was in Nigeria, he would be heavily involved.

Chief nodded. 'I had it hand-delivered to the homes of all Heads of Section a few hours ago, apart from Edmund, who's still away – his went to Smale instead. Because you and Henry will be taking the lead on this, I attached invitations to your copies asking you to come round this evening. Station 12 told me you'd been out when they called round, which is why I rang you up myself.'

Station 12 was the messenger service. 'I see,' I said. 'Sorry about that – I was at a concert for most of the afternoon. Was Henry not in either, then?'

He shook his head briskly. 'No, he got it. I scheduled him for a bit later, though, because I wanted to talk it through with you first. See what you made of it.'

I stood up and walked over to the fireplace, trying to think of a suitable answer.

'Could Slavin be a plant?' I asked, but when I turned round I saw he was already shaking his head. It surprised me he felt so certain: several recent defectors were suspected of being Trojan horses, sent over by Moscow to make outrageous allegations so the Service would chase its own tail.

'It's something Slavin said in his interview,' he explained, seeing my confusion. '"In 1945, we recruited a British agent . . ."' He waved at the dossier impatiently. I walked back to my armchair, picked up the papers and scanned them until I found the place.

'". . . We recruited a British agent in Germany and gave him the code-name *Radnya*."' I thought for a moment, trying to see what he was getting at. 'Radnya is Russian for "kindred", or "related". They go in for clever code-names, don't they – perhaps this means he's related to the Cambridge gang? Recruited later, but part of the same network?'

He shook his head. 'Nothing to do with the code-name. Have a look at that part in the original, and see if you can spot anything.'

I sat down again and searched for the line in the Cyrillic. 'What am I looking for?'

'I think that sentence has been mistranslated.'

'Deliberately, sir?' Had he called me out to deepest Hampshire for a rant about the quality of staff in the colonies?

'I'm not sure,' he said. 'It's possible, but I think it's more likely to have been a slip-up. I wanted to hear your view. It's the phrase "*tajnaya sekretnaya sluzhba*". How would you translate that?'

'Secret service,' I said. 'Only . . .'

He leaned forward slightly. 'Yes?'

'Only *tajnaya* and *sekretnaya* both mean secret. A literal translation would be more like "secret secret service" . . .'

'Exactly!' He beamed at me. 'I suspect the translator thought that a British agent would by definition have been working for intelligence, so he dropped it. But that is precisely the point. What Slavin seems to have been suggesting is that this chap was a member of a *secret* intelligence agency. And as all intelligence is, by definition, secret, what could that mean?'

'I'm afraid I don't know, sir,' I said. I had a feeling he was about to share his own theory. Sure enough, he immediately leaned forward and pinched the knees of his pinstripe trousers, revealing two strips of pale skin above his woollen socks.

'Back in '45,' he said, 'I was chief of the British army's headquarters in Lübeck. A couple of months after the war ended, I was walking out of the mess and ran straight into an old friend from my days in Cairo: your father, Lawrence.'

'Father? You've never mentioned this before.'

He coughed into his hand abruptly, which I knew meant he was extremely anxious. 'No,' he said. 'And I'm sorry about that. I know how hard it's been for you, but I could never find a way to . . . It's very delicate, you see.'

My father had last been seen in the bar of White's in May 1945, just a few days after victory in Europe. Nobody had ever discovered what had happened to him.

'Did you talk?' I asked, and Chief raised his head and looked me in the eye.

'Yes, we talked. He seemed extremely agitated. He asked me to take a walk outside with him, whereupon he told me that he was on a vitally important job – extremely hush-hush. He didn't divulge any more details, but said that the entire operation had been compromised by a Russian nurse who was working in the Red Cross hospital in Lübeck.'

'He wanted your help?'

'Yes,' he said after a few moments. 'He asked if I could take some men round to the hospital under cover of darkness, detain the nurse, and have her transported to the War Office's interrogation centre over in Bad Nenndorf.'

'That's quite a favour to ask,' I said. 'Did you oblige?'

Chief carefully placed his glass on the nearest side table. 'Well, I tried. He provided me with a dossier containing her photograph and particulars – her name was Maleva – and I assembled a small team immediately. We took a jeep round to her quarters that same night. Unfortunately, when we arrived we discovered that she was already dead.'

I paused for a moment to take this in.

'Suicide?'

He shook his head. 'Shot through the chest. Quite messy. Of course, I got my men out of there as fast as I could. British officers kidnapping a Russian nurse would have been bad enough, but if we'd been caught with murder on our hands there would have been all manner of problems.' He looked down at his drink a little mournfully. 'And that was that. I never saw Larry again. I've often wondered whether I was the last person to see him.'

'I'm glad you told me,' I said. 'And it sounds like this operation he was on may be the key to his disappearance. But I don't quite see how it relates to the situation in Nigeria.'

'Oh,' he said. 'Didn't I mention? The nurse Slavin's claiming recruited the double – it's this same damned Maleva woman!'

I stared at him uncomprehendingly. 'But how can that be?' I asked. 'I mean, if she was shot in the chest . . .'

'I know,' he said. 'And it had me stumped for a bit. But SOE had a section for camouflage and make-up techniques – perhaps the Russians had similar expertise.'

'Perhaps,' I said. 'But what about her pulse? Presumably she wasn't just lying there with her eyes closed, holding her breath.'

Chief took another sip of liqueur. 'That had me stumped for longer. In the end I rang Bill Merriweather and asked him how he would have done it.' Merriweather was our man at Porton Down, the Ministry of Defence's chemical laboratory – back in '56, he'd developed a nerve gas to use on Nasser. It would have worked, too. 'He told me about a discovery someone on his team made a few years ago. Using a very strong tranquillizer called haloperidol, they found a way to stimulate what he referred to as "a temporary state of death". The Russians have apparently been using the stuff on uncooperative prisoners for years, but if it's administered correctly, it can induce catalepsy, which looks like death even to a trained eye. Bill thought there might be other drugs that could produce the same effect.'

'I see,' I said, although it all sounded a little fantastic. 'But I don't understand why you think this is the same woman Slavin is referring to. He doesn't mention what name she was going under in 1945 . . .' I picked up the folder again and found the place on the page. '"During and after the war, Irina Grigorieva, currently the assistant third secretary at the embassy here in Lagos, worked as a nurse in the British Zone of Germany. There she fell in love with a British officer, according to her the one true love of her life. She succeeded in recruiting this man into the NKVD . . ." It doesn't say which hospital she worked at, and there must have been dozens in the Zone. Lagos Station's photograph of her is also a little blurred – what makes you so sure she's this Maleva?'

'Instinct,' he said. 'Instinct and experience. I've spent half the afternoon examining her photograph – I can't be one hundred per cent certain it's her until I check its counterpart in Registry tomorrow morning, but I'm fairly close to that. It has to be her.'

He was looking at me expectantly. And that was when I saw what had been staring me in the face since he had answered the door. Why he'd called me out here tonight instead of leaving it until tomorrow morning. Why he was drinking more than usual. And why I had to act now.

'You needn't worry, sir,' I said.

His broad face reddened immediately, and I knew I'd hit the mark. 'Worry? What makes you think I should do that?'

'You're quite right about the interview,' I said. 'Whoever translated it got it wrong. In the original Russian, Slavin quite clearly states that the double was recruited while involved in some sort of black operation in Germany at the end of the war. It sounds like he might have been part of Father's junket and become entangled with this woman. Did Father give you any idea how many people he had out there with him, if any?'

Chief shook his head. 'He didn't tell me anything at all about the operation – just that it was vital it continued.'

'All right. Still, the fact that you were openly working at British headquarters clearly rules you out as the double. I'll explain the whole thing to Henry as soon as he gets here. When was it you said he was coming over, again?'

'Henry? Nine.'

I glanced at my watch. It had just gone half eight. Pritchard might even be early, knowing him.

Chief was taking a congratulatory draught of Becherovka: he was in the clear now. He must have read the file this morning and panicked – not that another traitor on his watch would lead to calls for him to resign, but that his being stationed in the British Zone in '45 might bring him under suspicion of actually *being* the traitor. His position as Head of the Service was no guarantee of protection: Five's Deputy Head had almost lost his mind after being investigated by other officers in '66. Even a Chief could be brought down. He had probably spotted the omission in the translation some time during the afternoon. It exonerated him, but he knew it would cut more ice if someone else pointed it out. Of the officers who would be hunting the double agent, I was the only one with good enough Russian to spot it – outside Soviet Section, 'Tolstoy' and 'Turgenev' were about all anyone could muster. Additionally, I would have good reason to protect him, as he was a family friend and my father had apparently asked for his help. So he had called me in to get his story straight before tomorrow's meeting. 'It can't possibly be Chief,' I'd tell them. 'There's been a translation cock-up.' Good old Paul.

'Of course,' I said, 'Henry won't be the only one who will need convincing.'

He looked up, alarmed. 'What do you mean?'

'Osborne and Farraday,' I said.

'Yes, yes, of course. I see that. But can't you explain it to them, too?'

'I thought you'd already discussed it with them,' I said lightly, raising my glass. It was empty, and I made sure he noticed.

'What? No, not yet.' He stood up and walked over to the drinks cabinet. 'I thought it best to sound you and Henry out first.'

'Very wise,' I said, lifting my glass. He poured a generous measure, and as he stepped away I took out the Luger, disengaged the safety, aimed between his eyes and fired in almost the same moment. The kick pushed me into the armchair and I felt one of the springs dig into my back as the crystal shattered on the floor and his body slumped to the ground and the liqueur began to seep into the carpet.

It was very quiet then. I could hear the wind whipping against the trees outside and a joist creaking somewhere in the house. My head was pounding, the blood careering around it. There had been a moment, a fraction of a moment before I had fired, when he had stared into my face and I'd thought he might have understood what was about to happen to him – that he had realized who I was.

I replaced the Luger and stood up. Pritchard was due to arrive in twenty-eight minutes, and I had to clear up the mess and be well away before then.

I set to work.

II

Sunday, 8 July 1945, British Zone, Germany

I reached the farmhouse about an hour before dawn and hammered on the door. After several minutes it opened, and a tall, lean figure with piercing blue eyes peered out at me.

'*Kann ich Ihnen helfen?*' he said, in an unmistakably English accent. He looked exactly the same as he had the last time I'd seen him.

'You're English,' I said, searching his face for a reaction but getting none. 'That *is* good news. I'm afraid I'm lost. I'm looking for the British headquarters at Lübeck.'

'You *are* lost,' he said, placing his emphasis equally carefully. 'It's a good distance from here. Come in and I can show you on a map.'

It was typical of Father: the war in Europe had been over for two months and there wasn't a soul for miles around, but he had still insisted on keeping to nonsensical recognition codes with his own son until we were inside the house. As soon as we were, he shook my hand and asked if I had had a safe journey. Barely pausing to listen to my reply, he led me through to a cramped, low-ceilinged room and told me to take a seat. He didn't ask about Finland, or Mother, or anything else. He had business to attend to.

The area looked as though it had once been a sitting room, judging by the elaborate floral pattern on the wallpaper and armchairs, but it was now inescapably the domain of a military operation, with most of the space given to a row of card tables that had been pushed together and covered in maps and papers. The room was lit by candles – there was no electricity in the house, and wouldn't be for several weeks.

Against one of the walls was a dilapidated-looking wardrobe, next to which stood a ramrod-straight officer-type. Despite a neat moustache and severe spectacles, he looked only a few years older than me. I guessed that this was Henry Pritchard, a Scot who had been Father's second-in-command on several operations early in the war. Father confirmed this, and Pritchard extended a bony hand to shake mine, but said nothing.

Father seated himself in one of the armchairs and I did the same. Pritchard remained standing.

'The first thing I wish to make clear,' Father said, 'is that this job is completely off the books. And I mean completely. Only one living soul outside this room knows what we are doing here, and that's the Prime Minister. Nothing is on paper, nor will it ever be. This goes with us to the grave, or we shall have done more damage than we are trying to rectify. In the hands of our enemies, this information could create the next war. I gave the PM my word, and I intend to stick to it. Do you understand?'

I glanced over at Pritchard to see if it was some sort of a prank. His face was set like stone. Father didn't go in for pranks, I reminded myself.

'I visited him in London a couple of weeks ago,' Father continued. 'It wasn't easy to pull off, but I called in some favours. He gave me ten minutes to outline what I had in mind. He didn't like it at first. Said it would get out, one way or another, and that that would put us in a terrible position.' He smiled, the first time I'd seen him do so since arriving. 'He asked me to leave the building and never come back, actually.'

'What changed his mind?'

He nodded at Pritchard, who turned to the wardrobe and unlocked it. Inside, someone had placed a shelf where the coat-hangers would normally have been, and on it were several stiff-backed folders. Pritchard took one of these out and handed it to me.

It contained a sheaf of documents telling of the execution of two British commandos at a German concentration camp in November 1943. There were photographs of the corpses and eyewitness accounts, all of which pointed to one man as having ordered the deaths. Bodhan Shashkevich was a Ukrainian who had led an Einsatzkommando—an SS mobile killing unit—that had been responsible for the deaths of hundreds of women and children. The British commandos had interrupted some of his fun and games, but had been made to pay.

I looked back at the wardrobe, and at the other folders in it. 'Why do you need me?' I asked. 'This isn't my field.'

Father smiled tersely. 'Since May, SAS have been building up dossiers on suspected war crimes committed against their men and other British commandos. Last month a team moved into a villa at Gaggenau, over in the French Zone, and started trying to track down the perpetrators in order to bring them to trial. Henry is part of that team.' He nodded at the younger man, who smiled at me: for some reason, I wished he hadn't.

'Henry contacted me while he was on leave in London last month,' Father continued. 'He was concerned that some of the guilty parties could evade justice even if they were to be brought before a court. In cases where our men were out of uniform, their lawyers are bound to argue that the conventions did not apply. As a result, they may escape with light sentences, perhaps as little as five or ten years. Worse, some may not even come to trial at all: under the terms of Yalta, most Ukrainians, for example, are being sent back to the Soviet Union. Many of them will be killed on arrival, but the likes of Shashkevich survived the war against strong odds – if they have enough money or other influence, they may yet slip through the net.'

He stood up and walked over to the window. It looked onto a small garden, surrounded by a high wall. He turned back to face me.

'Henry showed me six files, concerning the very worst offenders. As soon as I read them, I realized it was an intolerable situation: many of the victims were British officers, and we should do everything in our power to see they receive justice. I set about trying to get in contact with the PM, and when he gave the go-ahead, came out and secured these premises. Henry has helped prepare a lot of ground for the job I have in mind – unfortunately, his leave ends on Wednesday, and his absence from Gaggenau would be too conspicuous if he did not return. You, however, are off everyone's radar, and that, to answer your question, is why you're here. We will be working very much along the same lines as the team at Gaggenau, with one major distinction: we will not be bringing any of these men to trial. We will have very limited access to supplies, fuel and transport, but Henry has put together papers identifying both of us as members of a British war crimes investigation team, and those should be accepted everywhere apart from the Soviet Zone. Once Henry leaves, though, we are on our own. Do you have any questions?'

I wondered if the two of them had lost their minds and begun weaving fantasies; many were these days. But they didn't look mad: that was the frightening thing.

Although barely in my twenties, I was already an old hand at the spy game, having been attached to several cloak-and-dagger units over the course of the war. This was something else entirely – an execution squad, pure and simple – and the war in this part of the world was meant to be over. But as I looked into Father's grim face flickering in the candlelight, I knew I had no choice in the matter, and shook my head meekly.

'Good,' he said. 'We start tomorrow – Henry's located Shashkevich.'

*

It was a beautiful morning. The air was crisp and clean, and the fields seemed almost to be glowing as the sunlight travelled across them. Somehow it made what we were about to do even worse. Father had briefed me on the day's job, but he hadn't told me how I would feel: as we cut our way through the countryside, a chasm of despair opened up in my stomach and I became terrified I would have to ask him to stop driving so I could vomit. For the first time in my life, I felt like a child playing at soldiers.

When we reached the camp, the guard on duty hardly glanced at our papers, waving us through at the sight of our jeep. In the central reception hall, Pritchard showed our papers again and we were led through to an area of stone cell blocks. A young American corporal marched us down a dimly lit corridor, unlocked one of the doors, saluted us, and marched away again without a word.

Shashkevich was seated on the bed, shivering under a rough grey blanket despite the morning sun filtering through the small window set high in one wall. He was still a large man, but the imperious-looking officer of the photographs in his dossier had been all but extinguished. His eyes were now deeply sunken and his skin pitted and sallow. He looked up at us, confusion spreading across his face as he registered our uniforms and berets. He wasn't shivering, I realized then, but rocking back and forth and mumbling something to himself in his own language. Whether he was reciting a prayer, a list of everyone he had ever met to keep his mind active or the defence he planned to use when he reached court I do not know.

Father told him to get up in Russian, and the fear turned to defiance.

'Who are you?' he said.

'Get up,' Father repeated, gesturing with his Luger.

After he and Pritchard had cuffed him, I held the door open as they marched him into the hallway and out to the jeep.

We headed out towards Frankfurt, taking small lanes to avoid the delays on the crater-heavy *autobahn*. It was mid-morning now, and the lines of refugees tramping across the fields, either on their way to DP camps or simply foraging for food, had grown. On the outskirts of the city, we took a turning into deep woods and kept going.

I breathed in the fresh air and tried to fix the moment in my mind: the birdsong, the smell of the trees, the strange emptiness of the sunlit ruined land. The engine stopped. We walked into the middle of a clearing and Father handed me the Luger. I released the safety and pressed the muzzle against the back of Shashkevich's pale neck. The coldness of it woke him up, and the fear came over him in a rush. His hands started shaking violently and I had to clutch him towards me to restrain him. I called out to him in a voice that sounded surer than the one in my head to stop moving or I would shoot. It was an absurd thing to say, because by now he knew I was going to shoot him anyway, and something in me realized this, but I suddenly couldn't stomach the position I was in, shooting him from so close. Without even considering it, I let go of him and stepped away, at the same time jerking one of his arms towards me so that he swivelled around as though it were a ballet. It all took place very fast, and contrary to everything we had planned – we hadn't considered the possibility he might lose control. Shashkevich's hair was plastered to his forehead with sweat and his eyes were staring out of his skull like a maniac's. I thought hard of the photographs I had seen in the dossier and squeezed the trigger.

'Pockets,' said Pritchard after. 'Don't forget his pockets.'

I leaned down and ripped away some papers and trinkets, then handed them to Father and staggered off into the trees.

*

Pritchard returned to Gaggenau a couple of days later, leaving Father and me to work together. We had five more men to find, and it didn't appear that any of them were in custody. We began following the clues contained within the dossiers, re-reading the testimonies and tracing possible escape routes on large-scale maps in the make-shift operations room set up in the house. The pace was furious, and we worked all day, every day, and often through the night. We visited scores of rundown barns and cellars all over the Zone, and I grew accustomed to the look in the eyes of children as we questioned their parents and grandparents. On one occasion, a young boy tried to rush us as we entered a disused stable where he and his family were hiding, and Father very nearly shot him. I began to know what it felt like to be part of an occupying power, and it frightened me. Sometimes I would lie awake in my bed in the attic of the farmhouse and watch the spiders making webs in the beams, thinking back to before the war and dreaming of a future when it would finally be over for me.

Father had no such doubts about the mission, of course. It was his crusade: there was a light shining in his eyes and a spring in his step. He was meting out justice. Although we never spoke of much aside from the work, I was initially pleased that he had felt the need for my assistance, and did all I could to show him I was worthy of his trust. He never mentioned Shashkevich again, and in time I forgot that I had almost botched it and was pleased that I had at least contributed to getting rid of one of them.

It took me several weeks to realize the true nature of my role in the operation. As well as helping him in the field, it was also my job to polish our boots, care for our uniforms and, once we had got the electricity back, cook from the stores in the larder. He never thanked me for any of it, and it slowly dawned on me that this was the primary reason he had wanted me with him. It was his operation, but he needed someone to deal with the household chores and offer support – I was effectively his batman. I felt like I was twelve years old again, lugging his gear around Brooklands. Did he not know what I'd been through in Finland? Hell on earth! Only to be followed by weeks underground in Sweden. And for what? I'd thought he had finally realized that I was now an officer, and a highly capable one at that – but he still saw me as a boy.

My resentment was muted by fear, however: I couldn't shake the feeling that it was a dirty job. With the war over, there were no longer any hard and fast conventions to follow – or if there were, we certainly weren't following them. I remembered the right-eous anger that had overtaken us all the previous year when we'd heard about Hitler's Commando Order, which said that we could be shot without trial. In avenging the men killed under that order, weren't we committing the same crime?

By the end of August, four of the targets were dead. But the final name on the list was the one Father wanted most: Gustav Meier. He was an SS officer, and there was compelling evidence that he had raped and tortured the families of suspected members of the Resistance in France, including children. We hunted for him throughout September, but with no luck. Father was acutely aware that the chances of finding him were fading with every day that passed: he might have jumped on a boat to Argentina by now. But in the last week of September, there was a breakthrough. Father returned from a long excursion and barged into my room. 'I've found him!' he shouted. 'I've found the bastard!'

He had discovered from the papers of one of Meier's colleagues that he had relatives living near Hamburg, right across the road from a British army barracks. We had conducted surveillance on the area for several days, but to no avail. But Father had returned for another look and had chanced to spot Meier as he had driven through the nearest village. He was working as a gardener, and further enquiries revealed he had been living with the family under an assumed name.

Father had come back to the farmhouse for a very particular reason. On the two previous targets, he had found pea-sized suicide capsules hidden in their clothing, similar to the potassium cyanide 'L-pills' SOE gave its agents. Himmler had bitten into one when he had been captured in June, and Father was determined not to allow any of our targets to take the same way out: he didn't want them to have that control, and I suppose also felt they deserved to know that vengeance was being served on them. Some reports had claimed that Himmler had been equipped with *two* capsules – one in his clothing and one that he had kept in his mouth. Although they were rubber-cased to avoid accidents – they could be swallowed with no harm done – there was clearly a danger that in a tussle someone might bite down without meaning to. Father wanted very much to deal with Meier on his own terms, so to be doubly sure no accidents happened, he needed another pair of hands: mine.

That evening, he came up with a plan. It involved me dressing up as a displaced person and him as a policeman. We would approach Meier and I would accuse him of some crime – a petty theft. Meier would naturally protest and, taking the opportunity of surprise, I would pretend to fly into a rage and pounce on him: in the resulting mêlée, either Father or I would retrieve any capsules he had on his person. As soon as this was done, Father would 'arrest' Meier, and it wouldn't be until we were some distance away that he would realize what had happened.

After going over it several times, we set out for Hamburg the next afternoon. We found Meier soon enough, working in one of the gardens as he had been the previous day. We approached him in our respective garbs and I claimed that the tools he was using were mine, stolen from me the previous week. But either Father's plan wasn't as clever as we'd thought or my acting was poor, because he saw through it at once and made a dash for it across the garden and into a nearby field. We had no choice but to go after him, but when I caught up and leapt on top of him, I found that he didn't have any capsules on him – but he did have a knife. Where he had hidden it, I don't know, because he had been dressed in very little in the afternoon sunshine, but I felt it go in, and it was the last thing I remembered when I woke in the sanatorium.

*

I have very little recollection of the first few days after the stabbing: I was blacked out for most of it. I do remember being forced to drink endless amounts of a tepid broth that seemed to stick in my throat. And I was occasionally lucid enough when being given a bath or being taken to the bathroom to feel enough residual shame at the indignity of being exposed to strangers that I lashed out at a few people who, after all, were only trying to help me.

One of those was Anna, but I only became aware of her once I had fully regained consciousness and was already a fair way along the road to recovery. She had explained how I had been brought there by a British officer one afternoon with a great gash under my kidneys, and had given me the letter from Father, still sealed in its envelope. The letter enraged me, because he had couched his abandonment of me in a mixture of military jargon and euphemisms: I was now 'on the bench for the remainder of the game' – that sort of thing. As an emergency measure, he left encoded directions for a dead drop near an abandoned well a few miles from the hospital. He said he would check this each day as long as he was in the area, which should be a few weeks more. But the main message was clear: recover, return to England, and forget I'd ever been to Germany.

I disliked Anna at first – or rather, I disliked myself for finding her attractive. Although not long out of boyhood, I was no stranger to the opposite sex, and had had my share of flings along the way. But none of the girls I'd known were anything like this. She was twenty-six, a Georgian with dark, rather flamboyant looks, but there was an unforced grace to her manner that set her apart. After five years of blood and battle, this fit, efficient woman, with her tanned arms, long lashes and perfectly set features seemed almost like a goddess to me. She seemed to belong to another world, where everything was bright and calm, and I wanted to jump through the looking glass and join her in it – but what hope had I of that? I knew that her beauty and job would mean she had probably long become tired of being mooned over, especially by patients, so I resolved not to fall for her, while, of course, at the same time hoping that my aloofness would make me more attractive than more obvious suitors.

My resolution barely lasted a couple of weeks, partly because my wound was so messy that it required almost constant attention, and I was isolated in my own room. While she administered medicine and changed my linen, I had discovered she spoke excellent English. After a few tentative exchanges, I dared to ask if she would mind arranging for me to have some books from the mess library. This she did, and I soon discovered she was very well-read, so after that we began to discuss literature: she was shocked I had never read any of the Russian greats, and proceeded to feed me all the English translations she could find.

I soon found that she was also passionate about the state of the world – when I asked her what she thought the future held for the new Europe, she openly condemned the British for pursuing what she saw as an openly anti-Communist policy so soon after the Soviet Union had, as she saw it, almost single-handedly defeated the Nazis. 'It's not you, Paul,' she would smile, 'but your government is really doing some despicable things. I thought we were allies.'

I tried to steer us away from such topics at first, but she was clever and eloquent – and I was happy just to be able to talk to her. We wrangled good-naturedly, with her usually taking the line that Marxism was the only way ahead and me desperately trying to remember all the reasons I'd been taught that that was wrong. But I couldn't catch her out: her answers were always lucid and thought-provoking. She was very good at sticking to abstract concepts. Whenever I brought up problems, such as the Moscow show trials and executions, she would fix me with her calmest gaze, concede that humans had misunderstood and abused the ideology, then solemnly insist that the world would only be bettered when class and states had been completely abolished and the dictatorship of the proletariat had taken their place. She used the language of Communist ideology with such a straightforward faith in Peace and Brotherhood that most of the time I acquiesced, simply not to appear a cynical beast and thereby lose her friendship. But when I felt particularly bloody-minded and pursued her on such points, her apparent innocence and naivety vanished and she would counter-attack, questioning British policy in India, for example, or picking out some other apposite situation to prove her point. I realized with growing surprise and admiration that her view of the world had rather more consistency and logic to it than my own, and over time had to concede that, in many areas, I was far more naive and ill-informed than she.

But politics was only one subject of our many conversations that autumn. Anna taught me about Russia, but also about herself. She was a born storyteller, giving vivid and moving accounts of her upbringing and her experiences in the war: she had been with the Red Cross all the way through it, which was why she was now working in the British Zone, rather than the Soviet one. Our friendship soon developed into one of those intimate affairs where you stay up all night talking; we ranged over every subject imaginable, skipping from one to the other like pebbles skimming across a lake. She would often visit me for an hour or so between her shifts on the wards, and it was on one of these occasions that I first kissed her.

Love is a fast worker, especially first love, and so it was that, barely three months after being admitted into the sanatorium, I found myself in bed contemplating proposing marriage to my nurse. I could scarcely imagine how Father would react at the news! The instructions in his letter had been clear: I should not visit the farm-house again unless it was an emergency, but I was past caring – and well enough to leave the hospital. I had been well enough for a couple of weeks, in fact, but had been loath to leave for fear of letting go of Anna. Now I knew she loved me, I made up my mind to propose to her and, if she agreed, journey out to see Father and tell him the news before taking her back to England.

All my dreams evaporated later that evening, however, when she came to visit me after her usual rounds. I was sitting up smoking a cigarette and I sensed the change in her the moment she entered the room.

'What's wrong?'

'Paul,' she said, looking up at me with a strange panic flooding her eyes. 'I am so sorry.'

I gestured for her to take a seat next to me. 'Why? What's happened?' She was usually so controlled.

She walked into the room and closed the door, but didn't move any nearer to the bed. 'I have lied to you,' she said simply.

'What have you lied about?' A cold feeling had begun creeping through me.

She looked down at her hands. 'My name is not Anna Maleva,' she said quietly. 'My real name is Anna-Sonia Kuplin, and I am an agent of the *Narodny Komissariat Vnutrennikh Del*. Two months ago, I was instructed by my superior, a man in the DP camp at Burgdorf, to seduce you and recruit you to our cause.'

She seemed to be talking at me through a fog or a dream. I looked at my hands and was surprised to see they were shaking. I couldn't seem to stop them. 'Why?' I asked, eventually. 'Why . . . were you asked to recruit me?'

She walked over to the bed and stood by the edge of it. 'My superior wants to know about all my patients, but he was particularly interested in you,' she said. 'He knew of your father, and of his hatred for Communism. Your experience in intelligence and your youth were also seen as . . . attractive qualities.' She grimaced at this, but made herself continue. 'I was told to work on the bitterness you feel against your father to persuade you to join us.'

The blood was rushing around my head, and my chest was heaving.

'So all of this . . .' I said, gesturing futilely at the room where we had spent so much of our time together in the previous weeks, where we had made love, even. 'All of this was because you wanted me to *spy* for you?'

'It was also thought that once I revealed the true nature of your work here, you would be more interested in hearing our proposals.'

'What work?' I said, rage suddenly sweeping over me. I leaned over and grabbed her by the wrists, then thrust my face into hers. 'You can't possibly know what my bloody work involves, you . . . you little Russian whore!' I brought up my hand to slap her, then stopped myself. She hadn't flinched.

'I know more about it than you,' she said quietly, her eyes facing the floor. 'You have been deceived by your father. He was a prominent member of several British fascist groups before the war, and is now part of a secret movement intent on waging a new war against the Soviet Union. The men you were hunting down and murdering were not Nazi war criminals, but Soviet agents.'

She looked up at me for a moment, desperately trying to hold my gaze. But it was too late. There was nothing there for me any more: she wasn't my Anna. I had an almost overwhelming desire to take the pillow from the bed and place it over her face so she wouldn't be able to utter any more lies. 'So that was meant to be enough to turn me, was it?' I said, finally. 'A few fireside chats about politics and a half-baked story about a fascist conspiracy and you thought I'd sign up for Uncle Joe's brand of storm-troopers? How *dare* you accuse me of such a thing? And did you really expect me to believe that our side's made up of blood-thirsty savages and you're all pure as the driven—'

'Oh, Paul,' she said. 'Don't make me tell you it is true.'

'It is not true,' I said coldly. 'And you are the one who has been deceived. I read the orders given by these men. I read the witness reports.'

She had recovered something of her old composure now, and was prepared to fight back. 'Such documents can be easily forged, as you must know. Would anyone else be able to confirm that your mission was legitimate, or did your father perhaps tell you it had been deemed too secret to go through the usual channels?' She looked up, saw the confirmation in my eyes, and continued. 'The first couple of men would have been bona fide, to persuade you. But after that, did you see all the files of the men you killed?'

I didn't answer.

'Meier,' she said. 'Did you read the file on him?'

'Yes, Anna, and he was a rapist! He raped children. How can you do this?'

'I can't!' she said, and her eyes began to well with tears. 'Don't you see? I told my superior to go to hell. I love you, Paul, more than I ever thought it was possible to love someone, and I want us to start again. To forget this.' She stood up and walked towards me. 'I thought at first not to tell you, just to ask that we leave this place, with no explanations. But I don't want any secrets between us, Paul, none at all. Don't you see? I *had* to tell you.' She let her arms open, beckoning me. 'Please.'

I looked at her and part of me wanted more than anything to take a step forward. But that, I knew somewhere deep in the core of me, was weakness, and the kind of immature sentimentality that had led me into this situation. Without looking at her, I told her to leave. She refused at first, continuing to plead with me to listen to her. But I had detached myself, and after a few minutes she saw it. She ran from the room, and I listened dispassionately to the sound of her sobs echoing down the corridor. Then, taking great care not to lean on my wound, I manoeuvred my way down from the bed and started dressing.

*

It was my first taste of fresh air in a long while, but I hardly noticed it. I stopped thinking about Anna's betrayal of me and started focusing on what it meant. She knew about Sacrosanct — and, presumably, so did her handler in Burgdorf. Father had said in his letter that he would continue the operation for a few more weeks. If he had done so from the same location, as seemed likely, he could be in great danger.

As I started heading for the house, a terrible thought occurred to me. Anna's allegation that Father had mounted a rogue operation and was running around murdering Russians was clearly fantasy, but she had still known a great deal about the operation: the name Meier, for instance. Only two other people had access to that information: Pritchard and Father — and Pritchard had left months earlier. Perhaps Father had risked venturing into the Soviet Zone, and been taken into custody. Under interrogation, he could have revealed Pritchard's and my involvement, and even our locations. Pritchard was surrounded by commandos in the French Zone, so they wouldn't pursue him, but I was alone, and injured. Anna had been assigned as my nurse a few days after I had entered the sanatorium – perhaps the idea for her to recruit me had stemmed from knowledge they had gained from questioning Father.

It all seemed horrifyingly plausible: I couldn't think how else she could have known about the operation. And if I was right, Father was almost certainly dead, and they would soon be hunting me. They would probably be waiting for me at the farmhouse, in fact.

I slowed down, and started walking in the other direction. Father's letter to me had still been firmly sealed, and I guessed Anna had not dared open it for fear of losing my trust early on. The drop, then. I headed for it at once, and left a message that Anna Maleva, a nurse in the Red Cross hospital in Lübeck, was an NKVD agent, and knew about Sacrosanct.

*

A few hours later, I was holed up in a cabin halfway up the mountains, shivering in a wooden cot in the dark. Father had come across the place one day when we had been tramping across the Zone looking for clues. It had been used before the war by local mountaineers as a resting stop on their way to higher climes. Later, the Hitler Youth had taken it over for their excursions, and there were still signs of their occupation, from the insignia above the entrance to graffiti they had carved on the walls: the same sort of obscene phrases and drawings teenage boys make all over the world, for the most part, but disturbing nonetheless. I had immediately thought of the place, because it was well away from the main paths and still within easy walking distance of the nearest town if I needed food. There were no amenities for cooking, or anything else, and it was a lot less comfortable now than it had been during July, when we had come across it. But it was shelter.

I had placed my clothes in one of the cots for padding and tried to sleep as soon as I had reached it. But it was no use. Although still seething over Anna's betrayal, I couldn't shake the feeling that I had missed something in her allegations against Father, something in the tone of them. As daylight began to seep through the wooden slats of the walls, I finally realized what it was: despite trying to resist it, part of me could not help recognizing the ring of truth. He *had* been a fascist before the war, and was ardently, even fanatically, anti-Communist. And even if the Ukrainians had been guilty of the most horrendous crimes, we had nevertheless murdered them – did it make any difference in what cause? But the thing that kept pushing to the front of my mind was Father's obsession for protecting the operation at all costs: his insistence that nobody could ever learn of it.

Had I just signed Anna's death warrant?

As soon as I thought it, I knew I had to reach her again. We would do just as she had said: leave here and start again. I had an image of her in her nurse's smock in a clinic somewhere in England. She loved me – how could I let her go?

*

After eating a handful of wild berries to give me energy for the journey, I walked back to the outskirts of Sankt Gertrud, then ran the remainder of the way to the sanatorium. The other nurses seemed perturbed at seeing me, and after I had managed to push past some of them into the ward area I saw why. One of the doctors was talking to a group of men in uniform. *Russian* uniform. As one of the men saluted, he turned away and I saw the stretcher. Blankets had been placed over her body, but her head was still exposed and the features beneath the yellowish grey complexion and closed lids were unmistakable. One of the nurses told me in a hushed voice that she had been found in her quarters a few hours earlier, and that her body was being taken to the Russian Zone, and then back to Georgia. Apparently the soldiers were looking to trace a visitor she had had the previous evening: a man wearing the uniform of a British officer.

Father had received my message loud and clear, and had acted to eliminate the threat: nobody could know about Sacrosanct. I turned before any of the soldiers spotted me and started running for the farmhouse.

*

As I finally crested the hill two hours later, I saw the outline of the jeep and made a desperate effort to increase my pace. He was still here! I pushed open the front door and almost fell into the living room. 'Where are you, you bastard?' I screamed. 'Where the hell are you?' But there was no reply, to that or the other abuse that I hurled at him, and I found out why when I reached his bedroom. He was lying at the foot of the bed, still in his uniform. No pills – he hated the easy option. He'd done it the same way he had meted it out, with a bullet to the temple from his Luger. The left side of his face had been completely destroyed, and the wall behind him was splattered with blood. There was no note, so I could only guess as to why one more murder had woken his conscience. Perhaps she had begged for her life, or told him about her love for me.

It didn't matter any more. He didn't matter. I took him out to the garden and buried him. The wind was fierce – winter would be here soon. I had only one thought in me. I had to get to Burgdorf and find Anna's handler.

I had a proposition to make him.

III

Sunday, 23 March 1969, Hampshire

As I crouched down to take a closer look at Chief's body, there was a noise somewhere behind me and my hand flew to the Luger. But it was just the bleating of the telephone from the sideboard.

I let out my breath and placed the gun back in my jacket. I had taken it from beside Father's body twenty-four years ago, and kept it as my personal weapon all this time. Now I had learned that he had apparently not used it to take his own life, or Anna's: he himself had been murdered, as part of a squalid little conspiracy to lure me into serving Mother Russia. The British officer who had been seen visiting Anna's quarters hadn't been him, but Chief. And the soldiers carrying Anna off in a jeep would have been NKVD – they had probably driven round to the farmhouse minutes later. Had Anna been the one to pull the trigger, or had she still been in her coma? It didn't matter: she'd been part of it.

Now I had murdered Chief. I had had no choice. He had spotted something crucial in the Russian transcript of Slavin's interview: that the double had been involved in *secret* secret work – some kind of deep operation. He'd known that Father had been involved in just such an operation, because Father had told him, but he hadn't known who else had been involved: me. However, Pritchard, the only other surviving participant of Sacrosanct, did know that. If Chief had lived another half hour, he would have told Pritchard about the translation error and the rest, and Pritchard would have realized at once that I was Radnya.

I had had to kill him, but it had only bought me a little time, because I had no idea what else Slavin might know about me. Defections usually involved delicate negotiations, and Slavin would know not to use all his bargaining chips too early. He was due to be interviewed again at the High Commission in Lagos on Tuesday morning, where the deal would no doubt be done to exfiltrate him to London. They could also try to get hold of Anna – she wasn't offering to defect, but they knew she had recruited the agent. I had to reach both of them before anyone else did, otherwise . . . Otherwise what? I would either be jailed or hanged. But what was the alternative? The masters I had served for over half my life had killed Father: how could I continue to serve them now? I knew I couldn't.

The phone stopped ringing, bringing me back into the room with a jolt. Who had called? I knew from previous visits that Barnes usually rang just before Chief sat down to dinner, so it was unlikely to have been him. Pritchard, to say he couldn't come? It made no difference – I had to act on the basis that either of them might arrive at any moment. But I couldn't kill either: while I might still manage to make it look like Chief had disappeared, nobody would believe that the Head of Africa Section or his personal minder had also happened to go missing at the same time. I would have to make other plans.

Still, there was only one road leading into the property, so I couldn't leave until Pritchard had been and gone, or I'd risk meeting him on the way out. But I had to hide the car – if he saw that, I was done for.

I took the key from the front door and walked out, locking it behind me. The moon's dull glow illuminated the car. It was a sports model, and I remembered with horror that it had no boot. Still, it was futile blaming myself – it wasn't as if I could have considered where to store Chief's body when I'd bought the thing.

I didn't have time to waste on it now – something would have to come to me while I worked on other problems. As I turned the ignition key, I added another to the list. I was used to starting her up in London; out here in the sticks, the noise was deafening. I could drive out of here at 150 miles an hour, but the decibel level would bring Barnes running, if not everyone in the county.

Very gently, I took her deep into the shrubbery that backed onto the riverbank. Then I ran back up to the front door to examine the result. She was completely hidden behind a hedge, lying under the canopy of one of the larger beeches, but there were now marks across the gravel where I'd turned. I hoped it wouldn't be noticeable to a new arrival coming up the driveway.

I unlocked the door, went in and locked it again from the inside. Then I drew the curtains and switched the lights off in the living room and hallway. After rummaging around under the kitchen sink, I came up with a torch, a dishcloth, a pair of rubber gloves and some gardening bags. I took an empty bag, soaked the cloth, put on the gloves, picked up the torch and went back to the living room, where Chief lay on the floor, his eyes staring up at me.

I closed the lids, and tilted his head so I could inspect the damage. I'd used a full metal jacket, so the exit wound was small. Thankfully, the little spillage there had been had fallen on the spread of papers that had been under his chair. I placed these in the bag, and then got to work cleaning the wound thoroughly — I didn't want remnants of matter brushing against the carpet when I moved him.

Then there was the bullet itself: it was embedded in the wall behind where Chief had been standing, to the right of the Georgian fireplace. I managed to jimmy it out and cleared the resulting dust with the other corner of the dishcloth. Now I had to find a way to hide the mark. The bookcase would have done the trick, but I didn't have time to move it, and anyone who had visited Chief in recent weeks would spot such a large modification to the room's layout anyway. On the other hand, anything I could easily shift would be moved by an investigating team later on, if it came to that.

I settled on the piano, which stood about a hand's width to the right of the mark. It was on a carpet, one of Chief's finest Afghans. I got down on my knees and pulled it, a fraction of an inch at a time, towards the cornice. After a few minutes, I had it in place. I left it a couple of inches short of the wall to make it less obvious, but the mark couldn't be seen unless you were right above it.

I continued my tour of the room, searching for anything either of us had touched. I threw both tumblers and the Becherovka bottle into the bag, along with the ashtray, the unfinished egg sandwich and the Slavin file. As I executed the moves – pick this up, clean that, check this – another part of me circled over the scene and wondered how I was capable of it. Why I was doing it. What I had become. But the machine in me drove on . . .

I climbed the staircase and negotiated my way along the narrow corridor to Chief's bedroom. From a quick sweep with the torch, it looked cramped and rather untidy. I took a few summer suits from the wardrobe and stuffed them into my bag with a couple of lightweight shirts, underwear, socks and a couple of pairs of shoes.

The bag was now full to the brim, so I left it at that and carried my haul back down the stairs. I took my coat from the hook in the hallway, put it on and headed into the living room to collect Chief. I took him in a fireman's lift. He was heavier than I expected, and I could still smell the Becherovka on him. I picked up the bag with my spare hand and half-staggered to the hallway, taking care not to move too fast – the batteries in the torch were going and the last thing I needed now was to break a vase.

By the time I'd reached the front door, my shoulders were starting to ache. I rested for a moment, then switched hands on the bag so I could open the door. I nearly cricked my neck doing it, but I eventually managed to squeeze through.

I locked the door a final time, pocketed the key and stumbled down the stairs onto the drive. By moving the car, I'd ensured a longer walk for myself. I focused on the thought that had Pritchard arrived before I'd moved it, I would have had to kill him, too. And, as I had already reasoned, I couldn't stage disappearances for both of them.

It had started to rain: just a drizzle, but the wind was gusting it around. I got a sudden whiff of urine, and held my breath for a few seconds. There were some large beeches with plenty of shadow, and I headed for them. I had to stop several times, but then, somehow, I was there. I let Chief slide to my feet. I could see by the moon now, so I let the torch fall into the bag, then counted to ten before picking him up again, ready to attack the final few steps to the car.

Crunch.

Wheels on gravel. I froze. Then, in one movement, I stepped back a pace, deeper into the undergrowth.

A moment later, headlights flooded the drive.

I dropped the bag and laid Chief on the ground by my feet, then turned up the lapels of my coat and buttoned them across so that nothing of my shirt or jacket could be seen. It wasn't the best camouflage routine I'd ever executed, but it might make all the difference.

The car sidled up alongside Chief's Bentley. The driver craned his neck out of the window to check whether he was near the verge. I could make out a few features: silver hair, glasses, and a neat little beard.

Pritchard.

*

I stood in the undergrowth and watched as he stepped out of his car. He was wearing a close-fitting red coat, white breeches, and leather boots. I remembered he liked hunting – he must have come straight from the chase. He walked round to the rear door and opened it. A dog leapt out: a black, white and tan dog with a long muzzle. The sound of its bark came like a shot, travelling across the drive and negotiating its way through the branches until it reached my ears, sending my brain a simple, stark message: I was done for.

They started for the house, Pritchard striding as though he were measuring out a distance, the hound zigzagging manically around its master. As they passed, I caught the expression on Pritchard's face. Perhaps it was a trick of the moonlight, or one of those odd extrapolations induced by proximity to extreme danger, but I could have sworn he was smiling.

This baffled me. What did he think he had been called here to discuss? Chief had said he hadn't yet discussed the Slavin file with any of the others. At least, I thought he'd said that. If I'd misunderstood, I had no option but to kill Pritchard now. I thought of the old Service proverb: three people can keep a secret, as long as two of them are dead.

But killing Pritchard would mean an immediate murder inquiry.

As he took the stairs to the front door, I weighed the odds. It seemed clear that I should stay my hand and simply wait for him to leave, but the uncertainty of it nagged at me. It would have helped if I could have convinced myself I'd imagined his gleeful expression.

Then another thought occurred to me: could it simply be that, far from resenting having his Sunday evening interrupted – as I had, and as most people would – Pritchard *relished* the prospect of a late-night rendezvous with Chief? Was he simply aroused by the scent of intrigue? I didn't have many dealings with Pritchard these days – I tried to avoid him as much as I could – but thinking back to the safe house in Sankt Gertrud, I decided it was quite possible.

He was ringing the doorbell now, rather forcefully – the car and the barking would normally have been enough to bring Chief to the door, so perhaps he was already wondering why they hadn't.

'Hallo? Anybody there?' After he had called out a few times, he checked the door was locked, found it was, and so walked round to the window and tried to peer in, the dog following at his heels.

The wind suddenly became stronger, whipping the branches to

and fro, and I stopped one with my arm before it took out one of my eyes. The gust had also hit the bag, spilling its contents over the ground. There was the unmistakable clank of glass, and the dog swivelled its head to locate the source of the disturbance.

Keep still.

Keep very, very still.

The dog started barking.

Pritchard chucked it under the neck. 'What's the matter, Fizz?'

Barking in my direction. There, master, the traitor and the corpse. In the undergrowth.

'What is it?'

Barking ferociously, pointing its head, trying to get its message across. Pritchard peered out at the drive.

'Find!' he shouted suddenly, and let go of the leash. The dog bounded down the steps and headed straight for me at a terrifying pace. Pritchard set off after it.

Keep still, and stay calm, I told myself. Foxhounds are trained to hunt foxes, not men, so it would not be looking for my scent, nor Chief's.

It was just a few feet away now. I could hear its rapid panting and see the wet glint of its snout foraging through the leaves. Pritchard came stamping up behind, talking all the while in a tender, singsong voice: 'What's eating you, you silly fool; what's wrong, eh?'

Foxes, not men, I repeated in my head, foxes, not men, trying to blank out the cramp, the fear, the ache in my jaw from the rain.

'There are no foxes here, you daft old thing.'

And then I could almost hear him thinking it: no, but there might be something else. And now he started to sniff the air, too, and my mantra no longer helped me.

Because Pritchard *was* trained to hunt men.

I breathed through my nostrils, as slowly and evenly as possible, and prayed that the rain and the mud and the foliage would mask any scents emanating from me, the bag or Chief. I closed my eyes.

He might pick out my whites from even the tiniest of movements, or see the reflection of the moon in my pupils. I shut down my brain and retreated inside myself, urging every fibre of my being to blend into the tree, the wind, the night, so that Pritchard would not register my presence.

I don't know how long I stood like that. Perhaps several minutes, perhaps only seconds. Then I heard a footfall and I broke back into full consciousness. He had moved into the hedge, a step closer to me. Could he sense me? If he came any nearer, he would *see* me. I wondered how quickly I would be able to draw the Luger. It shouldn't be a problem: I was younger, fitter and stronger than Pritchard, and he wouldn't be expecting it. Fizz wouldn't like it, but I could handle a few bites, if necessary.

Two steps more and I would have to kill him. I had killed Chief so that Pritchard would not suspect me of being the traitor. But if he discovered me now, with Chief and the debris from his murder beneath my feet, it wouldn't have helped me much.

The debris beneath my feet. I opened my eyes a fraction and looked down. I could see the Becherovka label, and a small greyish lump. Chief's sandwich.

Pritchard had his back to me now, turning to see where Fizz had gone. Taking care not to brush against any branches, I crouched down very slowly and picked up the sandwich. The rain had transformed it into a knot of mush. With my hand still an inch or so above the ground, I flicked the thing with my wrist, as though I were skipping a stone, in the direction of the riverbank.

Fizz barked at the rustle in the leaves, and ran over to see what it was.

Pritchard waited a few seconds, and then followed.

I stepped back another pace, deeper into shadow, and looked up to count the stars to calm myself. I couldn't make out much through the spitting rain, though, so I soon gave up and tried to peek over towards where I'd thrown the sandwich.

Where were they?

And then I saw Fizz emerging from the undergrowth a few feet down. The dog had a bird in its mouth, and Pritchard was laughing and calling it a stupid beast and then he took it by the scruff of the neck and they set off back up the drive.

Pritchard walked round the house and rapped on the windows again, then went back to try the front door again. He was puzzled and frustrated now, but finally he marched back to the car, the buttons of his coat clinking as he walked, stroking Fizz's ears with one hand.

The sound of the engine faded. I waited a few minutes, still breathing at the same slow pace, until I was sure he was not returning. Then I set about putting everything back into the bag. I picked it and Chief's body up again, and made my way through the bracken to the car.

*

There was some space for him behind the seats. Not much, but it might be enough. I put the bag on the passenger seat and set to work. First, I tried to squeeze him in with his knees folded to his chin. When that didn't work, I used a series of swift downward strikes until his legs broke at the knees. That helped me push him to the floor, at which point I heard a thin, sharp crack, which must have been his spine. An image suddenly flashed into my mind of the look on his face when he'd seen the gun. I forced it away. It wasn't Chief I was doing this to — it was just a lump of flesh that would soon become part of the soil, as we all did at some point . . . And as I would too sooner rather than later if I didn't focus.

I took off my coat and draped it over him, partly so he wouldn't be seen on the road, more to hide his unmoving stare. Then I walked around the car, stretching my legs, feeling the rain on my forehead, trying to rid my mind of bullets and broken bones and formulate a workable strategy to get me out of this hole. I had a rendezvous with Vanessa at midnight. Miss it, and I'd have some awkward questions to answer later on. Make it, and it would avert suspicion, although the idea made me queasy inside. The last person I wanted to see now was Vanessa — let alone use her as an alibi. I snapped out of it. I wasn't about to be hanged because of an attack of qualms.

I climbed into the front seat and put the key in the ignition. The house was in my rear-view mirror, dark and deserted under the sliver of moon. I had a sudden memory of school: holidays when I'd stayed behind, the gloom of empty dormitories in the dark.

I started her up, and began to move off slowly.

*

Winding through the empty lanes at about twenty miles an hour with the lights dimmed, the urge to push the pedal and leave it all behind was almost overpowering. But I couldn't yet risk it. I didn't want to wake people up.

I'd gone about ten miles when I came to a call box. I parked on the verge, went in and put in a collection of sixpences. Nothing happened. I cursed and was just about to hang up when I got through.

'Yes?' said a gruff voice.

'Something is going to fall like rain,' I said. 'And it won't be flowers.'

'Pardon?'

Oh, Christ.

'Something is going to fall like rain — and it won't be flowers.'

There was a long pause, and then a resigned 'Righty-ho' and he hung up. It's only when you're forced to rely on emergency measures that you see all the holes in them: a straight-faced 'Please pass the message on to Sasha that I need to meet at location four in two hours' would have sounded a deal less suspicious to anyone listening in. And what the hell had Auden been going on about? I wondered. Why would flowers fall like rain? Wouldn't rain be the more likely turn of events?

The spy games concluded, I climbed back in the car and set off again. I carried on weaving through the lanes until I reached the turn-off to the A32, and then put my foot down. It had already gone half ten, and it was going to be very tight getting everything done and still making Ronnie Scott's before midnight. I tuned the radio to some rock music on one of the pirate stations. I could barely hear it at this speed, but all I wanted was some noise. As the car tunnelled through the night, I wanted something chaotic to churn beneath it all, to keep me conscious that the soft years were over.

There was no way back.

*

I wound the window down to let some air in.

He was already there, which was a good sign. A no-show would have left me with all sorts of difficulties. I had given myself two hours from placing the call, but that was the absolute minimum: standard procedure was four hours, with an intricate set of checks and double-backs I'd developed over the years, but that clearly hadn't been possible tonight. This was an emergency, and I was working to a very tight deadline – Vanessa would be arriving soon, checking her coat, ordering a Cointreau – and it had been tempting to take a few more shortcuts on the security. I comforted myself with the fact that it was a Sunday night, which was probably the safest time of the week. I finished my cigarette, then got out of the car and walked across the street.

*

There were fewer people than I'd hoped for: some old men playing mah-jong; a couple of dockers. I breathed in the smell of fried rice, pork and incense. This was location four, the New Friends restaurant, one of the last surviving vestiges of the old Chinatown. A waitress with impossibly thick eyelashes drifted towards me, but I nodded in the direction of the man hunched over a table in the corner, and she moved off again.

He was pushing the remains of a chow mein around his plate and nursing a cup of tea. His postage stamps, our usual cover for conversation, were already neatly laid out on the table.

I seated myself beside him. I'd last seen him six months ago. His beard was a little greyer, his paunch a little wider.

'Hello, Sasha,' I said.

'Hello, Paul. I hope this is good.'

He was irritated at being called out to an emergency meeting: he'd grown accustomed to routine, as had I, and had started to believe he had a right to lead a normal life.

I pushed the barrel of the Luger into his thigh.

'Not here,' I said. 'Not enough cover.'

He quickly shuffled his stamps together, left some money on the table and followed me out to the car.

*

The streets were mainly one-way, and there were long gaps between the lamps. But I knew where I was going. I circled round the back of the restaurant and found the Horseferry Road turning.

I looked across at him. He wasn't doing a good job of hiding his fear: he couldn't keep his eyes still and rivulets of sweat licked his forehead. I put the gun away. I didn't want him to give the answers he thought I was looking for — I'd had enough of that.

'What happened?' he said.

'*Radnya.*'

It was the name Moscow had known me by for over twenty years, the name he had sat and encoded after every one of our meetings. The name I hadn't known before tonight.

He swore in Russian.

'Who?' he said. 'How?'

Who had betrayed me? How had I learned of their betrayal?

'Anna.' It answered both questions.

This time I got a different reaction: shock, and a seemingly overwhelming sadness. Apparently I'd underestimated his emotional range.

'I think you should explain,' he said, which was lovely. I composed myself as I dipped the headlights for an oncoming car.

'How long have you known she was alive?'

He looked down. Always, then.

'I never lied to you, Paul. You must—'

'Don't *Paul* me,' I said, and I felt the anger rise. 'No, you never lied, old friend. Just omitted a few things.'

'You're forgetting,' he said, and his voice wavered as I took a corner at high speed. 'We are both only pawns in this game.'

That made me laugh. My life falling apart, and he was feeding me B-film lines. Judging by the expression on his face, I was sounding a touch hysterical, so I carried on, out of spite. I felt sorry for him, too, of course: his longest-serving agent losing his nerve so spectacularly. But there it was – the taste of betrayal fresh in my mouth, and I felt sick with it and desperate to lash out. Perhaps I would use the gun again tonight. He deserved to die more than Chief. He had known of the plot – he had not only failed to tell me about it, but had continued to feed it to me.

'We're not pawns,' I told him. 'I told you at our very first meeting that I didn't want any more games – I had enough of that with Yuri. If you had told me the truth then, I would have accepted it.'

'No,' he said, regaining his composure. 'You wouldn't have. That, too, is horseshit.'

I ignored him. He wasn't answering my questions, and I needed answers to them, now.

'Why?' I asked him, my knuckles straining against the steering wheel. 'Why this way?'

'It shouldn't matter how you were recruited.'

A few hours previously I would have agreed with him, if we'd been discussing some other poor fool who had been lured in like this: yes, a clever little honey trap, very nice, the means justify the ends, and all that crap. Very nice — in theory. 'It matters to *me*,' I said, barely able to control my fury. 'The murder of my father *matters to me*, Sasha.'

'I am sorry,' he said after a moment. 'But you must understand that he would have been seen as a dangerous enemy.'

Yes, I understood, all right: eliminate a prime anti-Communist, and recruit his own son off the back of it. My code-name even gloated over the fact.

'How did it work?' I asked. 'How many people were involved? I want to know the details.'

'I don't have them,' he said. 'I was shown your file before I left Moscow, but the matter of your recruitment had only a very brief description.'

'Indulge me,' I said. 'I suspect it was fuller than the one I got.'

He turned to me, the shadows on his face shifting shape as we passed in and out of the fields of each streetlamp. 'You were admitted to a Red Cross hospital, where the agent you knew as Anna cared for you. Investigations established that you were the son of a leading British intelligence officer with links to fascist groups before the war.'

I kept glancing over at him, because I needed to match the meaning of his words with the way he said them. If he sounded a false note — if he was lying — I needed to know. I couldn't yet tell.

'So a plan was drawn up.'

'Yes. Anna was to persuade you of the rightness of our cause using her particular talents—'

'That's one way of putting it,' I said. 'Who killed my father?' I asked. 'Who pulled the trigger?'

'That I do not know, Paul.'

Narrow Street. I veered into it and Sasha lurched into the dashboard as we flattened a few cobblestones. Was this the truth — or more omission?

'And Anna disappeared.'

He shrugged. 'There was nothing else about her in the file. Perhaps you can tell me what you have learned?'

I debriefed quickly, leaving nothing out but embellishing nothing either. He didn't say anything, didn't react at all, even when I'd finished. He seemed to be more interested in the activity on the river: there were a couple of tankers moving silently about their business.

'Did you hear me?' I asked.

'Yes,' he said. 'You did the right thing.'

'The *only* thing,' I corrected. 'There wasn't anything right about it.'

He turned away from the river to look at me, and smiled thinly. He placed his palm on my shoulder, a pastiche of avuncular affection. 'I understand your distress,' he said, and it was all I could do to stop myself reaching for the gun again. 'That is something I can't help you with. You must look in your soul and examine the reasons things were done in this way. In time—'

'What do you know about Slavin?' I asked him. I didn't *have* any time – that was the bloody point.

'Slavin?'

'Yes,' I said. 'You remember – the KGB officer whose defection is threatening my life.'

'Only what you have just told me: that he is attached to the Soviet Embassy in Lagos. Considering the strategic importance of Africa, and Nigeria in particular, I imagine he is regarded highly by Moscow. But that is all I know, I'm afraid – that and I count my blessings that my services are required here, surrounded by beauty and art, whereas Comrade Slavin has the ill fortune of being posted to one of the world's most inhospitable cities during wartime.'

I looked over at the dirty black river and wondered about Sasha's definition of beauty.

'Forgive me if I don't share your sympathy for him,' I said.

'Oh, don't be so self-pitying, Paul! You have enjoyed more than your share of luck tonight. You weren't spotted by Henry Pritchard, for example. Although, of course,' he added, 'you will now have to be especially wary of him.'

Yes. Yes, I would. *'The control, at one remove from the action, may be able to offer the agent fresh insight into problems he faces in the field.'* It was from the Service manual, but I imagined Moscow had some similar gibberish printed up. I resisted the urge to tell him that it had already occurred to me that I might now have to be especially wary of Pritchard.

'Still, I don't think there's any need for you to worry yourself unduly,' Sasha was saying. 'Slavin will be dispatched tomorrow.' He gave a short chuckle.

I told him that nobody was going to lay a finger on Slavin, and after he had recovered from the savagery with which I had spat this out, he politely asked me why not. He even managed a sliver of bewildered amusement in his tone – I didn't like that. I wanted him scared.

'Volkov,' I said. 'It'll look too much like it.'

Konstantin Volkov had walked into the British Consulate-General in Istanbul in 1945 and asked to defect. He'd had information that would have blown Philby, but Philby had wangled his way into getting the job to fly out to interrogate him, and he'd taken enough time doing it for his handler to send some goons in to take the Russian and his wife back to Moscow. This was now known, thanks in part to Philby himself, who had published a slippery little volume of memoirs revealing just enough to push my colleagues into further paroxysms of paranoia. If Slavin suddenly disappeared, it would be clear he had been silenced by the double, and as the only men who knew about Slavin's allegations were Lagos Station and Heads of Section, that would narrow the field considerably. I had to get out to Nigeria as soon as possible, because I couldn't run the risk of someone else interrogating Slavin before me. But if anything happened to him, either while I was there or on my way out there, it would narrow the field to just one.

'You're safe,' said Sasha. 'Didn't you come through with flying colours last time? Nobody would ever seriously suspect you.' He patted the leather upholstery pointedly. 'Your cover is impeccable.'

'You're making me blush,' I said. 'But my last experience of being questioned was notably different, I think, don't you? I hadn't, for example, just killed the Head of the Service. If Slavin is mysteriously shipped off in bandages moments before I arrive in Lagos, I'll either spend the rest of my life in Pentonville or end up dangling from the end of a rope.'

'Let us be perfectly clear, Paul. What is it you are asking of me?'

'Keep your thugs away. Let me deal with Slavin.'

He took a sharp intake of breath, and gave a quick shake of his head. 'It is far too dangerous.'

'Reassuring to hear that you care, but I'll be the judge of that.'

'It's impossible.'

'It's non-negotiable.'

He gave me a long look. 'They won't let me.'

'Then don't tell them.' I leaned a little on the last word – his incessant passing of the buck was beginning to irritate me.

'I can't do that. There is another option, you know—'

I gave him a cool look. 'The flat in Moscow? Pissing away the rest of my life on cheap vodka like Philby and the others? No thanks.'

'I'm afraid I can't help you. I wish I could, I really do, but it's not in my power—'

I took the next corner, up a ramp to a space in front of someone's lock-up, 'Millwall FC' scrawled across it in blue spray paint. I pulled the brake and drew the Luger, then faced my comrade down the barrel.

He'd shut up now.

I leaned forward and placed the nose against his forehead.

'It's in your own interest,' I said. 'If they take me into the rubber room – which I can guarantee you they will if anyone touches Slavin before I get there – I'll give them everything I have on you before I bite down on the capsule.'

His expression remained blank – he didn't think I had enough on him for it to matter.

'They mightn't find you, of course,' I said. 'You mightn't even be here by then.'

'What do you mean?'

'If I come under suspicion, Moscow will almost certainly recall you.'

It had a more benign ring to it than 'dispatched', but it amounted to the same thing. His breaths had started coming short and fast now, and I thought I could see the logic gradually penetrate.

'All right,' he said, finally. 'You're on your own.'

'When's your next report?'

Hesitation. I twitched my finger a fraction.

'The second, barring emergencies.' He managed a smile, and I liked him a little for it. It brought to mind the Sasha I had known and worked with for so long.

But, then, that Sasha was a liar.

The second: that was ten days away. We drove on in silence for a few minutes, and then I pulled up at a yard filled with blackened barges. A sign on a wall proclaimed that 'DOGS LOVE VIMS'. The dirt in the air from the coal-loading wharf upstream was everywhere, impregnating the lamp-posts and the buildings, and the smell of tar and water was suddenly pungent. 'Your chief's body,' Sasha said suddenly, as I drew to a halt. 'You didn't say what you had done with it.'

I'd been wondering how long it would take him. I nodded at my coat behind his head. He glanced back over his shoulder and swore violently in Russian. 'You're going to dump him in the river.'

'No,' I said. 'We are.'

*

I parked the car close to the edge and we carried the body down, wrapped in the blanket. I took the arms, Sasha the feet, and we shuffled along to the end of the lock, stopping every couple of minutes — he kept complaining that it was tricky to keep a firm hold. Finally we were there, and we lowered Chief onto the moist gravel.

Sasha clapped his hands together, looking for a moment as though he would make a comment about the recent cold snap. I prayed he wouldn't — I didn't want to lose control altogether.

I began scouring the ground for stones and suggested he do the same. When I had a handful that were large enough, I stuffed them into Chief's pockets.

We carried on doing this for a few minutes, not saying anything. I think Sasha was afraid to — in silence, it was easier to pretend we were doing something else, so he busied himself with selecting the best stones for the job, delegating their placement to me. It was as though he were a child building a sandcastle, searching for decoration for one of the turrets.

When Chief was pretty much laden, I took his house-keys from my coat and placed them in his top pocket. No harm in being tidy. I signalled to Sasha. Chief's face and hands already looked grey in the yard's sulphurous light. Had I not pulled the trigger, he'd have been stirring his cup of cocoa and shuffling into bed about now — having just heard all about my involvement in Father's mission from Pritchard, and had me arrested for treason as a result.

I stopped looking at him and told Sasha to do the same; it wasn't making things easier. We lifted him again, shimmied to the edge and started swinging him until we had a reasonable rhythm and some height. Then I counted to three, and we heaved forward and let him go.

*

I was enveloped in a fog of cigarette smoke as I walked into Ronnie Scott's. Once I'd made my way through it, I saw that the support band was still on — three earnest young men sweating for their art in matching orange brocade suits — and the place was packed.

I usually savoured the atmosphere, but tonight I had to find Vanessa, and fast. I was close to half an hour late and I wasn't sure what kind of mood she would be in – our afternoon of lovemaking might have left her feeling the snub even more.

We hadn't visited the club since the previous summer, and it had expanded in the meantime, but I remembered that she liked to sit as close to the stage as possible, so I bypassed the bar and made for the candlelit tables up front. There was no sign of her. I scanned the crowd desperately: a handsome Indian gent in a pinstripe suit and white turban; a party of young women, all sporting the same outlandish hairdo; an elderly man enraptured by the band, playing along on an imaginary piano – every face in London, it seemed, but one. Perhaps she was in the lavatory, or had left a message with one of the waitresses. I was walking towards the bar, when I felt a tug at my sleeve.

'So there you are,' she whispered in my ear. 'I was about to give up hope!'

Her hair was down and her body poured into the turquoise shantung dress I'd bought her at Dior a few weeks earlier on a spree. She'd embellished it with a cream organza shawl and a necklace of ivory bones that showed off her tan. Her eyes were a little hooded, and one shoulder sloped oddly: she was either drunk, or high, or both.

I felt the tension leave me. 'I'm sorry, darling,' I said, raising my voice so I could be heard over a saxophone solo. She laughed gaily and offered me her hand. I took it and she led me away from the stage, towards her table.

'Yes, well, I'm sorry, too. Where on earth have you been? Killing Russians again?'

I forced a smile. 'Not quite. But something came up.'

'It's all right,' she said. 'I've been quite happy, really. I bumped into one of Daddy's friends and he's been entertaining me in your absence – such a charming man, and so knowledgeable. I believe he's also in your game?'

The tall, slender figure was seated at her table between a half-finished bottle of chilled Riesling and a plate of chicken curry, his jacket resting on his knees and his eyes fixed on me.

'Why, hello, Paul,' said Pritchard, with a wintry smile. 'Fancy seeing you here.'

IV

Monday, 24 March 1969, London

I woke to see the word 'BECHEROVKA' swimming in front of my eyes. My first thought was that I was still at Chief's house, but then the ringing in my ears and the coating on my teeth brought it all back.

Pritchard had left the club soon after my arrival. He hadn't mentioned that he had been at Chief's, though in a way I'd found that more troubling. But strangely enough, despite the fright he'd given me, I had almost been sorry to see him go, as I hadn't had much to say to Vanessa. I'd hung on at the club with her for another hour, wearing a death's-head grin and sweating inside my coat as the music spiralled out of control, before finally feigning tiredness and suggesting we leave.

I'd hailed her a cab – the longer I spent with her, the worse it would be. She hadn't been pleased, of course, but she'd taken it reasonably well and hadn't asked any questions. I had told her I'd call her in the morning, then I'd hopped in the car and driven back to South Kensington.

After parking near the flat, I had taken the bag from behind the back seat and thrown it into the bins behind an Italian restaurant. On impulse, I'd fished out the bottle of Becherovka and taken it up to the flat with me, hiding it under my jacket so the porter wouldn't see.

I'd slept very little, spending most of the night going through what had happened and getting to the bottom of the bottle. Now, as the dawn light fell on overturned chairs and shattered glass, I stripped and forced myself to work through the old fitness regimen. By the end of it, I was dripping in sweat and my mind was focused on the morning ahead. I had three objectives. Visit Station 12 and pick up my copy of the Slavin dossier — I didn't want to have to explain why I hadn't already received it. See if Chief's file on Anna was in Registry — as a Head of Section I had full clearance, although one didn't usually ask to see material related to Chief without a very good reason. I had several. But above all, I had to make sure I was sent out to Nigeria. I had no idea what else Slavin might have up his sleeve, and I needed to hear it before anyone else.

Resolved, I took a bath, shaved and put on a fresh suit. After a scratch breakfast, I packed an old canvas hold-all with a few clothes and took the lift downstairs. I left a message for George to give the car the full treatment, outside and in. Then I hailed a cab and asked the driver to take me to Lambeth.

*

'Gentlemen!' William Osborne's stentorian tones put a sudden stop to the murmuring around the table. 'I think it's time we settled down and got this show on the road, as our American friends like to say.'

He gave a slightly unconvincing chortle, and his waistcoat expanded in the process. Unblessed by the breeding or charm that had smoothed the waters for others, Osborne had clawed his way to becoming Head of Western Hemisphere Section by virtue of his prodigious intellect. A highly capable administrator, he had been widely expected to take over as Deputy Chief last year, but the job had instead gone to John Farraday, a smooth Foreign Office nob with no previous experience of the spy game but a penchant for hosting lavish dinner parties. Osborne had managed to isolate him within weeks, and nobody was in any doubt who really ran things when Chief was away. But he didn't have the title, yet — and it was by no means a certainty that he'd get it.

This meeting was held every Monday morning at this time, and was known as 'the Round Table', although none of us were knights and the table was, in fact, rectangular. Farraday had just arrived and taken his place in his usual corner; he was now busily checking that his cuffs were protruding from his jacket sleeves by half an inch. Seated immediately to his right, and directly facing me, was Pritchard. In a crisp, narrow-cut pinstripe suit and woven silk tie, he didn't look in the least as though he'd been sipping Riesling in a Soho jazz club less than nine hours ago.

After the war, Pritchard had joined MI5, where he had eventually become Head of E Branch: Colonial Affairs. When it had finally become clear to the Whitehall mandarins that it was suicidal to have intelligence officers posted in former colonies with no official links to the Service, which was responsible for all other overseas territories, E Branch had been taken over, and Pritchard had moved with it. Coming from Five, and being a Scot to boot, had initially made him a deeply suspected outsider, especially as many of the Service's old guard had been forcibly retired at the same time he joined. However, he was also a decorated war hero, independently wealthy, and staunchly right-wing, and within a few months of his joining the Service he had been taken up as a kind of mascot by its rank and file: their man on the board. While in Five, Pritchard had been converted to the Americans' idea that British intelligence was still penetrated by the KGB, and he'd devoted a great deal of time and energy to examining old files and case histories in the hope of catching another mole. He'd brought this zeal with him to the Service, and it had made him a lot of high-ranking friends. Chief and Osborne had initially been all in favour of Pritchard's 'hunting expeditions', as his periodic attempts to uproot traitors were known, but now felt that he and his clique were stoking an atmosphere of paranoia and distrust. I tended to agree.

Naturally, I had watched Pritchard's entry into the Service and subsequent rise in popularity within it with considerable unease – the tall bespectacled ghost I had met in a farmhouse in Germany in 1945 was, for obvious reasons, the last person on earth I wanted to work alongside, especially as he now seemed on a drive to find moles inside the Service. I had been appointed Head of Section at an unusually tender age, partly due to Father's near-mythical status within the Service and partly due to Chief's patronage. Now Pritchard had caught up with me, and although Africa was one of the smaller Sections, there was already talk of him in the corridors as a potential Deputy Chief, or even Chief, somewhere down the line.

Also seated around the table were Godsal, who headed up Middle East Section, Quiney, responsible for Western Europe, and Smale, who was standing in for Far East as Innes was on leave. They all looked harmless enough, with their schoolmasters' faces and woollen suits, but I was under no illusions: they could be lethal. One ill-timed gesture, one misplaced word, and they would pounce. Technically, treason still warranted the death penalty. If I were exposed, I had no doubt they'd apply every technicality in the book. So: tread carefully. I needed things to go my way.

Osborne pushed a garishly cuff-linked sleeve to one side to examine his wristwatch. 'I was hoping Chief would be able to start us off,' he said, 'but he doesn't seem to have arrived yet.' His piggy little eyes, buried behind thick black frames, darted downwards, as if he thought Chief might be about to emerge from beneath the table.

'Strange,' I murmured under my breath.

'Did you say something, Paul?'

'Sorry,' I said, looking up sheepishly. 'It's just that . . . No. Never mind, carry on.'

'What is it?'

'Well . . . it just struck me that it's very unlike Chief. He's usually in well before nine on Mondays, isn't he?'

Osborne inspected a fingernail, then nibbled at it viciously. 'Has he called in?' he asked Smale, who was performing his usual duties as the head of Chief's secretariat in parallel with his new role. Smale shook his head.

'Perhaps traffic's bad,' I said. 'God knows this place is hard enough to get to from the centre of town.'

Osborne nodded: the old buildings had been a short walk from his flat.

'It is a little peculiar,' said Pritchard suddenly, the traces of his Morningside accent amplified by the room's acoustics. 'He called me in to see him last night but wasn't there by the time I arrived.'

'Oh?' said Osborne, turning his head. 'What did he want to see you about?'

'The Slavin file — at any rate, his message was attached to that.'

'What time did you get the message?' asked Osborne.

'Around seven. I'd just come back from Enfield and left straight away, but the house was deserted when I arrived.'

'Perhaps he'd fallen asleep,' I suggested.

'I don't think so. I checked pretty thoroughly.'

Yes, I thought — you did.

'I was worried something might have happened,' Pritchard continued, 'but I couldn't for the life of me remember the way to Barnes's cottage and didn't want to call in a Full Alert without ample reason. I suddenly remembered Chief sometimes spends weekends in London with his daughter, Vanessa. I called her flat, and her roommate — a charming young Australian girl — told me she'd just left for a club in Soho, so I thought I'd drive in to see if Chief was with her — or if she knew where he'd got to.'

'And did she?' asked Godsal.

'No. She also thought he was out at Swanwick and was equally mystified. But I bumped into Paul there.'

The table's eyes turned to me.

'Caught red-handed,' I said, grinning sheepishly. 'I've a soft spot for jazz.'

'Oh,' said Pritchard, 'is that what it was?' Then, pointedly: 'She seemed quite taken with you.'

I did my best to blush.

'Perhaps we should give him a call,' said Osborne, rescuing me.

'Perhaps he's simply slept in.' He nodded at Smale quickly, before anyone could dwell too much on the unlikely image of Chief failing to set his alarm clock, and Smale walked briskly across the room and picked up a telephone sitting on one of the filing cabinets. As he dialled, I imagined the ring echoing in the empty house. To fill the silence, people conspicuously shuffled pieces of paper, fiddled with pen tops and suddenly realized they had lost their glasses cases, until Smale eventually replaced the receiver and shook his head, and we all went back to staring at him.

'Call Barnes,' said Osborne, and waved his hand to indicate he should do it elsewhere.

Smale nodded and slithered out of the door. And that was that: the ball was rolling. Within a couple of hours, a team of specialists would begin prowling through Chief's living room with dogs and cameras and ink pads. Looking for evidence, looking for blood. I'd carried out last night's work in a kind of concentrated trance. Now I was gripped by panic as the reality of it came back to me, and a series of possible lapses leapt through my mind. Had I swept every inch of the carpet? Covered the bullet-mark adequately? I had a sudden flash of Chief's dark, frozen eyes staring up at me from the floor – could I really have removed all trace of that horror?

Osborne clapped his great hands together. 'I think we should start. I know some of you have to prepare for the Anguilla meeting later. There is only one item on today's agenda – the Slavin dossier, which I trust you have all now read. All other matters will be covered in our next meeting.' He turned to Pritchard. 'Perhaps you could start us off, Henry?'

'By all means.' Pritchard walked over to the door and dimmed the lights, then fiddled with the projector in the centre of the table. After some clicks and whirrs, a magnified photograph suddenly appeared on the wall facing us. A man with stooped shoulders and a widow's peak was bending down to examine a wooden mask at a street market, a quizzical smile on his lips.

'Meet Colonel Vladimir Mikhailovich Slavin of the KGB,' said

Pritchard. 'Unmarried. No children. Walked into the High Commission in Lagos on Friday and asked for a British passport in exchange for information about a double agent. In an interview with Geoffrey Manning, the Head of Station, Slavin claimed that Moscow had recruited this agent in Germany in 1945, and that he was given the code-name Radnya.' He peered at the table over his half-moon spectacles. 'Needless to say, if true, this would be a monumental disaster. Twenty-four years is a very long time for a double agent to remain undetected, and Christ knows what damage he could have caused.'

With a click, another photograph filled the top half of the wall. This was of a woman, three-quarters in profile, her hair swept back, no make-up. She looked older, of course – but it was her. I focused on her eyes, trying to read anything in them, but she was squinting in the harsh light and it wasn't possible. An ancient line of poetry I'd last heard recited in a dusty classroom suddenly flashed through my mind, unbidden: *With them that walk against me, is my sun . . .*

'This is the other figure we're looking at. Irina Grigorieva, a third secretary at the Soviet Embassy in Lagos. According to Slavin, she recruited Radnya after falling in love with him. *Cherchez la femme.*' He allowed a brief interval for polite laughter. Once a couple of people had obliged, he continued: 'Both of these pictures, incidentally, were taken by the Station's watchers within the last couple of years, so we can take it that this is more or less how they look today.' He walked back to the door and turned the lights back up.

'Do we know what their duties involve?' asked Farraday.

'I had a look at our records this morning, and we have Slavin down as arriving in Nigeria in '65, under cover as a political attaché. Before that, he was in similar positions in Kinshasa and Accra, which makes him something of an Africa expert in Russian terms. Our educated guess is that his job is to formulate policy in the region – and, of course, to keep an eye on what everyone else is getting up to.'

'Everyone else meaning us?' asked Farraday. He seemed to be following the discussion, for a change.

Pritchard nodded. 'Among others. I presume everyone here's au fait with the situation in Nigeria?' He took some smart buff folders out of his briefcase and handed them round the table – the covers boasted the grand title 'THE NIGERIAN CIVIL WAR: A SUMMARY AND ASSESSMENT OF THE CONFLICT TO DATE'. 'This is a draft of a paper we'll be sending the Cabinet next week,' he said. 'I think you'll find we've covered a lot of ground.' Leafing through it, I could see he wasn't exaggerating: there was a section on the country's history, a detailed chronology of all the major events of the war so far, profiles of the leading personalities on both sides . . . I felt a pang of professional jealousy.

'I think you all know the basics,' Pritchard went on airily. 'But in case you've got sick of following it on the news, I'll quickly summarize the salient facts. Nigeria is our largest former colony. When it gained independence in '60, it was the great hope of Africa – a shining new democracy of thirty-five million people, with enormous potential both as a trading partner and as a political force for good in the continent. But independence was swiftly followed by chaos and violence. Pogroms against the Ibo tribe in the east eventually led to that region seceding from the rest of the country and renaming itself the Republic of Biafra. That sparked a civil war. So far, so Africa. From our point of view, however, it's been a complete mess, unfortunately compounded by our government's handling of the situation. We initially refused to take sides in the war, sitting resolutely on the fence. Then, in August '67, the Nigerians – "the Federal side" – took delivery of several Czech Delphin L-29 jet-fighters from Moscow. That sent us into a panic: nobody wants the Russians to be in control of one of Africa's largest nations once the war ends. As a result, we've now painted ourselves into a corner, and are effectively competing with Moscow to provide more and more arms to the Nigerians, in the hope of gaining favour with them after the war.'

'And what does Nigeria have to offer us?' asked Farraday innocently.

'Oil,' I said.

Pritchard flashed me a contemptuous look. 'You shouldn't believe everything you read in the papers, Paul.' It was a nice little dig – I was known for my contacts in Fleet Street. 'Contrary to public perception, the Biafrans never had *all* of Nigeria's oil.'

'They had rather a lot of it, though. Rather a lot of it that we would prefer remained in our hands. No?'

He leaned forward, glowering across the table. 'There's much more at stake here than oil. This is about the four hundred million pounds we've invested in the country – and the stability of the whole region. If Nigeria falls to Communism, the rest of the continent could follow.'

'The "domino" theory? I thought that was a Yank idea.'

He refused to be goaded. 'Even the Yanks are occasionally right.'

'And who are they supporting in this thing?' said Farraday. 'The Americans, I mean.'

Pritchard turned to him. 'Well, so far they've been officially neutral, but broadly on our side. They've left us pretty much alone, though – too busy trying to find ways out of Vietnam and beating the Russians to the moon. That may change now, though, as Nixon made a lot of noise about the Biafrans' plight during his election campaign. The Prime Minister has made much of the fact that he hasn't committed British troops in Vietnam, but the Americans aren't ecstatic about that arrangement and their good will may soon run dry. I don't think they are going to start supporting the Biafrans – yet. However, there are plenty of *other* powers already supporting them. France has been supplying them with arms through the Ivory Coast and Gabon in increasingly large quantities in the last few months. De Gaulle would like to protect francophone influence on the continent and sees the plight of "*les pauvres biafriens*" as a way to win back popularity after the mess of the student riots last year. He also wants access to Biafran oil, of course. Then there's

China, who are apparently lending the rebels their support simply to show up the Soviets as imperialist lapdogs for allying themselves with us and the Americans. It's hard to gauge what impact these skirmishes they're having with the Russians along their border might have, but it could mean that they step up their involvement in this conflict as well. Also supporting the Biafrans are the Israelis, who seem to believe that they're stopping the next Holocaust, and Haiti, who we have reports recognized the rebel regime this weekend — we're not quite sure what their reasons are. Finally, South Africa, Rhodesia and Portugal are all selling the rebels arms simply because they're happy to help one gang of wogs continue to butcher another.'

The room went quiet while everyone took this in.

'And the Biafrans, knowing all this, continue to buy arms from these parties?' Farraday asked.

'They have little choice.'

'Poor bastards.'

'Poor us, rather,' Pritchard replied. 'As a result of support from this motley crew, the Biafrans have managed to hang on by the skin of their teeth for nearly two years. We only agreed to supply arms to the Nigerians on the calculation that the whole affair would be over in a couple of *weeks*. The British public's disapproval of our involvement is now at an all-time high, partly because of "kwashiorkor". That's this disease the children get when they've not enough protein. It fills their stomachs with fluid — you'll have seen the footage, I expect. The Biafrans are now calling it "Harold Wilson Syndrome" and putting that on their death certificates, because they blame him in particular and the British government in general for not allowing enough food and aid through. We also have reports of the PM's name being used as a swear-word in Biafra.'

'Well, it's been that over here for a while!' said Quiney, eliciting a few quiet chuckles around the table.

Pritchard smiled. 'Yes, even his own party seems to be turning against him now. That's largely down to his stance on Biafra, and the pictures that are coming out of it. Liberal do-gooders don't seem so worried when the starving *look* like they're starving, but when they develop pot bellies it shocks them so much they feel compelled to organize jamborees and start marching on Trafalgar Square. Last week, *The Times* ran a series of articles claiming that the Nigerian pilots are deliberately bombing Biafran civilians. In response to increasing calls for him to resign, the PM announced he will fly out to Lagos this Thursday, supposedly to find out the facts of the war for himself and report back to Parliament.'

Of course. I'd seen it in the papers, but hadn't realized it was so soon. I asked if there was any ulterior motive to the trip, such as peace negotiations.

'Partly,' said Pritchard, 'although everyone's started playing that down in the last day or two. There was a similar plan last year for him to go out as a kind of super-mediator, but it was vetoed by the Nigerians, who are very touchy on the issue of outside interference. Ojukwu, the Biafrans' leader, has made it clear he will only meet Wilson within the borders he currently controls. Agreeing to that would enrage the Nigerians, though, because it would look like we were giving Biafra recognition – that's how the Biafrans would play it, anyway. Because of the pressure here, the government needs to be seen to be doing *something*, but our Nigerian sources say there's little expectation Wilson's visit will help matters beyond possibly improving the PR situation. But even that might backfire – he was going to go out there with some spades and agricultural tools until someone pointed out it might be reported he was smuggling in arms.'

'And the Biafrans?' said Farraday. 'What do our sources there tell us?'

'We don't have any reliable Biafran sources at the moment,' Pritchard replied, an edge to his voice. 'I visited Nigeria in December, and Lagos is still a little haphazard.' The colonial Stations had all been under Pritchard's control when he had been in Five, but they had been next to useless without the Service's input. Now they were finally under Service control, but it was clearly taking him longer than he liked to move things on.

'Are we informing the Prime Minister's office of the situation?' asked Godsal.

'No,' said Osborne. 'Nothing is to leave this room. That includes the PM's office, the FO, the Americans, and even our friends in Five.' He glanced at Pritchard. 'Especially our friends in Five. They might conclude that the PM is Radnya.'

Osborne had made a late play for the mantle of head jester. Some of the far right-wing officers in Five – a few of them Pritchard's cronies – had convinced themselves that Wilson was a Russian agent. I'd even asked Sasha about it. He wasn't. It was just another whispering campaign against him. The previous spring, there had even been rumours that Cecil King, owner of the *Daily Mirror*, had been plotting to overthrow the government with the support of Lord Mountbatten, Prince Philip's uncle. Nothing had come of it, of course.

Osborne waited for the tittering to die down before turning back to Pritchard. 'Isn't it a little convenient that a defector has turned up on the eve of this trip?'

'Slavin may be a plant, you mean?' Pritchard asked. I had asked Chief the same thing.

Osborne reached for the carafe in the centre of the table. Very deliberately, he poured some water into his glass, his eyes firmly on his task.

'It would be a pretty little trap,' he said coolly. 'Don't you think? Get us all running around for another traitor.'

Pritchard gave one of his soft smiles. 'But which is it, William? Either the Russians are so fiendishly clever that they've managed to keep one of their agents running in this organization for over twenty years or they're so fiendishly clever that they're sending us false defectors to claim that they have.'

Osborne sipped his water.

'Neither's an especially appetizing prospect,' Pritchard went on mercilessly, 'but considering that we have already discovered – at quite some cost – that we *were*, in fact, penetrated by the KGB, very successfully, it doesn't seem unreasonable to investigate the possibility that others remain in our ranks, undetected.'

'Hear, hear,' I said.

The two of them looked at me in surprise – my usual line, of course, was that it was divisive and paranoid to search for phantom Philbies among us.

'Look at the interview,' I said. 'If it's a ploy, it's not a very clever one. Slavin specifically states that Radnya was a British intelligence officer recruited in Germany at the end of the war. It can't be too hard to draw up a list of everyone we had involved in secret work in that area at that time. If we gave them all polygraph tests, we'd soon find out if Slavin's telling the truth.'

There was no response for a few seconds, and I wondered if I'd misjudged it. I got worried when Pritchard cleared his throat, but Osborne beat him to it.

'I'm not sure we're *quite* at the stage of deciding how to go about investigating this, Paul,' he said, blinking furiously as he pushed his spectacles up the bridge of his nose. He could usually rely on me to head off Pritchard's demands for more mole-hunts, so it was natural he'd be peeved. 'At any rate, I think it would, in fact, be rather difficult to draw up a list of everyone we had involved in intelligence in Germany in 1945. There were hundreds of people engaged on that sort of work. We also have no idea where the double is now – if he's become the Director-General of the BBC or Home Secretary, a request for a polygraph would need a lot of evidence to justify it.'

I nodded, conceding defeat, but he'd made the point I'd been angling for: there were hundreds of possible suspects.

'Can I just ask a silly question?' said Farraday, and everyone busied himself trying to look puzzled by such an idea. 'If this chap's not a plant and there really is another double, can someone give me a simple explanation as to why? I mean, why they want to betray us.

I can't really understand it – surely they read the news? How can they keep believing they're on the right side with tanks rolling into Prague and so on? Or did they all fall in love with Russian dolly-birds who turned them onto it?'

'Not all of them go for dolly-birds,' put in Pritchard archly. It was like *Hancock's Half Hour*.

'But seriously,' continued Farraday, turning to me, 'Paul, has your department done any sort of thinking about this, about what makes these people tick? Perhaps it will help us find this one – we could look at family backgrounds or what-have-you.'

They were looking at me intently so I took it they actually expected an answer. 'The only certain thing,' I said, after I had taken out a pack of Players and lit one, 'is that every double agent is different. The most common reasons for betraying one's country, as far as we can establish, are ideological conviction, disaffection with authority, pride – they get a perverse kick out of deceiving everyone around them – blackmail, and good old-fashioned pieces of silver.' I could have added a new one: hopeless credulity.

I took a drag of the cigarette. 'As to how a person can continue to serve a cause in the face of events that compromise its principles, which would appear to be the case with Philby and his friends, well, nothing's ever black and white, is it? After all, we all believe we're on the side of good, despite the fact that Henry has just given us a lot of information about how our government is contributing to the deaths of thousands of innocent people in a war in Africa because we don't want anyone else to get their hands on the oil there.' I put up a hand to stop Pritchard from interrupting. 'I know, it's not just about oil, and I'm simplifying, but hopefully you can still see my point. If you happen to think we're doing the wrong thing in Biafra – and most people in the country do – it doesn't mean you're suddenly going to abandon everything else you believe to be good about the way we do things and start working for the Russians.'

'But the Russians are supplying arms, too,' said Farraday, and a couple of others nodded.

'All right,' I said with a sigh. 'Bad example. Suez. Kenya. Aden. Take your pick of situations we've made a mess of one way or another in the last couple of decades. How do we continue to do our jobs in the face of this knowledge? We look at the wider picture, of course. I imagine it works much the same for the other side. And from what we know of the KGB's methods, I doubt it's all that easy to supply them with secret material for years and then one day announce an attack of conscience and ask if you can swap sides again, without them getting rather peeved, and perhaps sending a man with a silencer after you. The longer in, I suspect, the harder it would be to extricate oneself. And this chap seems to have been in for rather a long time.'

I paused. How could I possibly explain to these people, even in abstract terms, the ups and downs of my journey with Communism, from my tentative steps with Anna to my convert's zeal after her death – or staged death, as it now appeared – through to agonizing doubts and resulting confrontations with Yuri, and later Sasha, over everything from documents I didn't want to hand over to, yes, tanks rolling into Prague. I decided I couldn't, so I concentrated on my cigarette and waited to see if they had any more idiotic questions. But they didn't – they all seemed to have gone rather quiet.

'Thank you, Paul,' said Osborne. 'Most illuminating, and some food for thought for us all. I'm not sure what it is you think we did wrong in Kenya, exactly, but perhaps that's for another day.' He gave a slight nod to Farraday to indicate he was closing the issue. 'Perhaps you can tell us more about this woman who seems to be involved – Grigorieva? Do you have anything on her?'

'Actually,' I said, 'there is something.' I took my briefcase from the floor and placed it on the table. 'I had a look around Registry this morning and found this in "Germany 1945". I think it confirms that Slavin is very unlikely to be a plant.'

I'd read all of Father's files several times – I'd had to, for cover.

But Sacrosanct had been off the books, so they hadn't contained anything about that. I hadn't known he had asked Chief to take Anna into custody, though, or that Chief had written a report about the incident. Along with his other military records, it had been carried over to his Service file, and once I'd found the relevant bundle it had been easy to locate. I sprang the briefcase open, took out the photostats I'd made and passed them round.

'As you can see, this is extracted from the monthly reports that Chief wrote in September 1945, when he was head of the British army headquarters in Lübeck in Germany. If you turn to the top of the third page' – I waited for people to do so – 'you'll see the entry headed "Anna Maleva". Chief – or Brigadier Colin Templeton, as he then was – relates how he had been tipped off by SOE officer Lawrence Dark – my father – that Maleva, a nurse in the Red Cross hospital in Lübeck, was in fact a KGB agent. Chief took a small team to her quarters to detain her on the night of the 28th, but when they arrived she was dead, shot through the chest.'

A police car raced through the street below, its siren blaring, and I let it pass before continuing.

'Now, if you turn to page four of the dossier, you will find a photograph of Maleva, given to Chief by Major Dark for the purposes of identification. The photostat hasn't come out too well, so let's look at the original.' I walked over to the projector and placed it in the slot. I dimmed the lights, and the picture appeared on the wall.

The photograph had not aged well in the file. The edges were turning brown, and there were black spots across her forehead and her eyes. It had been taken outside the hospital: she was in her uniform, smoking a cigarette. I had naively thought that Father had simply abandoned me, but he had been keeping an eye on the hospital all along.

I pressed the lever to turn back, and the picture of Anna in Lagos filled the wall again. I flicked it forward and back a couple of times and then stopped. 'As you can see, it would appear that Maleva was not, in fact, killed in 1945, but is currently working in the Soviet Embassy in Lagos under the name Grigorieva.'

There was silence for a few moments. In my peripheral vision, I could see that Pritchard had his head down and was reading the file. I was taking a huge risk bringing this to the table, because I was revealing a direct link between Slavin's allegations and my father's work in Germany. As Pritchard knew what that work had been, and that I had been involved in it, he would naturally now suspect me. But there were no records on that operation – he could suspect me all he wanted, but if he couldn't prove it I didn't care. And I was fairly confident that he wouldn't be overly keen to confess to his part in an assassination squad, even after all these years.

'She was quite a looker, wasn't she?' Godsal was saying. 'The mouth's a touch thin, but still . . . she'd probably have got me to sign the Five Year Plan.' Nobody laughed. Godsal, I should note, has a face like a deranged horse.

'What would the Russians have had to gain by faking her death?' asked Farraday.

'I don't know,' I said. 'Perhaps Chief will be able to tell us more about the situation when he gets here.'

As if on cue, there was a knock on the door. All eyes swivelled as Smale entered.

'Well?' said Osborne.

'No sign of him,' said Smale: he must have been wondering why everyone in the room was staring at him so intently. Osborne nodded for him to carry on. 'Barnes went over and called me back. Says he seems to have packed his bags and left in the middle of the night. Didn't cancel his milk or papers.'

'Packed his bags?' asked Pritchard, his voice rising. 'Are you sure of that?'

'Well, it *looks* that way,' Smale backtracked. 'He said there appeared to be some clothes missing. Jackets, suits, that sort of—'

'What about his car?'

'That's still there. But the railway station's a ten-minute walk, with trains to London every hour.'

'Did Barnes talk to him last night?' asked Osborne.

'Yes — he made his final call at half past seven and says Chief answered as usual, with nothing to report. He was just getting ready to go over for his morning pass-by when I rang.'

Osborne harrumphed. 'Well, if Chief doesn't see sense now and let the chap have the spare bedroom, I don't know what we do. This system clearly doesn't work.' He turned back to Smale. 'What about neighbours? Has Barnes had a chance to ask around yet?'

'Most people are at work. But he said one local claims to have heard a car around nine last night.'

'What time did you leave, again?' I asked Pritchard.

'Around then,' he said, meeting my gaze. Yes, he suspected me, all right.

Osborne took his glasses off, decided they were dirty, and rubbed them on his tie, smudging them even more. He nodded at Smale, who scurried over to the trolley and put the kettle on.

Farraday was looking at Osborne. 'Chief received the Slavin dossier as soon as it arrived?' he asked.

Osborne glanced up, red indents from his frames on either side of his nose. 'Yes — he was sent it yesterday morning. Why?'

'Well, because within twenty-four hours of receiving it, he's disappeared, that's why!' said Farraday.

I asked him what he was implying.

'Oh, I'm sorry, Paul,' he said, turning to me. 'I know you're close to the old man. But there *is* a link with this Grigorieva–Maleva — you've just told us so yourself. Mighty suspicious, isn't it?'

'I'm sure there's a simple explanation,' I said.

But Farraday was on a roll. 'What could that be, though?' he pressed. 'According to this file you've dug up, which Chief himself wrote,' — he stabbed a long finger at the initials at the top of the page — 'she died in 1945. Either he's lying or the dame in the photo ain't her.' His attempt at hard-boiled American vernacular was painful, and thankfully he dropped it at once. 'But it does look rather a lot like it *is* her, doesn't it?'

The kettle whistled and everyone suddenly busied himself with passing cups and saucers around. Chief's empty chair suddenly looked very bare.

'I don't believe it,' said Godsal. 'It's unthinkable! I mean . . . I mean . . .' He searched for a way to get it across. 'We're talking about *Chief*, for God's sake!'

'The same Chief,' said Farraday, 'who conspicuously failed to catch Philby and fluffed the Cairncross business. And like them and the rest of the rotten bunch, he's a Cambridge man.'

Pritchard smiled at him generously. 'So's half the Service, John.'

'I'm not,' said Farraday. 'I was at Oxford. You were, too, weren't you, Paul?' I nodded. 'And you, William?'

Osborne pushed his glasses onto his nose prissily. 'Manchester. Look, we don't know where Chief is at the moment. But I don't think we can jump to the conclusion that he's a double agent simply because he's missed our regular Monday meeting.'

'I'm not concluding anything,' said Farraday. 'But surely we would all agree that no one – not even Chief – can be above suspicion in a case like this. That, after all, is how traitors survive.'

Osborne drummed his fingers against his glass, and we all watched him. 'With all due respect,' he said, finally, 'I've known Chief for a great many years and he has never given me a moment to doubt his integrity or patriotism. If the man has been acting, he's the best bloody double that ever existed.'

He'd meant it to be a throwaway comment, but as the silence stretched out, it took on an unintended resonance, and he began twiddling his thumbs.

'As I see it,' said Farraday, splaying his fingers out on the table as though he were about to start playing a piano concerto, 'there are only two options. Either Slavin's a KGB plant designed to get us running around for a traitor who doesn't exist or he's real and the traitor *does* exist. Chief has seemingly disappeared, and Paul has found the file on this woman who he says was killed but apparently wasn't, and whom Slavin just happens to mention as his source for the entire house of cards. Now if—'

'If I could just stop you there,' Osborne cut in, and his usual Billy Bunter tone had been replaced by overt aggression. 'I must insist that we wait for Chief to be present before we start flinging accusations around.'

'As you wish,' said Farraday. 'But this may be the last chance we have for an open discussion on this. Once Chief gets here — presuming he hasn't done a flit to Moscow — any such talk will be next to impossible on account of his position.'

'Nobody seems to have taken his position into much consideration,' said Pritchard. 'It's surely far more likely that the Russians or someone else have taken advantage of his abysmal security set-up and snatched him. I would suggest we give Barnes some support to search the area properly, and put out an alert to all ports just in case.'

'Should we circulate the names of Chief's known aliases?' asked Quiney. 'Or is that too delicate?'

'Far too delicate,' said Osborne, before Farraday could open his mouth.

'Perhaps your Section could look into the Slavin dossier,' Pritchard said to Quiney. 'See if your contacts in Germany can get a list of all the patients admitted to this Red Cross hospital in 1945.' He was talking to Quiney, but he was looking at me.

'Yes,' I said, meeting his gaze. 'Good idea. Perhaps you could also collate all the files of British military operations in the area at the time. I seem to remember there was some sort of a base in Gaggenau.'

Pritchard's mouth locked tight. I'd put forward a way of implicating him, but it was precisely what the other version of me, the patriotic British agent who had never gone near any Russian nurses, would have done. I'd have suspected Pritchard for the same reason he now suspected me: I knew he had been in the British Zone in '45.

'I'll do my best,' said Quiney. 'Though I can't imagine many of those records have been kept.' Good old Quiney – you could always rely on him not to do anything in a pinch.

'I would like to go out to Lagos and interview Slavin,' I said. 'It's been five days since he approached us, so time is of the essence – his colleagues could realize he's thinking of defecting at any moment and then we'd have lost any chance to find out what's really going on here. Henry has already as much as admitted that Lagos Station isn't up to the job, and I have a personal interest in making sure a thorough job is done. This operation of my father's occurred after he was last seen in London, so it obviously could provide an explanation for whatever happened to him.' I avoided looking at Pritchard, because he knew I was lying at this point.

'Perhaps Chief killed him,' murmured Farraday, at which Osborne's eyes nearly popped out of his head.

'*Killed* him?' he said. 'Please, John, let's try to keep the discussion sane. Chief's hardly a killer.'

'You have a point,' Farraday replied, nudging the photostat forward on the table. 'He last didn't kill someone twenty-four years ago, to be precise.'

Another silence descended, and people started shifting in their seats. This was a new side to Farraday, and no one knew what might be coming next.

'Paul has made an interesting proposal,' said Pritchard, in that fastidious tone of his. 'But let's consider it. I agree that Lagos Station isn't capable of dealing with something of this importance, and that it's vital someone go out there at once to do so. Because, of course, if the traitor's not Chief, then the real Radnya may be among us.' He paused to let that sink in, and then continued. 'But while I'm sure we all sympathize with your desire to discover the true cause of your father's disappearance,' – he looked into my eyes at this point, and I tried not to react – 'I'm not sure a matter of this magnitude should be influenced by individual officers' personal concerns — however troubling they may be.' He dropped a sugar cube into his tea and dipped his spoon in to stir it.

'Chief's an old friend of the family,' I said. 'If he's a traitor, or involved in my father's disappearance, I bloody well want to know.'

'We all want to know,' said Pritchard. 'But have you ever even been to Nigeria? Or Africa at all, for that matter? It's not quite *la dolce vita*, you know.'

It was another crack: my last posting had been in Rome. I didn't rise to it, just asked him if he had any experience of handling Soviet defectors. 'You don't even speak Russian,' I pointed out.

He laughed it off. 'There are people in Lagos who can translate,' he said. 'Someone translated Slavin's interview, didn't they?'

Not very well, I wanted to tell him. But I didn't have the chance to formulate another response, because there was a cough from the head of the table. It was Farraday.

'Gentlemen,' he said. 'Let us not bicker, please. I have come to my decision.' Osborne started turning puce and made to interrupt. Farraday shushed him and smiled, pleased that he was exerting control and, finally, rather enjoying this espionage business. 'Paul,' he said, 'you and Chief are very close — not just as colleagues but as friends. So I understand that this is something near to you. Believe me. And I quite see how the matter of your father's disappearance is something you would want to clear up.' He leaned back in his chair and spoke to a point on the ceiling, just left of the ventilator shaft. 'But I agree with Henry: I think it's probably best if he deals with this one.'

Then his head dropped down again and he smiled innocently at Smale. 'Any chance of putting some more water on?'

*

My office was cold and cramped. I turned the radiators on full blast and lit a cigarette.

Not good news. Not good news at all. I began pacing the carpeted cell. After several dozen crossings and two Players, I came to a conclusion: I'd have to go it alone — without back-up, without sanction, and probably with Pritchard in the same field.

The first thing to do was to write a note: something for them to get their teeth into, something that would appeal to their *Boy's Own* view of the world. When I'd prepared a few suitably indignant lines, I dug out the Service's Operations Manual from a drawer and looked up which vaccines and certificates were needed for Nigeria. These turned out to be yellow fever and smallpox, so I took out the forms and spent the next ten minutes carefully filling them in, making sure the dates were well within the prescribed time. Nigeria being a former British colony, no visas were needed. Then I placed two calls: one to a travel agent in Holborn, and the second to a number in Fleet Street, where I asked to be put through to someone in the newsroom.

'Dobson,' he answered. He sounded tired and a little angry. Not especially propitious.

'Joe!' I said, putting all the chumminess I could muster into my voice. 'It's Paul. Paul Dark.'

'Paul, me old china!' he said, more jovially. He liked to play up the old cockney wag act, even though his father was a barrister in St John's Wood. 'Long time, no hear. Got a scoop for me?'

It was a joke, of sorts — I wasn't a journalist, and he was reminding me of the absurd nature of our relationship — but at the same time he was being serious. He wanted to know if I did, indeed, have a scoop.

'I can get you one,' I said, 'if you return a favour.'

He laughed. 'You owe *me* a few, don't you, mate?' After a moment or two, he bit: 'All right. What can you get me, and what's the favour?'

'Something big is about to happen in Nigeria,' I said. 'I need to be there.'

'Nigeria? Since when was that your field? You been shifted to the Africa desk and not told me?'

'No, nothing like that,' I said. 'I just need accreditation – that's all.'

'Paul, old son, you do know there's a civil war on there?' I said I did, and he harrumphed. 'We've got three stringers out there already. I don't see how I could justify another. It's not like BOAC will just fly you into the jungle . . .'

'I don't want to fly into the jungle. I want to fly to Lagos.'

I listened to the sound of prolonged wheezing. 'Nice try, but April Fool's ain't 'til next week. There's bugger all fighting in Lagos – even I know that much.'

'Yes, but that's where the story is. Trust me.'

He laughed again. 'The PM's visit, you mean? Nobody's flogging that one. Unless you can give me a clue—'

'I've got everything else,' I said, trying to keep the desperation from my voice. 'I just need you to have me listed with the Nigerians that I'm one of yours – in case nobody buys my press pass, you see.'

'Robert Kane?'

It was the pseudonym we'd used for several stories I had sent his way. I'd had the documents made up months ago, as I did for all my cover names – now I was going to have to bring 'Kane' to life.

A sudden noise erupted in the background – the grinding of a machine. 'Hang on a tick,' said Dobson. The line went quiet and I chewed my nails. Outside my door, the secretaries chatted about boyfriends and pop stars' weddings, and further down the corridor Pritchard was in a briefing room, quietly going about making arrangements that might see the end of my days.

'Sorry about that,' said Dobson when he came back on the line. 'Bit of a balls-up on the press.' He took a deep breath, and I took it with him. 'All right, mate, I'll give it a go. For old times, as they say.' It was good of him – we didn't have any old times to speak of, unless you counted a few furtive meetings in the back room of the City Golf Club. I wanted to kiss him. 'All being well, I should be able to have you on the list by the end of the week.'

The kiss could wait.

'Can't you make it sooner?'

'Bloody hell!' he laughed. 'Give you lot an inch, you want a flipping hectare. Come on, then – let me have it. When were you planning on getting into Lagos?'

'Tonight,' I said.

V

Monday, 24 March 1969, Lagos, Nigeria

The heat hit me as soon I stepped onto the ladder – it was like someone throwing one of the airline's hot towels over my face. I walked towards the terminal building, shimmering in the evening haze. Along the tarmac, a large group of soldiers was silently unloading crates of ammunition.

Twelve hours previously I had rushed home to the flat to collect the Kane passport from the safe and then taken a cab to Heathrow – only for the flight to be delayed. My frustration had been slightly mollified by discovering the latest issue of *Newsweek* at a stand in the departure hall. As well as the dozen or so pages covering the trials of the Robert Kennedy and Martin Luther King assassins, there was an in-depth article on the civil war in Nigeria, including an interview with Ojukwu, the Biafrans' commander-in-chief. I read through it and Pritchard's briefing dossier over a cocktail in the airport bar. After committing as much of both documents to memory as I could, I went to the lavatory and spent ten minutes tearing the dossier to shreds and feeding it into the bowl.

The flight itself had been calm, and I had managed to sleep after we had refuelled in Rome. It was now 22.00 local time – the same as in London. But even if Pritchard moved very fast, he wouldn't be able to arrive until tomorrow morning at the earliest. My departure would almost certainly have prompted another meeting, which would mean more tea and banter until they reached a decision on how to proceed. He would already be inoculated against yellow fever and smallpox, so he wouldn't need to forge the documents as I'd done, but he would still have to complete his B-200, get it stamped and cleared – another meeting to debate what the procedure for that was in the absence of Chief and before the acting Chief had had his position confirmed – and then have his diplomatic cover arranged, flight booked by the secretariat, and so on. My flight was the last to arrive tonight, so I reckoned I had at least until dawn to try to swing things in my favour.

Before anything else, I had to get to Slavin and find out what more he knew, and how he knew it. The obvious move would be to track him down as soon as I got out of the airport, and kill him. But murder was a last resort: his death or disappearance would automatically bring me under suspicion with London, as I had run out here without asking their permission. There was also the question of Anna – I wanted to find her, too, and that would be much harder if Pritchard were actively hunting my hide.

The arrivals terminal was heavy with sweat and frustration. A solitary fan turned high above us at an agonizing pace, while passengers stood around an unmanned desk waiting for their luggage to be brought from the plane. Thankfully, I just had my one bag, so I walked straight through to the passport control area.

There it was even worse. The queues were enormous, interlocking and unmoving. I picked one of the lines at random and joined it. As on the plane, there were a handful of white people – aid workers and diplomats, I guessed – but the rest were Nigerian. All around me, conversations were being held, sometimes in local dialects but mainly in pidgin English, which Pritchard's dossier had told me was the lingua franca. I spent a few minutes tuning in, managing to pick out words here and there, accustoming myself to the tones in which it was used. It seemed an exuberant, rich language, a world away from the Pritchards and Osbornes of the world. The clothing was a mixture of African and Western, but there was exuberance in that, too. Businessmen in Western-style suits clutched important-looking briefcases, while matronly women in multi-coloured loose-fitting dresses sported thin Cartier watches. Soldiers wandered between the lines, looking over passengers and prodding their rifles into bags. They were young and arrogant, and just the look of them brought the reality of the situation home more than the endless statistics and prolix phrases of Pritchard's report. Something about them chilled the bones.

They seemed just as interested in me. Within less than ten minutes of my entering the hall, a pattern of surveillance had closed in around me: two by the gates, one by the toilets, and a small, neat-looking man in a beret operating them with nods from next to the telephones. There was nothing I could do about it. I was a journalist, and any move I made would only make things worse. They had probably marked me out because I was a white man they didn't recognize – the aid workers they would know. It was normal. Relax.

It was getting on eleven by the time I made it to the front of the queue. The clerk had a long, narrow face and thick glasses. Behind him was draped the country's flag – vertical strips of green, white and green. He picked up my passport and started to leaf through it slowly. I wasn't worried – the document had been made in precisely the same way as if it had been genuine. He stopped at the back page.

'Press?' he said.

'Yes.'

He looked troubled at this. He leaned down and took some papers from a drawer, then placed them in front of him and started reading, tracing the miniature lines of text with a finger. I had a mounting sense of unease. Had Dobson let me down? Surely my accreditation had come through?

The clerk suddenly glanced up at me, a pained expression on his face.

'What's wrong?' I asked. 'What's the—'

He was looking behind me. I turned. There were four of them. Quite a party. Broad chests and muscle visible under their uniforms, and patterns of scars down their cheeks. It was no use struggling – there'd be more of them elsewhere in the building, and I wouldn't have a hope. They'd shoot me in the leg, or send a car to get me. And then I'd have a real job explaining my behaviour.

'You come this way,' one of them said, and pushed a rifle into my back.

Do nothing. They just want money, beer, cigarettes. Pay them, get out of here and get to work.

Do nothing.

*

They took me down a narrow, unlit staircase and shoved me into a sparse, harshly lit room.

'Wait here.'

They slammed the door and I listened to their footsteps recede. I looked around the room: it contained two hard-backed chairs, a low table and some brochures advertising the International Year of African Tourism.

After ten minutes spent reading the brochures, the door opened and the small man in the beret walked in, followed by several of his men. His uniform was immaculate, his beret trimmed with a gold braid. In one hand, he gripped a riding crop.

'Good evening,' he said. 'I am Colonel Bernard Alebayo of the Third Marine Commando Division. Who are you?'

I took out my passport and offered it to him. He took it, but didn't open it. 'Your full name, please.'

'Robert David Peter Kane,' I said.

'That is more like it. Thank you. Cooperate with me and we will get along.' He smiled genially. He looked very young. 'Are you in Nigeria for business or pleasure?'

I examined his face. He appeared to be serious.

'Business,' I said.

'And what is your profession, Mister Kane?'

'If you look at my passport—'

'I am not interested in your passport at this particular moment,' he said, smiling sweetly again. 'I want to hear it from the horse's mouth, as it were.' He spoke English quickly and precisely, accentuating each word in an almost sing-song fashion.

I'd known who he was before he introduced himself: he'd been all over Pritchard's dossier. Alebayo, 'The Panther', was the Nigerian army's most famous commander. Trained at Sandhurst – like most of the military leaders on both sides of this war – he had a reputation for brutality and unpredictability. He was known to despise do-gooders, politicians and journalists.

'I'm a journalist,' I said.

He stroked his chin.

'For which newspaper?'

I told him.

'Ah,' he said. 'The famous *Times* of London.' He walked around the table, his boots squeaking. 'Of course, we have our own *Times* here.' He swivelled and faced me. 'Not perhaps as large a publication, or as renowned globally, but, nevertheless, quite respectable on a national level.' He looked down at his reflection in his boots for a moment. 'Yes, quite respectable.'

I murmured interest as best I could, and wondered where on earth this was heading.

Alebayo opened my passport, held it away from him as though it were contaminated, and squinted at my photograph.

'Do you know Mister Winston Churchill?' he asked, suddenly.

'My colleague, or his grandfather?'

'Are your articles as facetious as your speech, Mister Kane? Your colleague.'

'Yes,' I said, 'I know him. I wouldn't say we were friends—'

'Well, then,' he interrupted, 'as your newspaper has sent you to "cover" events here, you have presumably been "boning up" on what Mister Churchill has already written about this country in your newspaper? Yes?'

'Of course.' It had been Churchill who had alleged that the

Federal pilots were targeting Biafra's civilian population. His articles had caused such an outcry that Parliament had held another emergency debate on the war – the same debate in which Wilson had announced his trip.

'Your colleague appears to believe we are savages, Mister Kane,' said Alebayo. 'Cold-blooded killers, devoid of any moral sense.'

He suddenly held back his head and laughed, and his soldiers joined in, until he whipped the table with his crop, and the laughter abruptly stopped. It was like a very bad opera production.

'Can you imagine it, Mister Kane? The cheek of the grandson of Winston Churchill to write such a thing! Has he forgotten Dresden?'

'I don't know,' I said. 'You'll have to ask him.' The analogy didn't seem fair, somehow, but I wasn't going to get into it.

He leaned in again. 'Do you intend to file the same species of report as your colleague?'

'I don't think so,' I said. 'Lagos is four hundred miles from the fighting.'

'Quite so,' he said. 'You are a sharp one, my friend.' He was pacing around, confusing the flies buzzing about his face. 'So what will you be writing about? Expatriate dinner parties? Our local cuisine? What are your editor's orders?'

'Colour stories,' I said.

He bristled. 'I am so sorry, I didn't quite hear. Could you please repeat yourself?'

I reminded myself to choose my words rather more carefully. 'A picture of life in the capital of a country at war. What the feeling is in the corridors of power, how negotiations are going, that sort of—'

'Are those what you call "colour stories"?' he said.

I nodded.

'I could tell you a few others. But perhaps your readership wouldn't be interested in hearing the reverse side of the coin.'

'We're interested in the truth,' I said, and he laughed again.

'Let me be honest with you, Mister Kane. I do not like journalists. In fact, more often than not, I find them repellent – vultures circling around others' misery, looking for something to misconstrue.' He said the word beautifully, savouring its syllables. He was watching me very keenly. 'Are you certain you are a journalist? You don't look much like one.'

'What do I look like?' I asked.

'I'm not sure.' He used one hand to squeeze my right bicep through my shirt. 'But this arm has lifted more than a Parker pen in its time, I think. Perhaps you are a mercenary? I could use a few decent mercenaries at this particular moment. Were you ever in the army, Mister Kane?'

'Where's this going?' I said, cranking up my indignant civilian act. 'I demand to see someone from the British—'

'Were you ever in the *army*, Mister Kane?'

'Yes,' I said. 'A long time ago. But, look, I'm an accredited member of the press, I have all the necessary visas – why am I being detained?'

'Because I don't like the look of you,' he said. 'Your newspaper already has several correspondents in Nigeria, and I find it hard to believe it would suddenly have a need for "colour stories" hundreds of miles away from where anything of real colour is happening. So I want to know more.' He leaned in to look at me, his nostrils flaring.

'The British prime minister is visiting,' I said. 'On Thursday. I'm to report on that, too.'

'Ah, yes,' he said. 'Of course. Our dear and esteemed Mister Harold Wilson. I had heard mention of that. How fortunate for us all that he has decided to pay a visit. How newsworthy.' He tilted his head and looked at me as though I were a Picasso he suspected had been hung upside down. 'Do you know what the rebels call your prime minister, Mister Kane?'

'No,' I said, wearily. I was losing so much time it didn't bear thinking about.

'"Herod",' he said, grinning. 'Or sometimes "Herod Weasel".' He walked behind my back now, his heels clicking loudly. 'You maintain you are a journalist!' he suddenly shouted into my ear, making me jump. 'And yet your press accreditation only came through *tonight*. Please explain, Mister Kane!' He whipped the crop against the desk again, almost as though he felt he had to.

So that was it. I hadn't thought they'd be quite so hot on it.

'A colleague at the front was due to cover the trip,' I said, as calmly as I could. 'He cabled yesterday to say he was ill and wouldn't be able to make it back to Lagos in time, so my editor decided to send me out on the first available flight instead. That's why I've only just been accredited.'

Alebayo was silent for a moment.

'Are you perhaps a spy, Mister Kane?' he said, quietly.

I looked up at him. 'A spy?'

'Yes. A secret agent like your Double Oh Seven, saving the world from villains and foes . . . Amusing that you British have taken so long to realize that you no longer have an empire.'

'Isn't this approach unwise?' I said. 'My readers will be most interested to know how the Federal army treats the citizens of valued allies.'

'I think *I* will decide what is wise here – not you. There have been plenty of misleading reports about me in your newspapers already. I cannot imagine another will do any further harm. That is, if you ever succeed in filing a report on this little meeting.' He turned to the largest of his thugs. 'Is the transport ready?' The thug nodded. 'Good.' He turned back to me. 'Perhaps a visit to one of our prisons would provide some good material for your editor? Some "colour"?'

'This is outrageous!' I said, and now my indignation was only half-acted. 'Call my office in London! Call the British High Commission! I demand—'

'Please, Mister Kane, save your tantrums. They will not do you any good here.' He stood a little straighter and adjusted his beret. 'I must now return to Port Harcourt, where I have many things to attend to. There is the small matter of a war to win. But you will be well looked after by my boys here, I promise. And they may even discover what it is you came here for . . .'

There was a sudden banging at the door, and Alebayo glanced sharply in its direction. He nodded at one of the thugs, who walked over and opened it. Framed in the light was a large white man with a crumpled red face, wearing what looked to be a pair of pyjamas.

'Let this man go, Bernard!' he said in a booming English voice.

*

'Geoffrey!' said Alebayo through gritted teeth. 'How delightful to see you again.' He strode over to the door and gestured him outside.

The thugs eyed me warily – they were anxious for the order to tear me to pieces. I didn't much fancy my chances with them.

'Just follow your orders,' I told them. 'And we'll all be fine.'

They glared at me, and I wondered if I shouldn't try to make a run for it, after all. Then the door opened again and Alebayo shouted something at the thugs. They leapt up and ran out after him.

I looked in astonishment at the empty room. After about thirty seconds, I stood up myself, picking up my bag from the floor. At the door, I met the man with the red face. A hand was thrust out from a striped cotton sleeve.

'I'm Geoffrey Manning,' he said. 'Welcome to Lagos.'

VI

As we stepped out of the airport, a mob of taxi drivers swarmed around us.

'Where you go, mister?'

'I offer you best price!'

Manning waved them away and steered us to a blue Peugeot on the other side of the road.

'Did you catch the rugby on Saturday?' he asked as he unlocked his door. 'The Welsh seemed on good form.'

I climbed into the passenger seat. 'I missed that,' I said. 'Do they show the matches out here, then?'

'If only, old chap, if only. I caught the report on the World Service. Who's your money on to win the whole thing?'

'I haven't really followed it, I'm afraid.'

He grunted and locked his door, gesturing for me to do the same. When I had, he said: 'You're Larry Dark's boy, aren't you?'

I nodded.

'Fine fellow, your father. Never met him myself, but saw him break the land speed record in '38. Extraordinary day – were you there?'

I shook my head dully.

'Damn fine fellow.' He placed his key in the ignition and started her up. 'Anyway, glad you made it. Imagine you'll be wanting to get that suit off in this heat.'

He gestured at the back seat, on which an outfit identical to the one he was wearing lay folded.

'Pyjama party at the Yacht Club – any excuse for a booze-up.'

I told him I was fine as I was.

We turned onto the main road and he swore under his breath. 'Not our night. Bad go-slow.' He caught my look. 'Traffic jam in the local argot. Marjorie will be furious – she was expecting me hours ago.'

'Marjorie?'

'The wife. Super girl. Don't deserve her, really. Fine stock – Scottish blue blood, you know. Stuck with me through thick and thin.' He mimed swigging a glass and winked conspiratorially at me.

Pritchard had said things were a little haphazard, but I hadn't imagined they'd be this dire. I'd seen plenty of Manning's type before. He was a spook of the old school: stockbroker parents, minor public school, army, Colonial Service. Most of them had been swept away in '66 when the Service had taken over responsibility for the colonies from Five, but Manning had evidently managed to hold on.

I wound down the window and looked out. There was indeed a go-slow. The street was a mass of cars, trucks, motorcycles and bikes, the drivers of which were all either tooting their horns or yelling at the drivers around them. Many of the vehicles looked on the verge of collapse, either because they were overloaded with passengers and luggage or were missing vital parts: windows, wing mirrors, bumpers . . . The Opel Kapitän alongside us was short a door on the passenger side. Looming over the scene was an enormous billboard with a picture of a tyre: 'GO BY DUNLOP – THEY LAST LONGEST!' It seemed a little like trying to sell sticking plasters on a battlefield.

As Manning searched for an opening in the traffic, I considered once again his presence at the airport. I prided myself on my ability to think several steps ahead, but it had taken me totally unawares – I hadn't imagined my colleagues would be anxious enough to want me on a leash for just one night.

'When did London cable to say I was on my way?' I asked.

Manning glanced across at me. 'About half seven. I was just changing when the office called.'

Half seven. That was fast — it usually took them a month to agree to buy a lightbulb.

'I told the driver to take the night off and drove straight out here,' Manning was saying. 'Your flight came in, but there was no sign of you. Then I spotted a soldier standing guard outside one of the doors leading to the dungeons. Thought I'd better take a look-see.'

I told him I was glad he had; he waved my gratitude away. 'That's my job. Can't have our people thrown in the stocks the moment they arrive in the country! Especially not Larry Dark's boy. Not on my watch. You were unlucky — Bernard's only in town for a couple of hours. Well, I say unlucky. Depends on how you look at it, of course. A few months back a chap from the *Telegraph* thought it was a good idea to disagree with him. Bernard had the fellow's head shaved, got him to do press-ups for an hour, and then forced him to write out the words "I am a crappy Englishman and have no say in Nigeria" a thousand times.'

He roared with laughter at this, yanking the car into an opening in the traffic as he did so. '"*I am a crappy Englishman and have no say in Nigeria!*"' he bellowed out of the window at a startled motorcyclist, who nearly swerved into the drain as a result. 'Bernard was always a damn fool,' he continued calmly once we were safely ensconced in a line just as slow-moving as the one we'd left. 'Even at Sandhurst. That's where I first met him, of course, many moons ago. I was an instructor there. Know quite a few of the commanders in this war from those days, as it happens.'

'What's he doing in Lagos? I thought his division was miles away.'

'Yes, he's over at Port Harcourt. I asked him the same question myself, and he said he was picking up troops and supplies. Apparently he can't trust the other divisions not to steal his stuff unless he comes up and supervises things personally. Typically African way to run a war.'

I remembered the soldiers I'd seen on the tarmac. 'What's he up to? Preparing for the final push?'

Manning snorted. 'There's been a final push every blasted month of this war. They're calling this latest one the *final* final push – but nobody believes it.'

The traffic was at a complete standstill now, and it looked like we might be in for a long wait: Manning said it could sometimes take hours to clear. I took out my Players and watched as a mangy dog with great gaps of fur and a missing leg wandered up between the lanes of cars. Despite its limp, it had a strangely proud demeanour – almost as though it knew it would reach the centre of Lagos before us.

'What else did London say?' I asked Manning.

'Not much,' he replied, somewhat blithely. 'That Chief's gone missing. Reading between the lines, there's a flap on that he may have something to do with the double agent this Russian johnnie has told us about, and you've flown the nest to prove them wrong. Am I right?'

'Close enough,' I said. 'Did London mention when Pritchard would be arriving?'

'No, just to expect him soon. Good chap, Henry. Came out here a few months ago. Thrashed me at golf. Beautiful swing.'

'What were your instructions?'

'What? Oh. To pick you up at the airport, then provide you with any assistance you required.'

'I need to arrange accommodation,' I said. If they were going to assign me a nanny, I might as well make use of him.

'Of course. I'd have done it already, only nobody was sure what cover you'd be using.'

'Robert Kane. *Times* hack covering the Wilson visit.'

'Yes – so I gathered from Bernard. Well, we can check you in somewhere now if you'd like. Any preferences?'

'What's the best-known hotel?' I asked, and Manning glanced over at me. Most agents would have wanted somewhere discreet, but I wanted to make my presence felt in the city, fast.

'The Victoria Palace,' he said. 'It's the closest Lagos gets to the Ritz. Not that it's particularly close . . .'

I knew the name. Pritchard's dossier had mentioned it a couple of times, notably because an Ibo had tried to blow it up in advance of a peace conference a few years earlier. That it was enough of a landmark to be a target meant it was precisely the kind of place I was looking for.

'I'll drop you there,' said Manning. 'If this traffic ever gets going, that is. Oh, and before I forget . . .' He plunged a hand inside the pocket of his pyjama jacket and fished out a small package, which he passed over to me. 'You'll also need these.'

I opened the box and took out a dozen white tablets sandwiched between some cellophane.

'Paludrine. Anti-malaria. Take them once a day. It's all there in the instructions: "Best absorbed with evening G and T".' He had another chuckle, and I began to wonder if he might simply be drunk. He caught my look. 'Sorry. But see it from my view, if you can.' He gestured at the Lagos night. 'Stuck out here in the sticks miles from the bloody war and suddenly people start flying in looking for Chief – this is the most excitement we've had in yonks.'

I nodded, and packed the medicine in my hold-all.

'Seems we're in luck,' said Manning, pointing ahead. The cars were starting to move.

*

The hotel was a horrendous white modernist building that looked like a collection of giant window-boxes, but the car park was stuffed with diplomatic plates and flagpoles jutted importantly from the entrance marquee, so it was clearly the right spot. I told Manning to wait for me and walked through to the reception, where a sullen-looking young woman behind a marble counter sold me an air-conditioned double room for a hundred and eighty Nigerian shillings a night – the single rooms were all gone, she claimed. After filling in the registry and handing over my passport, I took the stairs to my room on the third floor.

It didn't quite live up to the picture I'd been given in reception, but it looked like it had the basics: the air conditioning worked, and there was a telephone and a radio. Was it secure, though? I threw my bag and jacket onto the mattress and checked the strength of the door from the outside. After a few minutes, I was satisfied that anyone wanting to break it down would have to make a hell of a noise to do so. The windows also shut firmly, and I rigged an elastic band across the two handles to make sure. They led out onto a fire escape, which would come in handy if anyone tried anything. I was directly above the swimming pool. Despite the lateness of the hour, there were still a few people lounging on deckchairs sipping from long-stemmed glasses: diplomats, or aid workers. Nice life. Not mine.

There was a tiny en suite bathroom with a sink that trickled lukewarm water, and a cracked mirror above it. After splashing my face and drying it on my shirt – towels didn't appear to be part of the service – I called reception and asked them to put me through to the Soviet Embassy. Amazingly, this took only a couple of minutes.

'*Da?*' The voice was cold. Night shift.

'Hello,' I said in Russian, but playing up my English accent. 'Could you put me through to Third Secretary Irina Grigorieva, please?'

'Everyone's gone home,' she said. 'Do you want to leave a message?'

'Yes,' I said. 'Tell her it's an old friend calling: name of Paul Dark. I'm at the Palace Hotel on Victoria Island, room 376. Did you get all that?'

She said she had, and I replaced the receiver. Slavin was my first priority, because he was planning to defect and might have more information that could point to me. But Anna could also expose me – she wasn't volunteering to do so, but she could – so I had to get hold of her, too. She would be unlikely to return to the embassy until the morning, and they wouldn't have given me her address, so I'd taken the next best option, which was to leave a message to try to bring her to me.

I locked up, and headed downstairs.

*

'Everything okay?' asked Manning.

'First class,' I said, fastening my seat-belt.

'What are you doing?'

'Tell me what you know about Slavin,' I said.

'Slavin?'

'Yes. Russian johnnie. Was there anything you didn't mention in the dossier you sent?'

He looked at me blankly. 'Like what?'

'How about the woman he mentioned – Irina Grigorieva? What's their relationship?'

'I have no idea,' he replied, irritated. 'I sent all the information we have.'

I smiled. 'Just double-checking. I'd like to talk to Slavin – see if I can make him open up some more.'

'You can do that tomorrow morning. He's due at the High Commission at nine . . .'

'I'd like to talk to him tonight.'

He tensed up. 'Sorry, old chap, I don't follow.'

'Tomorrow may be too late,' I said. 'Did he have any surveillance on him when he arrived at the High Commission?' He stiffened, but gave no reply. 'And when he left?' No reply. 'So you see, we have no idea how secure his position is, let alone how he's handling the pressure of being about to defect. He could already be under suspicion, or he could be getting horribly drunk and about to spill everything to one of his colleagues while we sit here discussing it. Have you put his home under surveillance?'

He shook his head defensively. 'Too risky. He was quite clear we should make no further contact until tomorrow.'

'But you know where his house is?' A nod. 'Well?'

'It's in Ikoyi, near the Russian Embassy.'

'Near, but not in?'

'That's right. Most of the Russians have their own villas, same as us. But I don't—'

'Right, then. We'll go and knock on his door, see if he's still alive, alive-oh, and then you can head off to your party and I back to my little rat-hole.'

He frowned. 'If he's under surveillance, we could blow him.'

'If he's under surveillance,' I said, 'he's probably already been blown. London told you to hold my hand, and that's precisely what you're going to do.'

After a while, he shook his head and let out a deep sigh. 'You'll have to think of something to tell Marjorie,' he said. 'She'll be livid.'

*

Like many others in the neighbourhood, the villa sat behind an imposing set of iron gates. 'Villa' was Manning's word, and was perhaps a little generous. It was a large but plain-looking bungalow, with mosquito nets on the windows and a jacaranda tree in the drive helping to mask the peeling paint.

Slavin's house.

We were at the easternmost edge of the city: Ikoyi was the last island. On the way over, Manning had told me that many of the city's expatriates, himself included, lived here. I could see why. Its houses, even the run-down ones, were spacious, its gardens neatly trimmed and, in comparison to the cacophony of traffic elsewhere in the city, it was eerily quiet: the only sounds I could hear were the mosquitoes buzzing around my ears, the ticking of my watch and the creaking of leather as Manning shifted his bum in his seat.

A Peugeot 404 was parked in the drive, so it looked as if Slavin was in. However, I had no way of knowing whether he was in there *alone*. I'd made Manning drive around the neighbouring streets to check for surveillance. I hadn't found any, but that wasn't conclusive: they could be watching us from inside the house itself. And so could Slavin. I'd told Manning that surveillance would mean he was already blown, but that wasn't strictly true. This man was a KGB officer and, if his work was important enough, he could be guarded around the clock as a matter of course.

Manning was also right to worry that this kind of approach might tip off Slavin's colleagues that he was intending to defect. If they were to get the slightest sniff of that, he would immediately be deported, and probably shot on arrival in the motherland. But that wasn't my plan: for the time being anyway, I wanted Comrade Slavin to stay alive. I had to find out what he knew, and how he'd discovered it. He had claimed that Anna had loved me, but had she been the source for that, or someone else? I had to get to him, but I had to find a way to do it without the Russians being alerted.

It wasn't looking promising. We'd been here for twenty minutes and there hadn't been a flicker of activity from inside the house.

'It *is* the cocktail hour,' Manning said, finally.

I looked at him. 'You think Slavin might also have a pyjama party on tonight?'

He shrugged. 'He might even be at the same one.'

'You socialize with the Russians?'

'Sometimes. Plenty of diplomats, from all over, are members of the Yacht Club. The Russian ambassador joined last year – chap called Romanov. Charming fellow, actually, and quite a good sailor –'

'Is Slavin a member?'

'Not that I know of. But anyone who is could sign him in. And it's quite a big bash tonight, so perhaps he'd want to go.'

I found it hard to believe Moscow would allow anyone important out on the cocktail circuit: it was almost an invitation to defect. Still, Slavin *was* planning to defect, so perhaps they had as tight a rein out here as the Service appeared to, employing buffoons like Manning. Perhaps Lagos was just one big pyjama party.

Or perhaps I was just tired. Manning was worried about the rocket he was going to get from his wife and was probably using the slightest possibility that Slavin would be at the same party as a pretext to stop my goose chase around Lagos. But it *was* a possibility, however slight, and now he'd put the thought in my head it was hard to dismiss. It would be too painful to bear if we were staking out his house while he was lording it up over the road in his night-gown and slippers.

'How far away is this party of yours?'

Manning jollied up. 'A fifteen-minute drive – less at this time of night. It's over on Lagos Island.' He pointed in the direction we'd come. As he did, I noticed the field lying in darkness by the side of the road.

'What's that? A golf course?'

'Yes. Part of the Ikoyi Club. I'm a member there, too. Not a bad little course, as it happens. Henry—'

I didn't want to hear about Pritchard's birdie on the ninth, so I opened the door and climbed out.

'Wait here,' I said.

*

As I approached the gate, I saw that behind it and to the right, partly shielded by bushes, was a small hut, wooden and painted blue. I pressed a buzzer, and after a few seconds a bulb went on and a man emerged from it. He was wearing grey flannel trousers and a sweater with cpaulettes.

'Who goes there?' he called. His handsome face was half-lit by the bulb, highlighting deep symmetrical scars down his cheeks. I could see the silhouette of his rifle: from the way he gripped it, he looked to be an amateur. Surely a KGB colonel would have more protection than this?

'Who goes there?'

'Is Mister Slavin in?' I asked.

He peered out at me. 'He expecting you, sir?'

That was good. 'Sir' was good.

'Yes,' I said. 'I'm here for the party.'

He didn't register either way, but he raised his rifle a little. I'd guessed wrongly: there might still be people in there, but he wasn't convinced it classed as a party.

'Listen,' I said quickly. 'What's your name?' I needed to change direction.

'Isaac,' he said warily.

'Isaac, could you do me a favour?' I patted my pockets absent-mindedly. 'Do you have a piece of paper I can write on?'

He went into his hut and came back a few seconds later with a newspaper. It was the *Daily Times*, Alebayo's read of choice. As he approached the gate, I saw that his rifle was now pointing towards the ground. His neck shone under the corona of the lamp. It would have been the easiest thing in the world to overpower him at that moment. But what then? What if I broke in and Slavin had company? At best, he'd be blown. At worst, I'd be dead.

Fifteen minutes, Manning had said. I looked at my watch: it was already half ten. I handed Isaac the note. 'Please give Mister Slavin this, and let him know I visited.'

*

'Any luck?' Manning asked, back in the car.

'Not much.'

'So what now?'

What now, indeed? It was getting on, and I was no further ahead. Come tomorrow morning, I was going to be in trouble. Even more trouble than I was already in. But I couldn't see a way past it – the odds were too high.

Manning was looking at me expectantly.

'All right,' I said. 'Just for half an hour.'

He turned the key in the ignition.

*

'The bar only opened last year, you know,' said Manning as he handed me my drink. 'Very controversial – the debate raged for years. A lot of us were worried the place would fill up with non-sailing types. There was even one chap – German, wasn't he, Sandy?'

'Dutch, I think,' said Sandy, who was a small elegant man in a long white nightshirt.

'Oh, yes,' said Manning, popping a peanut into his mouth. 'That's right. Dutch. Well, he came along one week and asked if he could join just to *socialize*. Brazenly admitted he had no intention of sailing at all! Put him right, didn't we?' He snorted, and Sandy nodded his head sagely.

'Oh, Geoffrey! I'm sure Robert isn't interested in the intricate workings of the Yacht Club.'

Marjorie Manning had been flirting with me outrageously since we'd arrived. She might have been a beauty twenty-odd years ago, but too much drink, sun, and Geoffrey had shaken most of it from her.

'What would you rather discuss, dear?' Manning asked her sweetly. 'The shops in London?'

'Why not?' she said. 'What's in fashion this season, Robert? Tell us, please. We have to rely on the local supermarkets to provide us with our clothes, and it's hardly Yves Saint Laurent.'

'I don't think fashion's quite Robert's patch,' said Manning, winking at me.

I'd been a bloody fool to listen to him, of course: there was no sign of any Russians, let alone Slavin. The party reminded me of dozens I'd been to in Istanbul and elsewhere: several dozen expats, mostly Brits, getting sloshed on brandy and sodas and munching stale crisps. We were seated at a table outside, making the most of the faint breeze coming in off the water. Stewards in white uniforms and guests in nightclothes milled about the lawn, giving the place a somewhat ghostly air. A group of men directly behind me discussed the merits of fibreglass hulls and wondered how long it would be until the rainy season. The consensus seemed to be that it would arrive any day now.

I glanced at my watch: twenty-five past eleven. My note had asked Slavin to meet me at midnight. Despite the needless detour, this was still marginally preferable to sitting in the car with Manning for half an hour, which was what I would have been doing otherwise: and staying on for that length of time might have been unwise if there had been any sort of surveillance of the street from inside Slavin's villa. I took a sip from my drink and wondered again if he was being guarded. Perhaps he was being questioned about my note right now: perhaps I'd blown his defection. And that would be disastrous, because I couldn't afford for him to be carted away before Pritchard arrived. But I was being too pessimistic, surely. The most obvious explanation was the most likely: he hadn't been at home. Perhaps he was working late at the embassy. Men about to defect often become conspicuously loyal to those they are about to betray. If he *was* at the embassy, it was stalemate – I couldn't get near him there.

'Mister Kane?'

I looked up. The man called Sandy was speaking to me. 'Sorry?'

'I said, "What is your patch, exactly?" I can't remember seeing your byline in *The Times*.'

I'd been wondering when he would pounce. Manning had introduced him as a property developer, but I recognized his name – he'd been a BBC correspondent in the war, and was now connected behind the scenes. Still did some work for *The Mirror*, I seemed to remember.

I mentioned a few of the stories that had appeared in *The Times* credited to Robert Kane in the past couple of years. Each had been written for short-term operational reasons, using the name as a convenient blanket – they hadn't been intended to build cover in the field. If Farraday hadn't suddenly fancied having a go playing at spies, Manning could simply have introduced me under my own name as a second secretary at the embassy. Instead, I was going to have to be on my back foot defending a half-formed legend.

'Out here for the PM's visit, I suppose?'

I nodded. 'My editor wants something about the feel of the place, how the Brits see the war, that kind of thing. Perhaps I can interview you at some point?'

'Certainly — just call my office. I was here for the Queen's trip in '56, so I'm quite used to the pomp and ceremony. Wilson's rather small potatoes, isn't he? Reminds me of a bank clerk in those silly raincoats he wears.'

'He'll have to ditch them in this heat,' said Manning.

We all laughed politely.

'Is Lagos as safe as everyone says it is?' I asked Sandy. 'It seems very quiet.'

'Oh,' he said, 'we haven't had any action here since one of the rebels' planes attacked the Motor Boat Club two years ago. Didn't do much harm, though everyone got frightfully excited, of course.'

'"Rebels"? You don't think secession was justified, then?'

'Not really. Ojukwu's a thug, and Gowon's doing his best to control a very difficult situation.'

'What about the accusations of genocide? I've heard there were seven thousand Biafran deaths a day due to starvation over the summer.'

He grimaced. 'A lot of do-gooders with no idea of how this part of the world works are swallowing the genocide line whole. Propaganda, of course — people throw around these enormous figures, but nobody really has the slightest idea. I think the Federals have actually dealt with the situation very well, considering the paltry support they've received from our government — and I'll be telling the PM that when I meet him at State House on Thursday. At the moment, we seem to be simply watching from the sidelines, as usual. Nigeria will carry on with or without us.'

'Wawa,' said Manning, nodding his chin.

'Sorry?'

'West Africa wins again. Another drink, old boy?'

'It's all right,' I said, 'I'll get it.'

I pushed my chair back and headed for the bar.

*

A steward in a gleaming white uniform and scarlet cummerbund stood behind a makeshift table crammed with bottles and paper cups. With all the poise of a Sotheby's auctioneer, he surveyed the small crowd gathered round him, eventually nodding to a man in khaki shorts and deck shoes.

'Star,' said the man, in the manner of someone who had been wandering through the desert for forty days and nights.

The steward leaned down, scooped a bottle of beer from an icebox, opened it deftly and handed it to the man.

And that was when I saw her.

She was sitting by herself on a stack of breeze blocks just beyond the bar, in a black bathing suit, a cigarette dangling from one hand. Her face was turned away in contemplation of the water, but the line of her jaw was unmistakable. I made my way through the crowd, stepped over the steward's icebox and tapped her on the shoulder.

'Anna.'

She turned and peered at me in puzzlement. And for a fraction of a moment, it was her – but her twenty years ago. And then the illusion faded, and I was apologizing for my error. What a fool I was! What a bloody fool to mistake the first dark-haired stranger for her. I was losing grip, and fast.

'You do not wear pyjamas,' said the girl. Her accent was French, as was her tone. I looked at her again. She had one of those androgynous cat-like faces that were so much in fashion, the effect highlighted by her lack of make-up and slicked-back hair. She was more conventionally beautiful than Anna had ever been, but there was something rather hard about her. She looked like she should be marching through Parisian boulevards holding a placard.

'No,' I said in answer to her comment. 'But neither do you.'

'I was swimming.'

I glanced down at the water — it looked filthy.

'It is not so bad once you have entered,' she said, white teeth flashing in the dark face.

I offered her my hand. 'Robert Kane.'

She shook it perfunctorily. 'Isabelle Dumont. Tell me, who did you think I was just now?'

'Someone I knew a long time ago,' I said.

She smiled softly. 'I see. So what do you do, Mister Kane? I haven't seen you here before.'

'I've only just arrived. I'm a reporter, for *The Times*.'

'That is a coincidence. I write for Agence France-Presse. Are you here for your prime minister's visit?'

I nodded, already bored of the pretext.

She grinned again, and lifted her chin. 'Look on the good side of it: you meet such very interesting people.'

I followed her gaze back to the table I'd left. Manning was stuffing his face full of peanuts, his wife was laughing like a hyena and Sandy was trying to fish a dead fly from his drink with a spoon.

'Yes,' I said. 'Why is it one can never stand one's countrymen whenever one meets them abroad?'

'One has no idea,' she said, curling her lip a little.

'Still,' I said, ignoring the crack. 'I've met you. You're interesting. Have you been out here long?'

'I grew up here,' she said. 'My father was the French ambassador.'

'Have you seen much of the rest of the country?'

There was a noise from further down the jetty, and we both looked up. A woman in a cocktail dress was squealing as a man lifted her over his head and threatened to throw her in the water.

People at other tables stopped their conversations to stare at the scene, but nobody did much, and a few seconds later there was a splash as her spine hit the water.

The woman swam to the shore and helped herself out, ignoring the man's insincere apologies. The steward ran over to offer her a towel, and she took it, wrapped it around herself and marched through the crowd into the clubhouse.

A few moments later, the man walked past us, a wide, innocent smile on his face.

'Kraut,' he said in an American accent. 'Can't take jokes.'

We watched him trudge up to the clubhouse, and then Isabelle took a puff of her cigarette and said in a very still voice: 'I was at the front in January. I must now get back. But it takes very long to obtain authorization to fly there.'

She was looking out at the sea instead of me, at the lights of the trawlers. Her brown skin, the sheen of her bathing suit, the lapping of the water behind her, the alcohol still warm in my throat . . . for a moment, I forgot about Slavin and Anna and Sasha and Pritchard, and felt like a human being. Then a ship hooted in the distance and I woke up. That life was an illusion, and I couldn't afford to slip back into it.

'I'm afraid I can't help you,' I said. 'I've only just got here.'

She turned, and shot me a withering look. 'I was not requesting your help,' she said. 'I make my own arrangements.'

I looked at my watch. It was a quarter to midnight.

'It was nice meeting you,' I said, and her looks softened for a fraction of a moment.

*

Back at the table, I took Manning to one side and told him I needed to borrow his car.

'Whatever for?' he said. 'Not that Slavin business again?'

'Well, he's not here, is he?'

'But how am I supposed to—'

'Sandy can give you a lift home,' I said, lifting the keys from his jacket pocket.

*

I stood on the eighteenth brown and looked around. Nothing.

Nigerian golf courses didn't have greens, Manning had explained to me. It was too hard to maintain grass in such a climate, so instead they had 'browns': they were made of a mix of sand and oil, which the caddies would sweep for you before your putt.

He was already ten minutes late. Had I just blown him? I had counted on his being senior enough to read his own messages without being challenged, but now I was having doubts. What if he was under such close supervision that his correspondence was read as a matter of course? I had no choice but to wait and find out.

Behind me were the banks of villas and embassies. I could see Slavin's street, but there didn't seem to be any sign of life in it. And then something moved in my peripheral vision, and I turned to catch it. It was just a shape in the darkness, but it hadn't been there before.

'Who's that?' I called out.

The shape stopped, and now I saw it was a man. He ran up the incline onto the far edge of the brown. He was tall with stooped shoulders and, I could just make out, a widow's peak.

Slavin.

*

I exhaled deeply. I had left London this morning with the aim of reaching this man before anyone else, and I'd succeeded.

'You are not Mister Manning,' he said, and I fancied he backed away a step.

I held up my hands. 'I work with Mister Manning at the High Commission,' I said in Russian. 'He told me to arrange a meeting with you.'

'Why? I thought it was clear that the interview was tomorrow.'

'It is,' I assured him. 'And I'm sorry we broke our promise not to contact you before then. But we had to. Some questions have come up in London.'

He took a couple of steps closer, and the moonlight struck his face. Anxiety was etched across it.

'Questions?' he asked. 'What questions?'

'Irina Grigorieva,' I said. 'We need to know more about her.'

He took another few steps, and now we were standing face to face, within touching distance.

'Irina?' he said, confused. 'But she has nothing to—'

He stopped, and I wondered if he had changed his mind about whatever it was he'd been about to tell me. But then I saw the dark red patch on his throat and my mind caught up with the sound, half-drowned in the wind.

Shot.

VII

Slavin fell into my arms. I dropped him and ran in the direction of the noise. As I clambered down the bank, I saw a figure on the fairway: a white man, running. I followed him.

Was he heading for Slavin's house? Had he been one of his guards? He looked to be heading for the road, certainly. On the drive here, I hadn't seen anybody on the streets – curfew descended at midnight, and expats were unlikely to wander around anyway. They had gins to drink, boats to sail, women to throw in the sea.

He still had the pistol in his right hand, and he turned to fire at me. It missed, and I wondered if it had been deliberate – he'd had no trouble with Slavin.

He was heading through a band of bushes to cut across to another hole, which sloped down to the gardens on Slavin's street. When he reached the crest of the hill, he stopped, staggering a little, standing back and bellowing at me. I couldn't understand it – the echo was too confusing. But it was a jeer. He raised his hand to fire again, and I dropped to the ground. He disappeared over the brow of the hill.

And now it started raining. It began gently, bringing the smell of the earth to the fore and refreshing my face, but within seconds it was a sheet. It attacked like hot needles, and the noise of it on the nearby roofs was deafening.

The rain wasn't good for the shooter, either, as he was stuck in weeds in the rough, bogging him down. I was on the fairway and started gaining ground. I saw that another mound was coming up, and from its position I guessed what lay behind it.

As he reached the brow, I shouted out at him, and he turned back for an instant. With a surge, I carried myself over and onto his back, tumbling us both into the bunker. He grunted and waved his arms around as though he were drowning, and I realized that I'd have to be quick; he was a younger, stronger man, trained, with a gun. I wanted him alive, but it might not be possible. I swung wildly at his head, trying to get at his eyes or nose. I felt the cracking of bone and heard him scream, so I immediately brought the other hand round in an axe-chop to follow through, but he rolled to avoid it and then he was climbing on me. A fist slammed into the small of my back, sending a wave of agony up my spine, and I tried to get the momentum to push back into him, hoisting my elbows towards his face, but I merely scraped his chin and he was grabbing me around the neck and pulling me towards him. His breathing was fast and I could smell him, could smell his sweat and his desire to kill me. As I started to lose control of my throat muscles, I freed one hand and grabbed at his groin. His grip loosened for a moment and I managed to turn enough to bring my other hand into play, gouging at one of his eyes. My fingers came away wet, but I lost my footing and fell face first into the mud. It took me a while to get back up, but I couldn't see anything and the nerves in my spine were stabbing at me. Where the hell was he? Everything was black, and the rain was hammering down. Suddenly I saw a glint of light. The moon? No, it was moving! I rolled away from it and heard a slashing sound behind me as I did. I leapt at the shape in the dark, lashing out with my feet and catching him hard in the stomach. He fell against the side of the bunker and I pinned him, locking my arms around his neck and squeezing. It was a thick neck: the neck of a KGB thug. Rage surged through me. Sasha had broken his promise.

'Who are you?' I screamed into his face in Russian, but he was incapable of answering, so I loosened my hold and concentrated on his left arm instead.

'Who? Tell me!'

He didn't answer, and after I'd asked him a few more times, I broke the arm in one movement. But there was no scream from the Russian, and I wondered what was wrong. His face suddenly looked pale; I realized what he was doing and frantically tried to prise open his jaw to get to the pill.

Too late.

I searched him. There were no identifying papers, of course, but there were some Nigerian shillings and a box of matches. The matchbox had something scribbled on it in pencil. I held it up to the moonlight. It was one very familiar Cyrillic word: "АЭРОФЛОТ".

I shunted it to one side of my brain, to deal with later, picked up the rake and started shovelling the mud over his body, as the rain kept coming down around us. Then I trudged back up to the eighteenth to look for Slavin and do the same thing.

VIII

In the front seat of Manning's car, away from the rain hammering into my back and drowning out my thoughts, I considered the implications of what had just happened. They were, all told, pretty bleak. The death of a KGB officer on the eve of his defection would trigger the order for an immediate investigation from London. I could have handled that if it had been run by Manning, but Pritchard would be in the city in a matter of days, possibly even hours, and he would be much harder to fob off. Especially as I had disobeyed orders to come out here, had then insisted on meeting Slavin ahead of the scheduled time – and had been the only witness to his murder.

There was nothing I could do about any of that now. If I went underground – moved hotels, cut all contact with Manning – I might as well paint a cross on my back. Pritchard would have a pack of hounds sent over on Concorde. No, my only option was to carry on the pretence I was searching for the traitor, even if that meant Pritchard breathing down my neck and giving me even less room for manoeuvre. It was precisely the situation I'd wanted to avoid – and precisely what I'd warned Sasha would happen if he got Moscow to send a hitman into Lagos.

Now I *had* to find Anna. The Service knew she had recruited Radnya, so would almost certainly investigate her next. I knew she was somewhere in this city – probably even somewhere in this neighbourhood. Perhaps that house, there, with the jacaranda trees swaying in the wind. Perhaps she was in that villa, wrapped up in pleasant dreams, while I sat here with my shirt dripping and my fingers caked in blood as the minutes wound down until Pritchard's plane landed.

I took the torch from the glove compartment and ran it over the assassin's effects. I wasn't expecting to find anything that would identify him: he'd been a professional. But there were clues. There were always clues.

The most obvious one was the word scrawled on the matchbox: 'AEROFLOT'. My first thought was that it was a reminder to book his ticket back to Moscow: after all, even hitmen need to organize their travel arrangements. But why would he write that down? It wasn't as if he would forget the name of the national airline.

Next thought: perhaps he had a contact at Aeroflot's office here. That made more sense – it was a common KGB cover. But again, why make a note of it? Bad form and, again, it wouldn't be too hard to remember.

I was missing something. I hadn't been in the field in over five years, and it was taking me time to get back into the old ways of thinking. Too much time.

I picked up the Russian's gun. It was a Tokarev TT. I had always thought it a brutish-looking weapon: unpainted and almost devoid of markings, it looked more like a cast of a pistol than the real thing. This one had been worn smooth with years of use, so that only one of the Cs in 'CCCP' arranged around the grip was still legible.

I emptied the chamber, because it had no manual safety and I didn't want to blow my knees off, and asked myself why a KGB assassin would be carrying this gun. The TT hadn't been produced in years – most KGB now used the Makarov. The army had continued to use it for a while, but I'd read a report just a few months ago saying that they had also abandoned it. Perhaps he had been in the army many years ago, and had kept the gun? I tried to remember his face, before its features had been contorted by pain. Late twenties – no older than that. So too young to have been issued with a TT even if he had been in the army. Perhaps someone he knew had been in the army and had given it to him. Or he had it for other reasons – like I had my Luger.

I wasn't getting anywhere. My thoughts turned to Slavin – were there any clues there? He had started to say something about Anna before the shots had interrupted him. 'But she has nothing to . . .' What? Nothing to do with this? Nothing to gain? Nothing to lose?

The shots. There was a clue. The first had gone through Slavin's windpipe; the second had nearly taken off my ear. But why had he wasted valuable seconds shooting at me? Simply because I was a witness to murder – or because I was his second *target*?

A chill went through me. Had Sasha ordered me 'dispatched', too?

I would have to make a move soon. I lit a cigarette with one of the dead man's matches. As I made to put the box in my pocket, I noticed that his scribbled 'eh' looked more like a stylized 'ehf'. That didn't help me much: so I knew he hadn't been an especially literate assassin. But then I saw that two other letters also looked wrong.

I flicked the torch across the surface again.

He hadn't written them down incorrectly – I'd misread them. The word wasn't 'АЭРОФЛОТ', but 'АФРОСПОТ'. I was so used to seeing the name of the airline in Section reports that my mind had automatically taken in a similar-looking word and jumped to the wrong conclusion.

So what the hell was 'Afrospot'?

*

At the Yacht Club, the party had moved into the bar. Manning was deep in discussion with his wife and Sandy: West Africa, no doubt, was winning again. When he caught sight of me, he nearly tripped over himself running over.

'Bloody hell!' he said. 'What happened? Did you get caught in the rain?'

'No,' I said. 'I decided to take a shower and forgot to undress.'

He coughed into his hand. 'Did Slavin show?'

I took him by the arm and led him down a corridor and into the men's changing rooms. I gave the place the once over, glancing into the WCs and the shower stalls to make sure nobody else was there. Once I was satisfied we were alone, I turned to Manning.

'Slavin made contact about half an hour ago,' I said.

'Did he have any information about the woman?'

'I don't know. Someone put a bullet through the back of his neck before I could find out.'

It took an instant for the words to penetrate, and then his face crumpled and his eyes lost their spark.

'Christ,' he said. 'That's rather a blow.'

'Yes,' I said. 'It is, rather.' I wondered if he was so comfortable out here that he'd forgotten what our game was about, or if he was just worried about Pritchard's reaction, and was seeing his pension float away. I walked over to a basin and washed some of the mud off my hands and face.

'Did you see the shooter?' Manning asked.

I took a towel off a nearby peg and dried myself. 'Not clearly. He got away very fast.'

'Ah. Pity.' He picked up a piece of tarpaulin peeking out from beneath one of the benches and stood it up against the wall. 'Terrible mess some people make,' he said. 'I'll have to raise it at the next meeting.' Then he looked up at me, as if he had suddenly remembered that his role in the Yacht Club was of secondary importance to a dead Russian. 'The office called,' he said. 'London cabled to say that Henry's flight lands at oh-eight-hundred tomorrow.'

On the drive over from Ikoyi, I'd held, somewhere at the back of my mind, the hope that Pritchard might not be able to make it out here for a few more days. Now it was settled: I now had less than eight hours before he arrived and started asking questions – and all I had to go on was a word scribbled on a matchbox.

Manning was shuffling his feet, anxious to get back to his drink.

'I'll meet you at the airport at half-seven,' I told him. 'But tell me something – does the phrase "Afrospot" mean anything to you?'

He considered it for a moment, then shook his head. 'Perhaps a local brand of pimple cream?' He chuckled, pleased with himself.

'Did you notice the woman I was talking to earlier on?'

He grimaced. 'Yes, I saw her,' he said. 'But don't you think you should leave the love life for later, old chap? Go back to your hotel, have a good night's sleep, and we'll sort all this out come morning.'

I counted out ten beats, timing them to a dripping tap somewhere behind me, letting Manning understand that I was not interested in talking sex, or rugby, or my father, and that this would be the last time I wasted valuable seconds on him. He coughed after the seventh beat, and I relieved him of the tension.

'Did you notice if she left?'

'I saw her setting out for the hard about ten minutes ago. Might still be there.'

'The hard?'

'Um – near the jetty – take a right and you'll see the path leading down to it.'

'Thank you,' I said, and headed for the door.

'What about my car?' Manning called after me. 'Sandy's already giving another couple a lift, and I'm not sure Marjorie and I will squeeze in.'

'I'll let you know in a couple of minutes,' I shouted back.

*

I checked the bar just in case, but she wasn't there, so I hooked my jacket over my head and headed outside. The chairs had been stacked up in columns and a steward was doing the rounds of the tables with a tray, picking up bottles and glasses and bowls while the rain blew against him.

I found Isabelle in a lifejacket, tethering her boat to a pole.

'Didn't fancy another swim, then?' I said.

She looked up, startled, and then smiled a little wearily as she put the voice to the face.

'You didn't say you had your own boat,' I said.

'I didn't have the chance. You left. Anyway, you have to be a regular sailor to be a member of the club. They don't . . .'

'Allow social members. I remember.'

'Are you angry with me?'

'Angry? What gives you that idea?'

'You left very quickly. As though I had said something wrong.' She finished tying the knot and looked up, her gaze challenging me.

'You didn't say anything wrong,' I said. 'I had a meeting to go to. An interview.'

'At this time?'

'I'm back now.'

'Do you expect me to bow down at your feet?'

So she was going to play it that way. 'Look,' I said. 'I'm sorry.'

She didn't answer.

'Have you ever heard of something called Afrospot?'

She stared at me for a few moments, and then gave a sudden, astonished laugh. 'You want to take me there?'

'No,' I said, 'I just want to know what it is.'

She jumped into the boat, and I thought for a moment that she was going to unmoor it and sail off. But instead she removed the lifejacket, then lifted one of the seats and took out a black hand-towel and a pair of boots.

'It is a nightclub,' she said, raising her arms and wriggling into the centre of the towel, which it transpired was a dress. 'In Ebute Metta.'

'Is that in Lagos?'

She nodded. 'About half an hour away by car. Do you have a car?'

I glanced up at the bar, and saw Manning standing at the window, looking worried. 'Yes. What road do I need to take?'

She smiled, and pointedly looked me up and down. 'They'll never let you in, *mon vieux*. Not without me.' And she jumped out of the boat.

IX

I steered us onto the main road and Isabelle indicated I should take a right. Manning wouldn't be too pleased when he realized I'd left, but he'd soon get over it: I was Larry Dark's boy, after all.

'It is not a new club,' she was saying. 'But it has a new owner recently, and more people visit. It is fun – you will see. Now it is your turn to speak: tell me why you are so interested in this place.'

'Oh,' I said. 'Just that I heard it mentioned and wondered if there might be a story in it.'

She laughed softly. 'I am not a fool, Robert! You didn't even know it was a nightclub. This means there already is a story. Something big, *non*?'

I had no idea. It was just a word on a matchbox. But the Russian had only written the name of the club – no date or time. That suggested he was confident he would meet his contact whenever he turned up there, which in turn pointed to that contact being either a regular at the club or, more likely, someone who worked there.

Isabelle was looking at me expectantly. 'There might be a story,' I told her. 'I'm not sure yet.'

She eyed me keenly and told me to take the next left.

*

We arrived at the club just after one. A ramshackle two-storey house, it looked like it was hosting a private party that had got out of control. An overpowering smell of marijuana wafted from the doors, along with the muffled sound of frenetic music. There were a few dozen people by the entrance, talking and dancing in the fug while they waited to be let in. A hand-painted sign announced that tonight's performance would be by 'the magnificent Black Chargers'.

As we approached the door, the Nigerians in the queue looked us up and down. A young man wearing a wide leather belt and an open-necked dress shirt shouted something to his friends, who all laughed uproariously.

I glanced at Isabelle.

'You don't want to know,' she said.

I asked her if she could try to find a way through the queue. If this was a dead-end, I didn't want to spend the rest of the night on it. She walked over to one of the doormen and started talking in very fast pidgin English with him. The man listened to her solemnly, then gave a nod and let us past, much to the chagrin of some of the crowd.

'I told him we are press,' she whispered to me. 'He said the intermission is coming soon and we can interview the owner. Is that okay?'

As there was a chance that the owner himself might be the Russian's contact, I told her it was fine. A group of heavies frisked us, Isabelle paid the entrance fee and I followed her onto a tiny but packed dance floor.

'Let's dance!' she shouted into my ear and, before I could answer, she had whisked me into the centre of the floor, where we were absorbed into the crowd of young Nigerians flailing their limbs around. The music was now deafening. On stage, at least a dozen musicians were playing trumpets, guitars and several sets of drums, all at a feverish pace. Every once in a while, a blast of notes emanated from a trombone attached to a small, wiry man in an iridescent suit, who seemed to be the chief Black Charger. It was like listening to a big band accompanying a voodoo ceremony.

Isabelle was swaying back and forth, her eyes fixed on me. I tried to play along with her, but my mind was too occupied to do anything other than shuffle my feet aimlessly and try to avoid colliding into others. The song was very repetitive, almost like a stuck record. With the heat and humidity, the frantic jostling crowd, the headiness of the marijuana and the nearness of Isabelle's body, I struggled to keep a clear head. After a few minutes, the song built to a dramatic climax, and my ears were left ringing in the relative quiet that came after.

Isabelle was smiling ecstatically, sweat dripping off her. '*C'est magnifique, non?*' she shouted in my ear, and I nodded. The band began making their way offstage, and were disappearing through an entrance covered by a beaded curtain. Isabelle found the doorman who had let us through. Money changed hands, and we were passed to one of his colleagues. Another swift transaction and we were shown through the curtain and led down a long corridor until we reached a door marked 'Artists' Green Room'.

*

'Welcome to the Afrospot, my friends!' said the trombonist, after he had been told by the doorman that we were press. 'My name is J. J. Thompson-Bola. Have you been enjoying the show?'

We nodded our heads like obedient schoolchildren. The room was almost as packed as the dance floor, with musicians and hangers-on chatting and smoking and laughing. Standing in one corner was a rather stern-looking middle-aged woman in a traditional dress and headgear made from the same material. She was looking at me with an expression I couldn't place – it was almost as though she knew me, or thought she did.

J. J. was now bare-chested, and a couple of young women were wiping his torso down with a sponge: he looked like a boxer limbering up for another round. As he rotated his shoulders and rolled his head around, his eyes fixed on Isabelle. 'You are reporter?' he asked her. 'For which newspaper?'

'Agence France-Presse,' she said. 'It's a news agency . . .'

'I know what it is,' he snapped, bringing his head back to its natural position. He paused, perhaps realizing there was little point in antagonizing the press unduly. 'I think I have met you before. Is that so?'

'Yes,' she said. 'I wrote an article on the cultural festival last year—'

'Ah, yes, I remember.' A woman handed him a bottle of Fanta orange squash and he gulped down a few swigs. 'So why have you returned? Could you not resist my charms?' He grinned impishly, and the middle-aged woman smacked her lips in mock disapproval. Could she be his mother, come to cheer on her son's performance?

Isabelle smiled at the flirtation. 'I told my editor about how your brand of high life is becoming more popular, and he was interested in another story, but this time to be centred around only you.'

J. J. beamed. 'Is that so? Well, tell your editor that he is a fine person with wonderful taste.' He laughed suddenly, and looked around the room for approval – some of the hangers-on joined in the laughter. He held up a hand and the laughter stopped. He turned to me. 'And who are you?' he asked.

'Robert Kane,' I said, stepping forward. '*The Times* of London. I'm also writing a piece on Lagos nightlife.'

'*The Times*!' he exclaimed. 'I know it well.'

'Oh, yes?'

'Certainly – I used to take it when I lived in London. Last year you ran an excellent article about my cousin. He has been imprisoned by the government on bogus and trumped-up charges for the last eighteen months, and he is rotting in a cell in Kaduna at this very moment.'

'I'm sorry to hear that,' I said.

'But how is London these days? I often think fondly of the nightclubs I used to visit there. I am trying to recreate a certain aspect of them here in Lagos. The Flamingo, the Marquee, Ronnie Scott's . . .'

'Ronnie Scott's? I was there last night! I saw a very good American group.' I struggled to remember the name, but my mind had gone blank.

'Dexter Gordon? Ben Webster? What instruments? I saw all the big names when I lived there. But now these Americans, they try to take over our country with this new soul sound. It is not real music. Our audience here' – he gestured dismissively in the direction of the dance floor – 'wants us to play James Brown, James Brown, all night. That does not interest me – to be James Brown in my own place. I studied for three years at the London College of Music. It was an excellent grounding in the kind of thing I am trying to achieve here.'

'I've heard they have a very good course,' I said.

'Ah, so you know it?'

'I know of its reputation,' I said, which seemed to satisfy him. I wasn't sure how far I could push things. The Russian probably had an introductory phrase to feed his contact – without it, I was lost. I didn't even know if this man was the contact. But it was moot: before I could think of anything else to say, he abruptly announced that it was time to go back on stage, and everyone began shuffling out of the room.

'Did you get your story?' Isabelle asked me as we moved back through the crowd.

'Not really. I might try to talk to him again after the show. Do you mind staying on?'

'No,' she said. 'I haven't danced in a long time.'

As J. J. and his band settled into another of their numbers, and Isabelle started twisting and turning round the floor, I considered the encounter. I wasn't sure what I had been expecting, but it hadn't materialized: I was no nearer to discovering who the Russian had wanted to meet here. J. J. ? One of his musicians? One of the bouncers? It could be almost anyone. Or perhaps he hadn't been due to meet anyone. Perhaps it was just somewhere he had heard about and intended to visit, or had visited, as recreation. Because it was a terrible choice for a meet. Any cover that might be offered by the crowd was completely offset by the fact that, apart from Isabelle and me, everyone in the place was black. Not ideal if you were a Russian looking for a secret rendezvous. If I were the contact, I'd certainly not have agreed to it.

Unless, of course, the contact wasn't actually supposed to make contact. What if the Russian had instructions to come here to find some*thing* rather than some*one*? That would explain why he hadn't needed a date or time – whatever he was after would simply stay here until he came to collect it.

I was suddenly wishing I had paid more attention in the green room.

I looked over at the entrance we'd come through from backstage. Two of the heavies were meant to be guarding it, but they had both advanced into the hall too far, and were now out of visual contact with each other. I shuffled round the back of them, waiting for my chance. It came a few minutes later, when J. J. had the crowd moving their arms up and down with the horns – the heavies got swept up in it, and I quickly slipped through the curtain and into the corridor.

*

There was no answer when I knocked on the green room door, so I stepped inside. Empty. I got to work at once, pulling out drawers, looking in bags and boxes, scanning every inch of the room as I moved around it. I found a collection of J. J.'s garish stage outfits, a sizeable stash of marijuana, and a few bottles of whisky and rum. The papers on the table were either posters for upcoming concerts or set lists. I didn't even know what I was looking for, and God knew what I would do if one of the heavies were to walk in now. In desperation, I turned to some larger cases for instruments that had been propped up against the wall, shoved in a small space behind a rickety bookcase. I squeezed past the bookcase and ran my finger down the line, clicking open their latches one by one. Empty. Empty. Empty . . .

A piece of sacking fell towards me. I caught it with both hands and sat it upright immediately. It wasn't sacking, in fact, but a soft canvas bag with leather straps. A gun bag. I undid the straps and saw the curved magazine. An AK-47? I leaned forward. No – it was a sniper rifle. As I took this in, I heard something move behind me. I snatched the rifle out of the bag and swivelled round, pointing it at the figure in the doorway.

'You should leave this room now,' said Isabelle. 'The police have arrived.'

X

The music in the club had stopped and I could hear the clatter of boots coming down the corridor towards us.

'What the hell are they doing here?' I asked.

'I don't know. Perhaps looking for drugs. Raids are frequent in this city.'

Or they'd found the bodies on the golf course and I was the focus of a manhunt. But how had they known who to look for – and where to find me?

The questions could wait.

'We need to get out of here,' I said. 'Try the window.'

She ran over and started trying to prise it open. It was jammed. There was no time to fiddle with straps, so I just put the rifle back in its bag and threw that into the trombone case, then joined her. The footsteps in the corridor were now accompanied by shouted commands, and sirens had started wailing outside. I smashed the case against the glass. Now the sound of the steps shifted in our direction. I swept away the shards with the back of my arm, then helped Isabelle crawl over the frame. Once she had jumped to the ground, I passed the case to her and followed her over. The door of the room crashed open as I was landing and a voice called out: 'Federal police! No one leave the building!'

I took the case back from Isabelle and we started running. Several policemen jumped down from the window and started pursuit. As Isabelle and I reached the front of the building, I glanced to the right and saw people streaming from the club in a panic. They were being greeted by a large contingent of police, all of whom were armed with machine guns. I could see J. J. and his entourage engaged in furious debate with them, and the man in the dress shirt who had laughed at us earlier was being pushed into the back of one of the unmarked cars that were parked behind the police line.

Those cars stood between us and the Peugeot.

I shouted to Isabelle to follow me, and headed towards the garden of the neighbouring house. The fence was already half-trampled and bent in on itself, so it was easy enough to leap over. I could hear Isabelle right behind me and, just behind her, shouting and gunfire.

We ran through the garden, passing a couple of frightened club-goers crouching behind an empty bathtub, and navigated the next fence, and the one after that. I carried the trombone case above my head – it made running easier, and protected my eyes from the hammering of the rain. At the fourth or perhaps fifth garden, I gestured to Isabelle that we should move back towards the street. Manning's car was directly opposite, and we headed for it. A few seconds after we emerged onto the road, the men following us reached it, too. They alerted their colleagues down by the club's entrance, and we won a few seconds as they shouted about us to each other. Then some of the men by the entrance headed towards their cars.

Isabelle reached Manning's car just before me.

'Let me drive!' she called out. 'I know the city.'

I threw her the keys. She jumped in and started it up, and I ran round to the passenger side and leapt in just as she was moving off. She reversed a few yards, making the men behind us stop in their tracks, and then headed straight for the police cars now hurtling down the street towards us.

There was a succession of shots from both directions. Nothing hit us, but it wasn't for a lack of trying. Struggling in the enclosed space, it took me a few seconds to get the rifle out of the case and find the ammunition. Then I wound down the window and leaned out to fire at the cars coming our way. I didn't hit anything, either: it was a self-loading semi-automatic, and although it could manage twenty to thirty rounds a minute, it was designed for accurate shooting at close quarters – not against moving targets while moving oneself. Isabelle pushed the accelerator down as far as it would go, and several of the cars veered out of the way. We caught two of them as we passed, and for a few yards we skidded on the wet tarmac and I thought we were going to end up in one of the storm drains that lined each side of the road, but she brought it round and pulled us back into the centre at the last moment.

Some of the group who had chased us through the gardens had reached their cars and were now coming up fast behind us. The man in the car closest was leaning out of the passenger window and firing his Kalashnikov, and he aimed well because there was a dull crack and thousands of tiny tributaries suddenly filled the rear window, before the whole surface gave way and fell into the back seat like a sheet of crushed ice.

As Isabelle took a sharp left turn, I carried on firing, but my knuckles were under assault from the relentless needles of rain and there were no streetlights, making my view through the sight next to useless.

There were now five cars on our tail: three dark, two lighter-coloured, all Peugeots of various models. Bullets were now peppering our bodywork every few seconds, and I realized we had to do something fast, before they hit a tyre, or the engine, or us. There were hardly any other cars on the street – it was well after curfew – which meant we couldn't easily create a diversion or block them. But the lack of lighting might help: if we got far enough ahead in a residential area, we could lose them in the darkness.

As if reading my thoughts, Isabelle took a late left turn, dimmed the lights for two streets and then swerved into a sudden right. Now we had just three cars in pursuit, the other two not having been tight enough on the turnings and skidding past, the Doppler effect of their sirens echoing after them.

I had run out of ammunition, but our pursuers didn't seem to be holding off on the shooting. It seemed unlikely they would have brought this much firepower with them had they just been out on a routine raid of the club. But I still couldn't figure it out: if they were chasing me for the Russians on the golf course, how had they known where to look? They clearly hadn't followed us out here. Did they think we were someone else? Alarm bells were ringing in my head – and most of them involved the person sitting at the wheel next to me.

I threw the rifle onto the rear seat, then grabbed the Tokarev from the glove compartment and leaned back out of the window. We passed, finally, a lighted building – another club? – which gave me a clear view of the driver of the nearest car for one vital second, and I managed to shatter his windscreen. There was a scream and the car swerved wildly – another of our pursuers was lost to the drains. But the remaining two cars suddenly loomed out from the darkness. As a series of shots thudded into the dashboard, bringing up a storm of sparks, Isabelle momentarily lost control, and then there was a horrific scraping sound as both cars came alongside us, squeezing us between them, and I was looking right into the face of one of the policemen as he raised a pistol and fired.

Isabelle slowed the car at the same moment, trying to gain control, and the shot went wide, but as a result both cars drew ahead of us and they immediately started turning to block off the road. I leaned over Isabelle and, shoving her away, grabbed hold of the wheel and spun it towards with me with as much force as I could manage, one hand over the other. The next few seconds were a havoc of screeched tyres and broken headlights and gunfire as we bumped across open ground, until finally, by some miracle, we hit tarmac again, and Isabelle put her foot down and I fell back into my seat. Through the rear-view mirror I could see that the police were busy trying to disentangle themselves from their roadblock, so I shouted at her to take a quick turn, then another, then another, until eventually I couldn't see any headlights behind us and my breathing slowed and I put away the gun and told her to keep driving.

They couldn't have been after me: they wouldn't have cared enough about a couple of dead Russians to shoot to kill. They must have been looking for something else.

'Do you know the Victoria Palace Hotel?' I asked Isabelle.

She nodded, and we headed for it.

*

The street was dark but for a shimmering yellow pool where the moonlight struck the rain-soaked macadam. I stepped back from the curtain and looked at Isabelle. She was sitting in the easy chair by the bed, her chin resting on one hand.

'Strip,' I said.

She looked at me from out of the darkness, but didn't move.

'Are all Englishmen this romantic?' she said, tilting her head.

'It's not a come-on,' I said. 'Strip now, or I'll do it for you.'

'Do you enjoy the rough stuff, is that it?'

'No,' I said. 'That's not it. It's that I don't like being taken for a fool.' I took the pistol from my holster and pointed it at her.

Her eyes widened. Then she stood up, shrugged and started to unlace her boots.

'How did you know I was in the green room?' I asked. 'At the club.'

She looked surprised. 'I saw you slip away. I guessed you had seen something backstage and wished to return for another look.'

'And the police?'

'Yes?'

'I don't believe, even in wild and woolly Lagos, that the police fire on people just for fleeing a raid. There were five cars chasing us, and they were shooting to kill.'

'So were you, *non?*' Her boots off, she started unbuttoning her tunic.

'How long have you been with French intelligence?' I said.

She stretched out her arms so the dress fell to the floor, leaving her in her bathing suit. 'How long have you been with British intelligence?'

She hadn't even denied it. I walked over and slapped her across the face. 'Where is it? Where's the transmitter?'

She grabbed my forearm — she had a strong grip — and wiped her face. '*T'es fou, ou quoi?* Why would I let the police know we were at the club? I came to warn you they were there, remember?'

That was true. But her story stank nevertheless. Nobody else had known where I was going, and I didn't believe that the police were acting on their own initiative. We were white: if they hadn't known who we were, they should at least have been worried about causing a diplomatic incident. They hadn't looked in the least bit worried.

I turned my attention back to Isabelle. 'What are your instructions regarding me?' I asked her.

'None,' she said. 'I haven't been in touch with my people yet. And as you can see,' she added sarcastically, 'I don't have any transmitters hidden on me.'

'So why are you here?'

'When we met at the Yacht Club, I thought you were British intelligence—'

'Why?'

She shrugged. 'Instinct. Then, when you asked to go the Afrospot, I decided to come with you and see. I always enjoy an adventure.'

Despite the slap of a few moments ago, she was smiling. I recognized the sort: she was still under the misapprehension that espionage was a glamorous business. She'd learn the hard way; everyone did, eventually.

'We were good, weren't we?' she said, bringing my hand back up to her face, where I'd hit her. 'Me driving, you shooting . . .'

'Is that your idea of kicks?' I asked, but she was good, better than she could possibly know, because my mind was moving without me being able to control it, moving back many years, to another room.

She started moving my hand across her cheek, making me caress her, and I didn't resist, just stood there as she did it. One of my fingers brushed against her mouth, and she grabbed it with her lip, and then her hands were in my hair and she was leading me over to the bed, where she kissed me. I could taste the sweat on her, from the club, from the car. She moved her hands across my sodden shirt and lifted it, touching my stomach, and there was a fluttering there that I hadn't felt in years, and I let myself be transported back, let myself drift away in her skilful arms. As she unhooked her bra and I bit into her flesh, we fell into the cool grey sheets and she cried out to me — 'Robert! Oh, Robert!' — but I wasn't there. I was in another place, many years ago, and so I couldn't speak, couldn't *do* anything but lie there as she rubbed her body against mine, two animals in the dirt and the heat, and my mind cried back, shouting out in its little cell, again and again, despite everything: 'Anna! Anna! Anna!'

XI

Tuesday, 25 March 1969, Lagos

I woke with a start and reached for the gun. The room was pitch black and my chest was soaked in sweat. There was a sound, and it took me a moment to locate and identify it. It was coming from the woman lying next to me: her body was rising and falling in a gentle rhythm, and a low whistling was emanating from her nostrils.

The previous night's events flooded back. I flicked the bedside light switch, but nothing happened. Taking care not to wake Isabelle, I climbed out of bed and walked over to the door. The main light wasn't working either. That explained why I was drenched – there'd been a power cut, so there was no air conditioning.

I looked at the luminous dial of my watch. Twenty past five. Pritchard's plane would be here in just over two hours. I had to get dressed and get outside. But to where, and to do what, exactly? It was too early for Anna to be starting work at the embassy, and I would be too conspicuous hanging round there at this time of night. There was nothing more to do until dawn.

The wind was shooting volleys of rain against the window, making an eerie fluttering noise every few seconds. I went over, parted the curtains by a finger's breadth and peered through the mosquito net. I couldn't detect any movement, either in the street or in the cars parked by the entrance. The rain was beating furiously against the surface of the swimming pool – no diplomats sipping cocktails now. Across the dark water, the lights of the trawlers pulsed softly.

I took a seat in the corner of the room and considered the naked woman sprawled carelessly across the bed. I'd deliberately brought her back here, blowing my base, because if she was working against me that was the quickest way to force her hand. It had been my strategy from the start, and in some ways it seemed to be working. Since my arrival in Lagos less than twelve hours previously, Slavin had been killed, his assassin had taken his own life, and I'd been shot at by the local police. Someone was working against me, and pretty effectively. Was it Isabelle, though? I was starting to have second thoughts. She hadn't been out of my sight since leaving the Yacht Club, except for those two minutes in the Afrospot when I'd left her to return to the green room. But even if she had found a telephone in that time, the police couldn't have reached the club so fast. There had been close to a dozen cars. Perhaps she had given a signal earlier — to one of the bouncers, or even someone at the Yacht Club.

But none of this seemed to fit the woman sleeping so easily a few feet away from me. After we had made love, I'd feigned sleep with one hand gripping the Tokarev, waiting for any sudden movement. But she had drifted off faster than most husbands. If she had wanted me dead, would she have slept naked and unarmed in the same room as me, knowing I had a pistol and rifle within easy reach?

It wasn't just Isabelle that didn't add up. In the turmoil of the previous evening's events, I'd made several assumptions on the hoof — as light began to seep into the room, I went through them again.

I started with the killer on the golf course. My first reaction had been fury at Sasha: I had presumed that, despite my threats, he'd sent someone out to kill Slavin. But that couldn't be right. The rifle had been left at the club for the Russian, but it had not been involved in the killing of Slavin — that had been accomplished easily enough with a pistol. A cold thought swept through me: Slavin's killer had to have already been out here.

But why?

I thought back to the Afrospot: had I missed anything? Quite possibly – I'd had very little time to investigate. I tried to picture the green room again, but nothing new came to mind. What else had been there – and why had that woman stared at me like that when she'd first seen me? Perhaps she was the contact, and had thought I was the Russian. When I hadn't quoted poetry at her, she'd realized her mistake and retreated.

My immediate instinct was to return there at once and forget meeting Pritchard, but I rejected the idea just as quickly. Slavin's death implicated me as the traitor, and unless I gave a plausible explanation for it, Pritchard would come hunting my hide with the full might of the Service. I'd have to give him the impression we were working together, while at the same time not allowing him to draw too close. It would be a delicate balancing act, especially if my thoughts about the rifle were correct, in which case he'd stick to me like glue. I could, of course, neglect to tell him about the rifle. But Pritchard had clout, and I might be able to use some of it to get some more answers.

I picked my shirt from the carpet and reached for the cigarettes in the pocket. There were twelve left in the pack. I wondered if I would find Anna before they had all been smoked. I changed the focus of the thought: I would find Anna before they had all been smoked. The phrase from Slavin's interview that I had been trying to avoid thinking about once again slipped into my mind: 'the one true love of her life'.

A muscle in my stomach tensed. It was partly hunger – except for a handful of peanuts at the Yacht Club, I hadn't eaten anything since getting off the plane. It was partly fatigue – I'd been under huge strain and had only managed a few hours' sleep. But I knew that it was also partly a sudden, overpowering longing for Anna. Something had awoken when Isabelle had touched me, but I had to put it to sleep. It didn't matter if Anna had loved me, or I her – that was over twenty years ago, and a lot of blood had passed under the bridge since. She was a highly dangerous professional who had gone to extraordinary lengths to betray me, and who had almost certainly had a hand in murdering Father. This was not a woman to long for. This was a woman I had to find.

I finished my smoke, then felt for the case beneath the chair and lifted out the rifle. The night hadn't been a complete waste, after all: I had found this. Perhaps, if I looked hard enough, it might offer up some clues as to what was going on.

It was in perfect condition. Even in the dim light, the laminated hardwood had a noticeable sheen. That meant it hadn't been used yet – gum would have been applied to lessen its visibility in the field otherwise. I wasn't sure if that meant anything, but I stored the thought anyway.

Then I started to feel my way around the weapon, figuring out how it fitted together. It was a very different beast from the Enfields I'd used in the war. The sight, as I had already discovered, was mounted over the receiver instead of the buttstock, which was itself unusually long and sleek. Hard to transport something this size. How had it been brought into the country? Diplomatic bag?

I spent several minutes sorting through all the thoughts that came to me. When my eyes had fully adjusted to the dark and I thought I could see how the rifle worked, I began a field-strip.

I detached the magazine, then lowered the safety and emptied the cartridge chamber. Then the sight. The eyepiece was still a little wet, so I took hold of a corner of curtain and dried it as best I could. Finally, I detached the cheek plate, followed by the receiver cover and retracting mechanism . . .

'What you are doing?'

I looked up to see Isabelle staring at me from the bed.

'Good morning,' I said. 'I'm cleaning the rifle. There's been a power cut.'

She sat up and rubbed her eyes. 'It is what time?'

I told her. She picked her damp dress from the floor and slipped it over her head with a shudder. It was a shame to watch her body vanish beneath the fabric – I had an urge to get up and help her take it back off.

I placed the rifle back in its case and walked over to the bed.

'I'm sorry about last night,' I said, seating myself beside her.

She pushed her hair behind her ears and smiled, her teeth gleaming in the soft bluey-greyness of the room. 'You have nothing to be sorry about.'

'Not that,' I said. 'Earlier, when I made all those accusations. Mistaking you for a spy.'

She tilted her head up sharply. 'Why do you say that?'

It was my turn to smile. 'Last time I checked, French intelligence still insists its agents have basic driving skills.'

She punched me in the shoulder. '*Connard!*' But it was said with affection. 'Did you also search my clothes for transmitters after I fell asleep?' I didn't react, and she punched me again.

'What story did they give you?' I asked. 'They didn't say it was your chance to help *la patrie*, I hope?'

She shook her head. 'That wouldn't have worked.' She paused, wondering whether or not she could trust me. Then, perhaps realizing she now had little to lose, she shrugged her shoulders and continued. 'Before I was due to travel to the front last year, an old colleague of my father approached me. He said they were doing everything they could to end the war here, but if I could provide any information on what I saw it might help end it sooner.' She narrowed her eyes and looked at me straight on. 'It might save lives, you know?'

I nodded. 'The usual lie.'

It was too quick for her and she bristled. 'I forgot – you are British. Of course you say this. Your government arms the Nigerians so they can isolate Biafra and starve innocent women and children. How could you think any differently?'

I smiled tolerantly. 'I never discuss politics before breakfast.'

She looked at me with all the scorn she could muster. 'Do you treat all questions you cannot answer this way?'

'No,' I said. 'I treat all questions asked by people who have already made up their mind this way.' She stared blankly at me. 'All right,' I said. 'We're supplying the Nigerians with arms. So are the Russians, and others. Guns, tanks, planes . . .'

'That is your justification? That you are not alone?'

'Your government only started selling arms to the Biafrans last year,' I went on. 'Its contribution is still tiny compared to what the Nigerians receive from us and Moscow. And no heavy weapons. At its current level, France's support isn't enough to give Biafra even the slimmest chance of victory. That's because the idea isn't to help Colonel Ojukwu win the war — it's to help General de Gaulle win votes. Your government doesn't give any more of a shit about starving Biafrans than mine, and any information you've given your father's friend has, like the arms he has supplied, merely prolonged the bloodshed. You haven't saved lives — you've helped take more of them.'

I saw the slap coming, and steeled myself for it. Now we were even.

She started crying soon after, so I took the rifle case into the bathroom and sat on the edge of the tub. I reached for the collapsible rod tip: the bore looked filthy.

She didn't know anything about Anna, or Slavin, or any of it. She was just an amateur, a hopeless idealist caught in the crossfire.

'I have to leave soon,' I called out. 'Can you get ready?'

I went over to the basin. A dead rat lay face up in it, its eyes staring glassily at me from the darkness. I opened the window and threw it into the street below. Perhaps that's what I am, I thought: a dead rat flying towards a gutter, where larger creatures wait to devour me.

Melodramatic fool. I was as bad as she was. Nobody was going to devour me. I'd devour them first.

The water from the tap was tepid, but I splashed it all over my face and body anyway.

'I leave now.' She was standing in the doorway.

I dried myself, and she waited for the words of kindness that were not going to come from my lips. I suppose she was used to men begging her to stay.

'If you have to pay any traffic fines, the AFP office has my details.'

There was no need to humiliate her, so I smiled. 'You're heading back to the front, then?'

She nodded. 'This afternoon.'

The phone started ringing in the main room, and I went through to answer it. Could this be it? Could it be her?

'Paul,' said the man's voice on the other end. 'It's Geoffrey. Have you seen this morning's *Daily Times*?'

I looked up to see Isabelle walking past the bed. 'Best of luck,' I said to her. She nodded, but didn't make eye contact. The door made barely a click as she closed it behind her.

'Who are you talking to?' Manning was saying. 'Hello, is anyone there?'

'Hello, Geoffrey,' I said. 'No, I haven't read the papers yet – it's barely dawn. Why?'

'The entire front page is about bodies being dug up from bunkers on Ikoyi golf course, that's why!'

Alebayo had been right – it wasn't a bad paper. They'd put the story together in just a few hours. I told Manning we could discuss it at the airport.

'I'm not sure you should come,' he said. 'I don't think we should be seen together. It might—'

'What?' I asked. 'Blow my cover? You've just used my real name on a line that may well be tapped, so I think it's a bit late to be worrying about that, don't you? I'll be at the airport at half-seven, as agreed. I'm leaving your car here – the police will be looking for it. Send one of your secretaries to come and pick it up.'

'Looking for it? Are you pulling my leg?'

'Unfortunately not.' I didn't tell him the back window had also been shot off, but he'd find out soon enough. Instead, I told him that the Afrospot had turned out to be a club, and that the owner was a certain J. J. Thompson-Bola. I spelled it out for him, and when he'd got it I told him to see if there was anything in the files.

Then I hung up and called the Soviet Embassy again. It was a different clerk, but much the same message: Third Secretary Grigorieva had not come into the building yet and no, he had no idea when she was due. I left my details again, then dressed, reassembled the rifle and called reception to order a taxi. Part of me wanted to direct it to the embassy, so I could sit and wait for her to turn up, but I knew I couldn't. There was something else I couldn't put off: it was time to face Pritchard.

*

The rain had finally stopped, and the sun was rapidly climbing the sky. It looked as round and yellow and artificial as a child's drawing up there, but its effect on me as the taxi sped along the main road was real enough: my cheek facing the window felt like a branding iron had been placed on it. The city outside seemed flat and colourless in the glare and the haze, and I felt a little dizzy and nauseous – perhaps the previous night's activities had taken more of a toll than I'd realized. Luckily, there were few cars on the road, so we arrived at the airport in good time. The driver charged me two Nigerian pounds, despite a sign saying it was a fixed fare of one and ten bob the other way. There were more important arguments to be had, so I paid him.

'Robert!' Manning shouted at me as I entered the arrivals terminal. He was keen to rectify his earlier mistake, even if it meant making a few more in the process. He marched towards me, waving away a small collection of flies buzzing around him. He'd traded the nightwear for a khaki linen suit and deck shoes – it made him look only slightly more trustworthy.

I asked him if Pritchard had landed yet, and he shook his head.

'Some sort of a hitch in Madrid, apparently.' He dropped his voice to a whisper. 'Look, Paul, I really think this situation—'

'Did they say how long the delay was?' Perhaps there was time to go to the embassy and come back – it wasn't so far away. Perhaps Pritchard's flight would have to turn tail to London, and he wouldn't come out at all.

Manning dashed the thought: 'An hour at the most.' He suddenly noticed the case. 'I do hope that's not what I think it is.'

It admittedly wasn't ideal, carrying the thing around in the airport, but it wasn't safe leaving it at the hotel either. I wasn't in the mood for a lecture on tradecraft from Manning.

'Perhaps I wasn't clear enough on the phone,' I said, keeping my voice even. 'Everything that happened last night was necessary. Everything except for the police shooting at me, that is. That might have been because the nightclub you'd never heard of was a KGB drop.'

He quietened down then. 'Sorry about that,' he said. 'Jungle dancing's not really my thing, you know.' He tried to get a smile out of me, but when he realized it wasn't going to happen he swivelled his head around the hall theatrically, then leaned over and handed me the newspaper, from one end of which peeked a plain brown dossier. By the time he'd finished the manoeuvre, even the woman cleaning the floor was watching.

'Turns out we have a dossier on the family,' he said.

'Anywhere in here sell food?' I said, trying to move the conversation to a safer subject. There didn't seem to be any police around, but I didn't want to attract more attention if it could be helped – one trip to the dungeons had been enough.

'There's a stall in the car park,' said Manning. 'Nowhere else is open yet.'

I fished some coins out of my pocket and handed them to him. 'Fruit if they have it,' I said. 'Bananas or citrus. Failing that, anything with sugar in it.'

He didn't disguise his anger at being ordered around, but I was London – I might be in trouble with Pritchard, but he knew that a few choice words about his cock-up over the Afrospot could force him into early retirement. So he chewed his lip and waggled his eyebrows, and walked over to the exit.

I found a seat and examined the front page of the *Daily Times*. 'CORPSES ON THE GOLF COURSE!' was the headline, and the story contained full descriptions of both men and some lurid speculation from unnamed sources about their manners of death – but no clue as to the perpetrator. I read it twice and decided I was fairly safe: it would be very difficult for the police to prise anything out of the Russians, and judging by the number of other crimes reported in the city on the inside pages, they already had a fair amount on their plate.

I turned to the dossier. It was a dull affair, by and large, filled with lengthy accounts of impossibly trivial matters relating to seemingly every member of the extensive Thompson-Bola clan. After struggling through it, I came out with two files of interest. One involved a Daniel Talabi, the cousin Thompson-Bola had mentioned at the club: he was a writer who had been imprisoned by the government for aiding the 'rebels'.

But by far the most substantial dossier was on Thompson-Bola's mother, Abigail. The harmless-looking woman in glasses and head-dress was apparently something of a firebrand. She had a decades-long history of anti-colonial protest – and was, according to the file, a hardened Communist. She had been one of the first African women allowed behind the Iron Curtain, where she had met Mao. If there had been any doubts in my mind about the family's knowledge of the drop, this put paid to them, and she was now my prime suspect for the contact.

Manning returned with my breakfast: an unripe banana and a bottle of Fanta.

'I checked on the flight's progress,' he said. 'No news.'

The hour had passed – the delay was now edging up to two. I

decided enough was enough, and told Manning to set up a meeting with Pritchard for the afternoon — I had a few errands to run.

'Are any of your safe houses near the Afrospot?' I asked. But he wasn't even listening to me — he was focusing on something over my right shoulder. I asked him if he had heard, and his eyes flicked over to meet mine. He pointed across to the customs official taking down the barrier in front of passport control.

'They've landed,' he said.

*

Pritchard came through ten minutes later, striding confidently past his fellow passengers. In his dark suit and tie, white shirt and dark glasses, he looked like an upmarket funeral director. He caught sight of us and walked over.

'Hello, Henry,' said Manning, beaming. 'Welcome to Lagos.' It was evidently his line for airports.

'Hello, Geoffrey,' said Pritchard. 'How's Marjorie?' They shook hands and exchanged a few more pleasantries. Then Pritchard turned to me, and gave me the kind of look I saved for dead rats.

'Paul,' he said, dipping his head.

'Henry,' I nodded back.

Manning lifted Pritchard's bag and we walked back outside and hailed a taxi.

*

The return journey was conducted in silence, save for Manning's barked instructions at the driver. Pritchard sat next to me, staring sullenly at the landscape. It made sense that he didn't want to talk shop with others present, but what was he thinking in the meantime? I ate my banana and tried to clear my mind.

About forty-five minutes later we reached a large square, in the centre of which a street market was setting up. Manning paid the driver and led us through the aisles, past traders laying out their wares. One stall was apparently a grocer's, but although the fruit and vegetables were abundant, they were rotten and already covered in flies. A handful of Westerners were wandering around, waving their money and cameras, and I realized that this was probably where the photograph of Slavin had been taken.

Manning made a show of haggling over an intricately carved knife for a couple of minutes, before leaving off and pointing us to a grand colonial house on the corner of the square. He led us through a side entrance and down a narrow dirt path until we came out at a small garden in the rear of the property. He pushed open a rickety door and we followed him through several rooms. Chandeliers, chaises longues, candelabra: it was like walking onto the set of *The Forsyte Saga* after hours. Some of the furniture was in covers, and fat balls of dust sat contentedly in the corners. Manning explained that the local building industry had long been dominated by the Ibos, but that most of them had returned to the East when it had seceded, leaving dozens of unfinished and unsupervised buildings dotted around the city.

It was an unconventional choice for a safe house, but I had to admit he wasn't quite as daft as he looked. The market was popular with tourists, meaning that white faces were less likely to stick out, and the building was so conspicuous that nobody would think twice about anyone who entered it.

We climbed a flight of stairs to the second floor, which was home to a large ballroom that Manning had cleaned up a bit. I sat in an easy chair by a large electric orchestrion, and Pritchard walked over to the window and looked out at the rooftops.

'Depressing-looking country, isn't it?' he said. He swivelled on his heels and inspected his Patek Philippe. 'So. What time did you tell Slavin to get here for?'

Manning looked over at me anxiously.

Pritchard registered it. 'Problem?'

I broke the news. He didn't react for a long time, just stared at a spot on the floor in front of his shoes. Then he looked back up at Manning.

'Thank you, Geoffrey,' he said. 'You've done very well. We can take things from here.'

'Oh,' said Manning. 'Right-oh, then. I'll be at the office if you need me.' He gestured to a phone on a mahogany dresser, then scuttled away, leaving me alone in the room with Pritchard.

XII

'So,' he said, removing his sunglasses and placing them carefully inside his jacket. 'You came to meet me. You've got balls, Dark, I'll give you that.'

'You're still angry I left London ahead of you, then,' I said.

'Angry?' He tilted his head and considered the idea. Then he walked over to me, the heels of his brogues clicking loudly across the floor. He came right up, until his face was just a couple of inches from mine. 'Put it this way,' he hissed. 'If you ever do something like that again, I will *destroy* you.' He rocked back on his heels, pinching his nose as though trying to stop the rage from bursting out. 'Do you understand?'

I said I did, and let silence consume the room for several seconds. 'But you decided to run me anyway.'

He stepped away and laughed a joyless laugh. 'Believe me, this wasn't my idea. I pushed for them to recall you, but Farraday told me to make the best of the situation and come out as your control.'

'Farraday is a fucking fool,' I said.

He sighed. 'He's also our fucking Chief at present, and unless you're tendering your resignation we are going to do precisely what he fucking says.'

'What if I refuse?'

'Apart from getting the sack, you mean?' He smiled. 'I'll blow your cover to the Nigerians and you'll be locked up and being buggered by the natives before you know it.'

He took off his jacket and placed it over the back of a nearby chair. Then he rolled up his shirtsleeves, revealing pale but muscular forearms. It was a clear signal: beneath the funeral director's garb was a man it would be wise not to mess with. But I already knew that.

'Now before you give me a thorough explanation for the complete *shambles* you seem to have created since arriving here,' he said, 'I'd like you to tell me what really happened in Germany in '45. You can start with Larry.'

He'd thrown it out fast, but I'd been expecting it. 'I wish I knew,' I said, and ignored his open look of disbelief. 'He disappeared looking for Meier,' I went on. 'Remember him?' Pritchard nodded slowly. I took out my pack of Players, lit one, and sucked in the rich welcoming glow. 'We'd found all the others, but Meier had been much harder. We just hadn't seemed to be able to pick up his trail. Then, in September, Father announced he had traced him to some-where near Hamburg. He left in the jeep that afternoon – and never came back. Obviously, something happened with this nurse, and I mean to find out exactly what.'

He pondered this for a moment, then sprung: 'Why did he leave alone? Why didn't you go with him?'

'You remember what happened with Shashkevich,' I said, and did my best to look ashamed.

'I see. But why didn't you mention at the Round Table that you were in Germany at the end of the war?'

I took another drag of my cigarette, and said I could well ask him the same question.

He ran a finger along the mantelpiece, then inspected the dust that had gathered on it. 'So you were just waiting for me, is that it?'

'You heard William: there were hundreds of people working in intelligence in Germany at that time.' I let a note of righteousness creep into my tone. 'Anyway, we were discussing a traitor in our midst. Your theory was that he might even have been in the room, so it hardly seemed like the best moment to reveal it.'

'You could have told Farraday after the meeting, surely? Unless you think *he* might be the traitor?'

'Why, after all these years, would I tell Farraday about Sacrosanct and risk—'

'Incriminating yourself?' he inserted. Then he relaxed a little and smiled. It looked painted on. 'I can see your point. I felt the same myself. But perhaps Farraday should be let into the secret now. It might look worse if he learns about it later and neither of us had mentioned it.'

I couldn't read his tone, but I didn't like the sound of that one bit.

'How could he learn about it?' I asked. 'Seeing as you and I are the only two who know? Anyway, I'm not sure he would understand even if we did tell him.'

'Oh, don't underestimate Farraday,' he said. 'He's sharper than he looks.'

Sharper indeed, I thought, remembering the way he had steamrollered Osborne at the meeting.

'Tell him, then,' I said. 'I suppose it's too late for all the repercussions you and Father were worried about, anyway.' I ground out my cigarette on the floor and opened the bottle of Fanta by tilting the top against one of the arms of the chair. It tasted warm, flat and oddly metallic. 'Perhaps you could also give him a thorough account of your operations in Gaggenau at the same time.'

His eyes were tiny marbles devoid of recognizable emotion. 'I think,' he said finally, 'that you could now debrief me on the current situation.'

We left it at stalemate, and I did as he had asked. It didn't take me long: one pyjama party, two dead Russians and a car chase.

'What about the bodies?' he said when I'd finished. 'What did you do with them?'

I handed him the newspaper. He read through it quickly and then put it to one side.

'Well, that's sure to enrage the Russians – let's see what they do.

Have you looked into Grigorieva yet? Slavin claimed she recruited the double, so she would appear to be key to the whole thing.'

'I haven't had time to stake out the embassy yet, but I imagine they've trebled their guard now. What do you have in mind? Approaching her as a possible defector herself?'

He nodded. 'Yes. Although if she was recruiting double agents twenty years ago, I imagine she'd be a fairly hard nut to crack. And I'd like to have at least some idea beforehand of why her death was staged.'

'What about Chief — has he not turned up yet?'

He walked back to his position by the fireplace and shook his head.

'That's a pity,' I said. 'I'm starting to wonder if Farraday might have been right. This hit on Slavin makes me think he might be involved in this, after all.'

Pritchard turned and faced me. 'Oh, no,' he said. 'We know Chief's not the double. He was murdered.'

*

I took out another cigarette. I was down to ten, but it didn't matter. I needed something to calm me down — and something to keep my hands from shaking.

I'd allowed Chief's death to drift to the back of my mind in the last few hours. I should have known it wouldn't go away for very long. I took a deep draught of the cigarette and asked Pritchard why murder was now suspected.

'Five have found traces of blood and matter in his living room,' he said. 'And a bullethole in one of the walls. The killer had tried to conceal it by moving the piano. They're looking into what kind of gun might have been used. At any rate, he was shot. Most probably by the real traitor. By the way, are your fingerprints on file?'

Despite the sunlight streaming into the room, I suddenly felt very cold. I shook my head. 'Why?'

'Oh,' he said. 'Five are planning to take prints of anyone in the office old enough to have been turned in '45. It's more so they can rule people out than anything. Lift any clouds of suspicion. You can have yours taken when you get back.'

'Of course.' I made the extra effort to keep my voice steady. 'Why would the traitor want to kill Chief, though?'

Pritchard shrugged. 'Perhaps he knew something that would give him away. Perhaps . . .' He stopped. 'I must say, you don't appear too surprised.'

'That Chief was murdered? Of course I'm surprised. I'm just trying to think it through.' I thought I had sounded flabbergasted, but Pritchard was evidently now viewing my every utterance with suspicion. 'Has Vanessa been told?'

'Not yet. But they'll have to do it soon, because she's already going spare. Osborne's speaking to her tonight.' He gestured at the case lying by my feet. 'Is that the item you found in the nightclub?'

I nodded, relieved to be moving onto safer ground. I took out the rifle and positioned it on the floor so he could have a good look.

He walked around it, twice. 'Looks like an AK-47,' he said. 'But it's not, is it? It's a sniper rifle.' There was no visible reaction on his face, no sudden dawning realization.

'Yes,' I said. 'It's a 7.62 mm Dragunov SVD. First produced in competition with Kalashnikov, in fact. It was adopted by the Red Army six years ago.' I picked it up and placed Pritchard in the crosshairs. He didn't flinch. Once again, it crossed my mind that I should kill him while I had the chance. But I was on a knife-edge already – another corpse would leave no doubt in London's mind. I didn't fancy running for the rest of my life or rotting away in Moscow, so I leaned down and placed the rifle back on the floor.

'Why didn't your man on the golf course use this to kill Slavin?' Pritchard was saying.

'I've been wondering the same thing myself,' I said. 'I reckon killing Slavin must have been a last-minute idea. The killer was out here on another job when he was told he had to take care of a defector as well, and fast. He didn't have time to go to the club to pick up the rifle, so he used an unmarked pistol instead.'

'"Another job"?'

'He had an L-pill on him and he *used* it. He had to be protecting something pretty major to take his own life.'

'Perhaps he was simply a well-trained servant of the Motherland.'

'I don't think even the Russians are that brainwashed,' I said.

'All right. If he didn't need a rifle to kill Slavin, what would he need it for?'

I nodded. 'I thought of that, too. What if Slavin was killed, not because someone was afraid he was going to reveal the identity of Radnya, but because he might reveal the identity of *another target*? The man on the golf course was no ordinary thug – he knew hand-to-hand combat, and he was a crack shot. Ever heard of SMERSH?'

He nodded. SMERSH had been the Russians' method of dealing with those they felt might escape justice after the war. They hadn't bothered burying their bodies.

'Officially, they were wound up in '48,' I said, 'but we have some evidence that the new KGB chief, Andropov, has reformed them. Remember those chaps who took over Prague airport last year? Very similar m.o.'

'I don't remember seeing any reports on this,' said Pritchard.

'We've not had solid proof of it. I've mentioned it to Chief a few times, but he keeps – kept – putting me off.'

'Assassination units in peacetime? Isn't that stretching it a little?'

'Have you forgotten, Henry?' I said. 'You helped my father set one up.'

He didn't say anything to that.

'Slavin was shot with a pistol,' I went on. I pointed at the rifle. 'So why was *that* waiting for him in the Afrospot?'

'Could be a number of reasons,' he said. 'The country is at war, after all . . .'

'Fine,' I said. 'Leave it, then. Let your petty hatred of me get in the way of you doing your job, and watch the PM have his guts smeared all over the street. Hell, you don't agree with his politics anyway, so perhaps you're ecstatic about it.'

He frowned. 'My personal feelings don't come into it. My problem is simply that what you're suggesting doesn't sound plausible. What would the Russians have to gain by killing the PM?'

'Nigeria, of course. If he were assassinated in Lagos, it would be seen as a direct result of his policy to provide arms to the Federals. Whoever succeeded him as prime minister would be under enormous pressure to end Britain's involvement here. That would leave the Russians free to step up their arms sales, end the war and move their men into the presidential palace shortly after. And with one of the largest countries in Africa in their grip, they'd soon start exerting influence elsewhere.'

'You didn't like the domino theory yesterday,' he said.

'I've learned a few things since then.'

He walked around the SVD, considering the implications of what I was saying. I needed him to conclude I was right, because the authority he had with Farraday might be useful to me – and could be very dangerous if turned against me.

'You're assuming too much,' he said after a minute or so, and I let my breath out slowly, trying to contain my disappointment. 'It's all rather circumstantial. Quite a lot of what you say is circumstantial, I find.'

I was getting sick of him. 'Look, Henry,' I said. 'I know you don't like me much. That's fine – I can't stand you, either. But if you would just listen—'

He put a palm up.

'You may be onto something. I was simply noting that you have no proof of it.'

He walked over to the dresser and rang Manning, asking him to get hold of a copy of the schedule for the Prime Minister's visit as a matter of urgency.

When he'd put the receiver down, I asked him what he thought he was doing.

'What do you mean?'

'I mean you just said I'm onto something. So when are you going to signal London and tell them to cancel the visit?'

He gave a sharp shake of his head. 'Can't do that. The PM has made quite a fuss about this visit. He'd have to have a very good reason to back out now.'

'A better reason than an attempt on his life?'

He ran his tongue along his teeth. 'If he pulls out now, it would be an enormous loss of face for the Nigerians, and it might lose us all the influence we've earned in the last couple of years. And it was hard earned, believe me. But more importantly, it would deprive us of the opportunity of finding out what the hell the Russians are up to – and perhaps finding this traitor. That's why we're both here, after all.'

'Doesn't the traitor become a slightly lower priority now that the PM's life is at risk?'

He tilted his head and let the way I had phrased it settle. 'If there was a plot to kill the PM,' he said, eventually, 'it would seem to have been extinguished.' He pointed at the rifle. 'We even have the weapon they were going to use.'

'They're not going to call it off because of that!' I said. 'Golf Course Man had written down the name of the place he was to pick up the gun. No professional would do such a thing unless they had to. He must have been the back-up.'

He considered this for a moment. 'Where's the original sniper gone, then? And what weapon will he use?'

'I've obviously no idea where they are, but weapons are easily replaceable.'

'Yes. So are prime ministers.' He misinterpreted my look. 'Oh, don't wet yourself. If I thought for a second we were endangering the life of the PM, I wouldn't joke about it. I agree that there seems to be a wider plot, but it can't be a coincidence: it's surely linked to Slavin's decision to defect. As Slavin is dead,' – he pursed his lips at me – 'he can't tell us how, but we need to find out because it may help identify the traitor. And that is paramount: as long as he is operating, we have no idea how much damage he has done, or even in what areas. If we tell Cabinet Office about this, they'll either whip the PM out of the country before we can blink, or wrap him so tight in cotton wool the Russians will immediately smell a rat. Either way, they will roll up whatever it is they've got going, and you'll be no closer to finding out what Slavin knew or how it connects to the double.'

It was a beautiful speech. The twist in it was lobbed in so elegantly that it took me a second to catch up to it.

'Me?' I said.

He nodded. 'The note you left in your office said you wanted to find the real traitor – so far all you've done is got our only lead killed. I'm not yet sure if that was cock-up or conspiracy, but here's your chance to prove your innocence. We now know Chief is not Radnya – I think it's time you earn your spurs and find out who is. If not,' he paused, 'well, I might be able to help the police in their investigation into the deaths of two Russian diplomats.'

XIII

In the harsh light of day, and without the wail of saxophones and trumpets emanating from it, the Afrospot was revealed as just another nondescript Lagos townhouse on just another nondescript Lagos street. The patch of lawn in front of the entrance was strewn with empty beer bottles and tin cans, and a gang of stray dogs barked at the young boys who were half-heartedly kicking around a punctured football.

'You're in Marjorie's bad books,' Manning was saying, as we surveyed the scene from a car across the street. When I didn't respond he turned to Pritchard, who was in the passenger seat next to him. 'He's in Marjorie's bad books.'

'Why's that?' said Pritchard, not moving his eyes from the entrance to the club.

'Because I've had to hide the car. This is one of the firm's spares. So you can imagine – she's not best pleased.'

It was a white Peugeot estate, and, if anything, it was in better condition than Manning's had been. But I didn't argue – there were other things to think about. I'd seriously miscalculated the way Pritchard would react to the idea that the PM might be the target of an assassination attempt. I had tried to convince him of it, partly because I didn't like the idea of sitting on information that someone might be about to get his head blown off, whoever he was, but also because it suited my own aims. I'd thought Pritchard would immediately arrange for the trip to be cancelled, which would tie him up in red tape and give me the space and time to get to Anna. I hadn't imagined he would be mad enough to use Wilson as *bait*. Still, I couldn't deny his logic – it was essentially the same strategy I'd used with myself: move close enough to the flame to be able to blow it out.

According to the schedule Manning had brought with him, the PM was due to arrive in just under fifty-one hours' time. I glanced again at the sheet of paper.

<u>Visit of the Prime Minister to Nigeria</u>
<u>27-31 March 1969</u>

Programme

Thursday 27 March
16.00 Prime Minister and British Delegation
       arrive.
20.00 Working dinner on board HMS *Fearless*.

Friday 28 March
09.00 Formal talks with General Gowon.
13.15 Depart Lagos by air.
14.30 Arrive Enugu. Visits to the ICRC
       Rehabilitation Camp at Udi and to the
       British Child Medical Care Unit at Enugu
       Hospital.
19.00 Arrive Lagos by air.

20.30 Informal dinner with General Gowon at
       Dodan Barracks.

And so it continued, until he flew off to Addis Ababa on Monday morning. In four days, he would visit dozens of buildings and meet hundreds of people. Without anything more to go on, narrowing down the time and location of an attempt on his life would be impossible. But Pritchard was right: there must be a connection with Slavin's move to defect, and as he had opened his negotiations by providing information about me, I wanted to know what it was.

'Why is he bringing the *Fearless*?' I asked Manning.

'Show of strength,' Pritchard answered, and Manning nodded vigorously.

'Precisely. The Russians have been building up a presence in the harbour over the last few months, so this will put them in their place.'

I ruled it out as a possible target — it would be far too heavily guarded. From Pritchard's dossier, I knew that Enugu and Udi were both former Biafran strongholds now in Federal hands. They also seemed unlikely; for propaganda purposes, Lagos seemed likely to be the Russians' first choice. My instinct, for the moment, was that they would be keen to strike as soon after he arrived as possible — perhaps even at the airport.

'Do either of you fancy telling me what this is all about?' asked Manning.

'Just stay here, Geoffrey,' I said. 'Look after the case, and if the police — or anyone else — arrive, come in and get us.'

*

'Remind me,' said Pritchard as we crossed the street. 'What are you hoping to find?'

'I'm not sure,' I said. 'I'm just worried I might have missed something.' It was partly the truth — it had been niggling at me since I'd read the files Manning had brought me on the family — but it was partly because Pritchard was now going to follow me wherever I went, so I couldn't go to the Soviet Embassy to wait for Anna. I wanted that meeting to occur alone. He hadn't been that easy to persuade, but I had insisted that the security situation there would make us too conspicuous.

The boys stopped their game as we approached. The tallest of the group ambled over and stood between us and the front door, legs akimbo and arms folded.

'We closed,' he scowled.

'Good morning,' I said. 'We're looking for Mister Thompson-Bola. Is he in?'

He looked us up and down, and slowly shook his head.

'It's important,' I said. 'We want to talk to him about Daniel Talabi.'

He wasn't convinced: perhaps the name didn't mean anything to him. But someone had been following the conversation, because there was a sudden scratching at one of the windows. The boy took a couple of steps back, listened for a few moments, and then gave a small nod of his head and stood to one side.

Pritchard and I walked into the Afrospot.

*

The room was a degree or two cooler than outside, but every bit as lifeless: there were beer stains on the floor, and smears on the windows. In the doorway stood J. J. Thompson-Bola. He looked tired, but otherwise the same as when I'd last seen him: he was still in his silver trousers, and between two fingers he held a marijuana cigarette so large it looked about to collapse in on itself.

'I remember you,' he said. 'The journalist. Where's your girl-friend?'

I could sense Pritchard stiffen beside me. 'She wasn't my girl-friend,' I said. 'But I have to apologize – I'm not really a journalist. I work for the British High Commission, as does my colleague here.' Pritchard showed his diplomatic passport: he was a second secretary, impressive cover to have set up in less than a day.

J. J. took a long drag of his joint. He didn't seem too surprised. 'What do you know about Daniel?'

'Is there anywhere we can sit down and talk?'

He nodded, and gestured for us to follow him. We walked down the corridor, past several doors, until we reached one, which he pushed open.

It was the green room. It didn't appear to have been touched since I'd been here – I supposed the police had occupied them for most of the rest of the night. It evidently also served as a dormitory of sorts, as there were a few mattresses on the floor, and as a dining room: several people sat eating at the central table, among them Abigail. She was wearing the same kind of traditional outfit as previously, but the headdress had gone. She looked up as we walked in, and immediately recognized me. She rattled something off to J. J. in their own language; they were Yoruba, I remembered from the file. J. J. replied in kind – I caught only 'Daniel'. She looked at him in surprise and, with a few words, immediately dismissed him and everyone else from the room.

When they had all gone, she addressed me: 'You want to talk about Daniel?'

I walked over and sat down at the table opposite her. Pritchard stayed put by the door.

'We believe we may be able to arrange his release,' I said. 'Would that be important to you?'

'How?' she said. The eyes behind the thick lenses were unflinching, proud and unafraid. 'How would you be able to accomplish that? I saw you run from here yesterday night. Run from the police. So I ask again: how will *you* arrange for the long-awaited release of my nephew from unlawful imprisonment?'

I could see how she could be trouble. Her voice was that of a natural orator – and she was no fool.

'Last night was a misunderstanding,' I said. 'I work for the British government, and we have called in some favours with the people who are dealing with Daniel's case. They are more than willing to cooperate. Provided,' I added, 'that you can help us with another investigation we are conducting.'

I scanned the instrument cases leaning against the wall. They looked untouched. The table was the same mess of glasses and bottles and musical paraphernalia, only now with a few half-finished plates of what looked like curry.

What was it I was looking for?

'You are not here to help Daniel,' she said.

Her tone was calm, but there was defiance in her face – a lifetime of defiance, against men who looked like me. I wished I could reach across to her and tell her that I was no enemy, that I shared her cause. But I couldn't – because I didn't think I did any longer.

'We're not here to help Daniel,' I admitted. 'But if you don't help us, things may become worse for him.'

She looked at me with disgust. 'You think you can blackmail me?' she said. 'I have nothing you can take. Nothing! Not even Daniel. I will not be forced against my will to do your bidding.'

I took out the Tokarev and leaned across the table.

'I think you will.'

She didn't avert her gaze. 'Why must men always revert to violence?' she said.

'I believe you've met Mao. The answer's in his book. "Power grows out of the barrel of a gun".'

'That is incorrect. It is *political* power . . .'

'This is political.'

'Shoot me, then,' she said, in the same calm voice. 'Shoot me with your gun. I don't think your masters would look kindly on it.' She glanced at Pritchard. 'Do you approve of this behaviour?'

Without moving the pistol, I glanced over my shoulder at Pritchard. He adjusted his sunglasses and gave the slightest of nods, either in answer to her question or to tell me to carry on.

I carried on.

'Tell me about the man who was meant to collect the rifle,' I said, placing a touch more pressure on the pistol.

And then she reacted. It was just for a fraction of a moment, but her eyes flickered to a spot a few degrees above my head. And in that instant I thought I saw something she'd not wanted me to see: not exactly panic and not quite fear. Confusion? And then she was staring straight at me again, expressionless, as though it had never happened.

I turned to follow the line her eyes had taken. Pritchard. But why would she look at him? And then I noticed that something was hanging on the back of the door, directly behind him. A white sheet, it looked like.

I placed the gun back in its holster and walked over. Pritchard gave me a puzzled look, but stepped out of the way. I unhooked the sheet, and found it wasn't a sheet at all. It was an apron. Embroidered on one sleeve was a small red cross. It also had a pocket across the front, out of which poked a small piece of white cloth, which I took out. A cap.

The roof of my mouth felt dry, and I could hear a drumming in my head.

They hadn't been expecting a man to collect the rifle.

They'd been expecting a woman.

*

I didn't find out how much more Abigail Thompson-Bola knew — perhaps it was just that there was a nurse's apron hanging in the green room of her son's nightclub. But even if she had known more, she wasn't going to give it to me without a long struggle, and I didn't have the time for that.

I had until Friday afternoon. Manning's programme didn't make clear the precise time the PM was due to arrive at the Red Cross camp in Udi, but the earliest it could be was half past two, so that was my deadline.

Anna had been due to pick up the rifle. She had been a Red Cross nurse in Germany; the assassin was to use the same cover. It couldn't be coincidence, and explained several other things. Abigail's odd glance at me when I had entered the green room of the Afrospot: she'd either been expecting a woman or wondered if I was her last-minute replacement, Golf Course Man. And why nobody had searched my room at the hotel, despite my doing everything to try to draw Anna out of the embassy. Because she wasn't in the embassy, but three hundred and fifty miles away.

But there was a lot it didn't explain. What had prevented Anna from picking up the rifle and the nurse's uniform? Why the sudden change of plan? Perhaps she had found out Slavin was about to defect. Panicking that he knew about the plot to kill the PM, she had left for Udi early, leaving one of her team behind to dispose of Slavin and pick up the weapon and apron.

These were all grim thoughts, though, because her involvement in something of this magnitude suggested that she had not only known about the plan to kill my father, but was more likely to have been the one to have pulled the trigger. I realized that a part of me had been harbouring the hope that she might have been almost as much of a pawn in the Germany operation as I had been. But this didn't look like someone who could have been used in that way. This looked like a ruthless professional assassin.

Pritchard had realized the ramifications of the apron within seconds, of course – I'd bloody given him the file in which it stated her cover in '45 had been as a nurse. That meant it was now more important than ever that I found her. Because if he got to her before I did, he had ample reason to put her in a room and squeeze her for everything she knew. And that meant I was dead.

As soon as we had left the club, Pritchard had headed for the High Commission with Manning to work on getting transportation to Udi, and had told me to check out of my hotel and get down to the Government Press Office in the centre of town to apply for a permit to fly to the front. We were due to meet back at the safe house for a progress report at 15.00 sharp.

It was now half past two. I had checked out of the hotel, but I hadn't been to the press office and I wasn't intending to go. Presuming that Anna had not changed her plans, there were now seventy-two hours on the clock, rather than forty-eight, but Pritchard had an awkward problem to solve: if he told London that the Prime Minister's life was in danger, they'd cancel the trip and he'd lose his chance to find out how the plot related to Slavin's defection. But any request for airborne transport would have to be cleared by the Federal side, and I already knew from Isabelle that the authority for that could take weeks. At any rate, they wouldn't let me on board, not after a British newspaper had just accused the Nigerian air force of deliberately targeting Biafran civilians. There were tank convoys, of course, but Udi was a hell of a long way away. Even in peacetime, getting across a country like this could take a while. In the middle of a war, three days would be pushing it.

I'd thought of a better idea. I had disposed of the rifle, dismantling it and leaving it in the wardrobe of my hotel room. Then I had taken a taxi to the Agence France-Presse offices, which were housed in a concrete office block opposite one of the Arab embassies in Ikoyi. I told the driver to wait and rang the bell. A tanned Frenchman in shirtsleeves answered the door, and I told him I was looking for Isabelle Dumont.

'I am sorry,' he said. 'She has already left.'

'Where from? What time was her departure?'

He smiled tolerantly — Isabelle and her lovers — and looked at his watch.

'Three o'clock,' he said. 'From the main airport.'

I shook his hand and ran back over to the taxi.

*

Through one of the windows, I could see that the Nigeria Airways DC-4 that had been on the tarmac when I'd arrived on Monday was still there — or perhaps it was another DC-4. But just one soldier stood beside it now, and as I watched he threw his cigarette stub to the ground and began to climb the steps of the ladder.

'That's my plane,' I told the customs official. 'If it leaves, prepare to receive a very stern note from Government Office headquarters.'

He was a small man with an oversize cap and a neat row of pens in his shirt pocket. 'I am sorry, sir,' he said. 'But I need to see your authorization before I can let you through.'

'And I've already told you that I don't bloody have it! It's on the plane with my colleague, Isabelle Dumont. There was a mix-up at the office, and she left without me. Call the control tower, stop the plane and ask her if she works with Robert Kane – or you can say goodbye to any chance of promotion!'

Something in that lot – perhaps the idea he'd be stuck talking to the likes of me forever – penetrated, and he hurried off to a back office. I lit another cigarette – forget my silly game, my body needed the nicotine – and watched the plane.

It was starting to move. Damn it, he had to hurry. I wondered if I should go in there and make the call myself. The plane was taxiing towards the runway, and with it my chances of getting to Udi. I had no other plan. I'd have to sit it out and wait for Pritchard to arrange something, but the chances were that they would allow only him to go, and that would be it . . .

The plane stopped. The official beckoned me.

XIV

The inside of the plane looked just like the one I'd flown in from London, only the seats were filled with sombre-looking soldiers instead of diplomats and aid workers. But it still bore many of the markings of civilian travel, right down to the emergency information card and sick bag in the seat pockets.

'Which division are we with?' I asked Isabelle a few minutes after we had taken off.

She gave me a puzzled glance. 'The first,' she said. 'Why?'

'No reason,' I said. I stood up and placed my bag in the overhead locker. 'Thanks again for your help, by the way – you needn't have.'

'It was nothing.' She rummaged around in her bag until she had found a camera. 'Take this,' she said, handing it to me. 'If you're coming as my photographer, you may as well take some pictures. That's a Nikon F – the best. Just point it at anything you think is interesting and press here.'

I strapped the camera around my neck and peered over at her window: the city was receding rapidly below us, the sun reflecting off the water as we swung inland.

'So what brings you back to me?' asked Isabelle. 'What is your mission in Enugu?'

'I'm not telling you that!' I said. 'I don't want it all over the French papers tomorrow.'

She gave a short, indignant laugh. 'So I risk my neck for you and you are not even gentleman enough to share with me the reason . . .'

There was a flirtatious upturn to her mouth, but anger lay just below the surface. She didn't realize that my not telling her was protection, for both of us.

'Perhaps later,' I said, picking the tourist map from the seat pocket in front of me. 'How long do you think it will take to reach Enugu?' I asked. It was very close to Udi.

'Get ready,' she said.

I glanced over at her: she was looking down the aisle. I raised my head a little and saw that one of the soldiers was walking towards us. He was a tall, lanky fellow, and from the way the others stepped out of the way as he passed, I guessed he was in charge.

'You are journalists?' he asked when he reached us. He wore a thick, sweat-stained camouflage jacket with a grenade dangling from each pocket, and the word 'GUNNER' was written across his helmet in white paint.

'Yes,' said Isabelle. 'I am a reporter.'

'And I'm her photographer,' I said, holding up the camera.

Gunner gave me a sharp look.

'You are English?'

I nodded.

'BBC?'

'No,' I said. 'We're with a French agency—'

'You want interview me?'

I looked at him – he seemed serious.

'I'm sorry?' I said.

'Interview. I give you exclusive,' he said.

I tried to explain that I was just Isabelle's cameraman. 'I don't do interviews,' I said.

He didn't seem to hear, and gestured that I follow him. I glanced at Isabelle, who gave me a nod and passed me up a notebook and pen. I squeezed past her and followed Gunner down the aisle.

He was heading for the rear of the aircraft, which was partitioned off with a grubby green curtain. Behind it, the seats had been stripped out and the space had been filled with crates of AK-47s and ammunition, lashed to the floor with ropes. Gunner seated himself on the floor between a couple of the crates and waited for me to ask him a question.

I crouched down beside him. The only thing I really wanted to know was how long it would take for us to get to Enugu, and how I could get to Udi from there. But that obviously wouldn't do. After a few seconds of silence, he gave me a look that indicated he wasn't impressed with English journalism so far.

'How long do you think the war will last?' I said – the first thing that had come into my mind.

He thought about this for a moment, and then replied solemnly: 'Hopefully, it will end soon. But first we must finish it.'

I dutifully noted down this pearl of wisdom, and tried to think of another question that might satisfy him.

'Do you think it is a just war?'

He looked up sharply.

'Just?' he snorted. 'Of course. Ojukwu tried to break this country into pieces. But to keep Nigeria one is a job that must be done.'

He was parroting Federal slogans at me – I'd seen the last sentence on a poster on a street in Lagos just a couple of hours previously.

'So you don't think the Biafrans have a case for secession?'

'What case?' He leaned forward and made sure I met his gaze. 'I am from the East. But I no agree with this so-called "secession". It no serve the interests of our region, and it no serve the interests of Nigeria. It only serve Ojukwu and his rebel clique.'

'You're an Ibo?' I said, surprised.

He held up one finger imperiously. 'Please, Mister BBC Journalist, do me the courtesy of allowing me to finish. I am Ibibio. I no like this Biafra idea from start, so I go leave the East and join the army to help crush the rebel movement.'

'That's an excellent quote,' I said, and he straightened his shoulders a little and jutted out his lower lip. 'Thank you very much for taking the time to talk to me.' He looked disappointed, so I asked him his name and rank to round the thing off for him.

'Captain Henry Alele,' he said, proudly, and I noted it down. He looked at me expectantly.

'And can I just ask, for our readers, how you got your nickname? Were you on anti-aircraft duty?'

He looked at me blankly, and I pointed to his helmet.

'Ah,' he said. 'Arsenal.'

I looked down at the crates. 'You make sure the weapons get to the front?'

'No, no,' he said, looking at me like I was a fool. 'I support Arsenal Football Club!'

I started laughing. It must have been a physical need welling up in me, because it wasn't the funniest joke I'd ever heard and yet tears were soon running down my cheeks. After a few moments, Gunner joined in, nervously at first, and then full-bloodedly. It changed the shape of his face, lighting it up, and I realized just how young he was. He couldn't have been more than eighteen or nineteen.

Then, abruptly, he stopped.

'Why you laugh at me?'

'I'm not,' I said, between heaves. But how to explain to him that I found his devotion to an English football team surreal without insulting him? And then something occurred to me. 'You lost the cup to Swindon . . .' But that thought just set me off again, and Gunner's eyes, which were starting to bulge with anger, only made it worse.

'Do not mention this word!' he shouted. 'I do not want to hear about these Swindon thieves!'

I waved a hand at him to stop, and he actually went quiet until I'd regained some control. Then he looked at me very seriously, and I wondered if he was going to ask to see my press pass.

'Tell me, honestly, Mister — what is your name?'

'Robert Kane.'

'Tell me, Mister Robert, have you ever heard of such a bunch of crooked sportsmen in your life as Swindon Town?'

'No,' I said, trying to match his tone. 'I haven't.'

My exclusive interview with Captain Alele came to an abrupt close just then, as the curtain was drawn and an anxious face peered out at us.

'Captain – we have some trouble with the plane. The pilot wants to know how to proceed.'

*

The trouble, Isabelle told me when I had returned to my seat, was that a message had come through from Enugu saying it was not safe to land there. Gunner and the pilot were now locked in heated debate about what to do. Isabelle's theory was that the Biafrans had coordinated one of their rare air strikes.

'What other airports do the Federals have?' I asked her.

'Not many,' she said. 'We already passed Benin City, so perhaps they will have to try Port Harcourt.'

I looked at the map. Suddenly the world wasn't so funny. Port Harcourt was a good hundred miles south of Udi. It looked like my strategy had completely backfired – we were now heading away from my target.

Things soon got worse. Over the next couple of hours, it began to rain again, after which we found ourselves flying through lightning. We were buffeted about in our seats, our stomachs churning, our fingers gripping the arm-rests. Just minutes before we reached Port Harcourt, the pilot decided to land in the bush.

And so, as night fell, we came down with an almighty bump in a muddy field somewhere in the forests of eastern Nigeria; I noticed a few of the soldiers crossing themselves when we finally came to a standstill.

Gunner moved swiftly into action. He might not have been the world's greatest interviewee, but he knew how to deal with his men. He picked out five of them to accompany him on a reconnaissance mission, and gave a short speech to the rest of us explaining the situation.

'We go see if we can find some transport for us to leave here.' He gestured at the two soldiers sitting in the aisle seats in the front row, and for a moment I thought he might point out the emergency exits, like in the safety demonstrations. 'In the meantime, Njoku and Otigbe, keep watch on your windows. If you see anything suspicious at all at all, raise the alarm. Everyone, stay close to your weapons. When we return, we knock four times on the door. Do not let anyone in who no knock four times. Understand?'

Everyone shouted that they understood, sir, and Gunner and his group started gathering up their weapons and backpacks.

'We're sitting ducks,' I said to Isabelle. 'A fully lit plane sitting in the middle of a field. What's to stop the Biafrans from attacking us?'

'Fighting is finished for today,' she said.

'You sound very sure of that.'

She nodded. 'There is a routine, followed by both sides. Usually, they fight in the morning, then have lunch and a siesta and then they fight for a few more hours in the afternoon. They do less during the rainy season – there is too much mud. In any case, it is very rare that there is fighting after dark, so we should be completely safe.'

Siestas? It seemed I had stumbled into a joke-shop war. Still, if what she said were true, then perhaps there was some hope. We had only been a few minutes from landing in Port Harcourt, which was a Federal stronghold. That meant there should be plenty of transport around. If we weren't under threat, I might be able to find some. I got out of my seat.

'What are you doing?' said Isabelle. 'Wait for me.'

I found Gunner and told him that we wanted to come along on the expedition. 'This could be a big story,' I said. '"Captain Leads Unit To Safety After Aircraft Downed By Storm".'

He considered the idea. 'You do as I say at all times,' he said eventually. 'Otherwise I tell my men to shoot you on the spot.'

★

The eight of us piled down the small staircase into the field. The rain whipped against us; I'd forgotten how strong it could be. Within seconds, my clothes were stuck to my skin.

The lights of the plane cast an eerie glow, but it made visibility easier. The field was surprisingly lush, although there didn't seem to be any crops in it – looted by soldiers, perhaps. Palm trees swayed menacingly around us, and the air was thick with the buzzing of mosquitoes.

'Be careful,' said Gunner, as we stalked through the field. 'There may be rebels close by. But there may also be our own soldiers – so look before you shoot!'

After about a mile, we reached a small dirt track, which Gunner decided we should take. It was the right move, as it led us straight into the centre of the nearest town.

If you could still call it a town. It seemed completely abandoned, and the unmistakable stench of decaying human flesh hung in the air – we all took care to breathe through our mouths. We walked through streets littered with spent ammunition, broken bottles and the occasional corpse, grey and inflated. The buildings were almost all ruined. One still bore a sign reading 'Bank of Biafra', while another had been a cinema: I glimpsed a poster advertising a showing of James Stewart in *It's a Wonderful Life* flapping from an empty window frame.

There were plenty of vehicles around, but they were either charred to a cinder or missing wheels. The lights of the buildings were all out – it didn't look as though there was any electricity here at all. My hopes of jumping in a jeep and driving off to Udi were looking pretty slim. The main road had been cut anyway, with trees laid across it at regular intervals, so even if I had found a working set of wheels, I'd have had difficulties getting anywhere.

Suddenly the wind intensified, bringing the rain up off the

ground. As I struggled to keep my footing, I saw Gunner raising his arms and gesturing at a nearby building, which looked like nothing but a small hut with an open entrance. I reached it just after him, with Isabelle following close behind me.

The hut seemed much bigger inside, a dark cavern that receded into nothingness. As I came further in, I was conscious of light, and with a start realized it was eyes: the whites of dozens of eyes staring at me from the silent gloom. The men were stick-thin. Their uniforms, if you could call them that, consisted of torn T-shirts and sweaters dyed green, and trousers that could barely hold themselves together. The women wore ragged cotton sheets and little else, their breasts bare and their ribs exposed so much it almost hurt to look. But it was the children that sent a shiver through me. Naked and pot-bellied, they stood there silently as the rain roared outside, calmly looking at the strangers entering.

'Nobody shoot,' said Gunner. But his men were frozen.

'The camera,' Isabelle whispered to me urgently. Perhaps Gunner's words had made her think of it. 'Give it to me now.'

And while we all just stood there, I handed it over and she crouched down on one knee and began photographing the scene, the sound of the shutter almost obscenely loud.

'Who is your leader?' said Gunner.

After a few moments, a stoop-shouldered old man shuffled forward.

'We just want food,' he said. 'We are all hungry.'

Isabelle stopped her clicking.

'We must take them back to the plane,' she said. 'We must help them.'

Gunner didn't say anything for a long time. Then he nodded, and we started taking them out.

*

'Order, order!' shouted Gunner from his position at the head of the aircraft. 'Now listen, men. I am glad to report that our recon-naissance mission has been a tremendous success.'

I saw a couple of the group glance at each other. There were now eighteen more bodies in the plane, and they were the enemy to boot.

'We are very close to a town that has recently fallen to our side,' Gunner continued. 'This is good news.' He looked out at us, and seemed to lose his train of thought for a moment. 'This is good news,' he stressed. 'This means our soldiers must be close by. Divisional HQ must not be far away. When morning comes, we go locate the HQ and proceed to Port Harcourt. We move at first light. In the meantime, please look after our . . .' He looked around at the Biafrans hopelessly, searching for the right word. 'Our guests. Keep them warm. Pass around blankets and cushions. Share your rations with them, please – there will be plenty of food tomorrow.'

He didn't say what would happen to the Biafrans tomorrow, and nobody asked. After water and bread had been passed around and some of the most severely affected and youngest children given as much treatment as the plane's first-aid kits could provide, some semblance of normality began to take hold. Guided by Gunner's skilful diplomacy, the Biafrans started to talk. One of the Nigerians recognized one of them from his schooldays, and soon they were comparing the fates of friends and family members. As the atmosphere warmed up, I told them how something similar had happened in the First World War – or 'the Kaiser War', as they knew it – when British and German troops had played football together in No Man's Land one Christmas Eve. It wasn't the same, of course – the men of the group were deserters, and had stayed in the bush when the town, which they told us was called Aba, had fallen months earlier. They had been trying to live off the land since. The field we were in had contained cassava, but it had long gone. But, despite the differences, my historical comparison went down well, and made everyone feel better for a moment.

It didn't last. A few minutes later, as everyone began preparing to bed down for the night, there was a loud banging on the rear door of the plane.

Everyone went quiet and listened to the sound. A few of the men quietly reached for their machine guns.

The banging came again, a dull but insistent thudding.

Gunner walked over to the door and stood a few inches away from it. 'Who goes there?' he shouted. Everyone tensed: fingers gripped around triggers, shoulders hunched and all eyes fixed on the door.

'This is Colonel Bernard Alebayo of the Third Marine Commando Division,' called out a familiar voice. 'Who goes *there?*'

XV

Alebayo stood at the front of the plane, his back and shoulders parade-ground straight. Although our encounter in the belly of Lagos Airport had been less than twenty-four hours earlier, it seemed much longer ago than that, and my image of him had changed in the interim. I was surprised at how small he seemed, and how young – with his short sleeves and slight frame, he looked more like a cadet than the most feared and celebrated commander of the war. But as he stood there, motionless, it was almost as though he were waiting for his presence to ripple around the cabin, and within moments I was remembering just how unpleasant he had been.

He was flanked by about half a dozen soldiers, all of them well-built and heavily armed. Rain dripped from their helmets, darkening the green and white Nigeria Airways logo that was repeated across the thin carpet. Alebayo's eyes slowly swept the cabin. As I followed the line of his gaze, the incriminating details seemed to leap out: the Nigerians in their smart uniforms; the rising sun insignia on the sleeves of the ragged Biafrans; the half-eaten loaf of bread.

When his eyes finally reached mine, they paused for a fraction of a second, and I fancied they glowed with a touch of triumph. He looked like he was about to say something, but if so he thought better of it, for he continued his visual tour. When he came to Isabelle, there was another flicker, but this I couldn't decipher. Concern, perhaps? Or just surprise to see a woman, and a young white woman at that, in these surroundings?

He jerked away. 'Who is in charge here?' he said, and his voice reverberated through the plane.

Gunner stepped forward and saluted smartly. 'Captain Henry Alele at your command, Colonel. This no be as it appear, sir. I apologize most heartily—'

Alebayo raised his hand. 'There is no need, Captain.' He extended an arm and patted Gunner on the shoulder, and at the same time a strange smile broke through his stern features. 'I applaud you, for you have done the right thing. We must rejoice, today of all days – it is only proper. It came as a shock to me, that is all. I hadn't heard, you see. When did the news come through?'

Gunner frowned. 'The news, sir?'

'Yes,' said Alebayo, his smile still fixed in place. 'It cannot have been long ago – I listened to the radio just before leaving my head-quarters, and there were no reports of a ceasefire then.'

Gunner lowered his head for a moment – perhaps to gather courage – and then looked up at Alebayo. 'I have not heard about a ceasefire, sir.'

'Oh?' said Alebayo, raising his eyebrows in a caricature of puzzle-ment. He slowly withdrew his hand from Gunner's shoulder and set his eyes travelling around the cabin again, in the manner of a lawyer making sure everyone in the jury appreciated that he had just caught out a witness. Then, in a louder, more menacing voice, he said: 'So why are you fraternizing with the enemy, Captain?'

Isabelle shuddered beside me. I knew how she felt – it had been a nasty little trick.

'I know it begin look that way, sir,' said Gunner. 'The truth—'

'Save it for afterward,' said Alebayo. He lifted his hand again, and as though he were signalling the start of a race, or were a Roman emperor ruling on the death of a gladiator, he suddenly brought it down, slapping it against the side of his trouser-leg. 'Arrest them,' he said quietly. And as his men moved forward to carry out the command, he looked across at Isabelle and me with something that looked very much like disgust. 'Arrest all of them.'

*

The rain beat against the tarpaulin above us, and I watched it bounce off the receding mud track, so thick it was almost impossible to see past. I was getting my ride, but it wasn't in a jeep and it wasn't to Udi. Instead, I was shackled to my seat in the back of a dilapidated lorry, headed in the direction, presumably, of Alebayo's headquarters in Port Harcourt.

Alebayo was in one of the vehicles ahead of us, along with Gunner, his men and the Biafrans. Before setting off, he had assigned three men to guard me and Isabelle. Our bags and the camera had been confiscated, and we'd been chained together and pushed into the truck with about a dozen soldiers.

So we sat, thighs touching — it was hard to tell where my sweat ended and hers began, even through layers of fabric. The smell of sweat was so heady in the confined space, in fact, that I was finding it a struggle to focus on our guards. They were seated on the opposite bench; all three had sub-machine guns aimed at our legs, and were keeping their eyes glued to us.

There was no reasonable hope of escape — I'd realized that at once. I was in poor shape to attempt it, anyway, as the last couple of days were choosing their moment to catch up with me: my eyes were stinging, perhaps because I'd only slept a few hours since leaving London, and I had a nagging ache in my back and down my left thigh, both of which were probably gifts from a nasty little Russian with a sand rake. None of this compared to my thirst, though; my tongue was working frantically in a desperate attempt to create more saliva. I hadn't had any of the water that had been handed round in the plane — I'd spent enough time in tropical climates to know not to drink from an open bottle — but now I was sorely regretting the decision. Thinking about it would only make it worse, I knew, but I couldn't help myself. My eyes only saw moisture: the rain outside; the sweat on the faces of my companions; even the polished metal poles that ran around the roof of the truck holding the tarpaulin up seemed to have a liquid quality to them.

I tried to empty my mind of such thoughts and concentrate on the problem at hand. The lorry's suspension was almost non-existent, and as we seemed to be taking dirt tracks through the forest, it felt like we were sitting on a drunk camel. The first time we had hit a sizeable bump, a couple of miles back, Isabelle had let out a yelp, and all three of our guards had tensed, as had a few of the other soldiers. But the guard on the left, the one with the scars on his cheeks, had let out his own cry, almost simultaneous with Isabelle's, and raised his gun, enough to make me think he was serious about using it.

I had no idea if Isabelle was aware just how precarious the situation was: a bigger bump, a bigger yelp, and one or both of us could get a round through the legs, or worse. I'd seen Alebayo give instructions to the men before they had taken us in hand, and I guessed he had told them that the two Westerners should not, under any circumstances, be killed — hence their aiming at our legs. And I was confident that they would try to carry out the order, because Alebayo had a reputation for rough justice: the report I'd read back in London had recounted how he'd had one of his soldiers executed by firing squad for shooting an unarmed Biafran. But would he take into account the bumps in the road, and Isabelle's nerves? If I were accidentally killed, the man responsible might also face a firing squad — but that wouldn't help my corpse.

'Do any of you speak English?' I said to the guards, in the clearest, calmest voice I could muster.

All three coiled in response, and I could feel Isabelle doing the same beside me. Coiled, but there was no harm done, yet. Fingers gripping triggers, but no shots fired, yet.

'Do not speak,' said the man with the scars. 'The colonel told us if you speak, we shoot you.'

'That's just it,' I said quickly, before he could think about it. 'I'm worried you might shoot us by accident. My colleague here is very nervous, and if we hit a big bump, I'm worried someone might . . .'

'Do not speak,' said the man. 'If I were you.' But he gave a tiny nod and kept his eyes locked on mine, as if to say he understood the problem. A few minutes later, he leaned over and whispered in the ear of the guard next to him, who in turn whispered something to the third man. And a few minutes after that, Scarface quietly put his gun onto safety, and the other two followed suit.

It was an opening. There was nothing now between me and the road – well, nothing but chains and a dozen armed soldiers. But supposing I could bound forward with enough force to break the chains? My hands were attached to the underside of the bench, meaning that if pressure were exerted at the right angle, I could use it as leverage. The bench was quite wide – I could press my feet back at least fifteen inches. It was perhaps even a little too much, but if I sat bolt upright, the distance shortened until it felt almost like a natural starting block.

And the soldiers? Most of them were not on their guard. This was just another journey back to headquarters. They would be looking forward to putting some food in their bellies, perhaps a beer or two, and sleep. They knew there were a couple of prisoners in their midst, of course, but they also knew that three of their colleagues had their weapons trained on us. We were not their responsibility. And unless they had been paying close attention, they wouldn't have known that those weapons were now on safety. I would have the benefit of surprise.

But, of course, the danger would not be over once I had left the jeep. It would take the fastest of the men only a few seconds to recover, if that, and I would be picked out even through the rain and the mud and the darkness in only a few seconds more. And nobody would face a firing squad for shooting a prisoner who had tried to escape.

My other potential lever was sitting beside me: Isabelle. If I managed to bring her with me, the soldiers would have two targets, rather than one, and added to the rain and the mud and the darkness that might just be enough to save me . . .

I stopped the line of thought. It was an exercise, that was all, an exercise I had hoped might reveal a way of prising open the chink. But I knew even as I went through the options that none of them was viable. Even if I managed to pull Isabelle and myself into the road, the chances of survival were too small to take the risk. The fact that escape was possible was no comfort — it had to be likely. In short, it was the kind of plan that looked good on a blackboard in the Home Counties, but when it was your life on the line in the middle of the night in the African bush, it was only good for keeping your mind distracted.

And right now I had more important things to think about. Chiefly: Alebayo. The good news was that I hadn't done anything I wouldn't have done had I, in fact, been a photojournalist. If he interviewed Gunner or any of the other men who had been on the plane, they wouldn't be able to report anything incriminating. And there was nothing in my bag that shouldn't have been there.

The bad news, of course, was that I had already crossed paths with him. He had been suspicious of my cover then, and it had changed since. Not substantially, but perhaps enough to be a problem. I'd told him I was working for *The Times*, assigned to follow the PM's trip in Lagos. If he remembered that (and I had a feeling he might), he would naturally want to know what I was doing several hundred miles away, and under the aegis of Agence France-Presse.

I decided the best thing was to bluff it out, and insist that I was still working for *The Times*, but simply teaming up with Isabelle. As long as she didn't crack and I stuck to my guns, there would be no easy way for him to prove otherwise. My trump card was that I was British. That meant he couldn't do too much without provoking an international incident — if I made enough of a noise, perhaps nothing at all. Hopefully I'd be away from here within a couple of hours, leaving me plenty of time to find my way to Udi.

More light was entering the jeep now, and the road had suddenly become much smoother. Peering through the rain, I saw rows of small houses, a few of them with lit windows, and then what looked like a grass tennis court. That must have been a mistake, though, because I couldn't imagine many towns in the area had a tennis club.

The truck started to slow, and our guards took their guns off safety with an audible click. It was our stop. Without a word, the soldier with the scars on his face released our chains, and we were pushed out onto a smooth asphalt surface. The truck sped away.

Where the hell were we? It didn't look like it could be a Nigerian town, or even an officers' mess – it looked like one of the new towns outside London. Neat, white Snowcem bungalows lined both sides of the road, and each had a small garden in the front fenced off by low hedges. There were even a few sun loungers, and I wondered for a moment if we had fetched up in some sort of luxury holiday resort; perhaps I had fallen asleep and we'd driven into some tropical paradise. But that wasn't right – it was quarter to ten, so we couldn't have been more than fifty miles from Aba, and probably less as the roads would have slowed us down. The smell of the swamp was still here, too, and every bit as fetid.

Before I could contemplate my surroundings any more, I was prodded in the back again, and Isabelle and I were marched towards one of the bungalows. We reached a small wooden gate and one of the men struggled with the latch for a few seconds before getting it open. We walked up the narrow path to the door.

A small plate was fixed next to the doorbell: '561. Sebastian Tilby-Wells and Family'. A former British army base, then? But why would the British have a camp out here? And looking down the street, it looked very grand for the military – even Fort Gosport didn't have this level of build. I tried to imagine Sebastian Tilby-Wells, and saw a very tall man with a neat ginger moustache and a burnt pate, bossing around his fat little wife and their fat little children.

Scarface fiddled in his shirt pocket and brought out a key with '561' stamped on it. He unlocked the door and we were pushed into darkness.

'Stay here,' he said. 'Do not try to leave, or you will be shot.' He cocked his trigger to make sure we'd got the message, then closed the door and locked it.

XVI

I ran my hand along the wall until I found the light switch. We were in a large living room: two armchairs, a divan, a coffee table, a couple of dead house plants. At the far end, an integrated kitchen, long metal windows — and an air conditioner. I walked over and switched it on, but nothing happened.

Isabelle slumped into one of the armchairs and asked me if I had any cigarettes left. I tossed her the pack and lighter, and walked over to take a look at the windows. They were unlocked.

That was interesting. I rolled them back to find a veranda, complete with deckchairs and flowers sticking out of what looked like old petrol drums.

'They had it good, didn't they?' said Isabelle.

I turned. 'Who? Where are we?'

She laughed, her face momentarily obscured by a cloud of smoke. 'You are very serious. "Who? Where are we?"'

'Fill me in,' I said, 'and I'll tell you all my knock-knock jokes.'

She sat up and ground out my sixth-to-last cigarette in an ashtray on the coffee table. 'We're in the Shell–BP camp at Port Harcourt. I thought you knew — Alebayo is using it as his headquarters.'

Of course. While I'd been feverishly fantasizing about throwing myself into the road, we must have been waved through some gates. The windows were unlocked because it didn't matter if we left the house: we wouldn't be able to get past the perimeter. I turned back to the window: the moon was dim in the rain, but I could make out a few more bungalows and, beyond them, the outline of a high concrete wall. I couldn't see any machine guns in turrets, but it amounted to the same thing.

I had another look at the room. The Tilby-Wellses appeared to have left the place rather quickly. Magazines and paperbacks were still scattered across the coffee table: a two-year-old issue of *Life* featuring the lost notebooks of Leonardo da Vinci shared space with *The Collected Short Stories of Somerset Maugham, My Family and Other Animals* and a booklet about West African birds. Apart from the standard pieces of furniture, the only unusual items were a drinks cabinet and an antique radio set. The kitchen was home to a disconnected fridge and a rusty stove. The cupboards were empty, except for a couple of cockroaches and several tins of Bartlett pears. No tin-openers, though.

It was like a safe house, I decided. The thought comforted me somewhat, and I made my way back to the drinks cabinet, where I found the dregs of a bottle of Drambuie, a sliver of Tio Pepe, and about a quarter of a litre of lime cordial. A not-too-dirty shot glass was resting on the board, and I poured the lot into it and downed the result. It tasted vile: my teeth felt as though they were rotting away as they came into contact with the liquid. But for one exquisite moment it relieved the dryness in my throat. I also hoped it might contain enough sugar to send some much-needed aid to the pain surging through my lower back and thigh muscles.

Behind me, Isabelle announced she was going to find the bathroom to powder her nose. I investigated the radio set. It was in working order, so I tuned it to the BBC's African Service. They were reaching the end of a bulletin – I wanted the headlines, to see if Pritchard had cancelled the PM's trip. I turned the volume up as loud as it would go, and the weather report blared across the room. Cairo was hot. Oslo was cold.

'What are you doing?' Isabelle called from offstage.

I walked towards her voice. 'The room may be bugged,' I said, taking a left at the kitchen. 'You might want to watch what you say.'

'You should check the plants. Isn't that where they usually hide them?'

If there were microphones, they could be anywhere — in the ceiling, the walls, the furniture. It would take at least an hour to turn over the place, and I didn't know how long we had.

'The radio is fine,' I said. 'Where are you?'

'Here!' she said, leaping out from behind the wall. 'So what do you think?' Instead of her usual Zazou black, she was now in a turquoise ankle-length dress.

'What the hell do you think you're doing?'

'You don't like?' she said angelically. 'I could no longer wear those wet clothes.' She scrunched up her nose in disgust, then raised a finger. 'I find something for you also.' She vanished behind the wall again for a few seconds, then reappeared clutching a pair of silk turquoise trousers and a white tennis shirt. '*Voilà!* You will match me perfectly.'

I took her by the wrist and exerted some pressure. 'We're not going to a bloody fashion show,' I said.

She pulled away. 'What happened to those jokes you promised me?' she said. She walked back into the living room, seated herself in one of the armchairs and pouted.

I didn't have time to waste on games — somewhere in this compound, Gunner and his men were being interrogated. And any minute now, it could be our turn.

'Listen,' I said. 'Do you have your press accreditation from Lagos?'

She looked up. 'No — it was in my bag. Why?'

That was what I'd been afraid of. 'Here's what we're going to do,' I said. 'I'm working with *The Times*, but at the last moment I got ordered to the front, and we decided to work together. All right?'

She took it in, then nodded. 'All right,' she said. 'But I think you should relax. We're not in danger now. It's a story for your friends back in London, I think. A story for myself also – my office will be very pleased to hear it. Some of the photographs I took in the hut may change the course of the war. This level of suffering – it will shock people into action.'

She looked so smug, I could have smacked her. I pointed out that Alebayo might not be too keen to let her call her office, or hand back her camera. She didn't hear me, so I moved closer and said it again.

She laughed, smoothing the pleats of her new dress with one hand. 'I think he will give it back. He can be tough when he's ordering his men to kill innocent Biafrans – I would like to see how tough he is in front of a member of the world's press.'

'These ones aren't all innocent, though,' I said. 'The men are deserters.'

She looked at me, aghast.

'Did you see the condition they were in?'

The silly bitch seemed to have forgotten we were in the middle of a war. It was bad news – if she tried to take Alebayo on, she'd really put the cat among the pigeons.

'Alebayo hates the world's press,' I told her. 'In fact, he hates anything that smacks of interference by the West. If you want to help the Biafrans, and yourself, you would do well to remember that.'

We listened to the football results in sullen silence for a few minutes. Finally, the familiar notes of 'Lilliburlero' whistled merrily into the room, and I turned it down slightly so we could listen to the bulletin more comfortably. Pakistan had a new president, there was fierce fighting in southern Vietnam, and John Lennon and his new wife were staging a protest in bed in Amsterdam. No mention of Nigeria or the British prime minister. I wondered where Pritchard was – probably a deal closer to Anna than I was.

'That was about your operation, wasn't it?' said Isabelle when the report had finished and I'd turned the volume back up. 'There was a coded message in one of the items!'

I shook my head. 'We don't do that any more.'

'What, then?' she said. 'You might as well tell me now.'

'The less you know, the better.'

It was a shame to have to treat her like a child, but she had a glint in her eye and it was worrying me. She was notching it all up for her exclusive report from the Biafran front, where she had been imprisoned in a bugged room with a British secret agent on a mysterious mission. It would make thrilling reading at breakfast tables across France — if we got out of here in one piece.

We listened to the radio for a while longer, and she cadged another of my cigarettes. I went over the story with her one more time, and then the door opened and Scarface marched in.

'Move,' he said, gesturing with his sub-machine gun.

*

The streets of the compound were quiet and deserted, but I caught a few glimpses of the site's new purpose: a couple of camouflaged armoured cars and a Land Rover parked outside one of the bungalows, and a small obstacle course that had been set up on the other side of what had once been tennis courts. It was still raining, and Isabelle was having trouble with her new outfit, which was sticking to her in all the wrong places. God knows what Scarface made of her get-up; he didn't say a word, just gestured which turnings we were to take and kept a close eye on our movements in case we decided to make a run for it. There was little chance of that, unfortunately — the only thing to do now was to talk Alebayo into letting us go as soon as possible. At one point, we passed a street that led to the entrance into the compound. It was a massive iron gate, and I managed to count eight guards before we had to make a turn.

After about a ten-minute walk, we arrived at our destination: a grand villa standing on the crest of a small hill. We walked up a path through the large and well-kept garden, passing jacarandas and palm trees. As we got nearer to the house, the sound of music spilled out onto the lawn, an American soul number with swishing drums and a plangent male voice singing about the end of the world. The doors to the place were open, and a handful of soldiers were pulling crates off a jeep in the forecourt. It looked a little like preparations were being made for a party – I half-expected to see a marquee being erected.

Scarface took us into the house, which still had the appearance of a private home – presumably this was where the managing director had lived. The paintings and mirrors still hung on the walls and there were vases filled with flowers. We walked down a short corridor, passing several soldiers on the way, their boots pinging off the tiled floor as they went about their business. Nobody gave us a second glance.

The music became louder with every step, and the instruments and voice started to mesh together. Scarface pushed open some double doors and we entered a large hangar-like room. It was dark, but I could make out desks, chairs, filing cabinets, telephones, several standard radio sets and a few SSBs. I could make out a faint glow from the rear of the room, and Scarface indicated we should head for it. As we got nearer, I saw that the light was emanating from a small area sunk a couple of feet into the floor. There was a campbed, a wardrobe and a mahogany table. On top of the latter was an antique gramophone player, from which the closing notes of the song blared, and a lamp, which cast a small pool of light on the tatty leather armchair in the centre of the 'room'. Seated in this was Colonel Alebayo, his head tilted back, apparently asleep. He was wearing a black and gold kimono-type number and matching slippers. His uniform lay folded neatly on the bed, his cap resting on top of it.

We stood at the edge of the pit for a few seconds, watching him. Then Scarface coughed. Alebayo's eyes snapped open, his head jerked upright and he jumped to his feet. Without looking at us, he strode the two feet to the table, stopped the needle and replaced the record in its sleeve.

'The prisoners are here, sir,' said Scarface unnecessarily, and gestured for us to walk down the three steps that led into the den.

Alebayo turned. 'Thank you,' he said, with a hint of a smile. 'I can see that.' Scarface thought about replying, but Alebayo waved him down. 'At ease, at ease.'

Isabelle and I took up position side by side in front of the armchair, like two schoolchildren summoned before the headmaster. As he and his men had done earlier in the aircraft, we silently dripped rain onto the floor.

Alebayo seated himself again and looked us over. It was very quiet in here, more noticeably so after the din of the music. Alebayo's face was as smooth and placid as a marble bust – it reminded me of the masks I'd seen in the market in Lagos.

'Mademoiselle Dumont . . .' he said, finally, and his voice was lilting, almost tender. 'I'm sorry – are you married?'

She shook her head. Alebayo stretched an arm out from the depths of a satin sleeve and plucked a piece of paper from the table. His voice rose: 'Mademoiselle, this is your authorization to be at the front. Is that correct?'

She glanced at it. 'Yes.'

'You have been a reporter for a long time?'

'Four years,' she said.

Alebayo nodded, and turned to me. 'And how about you, Mister Kane? Where is your authorization?'

'He's my photographer,' put in Isabelle.

Alebayo pursed his lips. 'Really?' He looked back down at her papers. 'But it says here that you work for Agence France-Presse. Mister Kane told me in Lagos just the other day that he worked for *The Times*, and that he was covering the visit of the British prime minister there.'

'That was true then,' I put in. 'But I got a cable from my editor this morning telling me to get out to the front and find a more interesting story. I proposed teaming up with Miss Dumont here. She agreed to it, as did my editor.'

Alebayo lightly waved Isabelle's authorization, as though fanning himself. 'They may well have, Mister Kane. But the Press Office of the Ministry of Information in Lagos did not. If they had, your name would also be on this piece of paper, or you would have your own.'

'Here's the thing,' I said. 'I did have my own, but we had a very bumpy landing and I couldn't find it afterwards. I must have dropped it.'

'How terribly careless of you,' said Alebayo, amused at the flimsiness of the excuse. He folded Isabelle's paper and placed it back on the table, then gave me a searching look. 'Do you know David Ashton of *The Daily Telegraph?*'

This game again. He'd tried it with Churchill back in Lagos.

'By reputation,' I said. 'I've never had the pleasure of meeting him.'

Alebayo pressed his fist against his chin as if thinking. 'How about Bill Turner of *The Express?*'

'Don't think so,' I said.

'Jack Stern? He's at *The Observer.*'

I shook my head apologetically. 'I'm afraid I'm not very sociable – I tend to stick to my work.'

He nodded. 'I quite understand. I am much the same.' He leaned forward in his chair. 'But here's the *thing*, Mister Kane. Those three gentlemen are all staying at a hotel very near here. So are several other British journalists. I took the liberty of calling earlier and asking if any of them had ever heard of or met a Robert Kane of *The Times*. And do you know – not a single one of them ever had?' He eased back into his chair. 'You must be *very* unsociable.'

There had always been the danger of my cover being blown. I hadn't designed it for use in the field, and I'd only had time to take the most limited of precautions, namely securing the initial accreditation for Lagos. So it was no real surprise it was coming under strain. I didn't say anything. It was his interrogation – he'd have to do the work.

'No,' said Alebayo after a few moments. 'I don't feel your story has a shred of credibility. But I admire your quick wits. The British Secret Service trains its agents well.'

'I was wondering when you'd get to that,' I said. 'I told you before I'm not a spy.'

'No?' he said. 'Do not play games with me, Kane.' I didn't like that – I'd been getting used to the 'Mister' bit. 'I am not buying the act.' His voice was now tinged with that familiar sharp edge. 'You are not an innocent journalist. You are a British spy, and you are in Nigeria to disrupt Russian involvement in this war.'

'That's absurd,' I said. It was, really.

'Is it?' He let the words hang in the air for a moment, and we locked eyes: his were openly triumphant. 'Do you deny that you have been monitoring our arms supplies?'

'What arms supplies?'

'The crates in the aeroplane you flew here on, Mister Kane. They contained weapons provided to us by the Soviets – as you well know.'

'How the hell would I know that?'

'They were all clearly marked with Russian identification. And Captain Alele has confirmed to me that you and he had a conversation in the rear of the craft . . .'

'At his request!' I said. 'He wanted me to interview him!'

'Come, come. Do you expect me to believe that if a trained British operative wants to investigate the hold of a plane, he cannot present himself to a junior officer in a certain way so as to ensure he gains the access he seeks?'

'Look,' I said. 'It's clear we've got off to a bad start. You didn't like me when you met me in Lagos and it's a shame we've run into each other again, because you seem determined to see my actions in the worst possible—'

Alebayo had one hand in front of his mouth, and it took me a moment to realize that he was quietly chuckling to himself.

'"Run into each other"?' he said. 'Is that what you think we have done? Do you think I just happened to be passing by Aba? Let me enlighten you, my friend – I was *looking* for you. Two Russian diplomats were murdered in Lagos last night, and this afternoon the police put out an alert at all airports for a British journalist by the name of Kane, whom they urgently wish to question. When you turned up again at Lagos Airport, a very efficient customs officer, Mister Igbaweno, a distant cousin of mine, as it happens, radioed through to me to ask what he should do. I advised him to let you on the plane and promptly contacted divisional headquarters in Enugu. They were very understanding, thankfully. We have had a few minor disagreements, our two divisions' – he offered a preview of a smile, then shut it off abruptly – 'but when I explained that there was a British spy and murderer flying in their direction, and that I had already come across him and would like the opportunity of dealing with him myself, they were only too happy to let the plane be diverted. When the winds came up and your plane failed to land as your pilot had announced to our control tower, I sent some of my men out to see what they could find. It didn't take them long to track you down. On arriving at the spot, I found that you had persuaded some of our troops to fraternize with the enemy. So you see,' he concluded, folding his hands in his lap, 'there is really no question of my misinterpreting your actions. They speak for themselves.'

Blown.

The police had known to look for Kane.

Blown by *Pritchard*.

What a fool I had been. I'd completely misread the man – desk work had killed my instincts. I was a fucking amateur, of no more use than Manning or, indeed, Isabelle. Because I should have – how could I not have? – realized what the bastard had been up to. When

I had suggested delaying the PM's trip, he had raised a few polite objections and then backed down, nodding that cadaverous skull of his at me. It was so obvious now that it felt like I'd been kicked in the stomach. He hadn't simply strongly suspected me: he hadn't bought my story for a moment. He'd realized I was Radnya the moment I'd fled London. Farraday hadn't told him to come out and run me; he'd told him to come out and find proof.

How terribly clever I'd thought I was being – but Pritchard had seen through my game from the start. He had *expected* me to run again, which was why he'd given me the deadline to meet him in town. Perhaps he'd had me tailed – in my rush to find Isabelle, I'd neglected to take the usual precautions – or he could simply have made a call to the Palace and discovered I'd checked out. That would have been confirmation enough, because there had been no guarantee he would find transport by nightfall, so it could only have meant a run.

He'd come out to Lagos certain I was the double, and I had confirmed it for him. So he had delivered on his threat, and blown me to the Nigerians. One anonymous call to the local police station would have done the trick. Result: I was in the middle of the jungle, surrounded by soldiers armed to the eyeteeth, in the hands of a man with a taste for sentimental songs and a hatred of journalists, spies, the West and especially, it appeared, me.

All of this shot through my brain as I listened to Alebayo's crowing little speech. There were a few cracks in his logic, though, and I leapt on them ravenously.

'With all due respect,' I said, 'your accusations don't make much sense to me, Colonel. If my mission had been to assassinate a couple of Russians, why would I flee to the front? I can think of safer places to hide from the police. And why would I also be checking your cache of arms and encouraging fraternization? My knowledge of espionage is extremely limited, but would any agent really be given so many objectives to complete?' I was surprised to find myself drifting into the same kind of cod-legalistic language he favoured, but decided it was a decent strategy: he might be more likely to free me if he felt we saw the situation in similar terms.

But he wasn't impressed. 'The precise nature of your operation does not concern me,' he said sharply. 'There is enough evidence of nefarious activity to condemn you several times over. As well as persuading Captain Alele to show you the weapons on board the craft, you also took photographs. Perhaps the Russians got in your way — or perhaps you decided to kill two birds with one stone.' He waved the argument away. 'In any case, you leave me no choice but to hold you here.'

I sensed Isabelle flinch beside me. Had she thought it would be so easy?

'What purpose would that serve?' I said, trying not to sound as though I were pleading. 'My editor will soon wonder where I've got to, and then he'll be in touch with the High Commission, and then you'll have to release me — and I'll have a very good story to publish.'

'You think you can negotiate because you are British? I told you in Lagos that I care not a jot for international incidents nor my reputation, which has been besmirched time and time again until we have all become tired of it. It would be more convenient if you were not from one of our so-called allies, and our one-time colonial masters at that. Of course, I admit that freely. It is a nuisance. However, we cannot deal in hypotheticals, but in the realities with which we are faced. The reality of this evening is that you are revealed as a spy, and as such I cannot allow you to leave here until the end of this conflict.'

'Until the end—'

'Allow me to finish, Mister Kane. It will do you good to listen. I am confident this war will not continue for very much longer, so you need not fear your incarceration will be a lengthy one. The rebels are on their last legs, as the sorry specimens you encountered today testify.'

'Will you also jail them?' asked Isabelle. 'After all, they may also be spies.'

Cat, meet pigeons.

Alebayo didn't take long to answer. 'I already have,' he said simply. 'They are enemy combatants. The women and children will be cared for by our medical staff, of course. What would you suggest I do in the circumstances?'

Isabelle nodded, but I could feel the anger surging within her. 'And me? Will you imprison me, too, Colonel?'

Alebayo inspected his slippers for a moment, then looked up at her. 'Yes,' he said. 'I am afraid I must. It is unfortunate, but I have no means of knowing if you are involved in Mister Kane's dirty work.'

Isabelle took a step forward, but Scarface was there at once, holding her back.

'*C'est un scandale!*' she shouted. 'My government—'

'Will be very angry.' Alebayo nodded at Scarface to let her go, and he did, reluctantly. 'Yes, Mademoiselle, I am well aware of it. My superiors will be equally concerned. There will be pressure on me from all sides to release you both. But I tell you now: I shall resist that pressure for as long as I am able. Because this is a war I am engaged in.'

'And my camera?' said Isabelle. 'Does freedom of expression mean nothing to you? Will you hide what is happening in this country from the world?'

Alebayo snorted. 'I will certainly hide military secrets from foreign powers,' he said. He tilted his head, and softened his tone again. 'Mademoiselle, if you are indeed innocent of any involvement with this man, please accept my apologies. But would you not agree it is a sound principle of war that if one finds a spy moving freely among one's troops, one jails him and anyone associated with him?'

She was shaking her head furiously, like a child who doesn't want to hear why she can't have any more boiled sweets. 'My father was ambassador to this country for fifteen years, and he knows people who will think nothing of ordering your dismissal from this disgrace of an army.'

'Mademoiselle—'

'*Non!*' she cried. 'You are a madman, and a bully, and a butcher!' And she leaned forward and spat in his face, a full globule that slowly ran down his cheek and onto his neck and disappeared into the lapel of his kimono.

Alebayo didn't react for several seconds. Scarface was trying to restrain her again, and eventually he shook his head and Scarface let go. Alebayo then stood up and walked across to the wardrobe. He took a handkerchief from one of the drawers and carefully wiped his face, before turning back to Isabelle.

'I can assure you, Mademoiselle Dumont, that I am no madman. I am in full possession of my faculties. As for being a bully and a butcher, that is for others to judge. But during these difficult days, I often think of my time in the Congo with the United Nations, and something one of my colleagues there shared with me. "When two elephants fight, it is the grass that suffers." I believe it is a Swahili saying. At the moment, there are several elephants fighting on the grass of Nigeria. But two of the largest beasts are Great Britain – and France.' He pointed a finger at Isabelle. 'Your government is providing arms to the rebels. It is you that is making a mess of the grass. My job is to minimize that mess.' He nodded at Scarface, who stepped forward and placed the butt of his gun into her back.

'Put them with the others,' said Alebayo. 'I do not wish to see them again.'

*

The rain had finally stopped, though it wasn't much comfort. Scarface prodded us through the Toytown streets. Whereas earlier I'd sensed a tiny measure of warmth in his manner, something I might have been able to work on, now there was no mistaking his open hostility. We were no longer Europeans summoned to see his commanding officer; we were foreign spies, and his prisoners to boot.

I inwardly cursed Isabelle and her little performance — it was a wonder Alebayo hadn't had us shot there and then. The worry was that she wasn't finished. Just as I could sense Scarface's hostility behind us, I could sense her seething as she trudged along beside me.

I tried to keep my mind on tracing our bearings in relation to where I'd seen the entrance earlier, and concluded that we were heading north-east from it. It was a pointless exercise — if I was going to make a dash for it, now was the time, because there would probably be more soldiers wherever we were being taken. But I wasn't going to run, because Scarface had a sub-machine gun and he might be inclined to use it. And even if he didn't, or missed me, I had already seen that the entrance was well guarded. All my options had closed down. So I marched on, turning when told to, hoping that Isabelle had got it out of her system.

After about a quarter of an hour of walking in silence, we arrived at a series of interconnected bungalows. Scarface jabbed us towards one of the doors and we stepped through and walked down a long corridor with doors on both sides. Each had a name-plate and a title — it looked as though we were in a former office block.

We were pushed through a door marked 'Walker, Godwin — Chief Accounts Officer, B-3', into a sea of familiar faces. Everyone from the plane was here, seated in chairs or lying on mattresses on the floor. They all looked up at the limping secret agent and his elegantly attired accomplice. Gunner had removed his shirt, and there was bruising on his chest — it looked like he'd had a rough time of it. The Biafrans were mainly sprawled on the mattresses, eyes closed, limbs sticking out of their thin 'uniforms'. I noticed with relief that the women and children were not here, and hoped that Alebayo had been sincere when he had said they would receive proper treatment.

I quickly surveyed the rest of the room. It was the archetype of an office: a massive square desk that looked like it had come in from a *Punch* cartoon, grey filing cabinets, dead pot plant. Perhaps the place was bugged. There were no other exits, no windows – and no guards. It was odd, but then why waste men? The prisoners would also have seen the gates and known the futility of trying to make a run for it, and they probably assumed someone was stationed outside the door anyway. They were also, of course, hardly in a fit state to escape. But still. It could be an opening . . .

'Do you think this is humane?'

It was Isabelle. She had turned to Scarface. Her hands were resting by her hips, but her glare was fierce.

'Do you?'

He stared back at her for a moment, his face expressionless, his arm clutched firmly around his gun.

'This is a war, Mademoiselle,' he said. 'You are enemy combatants.'

Isabelle was trying to hold back tears. 'That is what your superior said. What do *you* think? Do you think these people' – she gestured at the Biafrans on the floor – 'are a threat? They are starving to death!'

And then it happened. Scarface, perhaps about to launch into a more elaborate answer and wishing to make himself more comfortable, *lowered his gun arm*. And I saw the look in Isabelle's eye. It was sheer madness – you never attack a man holding a gun unless you really know what you are doing – but I saw what she had in mind. Too late, though, because she let out a terrifying scream and leapt at him and, Christ, it very nearly worked, because he stumbled backwards and she began scratching at his eyes and it looked, for the briefest of moments, as though she had managed to overpower him. But then the gun came up. My legs had barely started moving before the shot went off, and the two bodies crumpled to the floor, and there was stillness.

All told, it must have taken about five seconds.

I looked down at the floor. Scarface was clutching his eyes with one hand and using the other to try to prise Isabelle's body off him, but he was still holding the gun, so it was awkward. His first push managed to shift her a little, though, and as she turned I saw in one horrid moment the massive wound to her chest, the widening pool of blood, and the frozen eyes.

I placed my boot on Scarface's arm and took the gun from him. I knocked him unconscious with one blow of the butt, then looked around at the dazed faces and the walls spinning around me.

There was no time to waste — even in a rabbit warren like this, the sound of the shot would travel, and more men would be on their way. I had to find a way out of here, now.

XVII

I rubbed the butt of the gun against my trousers. When I looked again, the blood had gone. It was a Stechkin APS machine pistol — Alebayo's arrangement with Moscow clearly wasn't new.

Gunner was standing by the far wall. Like everyone else in the room, he was rooted to the spot. When I had 'interviewed' him on the plane, he had revealed that he was an Easterner who had specifically joined the Federal side because he didn't believe in secession. But he was clearly susceptible to their plight, because he had agreed to take the Biafrans from Aba and had fed them. However, I had no way of knowing what he might have done if Alebayo hadn't turned up — it seemed unlikely he would have let them go.

'Where are your ropes?' I asked him, and he looked up at me. His eyes were glazed, and he was having trouble focusing.

'What did you say?'

'The ropes they tied you with — where are they?' I said it a touch too harshly, a touch too loudly, because I was desperate to get through to him before more men came and the chance was gone, and that could be in five minutes or it could be in thirty seconds. As a result, some of the others started to stir, pulling their gazes away from Isabelle and Scarface as they realized that something new was happening in the room. I looked into Gunner's eyes and willed him to answer me. As every moment passed, my words sounded more and more like a mistake.

After what seemed an age, but which was probably less than ten seconds, he shook his head and pointed to the ground, where the ropes lay coiled against the inside of a table leg. I picked them up and looped them round one arm, then offered him the Stechkin.

He looked me over quietly. 'You are not a journalist.'

'No,' I said, forcing bonhomie and efficiency into my voice, trying to use the exchange of words as touch-paper. 'But we're going to pretend I am for just a little longer. I'm your prisoner. You're taking me to a hotel in Port Harcourt. Colonel Alebayo's orders.'

'Why?' he asked. 'You want me to desert my men?'

'What good can you do them if you stay?' I said. 'What good can you do anyone? If you want to help bring this war to an end, you have to get out of here. Now might be your only chance.'

He nodded slowly, weighing up the idea. Come on, man, come on! Somewhere in the room, a Biafran groaned, and the sound of it echoed against the walls. Taking his time, Gunner reached out and took the gun, and I became conscious of my breathing as he placed it in his waistband.

'I can only take two others,' I said, willing him to move faster. 'Your two most trusted men.'

That stopped him, and in the silence that followed I wondered if it meant the end of my trail and the rest of the war writing my memoirs on toilet paper. 'They will be here soon,' I said.

'I won't shoot my fellow soldiers,' he said.

'All right,' I agreed, thankful that that was all he needed to persuade himself. 'If we do this right, that won't happen.'

He spoke quickly to two of his men, and when they had saluted and gathered themselves together, we opened the window and climbed out.

*

As I landed on the grass with a thump, a wave of pain shuddered up my left thigh. A monkey that had been sitting a couple of feet away let out a series of ear-shattering shrieks before scampering back into the bush, his fading cackle taunting me. I stayed crouched for a moment, willing the pain to subside, then peered around the edge of the building.

There was no wind. It had stopped raining and the air was thick with mosquitoes – they whined past my ears, and I could sense them homing in on the spots of flesh exposed by the rips in my clothing. Above, a sickle of moon cut through a starless sky, and I wondered for a brief moment if Anna was looking at it, somewhere not so very far away.

Focus, Dark.

Directly ahead of me lay a patch of grass as smooth as a billiard table. Beyond that was the road, pools of which were illuminated by streetlamps.

There were no men. Yet.

On the other side of the road was the tennis court, and beyond that, if my calculations were correct, the street where I'd earlier seen the Land Rover parked.

The three Nigerians quickly took up position behind me. I whispered to Gunner to move to my left, towards the Nissen hut I'd spotted earlier. He nodded and scuttled off, disappearing into the darkness and re-emerging a few seconds later, a dim shape against the wall of the hut.

I looked at the other two men. One I recognized from Aba: he had a boxer's broken nose and split lip. The other was lean and tall, with skin so black and polished he looked almost blue, like a Senegalese. I suddenly felt very conscious of my whiteness, and wanted to scoop up a handful of mud and smear it across my cheeks. But there was no time, so I told Senegal to join Gunner, and took Boxer with me, towards the road. In darkness, it was best to spread out.

The surface of the grass was slick with rain, and I took care to keep my centre of gravity low and lift my heels after each step. In my peripheral vision, I could see Gunner and Senegal moving alongside us. There was still nobody else in view, but I didn't give it long: soldiers' ears are attuned to gunfire, and the camp was silent. They'd be putting on their boots and starting their engines. They'd be here, any moment now.

When we reached the verge of the road, I held out my hand and the three of them stopped. I told them to file behind me — we were approaching light, so we wanted to present a smaller target. When they had done this, I climbed up onto the road, and made for the space between two streetlamps.

This was no man's land, but there would be no football matches in it tonight. We were half-lit by the orbit of two lamps on either side of us. If they came now, we would be seen at once and they would just pick us off. After a few steps, my heart was pounding through my shirt, which was sticking to my skin after several soakings of rain, and the blood was drumming in my ears. But I could still hear the trickle of rainwater through the drains and the splashing of our legs through the shallow puddles. All my senses were alert: for sound, movement, smell, or any change in the environment that meant it was time to raise my arm a little and squeeze the trigger.

None came, and we made it to the verge of the tennis court, which was surrounded by a wire fence. We scrambled down the bank to the gate, and ran, still in single file, around the outside of the court. I saw some fuzzy grey spots on the ground and my muscles tightened on the trigger until my brain registered what they were: lost tennis balls.

We clambered back up the slope and flattened ourselves against it — it was something of a relief, so I tried not to relax the leg too much. It was still tense from my rocky landing earlier.

I peered over and scanned the horizon. And there, parked quietly by one of the bungalows, was the sight I'd been hoping for: the Land Rover.

I waved my hand to the others and we went over the top. The pain was now working its way up my body, but I used it as a spur, pushing myself against it to see how much it would hurt, knowing that every moment counted. We weren't out of here yet. At the halfway point, the others overtook me — it had been a long time since I was their age, running round the glens of Arisaig with only a compass and a dagger to guide me.

There were no lights on in the bungalow and no keys in the Land Rover. I told Gunner to get behind the wheel and Boxer and Senegal to jump in the back, then climbed into the passenger seat myself and looped the ropes around my arms so it looked as if I was bound. The fuel tank was two-thirds full, so that was all right. I reached under the dashboard for the solenoid and the hot wire.

'Is anyone coming?' I whispered to Gunner, and he had another look around and shook his head.

I bridged the two wires.

Ignition.

*

'Slow down a touch,' I said. A speeding vehicle might blow the whistle. We had cover now.

Gunner obliged. I remembered the way he'd walked down the aisle towards me on the aeroplane from Lagos — cocky, swaggering. He was a different man now — the sweat was streaming down his face. He had gone from fraternizing with the enemy to deserting with a suspected enemy agent — he knew he would face a firing squad if we didn't pull this off.

'Keep calm,' I said. 'We're nearly there. Just act as though you've been given urgent orders by Alebayo. They won't argue.'

He nodded, but his jaw continued to shake after he had done so. I placed the Stechkin under my feet and tore away a piece of my shirtsleeve.

'Here,' I said. 'Mop your brow. You need to stay calm.'

Without looking, he took it from me and held the rag to his forehead, as though it were a steak on a bruise.

I turned to Boxer and Senegal, crouched down in the back. 'If there's any trouble,' I said, 'just follow my lead.' I couldn't trust any of these men, of course, but they might now believe I could, or think it enough to delay their reactions for a fraction of a second if things got out of control.

'Next right,' I told Gunner, and he veered sharply, nearly taking us off a couple of the wheels. Waves of pain again, but now I could feel them stretching out their tentacles for my chest. I slumped back as far as I could in the bucket seat and tried not to breathe in too many mosquitoes.

We made the turning, and the gate came into view at the end of the road. The light at the end of the tunnel. I desperately wanted to tell Gunner to slow down, but I bit my tongue. I was in too much pain to waste words, and he needed these seconds to gather his confidence and remember he was in charge. I was just his prisoner now.

He slowed down a few yards from the gate, triggering a light in the hut. One of the guards came out a few seconds later, rifle at the ready and arm raised. There had been eight when I had counted – how many would be on duty now?

'Where are you going?' said the man, the barrel of his Kalashnikov lined up with my head. 'It is past curfew.'

'Let us through,' said Gunner with an admirable tone of authority in his voice. 'The Colonel just ordered me to take this man to Port Harcourt.' He gestured at me.

The soldier took a step closer.

'Who is he?'

'That is none of your business,' Gunner snapped. The guard's jaw tightened and Gunner pretended to soften. 'A British journalist. The Colonel wants him out the way – tonight.'

Too much. He'd said too much. The guard swivelled on his heel and leaned in to look at his face.

'Who are you? I don't recognize you.'

'Captain Samuel Johnson,' he said. 'I arrived from Lagos this afternoon on the Colonel's orders.'

The guard weighed this up, then looked at his watch. I could almost read his thought: 'Is it too late to call through to the main house and check?'

'Call the Colonel now if you like,' said Gunner, who was evidently on the same wavelength. 'But he will not be pleased by interruptions now – he gave me the express order to chop-chop.'

The guard nodded and saluted Gunner.

'Go on with one Nigeria,' he said.

'Go on with one Nigeria,' said Gunner soberly.

The guard turned his back and pressed the mechanism to open the gate, which slowly started to swing back on its hinges.

I felt the air move before I heard the shots. I looked in the rear-view mirror – they were coming over the far lip of the hill, bearing down the road. Dozens of men and a Ferret armoured car, its two lights blazing and its black snout rapidly growing larger as it came towards us.

As I reached for the Stechkin, I shouted at Gunner to put his foot down, but he already had – we were heading straight into the gates. The guard turned, took in the approaching men and car, and began shouting to alert his colleagues inside the hut.

I aimed for the ground just in front of him as I opened the car door and bundled out onto the tarmac. I saw him throw himself flat, and I rolled over and fired off several rounds into the lever controlling the gate until I saw sparks, and then the first flickers of flames. I could hear the others behind me as I got to my feet, then squeezed through the gates and pounded my feet down the tarmac, until I realized what I was doing and veered off to the left, down a steep bank towards the bush. I had no idea what direction I needed to go in, but that wasn't important now. They had a Ferret, and it was bearing down on us at a rate of knots. I could feel the heat of its lights on my back, and the shots were thundering in my brain.

I leapt through the grass, feeling plants and insects stinging my skin and prying my shoes away from the mud with each step. Two of the others – Gunner and Senegal, I thought – overtook me, clattering down the hill with their arms outstretched, and I followed them without thinking, blocking the rest of the world from my head and concentrating on my feet and the ground directly in front of me. Soon, I couldn't hear the Ferret — perhaps the lever had jammed and they were still trying to prise the gate open. I was running so fast that it took several strides before it hit home. I couldn't hear the Ferret, but I couldn't hear anything else either: no shots, no footsteps, not even my own breathing, which had been so strong just moments before.

I had gone deaf.

XVIII

I began to slow down. The pain in my upper left thigh was sharpening with every step, and I was shivering with cold. It felt like I was losing my balance, and my face was sticky with sweat. My brain also needed to absorb what had just happened. Which was that all the noises that had been registering in my head moments before — the squelching of my feet in the rain-sodden earth, the buzzing of the mosquitoes around me, the machine-gun fire from the men in armoured cars trying to kill me — had, without notice, been replaced by complete silence.

I had never experienced *true* silence before. It had a rather frightening beauty to it: every detail of the world around me was intact — the rank swamp smell, the curtain of sky framed by darkened palm trees, the shapes of the other two men skidding down the slope away from me — but with one element removed, it seemed unreal.

What the hell had caused this? Surely not the sound of the gunfire — I'd heard plenty of that in my time. Hunger and fatigue, then? I suddenly remembered all those horror stories people liked telling in the basement bar after hours of agents collapsing of exhaustion or going mad in the field. That poor sod Carslake who'd started having headaches in the middle of an operation just outside Bangkok. He'd gone blind before finding a hospital, and the opposition had simply picked him off on the street. His corpse hadn't been a pretty sight, by all accounts. Was that my fate, then? One second all my faculties intact; the next running through a sound-less world towards oblivion?

Run anyway – and then keep running. Think later. The car would break through the gate soon. Perhaps it already had. I forced my feet back into action, fixing on the path ahead and trying to block out the pain as I scrambled down the bank. I outstretched one arm to protect me from insects and branches, and kept the other hovering low in case I slipped. As I pushed aside some large fronds, glossy and greeny-black in the moonlight, I sensed some-thing in my peripheral vision, and turned to see a blurred ball of dark matter propelling straight towards my head. As I leapt away from it, I realized it was a mammoth insect – perhaps a dragonfly? – but that was as far as I got because I landed on something sharp, which cut into my right calf and shredded my trouser-leg so a flap of it now hung loose, leaving the wound exposed to the cool night air: a feast for the mosquitoes.

I tried to right myself and felt something solid pushing down on my head. I looked up to see a pair of gleaming bloodshot eyes: Gunner! What the hell was he doing coming back for me? His mouth was moving urgently, shouting something behind the screen between us. I gestured at my ears and shook my head, and he pushed my shoulders down roughly. I followed his lead and flat-tened myself against some muddy roots.

We looked up the hill. Flickers of red and yellow light flashed over the rim, and I guessed that the Ferret was heading down the road.

They hadn't seen us.

We lay there for a few minutes, or perhaps it was only seconds – time was getting harder to judge – and then I turned to see that he had gotten up and had started running back down the moun-tainside.

With a mighty effort I stood up and leapt after him, pounding my feet every step of the way. It was excruciating, but if I pounded hard enough, I could 'hear' the pulse reverberating through my body – not as a sound but as a physical sensation. Somehow it seemed comforting, so I concentrated on making it happen, again and again, all the while watching Gunner's silhouette ahead, weaving through the plants.

As the slope finally started to flatten out and we waded across a narrow rivulet of swamp water, I felt a closer shuddering. Had they changed their minds? Were they coming down the hill? I didn't dare look back, and at some point I realized that these new vibrations were coming from inside my own head – my teeth were chattering.

It was shortly after I realized this that the sound came back. Just as suddenly as it had been shut off, someone lifted the needle and placed it back on the record. My panting breaths, the rush of the wind and the sound of my trousers pushing through the brush burst into my brain at what seemed like double the normal volume, but after a few shaky seconds where I nearly lost my balance, I was almost insanely happy. The deafness had lasted just a few minutes, and now it had gone! The swish of my legs now spurred me on – create more swish, more noise, let the sounds continue for as long as you can enjoy them – and I leapt over rocks and eddies and kept running, full pelt, towards Gunner, until I slowly started to bear down on him, my heart thumping in my ribcage.

*

'I need to get to Udi. Do you have any idea which direction I should take?'

He shook his head. 'You no fit to go anywhere. You be very sick. You shake and sweat, and you no answer when I speak.'

'I lost my hearing for a couple of minutes,' I said. 'It's back now.'

He looked at me. 'This has happen to you before?'

I felt inside my shirt pocket and pulled out the soft pack of Players. So much for my little game – the remaining cigarettes were all sodden.

'Who the hell is Samuel Johnson?' I said.

He smiled. 'Someone I know at school. It was the first name that came to my mind.'

I nodded. 'Thanks for the help back there,' I said. 'I appreciate how hard it must have been.'

There was an awkward silence. When he'd seen that I was still visible from the road, he had realized it would lead the men down the hill – to me, but also to him. So he'd run back, made me duck for cover, and it had worked. But we'd lost Senegal and Boxer as a result – and who could blame them?

Now we were resting for a moment against a large palm tree he had picked out. He had found some of its flowers in the surrounding shrubbery and squeezed them open until a string of sap had dribbled from the stems, which he had offered me. Fermented, it would have become 'palm wine', but the sweet stickiness had been welcome enough and I had gained a little strength from it. My shivering had also subsided, although my thigh still pulsed with a dull pain.

'I sorry about your girl,' said Gunner.

I crumpled the cigarette pack in my hand. The tenses in his English were sometimes hard to decipher: the present was also used for the past. Did he mean that seeing Isabelle killed had helped persuade him to come with me – or was he sympathizing generally? Perhaps both. I had a sudden memory of her sitting and smoking in her black swimsuit on the breeze blocks at the Lagos Yacht Club, when I had mistaken her for Anna. And then later that night, her body glistening with sweat as she had called out to me in the dark.

'She wasn't my girl,' I said. I considered whether or not I wanted to know the answer to my next question, and decided it might be important. 'What's the procedure for prisoners' deaths?'

He nodded. 'It depends on the importance of the prisoner. I think they will bury her and the compound reverend bless the ground. But I don't think they tell anyone about it.'

'No.'

It would probably be weeks until her office became worried

enough to notify the embassy in Lagos, and then her parents – were they in France? I couldn't remember if she had said – would fly over and start trying to piece together what had happened.

'This war must end!' said Gunner suddenly, standing and spitting on the ground to emphasize the point. 'I want no more part of it.'

I wondered which part he meant – the shooting of Isabelle, or the fate of the Biafrans? Isabelle had not deserved to die, but she had chosen to be here, chosen this cause. And she had chosen, finally, to confront an armed soldier while a prisoner of war. The Biafrans, on the other hand, had had no choice, or very little. Fight for one side, fight for the other, or fight for none. Another image swam into view: their skeletal frames immobile on those flea-infested mattresses. The flies buzzing into the huge eyes of the children as they had stood in the hut. I pushed it down, as Gunner had pushed me down into the wet earth a few minutes before. Humanity coming over the hill. Don't let it spot you.

I must not make the same mistake Isabelle had, I told myself. This was not my war. Biafrans were being held prisoner across the country – so were Nigerians. Their fate wasn't my cross to bear, and there was no especial reason why I should have been concerned about the fate of a squadron of deserters, even with women and children attached. War was hell, and this one was no exception. Listening to Gunner talk about what he had seen and what he believed, I was reminded for a moment that I, too, had once been young and felt I could shake the world's foundations. Well, I hadn't done it. I wasn't sure it was even possible to do. Part of me wanted to argue against his young man's idealism, to tell him that he wasn't going to change anything by talking. But I forced myself to keep quiet: I still needed his help, and I'd soon have to persuade him all over again. I had to get to the nearest town and find transport. The scant cover that I was his prisoner was a lot more likely to get me there than going it alone.

And what would I find once I reached Udi? I wondered. From what I knew so far, it didn't look comforting. Anna was apparently not only still alive, but engaged on a mission to assassinate the British prime minister.

And yet, and yet . . . could it really be? I still had no solid proof of her guilt. There was no way I could even be completely certain about the photograph of her in Lagos: photographs could be forged. Perhaps they had found someone who looked rather like her, and Slavin's defection had been an elaborate operation to hook me in. But no, that couldn't be right. Why bother? Sasha was in touch with me whenever he needed. If they had wanted to cut me loose, they could have done so in London. But the assassination story didn't fit either . . . There were still too many unanswered questions. Had Anna really survived, and, if so, what had been her role in Father's death? How had Slavin found out about me? And how did the plot against Wilson fit into the situation?

I put these problems out of my mind – the answers lay in Udi, and I had thirty-seven hours and twenty minutes to get there. Perhaps the thing to do was to work our way back to the road we'd come from? Would they still have men posted on it? Possibly. It wasn't worth the risk. We'd have to find another road, or intersect the same one further along . . .

I realized that Gunner had stopped talking. His face was frozen, grim, and I looked up to see what had made it so.

There were five of them. They all had black beards, fierce expressions and were pointing rifles at us. The patches on the sleeves of their uniforms bore an illustration of an orange sun dawning – or was it setting?

Biafrans. But these ones weren't starving and there were no flies in their eyes.

'Come with us,' one of them said softly. 'You come with us now.'

XIX

We were led through the palm trees to a mud track, where a battered old Land Rover was parked, camouflaged by fronds and netting. Senegal and Boxer sat in the rear, guarded by about a dozen men, all of whom looked to be armed and – always a bad sign with soldiers – bored. None of their uniforms matched, and they wore an assortment of headgear: helmets, berets, caps and what looked like beach hats. A black metal pole was attached to the front passenger window of the vehicle, holding aloft a radio transmitter, and one of the soldiers held a receiver on his lap, the announcer's voice leaking out from it in an unbroken stream. We were pushed into the back, and then the jalopy stuttered into life and we started moving slowly down the track.

Pritchard's dossier had mentioned that Biafra had a guerrilla force. I wondered what Isabelle would have made of them – how they would have fitted with her idea of the Biafrans as utterly powerless victims. Their uniforms and weaponry were tattered and piecemeal, and half of them, I now noticed, seemed to be stoned. But they had crept up on Gunner and me without either of us noticing, and had sprung their trap smoothly and efficiently. With several rifles pointed firmly in my direction, I had little choice but to stay put and watch for an opportunity to escape. I wasn't all that hopeful it would arrive – I'd faced a similar situation just a few hours ago, when Alebayo's men had driven me to Port Harcourt under a similar armed guard.

Gunner, Senegal and Boxer were seated near me, all of them staring expressionlessly ahead, lost in their own thoughts. No doubt they were repenting their decision to follow me – if it came down to it, they would probably accuse me of kidnapping them or some such story. I wasn't sure what my own story should be. My thinking was impaired, by pain, fatigue, hunger, thirst – and the nagging thought that I might lose my hearing again. The smell of the marijuana was making me even woozier, and I hadn't stopped sweating since leaving the Shell camp. Every so often, my guts gave a sudden lurch, and vomit would rise in my throat.

After a few minutes, I decided I might as well try to make an opening, and asked the soldiers seated on the bench opposite me where we were going. 'I'm ill, and I need to see a doctor. Are we anywhere near Udi? There's a hospital there.'

They stared right through me.

'If you don't shut your mouth, old man, you will soon be much more ill,' said one.

That drew our cosy little chat to an end, and I concentrated on trying to keep my innards on an even keel instead. We bumped along the track for over an hour, past glittering lagoons and mangrove swamps, all the while rending the night air with the commentary from Radio Biafra. My ears pricked up as the announcer mentioned 'perfidious Albion' and, sure enough, he began to discuss the Prime Minister's impending visit. I couldn't follow it all due to the noise of the engine and a squabble that had started between two of the men near me, but the thrust seemed to be that the visit was a gimmick designed to deflect the world's media from a sudden and brutal attack by the Nigerians.

Twenty minutes later, we stopped. The radio was switched off, and the man in the passenger seat took out a walkie-talkie and spoke rapidly into it in his language. There was a pause, followed by a reply through a sea of static. After ten long minutes of this, we started up again, but at an even slower pace. Then I caught some movement a couple of hundred yards down the path: a cluster of men in camouflage were stepping out from the long grass. As we approached, I saw that they held bottles of beer and machine guns and that they were manning a checkpoint, which consisted of a bamboo pole across the path. Simple, but effective. We slowed and our driver leaned out of the window and handed over our papers, talking rapidly in the local language. They inspected them sullenly, then waved us through and trudged back into the long grass.

We passed several such checkpoints, each following more or less the same procedure. Finally, we reached a line of hardwood trees, some of which had been felled and used to create a crude gate. Documents were once more handed over and inspected, the gate was opened and we drove down a slightly larger laterite road.

This move was apparently unforeseen, because several of the men suddenly erupted angrily. Through the din, I figured out that they were urging the driver to take another route, but he was adamant that he knew what he was doing and would reach the destination in plenty of time. This assurance was greeted by derision and much pointing at watches. I looked at mine — it was a quarter to midnight. The captain in the passenger seat, who seemed to be in charge, quickly intervened, telling everyone to stop panicking and let the man do his job; as a compromise, he also chivvied the driver along, telling him to put his foot down. This forced us too fast over the next bump in the road and we all went flying, much to the driver's delight.

About ten minutes later, we came to a wide village square, which looked like it had once been the site of a marketplace. Unlike Aba, there were functioning cars parked on the street and strips of red, black and green cloth tied around the trunks of trees and pinned to some of the buildings: Biafran flags. We drove onto a wider road that proved to be even bumpier than the one we'd been on, until we came to a standstill in front of a large, squat building, which I guessed had been the town hall or something similar. A gruesome poster pinned to the entrance advised residents how to deal with

Nigerian paratroopers: 'Stake all open fields . . . leave skull-bashing to women . . . stab them to death . . .'

The atmosphere among the men had changed since they had decided to trust the driver's timekeeping: there had been the usual end-of-journey banter and stretching of limbs, but from the tone of their voices there also seemed to be tension in the air. Were they worried they would receive a dressing down from their commanding officer, perhaps?

I was prodded out of the vehicle along with the others, and the captain ordered a quick piss break – or 'pause for bodily relief' as he put it. Once that had been taken care of – and even at gunpoint, it was a mighty relief – the captain pushed open the door of the building, and we all filed in after him. I checked my watch again: it was exactly midnight.

The hall was empty and silent, with no seating and just a bare stone floor, although I could see some marks where heavy objects had previously been placed. The windows were all boarded up and there was an acrid smell I couldn't identify – something burning?

The door clicked shut behind me, and then the lights went out, plunging us into total darkness. As my eyes tried to adjust, my scalp wriggled with incipient fear. I could hear the fast, shallow breathing of the men around me: they were scared, too. So what the hell were we doing here?

'You have come.'

The voice erupted from nowhere, and resonated in my skull. It was male, booming, commanding. A few of the men started mumbling responses, but the voice quietened them.

'Please be seated.'

Groping in the dark, I lowered myself to the floor with the others.

'Now listen,' said the voice from out of the darkness. '*Listen.*'

After a few seconds, it began to speak again, but it was now talking in an African language, and the tone was completely flat, with equal stress on all syllables. An incantation of some sort? For the first few seconds, it seemed almost comical, like something out of a Rider Haggard story. But as the voice droned on, the words merging into one endless stream of sound, it started to gather force. Although I didn't understand a word of it, part of my mind began to enter the stream and try to decipher or imagine meanings, until I was drifting along, my eyes half-glazed, my face covered in cooling sweat, transfixed by this eerie, disconnected chant. The voice seemed to be talking to me about events in my past. Yes, that was right – Anna. I remembered now. That day she kissed me back. All the world blazing in light – the future stretching ahead of us. No war now. Home to England. 'What will you do in England?' she had asked me. 'What will you do now the great dragon has been slain?' And then the direction of the voice shifted a little, and I could see myself running into the clinic, the Russian soldiers, her body on the stretcher, the red wound and the closed lids. But her face wasn't her own, it was Isabelle's and at this horrific realization the floor started shaking and I looked up and the ceiling was, too, and there was light up there, light coming from the ceiling, three sources of light, and as they came closer, drifting down, I saw that they were in the shape of bodies – that they were bodies, in fact, humans in light form, and they reached the ground and one of them leaned in, and he had a strong face, a strong African face, and he asked me what my troubles were and I started crying because I couldn't tell him, I couldn't tell him all the troubles I had because I didn't know where to begin and he took me by the arm and told me it was all right, it would be all right in a little while, but I couldn't stop crying and it was taking me over, I was heaving and my lungs were on fire, and I couldn't get the next breath out to tell him, let go of me, don't hold me, I can't breathe, my back, hit my back, I can't breathe, let me breathe, help me breathe . . .

*

It was so warm in Germany, you see. I hadn't been used to the warmth, and it had taken me some time to get used to it again. A beautiful day for vengeance. But his neck, sweating. Sweating in the sun. I was unable, I had been unable . . . The wound had been warm, and there had been something comforting about that. No more ice. No more snow. Just a seeping warmth . . .

Sound.

It jolted through me.

What was it? A stream?

No, not that. Listen.

Animals! Geese, perhaps?

No, there was more to it, it was deeper. Listen again, closer this time.

Voices. That was it. Human voices. Criss-crossing. Now changing pitch, moving deeper. Singing. They lifted, somehow, and I felt myself carried away with them, on a tide . . . Not of water. Why was I thinking of snow? The voices seemed to be drifting down like snow, drawing me into their drift. And yet I was warm. Hot, even. Strange to have snow while I sat here sweating.

But there was a breeze. Hadn't there been a breeze just now? Yes, there it was again. It felt so good. It was almost as if I could follow every atom of it wafting across my face. Now it had reached the bridge of my nose, now onto my cheek. And then it had gone again. Why? How can it have gone like that? Now I felt drier than I did before. Wait. Here it came again . . .

I opened my eyes. A man wearing a white mask was waving something at me.

A banana leaf. So that was the breeze. Yes, keep waving it, I wanted to say to him. Give it to me. Let me wave it! He didn't. Instead he stopped waving. I could see the sides of some glasses frames through the peepholes of the mask, and behind the lenses lay dark watchful eyes. The man stood suddenly and moved away from me, out of my line of vision. The singing stopped abruptly, and as it did I placed the song. The snow falling outside on the black cars. The sky darkening. Cocktails at the consulate in Helsinki, all those years ago.

I was a long way from Helsinki. I tried to sit up, but all I caught was a glimpse of the man walking away, and the room I was in. It was very narrow and low-ceilinged. The walls were white and made of some kind of stucco or wattle, propped up with logs. The man was wearing a thin white coat, and there were shelves attached to the walls with small glass objects on them.

I felt dizzy with the effort so I closed my eyes again and tried to imagine the breeze washing over my face. It didn't come, but instead a cool wetness spilled over my lips, and I opened my eyes to see the man with the mask standing over me, his arm outstretched, a white cup pressed against my mouth. As with the sitting up, the fresh experience made me aware of the old one, and I could taste vomit, and it all came back. The hall. The voice. The bodies made of light.

'Good morning,' said the man. His voice was a little muffled by the mask. I couldn't place his accent — possibly American — but he was black; I had seen a strip of arm between a sleeve and glove.

He stood and raised his arms above me. I tilted my head and saw that he was adjusting some kind of a tube — I followed it and saw that it entered my arm.

'Where am I?' I said, and was surprised at the effort it took.

'You are in a clinic run by the Red Cross,' he said. 'You are very ill.'

A clinic. Of course it was a clinic — the tubes. That smell. Those objects on the shelves were bottles, I now saw. 'The Red Cross'. That phrase was also familiar. It meant something. More than what it normally meant. It was *connected* with something. Like a player of patience, I racked my brains to match the pair.

'"Finlandia",' I said, remembering another piece of the puzzle. 'I heard a choir singing "Finlandia".'

He nodded. 'The Biafrans have taken it as their national anthem. They often play it on the radio.'

A string of pairs suddenly matched up.

'Udi,' I said. 'Are we in Udi?'

The glove stopped the calibration of the tube, and the mask looked down at me. 'No,' he said. 'But we aren't too far away.'

'I need to get there.'

The mask nodded in understanding, while the gloves went back to their task. 'You need to recover first,' he said. 'You're very ill.'

'Malaria?'

The doctor finished his work and then sat down in the chair he had been fanning me from earlier.

'That's what we thought at first,' he said. 'But now we're not so sure. Do you feel you can talk?'

I nodded, and he took out a pad of paper and a pen from his coat.

'When did you arrive in Nigeria?' he asked.

It took me a few moments. 'Monday,' I said. 'Monday evening.'

'March 24th?'

'Yes.'

He wrote it down, adjusting his peepholes a little to make it easier. 'Have you taken any anti-malarial medication since arriving?'

I started to shake my head, but suddenly remembered the pills Manning had given me on the way back from the airport. 'Yes!' I said. 'Yes, I have!'

The eyes in the mask stared back at me. 'How did you take it?'

'What do you mean? Swallowed it, of course. A glass of water in my hotel . . .'

'From the faucet — the tap?'

'Yes,' I said, hollowly. 'From the tap.'

Silence, as his pen scratched the paper. My muscles ached; my innards gurgled; my head throbbed. Was it neon they were using for the light in here?

'Have you had any other contact with unfiltered water since you arrived? Have you been in any areas containing swamps, for example?'

Only waded through one. I couldn't bring myself to tell him, so I just nodded. He scribbled it down.

'Have you been in contact with any rodents since you arrived in Nigeria?' he asked, not looking up.

I stared at him and nodded. Of course. The rat in the sink. The same sink from which I had poured the water to wash down Manning's useless bloody malaria tablet.

'What do you think it is?'

'We're not sure,' he said. 'We've tested you for everything we could think of: malaria, typhoid fever, trichinosis . . . None of them fitted. Another candidate is yellow fever, but you don't look jaundiced and if you arrived Monday the incubation is still a little too fast. It could be a new disease: there was one discovered a couple of hundred miles north of here in January, in a village called Lassa. An American nurse in a missionary hospital fell sick very quickly. Then one of the nurses treating her caught it. Nobody's sure how it's transmitted yet, but one possibility is via rodent faeces. From monitoring you and talking to others, you seem to have had some of the same symptoms as the nurses: muscle and back pain, fever, nausea . . . Have you had any retro-orbital pain?'

'Meaning?'

'Behind the eyes.'

I nodded.

'That's another.' He looked down at his pad. 'Also intermittent loss of hearing, respiratory problems, hallucinations . . .'

His outfit was starting to take on a significance I didn't like. 'What happened to the nurses?' I asked.

'They died,' he said evenly. 'But that doesn't necessarily mean anything. That disease has only just been discovered, and we're by no means certain you've contracted it. It's just an idea. We've been giving you hydroxychloroquine and tetracycline, and now I am starting you on chloramphenicol. We're doing everything we can. In the meantime, I'd be very grateful if you could make a list of all the people you have come into contact with since arriving in Nigeria. We may need to start tracing them.'

I asked him how I had arrived at the clinic, and there was a conspicuous pause before he answered. 'Some Biafran soldiers brought you in. They said they had been at a meeting with Doctor Wise when you had collapsed.'

'Doctor who?'

'Wise. He's a well-known spiritualist in these parts. Many of the Biafrans are devotees of his – some of the soldiers insist that he has the final say on whether to go ahead with military manoeuvres.' The white cotton shoulders shrugged. 'It's crazy, of course. They think he can invoke spirits from the sky.'

It didn't sound so crazy to me. As he had been talking, I had managed to raise my head enough to have another look at the room. There was something I didn't like about it – there were no doors, just a flight of steps.

'Where are the doors?' I said. 'And why are there no windows?'

The doctor shifted a little in his chair. 'Because we are underground. This is usually a theatre for emergency operations, but we've converted it into an isolation ward to treat you.'

I looked around at the dank walls and low ceiling. The prognosis didn't look too good – I had already been buried.

The doctor closed his pad, placed the top back on his pen and placed them both back in his coat. 'Even though your fever has subsided somewhat, you are still in a critical condition,' he said, pushing his chair back and standing. 'I'll be back to check on you later. In the meantime, you have a visitor.'

As if on cue, there was a clanging sound and I looked towards the end of the room, at the staircase. Black boots tucked into khaki trousers appeared, followed by stocky legs, a stockier torso and, finally, the head of an African man with a bushy beard.

He walked over and nodded to the doctor, who turned to a trestle and picked up a white coat lying there. The newcomer carefully placed this over his uniform – it was a little tight on his shoulders. The doctor offered him a mask, but he shook his head and said something I couldn't catch. The doctor nodded and walked away, disappearing up the staircase.

The African approached my bed and leaned over me. I had never met him before, but I knew who he was.

'Hello, Mister Kane,' he said in a deep, velvety voice. 'Welcome to Biafra.'

XX

'A bearded Othello.' The phrase came into my mind, but I couldn't place where I'd heard it. Then I realized I hadn't – I had read it. I had been in an airport. That was it. The interview in the *Newsweek* I had bought at Heathrow.

As I watched him moving around my bed, I concurred with the journalist who had come up with the phrase. There was something of Othello about Colonel Chukwuemeka Odumegwu Ojukwu: a measure of dignified hurt, and an aura of self-importance. He was taller and broader than I would have expected; the photographs didn't get across how much space he took up. But he had a kind of lumbering elegance, a studied stillness, that seemed familiar from what I had read of him. Pritchard's briefing notes had referred to him as a 'power-hungry menace'. That, too, seemed a well-chosen phrase.

But this was all by the by. What the hell was the leader of the Biafran army doing here? And why did he want to talk to me?

After he had fidgeted with his coat a little, he sat himself on the chair vacated by the doctor, squeezing his frame into it as though it were a makeshift throne. Apart from a gloss of sweat on his forehead, he looked calm, well rested, relaxed. With one hand he stroked his massive beard. I'd read about that, too: he had grown it as a symbolic gesture after the pogroms against his tribe three years earlier, and many Biafran men had since grown their own in deference to him.

'I am sorry about your mishap,' he said. He made it sound as though I'd stubbed my toe in his swimming pool. 'My men are superstitious, you know. They had strict orders to bring you straight to me, but they didn't want to miss their rendezvous with their witch-doctor.' He smiled tolerantly at his charges' roguish ways. He struggled with his coat some more, eventually bringing out a pack of cigarettes: Three Fives. He slid one out and lit it with a worn gold lighter. 'The men responsible have been reprimanded.'

He took a puff of the cigarette. It looked like heaven from where I was sitting. He exhaled, and looked up at the low ceiling. I could sense him thinking, preparing his words.

'Do you have the message?'

I waited for him to continue, then realized that he had finished. 'What message?' I asked.

He laughed, a deep, hearty and utterly insincere bellow. It faded, and he closed his eyes and rubbed them with the palms of his hands.

'Please do not play games with me,' he said, letting out a sigh. 'Let's not go through the rigmarole of passwords. We are not children.'

'I don't have any message for you,' I said. 'I'm a journalist with *The Times*.'

His eyes snapped open and he looked at me as if for the first time. 'Is there a reason you cannot convey your message?'

'You've made a mistake,' I said. 'I have no message to give you or anyone else. Colonel Alebayo . . .'

'Alebayo?' He stood up suddenly. 'What does he have to do with this?' He leaned over the bed and stared into my face. He had very sad eyes, like a type of dog you want to adopt.

'Alebayo captured me,' I said. 'A French journalist died . . .'

'Oh,' he said, sitting down again. 'That. I know about that already. Let's not waste each other's time. Where does the Prime Minister want to meet?'

The Prime Minister? What was he talking about? Was this one of my hallucinations? I tried to block everything out and examine his words. Who did he think I was, and what did he want me to tell him? What was it he had said when he had come in? 'Hello, Mister Kane. Welcome to Biafra.' So he knew my cover name. That meant he had talked to Gunner – presumably that was how he had heard about Isabelle's death, too. But there was something else there, some clue. What was it? Why was the leader of the Biafran army in an underground hospital in the middle of the bush? He was apparently waiting for a message from the British prime minister to set up a meeting between them – presumably to talk peace.

Ojukwu was smoking, studying me.

'There is a plot to kill the Prime Minister,' I said. 'In Udi.'

He didn't react, just carried on smoking his Three Fives cigarette. Where did he get them from, I wondered, in the middle of a war?

'This is not the message I was expecting,' he said softly.

'It's the one you're getting,' I replied. 'The Russians are planning to assassinate him at the Red Cross camp on Friday afternoon. Help me get there.'

He examined me for a moment, then slumped back as far as he could in his chair, as mystified by me as I was by him. 'But why should I do that? Your prime minister is my enemy, and so are the Russians.'

I shook my head. 'You're not thinking it through,' I said. 'Think of the *effect* of killing him. Think of what it will do to public opinion in Britain. They are already opposed to this war. There are marches, petitions, debates . . .'

He nodded slowly.

'So how do you think they will react if their prime minister is killed out here?'

He opened his hands, waiting for the answer.

'They'll be furious!' I said. 'Not only are their taxes buying arms for this horrific war that is starving innocent children – now their prime minister has been murdered here. They will demand the immediate withdrawal of any assistance to Nigeria, and they will get it. The next prime minister would immediately withdraw from this war.'

'Good,' said Ojukwu, scratching his beard. 'But this is not . . .'

'No,' I said. 'Not good. Not good for you. As soon as the British have left, the Russians will step up *their* support. They will be the Nigerians' only hope, and make no mistake, they'll capitalize on it, and fast. They will flood the Federal side with weapons, and the war will be over before you know what's hit you. Then they will have their stepping stone in Africa . . .'

'This is all very interesting, Mister Kane,' said Ojukwu curtly, mashing out his cigarette on the floor with the heel of his boot. 'But I feel that we are drifting away from the main issue.'

He was looking up at the ceiling, and without his gaze to distract me, I was free to focus on his voice. And that was when it hit me.

'Take me to Colonel Ojukwu,' I said.

His head snapped back down and his eyes opened wide.

'What did you say?'

'You heard,' I said. 'I want to see Ojukwu. You're an impostor.'

*

My reading jag in Heathrow on Monday evening had been well worthwhile. Pritchard's dossier on the war had contained extensive briefing notes on the major figures of each side, and one of the Biafrans in particular had attracted my attention. Simeon Akuji, the Commissioner for Internal Affairs, was Ojuwku's second cousin and a possible means of communication with him via a personal cipher. Although it hadn't been spelled out, I had taken it that the link was overseen by Pritchard – especially as Akuji had been educated at Fettes, Pritchard's alma mater in Edinburgh.

As I had listened to 'Ojukwu' pontificating, something had bothered me about him. That he seemed to be performing an act was in character, but then I had realized why his little welcoming speech had jarred: there had been the faintest touch of a Scottish accent to it. My guess had been that Ojukwu had pulled a Monty and had Akuji impersonate him. Judging by the reaction, I had been right. But what was the reason for the subterfuge?

The answer, surely, lay with Henry Pritchard. Akuji seemed to be expecting a message from the PM, but according to the official programme no visit to Biafra was planned. Unless his entire trip to Nigeria had secretly been about meeting Ojukwu? Pritchard had denied that there had been a negotiating element to it back in London, but why else would the Prime Minister fly out here? So he could report to Parliament that he'd seen the war with his own eyes? To deflect attention from a Nigerian attack, as Radio Biafra had alleged? A peace mission made much more sense. He had even come with HMS *Fearless*, which he had recently used, albeit without much success, to hold talks with Ian Smith over the Rhodesian problem. A peace mission, then, with Pritchard the go-between setting up the meeting with the Biafran leader? Perhaps Akuji was the deal-broker; or perhaps Ojukwu was scared of being assassinated himself.

'You British have a most amusing attachment to conspiracies,' Akuji was saying, but I didn't have time for that.

'You read history at Lincoln, Colonel. I was there a few years before you, but I imagine they still had that marvellous portrait in Hall of – ah, who was it of again?'

He opened his mouth, and for a moment I thought he was going to try to bluff me, but then he dipped his head and sighed deeply. It hadn't been the most sophisticated ruse, and I'd been at Wadham anyway, but it had been enough.

'Is that why you're not wearing a mask?' I asked. 'So I could see how similar you are to Ojukwu?'

He nodded slowly.

'Quite a risk,' I said. 'If you lose your hearing, you know where to come.'

'The doctor warned me of the dangers,' he said, somewhat sniffily. Then, his pride hurt: 'How did you realize?'

'I'll come to that,' I said, though I had no intention of doing so. 'What made you so sure I was the messenger?'

'Who else would you be? The message told me to expect someone to turn up here on Wednesday, and here you are. Granted, you were waylaid for a couple of days, but I knew the reason for that – the men told me.'

'Waylaid?' I said. 'What do you mean?'

He gestured at the walls. 'You're ill, unless you hadn't noticed!'

'Not that,' I said. 'Not that. You said I was waylaid by a couple of days. But I'm not. It's still only Wednesday morning.'

He looked at me quizzically. 'Does British intelligence now train its agents to bamboozle its allies? Today is Friday.' He looked at his watch. 'Just after ten a.m.'

The walls suddenly seemed to be melting towards me, and all I could think of was Anna, on a roof, looking down at a black car with the Prime Minister in the back seat.

It wasn't Wednesday. It was Friday, at just after ten in the morning. I ripped the sheet off the bed and sat up. Then I set about trying to find how to disconnect myself from the feed.

'What are you doing?' asked Akuji, alarmed.

'Leaving,' I said. I had just over four hours to get to Udi.

XXI

It took me less than a second to realize my mistake. Our little chat had sharpened my mind but not my body, and I hadn't made enough allowances. I had deliberately stepped onto the floor with my back facing him, calculating that my apparent helplessness would delay him for a fraction of a moment in reaching for the gun he would inevitably be carrying. As I landed, I raised my right foot so it was in front of my left kneecap, then fired the right edge of the foot out towards Akuji, aiming at his thigh.

I'd executed this manoeuvre hundreds of times, and Akuji was no match for it: he crashed into a table on wheels behind him before I'd even brought my foot to a stop. I immediately followed up with a two-finger hand to his left carotid, after which he fell to the floor with a permanent-sounding thud. But by then I was also falling, because my stomach had suddenly been engulfed by a wave of nausea so intense I thought I was going to pass out. I managed to turn back to the bed and caught hold of the iron bars that ran around it for a second or two, but the nausea was overwhelming and I started slipping to the floor, automatically hunching myself into the fetal position as I came into contact with the concrete. My ears started ringing, and grey blotches were floating in front of my eyes, so I took to slapping myself in the face to stave off unconsciousness.

'Four hours,' I said aloud, partly to remind myself of the deadline, partly just to get my body and brain back on speaking terms. It was down to the wire now, and I couldn't afford to lose another minute. I couldn't wake up with the Prime Minister dead and Anna having fled the country, never to be seen again. Which would be worse, I wondered: Nigeria becoming a Soviet state, or the Biafrans continuing to be slaughtered in a war they could never win? Wilson dead or alive?

'Four hours.'

Akuji. You need to find him, make sure he's out, get his gun. You need Akuji's gun to get through this, so turn now, turn to your right . . .

If I'd had any voice then, I'd have screamed. I was practically on top of him: his eyes lolled obscenely, and blood was leaking from his mouth. He was out, all right, and would be for a while.

On his wrist was a slim gold watch: some fancy Swiss make. I managed to reach out and unclasp it and held it in my palm, staring at the second hand as it slowly made its way around a smaller circle set within the dial. When it gets to the top, I told myself, you must straighten your legs. I breathed in as deeply as I could, and the ringing slowly began to subside. The room was completely silent and I couldn't remember hearing anything since the thud of Akuji's landing, so I lifted the watch to my ear and was rewarded with a faint *tick-tick tick-tick tick-tick* . . . Another wave of nausea swept over me, and I longed to find a bathroom and shit all the bad stuff out of my system. In the shapes behind my eyelids, I suddenly saw the rat from the bathroom sink of the Palace Hotel tunnelling towards me, its claws outstretched, and the landscape it was tunnelling through was my bowels. I looked back down at the circle in the dial and saw that there were five seconds, four, three, two, move now, move your legs, and there we were, rest. Rest. Breathe. Now look at the dial again. Through the rat. Ignore the rat, look past him, there, at the hand inside the circle, concentrate on the shape of it, yet another circle at the bottom, so many circles, but this one is like a pivot, and then the arrow of the hand through it, sweeping slowly around the soft gold field. Now follow that, yes, there we are, no, ignore that, ignore that feeling, just keep watching, coming down, coming down, there, now it's going up, focus, focus, not long to go, fifteen, smooth sweep, thirteen, twelve, coming up, are you ready, get ready to move your knees, now, now, shift your knees up and move your feet, both of them, a bit more, there you are, there! You're sitting. Now you are sitting. Breathe slowly, not too much at a time, and take in your surroundings.

My heart jolted as I saw the rat scuttling across the floor. So I hadn't imagined it? It was a large, dirty-looking brute with yellowish eyes and a bright red tail breaking through the coarse brown hair. It scampered over the mountain of Akuji's body, past me and over to the other side of the room.

I watched the rat, following its movements obsessively, like a seasick passenger watching the waves. It placed me in the room and it made it easier to regulate my breathing and to hold the nausea at bay.

I gave myself a threshold of ten minutes' rat-watching time – any less and I'd be out cold again, any more and I'd be whistling down the seconds until her finger squeezed the trigger and it was all over. After seven and a half minutes the rat scuttled under a bed in the corner and started biting at a dirty piece of gauze, and I felt ready.

I leaned over and gently prised the gun from Akuji's hands. It was a version of the Tokarev: unmarked, but possibly Chinese, by the look of the barrel lug. China was supporting the Biafrans, so that made some sense. I checked the pistol – fully loaded – and placed it in my waistband. Finally, my lesson from Pritchard from all those years ago in a clearing outside Frankfurt: pockets. They had nothing in them but the packet of Three Fives in his jacket, which I decided to take. I slid a cigarette out and lit it. The nicotine burned my lungs and brought some fire back into my head.

After I'd taken a few drags, I grabbed hold of the table Akuji had crashed into for leverage and pulled myself to my feet. Several bottles had been smashed and thick, sharp-smelling liquids were flowing into each other across the metal tray. Taking care not to touch any of the broken glass or liquid, I examined the small bottles, turning the tops of them with my fingers so I could read the labels. Most had trade names I didn't recognize, but one I did. In bold black letters was a word that might save me: Benzedrine.

The small type on the bottle said it was 'fast-acting': I timed it as seven minutes before the tablet started to take effect. In that time, I found a white coat on one of the beds and put it on, and I was in the middle of ripping a sheet into strips so I could tie Akuji's hands together when the fatigue lifted and my senses came alive and I heard the footstep at the top of the stairs.

*

'Is he dead?' said the man in the mask as he surveyed the scene: Akuji on the ground and a half-crazed British spy shaking a pistol at him.

I took the cigarette from my mouth to answer, and promptly threw up all over my trouser-leg. There was blood in the vomit, and the man responded to his professional instincts and stepped forward. I waved the pistol at him and grunted threateningly, and he got the message and stopped, and I sorted out my throat and used some of Akuji's uniform to wipe off the stuff and then looked back at him again through stinging eyes, took another drag and tried again: 'He's just out of action for a while,' I said.

The doctor nodded. 'Please get back into bed now,' he said. I had to admire his sangfroid.

'How far is it to Udi?'

'We have all the facilities you need here . . .'

'I need to get to Udi now!' I said, banging my hand against the bed and making the bottles rattle on the shelves.

It must have come out stronger than it had in my head, because his eyes were wide now, through the slits.

'Please calm yourself,' he said. Then, slowly, reaching for the right words to pacify me: 'What medication have you taken?'

'A tablet of Benzedrine you had lying about.'

The white mask stared back at me.

'You are joking, I hope?'

'No,' I said, 'I'm not joking. Because in' — I checked Akuji's Longines — 'around three hours and forty-five minutes' time, something very bad is going to happen in Udi, and I need to be there to stop it. I need to be alert until then. After that—'

'After that you may die,' he said. 'There's no telling what Benzedrine could do to your system right now. And please put the gun away — soldiers threaten us all the time, and we're accustomed to standing our ground. You can threaten me all you want, but I can't let you leave here. It's just not safe.'

I started laughing then. 'Safe?' I spat at him. 'Half an hour ago you told me I might have caught this disease from rat shit, and there are rats in *here*, for Christ's sake!'

'I know. Unfortunately, they were here when we arrived. They were attracted by the smell of amputated limbs. But I didn't mean safe for you — I meant for everyone else. Your condition is probably highly contagious.'

'Yes,' I said. 'I didn't think you just liked masks.'

I walked towards him and pulled it down. A neat beard failed to hide that he was barely out of his teens.

'What's your name?' I asked.

'David.'

'David what?'

'David Kanu.'

'Born here and educated in the States, I presume? Wanted to come back to help out?'

He nodded. A trickle of sweat travelled down his left cheek.

'Can you drive, David? Do you have access to a car?'

'Why?'

I gestured to the body lying on the bed. 'Do you know this man?'

'No,' he said. 'He turned up in his car and asked if I had a British patient here. I said I had and he—'

'I mean do you know who he is?'

'Yes, of course.'

I waited for him.

'Colonel Ojukwu. The head of the Biafran army.'

'Wrong,' I said. 'He's an impersonator, name of Akuji. And, like me, he's a British agent. How far are we from Udi?'

'Sixty or seventy miles.'

'Right. Well, sixty or seventy miles from here, in a very short time, someone is going to try to kill the British prime minister. Do you understand?'

'We have a telephone,' he said. 'You could call your embassy.'

'They already know about it. But they might not get there in time.'

'You can't leave,' he said firmly. 'You might cause an epidemic. I can phone someone at the clinic in Udi. I have some connections with the American government.'

'Do you, now?' I said. 'That's interesting. But no, thank you. As for an epidemic, I may not be fit to pass a company medical but I'm not about to die either, and if I understood our conversation earlier the other people who caught the disease you think I have *did* die, and very quickly.'

'You've taken medication—'

'I've taken a tablet of amphetamine, which you've just told me should make me even more ill. So how is it that I am standing here talking to you about all the rats there are going to be scuttling around here if you don't help me?'

'What do you mean?'

'If the Prime Minister is killed,' I said, 'his replacement may decide to start providing arms to the Biafrans instead of the Nigerians.'

'Good for them,' he said, folding his arms.

'I thought the Red Cross were meant to be neutral.'

'We are,' he said, clenching his jaw. 'As much as it's possible to be.'

'I see,' I said. 'But it's not as simple as that. Strengthening the Biafrans may simply mean that neither side will be able to deliver the knockout blow. The war could last months, perhaps even years longer. In which case, you'll be treating a lot more amputees, and the rats will be the only ones happy about it.'

He considered this, and I tried to ignore the ticking of Akuji's watch.

'From what I hear,' he said, 'this war is very unpopular in Britain. If there is a new government, it might decide not to supply either side with arms, and that could lead to a ceasefire coming sooner rather than later.'

It was the same argument I had used on both Pritchard and Akuji, and the one I personally thought was the most likely to happen. I made a note that David Kanu was not as green as he appeared, and tried again.

'That may be the case,' I said. 'But I wouldn't like to have it on my conscience if it weren't.'

'You don't strike me as a man whose conscience often troubles him.'

'Perhaps not,' I said. 'But I think yours does. So, David, do you want to be kept awake at night because you have helped prolong the bloodshed among your fellow men or do you want to give me a lift and save a respected world leader from being murdered in cold blood by the Russians?'

He stared at me with hatred in his eyes, and I knew I had him.

XXII

Friday, 28 March 1969, Biafra, 11.30 a.m.

Emerging aboveground, my eyeballs throbbed as they adjusted to the glare of the sun. We were in a small clearing surrounded by dense forest, deserted except for two vehicles: a dirt-spattered Land Rover with a large red cross on its side and a white Mercedes estate in which were seated several heavily armed soldiers, all of whom were watching us keenly.

'Akuji's men?'

David nodded.

I got him to hand over the keys to the Land Rover and told him to wait for me.

There were six of them, all seated in varying postures designed to intimidate, all in crisp uniforms with the Biafran sun on their shirtsleeves and berets sitting on their heads at the correct angle.

'Hello,' I said. 'I'm Doctor Foster.'

'Where is the Colonel?' said one of the men, his thumb toying with the trigger of his machine gun.

'He's still downstairs,' I said. 'He wants to talk to the patient some more. Doctor Kanu and I are needed elsewhere, so he asked me to tell you to wait here for him.'

A few of the men sighed or rolled their eyes.

'I'm sorry,' I said. 'He should be up in about half an hour.'

David had told me that all the patients belowground had been moved to another clinic on my arrival. But they didn't know that, and I reckoned it would be at least another hour before they ventured downstairs to check up on Akuji. I turned to walk away.

'Doctor Foster!' one of them called out. I turned to face him and smiled through clenched teeth. 'Are you from Gloucester?' he asked.

A couple of the others broke into laughter, no doubt remembering the rhyme from childhood. Careless, Dark: you may be in the middle of the bush, but it's also a former British colony. If you're going to make this cover work, you're going to have to use your head a bit more.

I smiled wearily. 'Very funny,' I said. 'I've never heard that one before.'

Their cackles followed me back to the Land Rover. David was already behind the wheel, so I climbed in and handed him the key. As he started the ignition, he gestured at a small plastic container on the dashboard, which looked to be filled with yellow mush.

'*Garri*,' he said. 'Crushed cassava.'

I told him I wasn't hungry.

'That's because Benzedrine suppresses the appetite. But your body needs this. Eat.'

I did as I was told. The taste was coarse and bitter, but I was soon using my fingers to scoop out the last of it. When there was none left, I laid my head against the window and watched the landscape judder by.

I still had no idea why Akuji had been impersonating Ojukwu, but with an armed guard and a swish car, it seemed he had some pretty powerful backing. I had told both him and David that the PM's death would lead to Britain switching allegiance in this war, but that was because I thought it would persuade them to help me. I wasn't sure what the game was. Pritchard was still nagging at me: what was the message he had wanted to pass to Akuji?

I turned my head and was startled to see a man staring back at me from the road: sunken eyes, a few days' beard and a bloodstained white coat. It took me a fraction of a moment to recognize myself in the wing mirror, which was hanging at an odd angle. I felt light-headed and exhausted, but I couldn't sleep, not now. I caught David glancing at me, and I lifted my gun fractionally and met his gaze. He looked away and pushed his foot down.

*

Within twenty minutes of leaving the clinic we reached our first checkpoint. It was a distinctly unofficial-looking one, consisting of a gang of youths in unidentifiable uniforms and a few cleverly positioned oil drums. I had hoped that the large red cross painted across the side of our vehicle might speed us through such situations, but they signalled us to stop nevertheless, and I quickly slipped the gun into my waistband and covered it with my shirt. David pretended to brush some mosquitoes from the windscreen and in the same gesture brushed the *garri* container to the floor. 'They're looking for food,' he said. Sure enough, as we came to a standstill the group immediately headed towards the back of the Land Rover to investigate our cargo. Without turning my head, I tried to calculate the odds of survival if I had to make a run for it, but presumably there were no edible supplies under the tarpaulin because they quickly sauntered back and waved us through with their sticks and machetes. We passed two more similar checkpoints before reaching our first back in Federal-occupied territory, but apart from flicking through David's identity papers, which the boy held upside down, they were no more interested in us.

I was nevertheless getting anxious. I had to be there by half past two at the latest; it was now twenty to, so I asked David for an estimate of how far away we were. He pointed ahead, and as the haze lifted, I saw the concrete barriers, machine guns and ring of barbed wire reinforcing a solid perimeter fence.

'We're there,' he said.

Udi.

*

'Can I help you?' said the man in the uniform of the British military police, but his tone of voice suggested he couldn't.

'We're from the clinic over in Awo Omamma,' I said cheerfully. 'We were asked to bring over some supplies.'

The Benzedrine was really kicking in now: every pore on the Redcap's face was in focus and my fatigue had miraculously vanished.

He stepped back from the window and took a small notepad from his belt.

'Name?'

My stomach tightened, and a fresh supply of sweat broke across my neck and back.

'We probably won't be on there,' I said, lowering my voice. 'Has Pritchard arrived yet? I'm with his group.'

He looked at me.

'And you are . . . ?'

'Paul Dark. Government liaison.'

He frowned, and I knew why. Never change your story. I had started by saying I was with the Red Cross, before suddenly claiming to be a British government agent. I'd had to, because he had a list of authorized personnel and I wasn't on it and I didn't have time for the inevitable runaround that path would have led to: Snowdrop disappearing to fetch someone higher up the chain, bluster about phone calls received from people whose names I couldn't quite remember, and so on. No choice but to switch horses quickly and hope that the hint of top-secret hooha carried enough authority to sway him – and that Pritchard was curious enough to come out and get me, despite apparently warning every soldier in the country to lock me up on sight. I cursed myself for letting the local road-blocks lull me into complacency. The British prime minister was visiting – of *course* they would have something professional in place.

'Can't say I know of anyone by that name, sir,' said the Redcap, and put his pad away. 'I'm afraid I cannot allow you to come through here—'

'Oh for Christ's sake, stop mucking me around!' I said. 'It's vitally important I get through before the PM arrives. Find Henry Pritchard and tell him . . .'

I trailed off. A man with a jovial red face and a Saint George bow tie had made his way through the checkpoint and was striding towards us.

*

'Gosh – you have been in the wars, haven't you? So to speak.' He chuckled into his chins.

'Yes,' I said. 'I've caught some rare new disease, apparently.'

His eyes widened. 'Contagious?'

'Could be.'

He wiped his brow with a dirty-looking handkerchief. 'Best keep out of your way, then!' He squinted into the sun, which was almost directly above us. 'Mad dogs and Englishmen, eh?'

David had gone off with the Redcap to park the Land Rover, and Manning was leading me through the compound's main courtyard. All the usual pageantry and pomp of a state visit had been rolled out: Union Jacks hung from every available flagpole and a banner welcomed the British prime minister in foot-high letters above the main gate. Shirtsleeved photographers circled one another trying to find innovative angles to shoot it, while doctors in spotless white coats muttered abstractedly to journalists as they glanced anxiously at the wards that wrapped around the place like a quad.

It was easy to take the scene for granted, but I knew it could all change in an instant. I mentally replaced the Union Jacks with Hammer and Sickles and the black Rovers with ZiLs: one squeeze of a trigger and that could be the next state visit this place saw. So where could she be? The wards were very low-ceilinged, but there were three floors, so it wasn't possible to see into them all. Especially the corners . . . Manning was babbling something next to me, and I interrupted to ask him if he had heard from Pritchard yet.

'Yes, he arrived with Smale a few hours ago.'

'Smale? What's that little prick doing here?'

Manning looked offended. 'I thought he was rather a nice chap, actually. He's over there.' He pointed to a group of whey-faced men in suits standing by an armoured car at the other end of the court-yard. One of them seemed vaguely familiar, and I asked Manning who he was.

'Sandy Montcrieff,' he said. 'You met him at the Yacht Club, remember?'

I remembered: the ghostly figure in the nightshirt. Ex-BBC *Mirror* man.

'What's he doing here?' I asked. 'And Smale?'

'They're both with the PM's advance party. Making sure of secu-rity with Henry.'

'And where's he?'

'Oh, Christ knows. Last time I saw him he was about to head off to check the wards. Lord knows why he's so anxious: I'd have thought he'd have been used to this sort of thing, what with his connections.'

I stopped walking. 'What connections?' It sounded odd coming from Geoffrey: he was also a spook.

Manning turned to me, his piggy little eyes looking a little forlorn. 'Well, you know . . .'

'No, I don't know. Tell me: it could be important.'

'Ah,' said Manning. 'Did I not mention that Henry is Marjorie's brother?'

'No,' I said. 'You didn't.' It explained how the old fool was still working, though. 'So Henry is an aristocrat, is that it?'

'Well, yes – but not just any old Scottish aristocracy, old boy! They're second cousins to the Queen. I just thought with the number of state functions Henry's been to, he must be used to—'

I didn't hear the rest. I had already started running in the direc-tion of the wards.

XXIII

'Hello, Henry,' I said. The sweat was pouring off my right hand, the one clutching the pistol.

Pritchard turned and smiled at me. *Actually smiled.*

'Paul,' he said. 'I wondered when you might turn up.' He looked back at the window. As I had suspected, it was one of the corner rooms. 'Game's up, is it?'

'I'm afraid so.'

'"No sudden movements?"'

'That's the drill.'

It was dark in here: it seemed to be some sort of office-cum-storeroom, with filing cabinets and shelves of medical supplies. I mustered all the concentration I could to follow his arm as he dropped to his knees and placed the rifle on the floor.

'When did you find out?' said Pritchard, standing again, still affecting the absurdly casual tone, as though I'd walked in on him searching my drawers or reading my diary rather than preparing to shoot the prime minister.

'Just now,' I replied. 'Manning mentioned you were related to the Queen, and I wondered why I'd never heard that before. Where's Anna?'

Pritchard looked at me for a moment, then tipped his head back and gave a slightly deranged laugh. 'Oh, Paul!' he said when he'd managed to pull himself together. 'I thought you'd got a little further than that.' He adjusted his spectacles primly. 'Anna's dead.'

Something broke inside me. I don't know why, as it was what I had believed for nearly twenty-five years. But I had wanted to see her, just one more time. To hear her voice, just one more time.

'The photograph,' I said with the part of my brain that wanted all the details accounted for. 'In the marketplace . . .'

'Faked,' said Pritchard. 'Rather a good job, considering the time we had to put it together.'

'So Geoffrey is working for you?'

'Sometimes,' he said. 'He's not aware of the full ramifications, one might say.'

'Did you kill her?'

He dipped his head. 'In '45? No, that was also faked. Sorry, old boy. Anna changed her name and moved to Tunisia, where she died in '57. Lung cancer. Those unfiltered cigarettes she liked, do you remember?'

I remembered. 'So you and she . . . ?'

He nodded. 'Always. Yes, I was her one true love.' He saw the look on my face. 'You're lost, I know. I have a lot I need to tell you.'

I leaned against the wall. 'You can start with this' – I gestured at the rifle. 'Why kill Wilson? And why send a plant to London?'

He shook his head. 'I didn't send Slavin. Do you think I'd have given him my code-name?'

'What then?'

'Think, Paul. I'm no sniper – the chap you strangled on the golf course was meant to do the job. So why did I fly out here?'

'To protect yourself,' I guessed. 'To make sure Slavin didn't have anything else that could point to you being Radnya.' But even as I said it I knew I was wrong.

'To protect *us*,' he said.

So he knew about me. All right. Let that sink in for a moment.

'Slavin didn't know the double's name,' I said. 'So that meant either one of us could be blown.'

The corners of his mouth twitched. 'Well, you certainly seemed worried about the possibility. I must say I wasn't expecting you to kill poor old Chief. That's made life rather tricky for us, I think.'

'I had to,' I said, then stopped. I wasn't going to justify myself to Pritchard. 'So . . . Slavin was a genuine defector.'

Pritchard shook his head slowly from side to side.

'But why would Moscow want to expose a long-running double agent?' I asked. 'Possibly even two.'

'Moscow's a large city,' he said. My skin was prickling, but I didn't yet know why. 'Whom do we work for?' said Pritchard, and his pale blue eyes searched my face for a reaction. I realized that although he knew it was the end of the road, he was enjoying revealing the plot to me, like a conjuror finally able to show his audience how clever he had been. 'It's a simple enough question,' he said. 'Whom do we work for?'

'The KGB,' I replied, and winced; it sounded so childish suddenly, so cops and robbers.

'No, Paul,' said Pritchard. 'We don't. When Anna recruited me, it was into *Glavnoe Razvedyvatel'noe Upravlenie*: military intelligence. She had been persuaded of my good intentions by another of her agents – your father.'

He was lying. He had to be lying.

I knew he wasn't lying.

A dozen images flew through my head, but above them all I could see my father's body sprawled across the bed at the farmhouse, one half of his head a ruin.

'Did you . . .' My mouth was sewn up. 'Did you kill him?'

'But it was I who persuaded Anna to recruit you,' Pritchard went on, as though I hadn't spoken. 'Larry hated the idea – he felt you were too young. He always said that successful recruitment depended on the subject having a firm ideology. I thought you were at precisely the right age to foster that. I proposed we give you the ideology – through Anna.'

It was like listening to some macabre joke. The man whose views he was blithely referring to was unrecognizable to me — and yet, recognizable, too.

'Larry still wasn't satisfied,' said Pritchard. 'He desperately didn't want you spoiled by betrayal, as he felt he had been. He didn't want that life for you. In the end, he had no choice, though: Moscow demanded it. And Larry always obeyed Moscow. I never left for Gaggenau, of course — I was with Anna then. We knew it was only a matter of time before you were injured in one way or other. That cut you got wasn't much more than a scratch, really. Anna made certain you were isolated, and took care of your treatment. And you walked right into it, of course. Who wouldn't? She was young, beautiful, good in bed . . .'

I ran towards him then and hit him, smashing my fist into his mouth. He barely even flinched, just dipped his head a little, and I slouched to my knees, my hands falling uselessly into my stomach, where I clutched myself as though I were the one who had been hit.

I tried to stand up, failed, tried again. 'Finish the story,' I said, steadying myself by leaning against the wall.

Pritchard wiped the blood from his lip and smiled at me mock-affectionately. 'You always were too emotional,' he said. 'But the problem was you were stubborn, too — you refused to be swayed. You had your precious principles. So we came up with the idea of Anna's death, and that did the trick, finally, didn't it? You ran into our arms. Anna was taken out of the country. Larry . . . well, Larry didn't take it well. He could never really handle the hard decisions. He was weak.'

So well-spoken, this Scottish aristocrat. It was hard to believe that monsters dwelt inside him.

'So you killed him.'

He looked genuinely surprised. 'No, no. When he received your note about Anna, he immediately ran to his old friend Colin Templeton in Lübeck and asked him to take her away from the scene. But Chief and his men were too slow. When the soldiers brought Anna back to the safe house in her comatose state, Larry saw that he had failed and went, quite literally, mad. Said he couldn't live with the choice between betraying you or Moscow, so he was going to take the only way out he knew. He already had the gun – there was nothing I could do.'

He could have been lying – I was pointing a gun at him, after all, and confessing to killing Father might make me pull the trigger more readily. But somehow I knew he was telling the truth.

'And Churchill authorizing the mission personally – all a complete hoax.' I laughed at my own naivety.

'Yes – we were working to Beria's orders, in fact. All those men were traitors to the Soviet Union.'

'It's 1969,' I said. 'Tell me you don't still believe in all this.'

'Yes,' he said simply. 'I've always been a believer, ever since I read Marx at school. I'm still a believer, even with all this.'

'All what?'

'After the war, the foreign intelligence arms of the GRU and the Ministry for State Security merged. The new organization was called *Komitet Informatsii* – the Committee of Information.'

I nodded dumbly. KI. I knew it from a hundred dossiers: Molotov had been appointed chairman. 'It didn't last long,' I said.

'Indeed not. A couple of years later it was wound up and the GRU was once again an independent intelligence agency. So, what can we deduce?'

'That while the two organizations were merged, someone found out about you.'

'Bravo, that man! Yes, someone discovered that the GRU had recruited a British agent in Germany at the end of the war and given him the code-name Radnya. They didn't have my real name, but it was enough. They stored away this information – perhaps they had an inkling that the KI wouldn't last long. Then, a couple of decades later, as this same fellow sat at the head of some nasty little division of the KGB, he decided that Radnya would make the perfect ingredient for a grand plot against his counterparts in London.'

So I had been right about Slavin being a plant – albeit a very unusual one. Plants had to have a few secrets to hand over or nobody would believe they were genuine defectors. But that information couldn't be too valuable, or it would defeat the purpose. So you gave them lots of pieces of genuine but not very important information that you knew or suspected the other side already had. Barium, we called it: chicken-feed. But it had got trickier. With the paranoia over plants, all would-be defectors had come under pressure to produce much more than barium. The KGB officer handling Slavin had calculated that the details about a double being recruited in the British Zone in 1945 would be enough for the Service to unmask Radnya's identity on their own steam, thereby cementing Slavin's credentials and simultaneously sinking the British into a morass of recriminations over yet another traitor in their ranks. Slavin would then have been able to concoct the most outrageous untruths and have everyone hanging on his every word. At the same time, a body blow would have been dealt to the KGB's old rivals, the GRU, who wouldn't have known what had hit them.

It was a brilliant ploy. The only problem with it had been . . . me. The KGB hadn't known that the GRU had, in fact, recruited *two* British double agents in the same part of Germany at the end of the war, and that both of them – the Russian practice being not to tell agents their own code-names – would presume they were under threat of imminent exposure.

'Where does the PM come into this?' I asked.

'Ah, that,' said Pritchard, making it sound like a trifling affair. 'It's a long story.'

'We have time,' I said.

He smiled. I didn't like the smile, and it set alarm bells off in my head.

'Anna's here, isn't she?'

'No, Paul. Please let go of that idea. I told you: Anna died a long time ago.'

I could sense a false note somewhere. The eyes. His eyes didn't move — they were fixed on me. Because he was fighting the urge to look elsewhere. The window? Was it my imagination or was there some noise coming from that direction? What was it — cheering?

I glanced down at my watch. I managed to register that it was twenty-five past before I picked up the movement in my peripheral vision and looked back up to see Pritchard leaping towards me, his hands outstretched like claws. I pulled the trigger without even willing it to happen, and watched as the bullet ripped through his jacket and forced him back onto the floor.

'Where is she?' I screamed. 'Which corner?'

He whispered a word, and then was silent. His voice had been hoarse, and the word hadn't come out clearly, but I knew what it was instantly: 'Pockets,' he had said.

I searched them, and then headed downstairs and into the court-yard. A long black car was slowly approaching the gates, and some-where above me was Anna with one eye glued to her sniper sight, waiting for it.

XXIV

The courtyard was packed and noisy, with the crowd jostling against the ropes to catch a glimpse of the car that was now edging through the gates one yard at a time, presumably so the PM could wave at everyone. One of the Redcaps saw me and started racing over, so I dropped back to a brisk walk and made as though I were calling out to someone on the other side of the ropes. Manning had also spotted me and was heading in my direction, but I was just a few yards away from the next corner, and yes, there was the staircase. I took the steps three at a time, my ears hot and pulsing and my chest constricting. Then I was on the landing.

I took out the Tokarev and uncocked the safety. As there had been with the other staircases, two large open wards faced each other. All the patients who could move had thronged into the one facing the courtyard and were gathered around the windows peering down. All but one, a young boy with an artificial leg, who was leaning against the wall, watching me with large eyes. I had a sudden memory of a German boy of about the same age who had once looked at me like that, a lifetime ago.

At the far end of the landing was a door. If this staircase followed the pattern of the others, which it seemed to, it should lead me to a storage-room-cum-office. This was the door I'd travelled thousands of miles to open: behind it, almost certainly, lay the answers I was looking for. I grabbed the handle.

Locked.

I smashed my foot into the lower half of the door. A couple of splinters flew up, and after a couple more kicks the whole thing fell in.

The gun was the first thing I saw, a dark snake pointing out at me, the barrel gleaming. Then the figure in white behind it.

'Drop your weapon!' she hissed, and there was such danger in her voice that I immediately leaned down and placed my pistol on the floor, then kicked it towards her.

She picked it up and pocketed it, then backed away from me to the window. Thin bars of sunlight glowed through the shutters but much of the room was in darkness and it took my eyes a moment to decipher some of the objects. A mop and bucket leaned against one corner, a duffel bag on the floor nearby. On the windowsill, a tripod had been mounted. It wasn't until she started placing the rifle onto this that I got a good look at her.

She had changed. There was still the dark soulfulness in her eyes, the wide jaw, the wave of hair swept back. But the mouth that had been full and sensual was now thin and hard, and her skin was also somehow different: still bronzed, but now a little leathery. Perhaps Pritchard hadn't been lying about her having lived in Tunisia. She turned to look at me then, and it was almost as if her skin tautened under my gaze, until, like the surface of a painting being scratched away, the ghost portrait that had been hiding beneath was revealed.

It was her. Nearly twenty-five years after I had last seen her, here she was again, still in a nurse's uniform, and this time she was clutching a sniper rifle. I looked back at the duffel bag and saw the small white cap with a red cross on it peeking out of the top. It was just like the one I'd seen at the Afrospot. Or close enough: I noticed that the thread was slightly the wrong shade, and guessed she had taken the outfit from one of the Nigerian clinics and adapted it.

'Hello, Paul,' she said, and then she turned from me and lowered herself into position, crouching down on one knee and screwing her eye into the rifle sight.

*

I closed my eyes and swallowed the vomit that had risen in the back of my throat.

'I thought you were dead,' I said.

'You were wrong.'

I laughed involuntarily, though it came out more as a whimper. 'I was . . . Is that . . .' My breathing failed again and my legs nearly gave out from under me. Come on, get the words out! 'Is that the best you can come up with?' I said. '*I was wrong?*'

'We can discuss this later. Did you see Henry?'

I didn't say anything, mainly because my right thigh was jerking and I was trying to keep it under control with my arms, but she misinterpreted the silence.

'Did you see him, Paul?'

Her voice had a coldness that cut right through me. Even with everything that was happening, something told me not to let her know he was dead, and I shook my head, then answered, 'No' aloud when I realized that she still wasn't looking at me, but remained fixed in her position at the window. *With them that walk against me, is my sun.* Only she wasn't walking: she was staying put, waiting for the PM.

'Don't tell me you still intend to go through with this,' I said. She didn't reply, just kept on looking through the sight. I wanted to lunge across the room and rip her away from it, force her to stand and face me and answer me. But I was too weak, so instead I just stood there, clutching my leg uselessly. More seconds passed. What was going on down there? Had the car stopped?

There was too much flooding through me, and I couldn't slow it down or order it.

'How did you do it?' I asked, finally. 'Make-up and something to stop your pulse?' I had no idea what part of my mind had come up with the question, but another part approved. Keep her talking, get some answers, distract her. Distract yourself.

'Yes,' she said. 'Something like that. I was one of the first – they have done it many times since.'

'*Why*, Anna?' Here was the question. Here, finally, was the question I had wanted her to answer.

She didn't say anything for a while, and I wondered if she had heard me. Then she answered. 'Love,' she said simply. 'Love of my cause.' She lifted her head a fraction and glanced across at me, and the Anna I had known all those years ago receded once again. I searched her face desperately for the glimpse I'd had just moments before, but it was no use. 'I am sorry I hurt you,' she said, still talking in the same calm, slow way. 'I didn't want to. But I knew you were one of us the first time I saw you. I could sense that you wanted to do good, that you would be a strong soldier for us. Are you still a strong soldier for us, Paul? Can you keep fighting a little longer for me?'

The anger welled in my stomach. *Did she think I was a bloody child?* My legs started to spasm, and I fought back the dizziness. Please don't let me lose my hearing now! I closed my eyes for a moment and tried to find some stillness and regulate my breathing, but all I could see were dozens of tiny bursts of light, darting here and there, trying to make connections with one another. I placed a hand behind me and let myself slump slowly to the floor, leaning my head against the jamb. It was more comfortable here and, after all, it was where I belonged. How did the next line run? *The wheel is turned*, that was it: *'The wheel is turn'd; I hold the lowest place'*.

'I have paid a price, too,' Anna was saying, and I woke from my dreams of poetry in a distant classroom and strained my ears to make sure I heard her right. I wanted to catch every word of this extraordinary confession, wanted very much to know how she had paid a price for betraying me. 'I have sacrificed my career and a good part of my life to protect you,' she said. 'Because if anyone ever found out I was alive, that might have exposed you.'

Ah, well: that wasn't bad. One had to admit that that wasn't bad. So that was why she hadn't shot me yet – because of my value as an agent?

'But Slavin found out,' I said.

'Yes, that was unfortunate. Vladimir Mikhailovich had been out here too long – he was lonely. He became obsessed with me. I told him there was someone else. That was a mistake. I have spent much of my time away from Lagos in recent weeks, and on one occasion he must have broken into my quarters and found some letters I had never sent Henry. I had kept them – a weakness. I suppose he sent photographs of them to Moscow and someone in the KGB realized who I was. But he's gone now.' She smiled tersely. 'Nobody knows.'

'You're still a believer, then?' I said. A phrase she had often used in Germany came back to me. 'In the brotherhood of man?'

Her mouth tightened. 'Of course. Why not?'

I clawed my way up to a sitting position, but she heard me and lifted the rifle an inch so I stopped and she replaced it again.

'I don't know,' I said, as though nothing had happened. 'The gulags, the mock trials, the tanks in the streets? The use of assassination to sustain a civil war in Africa until you can install a puppet leader to further your own aims?'

The car must have stopped because she moved her eye away from the sight and turned to look at me. 'Henry warned me you might have lost your nerve,' she said. 'I didn't believe him. You've worked for us for over twenty years, Paul.'

'Based on what, though?' I said.

She went back to her previous position.

'I never lied to you about the big things. And you're hardly in a position to lecture me about sustaining a civil war. Your government—'

'My government. Not me.'

'So whose side are you on then?' she said, and the false politeness vanished for a moment.

'My own,' I said.

'I see. Just a neutral bystander, condemning everyone else from your position of complete superiority . . . and inactivity?'

'You're all as bad as each other,' I said. 'I refuse to take sides any longer.'

'But you must, Paul! Don't you see? You must! There's no room for sitting on the fence in this world. One side will win, and it will change how millions of people live. You have to take sides, and act on your beliefs. And I believe we will help this country.'

There was a mad glare in her eyes. I didn't want to hear how killing the PM was going to help – no doubt she had her answers. She'd always been good with the abstracts. 'So that's it?' I said. 'The cause above all, and screw anyone who gets in the way?' I forced myself onto my feet and began trudging across the room towards her. She didn't even flinch.

'What's to stop me from killing you?' I asked.

She looked up, surprised, then calmly put her eye back to the sight as though I were a child.

'Because you loved me,' she said. 'Perhaps you still do, in some way. I am what *you* have believed in for most of your life, and you can't destroy me. You will watch me finish this and then you will leave here, and we will never speak again. You will continue your work in London with Sasha.'

'No!' I said. 'I won't be—'

There was a sudden lift in the noise of the crowd outside.

'Here's the test, Paul,' she said. 'Here it is now. Which side will you take?'

I lunged forward, hitting her in the back. My pistol clattered onto the floor, out of reach, and Anna turned and lashed out at me, scratching at my face, but I managed to hook my arm around her right shoulder and brought her weight back and slipped the other arm around her neck and squeezed as hard as I could, trying to block out the pain, the sounds, everything. My hands were tingling and I looked down and saw that blood was flowing from the palms and I saw her face, her eyes fixed open, no drugs now, no clever injections, and I kept squeezing her even though I knew it was too late, because I could still hear the echo of the shot, and then I thought a flock of seagulls swept over the courtyard, but it wasn't seagulls, of course, it was humans, screaming. What a strange sound, I thought.

I looked down. I could see everything perfectly – the black car surrounded by a swarm of people, their shadows making everything seem to lean to one side: the black man in the peaked cap kneeling beside the body of the white man in the summer suit whose head didn't seem to be there any more. I let go of Anna, and she slumped to the floor. Releasing her seemed to do something to my breathing, because I started heaving uncontrollably.

There was a scraping noise and I looked up to see a small crowd of people tumbling into the room. I registered Smale first, then David the doctor behind him, and finally Manning, lobster-red in his tropical suit, his handkerchief the size of a windsail fluttering above the scene. Smale slapped me and screamed something I couldn't understand, and when I didn't answer he started shaking me. I wanted to tell him it was useless, he was wasting his time, I didn't have long to go. '*Murder!*' he was shouting, and I realized it was directed at me. '*I am arresting you for murder!*' It seemed like the wrong thing to say and I started counting aloud, for some reason. There was a lot of movement, a lot of panic, but I was perfectly conscious of it all, right until the last moment, the last breath. I was watching it all, right up until I died.

XXV

Nobody tells you you're dead – you have to figure it out yourself. It took me rather a long time. In fact, it was the presence of time that held me back. At the start, the idea didn't even occur to me. I seemed to be surrounded by an endless grey landscape, but that didn't mean death, surely: I was simply unconscious.

Only I wasn't. I could vividly remember everything, right up until when Smale had shaken me and I had stopped breathing. But still, the fact that I was thinking meant I was alive: probably in a hospital somewhere, recovering.

I clung on to that idea for a very long time. I thought it must have been at least a few months since I'd 'gone' and ended up . . . wherever I was. That was when it occurred to me that perhaps death wasn't what I had always thought it would be, but that it was a limbo state in which you had all eternity to reflect on the life you'd had, without being able to return to it.

My considerations of death were briefly interrupted by a series of extremely vivid hallucinations. One of these involved a tie I'd owned when I was a boy, a dark green silk tie with tiny red spots my father had bought me from Gieves when I'd turned sixteen, my last birthday in London before the war. The silk had been so thick and smooth it was like a river, and now it became just that and I dove deep into its comfort, luxuriating in its coolness and wishing I could stay there for ever, breathing bubbles up to the green, red-spotted surface. And then others started diving in after me, like the bodies in the ceremony I'd been at in Biafra, spirit bodies that cut through me and around me and seemed to keep diving further and further but never got any smaller or changed shape. And I wanted to climb up to the surface but I couldn't, because it was blocked by loose threads of silk, white and sticky, and I couldn't struggle past them and again I felt the weight on my chest and the trouble breathing, until I opened my eyes and saw a pair of disembodied eyes staring down at me from deep within a ball of white silk . . .

*

The lamps, though dimmed, had an unpleasant glare to them, and the walls a greenish tinge. I *was* in a hospital somewhere, but it was almost as bad as whatever I'd woken from. My food and drink were passed to me through a network of tubes, and I sat there, alone, imagining the fluid pumping into me and thinking back to what had happened, and what might happen next. I was in England, I knew, because the place smelled unmistakably of Dettol and every so often there was a hollow clanging, which I eventually realized was a radiator that was out of my line of sight.

I still couldn't move. There was a window, but like everything else it only changed from white to grey to black and back again. But I was in a hospital in England, recovering. Of that I was sure.

*

The disembodied eyes returned one day: now I saw they were attached to a man in a white coat, white gauze mask, white hood, white gloves. I couldn't speak to him, and he didn't say anything to me — just checked my tubes and wrote things down on a white pad. I thought that my hearing must have gone again at some point, because every sound was amplified. When he moved his foot on the linoleum, it was like a coin dropping in a well.

I no longer felt pain — physical pain, that is. I thought about

Anna every day, every hour. And grieved for myself, and the life I'd wasted.

*

Another man came to see me after that, wearing the same garb. It was Smale.

'You survived,' he said. 'They didn't think you would.'

I watched his eyes. Narrow and slanted, they seemed to me to be the kind of eyes that would belong to a small, ugly, grey fish. I tried to imagine the face of such a fish, and fitted it behind his mask.

'You were extremely lucky,' said the fish. 'You were in a medical facility when it happened. You were out for a minute and a half – your heart even stopped beating. The wog doctor you came with declared you dead. But then you came to – almost as if you had heard us and weren't willing to go.'

The fish paused. 'Of course, a lot of people have been hoping you wouldn't make it.' He looked away contemplatively. 'Not me, though. We'd lose so much valuable information.' He pushed his chair back. 'Let's get your clothes sent up, shall we? We've an important meeting to get to.'

*

London looked exactly the same: office workers jumped around puddles and struggled with umbrellas. We sploshed through the streets in the black Bentley. I sat in the back in my old suit, my hands cuffed to two soldiers sitting on either side of me. Smale was up in front. Near Piccadilly Circus Underground, we stopped at some lights and I glimpsed the headlines at a newspaper kiosk. 'THE PRIME MINISTER AND MOSCOW: LATEST REVELATIONS!' blared the poster for *The Times*, while *The Telegraph* had the more subdued: 'MOUNT-BATTEN SUSPENDS ARMS TO NIGERIA'.

'Mountbatten?'

Smale turned back to look at me, his eyes dead. 'He formed a government a couple of weeks ago.'

I couldn't think what to say. 'Wilson wasn't KGB' was what eventually came out.

'Really?' Smale replied, with a smile soaked in aspic. 'Did you believe everything your handler told you?' Then he turned away again and told the driver to take a right at the next junction.

*

They blindfolded me soon after that, and about twenty minutes later I was bundled out of the car and marched down a steep stairway. The room was cold and there was a slightly dank smell. Pipes gurgled in the background. Someone took the blindfold off. The two soldiers turned on their heels and took up station outside the door; Smale pushed me inside.

It was a familiar scene, right down to the naked bulb hanging from a coat-hanger. Beneath it, three men were seated behind a large desk that looked as though it were made from a solid block of steel. Two of the men were no surprise: Farraday and Osborne. The man sitting between them gave me more food for thought: Sandy Montcrieff, the *Mirror* reporter I'd met at the Lagos Yacht Club, and whom I'd later seen with Smale at the clinic in Udi.

We were in the 'rubber room', a space reserved for the interrogation of suspected double agents and other such undesirables; I'd sat in on a couple of sessions here before, during the renewed round of vettings after Philby had made a run for it. This gave me an advantage, of course. The bulb was burning through my eyes, but I knew it was a trick: it had been especially made by a company in Vauxhall to burn that bright, and the things were a devil to get replaced. Apart from the lamp, desk, chairs and a plastic bucket filled with dirty-looking water on the floor, the room was unfurnished, so as to enhance the subject's isolation and disorientation — but I knew that we were in the soundproofed basement of one of the smarter hotels in West Kensington.

Despite all of this, I was much more afraid than the poor souls I'd seen interviewed here before. Because I was guilty.

Osborne asked me to take a seat, which I did. The chair was cold and too low. I mentally stripped the three of them, visualizing Montcrieff's pale and bony legs, Osborne with his gut hanging over his belt and Farraday with unsightly moles across his back. It didn't help much.

'What's this about?' I said, selecting a tone somewhere between irritation and puzzlement. Might as well kick off proceedings. 'Are you holding me responsible for Wilson's death? I did everything I—'

'I'm sure you did,' said Montcrieff. 'Thankfully, it wasn't enough. But that's just between ourselves. If you don't tell us what we want to know, we'll announce that you were the assassin.'

The other two didn't flinch.

Montcrieff adjusted his cuffs and smiled innocently. 'What we want to know,' he went on, 'is how long you thought you could get away with playing us all for fools.'

'"Us"?' I said. 'Sorry, who the fuck are you again?' I turned to Osborne: 'William, I thought this was Service business.'

Osborne was stony-faced. 'Sandy's been with Five for years,' he said. 'And he was appointed Foreign Secretary two weeks ago.'

So. Not just a *Mirror* hack, then, but one of Cecil King's men in Five, and these two – along with Pritchard – had been plotting with him from the beginning. It was a repeat of King's coup attempt from last year, only this time the idea had been to have Wilson assassinated and then exposed as a Russian agent – and this time they had succeeded. Mountbatten was merely the figurehead: these three and a handful of other right-wing crackpots were in power now. No swastikas waving over The Mall – just a few desks moved. I imagined Chief would have been given the option of carrying on under the new regime or being shunted into retirement.

'You know I didn't kill Wilson,' I said. 'The Grigorieva woman pulled the trigger before I got to her.'

'We only have your word for that. According to Smale, you were holding the gun when he came in.'

'And he's willing to testify to that, is he?'

Montcrieff laughed. 'I don't think you fully understand the situation,' he said. 'We don't need to *try* you. The public is distraught, and crying out for revenge. We could have you hanged in Wembley stadium and sell tickets if we wanted.' He leaned down and took a rolled-up *Standard* from a briefcase by his legs. He slapped it onto the table and pointed to the headline: 'BRITAIN BACKS UNITY GOVERNMENT'. It was the twenty-eighth of April, I noticed – exactly a month since Udi.

'What do you want?' I asked, though I had a fair idea.

'We found Templeton's body,' said Osborne, referring to Chief by his surname; presumably he had the title now. 'Washed up near Limehouse.' He threw some photographs onto the desk. I picked them up and forced myself to look at them. They were as grim as could be expected.

'Well?' I said. 'It's obvious, isn't it? Henry killed him.'

'And why would he do something like that?'

'Because he was Radnya, of course.'

'We also found this in the clinic in Udi,' said Osborne, making the recommended sudden leap of subject to disorient me. He placed the Tokarev on the table; it spun for a moment on the surface before coming to a stop. 'Do you usually favour Soviet weaponry?'

'That's not mine,' I said. 'It belonged to a man called Akuji.'

'Yes, we know about him – Henry's contact with Ojukwu. We received his report a few days ago. He has shown no signs of developing the disease you had, thankfully.' He nodded at the gun. 'So what do you normally use, then? Henry told us you shot someone on a golf course.'

'I didn't shoot him,' I said. 'He took a pill.'

Osborne turned down the corners of his mouth. 'What weapon do you use?'

They had me. They must have searched my flat, found the safe, cracked it open.

'A Luger P08,' I said. 'As I presume you already know.'

'Indeed,' said Farraday, and he took it out and placed it next to the Tokarev. 'Did you get a chit from Armoury for this? Because I wasn't aware we kept a stock of antique German pistols.'

I smiled tolerantly. 'You haven't brought me here for carrying a non-regulation weapon. Presumably you're about to tell me that Chief's bullet-wound is consistent with it being fired from this gun.'

'Bingo,' said Montcrieff.

'Most officers have their own weapons,' I said. 'No doubt you all have your own, somewhere, in case of emergencies.' None of them reacted, so I went on. 'These little things' — I gestured airily at the Luger — 'were highly prized in their day, and are still very efficient. It wouldn't surprise me in the least if Pritchard also had one.'

'So where is it?' said Farraday.

'How the hell should I know?' I asked. 'Have you tried searching *his* home? It's interesting that he told you about Akuji, though. "Henry's contact with the Biafrans", my arse — don't you remember Henry told us we didn't *have* any contacts on the Biafran side? That's because we don't: the KGB does. Akuji is a Moscow man. He's closely related to and physically resembles Ojukwu. His role was to pose as Ojukwu to any British representatives sent to try to arrange peace talks with the Biafrans — I suspect Geoffrey Manning had just such a meeting arranged on the day I met him. My guess is that Akuji was to agree to whatever Manning proposed regarding talks, naturally without informing Ojukwu or anyone else in the Biafran hierarchy about it. Then whoever from the PM's party had gone along to meet him would either have found themselves stood up or wasting a lot of time trying to negotiate peace with an impostor — all of which would have drawn away vital resources and attention from the security arrangements for the visit to Udi.'

They just stared at me, and I kept looking from one to the other. 'For Christ's sake!' I said. 'I'm not the double. Look, it's obvious, isn't it? Chief must have called Henry out to Swanwick to discuss Slavin, and during their conversation twigged that he was Radnya. So Henry shot him, took a few of his clothes, dumped his body and pretended he'd gone missing.'

Osborne sighed. 'No. That is precisely what *you* did.'

It was my turn to stare. He sounded certain of it.

'As well as the gun, we have three witnesses. The firmest is a local solicitor, who lives in the village and was passing on the way into town. But all three described a black sports car very much like your little toy.'

'Impossible,' I said. 'It was in my garage. Did they get a licence plate?'

Osborne spread his hands on the desk.

'Well, then!'

'But they did identify the car in other ways. Our solicitor friend told us that it had no boot. There are very few models with that feature. Yours is one.'

'Who questioned him?'

'That is immaterial.'

'No,' I said, 'It's not. I'll wager that whoever questioned him had already come up with the theory that the car was mine, and the solicitor was just doing his best to give the answers he thought would satisfy the man from London. It's a classic investigative error.'

'Don't be so bloody patronizing,' said Osborne, and I knew he'd done the interview. Farraday's scornful glance in his direction confirmed it.

'Henry admitted to going out there – and admitted to the timing of the witnesses, if I remember rightly,' I said. 'It was also in the middle of the night, so anyone who saw a black car would have had to have been looking very closely. And as none of your "witnesses" took a number down, that seems unlikely.'

'Then,' said Osborne softly, 'there are the fingerprints. We took yours when you were in your coma. And then we compared them to all the sets we found in Templeton's house. Care to hazard a guess at what we discovered?'

'That some of them matched. Bravo – I've probably visited that house fifty times in the last three years. I was there the weekend before Chief disappeared.'

'Can you prove that?'

'I don't have to. You have to prove I wasn't.'

He raised his arm and for a moment I thought he was going to try to punch me, but he brought the palm of his hand down on a small bell on the table, the kind you see in hotel receptions, and a few seconds later the soldiers marched in. They aimed truncheons at my solar plexus, sending a jolt of pain through me and making me vomit. I tried to reach Montcrieff's shoes but he was too far away.

'Get him a towel or something,' said Farraday. I wondered what his reward had been − one of the more important ministries, no doubt. I remembered his little spat with Osborne over whether Pritchard or I should be allowed to go out to Lagos. They'd played it well, the three of them. If the coup hadn't come off perhaps they could have set up a small theatrical company.

I raised my head. Osborne was consulting a small leather-backed notebook. 'You hadn't visited Templeton in months,' he said. 'According to his daughter.'

I wiped my mouth with the cloth that had been handed me. 'How would she know?' I said.

'Well, you were sleeping with her, weren't you?'

'Where do you get these absurd—'

'She told us all about it,' said Farraday, chipping in.

'I hardly know her. She isn't my type.'

'Very suave,' said Montcrieff. He pushed forward another set of photographs. 'How do you explain these, then?'

In the car, rehearsing all the possible questions they could ask me, traps they could set, paths I could and could not take, this was one eventuality I hadn't envisaged.

She'd hanged herself, the poor cow. Her final few hours must have been hell. I remembered the look on her face as she had stood on the steps of her flat. Sorrow and despair. I had known it − and done nothing, too wrapped up in my own problems.

'Did she leave a note?' I asked, my lips tight.

Osborne nodded solemnly. 'Something about not being able to live with the fact that her boyfriend had killed her father.'

I leapt towards him, something like a scream coming from deep down in my throat, but I hadn't even reached the desk before I felt the thump. The soldier helped me back into my seat.

'So you *were* sleeping with her,' said Osborne, taking the cap off his fountain pen and noting it down neatly in his book.

'You really are a shit, Osborne,' I said, once I'd got my breath back again. 'Did you know that?'

He didn't look up from his writing. 'Murder and treason are more serious crimes.'

'Indeed,' I said. 'Conspiring to kill the prime minister is about as serious as it gets.'

That hit something. He pushed back his chair and stood up: his body may have been encased in finest Savile Row wool, but it did little to hide his bulk. He walked over to the plastic bucket and pushed it across the floor with a pointed little shoe, until it was just by my chair.

He yanked my head back by the forelock and brought his face up to mine. 'Did I ever tell you what we used to do with the Yids in Palestine back in '47?' he said, his eyes glazed over. 'The ones who wouldn't talk?'

He gestured at the soldiers again, and they stepped forward, took me crisply by the arms and shoved my face into the water, holding me down. I'd counted to twenty and was starting to panic when they jerked me out and dumped me back in the chair.

'Could we get some sandwiches or something?' said Montcrieff. 'I'm starving.'

'Yes, good idea,' said Osborne, whose face was flushed. He turned to one of the soldiers. 'Anderson, see if they have any decent food they can send down. Sandwiches or something.'

'Sir!' The soldier saluted and he and the others turned on their heels and left the room.

There was silence for a moment, then Farraday cleared his throat.

'Listen, Paul,' he said reasonably. 'We don't want to spend all day on this. We know you're working for the Russians. We just want the details. The name of your handler, where you meet him, how often. What information you've passed over. You know the drill. I can't guarantee immunity, but if you cooperate now it will be a lot better for you.'

I'd got my breathing back now, and I summoned up my energy to look up at him. He was busy adjusting one of his shirt-cuffs, which had unpardonably jutted against the bevel of his wristwatch. It was twenty past one. So I could at least place myself: it was twenty past one on the twenty-eighth of April.

'The smoked salmon and cucumber ones are good here,' I said. 'Could we have some tea as well?'

'This isn't funny, Dark,' said Osborne. He held out his hand in a fist and then opened it, like a child playing a game. 'Do you recognize this?' he said. It was a small green booklet about the size of a box of matches. He flipped it open, revealing a string of numbers and other figures. 'A one-time pad. To be used in conjunction with a radio transmitter. Care to explain?'

I was still catching up with a thought I'd had a few seconds earlier. I wasn't certain of it, but I played it anyway.

'By all means,' I said. 'But before I do, perhaps you can all answer one question that has been troubling me. Who was the poor chap who had his head shot off in Udi — one of the PM's bodyguards? I presume there's a D-notice on it.'

Osborne made to stand up, but Montcrieff gestured at him to stay seated.

'What are you talking about?' he said.

'It was bloody good,' I said. 'I'll give you that. The posters at the traffic lights were a nice touch. How long did that take you to put into place? Was it just the one kiosk, or did you set up several along the route between here and the hospital?'

None of them answered.

'It was this that gave it away,' I said, tapping the copy of the

Standard on the desk. 'You're a newspaperman, Sandy, so I'm a little disappointed. I'm sure all the details in it are perfect, but you over-egged the pudding making it today's West End Final. That edition doesn't come off the presses until two o'clock, and according to John's watch we're a good half-hour away from then. Careless, really – yesterday's edition would have done the trick just as well.'

They stared at me for a moment, and I savoured it.

'Fuck you, Dark!' spat Montcrieff, the first time I had seen him angry. 'This doesn't change that you're a traitor. Confess now and . . .'

'And what? You won't arrange my hanging at Wembley? Something tells me the PM might not be too keen to sign the chit for that whatever I say, and even if it were signed by the real Foreign Secretary.' I turned the screw. 'Perhaps he'd be more interested in hearing how you planned to kill him. I bet you all loved it when Henry proposed the idea – it was Henry's idea, wasn't it? Kill Wilson, then pin the blame on Moscow and claim he had double-crossed his masters at the KGB. Masterful. Did he tell you an actual KGB agent would do the job, though?' They didn't respond. 'How do you think he got her to do that? Did it not occur to you that his more-fascist-than-thou act might have been just that – an act – and that he was, in fact, leading you straight into a position in which the KGB could send a sniper to assassinate our prime minister?'

I let it sink in for a moment. Osborne rallied from the shock of me discovering their little subterfuge and waved the one-time pad at me. 'This was found in your pockets when we searched you . . .'

'And I took it from Henry's pockets moments after I discovered he was Radnya and shot him,' I said. 'Radnya means "related" in Russian, and just as you were all delighted Henry had access to the Queen – who you would need to form a government – so were the KGB. What could be more precious than a double agent with blood ties to the throne?' Their faces were turning white, so I closed in for the kill. 'I suggest you send a team to Henry's house and search the basement. Once you've found his transmitter, perhaps we can stop this charade and get down to the serious business of trying to assess just how much the bastard has compromised over the last twenty-five years.'

*

He was wearing a green tweed coat and a polka-dot bow tie. It had taken me four and a half hours to get to the meeting, and he'd turned up in an outfit a child could describe.

I wasn't in the best of moods. I'd spent most of the day with a team from Five, searching every inch of Pritchard's enormous flat in Belgravia. He'd made me sweat — for several hours I had seriously wondered if I might still be looking at the rope. In the end, it hadn't been in the basement, or the attic, or under the floorboards, but in a compartment concealed in one of the bookshelves.

'I want out,' I said to Sasha. 'I mean it.' But it sounded weak, even to my ears.

He leaned over and placed a hand on my arm. 'Please, Paul,' he said. 'Is that any way to greet an old friend?' We were in the Mayflower in Rotherhithe, which he had once confided in me was his favourite meeting-place. I assumed it wasn't for the beer or because you could visit the stairs where the Pilgrim Fathers boarded the ship, but because it was dark and cosy. The place was about half-full, with a good deal of background noise, and we were seated at a remote corner table, next to a mantelshelf filled with the usual assortment of books gathering dust: Lloyd's *Shipping Register* for 1930, *Bernard Spilsbury — His Life and Cases*, Foote's *Handbook for Spies* . . .

On the way over, between checking for tails and hopping on and off buses, I'd bought a paper — a real one — and seen that de Gaulle had resigned over a referendum on the Senate: it looked like the events in Paris the previous year had finally caught up with him. The editorial on page nine opined that his 'ideas and presence would nevertheless continue to play a part in French affairs', while the item beneath it discussed the fall of Biafra's stronghold, Umuahia. Would his idea of supporting the Biafrans continue, too?

I'd thought of the deserters and their families huddled in the hut in Aba; and of Gunner, ranting in the field at the futility of it all.

'I'm no use to you any more,' I said. 'I don't believe any of it.' And too many people were dead, I could have added – most of them because of me.

He pursed his lips, then placed his forefinger and thumb on either side of his mouth and stroked his beard. It meant he was thinking.

'They have questioned you?' he said, drawing his head a little closer to me. I gave him a look. 'What did you tell them?'

'I thought of something.'

He stopped stroking his beard. 'What?'

I took a sip of my pint. 'I blew Henry's cover,' I said. 'And I don't care what you say, it won't scare me. Trust me, nothing you can say will scare me.'

He didn't move for some time, and then he suddenly leaned back in his seat and started laughing. I asked him if he would mind explaining the joke.

He slowly wound down the merriment. 'You were worried about how I might react?'

I shrugged.

'This was foreseen, Paul,' he said pompously. 'This was always the endgame.'

'What was?' I asked. 'For me to blow Henry's cover?'

'Of course. If he was not going to survive, you had to remain protected at all costs. It does not matter that you have exposed him now. They can't question him, and you are clean.' He frowned. 'You told them about Anna also, I presume? I mean, that she was . . . working with Henry?'

I noted the hesitation and tried not to hate him too much for it. 'Yes,' I said. 'Was that also part of the endgame?'

Sasha raised his hands in a very Russian gesture. 'Perhaps. It is possible. I was never in contact with her. It was always Henry.'

It was always Henry. 'So Pritchard was running you?' I asked. He nodded. That explained a lot – why he'd had the transmitter, for a start. He had run Anna, he had run Sasha and, although I hadn't known it, he had run me. That night he'd left Vanessa's table at Ronnie Scott's — he hadn't gone home. He'd gone to meet Sasha and *then* home, where he had sent a message to Anna in Lagos. She had immediately upped sticks for Udi, telling her back-up man to find Slavin and kill him — and me if I tried to get anywhere near? Yes, that was how it must have been, or something like it.

I shivered inwardly and turned back to Sasha. 'If Henry was Radnya,' I said, 'what was my code-name?'

He pretended not to hear the tense I'd used. 'You really want to know?' he said. 'It's an ugly one. "Nezavisimyj".'

'"Independent" — why that?'

'Because we had to keep you separate from the rest of the cell, for . . .' — he looked around for a suitable phrase — 'personal reasons.'

'You mean because if I had discovered that Anna was alive, Henry had pimped her to me and Father had shot himself over the whole affair, I might not have been so cooperative.'

He smiled tolerantly. 'If you prefer. But from the start you were seen as an independent operator. A free agent. Someone who had to be nurtured, but who was his own man.'

'And now?'

He leaned over and grabbed a handful of peanuts out of a tinted glass bowl I hadn't noticed on the table between us, and dropped a few into his mouth.

'Now we need you more than ever,' he said, and crunched a few of them down noisily.

'Not interested,' I said.

'Paul, listen. I understand you are no longer a Communist. In truth, I sometimes wonder if I am either.' He caught my look. 'It is the truth. But times and circumstances change. Look at what you distrust about us. About me, if you wish. Do you really believe I am a worse master than the men now running your country?'

'The coup failed,' I said. 'They're not running it any more than they were last month.'

He tilted his head a little. 'No? With your old Chief gone, I think you will see some changes. These men have a lot of ambition, Paul. That is why Henry thought of the coup: he felt it would be less dangerous in the long term to let them into the open, with the illusion of victory, than to continue their games behind the scenes. The plan was for him to control them from the inside – and in doing so slowly immobilize them.'

'Hell of a risky plan.'

He shrugged: he could wear as much tweed as he wanted, but his shrugs were more Russian than vodka. 'I think it was well calculated. Britain would have been in a state of shock – look at what happened with the Americans – and a traumatized enemy would have suited us well. But, as you say, the coup failed. And Henry is dead. The faction is in a more powerful position than ever, however: far from being under suspicion for the attempt on the Prime Minister's life, they have used it to call for more financial support, which I think they will receive. They have a hold of the reins, and we need a way to control them.'

'Did I mention that they offered me Deputy Chief?' I said. 'Same as Pritchard would have got – isn't that funny?'

Sasha swallowed his peanuts. Very slowly, he let out a wide, car salesman's beam. Then there was the faintest quiver in his lower lip.

'You accepted, naturally.'

'I told you,' I said. 'I'm retiring.'

His face froze for a moment, but almost at once he decided I was joking. 'You can't *retire*! You are finally coming to fruition!'

I didn't like it – being talked about as though I were a wine.

'I'm going to teach English at a prep school in Berkshire,' I said. 'Read Bulldog Drummond to the boys before lights out and learn to smoke a pipe.'

He gazed at me with puzzlement. 'I've lived here nearly twenty years and I still don't understand your sense of humour,' he said. And then he reached inside his coat and took out a slim leather wallet, from which he removed a group of postage stamps. He placed them on the table, taking care to hold the corners down with the tips of his fingers. 'But just in case you have misunderstood the situation . . .' he said, inviting me to lean across for a closer look. As I did, I realized that they weren't stamps, but negatives. He held one up to the bulb for me, but I could already see what it was.

I had been wrong. He could still scare me.

*

Outside, I lit a cigarette and thought about the arrangement we had made. Arrangement is perhaps the wrong word: I hadn't had any say in the matter. The photographs of Anna and me covered every conceivable angle. I wondered who had taken them – Father? Pritchard? Well, it hardly mattered now.

I wandered down the street, looking for a cab but not seeing any. It was getting late, and I was on the wrong side of the river. A free agent, I thought bitterly, as I buttoned my coat.

Far from it.

Author's Note

The background to this novel is real. The Nigerian civil war took the lives of hundreds of thousands of people, and was a superpower conflict by proxy. It was waged for over two and a half years, until Biafra finally fell in January 1970. The British Prime Minister, Harold Wilson, was vilified as a result of his government's support for the Federal side, and did visit Nigeria in March 1969. I am grateful to the National Archives of the United Kingdom for providing me with copies of several Cabinet Office records related to his visit, including the programme (reference CAB 164/409 105669), an excerpt of which is quoted on page 156.

There is no record of an assassination attempt against Harold Wilson in Nigeria, but there were extensive and bizarre conspiracies against him, and by members of the British establishment and intelligence community. I am indebted to the work of Stephen Dorril and Robin Ramsay, whose *Smear! Wilson and the Secret State* is an impeccably sourced primer on that subject. Cecil King did meet with Louis Mountbatten and others in May 1968 to discuss a coup against the Wilson government.

Stephen Dorril is also the author of an excellent history of Britain's Secret Intelligence Service, which led me to many other works, and I am particularly grateful to him for his advice on Nigeria at an early stage. The atmosphere and details of life within SIS during the late Sixties were drawn from many sources, but chief among them was Tom Bower's biography of Dick White, *The Perfect English Spy*. Regarding Soviet intelligence, my starting point was *My Silent War*, the autobiography of Kim Philby, which was first published in 1968. It gave me few easy answers regarding the motivations of double agents, and even fewer details of tradecraft – although he does describe taking almost an entire day to meet his handler at one point! It is a frustrating but compelling book – I returned to it often. Robert Cecil's biography of Donald Maclean was similarly stimulating, as were several other books on the known double agents of this era. Christopher Andrew and Vasili Mitrokhin's works on the history of the KGB were also crucial stepping-stones for my research into Soviet espionage.

The SAS and others did search for Nazi war criminals in Germany in 1945; they did not engage in the nefarious work I have ascribed to my fictional trio, but I used their real working methods as a basis. Anthony Kemp's *The Secret Hunters* was my main source on that subject, but I was also lucky enough to interview veterans of 5 SAS who were involved in war crimes investigations – for which, sincere thanks. Some of the details regarding the Thompson-Bolas were inspired by the lives of Fela Anikulapo-Kuti and his mother but, again, I hasten to add that none of that family was ever engaged in the activities described in this novel. Thanks to Michael Veal for his advice on the intricacies of Nigeria's music scene during this time. I have relocated the Afrospot to a different suburb of Lagos, but kept its name – it is not meant to be an accurate representation of the real club at that time.

I read many accounts of the war in Nigeria, by soldiers, spies, doctors, priests, journalists and others, but I was probably most inspired by *The Nigerian Civil War* by John de St Jorre, which I remembered seeing on my parents' bookshelves as a child. I am honoured and grateful that John agreed to read various drafts of this book, and for his encouragement and advice on it.

Many details in the book may seem incorrect at first sight, but prove not to be on closer examination. For example, Lagos is usually one hour ahead of London, but between 1968 and 1971 Britain experimented with something called British Standard Time, whereby the country remained one hour ahead of Greenwich Mean Time all year round. But any factual errors in the book are mine alone.

I would also like to thank William Boyd, John Boyle, Ajay Chowdhury, Jeannette Cook, Vincent Eaton, Lucy Elliott, Kathrin Hagmaier, John Hellon, Kim Hutchings, Alice Jolly, Renata Mikolajczyk, Iwan and Margareta Morelius, K. V. Ramesh, Andrea Rees, Marika Sandell, Loretta Stanley, Tim Stevens and Martin Westlake for their advice on various drafts; Dr Evelyn Depoortere for her guidance on Lassa fever; David Powell for information on snipers; Alex Haw for his twenty years of friendship and keen questioning; my parents and parents-in-law for their advice, stories and contemporary material; my agent, Antony Topping, for his wonderfully astute reading of the manuscript and able guidance through this process; my editor, Mike Jones, copyeditor Arianne Burnette and everyone at Simon and Schuster for their encouragement and advice; and finally, my wife, Johanna, for her honest opinions, steadfast support and belief in this project, and my children for going to bed on time, occasionally.

Select Bibliography

Chinua Achebe, *No Longer At Ease* (Heinemann, 1960)

Chinua Achebe, et al., *The Insider: Stories of War and Peace from Nigeria* (Nwankwo-Ifejeka, 1971)

A. B. Aderibigbe (ed.), *Lagos: The Development of an African City* (Longman Nigeria, 1975)

Kunle Akinsemoyin and Alan Vaughan-Richards, *Building Lagos* (Pengrail, 1977)

N. U. Akpan, *The Struggle for Secession, 1966–1970* (Routledge, 2004)

Christopher Andrew and Vasili Mitrokhin, *The Sword and the Shield: The Mitrokhin Archive and the Secret History of the KGB* (Basic Books, 1999)

Christopher Andrew and Vasili Mitrokhin, *The Mitrokhin Archive II: The KGB and the World* (Allen Lane, 2005)

I. A. Atigbi, *Nigeria Tourist Guide* (Nigerian Tourist Association, 1969)

John Barron, *KGB: The Secret Work of Soviet Secret Agents* (Bantam, 1974)

Saburi O. Biobaku (ed.), *The Living Culture of Nigeria* (Thomas Nelson, Nigeria, 1976)

Tom Bower, *The Perfect English Spy* (Mandarin, 1996)

Andrew Boyle, *The Climate of Treason: Five Who Spied for Russia* (Hutchinson, 1979)

Jean Buhler, *Tuez-les Tous! Guerre de Sécession au Biafra* (Flammarion, 1968)

Robert Cecil, *A Divided Life: A Biography of Donald Maclean* (Coronet, 1990)

John Collins, *Musicmakers of West Africa* (Three Continents Press, 1985)

John de St Jorre, *The Nigerian Civil War* (Hodder and Stoughton, 1972)

Pierre de Villemarest, *GRU: Le plus secret des services soviétiques, 1918–1988* (Stock, 1988)

Len Deighton (ed.), *London Dossier* (Penguin, 1967)

Stephen Dorril, *MI6: Inside the Covert World of Her Majesty's Secret Intelligence Service* (Touchstone, 2000)

Stephen Dorril and Robin Ramsay, *Smear! Wilson and the Secret State* (Grafton, 1992)

Peter Enahoro, *How to Be a Nigerian* (Spectrum, 1998)

Sam Eppele, *The Promise of Nigeria* (Pan, 1960)

William Fagg (ed.), *The Living Arts of Nigeria* (Studio Vista, 1976)

M. R. D. Foot, *SOE: The Special Operations Executive, 1940–1946* (BBC, 1984)

Frederick Forsyth, *The Biafra Story* (Leo Cooper, 2001)

Henry Louis Gates, et al., *The Anniversary Issue: Selections from Transition, 1961–1976* (Duke University Press, 1999)

Mike Hoare, *Mercenary* (Corgi, 1982)

Ian V. Hogg and John Weeks, *Military Small Arms of the Twentieth Century* (DBI Books, 1985)

Madeleine G. Kalb, *The Congo Cables: The Cold War in Africa – from Eisenhower to Kennedy* (Macmillan, 1982)

Anthony Kemp, *The Secret Hunters* (Michael O'Mara Books, 1986)

A. H. M. Kirk-Greene, *Crisis and Conflict in Nigeria: A Documentary Sourcebook* (Oxford University Press, 1971)

Phillip Knightley, *Philby: KGB Masterspy* (Pan, 1988)

Phillip Knightley, *The Second Oldest Profession* (Penguin, 1988)

John Le Carré, *To Russia, with Greetings (An Open Letter to the Moscow Literary Gazette)* (Encounter, May 1966)

Colin Legum (ed.), *Africa Handbook* (Penguin Reference Books, 1969)

Akin L. Mabogunje, *Urbanization in Nigeria* (University of London Press, 1968)

Alexander Madiebo, *The Nigerian Revolution and the Biafran War* (Fourth Dimension, 2002)

Jim Malia, *Biafra: The Memory of the Music* (Melrose Books, 2007)

Peter Mason, *Official Assassin* (Phillips Publications, 1998)

Martin Meredith, *The State of Africa* (The Free Press, 2005)

Bernard Odogwu, *No Place to Hide: Crises and Conflicts Inside Nigeria* (Fourth Dimension, 2002)

Bruce Paige, David Leitch and Phillip Knightley, *Philby: The Spy Who Betrayed a Generation* (Sphere, 1977)

Kim Philby, *My Silent War* (Grafton, 1989)

A. I. Romanov, *Nights Are Longest There: Smersh from the Inside* (Hutchinson, 1972)

Ken Saro-Wiwa, *On a Darkling Plain* (Saros International Publishers, 1989)

Ken Saro-Wiwa, *Sozaboy* (Longman, 2006)

Julian Semyonov, *TASS Is Authorized to Announce* (John Calder, 1987)

Kate Simon, *London: Places and Pleasures* (MacGibbon and Kee, 1969)

Wole Soyinka, *Ibadan: The Penkelemes Years* (Methuen, 1994)

Gordon Stevens, *The Originals: The Secret History of the Birth of the SAS in Their Own Words* (Ebury Press, 2005)

Viktor Suvorov, *Aquarium: The Career and Defection of a Soviet Military Spy* (Hamish Hamilton, 1985)

Raph Uwechue, *Looking Back on the Nigerian Civil War* (in *Africa 71*, Jeune Afrique, 1971)

Michael E. Veal, *Fela: The Life and Times of an African Musical Icon* (Temple University Press, 2000)

Philip Warner, *The SAS: The Official History* (Sphere, 1983)

Auberon Waugh and Suzanna Cronjé, *Biafra: Britain's Shame* (Michael Joseph, 1969)

Olivier Weber, *French Doctors* (Sélection du Reader's Digest, 1996)

Nigel West, *A Matter of Trust: M.I.5. 1945–72* (Coronet, 1983)

Nigel West, *The Illegals* (Coronet, 1994)

Nigel West and Oleg Tsarev, *The Crown Jewels* (HarperCollins, 1999)

Terry White, *Swords of Lightning: Special Forces and the Changing Faces of Warfare* (BPCC Wheatons, 1992)

SONG OF TREASON

For my parents

Preventive Direct Action in Free Countries

Purpose: Only in cases of critical necessity, to resort to direct action to prevent vital installations, other material, or personnel from being (1) sabotaged or liquidated or (2) captured intact by Kremlin agents or agencies.

Policy Planning Staff Memorandum,
Washington, 1 May 1948

I

Thursday, 1 May 1969, St Paul's Cathedral, London

'Sir Colin Templeton was the most courageous, patriotic and decent public servant I have had the privilege of knowing. During his long career, culminating in seven years as head of the organization many of us gathered here today are honoured to serve, he faced this country's enemies unflinchingly.'

I paused, and as my words echoed around the magnificent building, I glanced up from the lectern and was overcome for a moment by the memory of the last time I'd seen the man I'd come to think of simply as 'Chief'. The way he had nodded at me when he had seen that my glass needed refilling: no smile, no words, just a tiny nod of the head. I relived, in a flash, the shuffling walk he had taken across the room, the sharp clinking as he had lifted the bottle from the cabinet, the shuffle back to pour me out a measure. Then the widening of his eyes as I had raised the gun and squeezed the trigger . . .

He hadn't flinched in the face of *this* enemy – I hadn't given him the time.

I gazed out at the line of stern faces in the front pew, bathed in the white glow from the windows high above. John Farraday was seated in the centre, dapper and bored. He was acting Chief now, but had already announced that in a couple of weeks he would return to the Foreign and Commonwealth Office, whence he had come. He was flanked by William Osborne, owlish in spectacles and tweeds. Once Farraday had gone he would take over, at which point I would be appointed Deputy Chief.

I'd got away with it: I was in the clear. A couple of months ago, this might have filled me with a sense of achievement, even triumph. But in the last few weeks I had been stripped of everything I'd ever held dear, left a trail of blood in my wake, and was now being blackmailed into continuing to serve a cause I no longer believed in. The triumph tasted of ashes, and all that was left was the realization that I had made a monumental error, and that it could never be reversed.

I glanced along the rest of the front row, which was filled out with Section heads and politicians, including the Foreign and Home Secretaries. Behind them, the congregation stretched into the distance, two solid blocks of Service officers, former army colleagues and family members, parted by the checked marble aisle. Several Redcaps hovered discreetly by the entrance, turning tourists away.

It was an unorthodox memorial service. The reading from Ecclesiastes, 'Jerusalem' and 'Dear Lord and Father of Mankind' were all standard fare, but the eulogy was being given by the murderer of the deceased, while the men who had plotted the fall of the government a short while ago were brazenly sitting next to Cabinet ministers. And around us all spun Wren's conception, as it had for centuries, cloaking us in false majesty.

I had washed down a Benzedrine tablet before leaving the flat in the hope it would stave off the remnants of my fever, but while it had succeeded in dulling the pain and heightening my senses – I could make out the grain of Osborne's tortoiseshell spectacle frames – it also seemed to have filled me with a feeling of recklessness. As I read from my hastily prepared address, I fought a rising urge to blurt out the truth to the congregation. I remembered hearing about Maclean's drinking in Cairo, and how he had eventually cracked and started telling colleagues he was working for Uncle Joe. Nobody had believed him, of course, and on hearing the story I'd blithely asked myself what could have brought him to such a state. But now, with the enormity of my sins bearing down on me, I wondered if this was where my crack-up was going to begin. It was an oddly tempting idea, like the thought of jumping in front of a train as it came into the platform. It would be a story to fill the Service's basement bar for years to come: the man who had confessed to murdering Chief in his eulogy at St Paul's. Perhaps they could get Bateman to make it into a cartoon.

I reminded myself that I was feeling the effects of the Benzedrine. I took in the Corinthian columns, the Whispering Gallery, and higher still the frescoes stretching across the interior of the dome, then forced myself back to my address.

'But for some,' I said, raising my voice to counter my loss of nerve, 'Sir Colin was much more than the man charged with securing this country against foreign threats. He was a friend, a husband and a father.'

Christ, what had I been thinking when I wrote this? Other memories sprang into my mind: his delight at catching a large trout that summer in Ireland, after he had insisted on using his ancient 'lucky' bait; the way Joan had looked at him when we'd returned to the cottage with the tail of the fish poking out of the basket, knowing he'd want it for supper that night. And Vanessa, of course . . .

I stopped myself going any further down that track. I realized that my hands were gripping the sides of the lectern, and that they were coated in sweat. My voice had frozen in my throat. I couldn't do this – it was monstrous. My only sop was that it hadn't been my idea. 'You knew him best,' Dawes had said when the arrangements had been discussed. 'Nobody else was as close.'

I looked down at the rest of the address. It ran through Templeton's career, from military service to Cambridge to intelligence in Germany and beyond: his friendship with my father in Cairo, then Istanbul, Prague, London. His body in the Thames, thrown there by Sasha and me in the dead of night . . . Not the last bit.

I looked up again and was surprised to see Farraday standing by the lectern. He was fiddling frantically with his tie, whispering urgently.

'What is it?' I asked. He mounted the steps.

'You're making a scene,' he hissed, pushing past me. 'Return to your seat, or I'll—'

But I never found out what he'd do, because at that moment he fell to the ground, and blood started gushing from the centre of his shirt. The cathedral was filled with screaming, but my mind was now totally lucid. I looked up. The shot had come from somewhere in the Whispering Gallery – and it had been meant for me.

I started running down the aisle.

II

I reached the spiral staircase and began climbing it several steps at a time, the soles of my shoes clanging against the steps. From somewhere far above me, there was a further clatter of noise – was the shooter coming down? I plunged my hand into my trouser pocket and wrapped my fist around my car keys, the only weapon I had with me. How the hell had he brought a rifle into St Paul's? I kept climbing. The noises were fading, and my dizziness was increasing. Some long-buried memory told me there were 259 of the things, but I resisted the urge to count them and pushed upwards, upwards, trying not to think about what had just happened, regulating my breathing and concentrating on the task at hand: get to the top; find the sniper.

I reached the Whispering Gallery, but there was nobody there, not even a Redcap. I glanced down and saw that several of them were heading for the staircase, against the flow of the crowd. I looked around frantically. Had the sniper gone back down another way? Would he shoot again? And then I registered movement in my peripheral vision. It had come from the far end of the gallery: a slim figure, bearded and dressed in black. He had a case strapped to his back, no doubt containing the dismantled rifle. He was heading towards a doorway that led to the next flight of stairs.

I resisted the temptation to stop for breath and ran after him, willing my feet to move faster, using my arms to hoist myself along the narrow iron banister and ignoring the rising heat in my chest, until finally I came out of the staircase and felt the freshness of the morning air on my face. I was at the base of the dome now, the Stone Gallery. My trousers fluttered in and out as the wind whipped against them, and I could feel my cheeks beginning to do the same. Voices echoed in my ears, and they were getting louder: the Redcaps would be here soon. I realized I had to get to him before they did — who knew what he might say if he was taken into custody? If he told anyone I had been his target it wouldn't take long for them to start speculating why, and having just cleared my name that was the last thing I wanted.

I reached out for a moulding on the wall, and began edging my way around the gallery as quickly as I could. Without meaning to, I caught a glimpse of the Thames far below, a glittering snake swaying in the mid-morning sunshine. I forced my eyes away and continued my journey around the platform.

The dome of the cathedral had been covered in scaffolding for years — structural damage from the war — but all of it had been taken down a few months ago. Or most of it had: as I turned the corner, I saw that there was a ladder lying on the ground, and what looked like a small pile of workmen's tools. Was this what the sniper had come up here for, something hidden in this mess?

Finally, I saw him. He had climbed onto the balustrade, seemingly oblivious to the wind and the height. He was sitting astride a climbing rope, which he had tied around the balustrade, and was now busy looping it around one of his thighs. He glanced up at me, then went back to his task, bringing the rope across his midriff and over one shoulder. I was just a few yards away, and pushed myself to get closer. If he was going to do what I thought . . . He brought the rope around one of his wrists, and took hold of it with both hands, one above and one below. He pushed himself back and started to fall.

It was now or never.

I surged forward and jumped blindly. He'd gone further than I'd thought, so that for a few moments I thought I'd mistimed it, but then came the crump of contact as I smacked into his back. I immediately clasped my arms around his torso, gripping as hard as I could and hoping to Christ that the rope was tethered tightly enough and could take the load of two men. The sniper started shaking his shoulders in an attempt to dislodge me, and as the ground approached two conflicting urges were passing through my brain – the physical one, saying 'let go, you madman' and the other one, saying 'if you let go you will die, if you let go you will die . . .'

I managed to hold on and we landed with a crash, the two of us a heap of limbs and bones. My whole body felt numb from the jolt of the impact, but I seemed to be uninjured. I was still trying to regain my bearings when I saw that the sniper had already let go of the rope and was off and running. It took me a few seconds to get to my feet and begin pursuit.

And he was fast, bloody fast, spurting down the narrow road, weaving his way around dustbins and lamp-posts. There was no traffic about, and he rushed across the pavement and darted down a grass-patched alley. I hurtled into it after him, my breathing coming heavily, half my brain still catching up from the fall. There was a thickening burr of noise, but it wasn't until I made it to the corner of Cannon Street that I saw the crush of people. Two massive placards bobbed above the crowd, reading 'PEACE AND SOCIALISM' and 'ALL OUT MAY DAY – SMASH THE WHITE PAPER'. The latter slogan was also being chanted by members of the column, the words echoing off the buildings.

Of course. The May Day march. It had turned violent last year, when it had been about Powell and immigration. This time Wilson and Castle seemed to be the villains, their crime being to propose trade union legislation. I caught the tinny strain of a loudhailer from somewhere in the direction of Lincoln's Inn Fields, and then there was the wail of a police siren seemingly very close by, and a clump of the column began moving off at a faster pace. The group behind were momentarily caught off guard, and I squeezed past a man in a checked shirt and jeans and squinted up Ludgate Hill, searching for a glimpse of the sniper. A sea of heads stretched into the distance. I looked for any unusual movement within it, for anyone running. Nothing. I turned and saw police and security staff massing around the entrance of the cathedral. Some of the Redcaps had seen me and were heading in my direction. I ducked back into the crowd and checked down Cannon Street again. Still nothing. Where the hell had he gone?

Then I saw him: a dark figure running up Ludgate Hill to Farringdon Street. Was he heading for the station? I pushed forward and began chasing him, calling out as I did in the hope that someone might stop him, but my throat wasn't working properly, and neither were my legs, and by the time I'd reached the end of the street he had already vanished. If he got on the Tube and I wasn't there with him, that would be it.

The drumming in my head and throbbing in my chest were telling me to stop to take some rest, but I forced myself to keep going and even made up enough ground to see him heading into the station entrance. I reached it less than thirty seconds later, and raced into the booking hall. He'd vanished again. And now I had to make a decision: under- or over-ground? The Underground seemed the better bet, as trains left much more frequently. There was a queue at the ticket office, but a quick glance told me my man wasn't in it. I couldn't see any inspectors and I guessed he had jumped over the barrier, so I did the same, pushing past people to try to catch sight of him.

As if by telepathy, he looked back at me the moment I spotted him. He was already on the footbridge, and I made my way towards him, keeping my eyes fixed on the rifle casing on his back. Behind him, a field of grey sky spread across the glass roof.

I reached the bridge and saw that he had ducked to the right, heading for the eastbound platform. I followed, shouting: 'Police! Stop that man!' This time the tactic worked. People stopped and turned to see who I meant, and the sniper slowed to avoid the attention. But he was confused, and an old lady with a bag of shopping bumped into him. There was a group of people coming across the bridge, and I noticed that they were carrying banners: reinforcements for the march, I guessed, or perhaps they'd had enough and were going home, but there was a crush and we were both finding it hard to get through. If only I could get a few steps closer to him . . .

A train started rumbling into one of the platforms below, and I looked down. It was the eastbound. I called out 'Police!' louder, pushing my way through until I reached the staircase, but it was like swimming in mud. The train grated to a halt and as I reached the foot of the stairs the doors juddered open and a crowd of people moved forward and into it. I couldn't see the sniper, but I had to gamble that he would get on board. My feet hammered down the platform and made it through the doors as they were closing.

I took a second to recover my breath again, my chest heaving, and then looked around. I saw him at once. He was in the next compartment, just a few yards away from me. He was standing there quite casually, partly obscured by a woman reading a paperback. I pushed the doors apart and stepped into the compartment. He looked up, and a smile broke out across his face, almost a leer. His right hand was thrust into his jacket pocket, and I could make out the outline of what looked like the barrel of a pistol. Just inches away, a man wearing a fisherman's sweater, canvas trousers and boots was seated next to a young boy, perhaps eleven or twelve years old, who was dressed almost identically in miniature. The boy's head was directly in the line of fire. The sniper raised his eyebrows at me and I nodded to show that I understood: not a step nearer.

This was my first chance to examine the sniper at close quarters. He was a youngish man, in his mid to late twenties, wearing a black suit with a dog collar — so that was how he had managed to get into the cathedral. He was of average height, but well built: unsurprisingly, considering the acrobatics he'd just pulled off. He had a wolfish look about him: a long handsome face, olive skin, thick shoulder-length hair, greasy with pomade or something similar, and a wild beard. The Christ-meets-Guevara look. No doubt it went down well with female revolutionaries, but he looked fake to me, like a fashion photograph. Despite the fixed smile he was sweating profusely, and I didn't think it was entirely due to physical exertion – every couple of seconds the muscles in his jaw twitched. Was he injured somewhere? Got it: his jacket was torn just below the left shoulder, a sliver of half-dried blood just visible against the dark fabric. Probably where the rope had burned him – I wondered how his hands felt.

I looked around the carriage, and saw that most of the passengers were clutching banners or sheets daubed with slogans. They weren't the students and flower children you typically saw on protests, but labourers and factory hands. A man in a boiler suit and boots caught my glance, and stared at my suit with open aggression.

'Been on the march, 'ave you?'

I shook my head, and looked intently at the sniper.

''Ark at 'im!' the man announced to the carriage. ''Is Lordship 'ere don't want nothing to do with the likes of us.'

'I've been at a funeral,' I said coldly. The man went quiet and started looking at the toothpaste advertisements.

The sniper smiled softly to himself. If he were to show his gun, panic would ensue and it would probably be to his disadvantage: the train would be stopped, transport police would board. But he knew I would try to avoid him taking that route, so as long as he kept his threat discreet he had the upper hand. Perhaps I could pull the emergency cord – that would flush the bastard out. I thought better of it. The gun could end up going off. On the other hand, if it were an automatic it wouldn't be able to cycle in his pocket, meaning that for the moment it would be a one-shot gun. I put it out of my mind: I had no idea whether it was an automatic or not, and one shot was too much to risk anyway.

I turned my attention to his intended targets. The man had a ruddy face, calloused hands and a broken nose: a docker, I thought. The boy, no doubt his son, looked like he'd already spent a few years on the docks himself. He was skinny, gangly-legged, with sunken cheeks and a glazed look in his eyes. At his age I had been wearing a tweed jacket and tie at boarding school. Father had been in Singapore then, and I'd never worn long sleeves before, let alone a jacket or tie, but I had soon got used to it . . .

I wondered what they were doing on the Underground. Perhaps the boy had been too weak to make it through the march? Then I noticed that the father was wheezing every few seconds. It wasn't that he was looking after the son, but the other way round.

The fluorescent lighting panels in the ceiling started flickering – and then, just like that, they went out, and we were plunged into darkness. The train screeched to a halt, and there was a collective gasp from the passengers, followed immediately by groans of frustration and anger and the murmuring of voices. Someone near me swooned and a few people lunged forward to help them – Blitz spirit and all that. I didn't have time to be chivalrous because the sniper might try to do something. He couldn't open the doors, but he could move between the carriages.

I made to step forward, but as I did the lights flickered back on. The train started moving again and the carriage returned to normal. Someone gave the woman who had fainted a thermos flask and she took a drink from it, gulping it down.

I turned my attention back to the sniper. He didn't look Russian, I realized. There was something about the way he was staring at me – he was enjoying it. There was also a bravado about him, and I put him down as a southern European. His enjoyment sent a fresh wave of anger through me. I had given Moscow more than two decades of my life, and now they had sent this thug to shoot me down like a dog. If he were taken in for questioning, he might reveal I had been his target, so I needed to kill him, and soon.

But first I wanted some answers.

The clacking of the train began to slow. The boy squinted up at the Tube map on the wall of the carriage, talking to his father. It looked like the incident with the lights had scared him, and they wanted to get off at the next stop. They started to busy themselves – they had a hold-all with them, presumably for drinks and sandwiches.

The boy helped his father up and they moved to a spot in front of the door. The sniper took a step back, but kept his aim fixed on the boy, at his midriff. I glanced at his face: he was watching me watching them. In some situations I might have tried to rush him, counting on the fact that he would hesitate before killing an innocent child. But this was not such a situation: this man had just killed the head of the Service in a very public place, and would stop at nothing to get away from me. The boy was expendable to him, and I had to act with that in mind.

We came into Barbican, and the doors opened. People rushed forward to get off the train. I made to move, but the sniper was fixing me with a frantic gaze, his nostrils flaring. The father and boy were oblivious to the danger, and were not moving. Had they simply got up a stop early to prepare? No, the father was leaning down to adjust the hold-all – it wasn't entirely closed.

He stood up, and as the boy held out his arm to help him off the train, the sniper made his move. He leapt onto the platform and took the boy under his arm, then started running, dragging the startled boy with him. There was a shout from the father, from others on the platform. For a moment, I froze. Then I jumped forward, too, but the doors were already closing. I squeezed through and onto the platform, but the two of them had disappeared among the passengers emptying from the other carriages, and I pushed past people, furious with myself for reacting so slowly. A mother was trying to get her pram off before the doors closed and people were helping her, blocking off the entire width of the platform. By the time she had made it out I had lost several valuable seconds. I looked up the platform. There they were, at the far end of it, the sniper running towards the tunnel we had just come through, the boy's head cuffed under his arm.

I followed, but then the sniper did an extraordinary thing – he let go of the boy and ran down a ramp at the end of the platform and *into the tunnel*. For a moment I thought it was suicide, but then I remembered that there was some space next to the tracks for the Underground staff to use. As I reached the end of the platform, I could see that he was running down it. The boy was standing there, frozen in shock. I told him not to worry, to stay where he was and his father would reach him soon, and then ploughed down the wooden ramp and into the tunnel, following the sound of echoing footsteps ahead.

I had been running for only a few seconds when I stopped. The bastard had disappeared again! Up ahead, I could see the tunnel curving away towards Farringdon, but he couldn't possibly have reached the bend already. Was he hiding somewhere in the tunnel, waiting for me? I peered into the darkness, but all I could see were occasional pillars and columns at the side, and the faint glimmer of the tracks running down the middle.

Then I heard footsteps again. They were distant, but recognizably the same rhythm. He was running down a tunnel, but it wasn't this one: he was *parallel* with me. I ran back a few yards and searched the walls. There it was: another train tunnel leading off to the left, the entrance a dark chasm. I jumped over a fence at waist height and started running down the tunnel. The sound of footsteps became louder. There was hardly any light at all here, and the walls felt clammier, the air staler. The tunnel was clearly disused, but where did it lead? I put the question out of my mind and kept running, peering ahead to see where the sniper was heading. But now I couldn't distinguish any movement or sounds apart from my own breathing and the crunch of my shoes on the gravel. Had he taken another tunnel?

I registered the glint of metal a fraction of a moment before he kicked. I tried to move but I had no chance, and he caught me full square in the stomach, sending me flying to the ground. I couldn't see straight but I knew I had to keep moving whatever happened because the glint was the gun and he intended to shoot me at close range. I rolled into the wall, scratching myself against something, and screamed as loudly as I could, hoping to distract him even fractionally, because a fraction could make all the difference.

This tactic seemed to work, because he fired blindly. The shot nearly deafened me and sent a great scatter of dust and debris and Christ knows what into my eyes, but I was alive, and I had a sliver of time on my side. He was still dealing with the recoil when I grabbed his wrist. I had to get the gun away from him, because I might not be so lucky a second time and now we were very close to each other and it was very dangerous, so I didn't scream because I didn't want to panic him. I wanted him alive a little longer – I needed to know who he was and why he had been told to kill me, so I kept the pressure on his wrist and fended away his other arm as he tried to punch me, and eventually it was too much for him and he jerked free. The gun fell to the ground and I tried to follow its trajectory but it spun into the darkness, and the sniper stumbled away and the chase was on again, only now I was closer, and my blood was up, and I felt I could get him.

There were no lights, but my vision was adjusting and the tracks had a dull sheen to them. I didn't dare move into the centre of the tunnel – I didn't trust the sniper enough to know whether or not a train could come whistling down here and carry us both off to Never-never-land – but the walkway was becoming narrower. There was the sound of dripping water close by, but I could still make out the faint echo of his footsteps ahead of me, and I focussed on them.

I had been running for about five minutes when the darkness began to lift fractionally. Soon, I was entering a cavernous space, which I guessed had been some kind of goods depot. There were small trolleys and wagons filled with sacks, but everything smelled dank and part of one wall had fallen away. As I came through, I saw the sniper at the far end, racing up a cobbled ramp. I reached it a few seconds later and as I did I realized where we were: Smithfield Market. He must have taken a tunnel that had been used to transport the meat here. The familiar open space of black and green ironmongery rose in front of me, almost like a cathedral itself, and the vista of the city's life returned as I glimpsed white-coated butchers through the archways and pillars.

It was icily cold here, and I realized we had come out at an alcove away from the main body of the market – some sort of storage area. Frozen carcasses lay slapped on top of one another in metal trolleys, glowing under the neon lamps. The sniper was bounding ahead of me, but he seemed to be flagging now. He crashed into one of the carts, sending the contents flying, and I slipped on a carpet of livers and entrails. He took the opportunity and grabbed me, dragging me through the slops and the sawdust. In the distance, a butcher shouted out his last prices. But that was another world away.

The sniper kicked me several times, and then began to choke me, his hands sticky and warm. I started seeing double, Christ and Che swaying above me, and I knew that I had only a couple of seconds left before I blacked out. I had to get him away from my throat. I lunged desperately with my left arm, and caught him on the ear. His grip loosened for a fraction of a moment and I used the momentum to topple him and reverse the hold, so that I now had my hands clasped round his throat. He kicked beneath me, but I was in a strong position now and I kept pressing down. He was trying to grab something with his arm, and I realized we had moved closer to one of the metal trolleys. My eye caught sight of an object on the lowest shelf: an electric saw. I placed my knee over the man's throat and reached out for the saw with my left hand. I flicked it on. The whine had an immediate effect on him, and the sweat started pouring off his face like a waterfall. I screamed at him to tell me who had sent him and why, loosening my grip the tiniest of a fraction for his response. After a few moments, he began repeating the same words over and over. I leaned down to catch them.

'*La prego non mi uccida . . .*' he said, and his face was creased with pain. '*Madonna mia, non mi uccida, non mi uccida . . .*'

He wasn't getting any further than that, so I slapped him, hard, and screamed at him again, but he couldn't hear over the sound of the saw, so I switched it off and tried once more, directly into his face this time, but his jaw muscles suddenly tightened and then went slack and as I watched the fluid dribble from his mouth, I realized he'd bitten into a pill and I'd failed. His eyes froze. He was gone.

*

I searched his pockets, but found nothing in them. Dazed, I staggered out of the alcove and through the market until I came to the front gates, where there was a call box. I dialled the emergency contact number, waited for the pips and then thrust sixpence in the slot. Nobody picked up. The sweat started to cool on me, and I began to shiver. I tried the number again, and then the second number, but there was nothing, no answer, nobody home.

After a while I gave up and called the office instead, telling them to send a squad down and to look for the man in the storage area with a rifle strapped to his back. I left the booth and stepped into West Smithfield. It had begun to drizzle, and a newspaper vendor across the way was dismantling his stand. I looked up for the familiar sight, but it wasn't there. Panicking, I ran down King Edward Street, desperately searching the skyline. It wasn't until I'd reached the end of the road that I saw it: the dome hovering above the city, just as it had always done. For a moment, I'd thought it had disappeared.

III

'So you will take the job?'

  'It doesn't look like I have much choice, does it? If they offer it to me, of course.'

  'But you said they had already——'

  'It still has to be approved. The formalities won't take place for at least a couple of days. They're holding a service for Templeton in St Paul's on Thursday, and they'll push through the new appointments after that. Does that satisfy you?'

  He nodded, and replaced the negatives in his pocket . . .

As the Rover skidded through the streets, I remembered my last conversation with Sasha, just three days earlier. I had told him. I had bloody *told* him where to find me.

'And he was definitely Italian?' asked Osborne, interrupting my thoughts. He was staring through the passenger window, looking rather pale and drained, as I imagined I did, too.

I followed his gaze. It was raining heavily and storms had been forecast: England's green and pleasant land was suddenly looking rather grey and sinister. The Cabinet had raised the alert level to Four: much higher and we'd have been taking helicopters to Welbeck Abbey – but that was strictly for when we were facing an imminent Third World War. Political assassination didn't require a subterranean command centre, but it did require an immediate meeting. I prayed it wouldn't go on too long. I was in desperate need of a shower, something to eat and a long kip.

Osborne had asked me about the sniper's nationality several times, perhaps because it was all we had to go on, or perhaps because Italy was a NATO ally and he was wondering about the diplomatic ramifications. I told him again that I was fairly certain of the nationality because he had spoken fluent Italian on the verge of death, at which point instinct tends to take over. But it was baffling me, too, albeit for very different reasons. Had he just been a hired thug, untraceable back to Moscow? I ran through the scene in my mind for the hundredth time: Farraday's head jerking forward, the shot ringing out. There was no doubt that I had been the intended target – if he hadn't suddenly stepped in front of me, the bullet would have gone straight through my chest. The fact that nobody had picked up either of my emergency numbers confirmed it: one of those lines was supposed to be manned around the clock, without fail. I had been cut off.

'How did they know about the memorial?' Osborne asked. 'We didn't announce it.'

He was like a schoolboy heading into an exam he hadn't prepared for, and I was the swot he was desperately hoping might help him out.

'I don't know,' I said. 'Perhaps Fearing will have something.' Giles Fearing was head of Five, and had also been invited to the meeting.

Osborne nibbled at a fingernail. I suspected he was torn between wanting any information he could get his hands on and hoping that he wouldn't be shown up by our rival agency. Five were responsible for domestic threats, while the Service dealt with everything overseas. That could be another reason he wanted to be sure of the sniper's nationality: it offered a chance for us to head up the investigation.

If so, he'd have to manoeuvre himself sharpish, because Five had a head-start. They'd been all over the cathedral when I'd returned from Smithfield: a team had already begun examining the building from top to bottom. Farraday had been killed instantaneously – the bullet had entered just above his heart. His body had been taken to the nearest morgue, while most of the congregation had retreated to their offices to contact colleagues and plan a course of action. The corpse of the sniper had also been removed from the market.

After telling them most of what I knew, I had taken a cab to Lambeth, but Osborne had already been leaving for Whitehall when I'd arrived, so I had climbed in and was now debriefing him on the way. He was biting his nails for good reason. For two Chiefs to be murdered within two months looked worse than a lapse in security: it looked like a declaration of war. And, of course, Osborne was now worried that there might be someone training their sights on *him* – not for nothing were we travelling in one of the bullet-proofed models. I had even asked if we should travel separately, as the formalities had been overruled and I was now acting Deputy Chief and he Chief. I wished I'd kept that thought to myself, though, as it had made him even jumpier.

I was also jumpy, but trying to keep my head. The sniper had been Italian, but the whole affair had Moscow's fingerprints all over it. I had been so intent on avoiding the suspicions of my colleagues in the Service that I hadn't noticed the threat looming from the other flank. But I still had no idea *why* they wanted me dead. This should have been the pinnacle of my success, with their long invest-ment in me finally paying off: even Philby hadn't made it this far. I thought back to my conversation with Sasha on Monday evening. He had told me that the Slavin provocation in Nigeria had been the work of the KGB, and that for the last two decades I had, in fact, been working for the GRU: military intelligence. I'd come away with the impression that the KGB hadn't wanted to give up control of me. Could it be that they now wanted to take revenge for my having messed up their operation? It seemed far-fetched, but there had been no mistaking the trajectory of that bullet. And Slavin had been one of their agents; perhaps they blamed me for his death. But why try to kill me in public, then, rather than simply ambush me at home? Perhaps the GRU had been behind it, after all, and someone had simply decided that I had served my purpose and had come too close to being exposed. I had taken Sasha at face value when he had told me that I was the hero of the hour, but perhaps he had just been stringing me along, keeping me sweet until a sniper could be found to deal with me. If the bullet had found its intended target, it would have made me a martyr in the eyes of the Service — and extinguished any questions about my loyalty once and for all. The Service would have closed the book on Paul Dark, and remained oblivious to the extent that I had compromised them. But as long as I was alive, I could be exposed, and if that happened I might crack under interrogation and make a list of everything I had handed over, rendering most of it worthless to Moscow in the process.

Or perhaps it was even worse than that. What if someone in the higher echelons of the GRU had decided, as a result of the events in Nigeria, that Sasha's entire network should be closed down? Or not just closed down, but terminated? What if Sasha and his whole crew had all been killed — and I was the only one left standing?

On reflection, the motivations for doing me in seemed almost infinite. But one thing was for sure: *someone* wanted me dead, and they'd gone to a lot of trouble to try to make it happen. As the car came into Whitehall, I wondered when the next attempt would come.

*

The conference room was large and well appointed, with the usual Regency furniture and chandeliers, but the blacked-out windows and whey-faced stenographer in the corner deadened the grandeur somewhat. In the centre of the room, three men were seated around a large polished teak table. Fearing was fair-haired and stoutly built, with heavy jowls; Pelham-Jones, his deputy, was a few years younger and two stone lighter; and finally, there was the Home Secretary, Haggard.

Haggard lived up to his name: a giant skeleton of a man with dark circles under his eyes and a cigar perpetually glued to his thin lips. He was considered the Prime Minister's closest ally — the two of them had risen through the party ranks together. His public image was of a straight-talking man of principle, and he was warier of spooks than everyone else in the Cabinet, with the possible exception of the PM.

As soon as Osborne and I had seated ourselves, Haggard stubbed out his cigar, scraped back his chair and walked over to one of the alcoves, from where he surveyed us like a hawk might a small cluster of overfed mice. 'Thank you for coming,' he said, not bothering to make it sound even remotely sincere. 'As you may know, John Farraday was a good friend of mine, and godfather to my eldest daughter. I also strongly recommended him for the position of Chief, and so view his murder not only as a national but as a personal tragedy.' He stepped forward and looked at us all in turn, and his voice rose fractionally. 'I also view it as a cock-up of monumental proportions. As you will remember, when the idea was mooted to hold this service in St Paul's rather than the Foreign Office chapel, my immediate concern was security. And I was assured that the place would be under closer scrutiny than the Crown Jewels.' He reached out and banged the table with the palm of his hand, making the glasses jump. 'Well, it was hardly the Crown fucking Jewels, was it, gentlemen?' he shouted, his face flushed.

He glared at us, daring anyone to reply. Fearing looked like he was considering it for a second, but then thought better of the idea. Haggard adjusted the knot in his tie and took a long, deep breath.

'The PM is currently suffering from gastroenteritis,' he said, his voice reverting to its usual chilly calm, 'so he can't be with us this morning. However, he has been fully apprised of the situation and has called a Cabinet meeting for his bedside at two o'clock, at which time I will report on the results of this meeting. He is already not best pleased with your lot as a result of the incident in Nigeria, and I need hardly remind you that John's murder came while we were mourning the death of the last man to occupy his position. So . . . can anyone tell me why I shouldn't recommend that he sack the whole bloody lot of you?' He picked his glass of water from the table and took a few gulps of it, his Adam's apple bobbing wildly. 'I want an explanation for this,' he said, sitting down again, 'and I want it now.'

Osborne glanced across at me and I debriefed for the third time, taking it from the moment of the shot until the sniper's death in Smithfield.

'What a pity you couldn't bring him in alive,' said Haggard once I'd finished. 'A capsule, you say?'

I nodded. 'He bit down on it within moments of my reaching him.'

'I see.' He took another cigar from his jacket and lit it, and a spiral of smoke wafted across the room to clog itself in the curtains. 'At any rate, thank you: we all owe you a debt of gratitude for at least trying to apprehend the killer. Perhaps your colleagues from Five can now tell us how this was allowed to happen in the first place?'

Fearing bristled at the scarcely veiled accusation. 'We took all the usual precautions and more,' he said. 'We had sixteen Redcaps stationed inside the cathedral—'

'Who were a fat lot of use,' said Haggard.

Fearing paused for a moment and decided not to pursue it: 'And we conducted a thorough sweep of the building before the service began. There was no indication—'

'"A thorough sweep"?' Haggard jumped in again. 'How on earth did the sniper get in, then? And what about the climbing ropes Paul's just told us about – how did he manage to bring them in unnoticed?'

Fearing's nostrils flared. As the head of Five, he was unused to being given a carpeting. But he deserved it: it had happened on his watch. 'We're looking into the first matter urgently, sir,' he said. 'But he may simply have walked in during the service.'

'I'm sorry,' said Haggard quietly, 'but did you just say that he might have *walked in?*'

'Yes. He was disguised as a priest. We did consider the security situation extensively, but St Paul's is a public place of worship. If we'd closed it off completely, we would have created an enormous problem with local parishioners, so some access was a condition of holding the service there, as it has been in the past.' He glanced at Osborne to make it clear that he had raised these issues beforehand. 'The Redcaps turned tourists away at the door explaining it was a private funeral service, but there was still some toing and froing. As for the climbing ropes, the scaffolding was taken down from around the dome last year but there were still a few bits and pieces on the galleries. We checked with the Dean beforehand that this was all in order, and he told us to leave it. But it appears that he had hidden his ropes among these—'

'Pathetic!' Haggard snapped. 'I don't want to hear any more of this tripe. You should, of course, have taken the Dean or whoever was responsible up there to check. And as for creating problems with parishioners . . .' His shook his head. 'Pathetic. Do we at least have any idea who was behind it? Paul said he was Italian – are we sure of that?'

'I think we can be reasonably confident, minister,' Osborne broke in. 'He spoke the language fluently as he was dying, at which point instinct tends to come into play.'

He had a good memory, Osborne; I had to give him that. Probably why he'd made it so far.

'But why on earth would the Italians want to kill John?' asked Haggard.

Pelham-Jones took it. 'The sniper may just have been a gun for hire, sir. We don't have anything further on his identity yet, although we've shared a detailed description with Interpol to see if they can help. But we have had a claim of responsibility.'

Osborne and I both looked up. 'Really?' I said. 'When was this?'

'About two hours ago. A call to Holborn police station from a group calling themselves the "Movement for International Solidarity".'

'Credible?'

Pelham-Jones nodded. 'There is no way of concealing that something happened this morning – there were simply too many people involved, and it will get out whether we like it or not. But this was still a very quick response, and at the moment we're inclined to think it was genuine.'

'I wish you'd told us this before the meeting,' said Osborne, and I felt his shoe kick against mine under the table. I glanced across at him but he was making notes intently on his pad. I squinted at the scrawl at the top of the page: *KNOW ANYTHING ABOUT THIS OUTFIT?*

'We've been rather busy,' Fearing said icily.

I picked up my pen and wrote *NO* on my pad. It rang a bell, vaguely, but I didn't have any facts at my fingertips.

Osborne scribbled again. *EDMUND MIGHT.*

He asked Haggard if I could briefly be excused to check whether or not we had anything on the group in our files. Haggard agreed, and I asked one of the private secretaries to show me to a telephone. It took a while to get hold of Innes, but once I had I quickly explained where we were. He perked up as soon as I told him the name of the group.

'I'll be there in fifteen minutes,' he said. 'I think I might have something.'

When I came back into the room, Pelham-Jones was handing round dossiers. I nodded at Osborne, who looked relieved, then picked my copy off the table. It was titled 'INTERNAL SUBVERSION: ANARCHIST AND COMMUNIST GROUPS'.

'If you turn to page twenty-six,' said Fearing, 'you'll see the chaps we think we may be dealing with.'

I turned. The page was largely taken up with a photograph of a hand-scrawled note, which read: *'Yankee fascism all over the world – no to racism – freedom for American negros!'*

Haggard snorted. 'An educated bunch.'

'Quite,' said Fearing. 'This was found in Grosvenor Square when the American embassy was machine-gunned two years ago. They managed to ruin three of the glass doors. As you can see, it's signed the "First of May", but we think John's assassination may have been carried out by a breakaway faction from that group – perhaps even more fanatical. The First of May have sometimes claimed to operate under the banner of something called the International Revolutionary Solidarity Movement, which was founded back in '61 by some anti-Franco Spanish militants. We think the Movement for International Solidarity may be a new version of that. As best we can tell, they seem to be mainly made up of anarchists and Maoist Communists, several of whom have been involved in trying to stir up violence at Vietnam demonstrations and the like.'

I wondered if this was the information Innes was racing over here to present triumphantly to the Home Secretary as our contribution to the investigation.

'All very interesting,' said Haggard, grinding the remains of his cigar into an ashtray, 'but flag-burning and chucking Molotov cocktails about are one thing, political assassination quite another. Are you sure this lot are capable? It's a long way from occupying the LSE.'

Fearing smiled tightly. 'This isn't a lot of student rebels, sir. There are some very dangerous people in this bunch. Some may have "graduated" from other movements, such as the CND, the Committee of 100 or the Spies for Peace, but we're talking about the hard-core well beyond the peace movement. Perhaps you remember last autumn, when we were warned that extremists were plotting to use home-made bombs and the like to take over sensitive installations and buildings during one of the London marches?'

'Yes – nothing came of it, though.'

'Indeed, but only because Special Branch set up barricades at strategically important points, and because we leaked enough material to the press to scare them off. Anyway, this is the same collection of people. We think they may have also had a hand in blowing up one of the pipes carrying water to Birmingham in December. But yes, in answer to your question, this would be their first assassination. They probably had outside help.'

'Any idea who?'

'I'll leave that to my colleagues,' he said, nodding towards Osborne and me.

Haggard turned to us. 'Well?'

Osborne fiddled with his tie and made eyes at me.

'Well,' I said. 'Let's look at how it was done. His rifle was some sort of custom-made job, and he picked off his target with one shot at a distance of over a hundred yards, which I'd have found difficult fifteen years ago. We know he hid the ropes on the Stone Gallery, but when and how did he do that – was it this morning, or earlier, disguised as a workman or some such thing? Either way, he ran circles around our security measures. He was also extremely fast on his feet and knew how to lose a tail, or at least try to – I was very lucky to catch up with him. Finally, he had a capsule on him, and he used it. So I don't believe he was some two-bit revolutionary, but an elite special forces operative – and my money is firmly on Moscow.'

Osborne took a sip of water and smiled coolly at Fearing. I had decided to go hell for leather in pinning the blame on Moscow because I knew they'd come to that conclusion themselves soon enough anyway, and it might be useful to be able to remind them later that the idea had come from me first, especially if there were any renewed suspicions about me. I also wanted to stress my expertise on Soviet affairs so I would be put in charge of the entire investigation. The next step was to undermine Five.

'I think the climbing stuff also gives us a possible angle of enquiry,' I went on, looking at Fearing and Pelham-Jones to make it clear that by 'us' I, in fact, meant them. 'He was clearly an accomplished abseiler: it's quite a height, and he didn't use a harness or any other equipment – just a rope. I wonder if he might have been a night-climber.'

'Is that a euphemism for something?' said Haggard.

'It's a sport,' I said, 'popular at Cambridge. I'm surprised you didn't think of it, Giles, what with you being a King's College man. Don't you remember those undergraduates rusticated a couple of years ago for placing an anti-Vietnam banner between the pinnacles of the chapel? If I might humbly suggest, why don't you call up some of your old chums and get hold of whoever runs the society? See if they've had any Italian members in the last few years, or if they know of any similar clubs in Italy that do this sort of thing. That sort of knowledge is fairly specialized, and there can't be many people who know how to do it.'

Fearing was flustered now. 'But he used a rope, you said. I thought the whole point of night-climbing was not to use any equipment at all? And the society is anonymous. How do you propose we find out who runs it?'

'Oh, sorry,' I said. 'I thought you were the Security Service.' He scowled. Careful, or he'll explode. I softened my tone. 'It's true that they don't use ropes, but many of them go on to become mountaineers. Perhaps start with the Alpine Club or the Mountaineering Council, then, and work back.'

I was about to suggest he also contact London Transport to see if they'd had anyone suspicious working on the freight line that led to the goods yard under Smithfield Market – it couldn't have been closed that long, and he hadn't looked twice running in there. But, thankfully, Innes arrived then, a little out of breath but clutching a briefcase.

*

We all made room for him, and he unclasped the case and took out an impressively thick wedge of papers. He was halfway to the projector when Fearing told him that it wasn't working.

He stroked his moustache. 'Never mind. I'll do it the old-fashioned way.' He was a dapper little man, bespectacled and balding; he tried to hide the latter by arranging his few remaining strands of hair carefully across his pate. He looked like an Edwardian banker, but he was as sharp as a commando dagger. He headed up Western Europe Section, although he'd also been holding the fort at Soviet Section while I'd been away.

He laid his papers on the table and cleared his throat.

'As you have no doubt just been hearing from Giles, the Movement for International Solidarity is an offshoot of a group that has also operated under the names the International Revolutionary Solidarity Movement and the First of May.'

Osborne smiled: Innes knew his stuff. We were in the lead again.

'This group has several splinter groups across the Continent, and they seem to be particularly active in Germany and Italy. This is partly the result of wartime allegiances: some members of the younger generation are rebelling against their parents' devotion to Hitler and Mussolini.' He turned the page on his notes. 'One of the group's first attacks took place in Rome three years ago, when they kidnapped the Ecclesiastical Counsellor to the Spanish embassy to the Vatican. In August '67, they machine-gunned the American embassy in London, which I imagine you've covered . . .' He looked up at Fearing, who nodded. 'Right. And, eighteen months ago, they claimed responsibility for bomb attacks on the Spanish, Greek and Bolivian embassies in Bonn, the Venezuelan embassy in Rome, a Spanish tourist office in Milan, and the Spanish, Greek and American embassies in The Hague. Quite a shopping list. Communiqués received after those attacks indicated that they were all in protest at what they called "fascist regimes" in Europe, and in solidarity with guerrillas in Latin America.'

'I've heard enough,' said Haggard wearily. 'Paul seems to think they're Moscow-sponsored. Is that plausible, and if so why are they targeting us?'

'I'm getting to that, sir, if you'll give me a moment,' said Innes, gloriously oblivious to the tensions that had been building in the room. 'The man who shot John appears to have been an Italian, and Italy is currently experiencing a huge amount of this sort of activity. There have been fifteen attacks in public places already this year. Two of them took place in Milan just last week, with bombs going off at a trade fair and the central railway station. Nobody has claimed responsibility yet, but we believe the First of May and factions associated with it were involved in both attacks, along with Italian Communists.' He flashed a little smile at Haggard, which was not returned. 'Between October '67 and last May, three members of the Italian Communist party travelled to Moscow for what we think was a four-month training course with the KGB in clandestine radio communications. We have reason to believe that other Italian party members have been trained by Moscow in how to prepare forged documents and other espionage-related activities.'

Haggard had turned a few shades paler than usual. 'Are you saying that the official Communist party in Italy is working hand in glove with terrorists?'

'We've no *hard* proof of it, but we suspect some members of the party may be, yes. Our colleagues in Italy are worried that Communists and sympathizers may be planning a campaign of attacks across Western Europe to force a sort of "wave of revolution". The idea would be to bring down governments – including our own, I might add – through violent means. The student movement would get caught up in it, and before you'd know it there'd be anarchy.' He pursed his lips. 'Which would suit Moscow down to the ground, of course.'

'Do the Italians have any evidence for such a plan,' said Haggard, 'and if so why haven't I heard of it before now? It sounds fairly extraordinary.'

Innes smiled sweetly. 'Well, this is just informal intelligence-sharing. It's something that's been a background concern of theirs for a while, and it's why we have stepped up our own interest in this area. About six months ago my Section started looking at a faction of the First of May in Italy called Arte come Terrore, or "art as terror". The name is taken from the title of a series of articles that were published anonymously in a magazine called *Transizione* last year, which argued that violence against the state was a form of performance art that cleansed society, which was in sore need of cleansing. Some of the ideas espoused were simply nuisance provocations along the lines of those in Holland a couple of years ago, but others seemed to be much more serious, which is why we were interested.'

'Do you mean to say that John's murder may have been intended as a piece of . . . performance art?' He looked as though he were about to choke.

'Possibly, sir, yes.'

Haggard looked around the room. 'I've heard some nonsense in my life, but this takes the cake, gentlemen. We are being outgunned by a bunch of art students!'

'Hitler was an art student,' said Pelham-Jones.

Haggard ignored him. 'Do we have any idea who the leaders of these jokers are?'

Innes cocked his head: he was coming to that. 'Rome Station has recently managed to infiltrate an agent into Arte come Terrore, a man called Barchetti, and he's given us an outline of the basic structure. It seems there's a central committee made up of a dozen members, all based in Rome. This is the leadership of the group nationwide, of which there are a few hundred members – we're not sure how many exactly. There are several people who we either know or strongly suspect are members of the group, but Barchetti hasn't been able to discover the identities of the leaders – he's not yet trusted enough with that information.'

Haggard slapped his hand on the table again. 'Well, he'd better bloody hurry up and *become* trusted enough!'

'Yes, sir. In fact, he seems to have made something of a breakthrough. Last night he filed a report, via dead drop, in which he said he'd heard rumours that a faction connected to the group were planning something big – imminently.'

'Obviously a warning about this morning,' I said.

Innes shook his head. 'He mentioned attacks "across Europe".'

There was a brief silence as we took this in.

'Christ,' whispered Haggard. 'That's all we need.' He took another slug of his water and scraped back his chair.

'When is Barchetti next due to report?' asked Fearing.

'First thing tomorrow morning.'

'Hold on,' I said. 'Not *Edoardo* Barchetti?'

Innes looked up. 'Yes. Do you know him?'

I nodded. I had run him when I'd been stationed in Rome in '64. I hadn't recognized the name at first because he'd been known to everyone as 'Bassetto', Italian for 'shrimp', on account of being about five foot tall. He had worked for the Service since shortly after the war, and I'd inherited him from my predecessor. He had hung around the fringes of Rome's underworld for years, mixing with thieves, gangsters and the sort of criminal not too scared to get his feet wet in the spy business. Sometimes he had picked up snippets of information on blackmailed politicians and suchlike, which he'd passed on to us, no doubt after some judicious elaboration on his part. He hadn't been terribly useful, but I had liked him: he had been lively company and I'd always looked forward to meeting up with him. But it was one hell of a move from occasional source to deep-cover penetration agent.

'How long has he been infiltrated, and how has he been coping?' I asked. When I had known him, Bassetto had been a heavy drinker, and had been so scared of being discovered passing information by one particular *mafioso* that it had sometimes taken hours to arrange meetings with him just to receive the tiniest scrap of gossip. I struggled to imagine him as a plausible anarchist agitator.

'He's holding up well,' said Innes, and Osborne gave me a fierce look — we were ahead on points, and I was in danger of sabotaging the victory. 'Apparently he always wanted to do this sort of job.'

That was even more worrying, if he'd *wanted* to do it: a Walter Mitty type. I didn't like the sound of any of it.

'You seem familiar with this man,' said Haggard.

'I ran him five years ago,' I said, 'but as an informant.'

Nobody said anything. I looked around the room and wondered

who would break the silence. Then I realized that they were all looking at me. They had to be joking.

'It sounds as if he's in very deep, and I don't think sending in someone new at this stage would help. Besides, my face is too well known in Rome.'

'Not by these people,' said Haggard. 'And it's an advantage that you already know the city: you know how it works. We need to find out whatever it is Barchetti knows. What if John's death is just the start of something much bigger?'

I didn't give a stuff about Farraday, and if there had been a project to assassinate intelligence bureaucrats across the globe I'd have been all in favour of it. But I knew that there wasn't, and that Farraday had been killed in my place. I didn't want any of them to discover that fact, so I needed to stay here and manoeuvre myself into taking over the investigation. If I were in Italy, Christ knew what they might dig up.

'Of course I care,' I said. 'But I'm afraid I'm under doctor's orders not to travel anywhere for the next two months. I only came out of isolation a few days ago.'

'Yes,' said Osborne, 'Paul picked up some dreadful disease in Nigeria. Have they figured out which one yet?' I shook my head. 'He's not fully recovered, and I agree it would be extremely dangerous to send him out in his current condition. We also need him here. We need to reorganize in the wake of this, and I'll require his help.'

Haggard leaned back in his chair and cracked his knuckles together. 'Well, I'm afraid I'm going to require much more than this to take to the PM,' he said, gesturing at the dossier in front of him. 'What we need is action. If these people are connected with John's death, I suggest we do something that hits back at them.'

'Were you thinking clandestine or covert, sir?' said Osborne.

He squinted at him. 'Remind me of the difference.'

Osborne smiled softly and spread his hands along the table. 'Clandestine is when you don't want anyone to know what you're doing; covert is when you're pretending to do something else.

Helping to instigate a coup is usually clandestine; sending an agent into a country and calling him an embassy official is covert.'

'I don't care,' said Haggard, 'as long as it can't be traced back to us. Perhaps send in the agent under diplomatic cover, as you say, and then get him to work clandestinely — is that possible?'

Osborne inclined his head, thinking about it. 'It depends on what you want done.'

'I want whoever was responsible for this to be found and killed, as quickly as possible,' he spat out. He nodded at the stenographer. 'Leave that out, please. I will inform the Prime Minister myself later today. I'm happy to take the consequences. John was a dear friend of mine, and you have my unquestioned support to do whatever it takes to find those responsible and . . . *act*.'

I looked at him. Had he gone quite mad? The target was widening by the second. 'Is that wise, minister?' I said, and I could sense the others' anger directed at me as I said it. 'I'm all for justice, too, but if these people are planning further attacks, surely it's best to find out as much as we can about their actions first, rather than go in with all guns blazing?'

'Don't give me that! Where are your balls? The head of your outfit has just been murdered in cold blood, in front of your very eyes, while you were *worshipping*. Are you going to take it lying down, or are you going to retaliate? You have a man infiltrated into the Italian division of this group, and even know the identities of some of its members. Let's find out who the leaders are, send in a hit-man, and pay the bastards back.'

'It's not quite that simple, sir,' said Osborne. 'First of all, discovering the identities of the leaders is no easy task — it may take years before Barchetti is trusted with that information. Secondly, we don't have "hit-men", and haven't for some time. There's the SAS, of course, but I hardly think—'

'What about Paul here?' said Haggard, puffing out his waistcoat and looking me over as though I were a gladiator he was considering sending into the arena. 'Can't you do it? You chased down John's killer, ran this agent in Rome. And the report I read on the Nigerian affair said you single-handedly managed to stop this Red Army sniper getting the PM.'

I coughed into my hand. 'Stopping a sniper and doing the sniping oneself are very different jobs,' I said. 'And I got rather lucky in Nigeria.' But it was no use – I could see he thought I was being the modest English hero. I tried another tack: 'I think it's perhaps not a very good idea for us to risk too many senior officers at this juncture.'

'Nonsense! They won't see it coming, will they? Element of surprise and all that. Go out to Rome under diplomatic cover and the Russkies will sit back and relax: a fact-finding mission from the top brass. Little do they know, our top brass is rather lethal with a telescopic lens and – bang! – you give the little Eyetie who planned this whole thing a bullet to his brain. An eye for an eye. No messing. They'll get the message then, all right.'

There was an uncomfortable pause.

'If we could find the leaders,' said Osborne finally, 'it might well be an idea, sir.'

IV

'There's no need to be like that,' said Osborne once we were in the car heading back to the office. 'Nobody seriously expects you to go out and *kill* anyone – he only put it in those terms because he was upset.'

'Quite understandable,' said Innes. 'We all are.'

I didn't reply. Haggard hadn't been in the mood to be dissuaded, I knew, but Osborne's intervention had really landed me in it. The meeting had ended with the decision that I would leave for Rome at once, subject to medical approval. I wasn't sure which would be the worse result to get back: that I was still suffering from a potentially fatal and highly contagious tropical disease that nobody was sure how to treat yet, or that I was healthy enough to be sent on a wild-goose chase of a mission to slaughter an as-yet-unidentified terrorist leader in Italy.

I had wanted to be put in charge of the investigation, but this hadn't been quite what I had in mind. Even ignoring the half-cocked assassination element, I didn't like it. Parachuting an outsider into an operation was fine: that sort of thing happened occasionally, and could help speed things along. Someone with Italian experience made sense, too. But I had last been in Rome under diplomatic cover, meaning that there was no choice but for me to go in that way again or risk being easily blown. That meant that, despite Osborne leading Haggard on, the potential for clandestine activity was, in fact, extremely limited – I wouldn't even be able to take a weapon into the country, for instance. And even if there had been any opportunity for me to take part in that sort of thing, I didn't believe there was anything I could do that couldn't have been performed with greater ease and efficiency by the local Station.

There was no way around it, though. Haggard had handed down his ruling, and to refuse to go now would only raise suspicions about my motives. Perhaps the worst thing about the development was that it took me away from London at a crucial moment. Because the other conclusion of the meeting had been that Innes was now to investigate whether or not there were any links between the deaths of the two Chiefs and 'the business in Nigeria'. That filled me with dread: given the run of Registry, and with me out of the country and unable to influence matters, there was no telling what he might dig up.

The office was in a state of turmoil, and Osborne and Innes both ran off to try to calm their respective troops, while I told my secretary to get onto Urquhart's to set up an immediate appointment, giving her the emergency authorization phrase.

As I flipped off the desk intercom, there was a knock on the door of my office and Barnes poked his head around.

He was a quiet Londoner of indeterminate age, with greying close-cropped hair and a heavily lined face. After stints in Kenya and Malaya, he had become one of the Service's bodyguards, most recently for Colin Templeton on weekends in the country. Templeton's insistence that Barnes live in the neighbouring village rather than be installed in his home, as he had been urged when he had been appointed Chief, had given me a free hand on that crucial night five weeks ago. I would never have risked killing Templeton if Barnes had been in the house that evening, and as it had been the only action available to me to head off my imminent arrest, I had a lot to thank him for.

'I'm your protection, sir,' he said. 'I'll be accompanying you to Italy.'

'Under what cover?'

'Third secretary, sir. It's already been arranged.'

My desk intercom buzzed: it was Mary, saying that Urquhart's were expecting me. I told Barnes to get his coat.

*

I sat in the waiting room in a very expensive but uncomfortable leather and chrome chair, flicking through a copy of *Country Life* and wondering who still lived it. Barnes was engrossed in a cheap paperback biography of Churchill he'd brought with him: he had told me on the way over that he was a lover of military history. I'd refrained from mentioning that he had probably lived through most of it. He was more talkative than I'd expected, and had spent much of the journey trying to reassure me that Templeton's death had been a once-in-a-lifetime lapse and that I was perfectly safe in his hands. It hadn't cut a lot of ice, because he hadn't seemed to notice the navy-blue Ford Anglia three cars behind us, driven by an intent, squat-faced man. I'd managed to lose him somewhere in Battersea, but that hadn't done anything to calm my nerves. They knew I was alive now, and that meant they could try again.

The receptionist walked over and gave me her best Harley Street smile: 'Doctor Urquhart will see you now.' Barnes followed, and the receptionist nodded at him — presumably she was used to such nonsense. I wasn't: it was like having a bloody dog.

Urquhart had been a medic with the Service during the war, and when he had set up his practice afterwards he had bagged the prestigious and, I suspected, rather well-paid job of looking after most of its senior staff. Some of his patients were bankers and barristers, but the Service was his bread and butter, and as a result there was a certain discreet level of security about the place — we had come through an unmarked entrance from a side street, and would leave by another one.

So far I'd been dealt with by his assistants, but today the man himself was there to look me over — I was definitely moving up in the world. I remembered him from previous check-ups as somewhat wizened, but he was looking almost obscenely healthy, with a glowing tan under his white beard; he looked a little like Father Christmas. I asked him if he'd been on holiday, and he surprised me by saying that he'd been to Jamaica.

'I go every other year,' he smiled. 'I love the vibrancy of the place – and the music.' I tried not to imagine Urquhart in the night-clubs of Kingston, and mentally cursed myself again for not choosing an easier, more profitable profession. Jamaica in May. What a life.

He tested my reflexes and took some blood, then gave me a test tube and asked me to go behind a screen and fill it. Barnes made to stand up to follow me, but I gave him a look and he sat down again, somewhat sheepishly. Urquhart covered the awkwardness by asking Barnes when he'd last been out to Gosport, which was the Service's training establishment. Barnes started gassing back immediately, and I peed in peace.

Urquhart took the tube from me and walked to an adjoining room. Barnes lapsed back into silence, and was no doubt hoping to get back to Churchill's preparations for D-Day.

After a couple of minutes Urquhart came back in, smiling. 'Good news,' he said. 'It looks like you've made good progress. You're not entirely out of the woods, mind you. Have you had any muscle pain since you were last here, or sore eyes?'

'Quite a lot of muscle pain,' I said. 'And my eyes sometimes throb.'

He nodded.

'How about your hearing? Have you had any more bouts of deaf-ness?'

'No, but . . .'

'Good, good. When any of the symptoms return, take one of these.' He handed me a plastic tube containing several small blue capsules. 'Don't take more than two a day, though. And if you lose your hearing again, stop whatever you're doing, get to a hospital and contact me through the Service switchboard. I'll let them know what to give you.' He picked up a clipboard from his desk and peered at it. 'I also see from your file that you're a smoker – a thirty-a-day man.'

'I've cut down,' I said.

'To . . . ?'

'About twenty,' I admitted.

He grimaced. 'Better make it ten. And go easy on the booze as well, if you can. Otherwise, I think you're basically in good shape.'

I stared at him. 'Is that it? You're clearing me for active duty?'

'Yes. It's a bit touch and go, admittedly, but I had a call from the Home Office earlier outlining just how important your work will be in Rome and I certainly don't think you're in *that* bad shape. In fact, I'm sure you'll be fine.'

Of course – Haggard had fixed it. Urquhart gave me a couple of swift jabs with whatever medication they were trying this week, before ticking off all the necessary forms for the Italian embassy. Then I drove back to the office with Barnes to let them know I had the all-clear, stopping off at my flat for a few minutes to throw some clothes and a toothbrush into a hold-all. The office had quietened a little, and Mary booked the tickets and made all the necessary arrangements, with Smale supporting her by speeding up the red tape with Accounts and Personnel. It was all very efficient – lots of bowing and scraping. Partly the promotion, partly the order from the Cabinet, and partly, I supposed, a desire to avenge Farraday's death, or at least get to the bottom of it. But somehow the likes of Smale kow-towing made me feel even more uncomfortable, and I realized that in an odd way I missed being under suspicion, because I deserved that and could concentrate on getting through it. Now that I was in the clear, the extent of my deception was getting much harder to take. Smale was almost looking up to me – and it was a little chilling.

I grabbed a quick lunch of gristle-laden beef and boiled potatoes in the canteen and then Mary came in with the tickets, and Barnes and I headed for Heathrow.

*

We were booked on a BEA flight out of the newly opened short-haul terminal. As we sat in one of the cafés on the first floor, I wondered how long it would be before the immaculate Conran furniture would be sticky with grease and lollipop stains. At least the coffee already tasted as reassuringly foul as it did in all British airports. A Pakistani cleaner placed our cups and saucers onto his gleaming chrome trolley with a clatter and moved off, his mind elsewhere. Barnes was reading his paperback, smoking one of my Players — he didn't seem in a rush to buy his own, I'd noticed.

I replaced the dossier in the hold-all by my feet. Its seven pages contained everything the Service had on Arte come Terrore. Part of me had wondered how much Innes had been showboating, but while the evidence against them was mostly circumstantial, it was also fairly overwhelming.

In July 1962, there had been an explosion at St Peter's in Rome – no one had been injured, but the base of the monument to Clement X had been chipped. Nobody had claimed responsibility for the incident, however, and the investigation had soon dried up. Then, three weeks ago, there had been another bomb scare at the Basilica, and this time two men, Paolo Rivera and Giuseppe di Angelo, had been picked up in the course of routine enquiries. Rivera and di Angelo were suspected by Italian military intelligence of being members of Arte come Terrore: the excerpts from their dossiers that had been shared with the Service showed that both had long histories with Marxist and similar-minded groups. Both had been released without charge, but subsequent investigations had revealed that di Angelo had also been in the area of the Vatican on the day in question in July 1962, and that Rivera had visited London six times in the last year and had attended an 'International Anarchist Commission' in Tuscany in August.

The Pope had responded to the bomb scare by calling for calm and the need for brotherhood. So far, it wasn't being heeded. Since the start of the year, the Italian press had been predicting a wave of industrial action, and it seemed to be coming true, with dozens of strikes, prison riots and street clashes across the country. Last month had seen a major strike at a tobacco factory near Salerno following rumours that the place would be closed down, and the police had shot and killed one of the strikers, and then a school-teacher who had been unlucky enough to see it happen. The government had claimed provocateurs from outside the city were trying to foment trouble, while the media had pointed the finger at Maoists and anarchists. But the authorities were still taking the brunt of the blame, and the Communist party had proposed legislation to disarm the police while on public order duty. As a result, there had been strikes against police repression in both Rome and Naples. The Communists' bill had been due to be debated in Parliament on April 28th, but on the 25th – Liberation Day – there had been the two explosions in Milan that Innes had mentioned in the meeting: one at the Fiat stand at the city's annual trade fair and another at the bureau de change of a bank in the central railway station. Twenty people had been injured, and the Italians strongly suspected Arte come Terrore's involvement.

So, the group looked to be both involved in attacks and interested in cathedrals. None of it would stand up in a court of law, perhaps – but it was enough. I looked out at a jet taking off and shivered inwardly. I usually enjoyed flying, but today the idea didn't appeal at all. As well as the fact that the dossier seemed to confirm that Moscow was trying to kill me through a proxy Italian cell, I was sitting here about to leave the country while Innes was rummaging through the files in Registry with those long pale fingers of his.

And there was the small matter of the tail: the man in the dark green suit and scuffed brown brogues sitting at one of the other tables, reading Le Monde a little too intently as he devoured a cheese and ham sandwich. The suit was a size too small for his paunch, which along with its colour gave him a striking resemblance to Toad of Toad Hall. It was the driver of the Anglia that had followed us to Harley Street. I hadn't seen him on the way here, but he'd evidently managed to follow us.

His presence was precisely why bodyguards tended to be a waste of time in this business. I had no doubt that Barnes was a tough nut, and useful to have on one's side in a fight, but he was pure muscle, and hadn't the first idea about surveillance. He wasn't acting, either, trying to make me think he wasn't switched on or some game of that sort; I'd watched him for several minutes now, and he hadn't looked up from his book once. It just wasn't in his training. He wouldn't know a Russian spy if his life depended on it.

And the man was unquestionably Russian, despite the paper he was pretending to read. It wasn't just the cut of his suit; even his face was unmistakably Russian: a pasty complexion from too much potato in the diet, blue-grey pupils glinting through narrow eyelids, a pugilist's nose and the mouth of a coelacanth. Straight out of Central Casting. He was from one of the northern republics, I thought, Lithuania or Byelorussia. Was he going to try to kill me here, in the airport? He hadn't tried to do anything on the road, but perhaps he had been waiting for the chance.

I pushed back my chair and told Barnes I was going to the lavatory.

He made to stand up and I stared him down. 'Right you are, sir,' he nodded. He went back to Churchill.

I followed the signs to the Gents' until I was out of sight of Barnes, then headed for the WH Smith stall and took up position behind a stand of paperback thrillers. It was a perfect spot: I could see the whole concourse, so would have ample warning of his approach, and there were two entrances, so I could make my escape whichever way I chose, depending on the direction he came from. I wondered what he would be thinking now. He could either sit it out and hope I would be back shortly, or come and investigate immediately in the fear that I had spotted him and done a runner.

It took him less than a minute. He ambled over, pretending he was looking for a bin to dispose of the wrapper of his sandwich. I slipped out the other exit to the gallery of duty-free shops, stepping into the aisles of alcohol, tobacco and perfume laid out to tempt.

I glanced into a display of Swiss wristwatches to see if I could catch sight of Toadski in the reflection. He was at the same thriller stand at Smith's I'd just vacated, apparently engrossed in the selection.

I turned and walked into another shop, selling overpriced knitwear. Toadski suddenly lost interest in Margery Allingham and came bumbling out into the gangway. He looked around frantically, trying to see where I had got to, and then he caught sight of me and our eyes met. He looked down, embarrassed, then tried to mask it by glancing at his watch and feigning distress that he was late for his flight. An announcement was being made, and he made a show of listening to it. He started to scurry away, but I leapt in front of him and grabbed him by the arm. A few yards further along there was a door marked STAFF. It was slightly ajar, and I caught a glimpse of a mop handle. I looked around, and saw that the cleaner was still circling the restaurants. I shoved Toadski inside and stepped in after him. There was an overpowering smell of bleach. I grabbed him by the throat and quickly searched his pockets. He was unarmed.

'What do you want?' I said. 'And make it quick.'

He gulped, his Adam's apple throbbing wildly. I loosened my grip a little.

'"The chairs . . . are being brought in . . . from the garden."' His accent wasn't bad, sort of stockbroker London. But he still looked like he'd just stepped out of the Minsk Players.

'Why am I a target?' I snapped at him, but he merely looked at me with glazed eyes and repeated the Auden line.

I removed my hand. He didn't know anything. He was a messenger, that was all: he had given me the arranged code-phrase for 'Danger: keep a low profile until further contacted.'

'Tell Sasha to screw himself,' I said. The shot had missed me by less than an inch and he thought he could reel me back in by sending this buffoon to tell me I was in danger? What the hell did he take me for? I was going to need a little more information before I turned up for a meet and risked having my head shot off by the next sniper hired for the job.

I pushed Toadski back out of the door, smiled at the Pakistani cleaner as he came rumbling towards us, and smoothed myself down.

*

Barnes was waiting for me outside the lavatories. 'There you are, sir,' he said. 'I was getting worried. Our flight has just been announced.'

'Thought I'd have a look at the duty-free liquor,' I said as calmly as I could. My heart was still thumping from the fury I'd released. 'The prices didn't seem anything special, though.'

Barnes smiled and we set off for the departure gate.

V

Thursday, 1 May 1969, Rome, Italy

My heart rate didn't have much of a chance to recover once we were on the plane: we sat for over an hour while the ground crew worked on a frequently referenced but unspecified technicality. We eventually touched down in Fiumicino at just after seven. The air was still warm on the skin as we trooped across to the terminal building, and despite the circumstances I had to admit that there was something pleasing about being back in Italy. Perhaps it had been the double Scotch I'd had once the plane had finally taken off.

Fantasy turned to reality again the moment we stepped inside: the queues snaked around the entire Customs area.

'Doesn't look too good, sir,' said Barnes unnecessarily, as a trio of small boys in sailor suits ran straight towards us, shooting each other with toy pistols. We sidestepped them and walked towards the queue that looked the shortest, but as we were taking up position behind an extremely noisy German family, someone tapped me on the shoulder.

I turned and was greeted by a beautiful young woman: a late-period Modigliani in a green blouse and a maxi skirt. She had a badge identifying her as an employee of the Italian airport authority.

'*Signor* Dark?'

I nodded, and gestured at Barnes to hand her our passports, which he did. She inspected them for a few moments, then handed them back.

'*Da questa parte, prego,*' she said.

It had slipped my mind that there were compensations to travelling under diplomatic cover, and that this was one of them: you didn't have to waste time going through the usual checks. We followed her over to a bench, where our bags were already waiting. She briskly chalked them, before giving us each a chit to sign and handing them over.

'Enjoy your stay in Italy,' she said, flashing perfect white teeth, and then her hips were swinging away from us and she was gone.

We walked through to the main concourse and were immediately accosted again, this time by a tall, fair-haired man in a dark blue suit: Charles Severn. He was a little broader round the belly, but otherwise looked much the same as I remembered: a good tan, slightly ruddy, a firm jaw and an open, earnest look about him. The only wrong note was his eyes, which somehow didn't fit the rest of his face. One expected them to be blue, but instead they were a peculiar grey, like the colour of gunmetal.

'*Buongiorno*, Paul,' he said, taking a grip of my hand. 'Long time no see.' He gestured that we head towards the exit. 'We should send a letter to The Trusty Servant,' he said. '"Two Wykehamists held a hot in Rome airport . . ."'

I groaned inwardly. We had been in the same house at Winchester; he was a few years below me. He had joined the Service after the war, and our paths had crossed a few times over the years, in Istanbul, in Paris, briefly in London. I never much enjoyed encountering him. He was bright and efficient, and generally rather charming, but he could also be very brash. I hated our shared past: the fact that he had stood next to me at Preces, knew the nicknames I had been given and so on. The Trusty Servant was the school paper, and it often featured inane letters from old boys re-enacting 'hots', the school game's surreal brand of scrum, in exotic and therefore supposedly hilarious locations. My pleasure at having made it through Customs so smoothly suddenly evaporated.

We walked out to the thick warmth of the street, where a throng of recent arrivals were negotiating fares with taxi drivers to take them into the city.

'You must be Reginald!' Severn shouted across at Barnes, the first time I'd heard anyone use Barnes' first name. 'You were in Nairobi, weren't you?'

'Yes, sir!' he shouted back. 'Among other places.'

'Capital. Wonderful to have you here. I'm afraid my car's a two-seater so there's not room for all of us – would you mind too much catching a taxi to the embassy and we'll meet you there?'

Barnes gave me a questioning glance, and I nodded my assent to the scheme. He asked Severn for the embassy's address, repeated it back to him, then took my bag from me and headed into the fray of the taxi queue without another word.

'Sorry about that,' said Severn, as we crossed the street, now Barnes-less. 'No pool cars were available. How was the flight? Shame about the delay, but you know what they say: Bastards Eventually Arrive.' I forced a smile at the stale joke. 'How are you feeling, by the way? I heard you came down with some awful bug in Nigeria.'

'I'm fine,' I said. 'Got the all-clear just a few hours ago, in fact.'

'Quite a turn-up, all that, wasn't it? I heard they even suspected you of being the double at one point – what on earth were they thinking?'

'Yes,' I said. 'It was unfortunate.'

'Desperately sad news about the Templetons. Although the last time I saw Colin he gave me a bollocking for daring to talk to Vanessa!'

I gave a tight smile: it wasn't quite how I remembered the incident.

'And everyone's very sorry about John, of course,' he said.

I doubted many out here had known Farraday, and if they had they probably wouldn't have liked him much. But I noted that Severn's diplomatic skills appeared to have improved over the years.

His car was parked precariously on a verge, although calling it a car seemed something of a disservice: I'd never seen anything like it. It was an Alfa Romeo, almost absurdly low slung and streamlined to perfection. The front window merged seamlessly into the roof, giving it the appearance of a prototype spacecraft. Instead of the traditional *rosso corsa*, the bodywork was British racing green.

'New toy?' I asked.

'Just delivered,' he smiled, unlocking an extraordinary pair of doors that swept up vertically, meeting in the middle like the wings of an enormous metal butterfly. 'Isn't it a beauty? It's a "33 Stradale" – only a dozen or so have been built. It's nearly identical to the racing version: top speed 175 miles per hour.' He climbed in and patted the white leather. 'Custom-built coachwork.' He opened a compartment and pulled on a pair of matching kidskin gloves.

I made some appreciative noises, and remarked that he seemed to be doing well for himself.

'Look who's talking,' he laughed. 'Deputy Chief at forty-five!'

I manoeuvred myself into the front passenger seat.

'Forty-four,' I said.

For a moment I wondered whether he was on the take in some way, but immediately dismissed it: he was from an old banking family, and he'd always been a flashy bugger, even at school. As he brought us out onto the street, he veered out behind a rusty-looking Fiat, then brought the wheel round and squeezed through the gap to overtake it moments before a lorry came hurtling the other way. It was a terrific piece of driving but he hardly seemed to notice, and even accelerated. I looked on in admiration. Although the coachwork and exterior of the car were beautiful, there were few creature comforts: no radio, no carpet on the floor, no luggage space. It was a pure, brutal speed machine, and it certainly replicated the feeling of being in a race car. It took me back to Father's sorties round Brooklands. I'd done a bit of racing myself in my teens, but had never really developed the taste for it: there didn't seem to be enough of a purpose.

As we approached the centre of the city, Severn finally switched down a gear and I asked him for a situation report, which he gave as fast and as fluently as he drove.

'There have been no further attacks,' he said, 'but the police took a call on Monday from someone claiming there was a bomb in the Finance Ministry – nothing was found, though. In Milan, the *carabinieri* have questioned fifteen anarchists and trouble-makers about the bombings there, and they've charged eight of them, including di Angelo and Rivera.'

I looked at him. 'I thought they were based in Rome.'

'They were both in Milan a few weeks before the bombing. The Italians think they might have been scouting around.'

'I see.' Well, that put paid to Haggard's little idea, at least – I could hardly storm Milan's police station and bump off a couple of their prisoners.

'But it's hardly over,' said Severn. 'Tensions are rising all over the place, and strikes and protests have now become almost the norm. Teachers, civil servants and railway workers have been on strike for the last few days, and a few hours ago several thousand Maoists stormed a Soviet May Day celebration and all hell broke loose, apparently. There are also rumours flying around that there's a coup in the works. It's a fairly explosive situation.'

I looked out of the window. An Agip dog whipped past, and then I started noticing the trees: ilexes, pines, even the occasional palm. In the blocks of flats lining the street, bougainvillea caught the evening sun in the highest trellises, and as we approached the next set of traffic lights I spotted a market stall selling fruit and vegetables in one of the side streets. Not much seemed to have changed in Rome, and I wondered if there was anything particularly out of the ordinary in Severn's summary. Analysis this close to events was often prone to exaggeration, and he was, of course, trying to show me he was on top of things. Coups were forever being rumoured in Italy – one had very nearly taken place when I'd been here last – and I'd just seen London's May Day march at close quarters, and that hadn't been pretty, either. Britain had more than its fair share of strikes at the moment, and army units had even been posted to Northern Ireland after a recent spate of fire-bombs . . . One could probably give a similarly grim sit-rep for most Western European countries, if one chose.

'And Barchetti?' I asked. 'When's your next scheduled meet with him?'

'Oh-ten-hundred tomorrow. The National Gallery of Modern Art.'

'Good. You can brief me over breakfast.'

He didn't say anything for a moment, and I tensed.

'There's good news and bad news,' he said. 'Which would you like first?'

I didn't reply.

'The Italians say they have more information about Arte come Terrore, and are happy to share it with us.'

'And what's the good news?'

He laughed. 'That *was* the good news, Paul!' I glanced at him. 'Marco Zimotti wants to brief you at dinner this evening.'

'Dinner? Not on – I need to get some kip. I've had rather a long day.'

He smiled at the understatement. *You don't know the half of it*, I thought.

'I'm afraid Lennox is insisting – visiting dignitary and all that.'

Christ, that was just what I needed. Lennox was the ambassador, a pompous fool I'd encountered several times before, and Zimotti was the new head of Italian military intelligence, Giacomo's replacement. I had never met him, but knew him by reputation: a tough customer, by all accounts. It sounded like he'd strong-armed his way into a meeting once he'd heard I was on my way. Still, if he *did* have anything useful on Arte come Terrore's plans, I might be able to tie up everything for Haggard and get back to London faster.

'All right,' I said. 'Dinner it is, but let's try to make it fast, shall we? But tell me about yourself, Charles – are you enjoying Rome?' I didn't care, especially, but it might help to show I was friendly: I was invading his turf, and he'd naturally be a little nervous.

He beeped at a passing motorcyclist and made a face. 'Can't say

I do, much,' he said. 'The summers are too bloody hot and the winters aren't much better than London. Nobody ever gets anything done and, frankly, once you've seen the monuments there's not a lot to *do*, other than get hassled by beggars and cats in the street. One might as well be in Africa. Didn't you find?'

I smiled. I suspected that in a few years' time he would be attacked by a pang of longing for the place, and would have forgotten all about the beggars. I considered telling him about what was going on in at least one corner of Africa that I knew of, but decided it wasn't worth it.

I looked out of the window again. We were approaching the centre of town now, turning into Via Cristoforo Colombo. Traffic was light on account of it being Primo Maggio, and I spotted a few students with banners wandering along the pavement. We passed a bar, and for a moment I caught the eye of a pretty young girl, who flashed a mouth full of gleaming teeth at me. It was an infuriating country, no doubt, and God knew I didn't want to be here on Haggard's wild-goose chase while Innes was asking awkward questions in London. But there was something about it I couldn't help liking. It was carefree, even in the face of political strife and bloodshed. There was something *living* about the place, and you could feel it pulsing around you, in the tooting of the horns, the policemen strutting about in their spotless uniforms, the mothers slapping their children around the head. Cooped up in that office in London I'd forgotten what living was. I'd remembered it in Nigeria – there was nothing like nearly losing your life to make you appreciate it all the more – but this was more like it. This was a place where life was appreciated. Perhaps it was time to get out, retire, buy a little villa somewhere in the south . . .

I caught myself and laughed inwardly. It was a line of thought I might have pursued a few months earlier – not any more. I glanced in the rear-view mirror to see if the girl was still visible, and it was then that I spotted the tail. It was four cars behind us, a small white Fiat with Rome plates. The driver was wearing a pair of oversized dark glasses, but it was definitely him: Toadski. I looked across at Severn, but he didn't appear to have noticed, and I wasn't about to set him right.

What the hell did the man want now? And how had he got here? I'd checked every seat on the plane. Presumably, he had watched Barnes and me walk off to our gate at Heathrow – careless of me not to notice – seen where we were headed and taken the next flight out. He'd had a stroke of luck that my flight had been delayed, but then again I had flown BEA so perhaps it wasn't so much luck as fate. But what did he want? It was a long way to come to tell me to keep a low profile again. He hadn't looked like an assassin, but perhaps I'd misjudged him and the message had been a diversion. I should have drowned him in a bucket of bleach when I'd had the chance.

As Severn drove through the embassy gates, I looked in the mirror and saw the Fiat pulling up to park about halfway down the street. Severn slipped into a space at the top of the driveway under a palm tree, and I opened my door and stepped out.

VI

We walked up to the entrance and I looked out at the grounds.

'Staff still in the sheds?' I asked, as he rang the bell.

He gave a curt nod. The original embassy in Via XX Settembre had been bombed by Zionists in '46 as part of their terror campaign against the British. Twenty-three years later, work had finally begun on rebuilding it on the original site, but most of the staff were still based here at Villa Wolkonsky, the 'temporary' embassy that had been set up after the attack. Although the ambassador's quarters were rather grand, when I'd been here most of the staff had worked out of prefabricated shacks and outhouses in the grounds of the building – and apparently still did.

'Sarah's found you a room,' Severn said. 'Not terribly opulent, but I hope it will do.'

'Sarah?'

'The Station's radio officer. We married last year.'

I remembered. I'd even been asked to sign off on it by Personnel, which I had done, naturally. 'Keeping things in the family' was approved of: it tended to make life easier. From past knowledge of Severn's girlfriends, I imagined she would be very pretty and very pliant.

A butler in tails came to the door and led us inside. There was no lighting: there had been a power cut. 'You see?' Severn muttered to me under his breath. 'Africa.' The butler gave us each a torch, and we walked past the copy of Annigoni's portrait of the Queen to the reception desk, where a young man asked for our passports. Severn handed over his, and I remembered that Barnes had mine. Severn vouched for me, and the guard produced a form for him to sign to that effect. As well as having worked out of temporary quarters for over two decades, the embassy had a giant chip on its shoulder about security that dated back to the Twenties, when one of the local employees had passed hundreds of documents to the Soviets because he'd been trusted with keys to all the safes. As a result, the security precautions were often insufferable. They had annoyed me intensely in '64, but right now I was delighted they were still in place: I couldn't have picked a safer place to stay.

We climbed the staircase to the top floor, where Severn led me to a room roughly the size of the broom cupboard I should have strangled Toadski in.

'Well,' he said, 'here we are.'

An iron bedstead had been made up with linen, and someone had sprayed cologne about, presumably to banish whatever unpleasant smell had previously occupied it. A rust-stained mirror and a washstand faced the bed, beside which sat my hold-all.

'Where will Barnes sleep?' I asked.

'His room's further down this corridor. Shall we go down now, or would you like a shave and a shower first?'

I walked over to the window and peered out. The street was largely protected from view, but I could just make out one corner of it. A tiny bubble of whitish grey stood out against the darkness: the Fiat.

I turned back to Severn. 'No,' I said. 'Let's get this over with.'

*

Downstairs again, members of the household were scurrying around lighting candles. From what I could make out, the place hadn't changed much: the same candelabra and carpeting, the same paintings of dead dignitaries and the same smell of varnish.

We walked through to the dining room, where twenty or so people were seated, their faces quivering in the candlelight and their voices merging into a low babble. Lennox, the ambassador, was at the head of the table, talking to an elderly woman I vaguely recalled was married to the French cultural attaché. On seeing us, he touched her lightly on the arm and stood, placing his napkin on the table. The room hushed, and he slowly began clapping his hands. A few moments later, the others followed suit, scraping back their chairs and facing me.

'Bravo!' Lennox called out. 'Bravo!'

It took me a moment, and then I realized that they were giving me a standing ovation for chasing down Farraday's sniper. I wished I were the man they thought they were applauding – but I wasn't. A wave of shame swept over me and I gestured for them to stop, but it only encouraged them to applaud with greater gusto. I quickly stepped over to Lennox and he shook me by the hand and, slowly, the circus died down.

'Welcome, Paul,' he said. 'It's a pleasure to see you again, although I wish it wasn't under such tragic circumstances.'

The last time we'd met had been at a particularly unpleasant meeting in London three years earlier, at which he had complained that my Section was interfering in his affairs – but no mind. 'We wanted to have something a little grander,' he was saying, 'but what with the dreadful news about John, not to mention all the demonstrations taking place in town today, it wouldn't really have sent the right message.'

I told him I quite understood and thanked him profusely both for the honour and for putting me up, and then let Severn lead me around the table. I shook hands with Cornell-Smith and Miller, two of the old hands at the Station. Then we came to Barnes, who looked up at me with evident relief that I hadn't been kidnapped on the way from the airport. It seemed that everyone was ahead of me: his taxi driver must have been luckier than us with the lights, or known a short cut. He was seated next to a good-looking man with brilliantined grey hair, to whom Severn now introduced me: Marco Zimotti. I shook his hand.

'A pleasure.'

'The pleasure is mine,' he said. He was wearing a crisp black suit accompanied by a white shirt that heightened a very dark tan, the whole outfit worn with a sort of studied nonchalance: he looked more like a film star than a director of military intelligence.

'I've been hearing about you from Reginald here,' he said with a disarming smile. His English was faultless, with just the faintest tinge of a Neapolitan accent. 'He tells me you went to the same school as Charles. Who, may I ask, was whose "fag"?'

I glared at Barnes. Severn was blushing to the roots of his hair – I wondered whether it was because he knew the American expression or because it wasn't the sort of thing one talked about in polite company.

'Charles was mine, in fact,' I said. 'Although we didn't call them that. He was my "jun man" – "jun" meaning junior. He had to make me tea and toast in the morning and that sort of thing.'

Zimotti raised an eyebrow meaningfully. 'And now? I imagine you could say he is still your "jun man" . . . no?'

Severn laughed rather too loudly and Zimotti joined in, and somehow we moved past it and everyone pretended it hadn't been said. Severn took me by the arm and indicated a woman seated to Zimotti's right.

'And this is my wife, Sarah.' She stood, and he leaned over to kiss her on the cheek.

Well, she was more than pretty. The few women I'd encountered in the Service who had escaped the typing pool had either been buck-toothed bluestockings or had done their best to appear so in order to be taken seriously. Not this one, though. She was in her late twenties or early thirties, tall and slim, with a sheet of honey-blonde hair that looked like it had been lifted from an advertisement for Sunsilk. She wore a white evening gown that had holes cut into it, discreetly revealing segments of golden-brown skin. It looked very expensive: the Gucci, Pucci, Cucci brigade. She had a high-boned face, with deep blue eyes heavily accented by kohl and a wide jawline leading into a perfectly shaped chin. Her lips were a little thinner than the fashionable Bardot pout, but otherwise she had the instantly recognizable look of the international jet set: one of the beautiful people for whom life was an endless round of cocktails and fun, fun, fun.

She offered me a hand sparkling with diamonds. 'You must be Paul,' she said. Her voice was low and cool, the accent Home Counties. 'Charlie's been telling me all about you.'

'You've got a head-start on me, then,' I said. 'He only mentioned you ten minutes ago.'

She tilted her head to one side and smiled. It was the sort of smile that managed to say a lot of things at once, and I imagined she used it often, and found it very useful. I took a seat between her and Zimotti, and Severn pecked her on the cheek again and squeezed past to make his way to the far end of the table.

A white-jacketed steward brought round some wine and bowls of cold asparagus soup, and I turned to talk to Zimotti. He threw out a few questions about my previous experience of Rome, and I answered some of them and parried a few more.

'I was sorry to hear about John Farraday,' he said after we'd exhausted the preliminaries. 'It is truly a tragedy, and I am deeply ashamed that one of my countrymen appears to have been responsible for it.' His jaw clenched, marking the bones in his cheek. 'But you have my assurance that we will discover who was behind this – and these Communist filth will be made to pay for what they have done.'

I thanked him for his support. 'Charles told me you may have more information about Arte come Terrore. Do you have anything that specifically links them to this?'

We paused as the waiting staff came round with the main course: over-cooked venison, by the look of it. Zimotti sawed into his meat, his eyebrows knitting at the toughness.

'We haven't heard from our colleagues in Milan yet,' he said, 'but there is no question in my mind that these people were behind it. We have been watching this group for some time. They spend a lot of time here, as well as in Sardinia.'

'Sardinia?'

'Yes, they have some kind of a base there, we think. We are working on discovering more about it.'

That was something, at least. I asked him who he thought was sponsoring the group.

'Moscow,' he replied without hesitating, 'although only the leaders of the group would be aware of that, of course.' He nibbled off another chunk of meat.

'Of course. But what makes you so sure it's not Peking?'

'All our evidence points to Moscow,' he said. I was about to ask him what that evidence consisted of when one of the stewards walked over and told him he was required on the telephone. He excused himself with a smile and left the room.

So much for his briefing me. Dessert was served: a rice pudding, of all things. I had a spoonful, then pushed it to one side. I called back the steward and asked him for a grappa. He brought it to me a couple of minutes later, in a rather large glass. I leaned across and told Barnes I was going to grab some fresh air, and then headed onto one of the balconies overlooking the garden.

*

There was a faint breeze, and I could smell the mimosa and magnolia trees. I looked down, trying to catch another glimpse of the street, but I wasn't high enough. Perhaps he'd gone home. Perhaps it hadn't even been him.

No. It had been him, all right.

I took a sip of the drink, welcoming the fiery sensation it caused in my chest, and gazed out at the lights of the Eternal City: the Alban hills were just visible in the distance. Somewhere not too far away teachers were striking, students were staging sit-ins and factory workers were planting explosives. Rome itself, so Severn claimed, was on the verge of burning. And here we were, watching and waiting . . .

My thoughts were interrupted as I became aware of someone behind me. I turned to see Sarah Severn standing in the doorway.

'Mind if I join you?' she asked.

'It's a free country.'

She stepped onto the balcony and flashed her Mona Lisa smile again. 'Is it?'

She took a pack of cigarettes from her purse: Nazionali, one of the more popular local brands, rather rough on the throat as I remembered. You could buy British tobacco everywhere here, so I took it she wasn't overly attached to home-grown products, as expatriates sometimes were. She shook a cigarette into her fingers in one graceful movement, and I leaned over with my lighter. She looked up, and as our eyes met I felt the familiar flicker of interest. I stopped the thought dead. No more women.

'Zimotti's back,' she said, and exhaled a stream of smoke in the direction of the Colosseum.

So that was why she had come out here – to shepherd me along. I didn't say anything and she glanced downward, showing off her long, dark lashes. 'Sorry,' she said with a hint of sarcasm. 'I just thought you might want to know.'

I placed my glass on a balustrade and lit one of my own cigarettes. 'Thanks.'

She looked up again. 'The head of the Service has just been murdered. Don't you want to find who was responsible?'

'I *know* he was murdered,' I said. 'He was standing a couple of inches in front of me when it happened. Perhaps you could let me decide how to do my job.'

She turned away and I immediately regretted my tone: my promotion was turning me into a pompous arse.

'Do you treat everyone this way?' she said. She paused for a moment. 'Perhaps the bullet hit the wrong man.'

She was looking at me calmly, brazenly, as though daring me to slap her, and I realized I was being a fool and smiled.

'Perhaps it did,' I said, reaching for my drink again.

The tension eased away. We finished our cigarettes in companionable silence and headed back indoors. But instead of returning to the dining room, she grabbed me by the arm and led me through a door and into a long corridor.

'Where are we going?' I asked.

'For a walk!' she laughed gaily, and I followed her, a hazy configuration of white silk and brown skin moving down the unlit hallway. I wondered if she might be drunk.

'I heard you were very brave,' she called out, 'chasing the sniper across London.'

'Not really,' I replied, dragging my eyes away from her figure. 'It was just instinct. I didn't find out much.'

We were heading into the heart of the embassy now. Candles had been placed in sconces along the walls, and I could make out the gatepost for the entrance to the Station at the far end of the corridor.

'Still,' she said, 'not many people would have risked their own skins like that.' She had slowed down and turned back to face me. 'And you found out something, or you wouldn't be here.'

What was she getting at? I didn't get the chance to ask her because there was a loud humming sound in my ears, and lights were flickering on.

'Finally!' she said. 'Now we'll be able to see where we're going.' She took my arm in hers and gestured ahead of us. 'Do you fancy a tour of the Station? It's changed a bit since your day, I think.'

'It's rather late,' I said, 'and I'm sure I'll see it tomorrow. What did you mean—'

I looked up to see Charles Severn standing a few yards ahead of us, a drink in his hand.

'Hello, lovebirds,' he said, stepping forward and placing a hand on Sarah's shoulder. 'Can I join, or is it a private party?'

*

I found Barnes hovering anxiously outside my room. Severn had said he'd become worried and gone looking for me. It was still early

– not yet nine o'clock – but I was shattered, so I had asked Severn to make my excuses to Lennox and he had headed back down to the dining room for coffee, his arm around Sarah's waist. He had seemed to believe her story that we had simply been stretching our legs, but I didn't. She had wanted to take me into the Station: why? She wasn't *that* forward, surely.

I told Barnes I was going to call it a night, and he nodded and headed for his room down the corridor. I walked into my broom cupboard and threw my jacket onto the bed. On an impulse I looked out of the window and down at the street, searching for the grey bubble. It was still there. Christ. Was he planning to stay there all bloody night?

I made a decision – sleep could come later. I drained the rest of the grappa from the glass and caught Barnes up in the corridor, making a show of patting my pockets. 'Damn it, I seem to have lost my cigarettes. They must have dropped out in the car on the way over. I'll just go and get them.'

'Yes, sir.'

I walked downstairs and headed outside to confront Toadski. This time, I'd make sure I got some proper answers.

VII

The street was quiet and deserted, and I ran down it looking for the Fiat. Yes, there it was. As I approached it, I smashed my glass against a wall, then yanked open the front door and pressed the jagged edge to Toadski's throat.

'Move over!'

He glared at me with a mixture of fear and fury and jerked his head desperately towards the back of the car. I looked: there was someone sitting there, hidden in the shadows.

I glanced down the street, then up at the windows of the embassy. No one. I pulled the glass away from Toadski's throat, opened the rear door and climbed in. There was a strong smell of cheap Russian tobacco, and something sweet I couldn't place.

'You've got two minutes,' I said, thrusting the glass forward. 'Why are you trying to kill me?'

I didn't know who he was, but I knew *what* he was: the head of Rome's illegal GRU station. Toadski would have called him on landing at Fiumicino and this, no doubt, was his car. He spoke to Toadski in Russian now, calling him Grigori Mikhailovich and telling him to take a walk and come back in five minutes. His voice was high-pitched – reedy and fluting, with a slight lisp. Without a word, Toadski opened his door and climbed out.

As the echo of his footsteps faded, the man in the shadows leaned forward, bringing his face into the orbit of the nearest streetlight. It was long and slender, with bloodless lips and watery eyes hidden behind large lids: it reminded me of the husband in the Arnolfini portrait. He was young, early or mid-thirties – one of the new generation coming out of Moscow's training schools – and he seemed to be chewing or sucking on something. I looked down and saw a small blue and silver box in his lap: *Baci Perugina*.

'Good evening, Mister Dark,' he said, inclining his head a little. 'My name is Pyotr Yurevich, and I currently have a pistol aimed at your heart. However, I assure you I have no intention of using it.'

There was no trace of a Russian accent except for when he'd said his name: I'd have guessed he was French or Swiss. Pedantic sort of tone, but that seemed to come with the manual. A black-gloved hand appeared in the small pool of light available in the car, and enclosed within its grip was the gun, a nine-millimetre Makarov by the look of it. Another hand appeared and swiftly unloaded it, and then the voice continued: 'Now, kindly remove that glass from my face and tell me why you think someone is trying to kill you.'

I considered for a moment, then opened the door, leaned down and placed the glass on the pavement.

'A bullet,' I said, closing the door again. 'About an inch from my face.'

There was silence for several seconds.

'How do you feel?' he said, eventually. 'I understand you recently suffered an ordeal in Africa.'

I stared into the darkness. I recognized the question from having run agents in the field myself. They sometimes lost it, either through fear or injury or simply fatigue. He thought I was still suffering from the fever I'd caught in Nigeria – and that it had made me delusional!

'You don't know what happened in London?' I asked.

He chewed his chocolate treat and waited for me to continue.

'At eleven o'clock this morning the new head of the Service was shot in the chest by a sniper in St Paul's Cathedral. The bullet was meant for me. The sniper was an Italian.'

He stopped chewing. 'No, I did not know this.'

His surprise sounded genuine, but then it would. Spying is acting, and acting of the hardest kind: you're never allowed off-stage to remove your make-up, never get to re-take a fluffed line, and your life depends on your performance. I'd been acting for over twenty years, and had become so good at it that I even managed to convince myself some of the time. Perhaps he did, too. Because if he were acting, he'd given a very good line reading, inflected with just the right degree of innocent surprise.

'What did Grigori Mikhailovich tell you?' I asked, jerking my head towards the empty driving seat. 'He must have given you a message from Sasha.'

'He did not tell me anything about this. Do you really think I would have come to meet you in front of the British embassy if I had just ordered your death?'

He had a point. As a deep-cover agent, he was taking an enormous risk just being here at all. Then again, so was I. Was it possible Toadski didn't know about St Paul's, either? He was a bit player, admittedly, an errand-boy, but surely Sasha would have briefed him nevertheless? Unless the GRU hadn't been responsible, of course . . .

'What about the KGB?' I asked. 'How are your relations with your colleagues there?' The infighting between the KGB and the GRU made the Service and Five look like something out of a Mills and Boon.

He hesitated for a moment. 'As far as I know, neither we nor any of our colleagues had anything to do with the incident you mention.'

As far as he knew — very reassuring. It was a legalistic sort of answer, and the hesitation didn't help make it any more convincing.

'Why don't you tell me what you *do* know,' I said, 'because I'm starting to wonder if I've stepped into the wrong car.'

He looked aggrieved, then sighed deeply, an Atlas of the spy world. 'I am a mere cog in the machine, Mister Dark. You cannot expect me to be privy to every operation we undertake.'

'We have a saying for that,' I said. 'The left hand doesn't know what the right hand is doing.' But, again, he had a point. The sniper had been Italian, but that didn't mean he had just flown in from Italy. I remembered how surely he had run into the tunnel at Barbican. Local knowledge? Pyotr here might not have been informed about a plan to kill a British double agent in London – especially if it were by another agency. Then again, if the KGB were out for me, he wouldn't want me to know that either. I glanced down at my wristwatch. I'd already been gone three minutes, and Barnes would soon be wondering where I was.

'I think we should start again,' he said. 'You are my agent now, and I would—'

'*Your* agent?' I laughed, and turned to open the door.

'If you leave this car,' he said, his voice immediately hardening, 'I will expose you.' His eyes glinted beneath puffy lids. 'Without hesitation.'

He reached inside his jacket, and for a moment I thought he was about to pull a second gun on me. He smiled at my panic and immediately opened his hand so I could see what it was he had reached for: the negatives. So it was that again.

'These are copies,' he said. 'The originals are in a safe in Moscow. If you do not do precisely as I say, my superiors will send them to your colleagues indoors. If I don't like the way you behave, they will send them. And if anything happens to *me*, they will send them. Is that clear enough for you?'

I let my hand drop from the door handle. He gave me a smug little smile and replaced the negatives in his jacket.

'Why are you in Rome?' he said. 'Is it because of Edoardo Barchetti?'

Another surprise. There were only two ways he could have known I was here to investigate Barchetti: either through a leak at the very highest level of Five, the Service or the Cabinet, or . . .

'He's been blown,' said Pyotr. 'He is a British agent, and he has infiltrated a little group of ours that operates here.' He unwrapped another chocolate and popped it in his mouth. 'We need you to kill him at once.'

*

There was a sudden sound from the street, but it was just Grigori coming back from his stroll and Pyotr sent him away again. *I should have heeded his advice in Heathrow – this was hardly low profile. Had Sasha known this assassination scheme was waiting for me in Rome and tried to warn me off?*

'Kill him?' I said, to buy some thinking time. Part of me noted that hidden in the absurdity of it all had been the admission that Arte come Terrore was a Moscow front: so Zimotti had been right about that. 'I think you've got the wrong man,' I said, finally. 'You're looking for an assassin.'

Pyotr pursed his lips. 'You had no such qualms in Nigeria.'

A lot of people seemed to have got the wrong end of the stick about what had happened in Nigeria. I suddenly missed Sasha. Oh, I hated him – his tweed suits and his stamp collection and his patronizing manner – but I missed him nevertheless. This chap was too smooth by half, and he was giving me the bloody creeps.

'Why me?' I said. 'Why don't you get someone in the group to do it?'

'That is our concern, not yours. But, as you ask, the group is not aware of our sponsorship, and we would prefer it remains that way. We also do not trust them to perform a job of this delicacy.'

So they were not just running Arte come Terrore, but they were doing so as a false-flag operation. Again, Zimotti had been right, although it was fairly standard procedure. Interesting that Pyotr felt they couldn't handle a hit, though.

'It doesn't add up,' I said, staring him straight in the face. 'You didn't know I was coming.'

He shrugged. 'That is true. But the man who was to have done the job is no longer available, and you are here in Rome to meet Barchetti – it is providential.'

I could think of other words for it. The man who was to have done the job was no longer available . . . because he had recently died in Smithfield Market? Was I being targeted by the GRU after all? And if so, why did this man not seem to know about it?

'Why do you want Barchetti dead?' I asked. 'You just said he'd been blown—'

'He was carelessly given some very important information, after which he immediately contacted London. Which is why they've sent you, I suppose – to find out what it is he knows?'

'Among other things,' I said. 'What was the information?'

He looked down at the box in his lap and started rummaging around in it. He wasn't in any sort of a rush, this fellow, and that was unfortunate because I was. I'd find it rather difficult to explain to Barnes what I was doing in this car. He was armed, but he'd put his gun away and I wondered whether I should rush him, try to strangle the information out of him. Dangerous: he didn't look like he could put up much of a fight, but there would be Grigori to contend with, too. And so far I didn't seem to be having much luck getting information out of people by force.

'Look,' I said. 'Could you just forget the fucking chocolates for a minute and tell me what's going on? I don't have a lot of time.'

He winced at the obscenity. 'It is information that could expose you,' he said.

'Then it's no dice. He'll run a mile the second he sees me – we used to work together.'

'He doesn't *know* it exposes you. But I will tell you no more. It is better for your sake.'

'I'll be the judge of that.' He didn't reply, so I tried another tack. 'Severn is scheduled to meet Barchetti tomorrow morning. If I insist on taking his place and Barchetti winds up dead, how do you propose I avert suspicion?'

'Tomorrow morning will be fine,' he said, though I hadn't been asking for his approval on that score. 'As for the other matter, you will find a way: the consequences of him remaining alive are much worse. Kill Barchetti, and you will be helping both yourself and us. Everybody wins.' He smiled.

'Except Barchetti,' I said.

He leaned forward. 'I understand your reaction,' he said, in what I think he meant to be a confidential tone. 'Believe me. I have only survived in this game myself through my ability to find opportunities where none seemed to exist, and for repeatedly turning the most hopeless-seeming situations into victories. I have studied your file, and I think the same could be said of you.' His tone turned cold. 'We have a saying in Russian: "Among wolves, howl like a wolf." Do not mistake us for puppy dogs, Mister Dark. We expect you to howl with us, all the way. This time it really is the end of the road: there are no exits, and we have the winning hand. If you do not do as I say, I will expose you. I am afraid it is checkmate. Kill Barchetti tomorrow morning,' – he patted his jacket pocket – 'or I will make sure Charles Severn receives these by lunch.'

*

Barnes was waiting for me at the top of the staircase, wearing a dressing gown.

'Everything all right, sir?'

'Fine,' I said, taking the pack of cigarettes from my pocket. 'They were in the glove compartment.'

I threw him a couple of sticks and he grinned. He went back into his room to smoke them, and I went into mine. I undressed and climbed into bed.

VIII

Friday, 2 May 1969, Rome, Italy

I woke with a start. Something had touched me. I opened my eyes and saw Barnes seated on the bed, his hand shaking my shoulder.

'I'm sorry, sir,' he said, looking embarrassed. 'But it's time.'

I thanked him gruffly and rubbed my eyes. He left, and I went over to the basin and washed my face. Slowly, the nightmare of the previous evening returned. Curiosity killed the bloody cat, I thought: if I hadn't left the building, I wouldn't have found myself blackmailed into an assassination job I couldn't see any way of completing. But I had left the building, and complete it I must. Pyotr had mixed a few metaphors but I didn't think he was bluffing, and deep down I knew he was right: I could rattle my cage all I wanted, but there was no way out. I'd read plenty of reports about blackmailed agents, but until now had never really appreciated what it meant, I suppose because I'd never believed it might apply to me.

I went through my fitness regimen, then bathed, dressed in a light linen suit, and collected Barnes from his room. Downstairs at the Station, Severn came to the barrier and told the man on duty to let us through.

'Good morning,' he said. 'Sleep well?'

'Yes, thanks,' I said.

I said hello to Cornell-Smith and Miller, and a couple of others who I'd glimpsed but not been introduced to at dinner the evening before. Sarah was seated at a desk in the middle of the main area smoking a cigarette, wearing a crisp white blouse and a dark skirt that showed off her long golden legs. She caught me looking at them and smiled, pushing a wisp of hair away from her eyes.

I looked around. She had been right: it had changed since I'd last been here. There was significantly more radio equipment, some fancy Scandinavian-style furniture – her doing? – and even a *cafet-ière*, from which Severn was currently pouring himself a cup. But the layout of the place was basically the same, with the heavy wooden doors to the offices. Severn was in my old one, I saw.

'There's been a change of plan,' I told him. 'I'm going to meet Barchetti.'

The cup clattered in its saucer as he looked up to see if I were serious. 'But you can't,' he said when he realized I was. 'You're under diplomatic cover.'

'So are you.'

He placed the cup on the table and wiped his hands against his trousers. 'Well, yes. But I've been running him . . .'

'I've run him, too,' I said. 'It's set for the modern art museum, isn't it? That's just by the Borghese Gardens, if I remember rightly.'

He started stammering about unorthodox procedures and prior notice, so I pushed a little harder, reminding him that I was Deputy Chief and claiming for good measure that the Home Secretary had instructed me personally to report 'from the spot'. It took me a few minutes to make him understand that he had no choice in the matter – the fact that I hadn't either made it easier to do.

'I also want you to send a telex to London,' I said. 'Message to read as follows: "Rivera and di Angelo in custody in Milan. Italians claim Moscow backing group, possible base on Sardinia, but as yet no evidence. Await further instructions. Dark."'

'Did Zimotti give you that bit about Sardinia?'

I nodded. 'But that's all I got, unfortunately. He disappeared to make a phone call just as we started talking.'

Severn pursed his lips. 'I see. Shame. Sarah, did you get all that, darling?'

'I'll send it at once,' she said, standing and walking over to the coding machine. I headed for the door.

'You won't be needing me, then, sir?' asked Barnes, and I shook my head. Slowly but surely, he was catching on.

*

I walked down Via Appia Nuova and found a small bar. The street was emptier than I expected for this time of the day, but then I remembered it was the Friday after a holiday. Many people would have *fatto il ponte*: made the bridge to the weekend. Half the city would be at the beach, or enjoying a picnic in one of the city's parks.

I felt for my money clip: ten pounds at the bureau de change in Heathrow had got me just shy of fifteen thousand *lire*. I went inside and bought a couple of bread rolls and a double espresso, then took one of the outside tables. It hadn't yet gone nine o'clock, but the sun was already blasting down and my eyes started to throb from the glare. I hoped it was a result of chasing snipers about rather than my Nigerian fever returning. I reached into my jacket pocket for a pair of ancient sunglasses I'd brought along, and as I did my hand brushed against the packet of capsules Urquhart had given me in London. I wondered for a moment if I should crack it open and take one, but decided against it.

I put the glasses on and looked around, just in case Severn had decided to be clever and send someone after me. I also scanned the roofs of the buildings opposite, checking for the glint of a telescopic sight. Whatever Pyotr said, the bullet in St Paul's had been meant for me, and I had no doubt that whoever had ordered it fired meant to try again.

But, at least for the moment, the coast looked clear.

I had my breakfast, savouring the rich flavour of the coffee and vowing never to have another one in a British airport. Then I left a few coins as a tip and walked over to a kiosk across the road, where I bought a copy of the *International Herald Tribune*. I rolled it under my arm and hailed a taxi.

As the driver manoeuvred through the morning traffic, I considered my old friend and informant 'Bassetto' Barchetti. Pyotr had been lying through his teeth about him, of course: whatever information he had managed to pick up, it didn't have anything to do with me. They'd already been planning to kill him before I arrived, and they couldn't care less whether I was in danger of being exposed; someone or other was intent on killing me, in fact. No, Pyotr had thrown in that bit about the information as bait to grab my attention. It must be something else, something big that they didn't want the Service to know, and it had got them into an almighty flap and desperate to get him out of the way for good, and sharpish. So sharpish that they had reached for their stash of negatives and tried to force *me* into doing the job for them.

I had agreed to report to Pyotr in the Borghese Gardens at noon, but I decided I would have to fob him off somehow, tell him it had been impossible to set up at such short notice. It was a plausible enough excuse, I reckoned. Assassination takes planning, and planning takes time. A museum was not a location I'd have picked, for example. I was not an assassin, but I had assassinated before, and I had studied my targets for weeks – in the case of Cheng in Hong Kong, months. If I had been doing the job I would have needed a weapon, preferably one that was completely untraceable. Thallium, for example, as the French had used with Moumié in Geneva, or a poisoned dart, like the Red Hand had done with Léopold in '57. Neither was readily available in the centre of Rome on two hours' notice.

The taxi arrived at the museum, and I paid the driver. As I was walking up to the entrance, a better way out flashed into my mind: discover what Barchetti knew, then use it to blackmail Pyotr! It was an unlikely scenario, but a possibility nonetheless, and I skipped up the steps with a little more gaiety at the thought.

*

From the outside, the Galleria Nazionale d'Arte Moderna looks like most other temples of great art around the world: a neoclassical façade with grand pillars and a general aura of solemnity and depth. Inside, however, the museum is largely taken over by the imaginings of the deranged fringe of the modern art world. I could understand why Barchetti had picked it. If he were being watched by his Arte come Terrore chums, they wouldn't be in the least surprised that he would visit this place. And it would be much harder to follow him through than a café or park.

I took off my sunglasses and checked for signs of surveillance. The immediate area looked to be clean, but no doubt Severn or one of the Station staff would be here shortly. Severn had arranged to meet Barchetti in the twentieth-century section of the museum, so I paid for a ticket at the front desk and followed the signs until I came to it.

I spotted him right away. He was standing between a sculpture that resembled a segment of a dinosaur fossil and a painting in which arrows from a large black 'Z' pointed towards the number 44 and an 'X'. Dressed in a dark suit and porkpie hat, he was peering at the canvas as though trying to figure out the solution to the equation – he looked more like a bank clerk on his day off than the infiltrator of a terrorist cell.

As I approached him, he turned and gave me a twitchy grin. His forehead was coated in sweat and his eyes were darting about to an unsettling degree. I recognized the signs at once: he was in far too deep.

'Hello, Edoardo,' I said, holding up my copy of the *Herald Tribune*. 'Long time no see. Charles couldn't make it today, so they sent me instead.'

'Not here,' he said. 'Follow me.'

No greeting, no memories of old times. All right. We walked through to one of the other halls, and he hovered by a velvet-covered bench before finally seating himself on it.

'I thought you worked in London now,' he said.

'So did I. What is it you've discovered?'

He looked around again.

'They know,' he whispered. And then, more urgently: '*They know!*'

'You're blown?' I didn't follow – why agree a meet, then?

He shook his head furiously. 'About the attack in the dome.'

'They know we suspect them, you mean? Or you have proof they were involved?'

His head swivelled and he looked up at me, his expression one of undisguised shock. There was a strange moment when our eyes met, and then I realized what he was going to do. He stood up from the bench and began walking away from me, fast but not so fast that he would attract attention. I had no choice: a shout would have ruined everything, and he wouldn't have turned back anyway. I walked after him.

*

He headed into the next room and then took a right through a curtained archway into another one. As I got closer I realized that it was a dark room – some sort of installation. A few people were straggling by the entrance, either waiting for companions to emerge or contemplating going in themselves. Barchetti had already gone through, so I plunged into the darkness.

An old jazz number was being piped through the space, but it sounded like it was being played through several amplifiers at the wrong speed, giving everything a woozy, underwater feel. After a few seconds, my eyes adjusted and I began to get my bearings. There were objects descending from the ceiling, coloured shapes. They looked like pieces from a child's mobile, sparkling as they turned through the air.

As I moved deeper into the room I started to make out the far end of it: there was a line of strip lighting running across the middle of the wall, half-obscured by some artificial fog spraying up every few seconds from the floor. I suddenly had the impression of being in a shower facility in a concentration camp, and had an urge to run back out into the main gallery. But I had to find Barchetti first. Did his information relate to me after all? Had he somehow realized who I was?

The floor started to shift gently, like a conveyor belt, adding a layer of nausea to the claustrophobic air: the artist was evidently some sort of sadist. A man wearing a hat moved past me, and I stepped forward to grab him. But he'd already gone.

The music was getting louder and louder, throbbing strangely, and I felt completely lost. I came across several treelike sculptures, their thin branches glowing and twisting around me. I reached into my pocket, hastily unwrapped one of Urquhart's pills and swallowed it whole. I immediately regretted it, as the thing tasted foul, bitter and chalky.

The music intensified, turning atonal: the sound of clocks ticking, crashing cymbals and a bass cello seemingly scraped at random. And then I saw him, just a foot in front of me, his face clearly lit for a moment by one of the fluorescent branches: Barchetti. I lunged forward and grabbed him by the arm.

'*Vattene, idiota! Sciò!*' he snarled, lashing out at me with his arms. There was a flash of light and I realized he had a knife. I leapt away and sensed the blade pierce the cloth of my jacket, but he'd missed *me* and I leaned forward again, kicking out towards his legs. I made contact with bone and he fell to the ground, cursing. The knife fell from his hands and I watched it skitter across the floor, the blade catching the light from the mobiles hanging from the ceiling. I immediately knelt down and grabbed it. He managed to get a foot under me and aimed it at my solar plexus and I was pushed back against a wall, winded.

But I had the knife.

There was more movement around us now: people were starting to become restless, perhaps wondering what the disturbance was. Through the speakers, a gospel choir had begun competing with the underwater whale music, and it was becoming louder by the moment. Barchetti leapt on top of me and started trying to scratch at my eyes and throat. My instinct was to use the knife on him, but I needed to get him away from here, alive. I tried to fend him away, but he was surprisingly heavy for such a small man. He was now sitting on my upper chest, restricting my breathing. The music was almost deafening, and I willed my mind to block it out. I reached out and managed to grab hold of Barchetti's shirt, and then pulled him towards me with all the force I could muster. It shifted him forward a little, but it wasn't enough and I could feel my lungs reaching their limit, so in desperation I threw my other arm up to his throat and squeezed it. He let out a scream and tried to bite me, but my chest was burning up and he didn't seem to be aware that I needed him to get off me, until there was no choice and I squeezed and squeezed and then his head jerked forward and his muscles slackened and I could roll him off me and, finally, breathe. I felt for his carotid and checked his pulse: nothing. The music took another unexpected turn, the woozy whale sounds switching to a jumpy jive, and I stood and reeled towards a sliver of light, my throat dry and my chest thumping and my hands wet.

I pushed the curtain aside and came into the adjoining room. I had to stop for a moment to gather myself, and someone came out right behind me, knocking my shoulder.

'*Esilarante, no?*'

I nodded dumbly, and then moved away, heading towards the exit.

IX

I walked down the stairs and onto the street, gulping fresh air into my lungs. Behind me I heard the muffled sound of screaming – someone must have stumbled over Barchetti's body. I looked down and my heart froze. The pavement was covered in spots of blood. I glanced back toward the entrance of the museum and saw a trail of it leading from the doors straight to my feet.

Panicking, I started running, but when I looked down again the blood had vanished: there were just a few small brown stones on the pavement. Was it a return of my Nigerian hallucinations? I slowed down again and reached into my pocket for another of Urquhart's pills. No. Leave them.

I picked up the pace again, and as I did I caught sight of a tall, slender figure striding up a flight of steps into a park on the opposite side of the road. Something about the way he was moving made me look at him again. He was wearing a dove-grey three-piece suit and pointed suede shoes, also grey – all rather well made. And he was taking something from his pocket and placing it in his mouth.

I hadn't seen Pyotr in daylight, but I knew instantly that it was him. My body felt as if it had been given a gigantic jolt. Had he seen me kill Barchetti? No, I thought. More than likely he had hung back in one of the adjoining rooms, watching, just to make sure I turned up for the meet. And when he had seen me coming out of the dark room, the installation or whatever the hell it had been, he had quickly made his escape. Not quite quickly enough, though . . .

I stopped for a few seconds to take some deep breaths and to let him get ahead: I didn't want him to see me. Interesting that he had come, I thought, rather than sending a lackey. Either it really was important or he didn't trust anyone in his team enough to handle it, or both. My God, I wished it had been his neck I'd wrung instead of Barchetti's. If it hadn't been for him I wouldn't be here at all – and what a damn fool I'd been for turning up on his say-so. I'd bought into the idea that he was some sort of master-spy pulling all the strings, but he was just a pathetic bloody amateur. Something I'd said back there had spooked Barchetti out of his skull, so much so that he had fled from me.

Well, enough was enough. I checked my watch. It was quarter past ten: I was due to debrief with him in the Borghese Gardens in an hour and three-quarters. So where was the bastard going now, then? I decided to find out.

It was time to rattle the cage.

*

I doubled back and made to cross the street, but the traffic seemed particularly chaotic on this stretch, and with a start I realized why – several police cars were trying to make their way down it, but were struggling against the flow. As their sirens grew louder, I started crossing and made it to the foot of the stairs I had seen Pyotr take – he had now disappeared over the top. I had to get as far away from the museum as possible, and I didn't want to lose him.

I walked briskly up the stairs, passed between a couple of fountains and finally saw Pyotr twenty or thirty yards ahead, his hands thrust into the pockets of his trousers. I breathed out and fixed my eyes on the top of his head as he wove among the pedestrians enjoying a stroll in the Borghese Gardens. He suddenly decided to cross the street, and as he did he glanced over his shoulder, and I

ducked into the midst of a group of American tourists, frightening
an elderly lady with a blue rinse.

'*Scusi*,' I said, and her anger softened at the manners of the
charming local.

I manoeuvred my way through the group in order to catch sight
of Pyotr again. He was striding ahead, more confidently now: he
hadn't seen me. I began walking a little faster, making sure to keep
several pedestrians between us in case he made any more sudden
movements. But I didn't think he was going to. He'd forgotten his
training, and had arrogantly presumed he wasn't being followed.
The thought stung me, and I suddenly remembered Severn – could
he have been at the museum as well? I stopped and looked around
me, more carefully than Pyotr had done. Tourists, businessmen,
students . . . I couldn't see Severn or anyone else who looked like
a potential tail, but that didn't mean a lot.

I had started sweating again, because I realized I was stumbling
into traps without thinking first, letting my anger guide me. I
wanted to follow Pyotr – but only if I was not being followed myself.
There are several ways to spot a tail, but I didn't have the time for
them: if I loitered somewhere and waited to see who came looking,
for example, I'd risk losing Pyotr.

I decided to take the chance that I was alone. If Severn were following
me, I could always tell him I had seen Pyotr in the museum and felt
that he might have been responsible for . . . Yes. Of course! Pin Barchetti's
death on Pyotr. It was perfect. I started after Pyotr again.

He was still walking straight ahead, down Viale Folke Bernadotte.
I had to pray he was headed somewhere nearby, because if he got
on a bus or tram I was done for. There was no way I would be able
to hide from him in such a small space. And if he hailed a cab, the
whole thing was off. Luckily, so far it looked like it was going to
be a walk away – he was still striding along purposefully.

He reached a roundabout at a grotto and I squinted to see which
turning he would take. A bus tore past me just as he rounded the

grotto and I lost sight of him for a moment. But then the bus was gone and I saw that he had taken a right into Viale Giorgio Washington and my pulse quickened – he was heading for Piazzale Flaminio, where there was a tram stop.

I walked a little faster, down a cobbled footpath shaded by over-hanging trees, past wooden benches on which young lovers were draped over one another. As I came into the crowded square, I saw that a couple of trams were already waiting at the stop. But Pyotr didn't even glance at them. It seemed he was walking to the end of the street, and I wondered if he was looking for a bar to find a telephone.

A tram at the front of the queue moved off, blocking my view of him again, and I leapt into the street and in front of a taxi so I could take up position on the pavement behind him on the other side of the road. But he had gone. I looked around frantically, but as I made it to the pavement I saw the outline of the back of his head and shoulders in the rear of the tram pulling out.

Damn. Damn, damn, damn.

I raced up to the next tram waiting, which was on the same line, and climbed aboard, paying the driver the fare and asking him when he was going to leave. Not for a few minutes, *signore*. I tried to calm myself and looked at the situation again. On the plus side, I knew where Pyotr was, and he could only go at a certain pace, on certain tracks. And I was still following him, from a vantage he couldn't see. But unless we left very soon, I wouldn't be able to see where he got off. What were my options: bribe the conductor to depart earlier? I dismissed it: he would be more likely to kick up a fuss or report me, and we'd probably end up leaving even later and I'd have lost Pyotr. I'd just have to hope I'd be able to see him when he got off.

I took a seat up front and kept my eyes glued to the tram ahead. After a couple of minutes, it slowed for a stop. An elderly lady disembarked, helped by a younger man. No Pyotr. It started back up again, veering in the direction of the river.

The driver of my tram started her up and we began following in leisurely pursuit. Soon we swerved around the corner, skirting the parked cars, and came to the same stop. A young mother tried to bring her baby carriage down the aisle, and berated a long-haired boy in jeans and an embroidered shirt who was standing in the way. Their argument became more heated, and the young man called the woman '*Fascista*'. I moved out of the way to avoid them, but they were blocking my view of Pyotr's tram, which was now slowing for the next stop.

There! He was getting off. I pulled the cord.

'*Scusi!*' I cried, and leapt out of the doors as they were closing.

He was walking at a normal pace down the street, and I followed him through a cluster of parked motorbikes and Vespas, past fruit stalls and newspaper stands and shuttered restaurants. A *gattara* glared at me as I passed her feeding crumbs to an emaciated tabby. We were now on the outskirts of Trastevere, a once very down-at-heel neighbourhood that was becoming increasingly visited by tourists. A man in a leather jacket and a cap approached me. '*Tabacchi,*' he said, as though it were a greeting. Black-market cigarettes sold for about two-thirds of the usual price here, and I was running low – but now wasn't the time. I shook my head and carried on walking. Where the hell had Pyotr gone? I looked around frantically, and finally spied him. He was at the far end of the street: he had stopped at the entrance to a restored medieval house. A block of flats now, it seemed. And he was letting himself in with a key. So he had gone home – perhaps to signal Moscow that I had completed the job?

It was approaching eleven now, so he would have to leave again reasonably soon if he wanted to make our appointment in the Borghese Gardens at noon. There was a bar across the street and I walked into it. Roy Orbison was wailing from a jukebox in the corner, and two old men in cardigans and twill trousers sipped cloudy aperitifs as they studied a wooden chessboard with great solemnity. The owner, moustachioed and stout, stood behind a long mahogany-effect bar polishing glasses with a cloth. Posters advertised Cinzano and proclaimed support for a local football team. There was no sign of Severn or anyone else.

I ordered a sandwich and an orange juice. I could have done with a cold beer, but this was no time for alcohol, and the sugar in the juice would give me energy. I found a table from which I could watch the front door of the block of flats through the reflection of a mirror, and waited for my quarry to reappear.

He emerged, looking a little flustered, twenty-three minutes later. He was wearing a different suit and his hair was wet – had he just gone home for a clean-up then? Perhaps the proximity to murder had made him squeamish.

He walked back up the street in the direction of the tram stop, presumably to head off to his appointment with me. I waited a few minutes to make sure he wouldn't double back, and then headed into the building.

*

I rang the doorbell and waited. Through an iron grate I watched as a stout old woman in black shuffled out of a back room towards me. She pressed her face to the grate and glared at me with undisguised suspicion.

'I am a plain-clothes officer of the Servizio Informazioni Difesa,' I said. 'We are currently engaged in an important investigation into a man who has just left this building.'

I spoke with a pronounced Milanese accent, because it is much harder to convince someone you come from the same part of the country as they. She asked me for my papers, and I patiently explained that it was not customary for plain-clothes officers to carry identification, for obvious reasons, but if she chose to call Marco Zimotti, the chief of the SID, at headquarters, he would be able to vouch for me. I gave her an invented number and smiled sweetly, praying she wouldn't call the bluff.

She looked me over for a few moments more, and then reached into the folds of her capacious dress and took out some keys. 'That will not be necessary,' she said, unlocking the door and letting me into the cool, dark vestibule. 'How can I help you, *signore*?'

I described Pyotr and she nodded. The Swiss gentleman, Pierre Valougny. I told her that was an alias and that he was, in fact, a Communist agent, and after her eyes had widened and she had howled a bit, she spat over her shoulder and said she had known there was something wrong with him all along. I nodded soberly and asked her to show me his rooms, and she took me up a very creaky lift and along a dank corridor.

There was a large, well-furnished living room, with a window looking out onto the street and a telephone – he must have lived here a while to have arranged the connection, especially in this neighbourhood.

'Three years,' said the landlady. 'Always paid the rent on time, and kept to himself. But I never liked him. I should have known. Please don't tell anyone of our misfortune here. Was he planning a coup?'

I told her that was state business and asked her to leave. Once she'd gone, I got to work: I wouldn't have too long before he realized I wasn't coming to the meet and started heading back.

I began by just walking around the place, trying to get a feel for who I was dealing with. He'd done well, either through Moscow's funding or his own business acumen, or a combination of the two. There were some hideous modern art paintings on the wall, but they were originals, and a few of the names were familiar. A desk by the window was home to an Olivetti typewriter and stacks of books – these were mostly hardbacks and, again, the subject was modern art. What was his cover, I wondered. Art dealer? That would bring him into contact with Arte come Terrore.

After rummaging around for a couple of minutes, I spotted a ladder next to one of the bookcases. Looking at the ceiling, I saw there was an attic. I pulled out the ladder and climbed up, pushing open the door.

I tugged a piece of string, and a naked bulb lit a small room containing a wing-backed leather chair and a rusty-looking filing cabinet. There was a mousetrap by the wall, loaded with a small triangle of cheese.

The filing cabinet was unlocked. The top drawer was filled with magazines, and I picked out a few. The first that came to hand was called *La Classe* and was dated today: the headline read 'LOTTA DI CLASSE PER LA RIVOLUZIONE': 'Class struggle for the revolution'. The rest of the pile contained other underground magazines, with names like *Carte Segrete*. Interesting. And slightly odd. Pyotr didn't strike me as a flower child, in or out of cover, so what the hell was he doing with these in his flat? I opened the next drawer down. More papers, but these were mostly invitations to showings at local art galleries: La Salita, Dell'Ariete. But there were also magazines here, and one of them, I saw, was called *Transizione*. Even more interesting – but not really enough to hang anyone for.

I turned to the bottom drawer and jerked it open. The radio transmitter stared up at me.

Bingo.

It was a simple short-wave set with a high-speed transmission converter, the kind you could buy from most electronics outfitters. He was presumably using it to communicate with the Station in the embassy here – they, in turn, would send out messages based on his information via telegraph or diplomatic bag to Moscow. Hidden behind the set was a Praktina camera and several neatly bundled wads of money: *lire* and dollars. I considered pocketing the lot – it would certainly be satisfying – but decided I would need all the evidence I could get.

As head of Soviet Section, I'd read the reports from Five on the Lonsdale Ring, which they had rounded up in '61. This wasn't quite as damning as the material they had found in the Krogers' flat in Ruislip – everything from cellophane sheets tucked away in a Bible to a microdot reader in a tin of talcum powder – but it was close. A radio transmitter, a camera and significant sums of money all spelled out 'foreign agent' in capital letters. He'd been caught red-handed − or he soon would be . . .

I stopped. There had been a noise. Was that him returning already? I stood very still for a moment, breathing as shallowly as possible, wondering what the hell to do. I wasn't armed, and he'd have his Makarov . . .

Then I saw the mouse, scuttling across the floorboards − the noise had merely been its nails scratching against the wood. The tiny creature paused for a moment, looking up on its hind legs with its snout twitching, before dropping back onto all fours and scurrying forward again.

Snap!

The trap sprung with brutal velocity, catching the mouse at the base of its neck. There was a tiny, almost inaudible squeak and then its eyes froze.

I made my way back downstairs and replaced the ladder next to the bookcase. A bookcase, I now noticed, that was built into the wall. I knelt down and inspected the skirting board. A few inches from the floor there was a sharp line in the board. I pressed the base of my hand against it and pushed. It slid upwards, revealing a small metal knob beneath, rather like a light switch. I flicked it, and the lowest shelf of the bookcase moved a few inches. I pulled it all the way out. Hidden behind it was a small space, inside of which sat a blue and silver cardboard box with the words '*Baci Perugina*' printed on it.

The chocolates had long since been eaten, but in their place was a sheaf of papers bound with an elastic band. The front page was embossed with a red star in a black circle, and a string of reference numbers lay beneath the typed heading: 'НЕЗАВИСИМЫЙ'.

The world around me suddenly hushed, and everything narrowed to the field of my gaze. It was as if a mouse had scuttled its way across my scalp, and that one word had snapped the spring shut. The last time I'd met Sasha I had asked him what my codename was, and he had told me: 'NEZAVISIMYJ', meaning 'independent'.

This was *my* file.

I picked it up and slowly turned to the first page:

```
INDEPENDENT was recruited in the British Zone
of Germany in 1945 - please see Appendix 1
for details of the operation . . .
```

Well, hadn't Sasha been clever? He'd realized I might not listen to his message at Heathrow, so he had given Toadski a copy of my file and told him that if I didn't come in with him he should follow me and hand it over to the local resident wherever I arrived. Presumably the photographs were in here, too? Yes, there they were, in a small plastic pouch beneath the file.

I shook them out and saw that, as well as the pictures with Anna that completed the nasty little honey trap that had brought me into this mess, there were around a dozen surveillance shots that had been taken of me over the years, in London, Istanbul and elsewhere. My anger at not having spotted the tails was somewhat mollified by the fact that I was now sitting in Pyotr's flat looking through their photographs.

I turned back to the file itself. The typeface was raised and glossy, almost like Braille, and the paper thick and crested. The pages were torn in places, with official stamps placed haphazardly over them and the words *Glavnoe Razvedyvatel'noe Upravlenie* everywhere. So I was under the control of the GRU: Sasha hadn't lied about that, at least. There was a long biography that focused mainly on my military service and relationship with Father, and detailed reports of every single meeting I'd attended. There was even a brief essay on my character, dated 12 December 1948, by one Nikolai Pavlovich Vasilyev – presumably Georgi's real name:

```
When meeting with INDEPENDENT, be advised to
choose your words carefully: he has a sharp
tongue and his temper cools slowly, so you
```

will waste valuable time antagonizing him unduly.
Do not make the mistake of trying to become
his friend or sharing your views on the wider
world with him. INDEPENDENT is intensely irritated by anything that he senses as prevari-
cation or skirting around an issue – you would
be much better advised to take a direct approach.
 INDEPENDENT is prone to questioning any statement he regards as unclear or euphemistic. He
is also insistent that he will only give us
information on matters of principle, so every
request for information must be framed in such
a way as to make him believe that it is of
crucial importance, not just to our own efforts
but to the benefit of all humanity. This is,
naturally, sometimes a difficult task . . .

Quite an astute assessment, on the whole. Had I really wanted
everything to be of benefit to humanity? I couldn't really deny it,
absurd as it looked in black and white. Still, Pyotr hadn't taken this
advice to heart: his approach had been direct, all right, but it had
certainly antagonized me, and unduly at that.

I checked my watch again: it had just gone half eleven. He would
be at the gardens soon, and wondering what had happened to me.
I calculated I had at least an hour before he would be back. I read
on, transfixed. There was a bundle of correspondence from early
in my career that made for very curious reading. Skimming through
as fast as I could, it appeared that Moscow had not initially believed
that they had succeeded in recruiting me. They had become
convinced that the Service had *knowingly* let me be recruited, so they
could then use me to pass disinformation over. This suspicion
appeared to stem from one of the earliest reports I had given. In
1949, Georgi had asked me to note down everything I knew about
the Service's efforts to recruit agents in the Soviet Union. As far as

I knew there were no such efforts, and so I had said so. But that hadn't been good enough for one Anatoli Panov, an analyst in the Third Department of the First Directorate:

> No British agents of note have been exposed
> as a result of INDEPENDENT's assistance, although
> he would certainly have access to such infor-
> mation. Are we expected to believe that he and
> others have chosen to fight for our cause, and
> yet the British have failed to recruit a single
> one of our men to theirs? Ours is clearly the
> more desirable ideology, but this is never-
> theless not a plausible assessment. The truth,
> of course, is that INDEPENDENT has come up
> against a piece of information he cannot divulge
> without hindering the British more than they
> would like, and has stubbornly insisted on this
> fatuous line in the hope that we swallow it
> whole. Let us not fall for such a simple trick.
> It proves comprehensively that he is a plant:
> a triple agent.

I read the last line several times, my temple throbbing. It seemed this idiot had been incapable of accepting that I might have been telling the truth. I was even more shocked to see that his report had been counter-signed by Stalin himself, who in the margin had even scribbled 'Исследуйте далее'— 'Investigate further'. It took me several moments to take it in, and I realized my hands were shaking. After the whole rigmarole they had gone through to recruit me, the extraordinary organization and time and resources that must have gone into that operation, after all the meetings in London and the precautions taken, and all the files I had passed over and reports I had written . . . After all of that, Uncle Joe hadn't believed I was a genuine double agent! Flicking forward, it wasn't until November 1951 – over two years later – that they had finally given me the all clear:

```
We are now satisfied that INDEPENDENT is secure
and that no disinformation is being passed to
us. Please renew contact with this highly valu-
able agent.
```

Thinking back, I realized that this coincided with Sasha's arrival in London. After several frustrating years of intermittent contact, I finally had a regular handler again, and he had pumped me for information in a way Georgi had never done. But, it seemed, to very little purpose. I searched in vain for reports on the operations I had betrayed at that time. It looked like Sasha had decided not to pass any of it on. But why on earth not, if I had been cleared? One reason immediately sprung to mind. Even in the Service, information that inconveniently contradicted a widely held theory – especially if it were also held by a Head of Section – was sometimes skimmed over or quietly dropped for fear of the messenger being shot. It looked like that might literally have been the case for Georgi: a brief note at the top of a file from 1949 explained that he had been classified as an 'undesirable'. He had been recalled and sent to the gulags, of course – perhaps Sasha didn't want to make the same mistake.

I didn't know whether to laugh or cry. So it had all been for nought, or as near as dammit. My recruitment and handling hadn't been some grand game of chess, but a muddle of crossed wires, paranoia and office politics. I'd spent twenty-four years deceiving everyone around me, but it seemed that for several years the men I had thought I was serving hadn't even been given the information I had obtained, let alone used it.

I straightened up. Did it matter, ultimately, that they had failed to take advantage of the material? Did I really need a tally of my own treachery, a count of the dead men? No. I had done it. I was a traitor, no matter what the cost had been.

But a terrifying thought suddenly occurred to me. The analyst Panov would have vanished from the scene long ago, of course, no doubt sent to the gulags himself for not having tied his shoelaces the right way. But his way of thinking had been accepted for two years, and clearly something of it had survived because it looked like much of the information I'd handed over subsequently still hadn't been passed up the ladder. What sort of an organization could have allowed that to happen? What if there was a new Panov in Moscow, or a group of them even, and they had decided that my actions in Nigeria proved I'd been a triple agent all along? After all, they had lost two long-serving agents at my hand. Could *that* be why I had been targeted? Yes, of course it bloody could.

I looked at my watch again. I'd been in here nearly an hour already, and Pyotr would soon be boarding a tram on his way back. I took the file and chocolate box and walked over to the desk by the window. There was an old Olivetti typewriter on top of it. I lifted the cover, took a sheet of paper from the drawer and rolled it into the machine. I began typing.

A couple of minutes later I scrolled the paper out, folded it, and placed it in my jacket pocket. I walked back to the bookcase and replaced the chocolate box, then glanced around the flat again, checking that everything was in order, picked my file from the desk, turned off the lights and quietly closed the door behind me.

*

I took the lift back down and thanked the landlady for her assistance. I warned her that I might return with some of my colleagues, but that whatever she did she should give no signal to Signor Valougny that he was under suspicion. She promised heartily to uphold her patriotic duty.

I went back into the bar across the street and asked for the lavatory. The barman pointed down a flight of rickety stairs. Once there, I locked the door and tore each page of my file into strips before feeding it into the bowl. Then I flushed it all away. There would be copies in Moscow, of course, but this would do for the time being. And there was a strange sense of satisfaction in watching the words dissolve and disappear. A plan of action had started to form in my mind. I went over all the scenarios I thought it could lead to, and decided that, while it was certainly a risk, it was one worth taking. Or perhaps I simply no longer cared.

I went upstairs again and asked if I could use the telephone. The barman looked at me, and nodded his head imperceptibly to the left. I gave him 100 *lire*, received two tokens and ten *lire* in change, and walked over to the machine. Severn picked up on the first ring.

'Where the hell are you? You've been gone over three hours, and Zimotti just called to say a body has been discovered in the museum—'

'It's Barchetti,' I said. 'But I've got him. I've got the bastard . . .'

'Slow down. Got who?'

'The man who arranged Farraday's assassination. The head of Arte come Terrore. Barchetti was scared at the meet, insisted I follow him into a dark room at the end of the gallery. But by the time I got in there, someone had already strangled him.'

There was a short silence, and I imagined Severn's face turning paler.

'Did you manage to get anything from him at all? What about his European lead?'

'Nothing. But I saw this chap leaving the museum in a hurry and he looked fishy, so I trailed him and he came running back to a flat in Trastevere. I waited until he left, and broke in. It's him,' I said. 'He's our man. Call Zimotti and tell him to bring a few of his men around to Viale Trastevere as fast as he can. Then jump in your car and come here yourself. I'm in a bar called' – I picked up a menu from the top of the telephone set – '*La Maddalena*, about halfway up the street. I'll tell you about it when you get here.'

X

'I demand to see a lawyer.'

Zimotti offered him an insincere smile. 'I'm afraid we can't extend you that right, *signore*.'

Pyotr glared back with contempt. I didn't blame him: his flat was suddenly looking rather cramped.

Severn had arrived in his race car fifteen minutes after my call, accompanied by his wife. Hot on their heels had been Zimotti, who had arrived with a couple of black Lancias containing two of his men, nasty-looking brutes in leather jackets and jeans. I had explained the situation in the back of the bar and shown them the note: Severn and Zimotti had glanced at each other in grim acknowledgement. Almost as if on cue, Pyotr had stepped off the tram, walked up the street and unlocked his front door.

And we'd pounced. The landlady had fretted over what the neighbours would think, but one of Zimotti's men had taken her to one side and explained that she was performing a great service for the republic, and her massive chest had risen with pride at the thought and she had waved us through, almost in tears. Pyotr had been brewing himself a cup of coffee when we'd broken the door down. He'd protested, of course, strenuously and in fluent Italian, but there wasn't a lot he could do about it: he didn't have diplomatic cover.

I looked over at Severn, who was standing by the door watching Zimotti at work. 'Let's get him,' was all he had said in the bar. Now he looked equally calm, but his jaw was clenched tight and he was drumming his fingers against his thighs. He sensed my gaze and looked across at me, then smiled unconvincingly. It sent a shiver through me. Woe betide anyone who got on the wrong side of Severn. For a moment, I almost felt sorry for Pyotr.

Almost.

Sarah Severn was standing next to her husband, smoking her third cigarette since we'd arrived. I wished to God Severn hadn't brought her along. She was a radio officer; there was no need for her to see any of this. She also seemed to be under the illusion that I'd been some sort of a hero in London, and I didn't like having to go through this grotesque charade in front of her. But go through it I would, of course.

We'd only been here a few minutes, but the flat was already halfway to a shambles. Zimotti's men had removed the drawers of the desk and shaken the contents onto the carpet, and they were now attacking the chairs, removing the cushions and tearing off the covers. Pyotr began objecting again and Zimotti pulled him up short, leaning over him and yelling at him to sit down. Pyotr glanced at the heavies and decided to do so.

'Will someone please tell me what is happening here?' he said, pouting like a child.

Zimotti smiled. '*Va bene*. We are representatives of the Servizio Informazioni Difesa, and we are here because we suspect that you are engaged in activities that may be harmful to the interests of Italy, Great Britain and its allies.'

'Only them?' said Pyotr with a sneer.

Zimotti ignored it. 'Specifically, we suspect that you are involved in terrorist activity, or are in contact with people who are. I am now going to hand you over to this man,' – he nodded at me – 'who is a very senior member of British intelligence. He has some questions to put to you.'

I stepped forward.

'Hello. My name is Paul Dark. Could you tell me yours, please?'

He didn't answer, just glared dully at me.

'The quicker you cooperate,' I said, 'the quicker we are going to get through this. If you are not involved in the way we think you are, we will soon clear this up and leave you in peace. You can have that coffee you were looking forward to.'

I tried to keep the tone relatively light, and glanced at Zimotti several times while I was talking. I wanted to hook Pyotr into believing that the Italians had somehow caught onto him but that I had engineered my way into handling the situation and was going to extricate him from it. That I was his friend, essentially.

There were a few seconds of silence, and then:

'Pierre Valougny.'

Hooked.

'Nationality?'

'Swiss.'

'Occupation?'

'I run a small printing company between here and Geneva.'

Someone had opened a window to let the air in and I walked over to it. The noise of the traffic drifted up. I strained to make out other sounds: birdsong, a dog barking, a fountain trickling in the *piazza*. I turned back to Pyotr.

'Edoardo Barchetti,' I said. 'Recognize the name?'

'No. I have absolutely no idea what any of this is—'

'He contacted us recently, concerning a small group he was a member of here: Arte come Terrore.'

No reaction, but there was no reason for there to be, yet.

'I say "was". A couple of days ago we learned that members of this group were planning a series of attacks in Europe. I went to meet him a few hours ago at the modern art museum to find out more, but I didn't get very far. Care to guess why?'

His nose twitched, but his eyes were glued to me. He didn't know where I was heading, but his instincts were telling him it wasn't the right way.

'Because by the time I reached him, Edoardo Barchetti was dead. However, I saw *you* leaving the museum in a hurry, so I followed you here. I'd like to know why you killed him.'

I didn't like myself for saying the last part, but in a way it was true. He had forced me into it, and now I was going to make him pay the price.

'I am a printer,' he said. 'My company prints art magazines. I was interested in the exhibition—'

'Is that an attic you have?' I said, glancing upwards. He made to stand up and I stepped forward and pushed him back down into the chair. I walked over to the bookcase and pulled out the ladder. Zimotti nodded at one of his men and he began climbing up.

I looked back at Pyotr. He was starting to realize the situation. The Italians hadn't caught onto him; I had framed him. His anger was rising and he was desperately trying to keep a lid on it. He was furious with himself for letting me get the upper hand on him. He'd wanted to play the big man with the compromised agent, and I'd responded by doing the unthinkable and he hadn't seen it coming. He was holding up well, considering, but I knew that he would go to the ends of the earth to pay me back if I didn't manage to pull this off. It was him or me now, and if he'd had no problem in blowing my cover earlier, he would now be itching to do it.

There was a noise from upstairs, and I knew the Italian had found the transmitter. A couple of minutes later and it was sitting on the desk, along with the magazines and gallery invitations. Zimotti and Severn both walked over and peered at the untidy-looking heap. Severn started leafing through the notes, his face set.

'How do you explain these items?' I said to Pyotr.

'The money is for emergencies – we Swiss are prudent people, and I always keep some at home, in all currencies.' He smiled sweetly, almost in recognition of his cleverness.

'And the transmitter?'

'I have a passion for amateur radio.'

'Why is it hidden in your attic?'

'My landlady does not like the idea – and it gets much better reception up there. It is not, as far as I am aware, a crime.'

'This is a spy transmitter, Signor Valougny, and you are using it to communicate with your colleagues in the Soviet embassy. And this,' – I picked up the Praktina – 'is a spy camera, used for copying documents.'

'I don't see why you use that term. I bought it in a shop in town, and I often use it to photograph pictures from my books here to take to the office with me. Books are unwieldy.'

It was weak, but then he wasn't playing to us. He was playing to a jury. We had to be a lot more solid than this to convict him; if we weren't, he wouldn't confess. He was skating on thin ice – I had to cut the ice away from his feet and make sure he fell in.

'You say you print art magazines.' I picked up the copy of *La Classe* and placed it on the table. 'But this is a Communist magazine, calling for class struggle – for revolution, in fact.'

'We print lots of different magazines. We are not responsible for the content. You must take that up with the editors and writers.'

Printer as a cover was a new one to me, but I could see the benefits. He could hover around the edge of the underground movement, but if pressed by the authorities – as now – could plausibly distance himself.

I pointed to a copy of *Transizione*.

'Did you also print this?'

He peered at it, then nodded.

'This is the same magazine that published a series of articles last year putting forward the case for violent acts against the state.'

'Yes, I read those articles. They were purely theoretical, of course. They weren't intended—'

'We don't think so. We believe that they constituted a kind of manifesto, in fact, and that they led to the foundation of Arte come Terrore. What do you know about the assassination of the head of British intelligence in London yesterday?'

'The assassination of who? I have no knowledge of this whatsoever. I demand that you leave my home at once. I am a respectable businessman, and I do not take kindly to this treatment.'

Enough cat-and-mouse. It was time to close in for the kill.

'All of this,' I said, gesturing at the table, 'is circumstantial. I
found this piece of paper on Barchetti.' I took it out of my pocket
and read it to him. It was only a few lines in Italian, but I'd packed
it with enough to damn him to hell and back:

We feel that the committee is now ready to
step up its actions, and recommend the targeting
of senior members of Western intelligence agencies. Details will soon follow of a public
event in Britain. Please choose an operative
for this task from among your number. We will
provide the necessary weaponry once they have
entered the country. Further operations in Italy,
France and elsewhere are in advanced stages
of planning.

I threw the letter onto the table and placed a hand on the Olivetti.

'How much do you want to bet that the typeface matches the
one produced by this machine?'

Pyotr licked his lips anxiously. Perhaps he was missing his chocolates. He was sweating now, and his face seemed to be turning an
ash-grey. It was doubly insulting to him, because only the sloppiest
of agents would have handed a contact such a note, in the clear and
typed up on their own machine. But he could hardly point that out.

'I did not write this,' he said coldly. 'I have never seen it before.'

I pressed it with my finger. 'Is this why you killed Barchetti? Did
you realize he was an infiltrator? Or was he perhaps blackmailing
you, threatening to tell someone about your plans?' I leaned on
the word 'blackmailing' and was pleased to see him flinch at it.
'Tell me!'

'This is an amusing game, Mister . . .'

'Dark.'

'An amusing game, Mister Dark. But how far are you prepared to take it?'

'All the way,' I said. 'I have no choice.'

He looked up at me sharply. 'What do you mean?'

I smiled – he thought I'd slipped up. 'A sniper killed the head of our agency in front of my eyes in London yesterday,' I said. 'It appears they have not finished their work. I can't let it go. I can't let you go until you tell us what you know.'

'So you're a patriot, is that it? You don't strike me as the type.' He glanced down at the letter disdainfully. 'I have never seen this letter before in my life.'

'Then why was it in Barchetti's—'

'Because you *planted* it there, Mister Dark!' His cheeks were burning now. 'You planted it there because you want to prove to your colleagues that I had something to do with the death of Mister Farraday in London.'

Trapped! Severn sprung forward. 'So you *do* know about—'

'I know because Mister Dark here told me,' said Pyotr, and I shook for a moment, realizing that he had decided to go all the way, dragging us through the whole charade. Well, so be it. I had a whole heap of evidence against him, and all he had against me was his say-so. 'Mister Dark told me when I met him outside the British embassy yesterday evening,' he said, his voice rising in pitch, 'because Mister Dark is a Soviet agent, and I am his contact here.'

There was silence for a moment.

'Are you confessing to being a Soviet spy, Mister Valougny?' I said.

He laughed derisively. 'No. I am confessing that you and I both are.'

Severn took a few steps closer. 'Do you have any evidence of that?' he asked, but I cut him off before he could go any further.

'Please, Charles,' I said. 'Let me handle this. It's a desperate gambit,

Mister Valougny, but I'm afraid it won't work. All you have to do is tell us what it is that Arte come Terrore is planning next, and we can take it from there. Perhaps we can make some sort of a deal if you were to work for us from now on. But please show my colleagues and me a little more respect. Throwing around melodramatic accusations is an easy game to play, but you're not convincing anyone and you're not going to disrupt this investigation.'

Pyotr smiled, but it was the grim smile of a man who knew he was defeated. Oh, he would be cursing the day he met me for a long time. It served him right. Don't blackmail someone unless you are very certain of your ground – and can lose a tail.

'Let's take him out of here,' said Zimotti, who was pacing around by the door. 'We need some time to crack this nut and this isn't the place for it.'

'What do you suggest?' I said.

'We have better facilities in town,' said Zimotti. 'Let's get this bastard into an interviewing room.'

*

We went outside and bundled into the cars. The Severns took the Alfa Romeo, Zimotti's men took Pyotr in one of the Lancias and I went with Zimotti in his own car. He didn't say anything as he drove through the early afternoon traffic, his face staring ahead grimly. I reviewed the situation. It had gone well, all things considered. Pyotr had thrown out the counter accusation, as I had expected he might when cornered, but the timing was a little awkward: I hadn't bargained on our being split up like this. No doubt he was now telling the others in the car behind that I had been recruited in Germany or some such thing. No matter – I'd disposed of all the evidence, and I doubted they would let him say very much: Zimotti's men looked like pretty tough customers. I would have to tread very carefully now to make sure none of the mud he flung stuck to me, but if I applied more pressure on him, and quickly, I reckoned I would be in a strong position . . .

We took a sudden lurch to the left, and I caught a glimpse out of the window. Zimotti had taken a minor road, and it seemed we were heading away from the city centre.

'Where are we going?' I said, but as I turned I felt a sting in my upper thigh and saw him removing the needle. I started calling out, but it was no use, because my world was fading to black and all I could think was: *I'm finished.*

XI

I came back to consciousness slowly and realized I was lying on the floor. After a few seconds, I remembered what had happened.

I did a quick inventory of my status. I was still in my suit, but my belt, shoes and socks had been taken, and my pockets emptied. Physically I seemed to be fine, apart from a small mark on my thigh from the hypodermic and some pain at the base of my neck and along my spine, no doubt due to having slept on the floor. I was drowsy, but not overly so: probably just a simple sedative, then. Mentally, nothing was damaged — yet.

The room was bare: nothing in it at all, not even a bed or a bucket. It was about fifteen feet across and ten wide. The floor and walls were white and appeared to be made from some sort of plastic material, smooth to the touch. A sliver of light crept in through a tiny window high in the ceiling. Was it dusk or dawn? My last meal had been the sandwich and juice in the bar in Trastevere, which suggested it was at least the next day, as my stomach was beginning to gnaw at me and my throat was very dry. What the hell was going on? And where the hell had they brought me?

I didn't have to wait long for answers. Within a few minutes, fluorescent panels in the ceiling flickered on and began to brighten, until it became almost painful to the eyes. A door opened in one of the walls and through it walked Zimotti . . . and Severn. Both of them were wearing dark glasses with mirrored lenses, and Zimotti was now in a tailored midnight-blue uniform and cap. He was head of *military* intelligence, I remembered. They must have brought me to a base or barracks.

A deeply tanned man with a sharp nose followed – I recognized him as one of Zimotti's men from the flat. He was also wearing dark glasses, and camouflage fatigues instead of the jacket and jeans he'd been in earlier. He carried a couple of rather tatty-looking wooden chairs into the centre of the room, planted them down, then swivelled and marched to one of the walls, where he took up station.

Zimotti and Severn seated themselves and looked down at me. Their entrance so soon after I had woken seemed unlikely to be coincidence, but how were they watching me? The room was as smooth and featureless as it was possible to be – I couldn't even make out the edges of the door they had come through – but presumably there were film cameras somewhere, monitoring every movement I made.

I looked up, and was shocked to see a frightened, cowering animal reflected in the lenses of their glasses. I struggled to my feet and started shouting at them, telling them they'd made a dreadful mistake, that I was going to have Severn dismissed, that if they wanted to believe a Soviet agent over the Deputy Chief of the Service they were out of their minds, and so on.

'Save it for someone else,' Severn said once I'd done. 'We know you're a double.'

It wasn't so much the words that scared me as the way in which they'd been said. The tone was of calm contempt, and there hadn't been a fraction of hesitation: he was dead certain. Think. The glance between him and Zimotti when I'd shown them the typewritten note in the bar . . . It hadn't been acknowledgement that Pyotr was guilty, but confirmation of *my* guilt. But how could they be so sure about it? It must have been something I'd done, because if the Service had known I was a double before now they wouldn't have let me get on a plane – they would have interrogated me back in London. So somehow I had just told them I was a double – but how? Simply because I had tried to frame Pyotr for Farraday's death? Yes, that must be it. They knew beyond a shadow of a doubt that he hadn't been responsible for it because . . .

Christ.

Of course.

'You killed Farraday,' I said to Severn.

His eyes didn't flicker.

'Not deliberately,' he said. 'You were our target.'

I shivered. If they had suspected me of being a double, they hadn't waited for confirmation of it – they had simply arranged my assassination anyway. But why would they . . . ?

Leave it for the moment. Now you need to fight back, before it's too late.

'I planted the evidence on the Russian,' I said. 'I admit that much. But that doesn't make me a double.'

'Why do it, then?'

'Because I wanted the glory, of course. Christ, you should see how they're acting back in London. Haggard sent me out here to sort everything out. I couldn't very well go back and tell him that not only had I failed to make proper contact with Barchetti but that he'd been *killed*. I saw this chap hanging around the gallery and he got careless, so I followed him. And I thought, well . . . it would be a good opportunity. I know how that must sound, but—'

'Pathetic is how it sounds,' said Severn, and my hopes lifted. Precisely what I'd hoped he would think of me. 'So, the great Paul Dark is just a little fraud. Tell me, what other triumphs of yours have you created this way? How about that business in Nigeria – was all that bravado and planted evidence, too?'

'I saved the Prime Minister, for God's sake – there were witnesses to it!'

'I don't believe him,' said Zimotti, and my hopes sank again. 'It was too calculated, too fast. He knew this Soviet, and I think the man was his controller.'

Evenly matched. Could I convince one of them to go the other way? Zimotti looked firm, but perhaps I could play Severn off against him?

'Let's find out,' said Severn, and then uttered three words that I knew meant I would never be able to change anyone's mind again. 'Let's break him.'

*

They left, taking the chairs with them. The chairs had been brought in from the garden, I thought, remembering Toadski's warning in Heathrow to keep a low profile. Well, I hadn't listened, and here I was.

The lights began to flicker, then dim, before extinguishing completely. There was a thin buzzing sound above me as a panel moved across and covered the tiny window. I was in complete darkness. I stepped forward until I reached the wall opposite – the door had to be somewhere here. I felt along the surface, but couldn't find it. It was completely flush. I made my way around the room, frantically running my hands across every inch of the walls I could reach. Finally, I came across the thinnest of seams – was *this* where they had come through? It must be. But there was nothing else there: no hinge, no handle, just the shallowest of grooves. I tried to dig into it with my hands, but I couldn't even get my nails in.

After several minutes searching the rest of the cell in vain for anything to get a handle on, I fell back onto the floor, exhausted from the effort. As I did, the lights flickered back on again. Had it just been a power cut? They kept flickering, and I realized that it was deliberate. The cell itself was an instrument of torture, a state-of-the-art environment that could be used to manipulate the occupant: me. I moved to one of the corners and seated myself as comfortably as I could, waiting for whatever they would throw at me next.

It came about ten minutes later. A blast of music suddenly erupted from hidden speakers in the ceiling. The song was vaguely familiar, the singer wailing about the world being on the eve of

destruction — a little joke on Severn's part? The song became louder
as it went on, until eventually I had to place my hands over my
ears to try to muffle it. Then, just as suddenly as it had arrived, it
was cut off. I realized I was breathing hard, and my heart rate had
shot up.

Over the next few hours they continued with this game, suddenly
introducing the song — always the same song — at a very loud
volume, only to cut it off again abruptly. Sometimes the song lasted
several minutes, sometimes just a few seconds. The result was that
the music became indistinguishable noise to me, and I began to fear
its return.

I knew they were trying to soften me up and that if I succumbed
now I would never be able to get back, so I put all my effort into
resisting, keeping my mind busy. I certainly had a lot to think
about. The one question nagging at me above all was: why? Why
had they tried to kill me? I'd cleared myself of being a traitor, and
Osborne had even approved my promotion . . . But no, that must
all have been for show, I realized, a front they had put on to lull
me into complacency while they made arrangements for a sniper
to take me out. They had evidently decided at some point that,
traitor or not, they didn't want to take their chances with me. I
could still expose the plot they'd cooked up in Nigeria, and that
alone was reason enough to have me swept out of sight.

They must have planned some of it while I'd still been in isolation at the hospital recovering from the fever. Where would they
have met, I wondered. The conference room on the third floor?
The basement bar? No, both were too conspicuous. Not everyone
could have been in on such a plot, and they'd have wanted to keep
any meetings not just discreet, but completely off the radar. So
they'd probably met at one of their homes after work — perhaps
even Farraday's. That would have been ironic. But no, Farraday
couldn't have been part of it, I realized, or he wouldn't have been
stupid enough to stand in front of me in St Paul's. Then again, he
hadn't been the brightest of men. But no, I reckoned Osborne was

the brains behind it, in which case his house in Eaton Square would have been their base. I could just picture the scene: Osborne, Innes, Dawes, perhaps Smale . . . the whole clutch of them drinking Scotch and smoking cigars and plotting into the night. The old guard, the robber barons, protecting the Service. I had never entered that little world, had deliberately stayed apart from it. That had been my undoing, I saw now.

At some point in the fug and the smoke, as they had debated what to do about the fact that Wilson was still alive despite their best efforts, the conversation would have swung round to me. *'What the hell are we going to do about Paul?'* Well, it wouldn't have taken them long to come to their decision — I was best out of the way. They could have just given me a swift injection, of course, and nobody would have been any the wiser. 'Yes, the fever took him. Dreadful affair. He caught it out in Nigeria.' But someone had been more imaginative than that, had seen a way to get more mileage from me, even in death. By doing the deed in St Paul's, in full view of two Cabinet ministers and half the Service, they would have killed two birds with one conspicuously Soviet-manufactured cartridge. I would have died a hero, a convenient martyr in the Service's struggle against anarchists and Communists, and the ministers, spooked at seemingly having come so close to being killed themselves, would jump to treble the Service's budget to deal with the menace. A nice fringe benefit. The Service would never come under suspicion, of course, and neither would Five. They were the investigators, so they could make certain the evidence showed just what they wished it to. And who would suspect them of plotting to kill one of their most senior officers? I hadn't.

They'd had to improvise, certainly, putting it all together in so short a time. Presumably the sniper had been one of Zimotti's men, completely unconnected with Arte come Terrore. Did Arte come Terrore even exist? Yes, I reasoned. Barchetti had clearly infiltrated them, and even with their elaborate plot to kill me I doubted they had the imagination to create something quite so outlandish out of whole cloth. They had simply used Arte come Terrore as a decoy, a convenient Moscow-backed group to pin the blame on. No doubt Five had been in on it, too: that was how the sniper had been able to 'smuggle' his rifle into the cathedral so easily. I added Giles Fearing into the scene at Osborne's house, his jowls wobbling with mirth as each of them had put successive ideas into the pot, stirring it until it came to a boil. I could just imagine how they had rubbed their hands with glee and patted themselves on the back when they'd come up with the thing. A bold and fitting move to counter the Nigerian disaster. Checkmate in one.

But it wouldn't have been easy. They'd had to find a sniper, train him, rehearse his getaway route in case something went wrong. Show him the tunnel leading to Smithfield, perhaps. And, luckily for me, something *had* gone wrong: Farraday had moved his head at just the wrong moment.

Worse, from the point of view of the conspirators, was that I had taken the initiative. I'd chased the sniper down, and he'd said something in Italian. They'd had to improvise anew then – Osborne biting his nails in the Rover – and they had decided to reveal their great foresight in predicting that this was the first of a wave of attacks across Europe, stemming out of a group in Italy. I thought back to the meeting in Whitehall, playing it again in my mind. Christ, Osborne had even had me call Innes to prepare their story!

I discounted Haggard as being part of the plot – there was no feigning that depth of outrage, and his suggestion that I go to Italy to hunt down and kill those responsible for Farraday's murder wasn't a script they would have wanted to play: it might have made me think a little more carefully about who had tried to kill *me*. I cursed myself that it hadn't; the thing had been staring me in the face. But I'd been sure that I was finally in the clear. The idea that they would try to assassinate me simply hadn't crossed my mind.

And, despite killing the wrong man, they'd got away with it: I hadn't suspected their involvement for a moment, and I doubted Haggard had, either. They hadn't intended for me to visit Rome, of course, but when Haggard had given them little choice in the matter they'd been happy enough to send me on a wild-goose chase – with Barnes watching over me to make sure I didn't stray too far. Barchetti must have wanted to meet about something else entirely. If I hadn't insisted on going in Severn's place, no doubt he would have returned from the museum and fed me a suitable story that would have led me somewhere else.

My thoughts turned to the here and now. Where had they brought me? I presumed from Zimotti's presence that we were still in Rome, or somewhere in Italy, at any rate. But why had they not already flown me back to London to face Osborne et al? Zimotti might want a piece of me, if the hatred of Communists I'd glimpsed at dinner were any indication – but that couldn't be the answer. There must be some other reason. It was also odd that they had waited for me to interview Pyotr first and then brought me in, instead of simply carting me off the moment I'd shown them the note. Perhaps they had wanted to see how far I'd take it. No, of course: they must have realized Pyotr was a Soviet agent, too – my handler, Zimotti had surmised. They had let me run ahead and lead them to him. Two for the price of one . . .

The music suddenly shut down, bringing me back to earth. There was a noise coming from somewhere outside the cell. It was dulled by distance and the walls, but there was no mistaking it: screaming. So they had brought Pyotr here, too, and were torturing him. How long before it would be my turn? I shivered, and my stomach clutched anew.

The record started up again, at ear-splitting volume, but after a few seconds it began repeating the same fragment over and over: '*Destruction . . . destruction . . . destruction . . .*' Either the record had become stuck and there was nobody manning the machine playing it, or they had put it on a loop deliberately to drive me mad. Probably the latter. How long were they planning to keep me here? There was no bucket, no slops . . .

Wake up, Paul. They're not planning to keep you here at all.

They're going to *kill* you. They had tried in St Paul's and narrowly missed. Yes, but they hadn't been certain I was a traitor then. It made little difference. They would squeeze everything they could out of me, then finish me off with a bullet through my skull. Severn would report back to London that the deed had been done, and Osborne would no doubt furnish a plausible story for Haggard. On reflection, perhaps I hadn't been so lucky that Farraday had moved his head.

The music stopped again, just as abruptly as the other times. This time, though, it didn't start up again. It was what I had been craving, but as the hours passed the silence became worse than the noise it had replaced: the room was suddenly twice as cold and lonely. I was desperately tired, and knew I needed to sleep if I had any chance at all of surviving. But the fear of being woken at any moment had blocked my brain, and all I could see around me was death, and death at my own hands: Colin Templeton's face as he handed me the drink, sometimes interspersed with the sniper closing his eyes on the floor of the market, or with Barchetti, choking. The images played in my mind on an eternal loop, and I tunnelled ever deeper into them.

XII

I jerked awake, my ears ringing. As the echo faded, I realized it had been a shot.

Had they just killed Pyotr?

I kept listening, but there was nothing else for several minutes. And then I heard the clacking of shoes. The door opened. I struggled to catch a glimpse of how the mechanism worked, but they had turned the lights up again and it was impossible to make out.

My eyes smarting, I squinted as Severn stepped into the cell. He was still wearing the mirrored glasses, and he had someone with him. Not Zimotti this time, but Barnes.

I'd forgotten about Barnes.

Severn took a pack of cigarettes from a pocket, shook one into his fingers and lit it, then slowly blew the smoke into my face. 'How are you doing?' he said. 'Ready to confess yet?'

'It'll take a bit more than a few flashing lights and some pop music,' I said. 'Try harder.' It was a stupid thing to say, and I don't know why I'd reacted that way. The cigarette, perhaps.

He smiled, almost jovially. 'Oh, we will. We will. You're forgetting that Reginald here worked in the camps in Kenya. He knows how to get information from a suspect, don't you?'

'Yes, sir,' said Barnes quietly. His jaw was locked tight, and his pale blue eyes drilled into me. No sunglasses for Barnes: he wanted to look at me unvarnished. 'We used to use a bucket, sir. Put it over their heads, then hit it with a club for a few hours. That was one trick we used to use, sir, with some of the harder-core elements.'

They'd told him, of course – that I'd killed Templeton.

'All right,' I said. 'I confess. I'm a double.'

It was a relief to say it after all these years, simply to say the words aloud. But it evidently wasn't what they wanted to hear. Barnes suddenly lunged forward and began pummelling at me, his fists crashing into my stomach and a deep animal roar bursting from him. As I tried to shield my head and body from the blows, I caught a glimpse of his face, his mouth in a rictus, the veins at his temples throbbing, and I just held my hands up meekly and waited for it to end. Fighting back now would only make it worse. Let him tire. Let him tire.

He didn't tire easily.

When it was finally over, my face felt like it had been inflated like a balloon. Through barely open eyes I saw him salute Severn and march out of the room. I prayed he wasn't going to fetch a bucket.

'Poor Dark,' said Severn, and laughed at the weak pun on my name. 'Got yourself into something bigger than you understood this time, didn't you?'

I looked up. Two versions of him floated in front of me. Part of my brain registered that this might mean a damaged retina, but the rest of it was busy trying to bring the two of them closer together, and failing.

I let my head hang down and wondered whether I could muster the strength to hit him, possibly even to kill him. It might be worth it, just for the cigarettes. I smiled at myself. I knew I didn't have it in me to pull it off, and what good would enraging him do? It would get it over with, perhaps. Make him kill me quicker. *No.* Hold out. What have they done? Music, lights, a beating up. You can handle that. Hold out. You might yet survive this, you might yet . . .

Severn threw his cigarette to the floor and crushed it with the heel of his shoe. Then he grabbed me by the hair and pulled me up until I was standing. It was his turn to have some fun now. He removed his glasses and I stared into his eyes. They were cold, dead: the gunmetal had turned to stone. I could smell his cologne — Floris? — but it was covered with the sharp tang of sweat. Anger — or excitement?

'I hate scum like you,' he sneered. 'I don't know how you can live with yourself, lying to your colleagues and friends day after day, for years. How do you do that, Dark, tell me?'

It was best not to answer that kind of question. And yes, true, I was scum. But there are grades of scum, and I was beginning to feel that he might be at least on the same grade as me.

'Betrayal, deceit . . . What a life. You *Judas*.' He spat out the word. The veins in his forehead were standing out, his throat muscles constricted. His body had released adrenalin into his system and he was beginning to experience tunnel vision, seeing red. He was seeing a Red, in fact: me. He seemed to have derived a vicarious thrill from watching Barnes beat me up, but he was no weakling himself.

'Tell me about school,' he whispered under his breath.

I stared at him, not understanding. *School?*

'You know about it,' I said slowly. 'You were there, too, remember?'

'Tell me about it anyway.'

It was then that I noticed his hand. Why hadn't I seen it before? It was gripping something I recognized, but had never expected to see again. A cat-o'-nine tails. He lifted it and I caught a closer look: it had a thin black leather grip, opening into the plaited thongs.

'Did you enjoy it?' he said, seeing that I had begun to understand where we were heading. 'Did you take pleasure from seeing me suffer?' His voice rose and he loomed over me, the cat waving in his hand. 'Oh, I know you didn't take part in the fun yourself, but you stood by and watched readily enough, didn't you? *You didn't do anything to stop it!'* The intensity of his rage seemed to be growing by the second. I had to calm him down before he completely lost control and killed me.

The cat's tails came down, and as the agony shot through me I finally understood what was happening inside the mind of Charles Severn.

In 1942, shortly before I left to join the army, I had been made a praefect at Winchester. One of my first duties had been to sit in on the 'Notions Examina', the school's initiation ceremony for new boys. Like most such ceremonies, it involved an element of humiliation: stupid games, coarse questions, name-calling. I'd experienced it myself, but had forgotten until this moment that Severn's test had gone horribly wrong: a few of the praefects had whipped him with a cat and somehow bones had ended up broken.

He had spent a few days in the San, but as far as I knew had suffered no lasting damage. Three months after sitting in on his Notions test I had gone to Oxford, before being sent to train with SOE. Just over a year later, I had seen men mown down by machine-gun fire in a village in Normandy. Severn's ordeal was small beer compared to what the rest of the world had gone through – though not, of course, to him. He had been recruited into the Service after the war, but would still have seen his share of men injured and killed over the years. But this had been his injury, and it had been deeper than anyone could have guessed.

I hadn't been one of the boys who had hurt him, but it didn't look like that was going to mean much now. And he had a point. He had been whipped brutally, and I hadn't lifted a finger to stop it. He had been thirteen then, and I had been seventeen: old enough to act. I hadn't realized how badly it had been going – none of us had – and I certainly hadn't enjoyed it. But it hadn't occurred to me to try to *stop* them. Severn had been having a worse time than most, certainly, but that was just hard luck. Someone had to. I hadn't felt ashamed of my inaction then, or in the intervening decades. I did now, although I suspected that if I had tried to stop them, they would have simply laughed, and quite probably turned on me.

But that was easy to say now, and not much of an excuse when it came down to it. That way led to mob rule, to Eichmann and his 'following orders'. I had stood by and let it happen. Yes. I was just as guilty as the others had been.

I became dimly aware of the sound of singing. It was Severn.

> *Domum, domum, dulce domum*
> *Domum, domum, dulce domum*
> *Dulce, dulce dulce domum!*
> *Dulce domum resonemus . . .*

It had always struck me as a strange kind of school song, one that remembered and glorified home. He was singing it very loudly, and flat. His face was scarlet and the tendons on his neck were bulging like tree-trunks. He had clearly gone quite mad, and the reason I was here and not in London was because he wanted to exact his revenge on me, in private. There weren't going to be any letters to The Trusty Servant about this particular reunion.

'What do you want to know?' I managed to gasp out.

He spat in my face and then leaned forward and kicked me in the stomach, winding me. I crashed to the floor.

He raised the cat again.

'What did she tell you?' he hissed.

I looked up at him, lost.

'Who? About what?'

'*What did she tell you?*'

His eyes stared out from his head as he screamed at me, and then he lifted the cat higher, above his shoulder. 'I'm going to destroy you, Dark,' he said. 'First I'm going to break you into little pieces, and then I am going to destroy you. Nobody . . .' he whispered, spittle foaming at the edge of his lip.

'. . . touches . . .'

His hand twitched.

'. . . my *wife!*'

He brought it down, and I let out a long scream. He kept going, bringing the thing up and then down, I don't know for how long, and then I started falling back into the abyss again, and my mind clouded over.

*

Something was terribly wrong.

That was my first thought as I came back to consciousness. The whole of my back throbbed with pain and, as I opened my eyes, my vision was still blurred. But I was *alert*. That should have been good news, but I knew it wasn't. Presumably they had drugged me again, but this time with some sort of stimulant.

I was strapped to a table. My arms and legs were in iron cuffs, making it impossible for me to move them. I couldn't lift my neck more than half an inch, but I could make out that we were in some sort of an operating theatre. Someone was hovering near the table, but all I could see was a slash of white sleeve.

I had spent twenty-four years in almost constant fear of being exposed, but I had never envisaged it ending like this. Interrogation, prison, perhaps even the chair, yes. Prolonged and sadistic torture, no. But it seemed fairly clear that that was their plan. Well, I didn't have anything to complain about – I *had* betrayed them. I'd had it coming to me.

I looked up. Neon lights lit a frame of steel instruments that was suspended from the ceiling, waiting to perform whatever form of punishment Severn and his friends had thought up for me. I tried not to think about water, food or cigarettes.

'He's come to,' said a voice I didn't recognize.

There was a delay of a few seconds, and then Severn's face loomed in front of me, his eyes expressing mild concern. They turned to stone again as soon as he saw I was conscious.

'Be brave, Paul,' he said with a grim smile. 'This will hurt you more than it will me.'

He patted me on the wrist, and I clenched it out of instinct, even though I couldn't move it away. Sweat ran down my forehead as I watched a hydraulic arm descend from the ceiling: it was clutching a needle, and I had a good idea that it would contain more than a sedative this time. Here came the squeeze of the syringe. Here came the part where I spilled out every secret I had ever betrayed. And after that they would shoot me, as they had Pyotr . . .

I looked up at the ceiling and then away, clamping my jaw as the needle plunged in, desperately searching for something in the room that would take my mind away from what was happening and give it something new to focus on as the drug pulsed through me.

Yes. There it was.

The room itself. The whole thing. Like the cell they'd kept me in earlier, it was immaculate, state-of-the-art. Glistening machines hummed, and the walls were made of the same strange plastic material. The thought leapt into my mind that it must have cost a fortune. Followed by 'Yes — but whose?' The Italians surely couldn't afford such a facility alone. Had the Service helped fund it? A stretch, I'd have thought: mechanical syringes and doors that disappeared into walls. The Americans, then? All three? I had been a Head of Section for four years but had never even heard mention of such a place. But to keep something like this so secret, it had to be operating at the very highest level. What was it Severn had said earlier? Something about me getting myself into something bigger than I understood.

And what had all that been about Sarah and me? He seemed enraged by jealousy, apparently for no other reason than he'd seen her touch my arm. But he also thought she might have told me something, which was interesting because it meant she had something to tell, and that he suspected her loyalty. I thought back to the Thursday evening, on the balcony. *'Perhaps the bullet hit the wrong man.'* Had she been trying to tell me something then? No, surely she had just been angered by my overreaction to her trying to help me. Help me, yes — she had wanted me to talk to Zimotti . . . But that didn't get me anywhere either, because Zimotti was in on the game. But she had said something else, in the corridor. That I had managed to find out something, or I wouldn't have been in Rome. Perhaps she'd been trying to warn me. Perhaps she had wanted to show me something in the Station. But what? Evidence of the plan to kill me?

'What is your name?' It was Zimotti's voice.

'My name? You know my—'

A shard of agony pierced my chest, and I realized they had wired me up to some sort of electric shock machine. In my peripheral vision, I glimpsed pieces of coil dangling from the table.

'That was just a warm-up,' said Severn, as though we were playing tennis and he'd aced me on the first serve. 'I will now increase the voltage. Please answer the question.'

I hesitated for a moment and another jolt shot through me, a sheer blast of pain that made my bones shudder and my heart palpitate madly.

'Paul Dark,' I said, gasping.

'Age?'

'Forty-four.'

'Where were you born?'

'London . . .'

They were softening me up, getting me to talk about innocuous subjects so my mind would offer less resistance. They wouldn't be innocuous for long. It was the standard technique. They would have asked me all these questions before they had injected me, but I'd forgotten what answers I'd given them. The drug was already starting to take hold and I could feel my thoughts drifting away from me like pieces of an ice floe. I had at most a couple of minutes before they disintegrated completely and I lost control of my own mind, after which I wouldn't be able to stop them probing it for every last secret they wanted. But there was something wrong, and I had to find out what it was. I had to interrogate *them*.

'Bill Merriweather told me about this,' I said. 'There are several phases to it, aren't there? The first—'

'Who's Bill Merriweather?' asked Severn.

'Porton Down,' I said. 'Don't you know him? Our chap there. Flaky skin, plays golf with Chief, used to anyway.' Steer clear of Templeton — you'll be confessing to murder next. 'Met him a few times, first in '65 after I'd been made Head of Section, and I went down to see him, took Vanessa's car, not that we were involved then' — steer clear — 'but I suppose it was the beginning of something because I took her car, and I visited Bill in his office and he told me all about how it works.'

Porton Down was the Ministry of Defence's chemical laboratory, and Merriweather was the Service's chief scientist on the staff. He had told me in gruesome detail about how the North Koreans had managed to brainwash American POWs. According to Merriweather, the Americans wanted to beat the Koreans at their own game, and had a project dealing with barbiturates that could break down the mind and render any subject helpless in the arms of his captors. Merriweather wanted a larger research budget, but admitted that there were ethical concerns.

Someone had obviously overruled them.

There was also Blake, of course, whose files I'd studied. One theory was that he had become a double after the North Koreans had captured him, and in the rounds of vetting that had followed his confession there had been a lot of discussion in the office about the plausibility of brainwashing, or 'conversion', as it was known. Could it really be the case, some had wondered. Wasn't all this conversion stuff simply fantasy? Let's not beat about the bush here, chaps, Blake was just a bloody Dutch Jew *traitor*. I had asked Merriweather about Blake, and he had explained in chilling detail how they might have done it, enumerating each phase, or 'plane', in the process. The first plane was to break down the mind so you got at everything there was in it, and that, I was sure, was what they were going to try with me now. I tried desperately to remember the other planes, because Merriweather had also said that no drug was perfect. The drugs simply 'opened up' the mind, enough to let the interrogator pry into it. But if you were prepared for it to happen, or knew about it, you could counter it. So I tried to counter it now by thinking about the very process I was going through, and blocking out the part of my mind that wanted to cooperate.

'What have you used?' I said. 'Amytal?'

Severn looked at Zimotti anxiously. He didn't know Merriweather, but he knew that a subject who was aware of mind control techniques was going to be a lot harder to crack.

'You met Barchetti,' he rapped out. 'Do you remember?'

'Yes,' I said. Volunteer nothing. It's his interrogation.

'What did he tell you?'

'He was scared,' I said, unable to help myself. 'He ran away from me. I followed—'

'What did he say to you?'

The voice was firmer, urgent, and it rang alarm bells. Why did they want to know this? Instinct warned me not to tell them.

'He didn't say anything. He didn't get the chance.'

There was silence, and then I thought I heard a fluttering sound far off in the distance: a helicopter in flight? There was suddenly fierce whispering between Severn and Zimotti. I couldn't make out what they were saying, but I knew what was wrong now. They were going about this all the wrong way. They were asking *the wrong questions*. I had been a double agent for over twenty years, but they hadn't shown the faintest interest in any of the secrets I'd revealed in that time. They didn't want a confession. Instead they were asking me about Barchetti, and what he had told me. That suggested that something was still running, that they were in the midst of some kind of operation. So the sniper in St Paul's was not the whole picture, just part of it — part of something wider. The wave of attacks Innes had mentioned back in London? Only Arte come Terrore hadn't been responsible for Farraday's death in the first place, *they* had, so why would—

Christ.

The bombs in Milan: the Fiat stand and the other one. They hadn't been Arte come Terrore either, of course. Zimotti's lot had been responsible, and they had framed Arte come Terrore and others for it, just as the Service had done with Farraday's death. It was part and parcel of the same thing, a continuation of the shenanigans Osborne had been up to in Nigeria. Italy had the largest Communist party in Western Europe: what better way to keep them out of power here than by carrying out attacks on civilians and blaming them on Red groups? The Communists' support at the ballot box would plummet, and any security measures Zimotti and his cadre wanted to introduce to counter the threat would be welcomed with open arms.

So there *was* a plan for a campaign of attacks: a campaign to be committed by Italian military intelligence. And the Service was providing the support – with American help, perhaps? As Deputy Chief, presumably they would have considered indoctrinating me into the operation, to stop me asking too many awkward questions if I came across material that didn't make sense. But in the end they had decided they couldn't trust me at all, and that I was better off dead. Better off, in fact, as another rung *in* the plan. Kill me and blame it on the Communists – perfect. Only they had missed.

And now? Now they wanted to know whether Barchetti had told me about any of this – but why were they so desperate? There could only be one reason, I realized: another attack was imminent.

I turned my focus back to Severn and Zimotti. I guessed they had tried to find out from Pyotr if he knew anything about the plan. Perhaps they hadn't been successful, but they had shot him just in case. Now all they wanted from me – apart from the personal satisfaction of tearing me limb from limb – was to discover whether Barchetti had unwittingly revealed the conspiracy to me, and whether or not I had told anyone else about it. Well, perhaps I should just tell them he had. What difference did it make either way? I couldn't stop whatever it was they were planning, for the simple reason that I didn't know what it was. But no – if I revealed I knew about the plan, they would kill me. The other night in the embassy Sarah had told me I was brave, that not many people would have risked their own skins chasing down a sniper. But, of course, the only reason I had chased him was to save my own skin. All I cared about was saving my own skin.

There was a noise and I looked up at Severn. I suddenly noticed another figure standing behind him. He was wearing flannel trousers and a dickie bow, and he looked very angry.

'Hello, Paul,' he said. 'Thought you could kill me, did you?'

It was Colin Templeton.

Ignore. It was a hallucination caused by the drugs, that was all: mental pictures fished from the parieto-occipital region of the brain, my visual mechanisms out of control, creating scenes that the subconscious had been avoiding, that the core of my psyche was terrified of confronting. Pink elephants occurring to a man terrified of elephants, a man in the pink . . .

I was entering Plane Three now – thoughts disrupted, difficulty in forming new thoughts. This was their access area, their point of penetration. But Plane Three only lasts a few minutes. It can be prolonged with further injections – how many had they given me, I wondered – but not for very long. I had to get through the next few minutes without giving away that I was on to them. I had to pretend to be . . . what? Well, they knew I was a double. Tell them about that, then. Bore them with it.

'I was recruited in 1945,' I announced. 'By a woman called Anna Maleva. She was a nurse at the Red Cross hospital in—'

'We know about all that,' snapped Severn. 'We want to know about more recent events. Why did you meet with this man Valougny?'

'That was his idea,' I said, unable to stop myself from blurting it out. 'He met me.' Change the subject. You're a double agent. Bore them. 'He's the local control, you see. Sasha couldn't make it in London. He didn't answer the call, nobody answered the—'

'What did Valougny want from you?'

'He wanted me to kill Barchetti.'

'Why?'

They didn't even care. Didn't care that I'd killed one of their own.

'Because . . .'

'Yes?'

Think.

'Because Barchetti knew about him.'

'What do you mean? That he had blown his cover?'

'Yes. Exactly. Pyotr – that's his name, or the name he gave me anyway – was worried, because Barchetti had discovered his identity and he was sure he was compromised, so he needed him killed. I told him you were due to meet him and he ordered me to go instead, said it was the perfect opportunity.'

Silence again. Then more whispering. The prick of a needle. And darkness.

*

I came back to consciousness to discover I was being dragged by my feet. I lifted my head as much as I could, as my back scraped against the floor. The man carrying me was panting and grunting, and I could hear shouting in guttural Italian. Above me swung a never-ending stream of lights, and I realized I was being dragged down a long corridor. Finally there was the jangling of keys, the clicking of a lock, and I was plunged into darkness again.

'*Bene*,' I heard a voice say. 'Leave him there.'

My body fell, bones crunching as my spine hit the floor.

I opened my eyes. My vision was still somewhat blurry, but I could see a fierce-looking brown face with a beak for a nose and bloodshot eyes. He was deeply tanned all over, like polished mahogany, and his eyes were sharp little pellets in his skull. Zimotti's chief enforcer and chair-carrier. Behind him was Barnes, gripping a brutish-looking sub-machine gun. They talked between themselves for a few moments, but too low for me to hear, and then they went out, leaving me in my private world of pain.

I managed to sit up, and touched the back of my head: it was sticky with blood. I was dizzy from hunger and thirst, although it was still the craving for tobacco that hovered utmost in my mind. I knew if I even thought about any of that I would go mad, so I rocked back and forth on my haunches, whimpering lines from a hymn I'd sung at Templeton's service:

> *O still, small voice of calm.*
> *O still, small voice of calm . . .*

My vision gradually began to clear, and I looked around. It looked very similar to the first cell, only the dimensions seemed slightly different: a little squarer. There was a pile of grey matter in one corner of the room, and I crawled towards it frantically, hoping it might be food or drink. But as I got closer, I saw with horror that it was a body, laid out like a corpse. At first I thought it might be Pyotr, but then I saw a curl of blonde hair, and realized it was her.

XIII

'Sarah,' I whispered.

No response.

I lifted myself onto my elbows and slowly crawled nearer, willing the pain in my neck and spine away. Her nostrils flared as the breath came in and out: she was alive, but either in a deep sleep or unconscious. She was wearing the same clothes I'd last seen her in, back at Pyotr's flat, only they were now torn and spotted with blood. Her skin was yellowish, and mottled and dark under her eyes. Finally, I saw the deep welts that criss-crossed her shoulders and neck. He had used the cat on her, too. A wave of revulsion swept over me, which swiftly turned to a cold rage. He had tortured his own wife.

I retreated slowly to the nearest corner to gather my thoughts. I wondered how many Severn and Zimotti would kill to get their way. Hundreds? Thousands? The goal would be a dictatorship, with Zimotti either the head of it or part of the leadership. It would be a coup, effectively, albeit a gradual and undeclared one. Italy had seen coups before, of course, but nothing like this. After a few large-scale attacks and swift arrests, Zimotti and his men would be able to introduce whatever measures they felt necessary, while a pliant and terrified public would greet them with open arms. And the British were apparently lending a hand, through their man in Rome. It seemed extraordinary, but I realized that I hadn't been paying close enough attention. There was a very powerful right-

wing faction operating within the Service. Perhaps more of a movement than a faction. They had tried to take control of the
government but failed — because of me. Perhaps they were planning
a similar series of attacks in England, blaming everything on the
First of May or similar groups. Perhaps Italy was just the beginning . . .

Something in me turned. This wasn't where my life should end.
I hadn't *helped*. I had spent it trying to divine the difference between
causes, but I hadn't seen the forest for the trees. East and West, I
now knew, were just two frightened children spurring each other
on to greater and greater acts of excess. But I was no better, standing
on the edge of the field pointing out their mistakes. I had to get
onto the pitch, into the game. I had to put aside all my cynicism
and stupid bloody English pride and admit that there were choices
here, and that I could make a difference to the situation. Where
was the shame in that? Why was I so afraid of it? Here was the
opportunity: a chance to save others, and atone for all the men I'd
betrayed.

No. That was still selfish thinking. I glanced across at Sarah, her
chest rising and falling. I wondered what she would think were she
to know who I really was. Utter contempt, I was sure. Nothing
could wash the blood from my hands or atone for those I had
betrayed — for Colin Templeton, or Vanessa, or Isabelle. But I could
save others from their fate, and stop a gang of power-hungry men
taking this country over, simply because *it was the right thing to do.*

Moscow hadn't tried to kill me, after all — but they would now.
I had deliberately exposed one of their men and got him tortured
and, it appeared, killed as a result. Even if they were prepared to
let that go and still wanted to use me, I didn't want them any more,
and they no longer had anything to blackmail me with: the Service
knew who I was now. I realized that I had become unmoored from
both sides and no longer had anyone to blame for my actions but
myself — that I was, finally, living up to my codename: independent,
a free agent. But what to do with that new-found freedom? Run

to ground? Or fight back — and create my own side? I had to, or I was lost forever.

I shook my head suddenly: the only thing that was unmoored was my mind. I wasn't free at all, and had no way of creating any *side*. I was not only imprisoned, but hours or perhaps minutes from death. The guards would return soon, and for the last time.

I looked across at Sarah again, and wondered why had they put me in here with her. On the face of it, it was a weak move, as we could conspire together, perhaps even help each other escape. On the face of it. In reality, of course, we were in a secured cell inside a military base that was doubtlessly manned by hundreds of soldiers; she was unconscious; and I was nearing the point of physical and mental collapse. There was no bucket or bed or food or anything else in this room, so it looked like they were only planning to hold us here for a short while before killing us. Severn had thrown me in here with her because it no longer mattered to him if she knew of his plans, or that she might tell me them. He had discarded us both.

So how would they end it, then? A bullet to the head, like Pyotr? That might well be the plan. But where had Severn and Zimotti disappeared to in the meantime? Perhaps they had left to oversee the next stage in their grand scheme, the next attack. Or perhaps it was now the middle of the night, and they were simply catching up on their sleep before returning for some more games in the morning. Yes, a bullet to the head would be too easy. They would have a slow and painful death in mind for me . . .

Perhaps it was the awareness that I hadn't long to live, or perhaps my nascent conscience, but my mind latched on to the idea that they had disappeared to execute the next attack, and refused to let it go. Hypothetically speaking, it asked, if you *were* somehow able to escape, how could you help, how could you stop them? What would the man you might have been do? What would the man Colin Templeton had believed you were do? Well, perhaps he'd try to get in touch with London, reach Haggard and tell him what was happening. No, I realized at once, that would be pointless. I was an exposed double agent. Haggard would never believe me. Yes, but exposed in what way? The only proof they had of my treachery depended on their admitting that they had murdered Farraday. A chink of understanding opened in my mind. Was that why they needed a confession from me — to block any remaining chance I could expose them? Was that why I was here, and not in London? They could extract a confession, then see that I didn't live much beyond it. And sort out the paperwork later.

Perhaps. But my confession hadn't seemed paramount. Regardless, I didn't trust taking this to Haggard, or anyone else. I would have to find out what they were planning and address it myself.

I stopped, and glanced at Sarah once again. I thought of her walking down the corridor, her hips swinging in front of me, asking if I wanted to see the Station. She must have wanted to take me there for a reason. Could it be that she knew what they were planning?

I crawled over to her and stared at her face, pale and gaunt from the stress and fear. I felt her pulse. She was sleeping, not unconscious. She needed her rest. I shouldn't wake her.

But somewhere outside these walls, a bomb might be ticking down.

I shook her shoulder gently, and her eyes opened. The moment she saw me she started sobbing.

*

It took some time for her to stop, but when she did it was almost frightening how calm she was, as if utterly detached from the world. I left her alone, fearing the worst, but eventually she called out to me. 'I think we need to talk,' she said, and I couldn't help smiling at the matter-of-factness of it.

At first I insisted we only communicate in whispers. I was afraid that the whole thing might be some sort of a set-up so Severn could learn what it was she knew – the place was almost certainly bugged.

But it soon became clear she had told him everything already. She didn't say what he had done to extract the information, and I didn't ask, but we both knew we had been left here to die, and therefore had nothing to lose from telling each other all we knew. Her voice was hoarse, as was mine, and we spoke quickly and frantically, uncertain how long we had before Barnes and his friend returned.

It transpired that Severn had used her as a courier, giving her packages to deliver to dead drops around Rome. She told me how she had gone about the job quite happily, not thinking too much about what it might mean – until the bombs had started going off.

'In Milan?' I asked.

'No,' she said, 'this was earlier than that. They were smaller scale. Charles had been frantic and nervous enough already, but now he was at fever pitch. I noticed one morning that he was reading the newspaper very intently over breakfast, and then rushed off to use the telephone. I looked at the page he'd been reading: it was about a bomb somewhere in the north of the country. A few people had been killed, and the thing had been blamed on some Marxist group. Bits and pieces of conversations I'd overheard suddenly seemed to make sense. The next time he asked me to do one of his late-night deliveries, to a churchyard in the south of the city, I opened the package.'

'What made you do that?'

'Well, he'd insisted so much that I never open any of them, and I was worried that they might have something to do with these bombs going off. I thought he might be involved in something . . . outside the remit of the embassy.'

'Working for someone else, you mean?'

She held my gaze for a moment. 'Yes.'

I considered this. 'All right, so you opened the package. What was in it?'

'Codes,' she said. 'Lots of documents in code: one-time pad stuff. I panicked because I couldn't find a way to reseal it so it didn't look like it had been opened. But eventually I did, and I thought the chap who picked up the message wouldn't notice. But he did, and he told Charles about it, and Charles went completely mad. He screamed at me, asking me dozens and dozens of questions until I just broke down and told him I'd been curious but hadn't understood any of it. That seemed to calm him down a bit. He made me promise never to mention any of it to anyone else or he'd . . .' She grimaced. ' . . . or he'd kill me.'

I tried not to think about what sort of marriage they had had, and what had happened to her in this cell. I asked her to carry on.

'Well, he never mentioned the packages again after that, and I tried to put the whole thing out of my mind. But then the message came through that you were being sent over from London, and Charles seemed to panic a little. Towards the end of Thursday afternoon I found myself alone in the Station: Cornell-Smith and Miller had gone home to get ready for dinner in the embassy, and Charles had left to collect you from the airport. Last year, he gave me the combination to his safe as a contingency – if anything ever happens to him, I'm to take everything out and burn it. So I went into his office and opened it. I just had to know what was going on. After looking through several dossiers, I found some one-time pads and documents that contained photographs of some of the drops I'd been sent to. And there were numbers – lots of them. Dates. I recognized them.'

'The dates when the bombs had exploded?'

'Yes. But the thing that really scared me was that some of the documents I saw had been stamped with Service seals. Charles isn't working for anyone else: it's an officially sanctioned operation, codenamed "Stay Behind".'

I stared at her, and let the silence envelop me for a moment. A chill crept through my bones.

Stay Behind. Was it possible?

Yes, I thought. Of course it was . . .

XIV

Saturday, 16 June 1951, Istanbul, Turkey

'Breakfast in Europe and lunch in Asia!' cried the ambassador's wife as the motorboat drew up to the landing-stage. 'I shall never get used to the decadence.'

'We do our best,' smiled Joan Templeton, stretching out an arm to help her ashore. She alighted with an unladylike squeal, but swiftly recovered and handed small bouquets of wild flowers to Joan and her daughter, Vanessa. The ambassador made the leap unaided, then turned back and muttered instructions to the crew, half a dozen young men in starched white shirts and matching pantaloons. They swiftly removed the Union Jack from its position by the wheel, folded it away, and seated themselves cross-legged on the cushions on deck – I guessed they would wait here until required for the return journey.

On land, everyone greeted one another with polite pecks on the cheek, and the ambassador asked Vanessa how she was enjoying her final year at Badminton. His wife, meanwhile, had caught sight of me standing to the side and immediately leapt over.

'I was *so* sorry to hear about your mother,' she said, taking my hands in hers and clutching them urgently.

'It was perhaps for the best,' I told her. 'She had suffered long enough.'

She tilted her head and gazed at me for a long moment, her eyes large and liquid with sympathy. I gave a tight smile in return: I knew this was one of many such exchanges I could expect to face in coming weeks. While we spooks were housed in the city's Consulate-General – the old embassy, a magnificent nineteenth-century *palazzo* – the regular diplomatic corps were based out in Ankara, an arrangement that suited us rather well. But in summer they descended on Istanbul, their arrival presaged by a flurry of thick crested invitation cards embossed with gold type. My usual existence, in which I saw less than a dozen colleagues regularly, was about to be overturned with two months of cocktail parties and picnics.

Today was the opening of the season, the Templetons' annual lunch party, which one had to take a ferry to reach as they lived in Beylerbeyi, a pleasant suburb on the Asiatic side of the Bosphorus. Like many others out here, the ambassador and his wife had known my parents in Cairo. I had spent much of the previous summer, my first in the city, fielding anxious enquiries over Father's disappearance at the end of the war and my mother's continuing ill health. But with Mother's death a couple of months earlier I had become an orphan, so I was braced for an even higher pitch of concern.

Had she known the truth about my parents, the ambassador's wife would probably have recoiled in horror. My mother had hailed from an old Swedish family that had settled in Finland in the nineteenth century. Father had been introduced to her at a ball in Helsinki in 1923 when she was just nineteen, and they had married soon after and moved to Egypt, where Father had been Head of Station. I had been born in London a couple of years later – I was to be their only child.

Shortly after my birth, it had become clear that beneath Mother's poised exterior lurked serious problems. She suffered from continual headaches, and became increasingly demanding, rude and, eventually, hysterical. Her father had been killed in the civil war by the Red Guards, and as a result she harboured a deep hatred of the Soviet Union. She was also virulently anti-Semitic, and would often refer to Jews in public as 'vermin'.

All this proved to be highly embarrassing for Father, whose career in the Service was flourishing. In 1936, he was posted back to head office in London. As the Nazis in Germany became more powerful, he had advocated closer ties with them, becoming one of the leading lights of the Anglo-German Fellowship. He was also an admirer of fascism – he was briefly Treasurer of the Nordic League – and argued strongly in favour of appeasement. However, he had swiftly abandoned this line once it had become clear that war was inevitable, and following the Molotov–Ribbentrop pact he had publicly cut all ties with fascist groups and become staunchly anti-Nazi as well as anti-Communist. But Mother's 'condition', as everyone had started to call it, was much harder to disguise.

Things had come to a head in early September 1939, when she had announced at a party in Belgravia attended by several government ministers that Hitler was the strongest leader Europe had seen in generations and that he was fully justified in his persecution of the Jews, who, she had added for good measure, were also natural enemies of England. Father had been advised by friends in the War Office that she was a liability, and that if nothing were done the three of us could be interned. As a result, he had had her shipped off to Finland, where she was cared for by private doctors at a remote estate. I came home from school to be told that Mother was ill, and that it might be some time before I saw her again. In the event, it wouldn't be for another five years.

In late 1941 Britain had declared war on Finland, and Father had had her shifted again, this time to a clinic in Stockholm. I had visited her there briefly early in 1945, but she hadn't even recognized me: either madness or medication had frozen her mind. She had remained in the clinic after the war, and had finally passed away after a series of strokes in April. Her funeral had been a quiet affair near her family's home in Helsinki. I had attended and spent a few days there, and then flown straight back to Istanbul.

The ambassador's wife let go of my hand, and Joan Templeton led us beneath some parasol pines and into the house. We walked through the cool shade of the living room and out to the sunlit garden, where several cane chairs were arranged beside a table laden with salads, cold cuts and a large dish of pigeon with rice.

'Colin's just upstairs with some guests,' Joan said. 'Colleagues from London. He'll be down shortly, I'm sure. Can I get you both a drink? Colin made some of his punch.'

'That sounds just the ticket,' said the ambassador, and his wife nodded her approval from beneath the brim of her hat. Joan headed towards the table to fix the drinks and everyone seated themselves. Vanessa settled into the chair next to mine and gave me a mischievous grin. She was seventeen now, and had blossomed into a classic English rose. She was lively company, but my thoughts were still entirely consumed by another woman: Anna, the nurse who had treated me in Germany six years earlier, whom I had loved and had planned to marry – and whom my own father had murdered before turning the gun on himself.

Anna had been a Russian, and over the course of our love affair had tried to convert me to Communism. She had come within a hair's breadth of doing so, but her revelation that she was an NKVD agent and allegation that Father was using me to execute Soviets rather than Nazi war criminals had been more than I could accept. I had coldly rejected her, and immediately delivered a message to Father denouncing her as a spy. Her subsequent death at his hands had overturned my mind: as well as the devastation of the loss, it had seemed to confirm everything she had claimed, and I had been plunged into shock, grief and rage. The rage had soon won out, however, and it had been directed not just at Father, but at all he represented. The thought of Anna's body laid out on the stretcher in the hospital, her skin already turning grey, tormented me. And so, as I had buried Father in the garden of the farmhouse in Lübeck, I had vowed to take my vengeance, by adopting Anna's cause as my own.

She had told me that her handler was based in the Displaced Persons' camp at Burgdorf, so I had taken Father's jeep and driven there. It had started snowing, huge flakes of the stuff, and by the time I arrived at the camp there was a blanket of it across the landscape. I presented the papers identifying myself as a member of an SAS War Crimes Investigations Unit and said I wished to interview residents of the camp as part of my team's enquiries. My uniform was a mess, but I had placed Father's leather jerkin over it, and after I had filled in a couple of forms, they had let me through with the advice to tread very carefully: several former SS officers had recently been discovered in the camp and nerves were particularly taut as a result.

I had walked around the main area for several hours showing the one photograph I had of Anna. Most people had clammed up as soon as I approached, but eventually someone recognized her and told me she had been an occasional visitor of Yuri, a Ukrainian doctor whose room was on the second floor of the old barracks. I made my way there and knocked on the door. After a few seconds, it was opened by a thin man wearing a greatcoat over a pair of pyjamas.

'Yes?' he said, peering at me. His face was cracked and leathery, as though he had spent most of his life outdoors, and he had tiny eyes, like sparks in a furnace. A snubbed nose gave him a faintly childlike appearance, but his hair was greying at the temples and I put him in his mid to late forties.

'I believe we have a mutual acquaintance,' I said.

He looked me over uncertainly, but then something registered in the eyes and I guessed he had recognized me from my file. He turned to speak to someone in the room, and a few seconds later a small figure scurried past me: a girl, fourteen or fifteen years old, wearing a thin nightgown. She looked up at me for a moment with startled eyes, then wrapped the gown tightly around her waist and disappeared into the corridor.

'My daughter,' said Yuri, his voice raspy. 'I do not like to discuss my work in front of her.'

He opened the door wider and I stepped inside. The room was sparsely furnished: an iron bedstead with a dirty mattress, a couple of wooden chairs, and clothes and books laid out on the floor. But he and his daughter had a room to themselves, which meant he was a very powerful person in the camp. I had seen rooms elsewhere that had been home to two and even three families. Presumably he was using his medical skills to gain favours and influence – and to seek out potential agents.

'Anna should not have told you about me,' he said, locking the door. 'Why have you come here?'

'Anna is dead.' At first I wasn't sure if he had heard me, but then he visibly crumpled, his body hunching over and his breathing coming in gasps. I made to approach him, but he held a hand up until he had recovered. When he looked up at me again, his eyes were wet with tears.

'It cannot be,' he whispered. 'Not my Anna.'

'Was she also your daughter?' I asked, suddenly shocked at the thought.

He shook his head slowly. 'But she could have been.'

He asked me what had happened and I told him, leaving nothing out. He listened very carefully, occasionally interjecting with questions to clarify a detail. When I had finished, he walked over to one of the chairs and perched himself on it.

'Thank you for telling me this,' he said. 'Anna was one of my finest agents, but she is not the first to have been murdered by the British.' He looked up at me sharply. 'Can you believe that earlier this year your country and mine were allies? Now one would almost think we are at war.'

'I know. There were even rumours after the ceasefire that we would join forces with the Germans and take up arms against you.'

His eyes widened a fraction.

'Why have you come here?' he said.

I had rehearsed a speech in the jeep, but suddenly I wasn't so certain of my convictions. I shut my eyes. The image of Anna in the stretcher swam back into my mind, and I forced myself to imagine Father squeezing the trigger, the bullet entering her . . .

'I want to work for you,' I said.

He stood up. 'And yet you did not when Anna was alive?' he said, a touch of anger in his voice. Perhaps realizing this, he stepped forward and placed a hand on my shoulder. 'I am sorry, but revenge is not a good motivation. It burns out too quickly. It does not persist. And I need people with persistence. With *ideals*.'

'I have ideals,' I said. 'You're right, I didn't want to do it when Anna was alive. But I didn't understand the situation, not fully. I . . . I'm afraid I didn't believe what she told me.' I stared into his face, at the curious snubbed nose and the glinting eyes.

'But you do now?'

I nodded, willing myself not to cry in front of him. 'Please,' I said. 'Have some faith in me. I am ready to serve . . .' But even then, even in that moment, I had been about to say 'Anna', not 'Communism' or 'the Soviet Union'.

Yuri paced around the room for a few minutes, his hands steepled together at his lips as he considered my proposal.

'I want to make sure we are very clear about this before we proceed any further,' he said, after a while. 'I need to be certain that you understand the consequences of what you are suggesting. There is no return from this point. Once you have committed to us, we will become your home. Your family.'

I thought of the family I had been born into: Father a murderer, Mother on the brink of insanity. And I thought of Anna, and the family we might have had together had she lived.

'I am committed,' I said.

Yuri looked at me for a long while. I held his gaze. 'You must go to London at once,' he said finally, and his voice had taken on a quiet hardness. 'Nobody must ever know you have been in Germany. You will be contacted shortly.'

I was filled with conflicting emotions: elation that he had agreed to take me on, disappointment and puzzlement that it wasn't to be at once. 'How will you know where to find me?'

'Don't worry,' he said. 'We will.' He walked over to the bed and picked a book from a pile leaning against it. I was surprised to see that it was a selection of poems by W. H. Auden. He opened it and read out one of the lines, then looked across at me. 'That will be your signal.'

It didn't seem as if there were anything else to say, so I had shaken his hand and left him. My frustration at his request for me to wait was tempered by the knowledge that I had now set out on the path Anna had wanted for me. I returned to London as instructed, and told everyone I had been visiting my mother in Sweden. A few people asked about Father, and I replied that I hadn't seen him in over a year. The story soon went around that he had disappeared just after the ceasefire – nobody knew where, or what had happened to him, but as time went by most presumed he had been killed. Eventually, I cleared out his things in Chelsea Cloisters and moved in there myself.

I had expected to find another job fairly easily, but it proved harder than I'd anticipated. This was perhaps partly because I felt very uncomfortable being back in England. After three years in foreign fields, the entire country now seemed to me an ugly braggart: delighted with itself for winning the war, but ignorant of the fact that without the Soviets and the Americans it would never have happened. I hated the glorying in victory, especially as I had seen the terrible state Germany had been left in.

I was a fish out of water in other ways, too. After joining the war late because of my age I had, almost as though making up for lost time, taken part in operations under the auspices of several organizations: the SAS, SOE and a few other irregular units. But all of them had either been disbanded or were about to be, and I wasn't sure I was cut out for the Service: I was a field agent, and most of the Service chaps I knew were desk men.

I nevertheless applied for a job in the Soviet Section, which was expanding almost by the day. Unbeknownst to me, it was headed up by one of Father's oldest friends, Colin Templeton. I was given the position, and started work at Broadway Buildings in early February, 1946.

The Section's entire focus was on obtaining up-to-date information about the Soviet Union: its scientific expertise, intelligence structures and, of course, military plans. Many were convinced that Stalin intended to invade Western Europe. As reliable information was extremely scant, real war crimes investigators in Germany, Austria and elsewhere were being thwarted: many of the senior Nazis they apprehended were swiftly judged by London to be crucial counter-espionage assets, and were exfiltrated, given new names, and pumped for everything they had. But the more I heard about the supposed Soviet threat, the more determined I became to counter it from within – and the more anxious I became about the fact that I had not yet been contacted.

Just as I was starting to wonder if Yuri had simply given me the brush-off, it happened. I was walking down Thurloe Street when I felt something graze my shoulder. Whirling around, I caught sight of a slim man in a grey herringbone coat heading in the opposite direction. As he walked away I felt my pockets, but to my surprise found that something had been added to them rather than subtracted. It was a small visiting card for a café a few streets away. And on the back of it, someone had written in pencil: '*It is later than you think. Saturday. 11.00.*'

The line of poetry seemed more ominous now than when Yuri had recited it to me a couple of months earlier. Perhaps as a result, I left the flat at eight o'clock that Saturday morning. The café was within walking distance, but instead I took a succession of buses all over town, repeatedly checking my watch. I had arrived, flustered but certain I had not been tailed, just before eleven, and waited for my contact to arrive. When he did, I realized it was the man in the herringbone coat. He shook me by the hand as though he had known me for a very long time, removed his coat, and ordered a pot of tea.

This was Georgi. He was in his mid-thirties, intelligent, cultured and charming. He had worked in France and Belgium, where he had been responsible for rooting out information about the Nazis' troop movements. We got on immediately, and over the next few months met regularly in locations around South Kensington. I once asked him if it wasn't unwise to meet so close to where I lived, and he had told me that it was by far the safest option: it would be easier to explain my presence if I happened to meet anyone, and the police were less vigilant because it was a genteel neighbourhood with few immigrants. As an additional precaution, we opened every meeting by establishing the cover story for it in the event of any interruption: most of the time he was a Finnish aristocrat who had known my mother in Helsinki. But we never had to use any of the cover stories we prepared: nobody paid us the least attention. We would sit in a corner and play chess or backgammon – he was rather good at both – and he would quietly question me about my work at the office. At that stage there was very little to report, and I had the feeling he already knew everything I told him anyway and was simply testing how much I would reveal to him, and how clearly I could relay information.

At our fourth meeting, Georgi announced that he would cut contact with me for six months, barring emergencies, in which case I was to leave him a message at a dead drop in a cemetery in Southgate. I had immediately feared that I had done something wrong, but he assured me that this was a positive sign, and that it meant that Moscow now trusted me enough to leave me to advance my career without having to watch over my every step.

'Bide your time,' he said. 'Go about your work efficiently, and when we meet again you will have more to tell me.' As I had watched the back of his coat disappear through the door of the café, I had felt strangely abandoned.

But I had followed his instructions. I had continued with my work in Soviet Section, and slowly but surely was given more responsibilities. Colin Templeton now often invited me to his home, where I met his family. The six months crept by, and then it was time to meet with Georgi once more. He asked about my work, and seemed pleased with my answers. Once again, I didn't feel I was telling him anything he did not know, but was happy I was finally of some use.

My meetings with Georgi continued in this way until late 1949, when Colin Templeton called me into his office and told me he was being posted to Istanbul as Head of Station, and that he would like me to come along as part of his team. I accepted at once, and left a message for Georgi in the cemetery in Southgate telling him the news. There had been no time for another meeting, as I was due to head out to Turkey immediately.

After nearly four years behind a desk in London I had been looking forward to heading into the field again, and Istanbul didn't disappoint. The city had been crawling with spies during the war, and it seemed little had changed since. The main concern was the Soviets, with the growing American influence a close second. Turkey had been neutral in the war, by and large, and was now cleverly playing the former combatants off against one another. Despite the plans for democratic elections, the possibility that they might turn to the Soviet Union had everyone worried, and strenuous efforts were being made to convince them to come into the new NATO structure. Britain's position was that this should happen in conjunction with it joining a separate Middle Eastern security alliance, but the Americans had other ideas. Despite Britain's efforts to persuade them otherwise, the Turks were coming to the realization that the balance of power was shifting in the world, and that the United States might be better able to provide them with long-term support.

I quickly settled into my position in the Station. I loved being away from London, with its pea-soupers and boiled beef, and immediately immersed myself in the hubbub and intrigue of the city's back alleys. After a year had passed without any contact from the Soviets, I began to panic. Perhaps Georgi had not picked up my message in Southgate, and they were unaware I had moved to Turkey? But surely he would have checked the drop.

My fears had finally been put to rest just three weeks earlier. I had been wandering around the Grand Bazaar when a small boy had placed a piece of paper in my jacket pocket and run away giggling. I had followed the address to a shop that sold antique silverware, where I had discreetly been led through to a back room. To my surprise, I found Yuri seated on a pile of silk cushions. He looked much the same as he had in Burgdorf, only his hair was a little greyer and the greatcoat and pyjamas had been replaced with a smart lounge suit.

He had wasted no time in getting to the point. There had been some commotion in Moscow: several agents in the field had been recalled to headquarters for further training. As a result, all the information I had given to date had been reviewed – and been found wanting.

'What do you mean?' I asked, reeling. 'Georgi was very pleased—'

'He was mistaken. Moscow feels you have not yet handed us anything significant.'

'But I haven't had anything significant to provide!' I said. 'Georgi told me to bide my time until I was more established.'

Yuri gave a thin smile. 'Moscow is concerned about the time and resources that have been spent on you for such little reward. Unless you can provide a higher grade of material, it is perhaps best that we discontinue our arrangement.' And with that he announced the time and location of the next meet, then stood, parted the curtains, and disappeared through them.

That next meet was now less than a week away, and I still had nothing of note to report. The simple truth was that, at twenty-six years old and with just five years in the job, I was still far too junior to be given access to any great secrets – and I couldn't see that situation changing any time soon.

I took a sip of punch and looked up at the villa, wondering again what it was that Templeton might be discussing with the 'colleagues from London'. They had arrived a couple of hours earlier, not by motorboat like the other guests, but in a scratched-up jeep they had parked in the driveway at the foot of the garden, on the Asian side. Templeton had immediately escorted them inside the house and up to his office, and they hadn't been seen since.

There had been three of them. William Osborne was one of the

Service's rising stars: having spent much of the war working in the Middle East, he was now establishing a reputation as an expert in deception operations. Charles Severn, the driver of the jeep, was a new recruit to the Service whom I had known at school, and not much liked. The final member of the party had not been from London at all: the head of Turkish military intelligence, a dapper man with a marvellous moustache who, for reasons I had been unable to unearth, we called 'Cousin Freddie'. He sometimes came by the office to meet Templeton – but what was so important that he had come to his house?

'Hello, Dark.'

I looked up to see a young man stretching out his hand. He was dressed in a dazzlingly white short-sleeved shirt and navy-blue Daks, and his fair hair was brushed back with pomade. Despite the addition of several inches in height and a short clipped moustache, he was instantly recognizable as the boy I had last seen nine years earlier.

'Severn,' I said, shaking his hand. 'It's been a while, hasn't it? Do you know everyone?'

Severn made his way around introducing himself, and Vanessa blushed as he kissed her hand.

'Is this your first visit to Istanbul?' she asked him.

'Yes,' he said, settling into a chair.

'How are you enjoying it?'

He wrinkled his nose. 'Not much. Rather a scruffy-looking place. I was expecting more, somehow.'

There was an awkward silence, and I wondered whether Templeton had sent him out of the meeting early because he was too junior to hear the rest, or because he hadn't been able to stand the sound of his voice any longer. Perhaps he was nervous. I asked him if he wanted a drink, and he looked up at me with gratitude. Yes, I decided, it must be nerves. Probably his first mission in the field – I remembered how I had felt on mine.

More guests arrived, most of them diplomats. Drink was consumed, and food eaten. Conversation turned to Korea, and the

King's health, and which mosques were worth visiting. Severn told me a series of anecdotes about old boys I had no recollection of, and I did my best to feign interest. But there was still no sign of Templeton, Osborne or Cousin Freddie. They'd now been closeted away for over two hours. What on earth could they be discussing?

'Pretty girl,' said Severn. 'Is she yours?' I turned to him, and he nodded at Vanessa, who was talking to a first secretary.

'No,' I said coldly. 'She is not.'

'Sorry. Didn't mean to offend.'

I decided to change the subject. 'How's London these days — do I take it you're working for Osborne?'

Severn laughed bitterly. 'That's one word for it. The man's a positive slave-driver, and I'm the one being driven. Or rather, it's the other way round — would you believe he's dragged me halfway across the world to be his chauffeur? Wish he'd got some local sod to drive him around the desert instead.'

I suppressed a smile. 'Why didn't he?'

He placed a finger to his lips. 'Hush-hush stuff. Although no doubt Templeton's given you some of the background?'

I shook my head. 'No,' I said. 'Sorry, I didn't realize. Templeton doesn't tell me that sort of—'

'Don't pull that with me. You should have heard him in there — he couldn't stop talking about you. You're his boy. Stay close to him, I would. Only reason I'm chumming up to Osborne is because I reckon he might go to the top. And his politics are sound. He says what he means, anyway.'

I made some assenting noises and went to help myself to more punch. I couldn't work it out: was something significant going on here, or was it just the pressure from Moscow that was making me believe there might be? I found Severn's attitude mildly surprising. His family were one of the richest in England, and I had presumed the Service was simply a hobby for him. But it appeared that he was, in fact, rather ambitious, and sharp enough at least to try to judge which way the wind was blowing.

I made a note to myself to keep an eye on him, and turned to see Templeton, magisterial in a straw hat, cream linen suit and a pair of battered leather sandals, marching out of the house. Osborne and Cousin Freddie followed directly behind him. The meeting finally appeared to be over.

'Hello, everyone!' Templeton said as he approached the gathering. 'Sorry to be the absent host. Is there any punch left?'

Everyone laughed, and he kissed his wife and daughter. More introductions were made; glasses clinked; the sun beat down. A *hookah* appeared from somewhere and Templeton offered it to Cousin Freddie, who nodded in appreciation at being given his own amber mouthpiece to use. Some felt that Templeton had gone native, but I suspected that this sort of thing was simply solid tradecraft, an extension of the idea that a good agent always listens twice as much as he speaks. Cousin Freddie certainly seemed to become more talkative as he inhaled from the water-pipe, and Templeton sat cross-legged opposite him, nodding his head every once in a while.

The shape of the party shifted, with separate circles forming. Osborne ambled over to speak to Severn, who noticeably stiffened as he approached. Osborne gave me a nod — we had met briefly during the war. He had put on a lot of weight since then, and the heat seemed to be getting to him: his hair was plastered to his forehead and his cheeks were flushed. I couldn't see his eyes, as they were hidden behind small dark glasses with gold rims.

'What's the story with the missing diplomats?' Vanessa asked him. 'Is it true they were spying for the Russians?'

I glanced across at Templeton to see whether he had heard, but he was still deeply engrossed in conversation with Cousin Freddie. Templeton tried to shield his daughter from any discussion of his work, but it had had the opposite effect: Vanessa was fascinated by the espionage world, particularly its more sensationalist aspects. She had been talking incessantly about the diplomats since they had vanished from their jobs at the Foreign Office a few weeks earlier.

She wasn't the only one. I had never met either man, but both were well known to the community here. Donald Maclean, the son of a Liberal MP, had been head of Chancery in Cairo, while everyone seemed to have a story to tell about Guy Burgess. He had been in the Service before the war, worked for the BBC during it, and afterwards had joined the Foreign Office, eventually being posted to Washington as a second secretary. The rumour was that he and Maclean were Soviet agents who had been on the brink of being exposed by Five. Their disappearance was the talk of the town, and as a result, several diplomats within earshot turned to see how Osborne would reply to Vanessa's question. Such subjects were not generally broached in public, but if ever you were going to pick up a titbit it would be at the Templetons' party.

'It doesn't look good,' Osborne admitted *sotto voce*. 'The bad news is that Five now want to interrogate Philby about the whole affair.'

'Really?' said Vanessa, placing her hand over her mouth. There was an almost audible intake of breath from people seated nearby. Kim Philby had been Head of Station here before Templeton, leaving for Washington in '49. We were sitting less than a mile from his old house: he had been the first from the office to live out in this neighbourhood, and several others had followed suit, the Templetons included. I knew Philby and Burgess had been friends: the regulars at the Moda Yacht Club still hadn't forgiven either man for the time they had become royally drunk in the bar on one of Burgess' visits out here. But that hardly seemed enough to hang him for.

'They don't seriously suspect him?' I asked.

Osborne removed a handkerchief from his jacket and wiped the back of his neck with it. 'Apparently, yes. They claim he's the only person who was in contact with Burgess and also knew Maclean was under suspicion. But the whole thing's absurd. Everyone's blaming everyone else, and it looks like Five want to blame us.'

'I heard they were queer,' said Severn, who was now on his fifth glass of punch by my count. 'Part of the Homintern.' He gave a braying laugh, and Osborne glared at him. 'Well,' Severn trailed off, 'they're snakes in the grass anyway.'

'We once had a snake in our garden in Cairo,' said Joan Templeton brightly, and polite titters rippled around the chairs. 'No, really, we did! What was it, Vanessa – a cobra?'

'No, Mummy, it was an adder! And the snake-charmer brought it there especially, remember?'

The conversation moved on. People began reminiscing about the embassy ball in '47, when the Fleet had visited, while Severn continued to knock back the punch and Osborne turned more and more scarlet. The heat was starting to get to me, too, and I excused myself to stretch my legs.

I wandered through the house and back to the landing-stage. The boat crew were busy chatting to one another, and looked up at me with surprise.

'Does anyone have a cigarette?' I asked, placing my fingers to my lips.

One of them smiled and produced a packet. Although disappointed I couldn't get hold of Players in the city, I had gradually become accustomed to the taste of Turkish tobacco. As I gratefully accepted the cigarette, I pondered the conversation about Maclean and Burgess. By the sound of it, they were indeed doubles. I had occasionally wondered whether there might be others, but had been grateful I didn't know who they were any more than I imagined they knew of me, working on the well-established principle that the fewer people who were in on a secret the more likely it was to be kept. But it seemed the two men had planned their flight together, so perhaps they had been aware of each other's secret beforehand – and then there was the extraordinary possibility they might have been aided by Philby. I had nobody to confide in but Yuri, or whomever else Moscow sent to run me. Once away from a meet, I was on my own.

I chatted to the boat crew for a while, then wandered back into the house. Joan had decorated it with her customary good taste:

elegant silk screens, mementoes from the family's time in Egypt and a few artfully placed carpets. I smoked my cigarette and eyed the staircase that led up to Templeton's study. I knew from the office that he often left the last thing he had been working with on his desk. Perhaps he had done the same now. Everyone was sitting outside, enjoying the party — would anyone be likely to notice if I were away for a few more minutes? I thought not. I headed towards the staircase and started walking up it.

As I reached the top, I heard raised voices — they were coming from Templeton's study. I pushed open the door and saw Templeton towering over Severn, his eyes bulging out of his head and his face flushed. He looked like he was about to hit him. He spun round on his heels at the sound of my entering, and I immediately hid my cigarette behind my back — he disapproved of smoking.

'Paul,' Templeton said, his jaw clamped together in quiet fury, 'I wonder if you would be good enough to put Charles up this evening? I fear we're a little short of room here.'

'Of . . . of course, sir,' I said, and Templeton bowed his head at me and stalked out of the room.

I stepped forward and helped Severn up — he had slipped to the floor.

'What the hell did you do?' I asked in wonder. I'd never seen Templeton lose his temper in this way.

Severn looked up at me with clouded eyes. 'Search me,' he said, slurring the words. 'I only placed my hand on her leg, I swear.'

After a decent interval, I took him by the arm and led him downstairs.

*

By the time we reached my flat in Pera, Severn's head was lolling against the side of the jeep. As I had helped him downstairs, Templeton had discreetly taken me to one side and given me the keys to the vehicle, telling me to return it to the Consulate-General transport park as soon as I was able. Then he had placed a hand on my shoulder, thanked me, and trudged back to the party. I didn't get the chance to see Vanessa before leaving to check if she was all right.

I managed to drag Severn up the stairs and hoisted him onto the couch in my tiny living room. I took his shoes off and went back down to the jeep to lock up. As I did, my eye fell on a flap of yellow material peeking out of the underside of the driver's seat. I jimmied the seat up, slid it out, and squinted at it in the glare of the afternoon sun. What on earth . . . ?

It was a large-scale fold-out map of Turkey, and someone had drawn small black circles at several points on it: I counted thirty of them.

I quickly considered my options, and came to the conclusion there were two: I could either make a copy of the map and give it to Yuri at our next meeting, or I could replace it under the seat and forget I had ever seen it.

My first instinct was to copy it, of course. Here, finally, was something substantial to give Moscow. But *was* it, and if so just how substantial? I had no way of knowing. It was a strange sort of morality, perhaps, but it was mine: I was uncomfortable with the idea of handing over a secret I didn't even know myself. And there would be nothing lost if I replaced it. After all, it was only thanks to Severn getting blotto that I had seen it at all. I might just as easily not have done – and it might not be important at all.

No, it had to be important. Osborne had come out here because of this, and Severn had obviously driven him, Templeton and Cousin Freddie to some or all of the marked locations.

Perhaps, it occurred to me, there was a third option. I could find out what the map meant myself, and then decide whether it was something I felt I could pass to Yuri. I glanced down at it again. The nearest circle was positioned just outside Izmit, a town about sixty miles away – if I took the jeep, I could be there and back in a couple of hours. Severn was passed out, and everyone else was still at the party in Beylerbeyi. I had a jeep at my disposal . . .

I walked back up to the flat and into the living room. Severn was snoring now, his head tilted back. I went over to the dresser and wrote a quick note explaining that I was returning the jeep and would be back shortly. I placed it by his head, then went into the bedroom and removed a metal case from beneath a floorboard. I took out Father's Luger, which I had taken from his body in Germany six years earlier, and held it in my hand. It was heavy and cold. I placed it in my waistband, then turned off the lights, locked up the flat and returned to the jeep.

*

Once I had crossed back over the Galata bridge, I took the road out of town, heading through a landscape of grey mosques and olive groves until I was driving along the coast, the wind blowing dust into my hair. The circle on the map was a few miles short of Izmit, and as I reached the spot I saw a wide earth track heading off the road and decided that it must be the location. I slowed to a snail's pace, checking for signs that the site might be occupied or under surveillance. There didn't seem to be any, so I slowly drove down the track, eventually coming to a dead-end at the crest of a hillock. I parked the jeep and got out to have a look.

It was late afternoon now, but the sun was still a glaring hole in the sky, and it beat down on my neck as I walked around trying to see what it was that Severn and the others had driven out here to see. I decided I had turned off too early, as there was nothing but scrub and a few beech trees. After several minutes of fruitless searching, I headed back to the jeep and started reversing back down the track to rejoin the road. It was probably just as well, I thought . . . But as I tried to angle one of the wheels, I saw something that made me hit the brakes: a tree stump.

If I hadn't been here with the map, it would never have given me pause for thought. But it was the only stump around, and it was setting off alarms in my head. I braked again and went to the back of the jeep, where there was a small bag of equipment: driving gloves, binoculars and a torch. I took the torch and walked up to the stump. Kneeling down, I placed my hands against the side of it, and pushed.

The stump lifted: it was on a hinge. I brushed away soil and leaves to reveal netting. Pulling that away, a dark hole about the width of a man appeared, and I saw a narrow wooden ladder leading down. I took a breath. There was still a chance to turn back, pretend I'd never seen the map, pretend none of it had happened. But Yuri's words came back to me: *'Unless you can provide a higher grade of material, it is perhaps best that we discontinue our arrangement.'* I reached out for the top rung of the ladder.

A few seconds later I landed in darkness. I grabbed the Luger from my waistband and turned on the torch. I was in a low tunnel. There was an opening to my left, and I crouched down and crawled through it.

The space was bigger than my bedroom in Pera. Most of it was taken up with wooden crates. I pushed aside a layer of plastic sheeting in one and shone my torch down on it: cold metal glinted up at me, and I caught a whiff of cosmoline.

I spent several minutes poking around the boxes, prying with my fingers and the torch. I found rifles, pistols, binoculars, a radio set and even commando daggers. The latter confirmed all my suspicions: this was a stay-behind base.

Early in the last war, several groups in England had been secretly trained and provided with underground arms caches such as this, the idea being that if the Germans invaded a resistance force would already be in place ready to counter them. The concept of the Auxiliary Units, as they had been called, had expanded as the war had progressed. Instead of waiting until a country fell to the Axis powers and then dropping supplies to hastily assembled partisan groups, as had happened in France, men in several countries were discreetly approached and asked to commit to staying on as part of resistance forces in the event of invasion. In Singapore, these groups had initially been called 'left-behind parties' until someone had realized that it might not be the best name to inspire volunteers, and changed it to the rather more inspiring 'stay-behind parties'.

But why would the Service need stay-behind parties in Turkey? The answer was obvious: the threat of Soviet invasion. If there were to be another war, as many were predicting, Turkey was an obvious flashpoint – the Russians could slip over the mountains along the long border and the army wouldn't know what had hit it. Britain didn't fancy that idea, so had set up these bases as a precautionary measure. That meant that there must also be men who knew where the bases were and had been trained in guerrilla warfare – that, presumably, was where Cousin Freddie came in.

I made sure there was no sign that I had been in the cave, then clambered back up the ladder and hoisted myself out of the hole. I carefully replaced the netting, the foliage over it and the stump, then headed back to the jeep and drove off, my heart thumping in my chest.

I arrived back at the flat around dusk. I replaced the map under the driver's seat and entered the flat. Severn hadn't moved from where I had left him, and his snores had only increased in volume.

I tore up the note I'd left him, and headed for the comfort of my bed.

XV

A lot had happened since that summer eighteen years ago. Turkey had joined NATO, and the Americans had soon taken charge of the place. All three of the Templetons were dead: Joan from cancer a couple of years ago, Colin more recently by my own hand. And Vanessa, whose love I had ignored for so many years, then tried but failed to return . . . she, too, was gone.

My dreaded meet with Yuri had been a wash-out: I had waited in the chill morning mist outside the warren of the Grand Bazaar for half an hour, but he had never turned up. I had tried again the following day, then three days after that and so on according to the schedule, but he had never shown his face again. Part of me had been relieved, as the prospect of blowing the stay-behind bases had made me very uneasy: if the Soviet Union *did* invade, the entire security of Turkey might depend on them, and that was a measure of influence I wasn't sure I wanted to have. But Yuri's vanishing act had also seemed rather final: it seemed Moscow had carried out its threat, and discarded me.

I had been posted back to London in September, where I was given a hefty promotion within Soviet Section. I had occasionally checked the old dead drops, but to no avail. Finally, one freezing December evening someone brushed past me as I left a cinema, and my double life resumed once again.

My new contact, Sasha, was in his early forties, with a neat beard and a penchant for tweed suits and bow ties. He claimed not to know why Yuri had failed to show in Istanbul, but assured me that Moscow's previous concerns about me were ancient history. He pumped me with questions about my work in Soviet Section, and I answered them as fully as I could. He never asked me about Turkey, and I decided not to mention the map or the arms cache.

Our meetings continued over the next few years, although after a while they became much more infrequent for security reasons. The Templetons' garden party had given me my first indication that I might not be the only double, and that had been confirmed in '56, when Burgess and Maclean appeared at a press conference in Moscow. A string of exposures had followed: Blake in '61, Vassall in '62, and then Philby's defection in '63, which had, in turn, led to the unmasking of Blunt and Cairncross. The newspapers were filled with talk of spy rings and third and fourth men. I was as agog as anyone at the extent of Soviet penetration.

I forced my mind back into the here and now: a prison cell, presumably somewhere in Italy. Now, finally, I too had been exposed, but I had to figure out what the hell was going on and get out of here and stop it. When I had been appointed Head of Soviet Section in '65, I had been given access to a lot more files, but I had seen nothing about a stay-behind operation in Turkey, and I'd presumed that it had been wound down: the threat of Soviet invasion no longer seemed realistic. The idea that Severn and Zimotti's plans were part of the same operation suggested a much larger scale than I had feared. There had been thirty arms caches hidden across Turkey in '51. How many would there be in Italy now and, more importantly, how many men had been trained to use them? If my suspicions were right, this wasn't just a few spooks idly plotting, placing a bomb here or there: they had a highly trained army prepared to do their dirty work.

I turned to Sarah sitting next to me in the gloom of the cell, and let my mind absorb the significance of it for a moment.

'So this is what you wanted to tell me at the embassy?' I said. 'Your suspicions about Charles, the documents you found in his safe . . .' She nodded. 'But why? How could you be sure I wasn't a part of the plot?'

She took a deep breath and smiled faintly.

'Charles had already told me about what happened in St Paul's: that you had chased down the sniper, discovered that he was an Italian, and were coming out to investigate. He seemed very jumpy about you, so I asked him about your history. He told me you'd been at school together, and also about what had happened in Nigeria, and after – that you had briefly been suspected of being a double. We still had files in the office from your time here, so I read up on you – your missing father and your wonderful career and so on – and suddenly it just came to me, I suppose.'

'What did?' I asked. But I knew what she was going to say.

'Well, that you *were* a double. That you had gone out to Nigeria to stop that defector exposing you, and chased the sniper halfway across London because *you* had been the target, not John Farraday. As I read the files, it seemed that everyone around you ended up dead, but there you were still standing at the end of it all, and . . .' She looked into my eyes. 'I was right, wasn't I?'

I stared back at her. It was ironic, of course: I had fooled Templeton and Osborne and everyone else for all these years, and finally with barely a glance at my file a cipher clerk in Rome had guessed at the truth.

'Yes,' I said. 'You were right. But if you were so sure I was a double, why did you decide to confide in me?'

She raised a smile. 'It was a risk – but I reckoned a Soviet agent probably wouldn't be involved in a conspiracy to smear Communists. I thought you might have already guessed at what they were up to, in fact, and that that was why you had come out here, or that you were at least somewhere on the road to finding out. So I thought I could be . . .' She looked for the right word. 'Indiscreet. Not tell you, exactly, but just give you a nudge in the right direction. If you realized what was going on, you'd tell Moscow, and then they'd have to stop it.' She shrugged her shoulders simply. 'I'm not a Communist or anything.'

'Neither am I. I was, once, but that was a long time ago, and I was . . .' What — young? Trapped? It was time to put my excuses away. 'And I was wrong about it,' I said.

We sat in silence for a while then. I wanted very much to tell her that everything would be better — to *make* it better for her, somehow. But there was nothing that could be done. For anything to move forward, we had to get those documents. Without them, this was all smoke and mirrors: nobody would ever believe it. Even with them it might be smoke and mirrors, because several governments would be very quick to discredit them as fakes, and it might be hard to prove otherwise. But the operational details would be in there, and if Sarah were telling the truth we were faced with the slaughter of hundreds, possibly even thousands, of innocent people.

Somewhere in the back of my mind, the seed of an idea was forming: Haggard. In Italy, the operation was designed to discredit the Communists and keep them from coming to power. But in Britain, the target seemed to be the Labour government. That meant Haggard couldn't be part of the conspiracy: he was one of its main targets. And as Home Secretary, he could act. Unmask the conspiracy to him and I had a sliver of a chance of not just stopping whatever bloodbath was being planned, but redeeming myself. My life as a double agent was over, but perhaps, if I could take on this lot and *win*, I could start afresh, in a new Service purged of the conspirators. A new life, a new page . . .

Well, it was a nice thought, but I couldn't unmask anyone without proof. And that was tightly locked up in Severn's safe in Rome. I squeezed Sarah's hand gently, and as I did I felt a hardness in her fingers. Her wedding band, no doubt. Only it was sharp. I glanced down. Her other jewellery had gone, but her engagement ring, dirty and bloodied, shone dully.

That meant two things. First, Severn had not discarded her

entirely. My watch and everything in my pockets had been taken from me, so it must have been a deliberate decision to leave this on her. Despite imprisoning and torturing her, it seemed he hadn't wanted to remove this symbol of love from her body. I remembered his screams as he had brought the whip down on me: '*Nobody touches my wife.*' Secondly, it was a weapon. Not an ideal weapon, by any means, but then prisoners with no other hope of escape can't be choosers.

'I have an idea,' I said. 'Can you run?'

She nodded slowly. 'I can try.'

'What would happen if . . . ?' I stopped myself. It wasn't the most gallant request I'd ever made. I tried to keep my voice even. 'What would happen if I kissed you?'

I thought for a moment she was going to slap me, but then she saw me nodding at the walls and felt me squeeze her ring finger, and understanding dawned on her.

'Charles . . . Yes, I see. But he might bring others with him.'

I held her gaze. 'What do we have to lose? They'll be here sooner or later anyway. Isn't it better if it's sooner?'

She didn't answer for a few moments, and then I thought I saw the trace of a smile cross her pale lips.

'"Was ever woman in this humour wooed?"'

My spirits lifted faintly: if she still had the wherewithal to make literary references, we might just have a chance. I took a deep breath, and she nodded. This was, I thought, quite likely suicide.

We stood and I moved closer to her, whispering in her ear to pass me the ring. She wriggled it off and I squeezed it onto my little finger. I made sure that the stone was facing outward: a very small, very expensive knuckle-duster.

We were inches away from each other now. I tried to keep my mind focused on the task ahead, and brushed a wisp of hair away from her face with my fingers. My stomach began to contract as the adrenalin began pumping through me. I leaned down and touched my lips gently against her collarbone.

'Does that hurt?' I whispered.

She shook her head. She was breathing rapidly now, whether in earnest or acting for the cameras I wasn't sure, and I brought my face up and gently pressed my mouth against hers. She didn't react at first, but then her lips parted slightly, and I felt the warm moistness of her tongue . . .

The door of the cell slammed open, and Severn rushed in, his face dark with rage and a low roar in his throat. I lunged at him, thrashing the ring against his face with every ounce of strength I had in me. Somehow I hit home, because he cried out and reeled backwards, stumbling into the wall and falling to the ground with a thick thudding noise. I stepped forward to finish the job, but he was already out for the count: his cheek was torn open and blood was gushing down it, but his mouth was lax and his head was resting on his shoulder.

I breathed out. It had worked. Against all the odds, it had worked.

But now we had to get out of here.

I quickly searched him: he was unarmed, but I grabbed the keys from his belt. Sarah picked the ring from the floor and threw it at him fiercely, then made to kick him. I pulled her away – we didn't have time. I opened the door and we came out into a long corridor, at the far end of which was a staircase.

We started running towards it.

XVI

The staircase led us out to a strip of concrete – we had been underground. The soles of my feet were already sore from the short run and my chest was still tight with tension. The light was bluish-grey and eerie, and I shivered as I breathed in the cool air. I could smell the sea close by. To our right, about a hundred yards away, were several Nissen huts and a line of low dark buildings, many with radio masts jutting from their roofs.

I turned to Sarah. 'Any idea where we are?'

'Sardinia, I think. Charles mentioned it once. A special base for political prisoners.'

Sardinia – I had spent a long weekend here with a girlfriend in the spring of '64, a lifetime ago. Zimotti had told me Arte come Terrore were based on the island. A strange sort of a bluff, but perhaps they'd intended to lure me out here all along. Perhaps torture had always been on the cards. Precisely how long had they known I was a double – and *who* knew, precisely?

To our left was a gate, surrounded on both sides by a fence, the top of which gleamed in the dim light: barbed wire. There was a small hut, no doubt for guards, but they would be more prepared for people trying to come into the base than trying to leave it – if we were fast enough. I reckoned we had a couple of minutes at most before Severn recovered and started coming after us. And, in a place like this, there was no telling how many he might bring with him.

There were several small military vehicles parked on the concrete: Volkswagens. We jumped into the nearest one and I reached under the dashboard, pushing against the panel to free it and quickly locating the two wires. I bridged them and the engine stuttered into life.

'That's a clever trick,' said Sarah, as I grabbed the wheel and headed for the main gate.

'It can come in useful,' I agreed. The engine was behind the vehicle's rear wheels and it felt very lightweight, almost like driving a dune buggy. I told Sarah to duck and then pushed my foot down and steered to the right of the gate, straight for the barbed wire fence, the engine squealing from the strain I was putting it under. There was a screech and crunching of metal and glass as the wheels trampled over the fence and crashed through to the other side, and then the shots started coming from behind us. They went wide, but they had reacted faster than I'd expected, and they wouldn't go wide for long.

I made to steer onto the main road leading out of the camp, but decided against it at the last moment. That would give them the advantage, as they would know where we were heading and could plan accordingly. So instead I yanked the wheel to the left. I glanced across at Sarah, and saw she had her fists curled up in her lap from the suddenness of the manoeuvre. 'Sorry!' I shouted, as we bumped across the ground and through a string of low shrubbery.

Glancing in the rear-view mirror, I saw that there were now several vehicles in pursuit: at least three, but there was a shroud of early morning mist so there might have been more behind them. There was a rough path through the brush straight ahead, but looking to my right I glimpsed a tiny segment of pale blue in the darkness and suddenly realized we were on a bluff overlooking water. There was our chance.

I started slowing the engine and shouted out to Sarah to jump out. She didn't hear me, so I told her again, screaming it out. She looked at me in terror, but nodded, and on the count of three I opened my door and leapt to the earth, hoping she was doing the same.

I landed badly, a stream of stones and grit cutting into my hands and face, but I was going very fast and managed to tumble my body for several yards, lessening the impact. Sarah had already got up and was scurrying over to join me: she must have had a better landing. The Volkswagen was already beginning to veer off course, but I reckoned our pursuers wouldn't realize we had bundled out for another second or two. We needed to get out of their line of fire in that time, and down into the rocks where they couldn't follow us on wheels.

The surfaces of the stones were ice-cold against the soles of my feet. I started clambering down the slope, taking care not to go too fast. My body was still aching from the beating Barnes had given me, and if I slipped and fell now I wasn't sure I'd have the strength to get up again. This was Maquis-type country, with the rocks interrupted by stiff brush, gorse and myrtle bushes. I picked out some scrub to step on, but it was spiky and I rapidly switched back to searching for stone surfaces. Sarah was just behind me and I could hear her panting with the effort.

We clawed our way down the bluff, conscious that we might be spotted at any moment. My hands were getting scratched and we were kicking up a lot of dust, which kept getting in my eyes. Above us the noise of engines died away and was replaced by the voices of men. I strained my ears to try to make out whether Severn was among them, but couldn't hear and didn't have time to linger. The further down we got before they realized which way we had gone, the harder it would be for them to find us. But they wouldn't give up easily, I knew. We had to get off the island entirely.

As we approached the bottom of the slope, the water stretched out before us in a small bay, and my heart lifted a little. I couldn't yet see any boats, but we should be able to swim far enough away to find one, or some other form of transport. But then I turned and saw Sarah staggering behind me, her chest shivering beneath the thin dress, and the panic rose in me again.

'You go!' she called out in a hoarse whisper. I shook my head and looked around desperately. The voices were still above us, but they didn't seem to have figured out which way we had gone yet. A large structure, a circular stone tower, suddenly loomed out of the mist on a plateau not more than a dozen feet away from us. My first thought was that it was another hallucination, but it looked far too real and it triggered something at the back of my mind. Yes, I had seen several of these on my previous trip. I couldn't remember what they were called, but they had been used by the island's prehistoric inhabitants, I seemed to recall, for shelter against potential invaders.

Well, we needed shelter now. If they hadn't seen which way we had come down the slope, we might just be in luck, as they would no longer have the chance to spot us and we'd also be able to catch our breath and perhaps get some strength back. There was, hopefully, simply too much ground for them to cover, and they would have to conclude eventually that we had got away from them. Then again, if they had already seen which way we'd gone, we might be making a fatal mistake by stopping, as they could simply come in and scoop us up.

I couldn't hear the voices any more, so decided to risk it. I took Sarah by the arm and we headed towards the narrow entrance of the shelter, and into a very dimly lit passageway. I remembered that these places were built from stones simply piled up on top of each other, and suddenly wondered how solid they were.

At the end of the passageway we came to a staircase, which we started to climb. The place was dank and cold, and the only light filtered through a few tiny windows. About halfway up I heard a faint buzzing in the background, which grew to a drone.

A helicopter was coming our way.

I looked through one of the windows. It was a camouflaged Sea

King, or an Italian version of it. I turned to Sarah, who had started shaking, her breaths coming out in sobs.

'It's all right,' I whispered. 'We'll be all right.'

But the obvious lie made her even more nervous and she started making more noise. I looked through a slat again — the helicopter had started to descend, and was now hovering a hundred feet or so away, like a giant and sinister wasp.

I took Sarah in my arms, letting her bury her head in my chest, stifling her sounds. 'You must be quiet,' I said, and held her as firmly as I could, willing her to stop shaking. The sweat was pouring off me now, and I prayed that the helicopter would leave. We stayed in that position for what seemed like an eternity, but then Sarah suddenly looked up from my chest. There had been a noise downstairs.

Someone had come in.

*

We sat, huddled, hardly daring to breathe, and listened to the footsteps below us. I realized we were on a level circling the exterior of the structure. It might take them a little while to figure that out, too, so perhaps once they started climbing we could cross to the other side, take the stairs back down and slip out. Only . . . I glanced through the slat again: the helicopter was still there, and would no doubt be equipped with machine-guns. Our only hope, then, was that they wouldn't realize we were in here, and would leave to check somewhere else. But the footsteps sounded very sure, and were moving closer to us by the moment.

I gestured at Sarah and we started moving away from the sound, to the other side of the floor. But we must have dislodged something as we ran, either a stone or some dust, because there was suddenly a shout from below, and when I next looked up, Barnes was standing in front of me with a machine-pistol in his hands and a murderous look in his eyes.

We raised our hands, and he gestured to the staircase with the weapon.

'Down.'

*

The helicopter was hovering several feet above the ground, flattening the surrounding shrubbery and kicking up eddies of dust. In the cockpit, headphones over his ears, sat the beak-nosed guard, while standing a few feet in front of it was Severn, his fair hair swept back by the wind from the blades and his eyes locked on us as Barnes marched us towards him. He wiped his hand against the gash on his cheek, and as it came away I saw it was dark with blood.

I looked across at Sarah: she was still shaking, and her back was hunched over. Behind us, I could sense Barnes' fingers twitching on the trigger of his machine-pistol, and realized that we were probably seconds away from death. But there was no way out. My chest tightened, and I could hear my heart drumming in my head.

'Here, sir?' Barnes called out to Severn. He was itching to kill me, to avenge Templeton.

Severn shook his head. 'Inside.'

A few seconds' reprieve, then. Probably because he didn't want the trouble of carrying our corpses aboard.

We were level with Severn now. The spinning of the rotors was deafening, and it was proving difficult to walk. Barnes yelled at us to enter the helicopter, and Sarah started trying to lift herself over the ledge. She fell on the first attempt, and Barnes roughly dragged her up and pushed her up and over with one hand, the other still clutching the machine-pistol. Now? The moment I had the thought the chance was gone: he swivelled back to face me, and gestured I should follow suit.

I didn't react. I knew he would shoot us as soon as we were both on board. Once the chopper was safely over the water, they would throw our bodies out. Barnes took me by the collar of my shirt and shoved me up and in, using the machine-pistol as a prod. As I collapsed at Sarah's feet, Barnes leapt aboard, and Severn after him, and I soaked in the smell and atmosphere of the cramped space, taking in the beak-nosed guard up front, the bank of equipment he was operating, and the fact that we had already started to take off. I glanced up and saw Barnes looking over at Severn, who nodded.

'Dark first,' he shouted, pointing at me, and Barnes grabbed me by the collar again and hauled me around until I was kneeling by the door, facing out and looking down at the ground as we rose up from it and away, now already above water, my heart in my lungs and vomit rising in my throat.

This was it. This was the end. I could hear Sarah sobbing behind me, begging Severn not to kill us. She was interrupted by a loud burst of noise, static from a transmitter, and for a fraction of a second Barnes moved to register it and without even thinking I reached back and grabbed Sarah by the wrist, then pitched forward, diving blindly into the sky. The wind yanked me down, and I lost contact with Sarah and went spinning through the air, my guts in my eyeballs and my brain in my toes and a choir of gunshots ringing in my ears, and then there was a smack and a deep boom, and the water was cold, freezing, salty, and I was plummeting further and further into it . . .

XVII

It took a few moments to catch up with what had happened: my head was dizzy from the fall, my chest burning from the impact, and every injury on my body was suddenly seared by the salt in the water. But my mind was singing, because I knew I was alive.

I clawed my way up to the surface for air, but the moment I broke through machine-gun fire split the water around me, bursts of green and orange flame kicking up through the waves. I grabbed a breath before submerging again, and saw that Sarah was just a few feet away, and seemingly in trouble, her limbs flailing about. My mind stopped singing. There was a helicopter with machine guns right above us, and we were sitting ducks. I squinted through the bluey-green world and saw a formation of jagged grey rocks in front of me: the coastline.

About halfway down the wall of rocks was a large hole: it looked like some sort of passage. I swam frantically towards Sarah and managed to twist her round so that she was lying atop my back, and then kicked as hard as I could towards the cavern. It was large, and I swam through, feeling ripples from fish and sea-creatures around me as I did.

I came up for air a few seconds later and deposited Sarah next to me on a large cold slab of stone. She spluttered out water and wheezed, her body racked from the experience. I looked up – had they seen us? Apparently not. Directly above our heads was a large overhanging rock formation, and just a few feet away its twin.

Between the two overhangs stretched a patch of pale pink sky. The hole was much larger than I would have liked: if the helicopter happened to fly over it, we were fish in a barrel. But if we had come up anywhere else, they would have already shot us.

The vital thing now was not to move and attract their attention. I explained the situation to Sarah, and we sat there, listening to the shuddering roar of the helicopter as it hovered over the area, circling back and forth, looking for us. With every increase in volume, my heart clenched, then subsided as the sound receded, only to clench again moments later. After a few minutes, the effort of staying still was starting to cramp my muscles, and I was worried that I wasn't going to be able to hold out much longer. If I fainted now, it could be fatal. Sarah was in the same position as I was, her muscles tensed and her stomach heaving. I suddenly noticed a line of small dark dots in the corner of the window of sky. Had they spotted us? But the dots weren't moving. My brain rearranged the perspective and I realized with a start that there was another overhanging rock between the sky and us, and that the dots clinging to it were, in fact, the heads of birds: vultures.

I squinted, and managed to make out a few of the individual heads. They were staring intently at us, and I knew why. We weren't moving: they were starting to wonder if we might be carrion.

Keep calm.

I looked beyond them at the patch of sky. No helicopter in it, but the noise was still there, so they hadn't given up yet, and were no doubt using binoculars to examine every possible hiding place we could have disappeared into. If we made any movement at all, they might catch it and then we would be finished. But if we *didn't* move, the vultures might decide we were worth investigating further.

I switched back to the line of dots. They weren't there any more! I caught a frantic flap of black feathers in my peripheral vision, and then saw them gliding down, seemingly not moving their wings, until they were circling directly above the nearest ledge. Any closer, and they might give away our position. But we were still exposed by the window, and any movement I made might alert Severn and the others.

The vultures were swooping nearer and nearer, a sinister sound emanating from their throats. An image flashed into my mind of their red eyes glaring glassily as their beaks pecked at our flesh, and I realized I had to risk it. The noise of the chopper momentarily fell away and I threw up a hand and retracted it almost as quickly, praying that the sudden movement would be enough to tell the birds we were alive but not enough to be seen by anyone in the chopper. There was a flickering of wings from the vulture at the head of the pack, and within a few moments they had disappeared from the window, no doubt moving on to the next outcrop. I looked up for any sign of the helicopter. Had they seen either the vultures' interest or my hands? It didn't seem so. The sound of the blades was fading into the distance.

Several minutes later, I realized they weren't coming back – at least not for the time being. I suddenly felt very tired. My eyes stung, my arms ached, my legs were in seizure – my whole body was racked with pain, and all I wanted to do was lie down and sleep and let oblivion do the rest. But now wasn't the time for such thoughts. We couldn't stay here – they'd have the police of the whole island awake to our presence within a few hours, which would mean we wouldn't be able to rent a boat or catch a ferry or do anything. We had to get back to the mainland, where we'd be able to slip through the cracks, and we had to do it now. I pushed myself up to a standing position and gripped the corner of a nearby rock. There was a narrow opening between two stones that led to more rocks. I helped Sarah to her feet, and we began crawling through.

It took us about an hour by my estimation, but we finally clambered through the rocks and found ourselves on a small strip of beach. The sun had come up now, and the heat was starting to beat down on us. Hidden high above the beach I could see the outline of a large white building: a hotel, perhaps, or one of the older villas.

We walked across the sand until we came to a tiny wooden jetty. Tethered to it was a boat. It was small, but it could get us off the island. I climbed up and threw off the ropes. There didn't seem to be a key anywhere, and I decided the best option would be to jump-start it. I hadn't done it since the war, but this didn't look all that different from a motor-torpedo. I was about to climb in when something stopped me dead. It was the click of a hammer.

I looked up. Standing directly above us was a man wearing a striped shirt and canvas trousers. And he was pointing a shotgun at our heads.

*

'*Che state facendo qui?*' he snarled. '*E' proprieta' privata.*'

He was young, in his early twenties I thought, and of much the same stamp as the sniper from St Paul's: long dark hair swept down over his forehead and the beginnings of a beard covering his deeply tanned face.

We raised our hands and walked towards him. He looked Sarah over in a way that made me feel queasy – her clothes hadn't completely dried and were still clinging to her in places – and then levelled the gun at my chest.

'*Abbiamo solo fatto una nuotata,*' I said. '*Non e' quello che pensa*—'

His eyes widened. '*E cosa penso?*'

'*Ascolti, mi dispiace molto di averla disturbata,*' Sarah broke in, surprising me. '*Avremmo bisogno di affittare la sua barca. In questo momento non abbiamo denaro con noi, ma lavoriamo per il governo britannico e mi accertero' personalmente che l'ambasciata la rimborsi*—'

'My God,' he said, lowering the gun. 'You're *British*! Why didn't you say so in the first place?'

Sarah and I looked at him with shock. The voice was pure Old Etonian.

'What the hell are you doing here?' he asked. 'You look a complete mess.'

'Help us up and we'll explain,' said Sarah, and gave her most winning smile. 'We come in peace, honestly.'

He hesitated for a moment, but a beautiful girl with an English accent can never be dangerous. He stuck out his hand, and helped her up, then offered it to me.

'Ralph Balfour-Laing,' he said. 'Pleasure to meet you. And yes, of *the* Balfour-Laings, before you ask!'

I'd never heard of any Balfour-Laings, and hadn't been planning on asking about them either. My first instinct was distrust, and it even went through my head that he might be a plant of Severn's, some sort of casual watchman for the base. But I dismissed it at once – he was just a rich young layabout, and Sardinia was one of their natural habitats. Gesturing at the villa, he explained that he was a painter and that the place was a private retreat where he sometimes came to discover his muse and, it seemed, host the occasional wild party with the island's jet set. He eyed Sarah up again and asked her if she had ever been painted nude. Before things got too out of hand I told him we were on urgent government business and needed to get back to the mainland immediately. Could he help?

'I can do more than that,' he said with a grin. 'I'll take you there myself. That's not my only boat, you know.'

XVIII

The face in front of me was covered in the beginnings of a beard, the bloodshot eyes staring out wildly. I looked like hell, and felt worse. There was a razor next to the basin, but I decided it wasn't a good idea: partly hidden under the beard, a long gash ran down the length of my right cheek, with grit visible inside it, and there were abrasions on my chin and throat. If I shaved, I might look even worse.

I picked up a monogrammed hand towel from a pile above the mirror and soaked a corner of it in the basin, then cleaned out as many of the wounds as I could, wincing with the pain, trying to remove as many of the surface problems as possible. Once I was satisfied, I picked up a glass from a mahogany sideboard, filled it with water from the tap, and drank down several glugs.

I walked over to one of the portholes and looked out at the island rapidly receding behind us. We'd made it. We were alive. But I couldn't help feeling it was just a temporary reprieve. The boat was going at a healthy rate of knots – but would it be fast enough? Severn would comb every inch of the bay looking for our bodies. When he didn't find us he would eventually come to the conclusion that we had escaped, and then his thoughts would turn to what Sarah might know, what she might have told me and what we might do next. Everything depended on how long he would keep up the search. He might start sending men into the nearby villages to look for us and ask around – or he might decide not to take any chances and immediately fly the helicopter straight to Rome. In which case, this would all have been for nothing, as he'd be waiting for us when we arrived.

I looked across at Sarah, obliviously asleep on a bank of padded orange seats in the corner of the cabin, beneath one of our host's works of art, a blotchy oil painting that I thought might be a Sardinian sunset gone askew. On the floor, the end of a cigarette smouldered in a terracotta ashtray.

Balfour-Laing hadn't had any food on board apart from some beans he'd found in a cupboard, which we had devoured straight from the tin, but the cigarettes had perhaps been more welcome. He had also offered us wine and beer, but neither of us was in any shape or mood for alcohol and had been more than grateful for water, and Sarah had soon fallen asleep. Some colour had finally returned to her face, and while the welts were still faintly visible on her neck, she otherwise looked in much better shape. Balfour-Laing had dug up a T-shirt and a pair of old overalls and, hunched over in them inelegantly, she looked like a child in hand-me-downs. I was wearing a pair of his trousers and a paint-flecked shirt – he hadn't had any spare underwear, but I wasn't about to complain. Both our outfits were completed by rather natty white plimsolls, part of a supply he kept on board for when the heat of the sun became too much for his guests to walk around barefoot on deck. Today was Sunday, he had told us: we had been imprisoned for nearly two days.

Perhaps feeling the force of my gaze on her, Sarah opened her eyes. She sat up and stared at me inquisitively.

'Are we nearly there?'

'Another hour or so.'

She nodded, and leaned over to pick up the pack of cigarettes from the floor. She slid one out and lit it. 'Thank you,' she said.

'Thank *you*,' I replied. 'You got us aboard.'

She took a draught of the cigarette and looked at me intently. 'That was nothing. You got me out of there.'

I changed the subject. 'We need to prepare. What more can you tell me about those documents you read in Charles' safe?'

'Nothing,' she said. 'I told you all I know. I could only risk staying in his office for a few minutes. I saw the Service seal and "Stay Behind", but there were hundreds of pieces of paper in the dossier and I didn't have the time—'

'I understand. Look, I have to stop whatever it is they are planning, so I'll need to get back into that safe and find those documents.'

'I know. I'll help you.'

'Good. I think it's best if you tell me the combination now, and that we part ways once we reach the mainland. They won't have put a stop on the airports yet and you'll be able to get a flight to London soon enough. As soon as you land, go straight to Whitehall and ask to see the Home Secretary, urgently. Tell him what you know—'

'But I don't really know anything!'

'You know enough. Tell Haggard everything you told me, and make sure to mention "Stay Behind". He'll understand. He'll ask you for proof, of course: tell him it's coming. Don't mention me.' It wasn't ideal, by any means, but I had to get her out of the country – and out of the reach of Severn.

She leaned down and crushed the remains of her cigarette into the ashtray. 'I appreciate what you're trying to do, Paul, but I want to stop this, too, and running away won't help. The Home Secretary isn't going to do anything without any evidence, and you know it. You need me to show you where the documents are – there were hundreds of them.'

'Describe them to me. I've a good memory.'

Her jaw was set. 'You're not getting rid of me.'

'Look,' I said, 'this isn't a time for heroics or impulse decisions. If this is what I think it might be, we're dealing with a conspiracy that a lot of very powerful men will do anything to protect. And I mean *anything*.'

'Don't you dare lecture me,' she said, her voice rising. 'I was already committed to stopping them, remember – I was prepared to show you the documents the other night, and I haven't found any reason to change my mind since. Quite the contrary.'

'Tell me how to get into the safe, Sarah. This isn't a game.'

She cut me off with a bitter laugh. 'Do you think I don't know that?' she spat out. She pulled the collar of her shirt down sharply, exposing one of the larger welts. 'Do you think I don't know who we're dealing with here?' Her gaze narrowed. 'I want to stop whatever it is he is planning, even it means I die running from him.'

Her voice had started to crack and she put a hand up to her face. I made to lean over, but she shook her head and stood up. She walked over to the other side of the cabin, next to a lifebuoy pinned to the wall with the name of the boat emblazoned on it: PARADISO. I could see her shoulders moving a little, and knew she was crying in both shame and fury.

I walked over and placed my hand on her shoulder, and eventually said something I didn't want to: 'All right, then. We'll do it together.'

She turned to face me, her face streaked with tears. 'Really?' She burst into unintended laughter, and I had a dreadful hollow feeling inside. But I had no choice – I had to get into that safe. For a moment, I wondered about abandoning the whole idea and just flying to London with her and going to Haggard. But I knew she was right, and that that wouldn't stop anything. I thought again of Colin Templeton and my vow to do some good finally, and my will hardened. I needed to get to the documents, and if she were prepared to take the risks I'd have to live with that, too. I didn't want her death on my conscience, but she had her own will and I couldn't force it – or I'd be as bad as her husband.

I nodded. 'Let's go upstairs and see Ralph. He might have some more of those beans.' I did my best to smile convincingly, and passed her a towel to wipe away her tears.

'Can't we stay down here for a bit?' she asked.

'I told you, it's perfectly safe. The deck area is completely shel-
tered and—'

'It's not that,' she said. 'I just don't feel I've thanked you properly.'

I looked at her sharply. Something in her tone – was she toying
with me?

'I don't need a reward,' I said. 'You've thanked me more than
enough.'

She stood up. 'At least let me return that kiss you gave me.'

She turned and needlessly drew together the curtains behind
her, affording me a glimpse of the outline of her backside through
the thin cotton of the overalls.

'Look,' I said, 'we're not out of the woods yet. Not by a long
chalk. And you've been through a hell of a lot and I think—'

She placed a finger to my lips, and then leaned her face over so
her mouth was by my left ear.

'I liked the way you kissed me,' she whispered. 'Do it again.'

She moved my chin across to her lips. I opened my mouth and
the hot wetness of her tongue jolted through me. I pressed against
her. She abruptly took her mouth away from mine and started
kissing my neck, then raised my arms and lifted off my shirt. We
stumbled across to the padded seats and she kissed my chest, rubbing
her chin against my hair there, and then flickering her tongue
against my stomach.

'Sarah . . .'

She shushed me, then placed her fingers at the waistband of my
trousers, and slowly slipped them down. She smiled softly at the
lack of underwear.

I couldn't resist any longer. I caught hold of her by the hips and
struggled to unclasp the overalls, cursing as I did. She laughed at
my ineptitude but finally the clasp was undone, and she removed
her T-shirt and bra while I ran my fingers down her body to her
panties. I eased them down over her thighs and she gasped, clamping
her eyes shut.

We stood there naked, gazing at each other, and then she pushed me down onto the seats. She leaned over me for a moment, breathing hard, and tipped her head back. Her neck and breasts glistened with sweat, and I pulled her closer to me, until we were locked tightly together. I clasped her shoulder to slow her rhythm and she cried out, then moved with me, rocking back and forth. She stared down at me, her hair covering her eyes, and I thought for a moment I could feel what she was feeling, her flesh parted by me, the shiver through her body. She began panting louder, gasping for air, and I moved more frantically, and she bit down on my hand as we rocked back and forth, faster and faster . . .

There was a fierce knocking on the door of the cabin, and we froze, our hearts thumping against each other.

'I say,' called a voice, 'everything all right down there?'

I glanced at Sarah, a film of sweat covering her forehead.

'Out in a minute!' I called back.

There was no reply for a second, then a 'Righty-ho!' and the sound of receding footsteps.

Sarah leaned forward.

'I do hope not,' she whispered, and then slowly ran her tongue along the underside of my neck. I grabbed hold of her and took her with renewed ferocity.

XIX

Sunday, 4 May 1969, Rome, Italy

We spent the rest of the journey above deck with Ralph Balfour-Laing: Sarah and he discovered that they had a few acquaintances in common, and I learned more about the London 'scene' and the Cresta Ball than I needed to know. We both declined several offers of marijuana cigarettes. But, as promised, he took us all the way to the mainland, dropping us at the main harbour at Civitavecchia. It was just coming up to eight o'clock in the morning. When we told him we needed to get to Rome, he unhesitatingly thrust a sheaf of *lire* into our hands and brushed aside all our thanks and assurances that the embassy would be in touch to reimburse him. He chanced his hand one last time by giving Sarah a card with his details, and then he returned to the boat and to the sweet life in his island retreat, and we jumped aboard a crowded bus on its way to Rome.

As the bus sped through the dusty roads, I opened the window so the sun could warm my bones. Our driver had the radio on, and sang along to the romantic ballads emanating from it in a loud and gloriously out-of-tune baritone, but about twenty miles outside the city, relief came in the form of a news bulletin. The first headline: someone had hurled a bomb from a passing car at the headquarters of the Communist party in the city the previous night, and the party had responded by pulling down the shutters and drafting in students and activists to guard the building.

'These damned Communists deserve what they get!' cried the

driver in Italian, throwing out an arm angrily, and rather danger-ously. Several voices in the bus grunted their agreement.

Sarah looked at me questioningly, and I shook my head. This wasn't connected, although it didn't help the situation much. Severn and Zimotti were going to use the current climate to stage something, and I had a feeling it would be more spectacular than a bomb thrown from a car. It would also, of course, be something they would blame on the Communists, rather than targeting them. She turned away, and as she did I took the opportunity to examine her profile. She looked like a Pre-Raphaelite painting, crossed with Grace Kelly. No . . . that wasn't quite right. She was like nobody else, of course – utterly unique. The line of her jaw, of her nose, the positioning of every feature was so simple, so fitting, that one wondered why God or whichever artist was responsible had not repeated the trick with all women, with all the world . . .

'Easy prey for any beautiful woman.' It was a phrase I'd read in my dossier at Pyotr's flat – part of the preparatory document for my recruitment in '45. But could this be different? I put it out of my mind. My attraction to Sarah was strong – frighteningly so – but it was simply being reinforced by the position we were in. We were both on the run, and we had only each other to turn to. I had to make sure I didn't get carried away. We hadn't talked much since our love-making on the boat, but perhaps she had simply needed a release, a way to prove she was still alive and banish the thought of Charles a little. I had simply been there, that was all – I had done the same myself many times.

*

About an hour and a half later we got off the bus at the main train station, and from there we took a taxi to the embassy – Balfour-Laing's money was disappearing rapidly. There were no cars parked outside. It looked like Severn had not yet made it here. We knocked on the large iron door and were led into the entrance by the same butler as had let me in three evenings earlier. He didn't seem surprised to see us, and I breathed a tiny sigh of relief. We hurried across the marble floor to the reception desk. The clerk did look a little surprised, but then it was Sunday, and we had turned up looking like a couple of clowns.

'Good morning, Mrs Severn. Mister . . . ?'

'Dark,' I said. 'I was at the reception here on Thursday.'

'Yes, sir. If I could just see your identification . . . ?'

'Don't be so absurd, Harry,' Sarah said. 'I'm here every day, and this is the Deputy Chief of the Service. We're going up.'

Harry's face flushed but he didn't move from his desk, and we quickly headed for the staircase and made our way up to the Station. The place was deserted, and it was odd to think I'd been here just two days earlier, about to go out to meet Barchetti.

'Are there any weapons in here?' I asked Sarah, but she shook her head.

'Charles has a Browning, but he had it with him in Sardinia.' She caught my look. 'There may be something hidden somewhere, but I've no idea where.'

I nodded. It was unfortunate, but we didn't have time to waste on it. She ran over to a drawer next to the *cafetière* and pulled out the key to Charles' office, which she swiftly unlocked. The morning sunlight streamed through the window and the sound of traffic came up from the street below. She went over to the painting above the desk – a portrait of the Queen, of course – and I helped her take it down, revealing a wall safe. That was new – I'd only had a locked filing cabinet when this had been my office. She dialled the combination, and then, with a click, it opened.

She hadn't been exaggerating on the boat: there were *hundreds* of dossiers, all arranged in metal shelves within the safe. Thank God I had her with me – I'd never have found the right one by myself. As the thought hit me, I noticed the look on her face.

'What's wrong?'

'It looks different,' she whispered. 'I think he's rearranged it.'

My heart sank. I considered taking the whole lot with us for a moment, but there was simply far too much to carry. I started removing the dossiers from the left-hand side of the safe and lifting them over to Severn's desk.

Anything you remember about the dossier?' I asked. 'About what it looked like?'

She was already bent to the task. 'Some of the pages had a black banner across the top,' she said. 'And the whole thing was paper-clipped together.'

I started going through them, wanting to set aside anything that didn't look right as fast as possible, but not so fast as to miss the crucial dossier. There were insurance papers, staff lists, files on Italian leaders . . . Some fascinating information, no doubt, but none of it threatening the imminent death of innocent civilians. I continued riffling through, looking for paper-clipped pages with black banners . . .

I had looked through and abandoned over a dozen dossiers when I froze.

'Did you hear that?'

Sarah looked up. 'What?'

I thought there had been a noise from outside. I leapt over to the embrasure of the window and peered down into the driveway. But there was nobody there. I hurried back to the desk.

'Got it!' Sarah suddenly shouted. 'I've got it!'

'Are you sure?' If we took the wrong documents, we'd be back where we started.

She nodded furiously. 'This is it.'

'Let me see,' I said, and she reacted to my tone and handed it across. I suppose part of me had refused to believe it possible, and I needed to see it for myself. By the look of it this was Severn's own copy, and I guessed it had come through the diplomatic bag to avoid being deciphered by Sarah. The whole thing was held together with a large and slightly rusty paper clip, and a black banner across the top read 'STAY BEHIND: STRATEGY AND EXECUTION'. Beneath that was the date: 18 June 1968. I read it almost in a haze:

> In previous papers, we outlined the proposed
> new aims for STAY BEHIND in the current polit-
> ical climate. In this paper, we will explore
> how those aims might practically be executed
> across Western Europe. We estimate that these
> plans would be put into practice starting in
> early 1969 . . .

I flicked through the rest — it was in sections, but I wanted to check that the whole thing was here. I needed to be sure that it contained the details of the operation, and that they hadn't been saved for another paper. The next section of the dossier was titled 'Targeting', and I turned to it anxiously.

> Targets should be as iconic as possible. Historic
> monuments are desirable, especially as many
> are poorly guarded. Smaller targets with signifi-
> cance to the local population are ideal, as
> one can cause less damage and thus not lose
> too much sympathy, but have a much greater
> effect on public morale . . .

That didn't help much. The country was littered with historic monuments. I hurried on:

> Whatever the target, we must consider whether
> to blame the attacks on Moscow or on local
> groups with particular grudges to bear, whom
> we can then associate with Moscow via falsi-
> fied documentation, communiqués, press contacts
> and other means. In our view, the latter is
> the preferable option, as newspapers and others
> will piece together a conspiracy of attacks
> across Europe of their own accord, without

```
seeming to have been fed the information. We
wish to give the impression that Moscow is
supporting several disparate groups, to the
same end . . .
```

Damning stuff, but there were still no specifics: there was no indication of *which* targets they had chosen or on what dates they planned
to attack them. I flicked to the end of the document, to the final
page:

```
Large-scale public events also provide oppor-
tunities for attacks. The Olympic Games, soccer
tournaments and similar sporting events attract
thousands of spectators, and the impact of an
attack at such an event would be enormous.
```

'Soccer', I noted, rather than football. The Americans were definitely
involved, then.

```
Cultural events, such as concerts or other
performances, should also be considered.
Transport to such events - such as train jour-
neys - could be easier targets. However, secu-
rity is usually extremely tight at larger events,
so it is worth looking for smaller ones appro-
priate to the message we want to convey. An
attack during a performance of a play critical
of Communism would clearly point to Communist
perpetrators. Taking a step further into the
symbolic, a sabotaged play about high finance
could also be plausibly portrayed as a Communist
attack. Going further still, an attack during
a ballet could be seen as an indirect comment
on Nureyev's defection, even if Nureyev were
```

> not in the production. This would require a
> more delicate touch, but planning an attack
> for a ballet in which Nureyev would usually
> be expected to perform but did not for some
> reason on that day could be particularly effec-
> tive. In the next part of the paper, we will
> discuss operational plans in greater detail.

Apart from the reference to soccer, it had all the hallmarks of one of Osborne's Section reports. I had misread him all along, seeing him as a little Englander, a rabid Mosleyite who thought 'the wogs start at Calais'. But even Mosley was a European these days, and it seemed Osborne's hatred of Communism was rather stronger than his distaste for foreigners. He evidently had some powerful friends, and together they had taken over the original stay-behind networks and planned to use them to forge a hard-right agenda for the Continent.

And it was as well I had checked: the report seemed to end here, followed by a sheaf of documents in completely different typefaces. So either this was merely the first in a series of reports about the operation or someone had removed whatever came next in it — either way, it seemed to be missing the details of what they were planning. I turned back to Sarah. 'Do you remember if this was the exact dossier you saw, or could it have been one of the others?'

She looked at me in despair. 'I'm sorry,' she said. 'I really don't know.'

'We need to find the next part of this dossier,' I said. 'We need to know the operational—' I stopped. A car had just driven past the window, followed by the sound of tyres screeching on gravel. Severn? I ran over and looked down.

Yes. He was parking the Alfa Romeo, and coming through the gates behind it were two black Lancias.

I glanced at Sarah, and nodded affirmation. A clanging of iron echoed up the stairs.

They were in.

I calculated we had less than two minutes. I scooped up as many dossiers as I could, about half a dozen of them, stuffed them under my shirt, and gestured to Sarah to do the same. We would just have to hope that the operational plans were among them.

We stepped out of the office, and Sarah pointed to a door at the end of the corridor. Behind it was a much narrower staircase, with no carpet and no paintings on the walls: the staff staircase.

'This way!' she said.

XX

As we reached the foot of the staircase, we met the man with the beak coming into the main hallway. He froze at the sight of us, then reached for the pistol in his waistband. I leapt towards him and aimed a kick at the lower half of his legs – several of the dossiers that had been in my shirt fell to the floor, scattering in a spread at his feet. He stumbled on one of them, but then managed to throw out his hands and catch hold of Sarah by the waist as she made to run past him. She screamed and lashed out with her feet, catching him in the jaw. He was knocked to the ground, but she had also lost a few dossiers in the meantime, and started to lean down to pick them up.

'Leave them!' I shouted at her, and she nodded and started running for the open doorway. I kicked the man in the stomach to make sure he stayed down, then started to follow her. But the commotion had already alerted the others, and as I approached the door I saw Severn coming down the main staircase, with Barnes and Zimotti directly behind him.

I leapt through the doorway as the shot scraped the nearest wall. They would be with me in a second or two. I saw Sarah running down the driveway, heading for the Alfa Romeo. Good idea. I raced over to join her. The key was still in the ignition.

'I'll drive!' I shouted, pressing the button to unlock the doors. They opened on their hinges and we jumped in. The machine growled as I started her up, and we tore through the gates. A shot fired behind us, wild. But they would come in the Lancias soon enough.

As I turned onto the street, Sarah cried out and I glanced across at her.

'Drive on the right!' she screamed.

Shit. I looked back at the road and pulled us onto the other side just as a heavy goods lorry came rumbling towards us.

Close call.

Sarah started looking frantically through the dossiers, throwing each one onto the car's floor as soon as she had discarded it. I hoped to God we hadn't left the crucial one behind.

My plan was to head straight for the centre of town, as fast as possible: the more people there were around, the harder it would be for them to shoot at us. I squeezed the throttle and the needle shot up, and kept climbing. We passed the Fontana delle Api, and then I turned sharply down Via Druso. The car took the corner beautifully, and part of my brain was involuntarily awed by the machine under my command. The other part was desperately trying to see the street ahead, control this beast and get away from our pursuers. One of the Lancias was already in my rear-view mirror, taking the turn. A bullet ricocheted off the bodywork, and I swerved into the centre of the road for a moment. I swerved back, and reached over to open the glove compartment. Perhaps Severn had left a gun in there, or a map — but there was nothing. I looked up just as a Fiat with an enormous exhaust swerved in front of me, and I jabbed at the horn manically until it got out of the way.

I took another hard turn, into Via dei Cerchi. The traffic was starting to thicken now — evidently not everyone had taken the long weekend off. The streets were packed with pedestrians milling about aimlessly: tourists and nuns and children slobbering ice cream. I realized it had been a tactical error to head this way, because even if it made our pursuers a little gun-shy, which I was now rather less sure of, it was slowing us down terribly.

We had to get *out* of the centre — but where to? By now Severn would have made sure that all the country's ports, airports and customs posts had been given detailed descriptions of the two of us, and even if we travelled separately I didn't fancy our chances. Ergo, we had to find a way of avoiding Italian customs. If we reached, say, Switzerland, we would then be able to fly to London with little trouble: even Severn's powers didn't stretch that far. Travel between Italy and Switzerland didn't require visas, so if we ditched the car, split up and took the train we might be able to get through the checkpoints.

Switzerland it was, then straight to Haggard in London. But we needed proof first.

'Any luck yet?' I called out to Sarah.

'Not yet!'

I saw a space in the traffic and turned down Via della Greca, taking us around the bank of the Tiber. The main train station was only a mile or so away, but I had to find a way through this bloody maze of a city to get back to it. A thought hit me: the conspirators might not have dared to commit the operational details of this to paper. The strategic document could be all we had, and we would have to figure it out from there. 'Check the document we read in the embassy again,' I told Sarah. 'See if it mentions any other targets, or dates.'

She leaned down and started rummaging in the files at her feet. We came into a boulevard shaded with trees: Lungotevere dei Pierleoni, but that would take us into town, not away from it, so I took the next turn and pushed the pedal down again.

Sarah had now found the original document and was reading through it hurriedly. 'How about this?' she said. '"*In some Western European countries, especially in the south, religious events should be considered for attacks, as they provide a large crowd, easily understood and revered symbolism, shock value and, in many cases, low security. As Communism is an atheist ideology, Moscow's involvement would immediately be suspected . . .*"'

A religious event – yes, that might make sense. Could that be it, rather than a ballet or a football match? I thought back to my meeting with Barchetti. 'They know,' he had whispered. And then, when I had asked him if his cover had blown, he had shaken his head: 'About the attack in the dome.' I had presumed he meant that Arte come Terrore knew they were the prime suspects for Farraday's murder. But perhaps I'd been wrong. The sniper had stored his climbing ropes on the gallery at the base of St Paul's dome, and used that as an escape route, but the attack itself had taken place down in the cathedral, not inside the cupola. A slip? Barchetti's English hadn't been perfect, but I didn't think so. I bit my lip and cursed myself. I'd missed his real message – he hadn't been talking about what had happened in London at all. He had wanted to tell Severn that Arte come Terrore already knew of the next attack, which was going to take place *in another church entirely*.

Sarah had gone quiet, still engrossed in the document.

'What is it?'

'Charles has written in the margins on this page,' she said. 'He's circled the part where it talks about religious events and written . . .' She squinted. '"4 May."'

I looked across at her. 'That's today.'

Forget Switzerland. Forget Haggard. I swerved to the right, taking the turning back into the centre of town.

'What the hell are you doing?' shouted Sarah.

'It's going to happen *here*,' I said. 'In Rome. The Pope's noon address in St Peter's Square. They've placed a bomb in the dome. They're going to kill the Pope.'

She went quiet, and the papers slipped from her grasp and onto the floor.

XXI

I pushed my foot down on the accelerator and adjusted my hands on the wheel: they were slipping from the sweat pouring off them, as I realized what we were up against. No wonder Severn and Zimotti had been so anxious to find out what Barchetti had told me. This was on a far greater scale than the attacks in Milan, or the attempt to kill me in the middle of St Paul's.

The assassination of the Pope would, of course, shock Italy, and shock the world. No doubt they had already prepared a way to pin the blame on Arte come Terrore, or some other Communist-linked group, as outlined in the dossier. Moscow could deny it as much as they wanted but nobody would ever believe that Italian intelligence had been behind such a thing. I could scarcely believe it myself. The foot-soldiers would not be aware of it, of course. Did anyone in the Vatican know about it? They had certainly made some shaky alliances in the past – but to assassinate the Pope in this day and age? Even if they were brutal enough to sanction such a thing, Zimotti would never have trusted them with the information: one slip of someone's conscience and the whole operation would fall apart.

So there was a chance, if I reached the Vatican in time and warned them. I looked at the clock by the speedometer: it read ten o'clock. We had two hours. That would normally be plenty of time to get to the Vatican, but of course we were being pursued, and heading straight through the centre of the city.

I cursed the car. It was a racing model, or close enough, but that wasn't much help in this situation: we were being chased on very short stretches in a built-up area by cars that were not that much slower anyway. Even if I could have increased my speed, it wouldn't have been a good idea, because I didn't want the *carabinieri* on our tail as well. But the Lancias, perhaps because they were being driven by the two Italians, were snaking expertly through the traffic. The one in front, driven by Zimotti, was now less than a hundred yards behind us, and the traffic was, if anything, slowing.

We crossed the Tiber, the Castel Sant'Angelo to our right, and came into Via della Conciliazone. And there was the dome, reaching up into a cloudless blue sky. It was tantalizingly close, but traffic in the street was at a complete standstill and in my rear-view mirror I could see the Lancia gaining ground. I decided drastic action was needed, and veered right into the nearest side street, Via della Traspontina.

A three-wheeled scooter loaded with flowers in the back cart squealed around the corner, and I swerved to avoid it, then took the next left down Borgo Sant'Angelo. I just needed to find a left turning somewhere down here to get ahead of the traffic in Via della Conciliazone and come into the square. The entrance to Via della'Erba was blocked by an idiotically parked van, and the tip of the dome had now vanished behind one of the buildings ahead, making it harder for me to judge the distance. But the next turning or the one after that should do . . .

I glanced in the mirror again and saw that one of the Lancias was now just three cars behind us. I took a sharp right. It was taking us away from St Peter's, but I had to lose them and if I could take a few quick turns I might be able to. The street was narrow, leaving barely enough room for us to squeeze by, so I put my foot down and tooted the horn like a born Roman. Pedestrians jumped out of the way, a few of them shouting or waving their fists at us.

I turned left onto Borgo Pio. It was slightly wider, but had an outdoor *caffè* in it. I swerved to avoid it, but just as I did the sun broke over a building, blinding me for a moment, and Sarah gasped as one of our rear wheels crunched against a metal chair.

To the left was Vicolo del Farinone. A sign read 'SENSO UNICO', but it was the wrong way. No matter. I turned in. Vespas and motor-cycles lined the left-hand side, while in the centre of the street a party of pigeons was flapping about a crust of bread. They scattered at the sound of the engine, and I hugged the car to the right wall. There was an archway at the end of the street, but as we approached it I saw the nose of a car just coming into view. It was one of the Lancias. *How the hell had they got there?* I glanced in the mirror: the other was now right behind us. And there were no turnings in the street.

I put my foot down, hoping that I might scare the Lancia ahead into reversing. But it kept nosing further into the archway. The walls on either side of us seemed to be closing in, and even the sky above was obscured by laundry hanging from windows: underwear and shirts. The sun was blazing – they wouldn't take long to dry. I saw that the street widened a little before the archway, and as I looked over to the right I saw why – there was some sort of gate there. Something sparked in my mind and I reached for the button for the car doors. The hinges clunked and began moving out and then upward, just avoiding the walls of the passing houses, until they were almost touching each other above the front windscreen.

Wind was rushing into the car, and I started slowing down. We were a couple of seconds from the end of the street now, but we had to get there before the Lancia could block us off completely. I slowed the car some more, and we hit a cobble or something and landed a little off course: a corner of my door sheared against a drainpipe and got caught for a moment, metal screeching against metal. I righted us, then unbuckled myself from my seat. Now we were coming up to the end of the street, and the gate. A sign above it read '*Proprieta Privata*', but I could see that it was slightly ajar.

We were now travelling at just a few miles an hour, and the Lancia behind us thumped into the rear of the car. Someone –

Zimotti? – took a shot, but it hit the metalwork. Even at this speed, we were a moving target. There was an awful whistling noise emanating from the engine, and one of our back tyres had gone, a victim to speeding over the cobbles.

I turned to Sarah and gestured at the documents in her hand. She nodded dully and thrust them into the pouch of her overalls.

'Now!' I shouted, and she bundled herself out of the door, pushing the gate open as she did. The Lancia ahead of us was now in the archway, but it was stuck – they had no room to open *their* doors. I let go of the wheel and dived after Sarah through the open gate. There was a crunch as the Lancia bulldozed into the front of the Alfa Romeo, but I was already racing up stairs and down a small alleyway, passing the backs of houses. A few feet ahead there was another gate, and it was closed. Was it locked?

No. Sarah reached it and opened it, and a few moments later I joined her. As I stepped into the street I was nearly run over by a horse-drawn carriage coming the other way. The horse whinnied and lifted its legs and the tourists in the carriage shouted abuse at me. I took a moment to catch my breath, then looked up at the street sign on the archway. Via del Mascherino. I had momentarily lost my sense of direction, so I took a few more steps into the street and glanced to my left – the Lancia was reversing out of the archway a few feet away. But to my right was a curving colonnade, and just visible above it was the ball and cross of St Peter's.

I took Sarah by the hand and we started running towards it.

*

I'd forgotten how vast the square was, and how crowded it could become. The first part of it was reasonably easy to cross, but by the time we reached the Obelisk we had been absorbed into a heaving mass of people, chattering, jostling and fanning themselves in the heat of the morning. Believers of every age, nationality and colour were here, wearing paper hats and sporting binoculars so they'd be able to get a better look at the action. I pushed past a group of

African nuns and squinted up at one of the clocks on the Basilica: it was coming up to half past ten. There was just over an hour and a half left before the Pope was due to address the crowd.

The great church stood in front of us, the dome now just visible, framed by a cloudless blue sky. It looked even more impressive than St Paul's – but was it any more invulnerable? Sarah and I elbowed our way through the crowd, muttering '*Scusi – emergenza!*' People let us pass, reluctant to show anger in such a place and perhaps sensing our urgency.

Sarah pointed towards a flight of stairs on the right-hand side of the colonnade, and we headed that way. Several Swiss Guards were posted as sentries around the entrance, their absurd costumes offset by the short rapiers holstered in them and the long halberds they held in their hands. I pulled away a low wooden barrier and we ran up the stairs. The nearest of the Guards turned to us, alarmed.

'We need to speak to someone on the Pope's staff immediately,' I said, still panting. 'It's an emergency.'

He gave us a frozen look, and I became conscious that we were bruised, battered and wearing Ralph Balfour-Laing's paint-flecked clothes.

'Do you have any identification, please?' said the Guard, a pug-faced man sweating beneath his ridiculous plumed helmet.

'We're from the British embassy,' said Sarah. 'Ambassador Mazzerelli will be able to vouch for us.'

He wasn't impressed. 'Ambassador Mazzerelli is not here, *signora*. Do you have any identification from your embassy?'

Sarah touched my arm, and I turned to see Severn and Zimotti making their way through the crowd, followed by Barnes and the beak-faced soldier. They were now just a few dozen feet away, and heading straight for us, holding up wallets as they made their way past: they had identification, of course.

I faced the Guard again. 'Please,' I said. 'We are representatives of the British government and we need to speak to someone on the Pope's staff at once. You must stop the address at noon.'

'*Signore*, I do not care who you are. We cannot allow anyone through simply because they claim to have an urgent matter. Please wait here.'

He made to leave and I leaned forward and grabbed his tunic by the sleeve. He swivelled round sharply, and I turned to Sarah.

'How are those documents keeping?' I said. She looked at me blankly, and for a terrifying moment I thought we might have lost them on the way, but then she reached into her overalls and removed the sheaf of papers. At my prompting she turned to the page she had been reading from in the car and thrust it into the hands of the Guard.

'Just look at this,' she said. 'It's a proposal by foreign governments to commit terrorist attacks in Italy and blame them on Communists. Here' – she pointed to the relevant paragraph – 'it mentions that ideal targets are religious events. May the fourth is circled in the margin—'

'And that's today,' I broke in. 'There may be a bomb in the church.'

The Guard's momentary anger seemed to have calmed: perhaps he was used to such claims and was now certain he was dealing with a couple of cranks. I glanced back into the crowd. Severn and the others had already reached the first flight of steps.

'This is not possible,' the Guard was saying, and he handed the documents back to Sarah. 'We have very good security measures here, and I myself was involved in the search of the Basilica this morning. But if you would care to wait here— '

'You don't understand! The life of the Pope and everyone in this crowd may be at risk.'

He wasn't budging, so I took Sarah by the arm and made to leave, then at the last moment turned with her.

'Come on!' We ran through the gap between the Guards, through the massive arched doorway behind them. They let out a shout and began running after us.

*

We were in some sort of a hallway, with a thick red carpet and glittering chandeliers. A tall man in flowing robes with a red sash was already bustling towards us, the slapping of his slippers echoing against the marble floor.

'What is this, please?' he said. He had a narrow, ascetic face: a thin mouth, high cheekbones and deep-set eyes. The Guards were now stationed behind us, their halberds drawn.

'These people just broke in—' our Guard started to explain, but I cut him off.

'We are from British intelligence. We have information suggesting that there may be a bomb in the Basilica.' I nodded at Sarah again, and she withdrew the papers and handed them over, pointing to the paragraph in question. The man took a pair of spectacles from his robe and began reading, but after a few seconds he handed the wad back officiously.

'I have no way of knowing if these are genuine or not. Do you have any identification?'

'That is what we asked, Cardinal—' the Guard broke in, but the cardinal silenced him with a glare.

'No,' I said, 'but there really isn't time for that. You need to tell His Holiness to cancel his address.'

The cardinal started. 'Impossible! Look at the crowd outside, *signore*. Many people have come a very long way to see His Holiness, and they will be very upset if he does not appear.'

'They'll be even more upset if he's killed. Send these Guards out to explain that he's not feeling well. The people will be disappointed, of course, but they will understand. What do you have to lose? If you find we have tricked you in some way, you can make a formal complaint to the British government and I assure you we will make a full public apology. But please – this is a very serious threat.'

He was quiet for a moment, then put out a skeletal hand to Sarah again. She returned the papers, and he looked down at them once more.

'Impossible,' he muttered.

I looked at him in despair, and started wondering if we could perhaps risk running past *him*. But then I remembered something. 'Last month,' I said. 'There was a warning about a bomb here.'

He looked up at me, surprised. 'Yes – but nothing was found.'

'Because they didn't know where to look. Someone *planted* it then, and it's due to go off today.'

His eyes widened. He looked back down at the document, and then he seemed to reach a decision.

'Do you know where they have placed it?'

I nodded.

He gestured to the lead Swiss Guard. 'Take this man wherever he wants to go – and quickly!'

'The dome,' I told him. He glared at me for a moment, then bowed to the cardinal and showed us to a door at the side.

'Follow me, please.'

*

The Guard took us quickly up a flight of stairs, then down a long carpeted corridor. We passed a magnificent statue of a horse and then pushed through a doorway into a small courtyard. There was a long queue of people waiting to take the lift up to the top. I had thought that the Pope's address would have thinned the crowd inside the church, but by the looks of things it hadn't made much difference. We rushed to the front of the line, and the Swiss Guard pulled aside the rope and asked the clerk in the ticket booth how long it would be until the next lift arrived. The clerk shrugged expansively.

'Five minutes?'

Too long. I nodded to the Swiss Guard, and the three of us raced ahead to the staircase. I reached it first and started climbing the narrow steps, turning past walls scratched with names and dates: tourists who wanted to leave their mark for posterity, I supposed. There were several other people making their way up the stairs, and I weaved my way around them, wondering how far behind Severn and Zimotti were.

I came out onto another courtyard, and there was the dome directly ahead, the cross and ball lit by the morning sun. To the left, beyond some pieces of scaffolding and canvas, the statues of the Apostles gazed out over the city. Could the bomb be here somewhere? I didn't think so – not enough impact. *In* the dome, Barchetti had said. Keep going.

I could hear a low burring noise behind me and realized it was the lift descending – Severn and Zimotti might soon be coming up in it. I crossed the courtyard to the next flight of stairs, which was surrounded by white railings. A short flight up and I reached a narrow balcony that gave spectacular views both down into the church and up into the dome. Tourists were pressed along the balcony deciding which to photograph first, and I squeezed past them to the next archway. The stairs led down, confusing me for a moment, but then I saw the archway on the right. The sign above it read 'INGRESSO ALLA CVPPOLA', and I leapt through it and saw the next flight leading up.

Christ, it was narrow. There was barely room to move, and as my leg muscles started to pulse with pain I regretted not taking the lift for the first part of the journey – I'd be lucky if I had any energy left by the time I reached the top. Then again, if we had waited for the lift Severn and Zimotti might already have caught up with us. I had to climb at a slower pace now because I was stuck behind an Australian woman complaining to her husband that she hadn't had any breakfast and couldn't climb on an empty stomach. I heard shallow breathing behind me, and turned to see Sarah, the palm of one hand resting against the wall for support as she climbed.

The staircase began spiralling, and through narrow slits in the walls I caught glimpses of pink tiles, white statues, green trees. The stairs straightened again, and then started angling to one side as we squeezed between the inner and outer drums of the dome. It was getting warm, and a surge of dizziness flooded through me – I blinked and shook it away.

There was another spiralling stairwell, now with a rope instead of banisters, but it was mercifully short and we came out onto another balcony, this one in the open air. A mass of tourists stood by the low railings, and beyond them the city stretched out in the sunshine. I turned to see both Sarah and the Swiss Guard and raised my chin. The Guard pointed ahead, and I saw an iron ladder a few feet away, hanging almost vertically. I pushed through the crowd of people and grabbed hold of it, my heart racing. How long did we have until the bomb went off? I climbed hand over hand, until finally I was right in the copper-plated ball. I took a few seconds to recover my breath, then looked around.

There was nobody here, just a wooden bench, smooth from a billion tourists' arses, and tiny slats looking down at the city. And somewhere, I was sure, a bomb. But where? Had I guessed wrong? Perhaps they had placed it in the church itself, or on the balcony the Pope would be standing on shortly . . . No. Barchetti had specifically mentioned the attack *in the dome*.

There was a clanging at the ladder and the Swiss Guard climbed into the space. Sweat was pouring down his face, and I felt a pang of sympathy – I hadn't made the climb in that outfit. He glanced at me and immediately registered my confusion.

'I told you, *signore*,' he said. 'We checked thoroughly this morning.'

My sympathy vanished. Triumphant little shit. But he was wrong. It *had* to be here.

There was another clang, and Sarah emerged, very out of breath.

'What's the programme now?' I asked the Guard. 'The Pope's address is at noon, and then what? Mass?' Perhaps they hadn't planted the bomb yet, but would do shortly.

The Guard shook his head.

'It is a much shorter Mass today, because at one o'clock there is a special service for the feast day of Santa Sindone.'

'How much shorter?' I asked. 'Will the Pope be . . .' I stopped. 'What was that? The feast day of what?'

'Santa Sindone.' I stared at him blankly. 'The Holy Shroud of Turin — the cloth Christ was buried in.'

May the fourth was the feast day of the Shroud. That was an iconic religious event, all right — even more so than the Pope's regular Sunday address.

'The Shroud. Where is it?'

'In Turin,' said the Guard, exasperated at my ignorance.

'In the cathedral?'

He nodded. 'The chapel attached to it. Every May the fourth, they remove the Shroud from the altar and—'

He stopped. There had been a loud noise below us. I glanced down the ladder and saw Zimotti emerging onto the gallery, holding up his identification wallet and shouting as he made his way through the crowd. The Guard turned to descend, but I grabbed him by the lapel and gestured for Sarah to stay where she was, too.

'Does it have a dome?' I asked. He looked at me uncomprehendingly, and I shook him. 'The chapel housing the Shroud! *Does it have a dome?*'

He nodded, and tried to move a hand towards his rapier. I pushed it aside.

'What time?' I shouted at him. 'What time is the service?'

There was more noise, and I could hear Zimotti's voice below us. The Guard stared back at me blankly.

'They begin at eight o'clock . . .'

The world slowed to silence, and I knew I had made a terrible mistake. I brushed past the Guard and reached for Sarah's hand.

We were in the wrong place — the wrong bloody *city*. The attack wasn't planned for here. It was planned for Turin, in less than nine hours' time.

XXII

Sarah began to climb back down the ladder, and the Swiss Guard and I rapidly followed. I could hear Zimotti making his way through the crowd, and I pushed Sarah the other way, cursing myself for leading us up here. I had foolishly presumed that the next attack would revolve around an individual. But it wasn't Christ's representative on Earth that was the target, but Christ himself — or rather his followers. The documents had mentioned that religious events had an 'easily understood and revered symbolism'. It was hard to think of anything more revered or symbolic than the Turin Shroud: millions of people around the world believed it to be the cloth Christ had been wrapped in after his crucifixion. It was perhaps the greatest icon of the Catholic Church, and an attack on its holy feast day would create headlines around the world. In Italy, the idea that the Communists were prepared to blow up innocent worshippers in a church would scare everyone away at the next election. And if they damaged the Shroud itself . . . but could they really be prepared to do that?

As we moved through the crowd looking for the stairway leading down, I spotted Severn coming round the other way, and froze. I grabbed Sarah by the wrist and ran in the only direction available, pushing through the crush of tourists until I reached the railing. The outside of the dome curved away, and I peered over to see the statues of the Apostles on the courtyard below, and beyond them the crowd in the square undulating like a giant moving carpet.

I turned my attention to the dome itself. A couple of feet down there was a horizontal ring of small windows, like portholes in a ship. And between the windows, vertical mouldings circled the dome, jutting out from the surface like giant white centipedes. Fixed to the roofs of the windows and running down the centre of the centipedes were dozens of small iron discs, reddish brown with rust. They stirred a dim memory – wasn't the dome illuminated on certain occasions? Perhaps these discs once held the torches. At any rate, they were fastened to the surface with iron spikes. I glanced over at Sarah, and her eyes bulged as she realized what I had in mind. But Severn and Zimotti were jostling through the crowd on either side of us, calling out that it was a public emergency. They would be here any moment. We had no choice.

I took a firm hold of the railing and hoisted myself over, ignoring the screams of a woman behind me. Once on the other side, I jammed my right plimsoll down and under the nearest disc. Would it take my weight? There was only one way to find out. I worked my way down to the bottom of the railing with my hands, flattening the front of my body against the side of the dome as I did. Close up, the surface was covered with threads of black grime and pigeon droppings. I lifted my left leg away for an instant and the disc didn't budge beneath my right foot, so I lowered myself once more and wedged my left shoe into the next disc down.

I took a breath, then looked up, expecting to see Sarah descending the same way. But she was still astride the railing, and she wasn't moving. She had frozen to the spot.

'I can't!' she said, almost sobbing with fear. 'I . . . can't move.'

But she was moving – her legs were shaking. Any moment now and she would lose her balance and fall.

'It's fine,' I said. 'But you have to come *now*.'

As if in answer to this, there was some sort of a commotion to the left, and I looked up and saw Severn leaning over the side of the railing, one hand raised to hold back frightened tourists. There was a pistol in the other, and he was aiming it straight at her.

'Everyone around you ends up dead . . .'

Not this time. Please not this time.

I shouted up to Sarah that she had to move and she shook her head violently, but then something made her realize she had no choice and she brought her legs over and lowered herself down onto the centipede to the left of mine, her shoe reaching the first disc as the shot came, sending a blast of sparks off the railing. This church might not be the target of the operation, but Severn and Zimotti clearly weren't squeamish about damaging it.

I looked up at Sarah, whose face was flushed from the effort. We had a moment's breathing space, because we were now out of Severn's line of sight and he couldn't shoot around curves. But only a moment: he had probably ordered some of his men to take the staircase and wait for us at the bottom, but the crowds would hold them up and there were several exits. His best chance to catch us now was to follow us over the railings, and I was pretty sure he'd realize it.

I started climbing down the rest of the way, my hands now clutching the spikes that kept the discs in place, which were blisteringly hot after a few hours in the sun. In principle it was easy, like climbing down a step-ladder. But the ladder was curved, and if we made one slip we would fall to our deaths.

We made our way down our separate ladders as quickly as we could and reached the rim of the dome, where there were plinths large enough to stand on. There was a jump of several feet to the next level, but I could see a relief of stone flowers jutting out from the wall between my section and the next plinth along. It looked like a safer bet, so I shimmied over to the next ledge, clutching at a thinner line of centipedes descending from the top, and then crouched and hung my legs over the side. I glanced down and saw that the relief wasn't protruding as much as I'd thought it would, so I let go and tried to angle my body in as I dropped.

My right knee crunched down on the top of the relief, and I let out a cry and threw my hands up to gain a hold before I slipped over the edge. My fingers gripped something, and I looked up to see that they had hooked around the lower lip of the mouth of a fierce-looking stone lion: a relief just above the flowers that hadn't been visible from my vantage point on the ledge. I pulled my other knee up until I was kneeling firmly on the top of the floral relief. Once I was comfortable, I turned around and prepared to lower myself again and jump the final few feet to the ledge beneath.

The pain came from nowhere. My throat felt thick and constricted, and I was being dragged back upward. He had his boots wrapped around my neck and he was trying to crush my windpipe. My eyes rolled upward and I saw a pair of boots and the first few inches of a pair of trouser-legs hanging from the ledge directly above me. The trousers were midnight blue – not Severn, then, but Zimotti. I suddenly felt very cold, and realized that my teeth were chattering.

Zimotti was shaking his legs frantically, trying to swing me out so he could drop me over the ledge and to the ground far below. My fingers started slipping as my breathing began to suffer and I tried to call out to Sarah, who I could hear was still in the next section along, but nothing came from my throat.

Above me, Zimotti was grunting and cursing, but his voice sounded peculiar and I realized that it *wasn't*, in fact, Zimotti but his hawk-faced hatchet man. I hadn't seen him on the gallery earlier. Among his curses, I heard the word 'Fratello' repeated several times and with a shock it hit me that he meant the sniper in St Paul's, who was either literally his brother or a brother in arms, and that he blamed me for his death and wanted vengeance for it. Vengeance for a man who had been given the task of assassinating me, and who had thought nothing of using a defenceless child as a shield.

Fury pulsed through me and I used the strength of it to jerk my head down violently in an effort to dislodge his boots from around my throat. But it didn't make any difference. They were locked there, and squeezing tighter by the moment. As I started to choke and felt my vision beginning to black out, I did the only thing I could think of: I lifted my left hand from the relief for a moment and punched up between the Bird Man's legs, towards his groin.

He screamed, and I quickly reached to grab hold of the relief once again. Stone scratched against my nails and then my fingers gripped tightly, and as they did, the pressure around my neck floated away, and I realized that the Bird Man was starting to fall. I gripped tighter with my hands, and the scream intensified and wind brushed against me and I looked down as his torso cracked against the rim of the ledge beneath and he spun towards the courtyard below, sending a group of tourists screaming.

For a moment I thought it might not have been enough of a fall to kill him, but then the stone beneath him began to turn red and vomit rose in my throat. I winced and gulped it down. My shirt was now soaked in sweat and clinging to my back. And I could hear the sound of someone moving above. It wasn't over. We had to get down before the others came.

My fingers started to slip, and finally I let go. I landed on the ledge and my thighs clenched with the pain, so sharp it took my breath away. But nothing was broken and I was safely in the centre of the ledge. I took a deep breath and looked up to see Sarah preparing to make the same jump a few feet away. Directly below us – within easy reach – was the white-railinged flight of stairs we had come up, and below that the courtyard with the dead man sprawled across it. We just had to reach that courtyard. After that, we could take the stairs down.

I could sense Sarah hesitating again and decided to lead by example, to show her how close we were. There was a tiled roof a couple of feet from the ledge. I scurried over, then levered myself onto it using the chimney, after which I began creeping down the tiles like a crab.

'See?' I called. 'It's easy.'

There was a thud above me and I looked up, expecting to see Sarah landing on the ledge. But instead I saw Barnes. Christ, they'd brought the lot of them. He was wearing the same fatigues he'd been in at the base in Sardinia, and his pale blue eyes were blazing with hatred. He stood to his full height and his mouth formed a grim smile: he thought he had me. He was grasping something in his hand, and it glittered momentarily in the sun. It had a long, thin blade: a stiletto knife? Severn must have given it to him, because he couldn't have brought it through . . . I stopped. We hadn't come through customs. He could have had it strapped to his leg the whole time.

I looked past him, trying to see where Sarah had gone, but she seemed to have disappeared and the move was a mistake because Barnes saw his chance and leapt forward, pushing me further down the roof and towards the line of railings that enclosed the flight of stairs. As he jerked the knife down, I threw my arms up and grabbed hold of his wrist, managing to stop the blade a few inches from my neck. He grunted, his mouth clamped shut and a hissing noise emanating from his nostrils, and the blade moved closer. I pushed back against him with every sinew and fibre, but I knew that I could only hold out for another second or two at the most. He was older than me, but he was fitter, better trained and, like the Bird Man, he wanted revenge – in his case, justifiably.

There was a blur of movement and his free hand came round in a tight fist, aiming low, and I recognized the old commando move and made to counter it with my forearm. I caught it just in time, but in the meantime the blade continued its descent. I pushed back again. Beads of sweat dripped into my eyes, stinging them, and I tried to blink them away, to no avail. Barnes grunted again, and as the blade dropped another fraction of an inch I prepared myself for it to pierce into me. But then I realized with a flash of intuition what I had to do, and I abruptly relaxed my grip and jerked my head away sharply at the same moment, and the surprise and momentum were too much for him to correct and as his arm came down he lost his balance and the whole upper half of his body tipped over with it, and then I was looking down at the cluster of railing spikes emerging through the top of his head, the tips covered in some dark slimy mixture I didn't want to think about. He moaned one last moan, and then his limbs went into a final spasm and he was still.

I wiped the sweat from my eyes and breathed in deeply to calm myself. Then I called up to Sarah to make the last leap. She did it, making a much better landing than I had done, and then she climbed onto the tiled roof and I helped her over the railings and we walked down the steps into the courtyard. I asked her if she felt she could continue. She nodded, and we left the bodies of Bird Man and Barnes and staggered past the open-mouthed and horrified tourists down the remaining stairs until we reached the square. There was no sign of Severn and Zimotti, but I had no doubt they were coming.

We stumbled through the crowd and into one of the side streets – but where to now? Hiring a car was out of the question, as their next step would be to contact all the rental places, so a description of anything we hired would immediately be sent to every police station in the country. The most anonymous form of travel, and I reckoned our best bet, was the train. A teenager on a bright red Vespa hurtled straight towards us, and I stepped out in front of him, putting my hand out officiously and yelling for him to stop. He slowed fractionally, and as he passed I yanked him by the collar and dragged him off the bike, hoisting myself into his place.

'Get on!' I called to Sarah. She hobbled over and clambered aboard, and I changed gears as the former owner shook his fists at our smoke. Needs must.

XXIII

I parked the Vespa in Piazza dei Cinquecento and we headed into the main hall of Termini railway station, past young people smoking and flirting and generally having the time of their lives. There was a swarm of people surrounding the ticket booth, to the extent that it wasn't clear where one queue ended and the next began. I looked up at the departure board and saw that the next train to Turin was leaving in less than five minutes: the Tirreno, a fast service that stopped at Pisa and a few other places on the way. It was our only chance. We would just have to pay on board, or hope the train was so crowded that the conductor didn't bother to check tickets.

We rushed across to the platform and, to my relief, I saw that it was indeed crowded. Dozens of men were calling to each other as they tried to coordinate an effort to bring all the luggage onto the train. Some were pulling their suitcases tied together with string through the doors, while others were lifting them to their friends and squeezing them through the windows of the compartments.

'What's going on?' I asked Sarah. 'Why are they taking suitcases to a religious festival?'

She shook her head. 'They're not going to the festival – they're heading north for work. The "economic miracle" has run out of steam down here.'

We made our way through the throng and climbed onto the train, then walked along the corridors looking for seats. We squeezed past students strumming guitars, tourists consulting maps, a monsignor cutting open a garlic sausage, and everywhere these wild-eyed men in their threadbare suits trailing their suitcases behind them. Finally we found a compartment with a couple of spare seats, which was otherwise occupied by an elderly Mother Superior and a gaggle of young nuns excitedly exchanging gossip and unpacking sandwiches for the journey. A whistle blew and we were off.

As the wheels started gathering pace, the tension within me faded a little. We had lost them. I turned to Sarah. She had circles under her eyes, and cuts and dirt were smeared across her cheeks. She looked much more fragile than when I had first met her in the embassy, but infinitely more beautiful. I leaned across and gently placed my hand against her cheek, and she gave a wan smile in return.

I glanced out of the window and caught sight of a clock in the station. It was coming up to noon, and the departure board had said that we were due to arrive in Turin at quarter past seven. But train timetables didn't mean much in Italy these days, and anything could delay us. Even if we arrived bang on time, we would have only forty-five minutes to get to the cathedral, and I suspected we would have a welcoming committee to evade first – Zimotti would have furnished the local *carabinieri* with detailed descriptions of the two of us. And even if we made it out of the station and to the cathedral, I had no idea what sort of explosive they would use. From what I remembered, the two explosions in Milan had been simple dctonators with sticks of dynamite – but my source for that information was the Service's file, and that had also claimed that Arte come Terrore were responsible. And I had a feeling this would be on a much bigger scale than the bombs in Milan. If we did find the bomb in time, the church authorities might listen, but they wouldn't have access to any bomb disposal experts of their own. About all we could hope for was that they would clear the area – but how long would that take at such a massive event?

I wondered if I hadn't just miscalculated horribly. Severn had told me I had got myself into something bigger than I understood, and I was starting to fear he'd been right. Well, we had several hours on this train. I decided to take the opportunity to have another look at the documents, and read them through thoroughly. I didn't expect them to tell me how to defuse the bomb, but they might contain other clues as to what we were up against. I turned to Sarah and told her what I had in mind, and she unbuttoned the pocket of the overalls and handed the bundle across. The cover was torn from our climbing adventure, but the papers inside were untouched.

I took them out and started reading, but after a few minutes the words began to swim in front of my eyes and my temples throbbed with pain. It was too bloody stuffy in the compartment. I asked Sarah to open the window, and it was then that I noticed the Mother Superior peering at me from beneath her wimple. I looked down at the documents and saw the seals exposed on the page. I doubted she could read them, but together with our overalls and bruised faces, her interest had certainly been piqued. I nudged Sarah again. 'Leave that. Let's go and see what they have to eat instead – I'm famished.'

She nodded, and we left the compartment and walked down the corridor, through first class and into the restaurant car. It was shielded from the sunshine by heavy curtains, and was empty: we had only just left the station and it was still too early for lunch. We took a table, and I seated myself facing the glass doors we had come through. A waiter ambled over and I ordered two steaks, a bottle of San Pellegrino mineral water and a pack of cigarettes; he nodded and disappeared.

I took out the bundle and placed it on the table. I decided to start from the other end, at the series of papers that came directly after the strategic document: I hadn't looked at them yet. The first one I picked up was in Italian, and was dated 1 June 1959. A slightly faded letterhead read 'Stato Maggiore della Difesa, Servizio Informazioni delle Forze Armate' – the old name for military intelligence – and under that was the title 'LE "FORZE SPECIALI" DEL SIFAR E L'OPERAZIONE

"GLADIO'": 'The Special Forces of Military Intelligence and Operation "Gladio"'.

The document was a briefing on the country's stay-behind operation, and I was shocked at how advanced it was. It seemed it had been – and perhaps still was – linked to the Clandestine Planning Committee, which itself was affiliated to the Supreme Headquarters of the Allied Powers in Europe. The base in Sardinia was mentioned at several points, and appeared to be used primarily as a training centre for the stay-behind army. In June 1959, this had been made up of forty cells: six for intelligence-gathering, ten for sabotage, six for propaganda, six for escape and evasion and twelve for conducting guerrilla warfare against the enemy. The guerrilla cells were described as having hundreds of units each.

I placed the document to one side and turned to the next on the table. This was dated much earlier, from 1948, and seemed to be a formal agreement of cooperation between the Service and the network in the Netherlands. I started looking through the other papers: Germany, France, Spain, Portugal . . . every country in NATO was here, and even a few outside it. The file from Turkey was dated June 1951, and was signed by Templeton, Osborne and a Turkish name I recognized as Cousin Freddie's. All the files related to the establishment of stay-behind networks, sometimes with British and sometimes with American support. I guessed the latter were providing most of the money behind it. The organization didn't seem to have one overarching name: it was simply called Stay Behind in Britain, but was known as Glaive in France, Gladio in Italy, Kontrgerilla in Turkey, and so on.

There were also files on individual Stay Behind officers, including one on Zimotti. It seemed that in the war he had been a member of La Decima, the elite commando frogman unit. After the Italian armistice in 1943, he and about 20,000 other men from the unit had continued to fight in the north of the country on the Axis side, under the command of Valerio Borghese, 'The Black Prince'. They had become infamous for their brutal acts against the partisans, including summary executions, torture and the burning down of villages with a strong partisan presence. In 1945, he was one of the many La Decima members arrested by partisans, but had been one of the lucky few who had been saved from reprisals and taken to safety by the Allies. The Black Prince himself had been rescued by the Americans, but Zimotti owed his life to the British: to William Osborne, in fact, who had been in charge of his case in England before he had eventually returned to Italy.

There was a file on Severn, too. Back in '51, he had felt Osborne was misusing him as a chauffeur, but his trip to Istanbul had merely been his indoctrination into Stay Behind. And just as the Turkish network had been controlled by Templeton, with Cousin Freddie as the local liaison, Severn was now the Service's Stay Behind commander in Italy, working in conjunction with Zimotti. I couldn't see a file for Osborne, but I guessed he was very senior in the whole set-up, if not in charge of it outright.

All of which was very interesting, but there was nothing here I could take to Haggard. Just because Zimotti and others had been fascists during the war did not prove that they had subverted the original networks in any way. The strategy proposal arguing the benefits of false-flag attacks on churches and football stadia was extreme, but it was, after all, merely a proposal. Many such documents were written, but the operations mentioned within them didn't always come to fruition. My throat suddenly felt dry. Had I got completely the wrong end of the stick? Were these simply documents about the original stay-behind networks, kept in the Station safe for perfectly innocent reasons?

The train swayed as it rounded a bend in the track, and I grabbed at the papers to stop them from slipping off the table. My thumb caught hold of one I didn't recognize. I tidied the stack, waited for the train to settle and then picked it up again. It was in English. I read it through, then placed it back in the pile and handed the whole lot back to Sarah, who replaced it in her pocket.

'Anything interesting?' she asked.

I nodded. The last document had been dated 1962, and bore the NATO seal. Its distribution list included senior members of French, German, Italian and British intelligence, including Osborne. And it was nothing short of a manifesto, laying out in detail the justification for resurrecting the original stay-behind networks as an 'anticipatory mechanism' – in short, instead of waiting for Moscow to invade or for the Communists to come to power democratically, to attack the citizens of their own countries and frame Moscow and others as a means of frightening the electorate and imposing strict law and order. It made it clear that national governments had not been informed of the operation – instead, it seemed, one politician in each country, usually a minister of defence, had been indoctrinated into the plan. I hadn't been wrong, after all. The conspiracy was real, and here was the proof.

I quickly explained the situation to Sarah, and she asked me what I planned to do.

'Let's start by getting to Turin and stopping whatever they have planned there,' I said. 'Presuming we manage that, I suggest that the minute it's over you call the Home Secretary, and then take the first flight to London you can.'

The waiter arrived with our meal, and we started eating. I hardly noticed it – the dossier had left a sour taste in my mouth that I couldn't seem to banish and my mind was too preoccupied. I opened the pack of cigarettes and lit one from the book of matches on the table.

'But what will *you* do?' Sarah asked, finally. 'If I go to Whitehall?'

I took a draught of the cigarette – the nicotine pushed deep into my chest and warmed it. 'I don't know,' I said, which was the truth. I hadn't made up my mind if I wanted to enter the lion's den of London again. Back in Sardinia I had been confident that Haggard would be able to deal with Osborne and the rest of his cabal if I could show him proof of what they were up to. Now I knew just how far-reaching the conspiracy was, I wasn't so sure. They had secret *armies* in every NATO country preparing to commit atrocities to stop the Communists. If they couldn't kill me, they would do everything in their power to prove to Haggard and everyone else that I was a Soviet agent. As I was one, they would probably succeed in that – and nobody in London would listen to the allegations of a traitor. Sarah had a much better chance of persuading Haggard without me. 'I might try to head for Switzerland,' I said. 'It all depends—'

I froze. Just visible through the glass doors of the carriage was the blue trouser-leg of a man. The conductor? Or Zimotti? I stubbed out my cigarette in the ashtray. It was Zimotti, and as he stepped inside the carriage I saw Severn standing directly behind him. They must have boarded at the last moment and been combing through the train looking for us. Zimotti's eyes met mine, and then he cried out and they started heading towards us.

I took Sarah by the arm and we started running down the restaurant car, crashing through the doors. To the left was a corridor leading to passenger compartments; straight ahead, the kitchens. On an impulse, I dived ahead. The place was tiny, and thick with steam. White-coated cooks and stewards scattered in alarm as a shot rang out, racing to a door at the far end of the room. I turned to see Severn and Zimotti right behind me. Sarah leapt towards Severn, trying to scratch at his eyes, and as he lifted his gun again I ran forward to help her. But Zimotti had seen what I was planning, and he picked me up and hurled me against one of the workbenches. Behind them I saw a line of steel cauldrons, and he lifted me by my shirt and pushed my head towards one of the vats. It was open, bubbling with boiling water, and I felt a blanket of steam engulfing me and lashed out blindly, trying to reposition myself, but he had a firm grip and the heat was becoming more intense as he pushed my face closer to the surface of the water. I remembered glimpsing saucepans and ladles hanging from the ceiling when I'd come in, and I reached up to try to grab one, but came away empty-handed. I kicked behind me desperately, and one of my legs caught Zimotti in the chest. He reeled back, screaming and cursing me in

Italian, and I ducked down as he ran towards me in a rage, grabbing him by the legs and lifting him so he flew over the bench.

There was a dreadful scream as he plunged headfirst into the boiling cauldron. Without even thinking, I grabbed him by his collar and lifted him out. His entire face was burned, a surface of red sores. I tried to push him back down but he was already reaching out for me, and I lunged for the surface of the workbench. There was a knife there, and I managed to pick it up. As he came towards me, I held the knife firm with both hands as it pushed into his chest. He crumpled to the floor, and his cries of agony sputtered into groans, and then whispers, and then silence.

I made my way through the steam trying to find Sarah and Severn. They were still over by the door, and as I approached them my chest clenched. He was aiming a gun directly at her head.

'Tell me!' he was screaming at her. 'Did you screw the bastard? *Did you screw him?*'

She didn't answer him, and he let out a howl at the realization. He was about to press down the trigger and I leapt towards him with the knife. He saw me and moved to avoid it but he was a fraction too late and the blade glanced across his jaw, and he lost balance and started falling. The gun fell from his hands and Sarah jumped down and grabbed it, then stood again. Her eyes were hard and cold, but her hand was shaking as she brought the gun up and aimed it straight at her husband.

'Don't shoot!' I yelled.

Severn looked up from the floor, the right side of his face soaked in blood and a strange smile on his lips. 'You didn't read it,' he said, and I realized he was talking to me. 'You don't know . . .' He wiped his hand with blood, and cocked his head at Sarah dismissively. 'Enjoy her while she lasts. It won't be long.' His mouth twisted into a grimace, either of hatred or pain, I couldn't tell, and then the shot rang out and there was a small red dot in his forehead. The blood oozed slowly from it and mixed with the blood from the knife wound, and his eyes were like glass.

Sarah had dropped to the floor, and I stepped forward and gently took the gun from her hands. It was a Browning, and it was still hot. I put it on safety and shoved it into my waistband. She looked up at me dully.

'You understand?' she whispered. 'I couldn't let him . . . I couldn't let him *own* me any more.'

I nodded, and pressed my hand into hers. I didn't blame her: he'd had it coming. What I didn't understand were his parting words. What hadn't I read? The documents, presumably. But I had read them all. Was there another dossier somewhere?

I leaned down and searched through his pockets, turning each of them out to see if he had any papers on him and padding him down in case he had secured them elsewhere. Then I took off his boots to check he hadn't hidden anything in the soles. But there was nothing. Nothing at all.

I turned to Sarah and asked her to pass me the sheaf of documents again. She didn't answer, so I knelt down next to her and repeated it and she nodded and unbuttoned the pocket and passed the packet to me. I flicked through the pages, trying to see if there were any clues as to what Severn had meant, but there was no mention of Turin, no specifics about this attack or its ramifications. Whatever it was I had missed, it would have to wait. We had to get rid of these bodies — the kitchen staff might be back any minute, and the conductor with them.

I jumped over to Zimotti and searched him. He didn't have any papers on him, either, but he did have a wallet containing his identification badge. I took it, then stripped the trousers, shirt and jacket from him and hurriedly put them on over my own. I took off my now-ragged plimsolls and replaced them with his thick-soled boots.

There was a cargo hatch for goods near the door, and I leaned over and slid the cover to one side. Sarah was still dazed, but I persuaded her to stand and we lifted Zimotti's body and heaved it through the hatch. There was a clump as it hit the sides and then it was gone.

We repeated the process with Severn, after which I cleaned up as much of the blood from the floor as I could with a rag. I threw it in the sink, then took Sarah by the hand and we ran back through the restaurant car, to the compartment with the nuns and the Mother Superior. Sarah stepped inside and I was about to follow her when I saw someone walking through the door at the far end of the corridor. It was the conductor.

He was a short, rotund little man with drooping shoulders and a ferrety moustache. I slid the door of the compartment shut and marched towards him. 'Di Angelo,' I said, flashing Zimotti's identification in his face. 'Servizio Informazioni Difesa. Have you seen my colleague? He's with a British agent with fair hair. We're looking for a couple of fugitives.'

He nodded eagerly. 'I saw them heading this way a few minutes ago. I thought I'd better come and investigate myself because half the kitchen staff just barged into my quarters and told me there was trouble at this end of the train.'

I gave him a puzzled look. 'I haven't seen anything. Tell them to get back to their stations. It was a false alarm.'

He hesitated. 'But one of them said he heard a shot.'

I looked at him, and his shoulders drooped a little more under my gaze. 'Do what you are told,' I said sharply. 'This is urgent state business, and I have no time to explain the situation. Do you understand?'

'Yes, officer. Shall I stop the train so you can conduct a search for the fugitives?'

If he stopped the train, it was all over. The *carabinieri* would come on board, and we would be delayed.

I gave him my coldest, most imperious glare. 'If I had wanted you to stop the train, I would have asked you,' I said. 'Did you hear me make such a request?'

'No, officer.'

'Well, then . . .' He looked up at me with ill-concealed resentment, and I pretended to soften. 'I apologize. You are a good man,

I know. We all have our jobs to do, and sometimes they're not easy. I appreciate the suggestion, but I don't think we need stop the train just yet — we'll find them soon enough. In the meantime, can you keep your eyes open for me?' He nodded gratefully, and I clapped him on the back. 'Good man. I'll start checking these carriages, and I suggest you go and tell the kitchen staff to return — there may be hungry passengers, and we wouldn't want them to make a complaint, would we? If you see anything suspicious on the way, come and find me at once.'

He nodded and trundled away.

*

As we slowed into Turin's Porta Nuova station, I braced myself for the next hurdle. There was a group of *carabinieri* waiting at the barrier on the platform: no doubt they were armed with our descriptions. I wasn't sure I could bluff them with Zimotti's identification badge — they might look a little more closely at the photograph than the conductor had done, and while there were a few flecks of grey in my hair, it wasn't nearly enough of a likeness. But a bigger problem was Sarah, who had no disguise: her long blonde hair stood out a mile.

The train came to a standstill, and we stepped off and joined the crowd heading for the exit. As I had feared, the *carabinieri* were examining everyone as they came through. I adjusted my collar and took a deep breath. We walked towards the barrier, shuffling through the crush. Any moment now someone would catch sight of Sarah's hair.

I swivelled on my heels to face the person behind me, a hollow-cheeked young man, and flashed my identification at him. Puzzled, he slowed down, and I quickly reached out and grabbed the cap from his head, then threw it to Sarah.

'Put this on!' I told her. 'Try to get through!'

She clamped the cap down over her head, tucking as much of her hair as she could into it, then pushed forward into the crowd.

My victim, in the meantime, had swiftly turned from puzzled to angry and started shouting at me. One of the *carabinieri* at the barrier flicked his head up and began moving towards us. I could see Sarah a few feet ahead, but she had not yet made it through to the other side.

'*Venite subito!*' I shouted. 'Someone has been stabbed here!'

The *carabinieri* froze for a moment, then shouted back at one of his colleagues and the two of them began thrusting their way through the crowd towards the imaginary scene of the crime. It left a gap on one side of the barrier. I pushed past a middle-aged couple and started heading for it. By the time the *carabinieri* had reached the perplexed man, who tried to explain what had happened, I was in the station concourse.

I ran across it and through the colonnaded exit, where Sarah was waiting for me. There was a queue for the taxis, but we didn't have time to wait. We ran to the front, holding up Zimotti's badge to the astonished line of customers. I opened the door of the front taxi and jumped in.

'*Il Duomo*,' I said.

The driver gave a curt nod and put his foot down.

XXIV

The city swept by in a blur, and my eyes fixed on the clock on the dashboard of the taxi. It read a quarter to eight — we had fifteen minutes to find the bomb and stop it. As we came into Piazza San Giovanni, the cathedral rose in front of us, the façade a mass of white marble glinting in the evening sun. And, just visible above it, the tip of the chapel pierced the evening sky.

I paid the driver and we got out and started running towards the square. The crowd was much bigger than I'd hoped, a great crush of people queuing to enter in advance of the service. I waved Zimotti's identification above my head, and people reluctantly let us pass, until we finally reached the doors and entered the cathedral.

Incense hung heavily in the air. A procession of purple-robed priests were walking through the central candle-lit aisle, their chanting echoing around the space. At the far end of the nave there were two massive stairways with signs indicating that they led up to the Chapel of the Holy Shroud. We took the one on the right.

The stairs were steeper than I had expected, and halfway up I was nearly overcome by dizziness. Sarah grabbed my arm, and I shook the feeling away. She gave a taut smile and we carried on climbing, until we were in the chapel. Black and white marble and gilded bronze gleamed, and light shone through the cupola above, striking the ornate altar in the centre like a spotlight. Inside the altar was a magnificent silver chest, and inside that lay the Holy

Shroud itself. I looked up at the frescos in the dome above. Barchetti had said 'in the dome', so that was where we had to go.

Sarah pointed to a staircase on the right. As we rushed towards it, I heard a disturbance from below. I looked down and saw one of the priests detaching himself from the procession. He'd seen us. He called out to us to stop, but we ducked into the staircase and started climbing, and then I heard him call out again and the sound of his footsteps echoing on the marble. There had been a tinge of panic in his voice, and I guessed that he was the inside man, the guard to make sure nobody came near the bomb.

There was a gallery directly under the dome, like the Whispering Gallery in London. I looked down and saw that the procession was entering the chapel below, heading for the altar with the Shroud. Ignore them. Concentrate. I looked around frantically. A large enough bomb here would not only destroy the Shroud, but might kill or maim people in the church — perhaps even some of the crowd outside. But where the hell had they put it? As in St Peter's, there was nothing but a bench, which Sarah was now sitting on, catching her breath.

'Stand up!' I told her, and she did so with a guilty start.

'You think it's here?'

'Perhaps.'

I knelt down and took a closer look. Yes, there was a lid to it — it was a chest as well as a bench. Perhaps this was where they usually kept spare parts or cleaning equipment or some such. It had a sliding lid, but I couldn't get it open. I looked for a lock, but there was none. It was simply jammed at one end, and it wasn't budging. I tried to place my nails into the tiny gap between the lid and the rest of the bench to lift it a fraction, but they weren't long or strong enough. Sarah shuffled over and tried with hers, but with no better result. It was useless.

Footsteps were now echoing up the stairs, and they were getting louder by the second. In frustration, I hit the palm of my hand against the lid. It moved. Just a tiny amount, but now there was enough space for me to use my fingers. I formed my hand into a claw and tried again. Slowly, the lid glided open.

I looked down into the chest. There was a bag inside, a faded leather hold-all. Perhaps it had tools in it. Or perhaps a chunk of plastic explosive connected to a timer. I leaned down and unzipped it.

There was nothing there.

I looked again, rummaging my hand around the sides and bottom. It was completely, mystifyingly empty. So where the hell had they planted it? I looked around desperately, at the columns and the pillars and the procession swaying below.

'Any ideas?' I asked Sarah.

She didn't respond, and I glanced up at her. She was sweating, shivering, with a panic-stricken expression on her face. That was understandable, but something about it seemed wrong, like she was terrified of something I wasn't aware of. She placed a finger to her head and said something, but her mouth couldn't seem to form the words, and my skin started to crawl as I realized why. She'd lost her hearing.

'Have you had any muscle pain since you were last here, or sore eyes? . . . Have you had any more bouts of deafness?'

There was no bomb here. Because they weren't using a bomb.

They were using *me*.

I looked up. There were three of them, all wearing black robes with masks over the lower half of their faces. The figure nearest to me stepped forward and I saw he had a syringe in his hand. I tried to stand to make a run for it, but I didn't have any strength left and there was nowhere to run anyway, not any more. The other two men held me down, and as the needle plunged into my arm I imagined I felt the liquid pulsing through my bloodstream. They stepped over and I watched as they performed the same task on Sarah, and then my vision started to blur and my eyes closed.

XXV

I was in my dressing gown, waiting. It was night, and we were all assembled in Library, waiting anxiously. Moonlight shone through the window onto the ragged armchairs, and I felt like sneezing from the dust of the books. Thousands of others had made their way through this process over the years – so would I, I told myself. We had been woken and brought down here hours ago. I stared down at the pattern of the carpet, which was brown and red with little flecks of white in it, curlicues, like pieces of gristle in a slice of salami, like sea-horses in an ocean of wine, and I tightened the cord of my dressing gown around my body. It was like a rope, the cord, and I pulled it tight, chafing my skin, already raw from the winter night – there was little heating these days. It was a navy-blue dressing gown, bought by Mother at Harrods before the war, with my label sewn inside the collar. Outside I thought I heard the drone of the planes in the night. Somewhere out there, Father was waiting for me to grow up and become a man . . .

And now the big door opened to reveal Mason, impossibly tall Mason with his great hooded eyes, and he pointed to me.

I stepped forward. He placed the blindfold around my eyes, and I followed him.

I ran through everything in my mind one last time, all the words and facts I had studied obsessively for a fortnight, in the hope that it would soothe my nerves a little.

Mason walked me round the building, took me up one flight of stairs and down another, spun me round, shouted at me from different directions and after a while I stopped trying to figure out where we were going. It didn't matter. Every so often I reacted too slowly to his instructions and felt a swish against my calves and heat rising through the prickles. He had some sort of a whip with him.

I was being lifted into light. There was a moment of release as the cooler air hit my eyes and forehead, the sweat evaporated, and then a terrific blast of heat. Move, look away. Swish.

'Whenever you look away from the light, we will use this,' I heard someone say. He was holding the thing up in front of my face, but everything was a blur.

'We call it the Cat,' said the voice, and I recoiled as it brushed against my face. 'Keep looking at that light.'

Just a lamp, a common or garden lamp. Fix on something else, not on the bulb, or you will damage the retina. Fix just above and to the left and let the light become the background. Then I caught a glimpse of the boy holding the Cat, and realized it was Charles Severn, and I sat up with a jolt, my lungs heaving, sweat pouring off my face.

A nightmare. It had been a nightmare. My Notions test had been fine. I had passed. No bones broken. I was an adult. Severn was dead. A nightmare.

I looked down. A grey blanket and white sheets covered me, but it didn't feel sturdy enough for a bed: a stretcher, then. I moved to step off it, but found that I was strapped down.

As I took my bearings, questions started to flood through my mind, but before I could order them I was pulled up short by the sound of movement very close by. I looked up to see a young man in the uniform of a *carabinieri* standing by the edge of the stretcher. He wasn't wearing a mask, which something told me was a good sign. He was flicking his hand against a catheter tube attached to the stretcher. I followed the line of the tube, and lifted the sheet to see it leading into my wrist.

The man scribbled something down on a board he was holding, and then started walking away from me. I made to call out to him, but then noticed in my peripheral vision that there was something in the place he had been a moment ago. It was another stretcher, and lying on it, her eyes closed peacefully, was Sarah.

'She's fine.'

I looked up, startled, to see a man ducking his head down and entering the room. My stomach tightened.

'Hello, Paul,' he said.

'Hello, Sasha,' I replied.

*

He looked much the same as when I'd last seen him in London — could it really have been only a week ago? — but instead of his usual tweed get-up he was also dressed as a *carabinieri*. I tried to untwist what this meant. They had donned these uniforms in order to get into the cathedral . . . so they could take us out again without arousing any suspicions. But the sheer scale of organizing that meant that they must have been following events very closely for some time. And that they had gone to a lot of effort to rescue us. Why?

Something about the ducking movement he had made suddenly alerted me to the rest of the space I was in. Glancing upward, I saw that the roof was rather low, as grey as the blankets, and metal, and I realized I was in the hold of a plane. There was a porthole in the wall, and I looked out of it with a sense of mounting dread.

But . . . no. There was a stretch of black tarmac. We were still on the ground. We hadn't taken off yet.

Sasha came over to my stretcher and handed me a glass of water, which I gulped down eagerly.

'How fine?' I asked. 'You have to tell me—'

'Better than we hoped,' he said quietly, taking the glass from my hands and placing it on a small trolley at the foot of the stretcher. 'You have both fully recovered and are no longer contagious. It was a fortuitous escape.' He paused for a moment, and something about the pause made my stomach lurch. 'But there are some . . . consequences to your having been infected.'

'What the hell do you mean?'

He ran his tongue around his teeth as he considered how to broach it.

'Sarah has not yet regained her hearing,' he said, finally. 'I am afraid she may never do so.'

I looked across at her, sleeping peacefully in her own world, and felt something break deep inside me.

'But if we had not reached you when we did,' Sasha was saying, 'you would both be dead, as might many others. We were monitoring the Italians' radio communications, and the message about Turin came in very late. But it seems we gave you the antidote just in time. Our doctors tell me that you were within an hour or two of optimal transmission, and that if we had arrived a little later everyone within a few feet of you would have been infected.'

'*Optimal* transmission? What about the people in the church, in the procession? How many feet do they need to have been away?'

He tugged gently at the tuft of beard under his lip. 'We will make discreet inquiries — but, as I say, we feel it was a fortuitous escape.'

He always sounded so reasonable, that was the problem. If you didn't catch yourself, you could get swept up in it and miss what was really going on.

'Let her go,' I said. 'This isn't about her.'

He paused and looked at me . . . sorrowfully? Can sorrow look reasonable?

'I'm afraid this is not about either of you, Paul,' he said. 'It's about what you know. If we allowed her to go, she would reveal everything — or be forced to reveal it — and the game would be up.' He smiled, pleased at his mastery of idiomatic English. 'The same applies to you. I'm afraid the only option is to put a brave face on it. After all, we have just saved both of your lives. Some would be grateful for that.'

I wasn't sure I was.

'*Why* did you save us?' I asked, making sure to sound resigned to my fate. If I could somehow get down onto the tarmac, perhaps we could reach a border – Switzerland, or Yugoslavia. It depended which airfield they were using. Think of that later. Find a way out of here first.

'Do you remember the tunnel?' Sasha was saying, and I had a flash of the Underground, the sniper's breath against my face as he tried to strangle me.

'In Berlin, I mean.'

I nodded dully, shaking the memory away. Back in 1955, in collaboration with the Americans, the Service had built a secret underground tunnel between West and East Berlin that intercepted the landlines running from the Soviets' military and intelligence headquarters in Karlshorst. As a result, they could listen in to a large portion of the East Germans' communications with the Russians. It was a highly protected operation and I had been far too junior at the time to be indoctrinated into it. But Blake had been given clearance for it and, being the good double he was, had immediately informed Moscow.

'It was a great reverse, of course,' Sasha went on, 'but also an extremely delicate one. It gave us the opportunity to feed disinformation to our adversaries, which would be very useful for furthering other operations. However, if we passed too much disinformation, the British and Americans would soon realize that we knew we were being listened to, and would begin looking for the leak. On the other hand . . .'

'. . . If you carried on as normal, you'd be giving away all your secrets.' I knew the story, and the conclusion to it: they had staged an 'accidental' discovery of the tunnel in '56 and closed it down. The Service had eventually cottoned on to Blake and arrested him, but he'd escaped from prison and defected to Moscow. 'What does the Berlin Tunnel have to do with this?' I asked.

Sasha smiled indulgently. 'I am trying to illustrate how the spirit of compromise can drive an operation, and how other priorities can become factors. With the tunnel, we compromised, continuing to pass important information through it even though we knew we were being listened to. We did this to protect our agent – but we made sure to keep our greatest secrets out of the traffic. Eventually it became too difficult to continue, so we broke it up. There is a similarity with this situation. But I think perhaps this will explain it more easily than I can.'

He leaned over and placed something in my hands. I looked down at it uncomprehendingly. It was a book, titled *The Tide of Victory*. With a start I realized it was the volume of Churchill's memoirs that Barnes had been reading. I remembered Severn's final words: *'You didn't read it. You don't know . . .'* I opened the book. There didn't seem anything unusual about it. I flicked through it, until I reached the end. Taped to the inside of the back cover was a small pouch, and inside it I could see a tightly folded bundle of papers. I shook them onto my lap and picked up the first page. I recognized the handwriting at once: it was Osborne's.

> *C. – see attached proposal. I initially vetoed but suggest we reconsider in light of this morning's catastrophe. U. taking next flight to S. with medication. See D. gets it.*
> *W.O.*
> *P.S. – Sort out your wife, for all our sakes.*

'C.' was Charles Severn. Osborne had inserted this message in Barnes' book and told him to deliver it to Severn on his arrival in Rome. If I understood the postscript, he hadn't wanted to risk sending a message in code to the Station due to Severn's suspicions about Sarah's loyalty, a matter he wanted Severn to sort out – although precisely how wasn't clear. 'D.' was obviously me, and so I turned to the attached document to see exactly how they had planned for me to get it.

It had the same heading as the other dossier – 'STAY BEHIND: STRATEGY AND EXECUTION' – and looked to be in the same typeface. But it had a different date: 29 April 1969, less than a week ago. And it was stamped 'W16', which was the Registry number for Porton Down.

Update on Nigerian virus, as requested.

The virus was isolated from acute-phase sera extracted from the blood of patient HANDSOME in a Red Cross clinic in Awo Omamma, Nigeria on Friday, March the 28th. Tests subsequently conducted at that clinic and laboratories here have confirmed that it is an arenavirus, and nearly identical to that found in two missionary nurses in Lassa, near Jos, also in Nigeria, which we isolated and examined in early March. There were also marked similarities to samples taken by the field team in Cameroon in November 1968 (see Annex 1).

This virus, which we have named Lassa Fever, is both potentially fatal and extremely infectious. It appears to be transmitted to humans via exposure to rodents, rodent faeces (transmitted via dust in the air), and possibly human-to-human contact, such as the exchange of bodily fluids. We believe HANDSOME may have contracted the virus either via exposure to rodents or sexual intercourse with ISABELLE DUMONT, who may have contracted it on her travels through the country as a war reporter. However, this cannot be confirmed, as DUMONT was dead before we arrived at the clinic, and we were instructed by you not to search for her body.

Jesus. I thought back to my time in Nigeria. I had slept with Isabelle only once . . . No wonder Severn had been so worried Sarah might have slept with me – he'd thought I was going to contaminate her with the virus. And I had.

I read on:

Tests on monkeys over a period of several weeks revealed the virus to be very easily transmittable via the exchange of saliva or blood: only a few droplets were needed. It is too early to give accurate figures for morbidity or mortality, but we would estimate it to be very high – possibly higher than other arenaviruses. As outlined in my report of March the 3rd, colleagues at the U.S. Biological Warfare Laboratories have already successfully adapted both Yellow Fever and Rift Valley Fever for warfare use. We felt that, on account of its lethality, virulence and lack of known antidote, Lassa Fever was a promising candidate and we adapted it in a similar manner on April the 23rd.

The adapted strain was so virulent that in some of the cases infection was achieved via the inhalation of respiratory droplets when subjects were over five feet from an infected specimen. Of the nine monkeys we tested, two began exhibiting significant symptoms twenty-four hours after exposure, and died within forty-eight hours. A further two specimens died within the following forty-eight hours. One further specimen began exhibiting symptoms consistent with early stages of the disease on

April the 27th, and we administered a strong dose of vaccine. The specimen appeared to recover fully within a matter of hours, although it remains to be seen whether or not there will be any long-term effects.

With such a small, non-human sample size, it is impossible to conclude whether this represents an accurate picture of the transmissibility or mortality rate of the adapted strain in the event of humans being exposed to it. However, we cautiously calculate that the incubation period of this strain is twenty-four hours, and that after that time human cases will reach an optimum level of transmissibility.

We believe that this strain could be packaged within a capsule that, on breakage, would distribute particles across a wide area. Although the estimated mortality rate of this virus is lower than in some of the others we have analysed, even with the adapted strain, the shock value of using it would be significant. Some of the symptoms of the virus, such as fever, headaches and chest pain, are similar to those of pneumonic plague, and we would expect that diagnosis to be widespread initially. This would, of course, result in a certain level of hysteria among the population.

That was putting it mildly. I turned away from the text for a moment and looked up at Sasha, who was picking lint off his jacket. I took a breath and forced myself to read the rest of the report.

However, such a weapon could take years to
develop, and would involve on-the-ground help
from the Americans, which is undesirable for
many reasons known to you. There is, however,
an alternative method of carrying the virus
that would lead to fewer fatalities than an
aerosol-distributing capsule, but that would
perhaps create a greater impact. This option
could also, we feel, be put into effect within
the next few months and with little cost to
ourselves. HANDSOME has already been exposed
to the original virus, has just woken from
unconsciousness in our custody in London, and
has been deemed *persona non grata*. It therefore strikes us that, by chance, we may have
the perfect 'live agent' with which to test
the transmissibility of the new strain . . .

Next to the phrase 'within the next few months', Osborne had scrawled '*Not fast enough. Stick to S.P.*', which I took to be his vetoing of the operation in favour of shooting me in St Paul's. I read the rest of the document in a haze: it consisted of a detailed technical description outlining precisely how they would engineer it so that my body would become the carrier of the strain, complete with dosage recommendations and tables comparing mortality rates.

The thing was signed by Urquhart, of course – 'U.' in Osborne's note. His had been the voice in Sardinia I hadn't recognized as I had emerged from unconsciousness on the operating table: '*He's come to.*' Yes, Dr Urquhart, with his tan under his Father Christmas beard, hadn't been holidaying in Jamaica, soaking up the music – he had been in Nigeria, looking into the disease I had caught and investigating whether or not it could be adapted for use as a biological weapon. The capsules he had foisted on me hadn't been to suppress my symptoms, but placebos.

It seemed they had improvised more than I had thought. When their plan to kill me in St Paul's had gone wrong, they hadn't just let me fly off to Italy. No, they had immediately put into action another operation to kill me — one that would helpfully make me a guinea pig for their future atrocities. Although Osborne had originally vetoed the idea in favour of shooting me at the memorial service, he'd jumped at the chance to put it back on the table. And to make sure I was under a tight leash, he had sent Barnes along as — what? — my warder? Or my nurse? I had a sudden memory of waking in the embassy with him leaning over me. What had he been doing? Checking my pulse?

At any rate, Barnes and Severn had been told to keep an eye on me while Urquhart flew out to the base in Sardinia — 'S.' in Osborne's note — to wait for his guinea pig to arrive. Zimotti had helpfully provided me with a lead to Sardinia. My insistence on going to the meet with Barchetti must have interfered with Severn's plans, but then I had led him to Pyotr and they had flown me off to Sardinia to inject me and begin their little experiment. In the last few days I had suffered muscle pain, hallucinations, headaches, constriction in my chest and many of the other symptoms I had experienced in Nigeria — but I had been so intent on stopping an imagined bomb that I had written them all off as after-effects of a whipping and some loud pop music. Worse, I hadn't noticed that the woman next to me had been developing precisely the same symptoms.

I turned to Sasha. 'How did you get hold of this?' I asked, pointing to the paperback.

He smiled softly. 'The butler did it. Despite some superficial precautions, money still talks, and we have a way into the British embassy. We removed it from Severn's safe just a few minutes before your arrival.' He took the papers from my lap and carefully folded them back into the pouch of the book. 'It will be returned soon enough.'

'After copies have been made, of course.'

'Of course.'

'And how am I alive? The document says there's no antidote.'

'No known one. Our scientists have been working on adapting this type of virus for several years, just as the Americans and British have been, and we have developed a range of antidotes. As you were already infected with the disease, it seems they only gave you a tiny dose of the new strain. We think they wanted to see what the effect would be in a controlled environment: to observe how transmissible their new strain might be to other humans before they tried it out on a larger scale at a later date . . .'

My mind jolted back to Sardinia, and my skin crept. They had put me in the same cell as Sarah because they had wanted to see how quickly she would catch the new strain from me. The plan had never been to attack Rome or Turin, but somewhere else entirely. Severn had scribbled '4 May' on the strategy document, but it must have been just a possibility, rather than anything they had yet planned. Once Urquhart was fully satisfied that the new strain could act as effectively as it needed to, they would have injected me anew, then found a football match in Naples or an opera in Venice or whatever suited them, planted me in it and stood back and waited for the crowd to become infected. No doubt they would also have prepared suitable evidence to leak to the press that the carrier of the deadly new plague had been a Soviet agent.

Now I saw why Severn had been so anxious about whether Sarah had slept with me: he had still loved her, and if she had only been near me for a few hours she would have been unlikely to have caught the disease already – the idea was that it took several hours to come into effect. But if we had *slept together*, the chances would have been far greater that she already had it. It was a monstrously warped kind of love, of course – he had still put her in a cell with me to test how fast the disease could spread without us sleeping together.

Only we had escaped before they had had the chance to find out.

The knife Barnes had pulled on the rooftop in the Vatican hadn't been a stiletto blade, but a needle. He had been trying to inject me with the vaccine, because my twenty-four hours were nearly up and I had been about to reach my optimum period of transmissibility, or whatever the scientific term for it was. And that explained Severn's valediction. When he had arrived at the embassy and we were there, he had realized that both the dossier and Barnes' paperback were missing from his safe, and had presumed that Sarah and I had taken both and so discovered the plan to use me as a weapon. But then I had confused him. Instead of trying to leave the country, either to defect to Moscow or head for London, I had inexplicably raced to the Vatican, and then to Turin. At some stage, he had guessed that I was running too fast to have discovered or read the documents in the back of Barnes' book, and was still acting on the basis of the strategy dossier and the various Stay Behind documents.

But those documents were still enough to damn them with – if we had reached Haggard or anyone else who hadn't been involved, the whole thing would have backfired. So they had run after us with needles, in the hope of stopping us before we reached optimal transmission and caused an attack they weren't able to manage, and to retrieve the documents and kill us before we told anyone about their conspiracy. Severn had told me that I didn't know what was happening, not out of any sense of remorse, but because he had realized he had failed to stop me and wanted to taunt me with his knowledge of what lay in store. *'Enjoy her while she lasts. It won't be long.'*

I turned back to Sasha. 'I take it you have known about this for some time,' I said. 'Like the tunnel.'

'The revival of Stay Behind? Since last year. A British agent in Stockholm revealed it inadvertently to one of our assets.'

That drunkard Collins. The Service should have sacked him years ago.

'And you're willing to stand by and let innocent people be killed – and to be blamed for their deaths – just to protect the fact that you know it's going on?' As well as being terrible operational logic, I wondered if it wasn't worse than committing the atrocities in the first place.

'But it is not *we* who will be blamed,' he said. 'Not exactly. It is British anarchists, the Italian Communist party, and similar groups throughout Western Europe. We support these people sometimes, but they are not our real friends. They are like the information we let through the tunnel – not the most important. We do not want to expose NATO's actions at this particular moment. If they kill a great many civilians and blame it on others, then we may do so. In the meantime, the more evidence we have pointing to their involvement, the better.'

They 'may do so' – he didn't seem too bothered.

'How many people count as "a great many"?' I asked.

He gave me another of his patronizing smiles – he seemed to have an endless supply of them. 'I think you have misunderstood the strategy of their operation,' he said. 'In Italy it is called Gladio, and that is an apt codename, I think. It is named after the *gladius*, one of the weapons used by the gladiators: a stabbing sword.' He thrust his fist towards me. 'The wounds it inflicted often looked horrific, but were not that deep – it was an ineffective weapon if you wanted a quick kill, in fact. But, of course, that was not what the organizers of the fights wanted: they wanted slow kills. Do you know why?'

'Yes. Because the longer it took for someone to die, the more entertainment there was for the crowd.'

'Precisely – nobody likes going to a boxing match to see one fighter knocked out in the first ten seconds. And so, too, with Gladio. They are not interested in killing many innocent people – but they want to *terrify* many people, with a superficial but spectacularly bloody wound.'

'That's a pretty poor salve for anyone's conscience,' I said. 'Would you say the same to the families of those who are killed? Or is that why you rescued us? A sudden attack of scruples because the virus would mean more deaths than you could justify?'

'I am sorry to disappoint you once more, but no. We were worried that you would reach London with the documents. That would have been . . . unfortunate. Osborne and the others will, of course, wonder how much you discovered, and what you will tell us. But once we have returned all the documents to the safe, there will be no reason to suppose that you discovered anything at all, and we are confident that the strategy will continue.'

He was actually boasting about prolonging the operation. It appeared that, from Moscow's point of view, the more people who were killed and blamed on proxy groups the better — it would be all the more effective when they held their press conference to reveal that NATO had been behind it. Unlike the Berlin Tunnel, this time they didn't appear keen to call things off and 'accidentally' discover the plot when given the chance.

When Barchetti had told me Arte come Terrore knew about the attack in the dome, he had meant the events in London after all — the 'in' had simply been a slip of the tongue, or because he hadn't known precisely what had happened there. What he had discovered, and what he had been desperate to tell Severn, was that the cell knew that they were going to be blamed for that attack. That meant that they knew about Stay Behind — and so did Moscow. So the whole thing was blown, and Barchetti had needed to warn the Service. When I'd turned up instead of Severn and asked if he thought Arte come Terrore were involved in killing Farraday, he had realized I didn't know about Stay Behind at all, and that something was therefore desperately wrong with my having been sent to meet him. So he'd fled . . . And that was why Pyotr had ordered me to kill him: Moscow not only didn't want the Service to know that they were aware of Stay Behind, but were prepared to kill for it.

A strange sensation ran through me. There hadn't been any attacks planned for Rome or Turin, but there would still be plans for attacks in Italy and elsewhere. And by killing Barchetti before he got his message to the Service, I had allowed the whole bloody thing to continue, just as London, and Moscow, had wanted.

Unless, of course, I could get out of here.

But how? Something told me they wouldn't take off until Sasha was seated and belted in and had given the go-ahead, so I tried to stall him some more.

'Why didn't you answer my call in London?' I asked.

He smiled tolerantly. 'Has that been bothering you? Let me put your mind at rest there, then. I had no idea about the attack in St Paul's, none at all. My radio man simply had a feeling that the safe house was compromised, and he and his team shut down and moved immediately as a precaution. As soon as I felt we were secure again, I sent Grigori to let you know . . . But you didn't seem especially open to hearing the message.'

So my paranoia had got the better of me. It hadn't been the first time they had moved safe houses – it was good practice to do so every once in a while, in fact. As there had been the risk that they would do so at the same time as I needed to contact them urgently, we had arranged that in such events Sasha would send someone to alert me within twelve hours. And he had done so. But he and his team had happened to move just as someone had taken a pot shot at me, and I had forgotten all about that arrangement and jumped to entirely the wrong conclusion. Perhaps if I had stopped for a moment in that call box in Smithfield and considered that, I might have heeded Toadski's message in Heathrow, and not taken the flight to Rome, and . . . but that way madness lay. Whatever I had done, that bastard Osborne would have tried to kill me. It was a miracle he hadn't succeeded – but at what cost?

I couldn't look Sasha in the face now, but I had one last question to ask him. 'This new strain . . .' I said. 'Is it more effective than the ones developed by your scientists?'

He nodded. There was a moment of silence, and then he understood what I was really asking. 'Yes. The doctors isolated it from you a couple of hours ago.'

I leaned forward to try to hit him, but the strap around my chest held me back.

He stood, and smiled down at me. 'I wish I could make you see how much I admire you, Paul. I've always felt you were a man of high ideals – perhaps too high. Sometimes they must be sacrificed for a greater cause.'

I didn't have any ideals to speak of, but in the land of the blind the one-eyed man is king – if he's not hanged by the mob.

'What greater cause?' I asked. 'Communism – or the Motherland?'

'Both, of course. The second is meaningless without the first. It is true that in this case the interests of the state have perhaps over-ruled strict ideology, because more important things are at stake. But you surprise me – did you really think you and your girlfriend were going to stop this war alone?'

'She's not my—' I stopped myself. It was futile. There was nothing more important at stake than a perpetual cycle of point-scoring, but he would never be able to understand that.

He gave me a thin smile. 'I think you should sleep now,' he said. 'We'll be leaving soon.'

*

He had left me here, alone with Sarah. Well, why not? We were strapped to our beds in the hold of a plane, about to take off.

But we hadn't taken off *yet*.

I started tearing at the strap, but it was no use: it was fixed tight. Panicking, I began clawing away at it in the hope my nails might break the surface. But I knew that wouldn't help. My eyes raced around the small space desperately looking for something that might help, and trying not to think of how little time I might have. I had to get moving before . . .

That was it. Movement. The stretcher was on caster wheels, albeit with brakes on each one. But if I could create enough energy to lift them . . . At the foot of the bed I could see the glass Sasha had handed me earlier resting on the trolley. But how to move myself towards it?

I placed a hand out of the stretcher and tried to reach down to the floor. I was several inches short. That wouldn't work. So I strained my chest against the belt again, but this time tried to jerk my entire body upwards as I did so. For a moment, the stretcher leapt a fraction of an inch in the air, and as it did I tried to use the momentum by pushing upwards again, and again, until it bounced. Praying that the noise wouldn't bring anyone running, I started jerking from side to side as well as upwards, and gradually the stretcher began to turn. It was infuriatingly difficult to control, but after a couple of minutes I had managed to move myself so that I was almost horizontal to the trolley, and less than a yard away.

I didn't think I was going to manage to get within arm's reach any time soon, so I reached down and removed the catheter from my wrist. Then I reached for the pole containing the intravenous drip bag and tilted it towards me. I quickly unhooked the bag, and then dipped the pole down and took a swipe at the trolley, missing by several inches.

I made it on the fourth attempt, snagging the pole perfectly around one of the trolley's legs. I pulled it towards me carefully and reached out for the glass. Shielding my face with my arm, I cracked the glass firmly against the side of the trolley, sending shards scurrying across the floor. But several shards had remained in the trolley. I picked out the largest and sawed away furiously with it at the base of the strap. Finally it started to fray, and then it broke away.

Gulping for air and soaking in sweat, I stumbled over to Sarah's stretcher and performed the same exercise. She woke while I was freeing her and looked up at me in a daze. I gestured for her to follow me, and she nodded. I knew it could be just moments before they started taxiing across the tarmac, after which we would have no chance. Coming out of the hold I saw that one of the doors was just a few feet away. I ran towards it and pushed the button. It shunted open, and a blast of air entered the plane.

I beckoned Sarah on and she reached the door, and then we started racing down the metal stairs until we were on the tarmac.

Wind whipped across my face, sending a dull ache through my jaw, and the sweat on my back suddenly felt chilled. We must still be in Turin, or nearby. That was good. France and Switzerland were close. I hoped we were nearer Switzerland: we had to get over the border, find a proper doctor . . .

I ran across the airfield, my chest burning and my head pounding with the desire to reach safety. We reached a fence, and beyond it was a road, a motorway of some sort. I glanced back for a moment: Sarah was a few yards behind me, but the plane was still sitting there in the darkness, and there was nobody coming for us. We had made it. We were going to be all right.

It was when we reached the road that I slowed down for a moment, and I felt a tug at my sleeve. I turned to see Sarah pulling at it.

'What is it? Are you hurt?'

I followed the direction of her gaze. In the distance was a line of buildings, shrouded in morning mist. But slowly I realized that many of them were domes.

Onion domes.

It hit me like a kick to the stomach and I knelt down on the tarmac and waited until they came to fetch us.

*

We didn't have to wait long. There were four or five of them: burly men in suits the same shade of grey as the tarmac. Now I saw that a couple of black Chaika limousines were parked on the other side of the plane, and as they walked us towards them I glanced over at Sarah. She gave me a look of sheer panic in return, and I felt numb inside.

Sasha was waiting for us. He stared right through me, then shook hands with the security men and headed into one of the Chaikas. We were led over to the other one, which had a flag pinned to the front grille. The door was opened, and we climbed into the rear. The interior was bright red — Soviet red — with fold-down seats on the side nearest the driver. The leather was cold against the back of my neck. I looked up and saw a man seated opposite us, wearing a uniform: gold glinted on his epaulettes. He was very old, and deeply tanned. He looked alarmingly reptilian, his eyes glinting through a network of wrinkles that spread like tributaries across the landscape of his face, and for a fraction of a moment I had the thought that it was Auden, the great poet revealed as Moscow's puppetmaster-in-chief, the final Russian doll in the collection. But it wasn't Auden, of course: the nose was snubbed, and the eyes were tiny sparks in the crumpled papyrus of skin.

'Hello, Yuri,' I said.

'Greetings,' he said, and smiled to show a collection of nicotine-stained teeth. 'But perhaps now you can call me Fedor Fedorovich.' His eyes flicked over Sarah. 'So this is the woman.' The tip of his tongue darted from his mouth and licked at his lips. I shivered inwardly as I remembered his 'daughter' in Burgdorf.

'Are you the maniac behind this idea?' I said. 'This . . .' I struggled to find a word. '. . . *game*?'

He turned his eyes to me, dipping his head in a mocking bow. 'No,' he said. 'I am not the "maniac" behind the strategy, as you put it, although I have had my input. But I am old now – the new guard do not listen to me as much these days.' He clasped his hands together. 'I know that our objectives have not always been clear to you. As I am sure you understand, we cannot always provide agents such as yourself with the full picture, so you could not know where our priorities lay in this operation. I nevertheless congratulate you for your efforts to save our Italian comrades from being wrongfully blamed for the deaths of innocent civilians, even if—'

'I was more interested in the civilians than your comrades.'

He gazed at me for a moment, then turned his head to look out of the window. 'Take a word of advice from an old man,' he said quietly, and his voice was a little colder now, a little stiff: 'When we arrive, adopt the line I have proposed instead. I think it will help you fit in better.'

He suddenly leaned forward, and I flinched. He smiled at my nerves and lifted a bottle of vodka from a compartment in the door, along with three shot glasses. He thrust a glass each into my and Sarah's hands, then poured out measures for each of us. 'I give you a toast,' he said. 'You must drink it *do dna*: to the bottom.' Then he cried out *'Mir i druzhba!'* – 'Peace and friendship!' – raised his glass and downed the contents, eyeing me carefully over the rim as he did.

I turned and stared out of the window, and saw the domes and spires looming out of the mist ahead. We were approaching Moscow: a new world. It was one I had been heading for since I had sought this man out in 1945, but my reprieve had finally come to a close – I had reached the end of the road, as another Russian had told me not long ago.

I forced myself to look across at Sarah. Her face was as cool and beautiful as the moment I had met her in the British embassy in Rome. But her mind, I knew, was flooded with confusion and fear. I had brought her to this point. Another life lay ahead of us now, and we would have to draw on all our reserves to survive it – and I must find a way to protect her. She met my gaze and stretched out her hand. I clasped her soft, ringless fingers in mine, then raised the glass in my other.

'Mir i druzhba,' I said, and as the liquid burned the back of my throat, Fedor Fedorovich's laughter echoed in my ears.

Among wolves, I thought, howl like a wolf . . .

Author's Note

This book is a work of fiction, but it is set against a background of real events. In the late 1960s, Britain and Italy both witnessed widespread industrial action, the springing up of terrorist groups, and plots against the governments of the day by senior members of their respective intelligence communities. The First of May group did machine-gun the American embassy in London in 1967, and carried out several other attacks and kidnappings until disbanding in the early 1970s, whereupon their mantle was taken up by the Angry Brigade and others. In Italy, several anarchist and Communist groups carried out attacks on civilians at this time, eventually flowering into the Red Brigades and other groups that terrorized the country for much of the '70s and '80s.

As with *Free Agent*, I was inspired by the investigative journalism of Stephen Dorril and Robin Ramsay, particularly a chapter in their book *Smear! Wilson and the Secret State* in which they described attempts to organize a coup in the United Kingdom during this period as part of a longer-term 'strategy of tension' against British Prime Minister Harold Wilson.

Arte come Terrore is fictional, inspired by Germano Celant's essay *Arte Povera: Appunti per una guerriglia*, published in the journal *Flash Art* in 1967, in which he wrote of a revolutionary existence that 'becomes terror' ('*Un esistere rivoluzionario che si fa Terrore*') – I took his metaphor literally and extended it. However, two explosions did take place in Milan in April 1969, and several anarchists were charged in relation to them. Some now believe that those and several subsequent attacks, such as the bombing in Milan's Piazza Fontana in December 1969, which killed 16 people and injured 80, and the bombing of Bologna train station in August 1980, which killed 85 people and injured over 200, may not have been carried out by anarchists or left-wing terrorists, as originally thought, but by right-wing groups with connections to Italy's secret services, NATO, the CIA, MI6 and others.

In 1990, two Italian judges discovered a document written by Italian military intelligence in 1959 that outlined the purpose and structure of a network known as Gladio. In a statement to Italy's parliament on 24 October 1990, Prime Minister Giulio Andreotti confirmed that this had been part of a secret NATO operation, known under different names in other countries, which had been set up shortly after the Second World War as a contingency plan in the event of a Soviet invasion of Western Europe. The plan had involved the creation of 'stay-behind nets': forces that could provide effective resistance to the Soviets, and which had access to hidden caches of arms, supplies and technical equipment in many countries.

The existence of British stay-behind networks and their offshoots had been publicized prior to Andreotti's statement. In 1977, Chapman Pincher wrote in the *Daily Express* of the existence of the 'Resistance and Psychological Operations Committee', which he claimed contained an 'underground resistance organization which could rapidly be expanded in the event of the Russian occupation of any part of NATO, including Britain' and which had links to the Ministry of Defence and the SAS. And in 1983, Anthony Verrier stated in a footnote in his book *Through The Looking Glass* that '*current* NATO planning' (his emphasis) gave the SAS a similar role to that previously held by SOE regarding stay-behind parties. Since 1990, little else has been revealed of Britain's post-war networks, although an exhibition at the Imperial War Museum in London in 1995 noted that junior Royal Marine officers in Austria had been detached from their normal duties in the early '50s in order to prepare supply caches and coordinate with local agents for stay-behind parties.

The CIA established the Turkish arm of the network in 1952, but I have speculated that the British had already done some work along these lines a year earlier. This is based in part on a paragraph in Kim Philby's memoirs in which he stated that SIS's Directorate of War Planning was busy setting up 'centres of resistance' and guerrilla bases in Turkey to counter a possible Soviet invasion while he was stationed there in the late '40s: in other words, a stay-behind network. If Philby were telling the truth, one presumes he informed Moscow at the time, meaning that at least part of the stay-behind operation was compromised from the start. If he was lying, the Soviets nevertheless knew about such plans by 1968, when his memoirs were published.

Following Andreotti's statement in the Italian parliament, many people questioned whether members of Gladio and the other stay-behind networks had turned from their original mission of protecting Western Europe from Soviet invasion to supporting, planning or executing terrorist attacks on civilians – attacks that were then blamed on Communists and others in order to unite public feeling against the Left and bolster the country's security structures. Since 1990, a great deal of information has emerged to support this idea, but despite parliamentary inquiries, arrests, trials, acquittals and retrials in Italy, Turkey and elsewhere, it remains unproven. Until NATO declassifies all its files on these networks, the truth may never be known – and perhaps not even then.

For the purposes of this novel I have presumed that NATO's post-war stay-behind networks were subverted for false-flag terrorist

JEREMY DUNS

operations, and have used some established facts in the hope of creating plausible fiction. My main sources were Philip Willan's *Puppetmasters: The Political Use of Terrorism in Italy* and Daniele Ganser's *NATO's Secret Armies*. I am especially grateful to Philip Willan for his comments on an early draft of the novel.

In Chapter XXIII, Paul Dark reads the Italian military intelligence document discovered in 1990, and the figures mentioned there are taken from it. The 'strategy document' he reads earlier is my own invention. Right-wing establishment figures in both Britain and Italy were plotting against their governments during this period and, according to Daniele Ganser, an SIS agent betrayed the stay-behind networks to the KGB in Sweden in 1968. Italian Gladio members were trained by British special forces instructors in England, but their main training facility was a secret military base at Poglina in Sardinia, near Capo Marrargiu. In two separate right-wing coup attempts in Italy, in 1964 and 1970, there were plans to detain left-wing leaders, journalists and activists at this same base. The area between Capo Marrargiu and Alghero is known as The Griffons' Coast, as it is home to the griffon vultures that Paul and Sarah encounter in Chapter XVII. Part of the area is now a reserve for this species.

In Chapter IX, Paul Dark discovers that his handlers in Moscow were initially unsure of the validity of the information he had given them. This is partly based on accounts of Moscow's scepticism towards Kim Philby and other members of the Cambridge Ring during the Second World War. Genrikh Borovik in *The Philby Files* and Nigel West and Oleg Tsarev in *The Crown Jewels* quote declassified Soviet intelligence files expressing these suspicions, including several reports concluding that Philby and the other members of the ring must have been discovered by British intelligence and were unwittingly passing on disinformation. The spies were not fully cleared of suspicion by Moscow until 1944.

The frontispiece quote is taken from a memorandum prepared by George Kennan that set out the case for the United States' use of 'organized political warfare', and is quoted courtesy of the US National Archives and Records Administration (RG 273, Records of the National Security Council, NSC 10/2. Top Secret). The United States' post-war influence on Italy and fear of the Communist party coming to power in that country is widely documented, and it is clear from former CIA chief William Colby's memoirs and other sources that the Americans were instrumental in setting up and running several post-war stay-behind networks, including in Italy.

It is thought that most of the superpowers investigated the use of biological weapons during the Cold War, often developing research carried out in the Second World War. In 1942, British military scientists detonated anthrax bombs on the Scottish island Gruinard: it was not decontaminated until 1990. As far as we know, Britain never 'weaponized' Lassa Fever, although the United States and the Soviet Union both suspected the other of trying to do so. In the 1970s, American scientists investigating the disease in Liberia encountered Soviet researchers looking for Lassa antibodies, reagents and samples. The darkened room in Rome's Galleria Nazionale d'Arte Moderna is inspired by a description of a work in that gallery in Kate Simon's *Rome: Places and Pleasures*, and on the earlier work of Lucio Fontana.

The ball at the top of St Peter's Basilica is no longer open to the public, but it was in 1969, and was large enough to accommodate sixteen stout-hearted tourists. The Chapel of the Shroud in Turin is still under renovation following the fire in 1997. From April 2010, visitors will be able to see it for the first time since its controversial restoration in 2002.

I would also like to thank the Confraternity of the Holy Shroud and the Museo della Sindone in Turin; the staff of the bookshops Ardengo, Tara and Open Door in Rome; Caroline Brick at the

London Transport Museum; Isobel Lee, Enrico Morriello, Sandra Cavallo, Francesca Rossi, Isabel de Vasconcellos, Sebastiano Mattei, Craig Arthur, Clare Nicholls, Evelyn Depoortere, Carla Buckley, Grant McKenzie, Helmut Schierer, Sharon and Luke Peppard, Nick Catford, Roger Whiffin, Blaine Bachman, Graham Belton, Ajay Chowdhury, Rob Ward, Phil Anderson, Phil Hatfield, Steven Savile and Tom Pendergrass for their comments, expertise and suggestions; my agent, Antony Topping, for his skilful shepherding of me to this point; my editors, Mike Jones at Simon & Schuster and Kathryn Court at Viking for their faith in Paul Dark; my parents and parents-in-law; my daughters, Astrid and Rebecca; and my wife, Johanna.

Select Bibliography

Christopher Andrew and Vasili Mitrokhin, *The Sword and the Shield: The Mitrokhin Archive and the Secret History of the KGB* (Basic Books, 1999)

Christopher Andrew and Vasili Mitrokhin, *The Mitrokhin Archive II: The KGB and the World* (Allen Lane, 2005) Charles Arnold-Baker, *For He Is An Englishman: Memoirs of a Prussian Nobleman* (Jeremy Mills Publishing, 2007)

Jeffrey M. Bale, 'Right-wing Terrorists and the Extra Parliamentary Left in Post-World War 2 Europe: Collusion or Manipulation?' (in *Lobster*, issue 18, 1989)

Luca Massimo Barbero (ed.), *Time & Place: Milano-Torino 1958–1968* (Steidl, 2008)

John Barron, *KGB: The Secret Work of Soviet Secret Agents* (Bantam, 1974)

George Blake, *No Other Choice* (Jonathan Cape, 1990)

Genrikh Borovik, ed. Phillip Knightley, *The Philby Files: The Secret Life of the Master-Spy — KGB Archives Revealed* (Little, Brown and Company, 1994)

Tom Bower, *The Perfect English Spy* (Mandarin, 1996)

Andrew Boyle, *The Climate of Treason: Five Who Spied for Russia* (Hutchinson, 1979)

Robert Cecil, *A Divided Life: A Biography of Donald Maclean* (Coronet, 1990)

Germano Celant, 'Arte Povera: Appunti per una guerriglia' (in *Flash Art*, 1967)

William Colby, *Honorable Men: My Life in the CIA* (Simon & Schuster, 1978)

Peter Collins, Ed McDonough, *Alfa Romeo Tipo 33: The Development and Racing History* (Veloce, 2006)

Nicholas Cullina, 'From Vietnam to Fiat-nam: the politics of Arte Povera' (in *October*, issue 124, spring 2008)

Guy Debord, 'The Situationists and the New Forms of Action in Politics and Art' (in *Internationale Situationniste*, No. 8, 1963)

Len Deighton (ed.), *London Dossier* (Penguin, 1967)

Pierre de Villemarest, *GRU: Le plus secret des services soviétiques, 1918–1988* (Stock, 1988)

Stephen Dorril, *MI6: Inside the Covert World of Her Majesty's Secret Intelligence Service* (Touchstone, 2000)

Stephen Dorril and Robin Ramsay, *Smear! Wilson and the Secret State* (Grafton, 1992)

Caroline Elkins, *Britain's Gulag: The Brutal End of Empire in Kenya* (Pimlico, 2005)

Fodor's Guide to Europe (Hodder and Stoughton, 1969)

Fodor's Guide to Italy (Hodder and Stoughton, 1969)

M. R. D. Foot (ed.), *Secret Lives* (Oxford University Press, 2002)

M. R. D. Foot, *SOE: The Special Operations Executive, 1940–1946* (BBC, 1984)

Alec Forshaw and Theo Bergström, *Smithfield Past and Present* (Heinemann, 1980)

Daniele Ganser, *NATO's Secret Armies: Operation Gladio and Terrorism in Western Europe* (Frank Cass, 2005)

Laurie Garrett, *The Coming Plague: Newly Emerging Diseases in a World Out of Balance* (Penguin, 1994)

Roland Gaucher, *The Terrorists: From Tsarist Russia to the OAS* (Secker & Warburg, 1965)

Ian V. Hogg and John Weeks, *Military Small Arms of the Twentieth Century* (DBI Books, 1985)

Harold F. Hutchison, *Visitor's London* (London Transport, 1968)

Alexander Kouzminov, *Biological Espionage* (Greenhill Books, 2005)

Bruce Page, David Leitch and Phillip Knightley, *Philby: The Spy Who Betrayed A Generation* (Sphere, 1977)

Kim Philby, *My Silent War* (Grafton, 1989)

Rufina Philby with Hayden Peake and Mikhail Lyubimov, *The Private Life of Kim Philby: The Moscow Years* (St Ermin's Press, 2003)

George Rosie, 'Integrated scheme for new Heathrow terminal' (in *Design*, June 1969)

W. Ritchie Russell, *Brain Memory Learning: A Neurologist's View* (Oxford University Press, 1959)

Kate Simon, *Italy: The Places In Between* (Harper and Row, 1970)

Kate Simon, *Rome: Places and Pleasures* (Alfred A Knopf, 1972)

Kate Simon, *London: Places and Pleasures* (MacGibbon and Kee, 1969)

Michael Smith, *The Spying Game: The Secret History of British Espionage* (Politico's, 2004)

David Teacher, *Rogue Agents: The Cercle Pinay Complex, 1951–1991* (Institute for the Study and Globalization and Covert Politics, 2008, online)

Richard Thurlow, *Fascism in Britain* (IB Tauris, 2006)

Anthony Verrier, *Through The Looking Glass: British Foreign Policy in an Age of Illusions* (WW Norton & Company, 1983)

Nigel West, *The Illegals* (Coronet, 1994)

Nigel West and Oleg Tsarev, *The Crown Jewels* (HarperCollins, 1999)

Terry White, *Swords of Lightning: Special Forces and the Changing Faces of Warfare* (BPCC Wheatons, 1992)

Philip Willan, *Puppetmasters: The Political Use of Terrorism in Italy* (Authors Choice Press, 2002)

'Of Dart Guns and Poisons' (in *Time*, 29 September 1975)

A Trip to Italy (Italian State Tourist Department, 1969)

THE MOSCOW OPTION

For Johanna, Rebecca and Astrid

A Note on the Background

This novel is inspired by real events that took place in October 1969, and much of the information in it is drawn from declassified material, some of which has never previously been published. The document quoted in Chapter VII is a translation of a dossier written by the head of Soviet military intelligence in 1964.

I

Late October 1969, Moscow, Soviet Union

I was asleep when they came for me. I was running through a field, palm trees in the distance, when I woke to find a man shaking my shoulders and yelling my name.

I sat bolt upright, gasping for breath, sweat pouring off me. The man was wearing a cap, and looked to be barely out of his teens. Part of my mind was still caught up in the dream: I was sure I'd been in the field before, but couldn't think when or where. But I didn't get the chance to consider it further because I was being hauled from the mattress by my arms. Now I could see that there were two men, both in the same uniform but one without a cap. Neither was part of my usual guard detail.

'Get up, scum!' shouted the one in the cap, leaning in so close that he was just a couple of inches from me. His face was squared off, with a wide jawline and a pug nose, and he was wearing some foul eau de cologne that seemed to have been impregnated with the scent of fir trees rolled in diesel. He shoved a pile of clothes into my arms.

'Put these on, old man,' he sneered. 'And make it fast.'

I looked at the bundle. There was a dark suit, crumpled and baggy, a white shirt with sweat stains around the armpits, and a pair of slip-on shoes. No belt or tie.

I started to dress, my eyes still half gummed with sleep. What the hell was going on? I'd been wearing the same grey tunic and trousers since my arrival here, so why the sudden change of clothes?

Perhaps they were transferring me to another prison, or to a court-room – Sasha had often mentioned the possibility of a trial. Or perhaps they were simply dressing me up to take me out to the woods to finish me off. I had a sudden memory of a summer's day in 1945 in the British Zone in Germany, the jeep riding through the burnt-out roads with Shashkevich manacled in the back, until we came to the clearing; the Luger heavy in my hand as I placed it against his neck; his sweating, shaking; and my finger squeezing down on the trigger . . .

I shivered at the thought, but found to my surprise that I wasn't afraid. There were worse ways to go. I wouldn't feel it, at least. I'd been here six months but it seemed much longer, and the future held nothing for me but the gradual disintegration of my body. I was forty-four, but already felt twice that. Rather a bullet through the head than the prolonged suffering and indignity of old age and disease.

'Faster!' shouted the man in the cap. He must be the senior of the two. I finished buttoning the shirt and, as I leaned down to pick up the trousers, realized that both men were armed with pistols at the hip. Judging by the size of the holsters, they were Makarovs. Despite their resemblance to the Walther PP, their combat effective-ness was comparatively poor, and I began gauging the distance between the men, the angles of their bodies and their respective weights to see if there might be any possibility of catching them by surprise, taking one of their pistols and turning it on the other. But it was just a habit, a tired old spook's reflex. I had no real inten-tion of attempting to escape. There was nowhere to go. Even if I were able to overpower these two, there would be dozens, if not hundreds, more of them.

I adjusted the lapel of the jacket and stood to attention, ready. The suit was a couple of sizes too large for me and stank of stale urine, but it felt almost civilized to be wearing one again. The guards led me through the door of the cell and marched me down a series of corridors, until we reached a large steel door I hadn't seen before.

Once it had been unlocked, we walked through it and, for the first time in nearly six months, I found myself outside.

*

We appeared to be on an enormous airfield. I took a deep breath, then exhaled. My breath misted: it was at least a couple of degrees below freezing.

The sky was the colour of slate, and the barbed wire and bare-branched trees formed a strange tracery against it. To my left, I could make out several large buildings. I recognized their outlines from dossiers I had read and memorized in London years before and knew, finally, where I had been held all this time. The building we had just left was nicknamed *Steklyashka* – 'the sheet of glass' – by its inhabitants, because two of its wings were encased in glass. A former army hospital, it now served as the headquarters of the GRU – Soviet military intelligence. It had been my first guess, but it came as a shock nevertheless. I suppose I'd made the place another world in my mind, away from the reach of dossiers.

My escorts gripped me by the arms again and we headed across the tarmac, buffeted by the wind. We passed several helicopters and armoured tanks, and I remembered that it was, by my calculations, the last week of October, and guessed they were destined for the annual parade in Red Square.

A car was waiting for us near the perimeter, its engine running. It was a polished black ZiL limousine with red flags attached to the mudguards. That was interesting: they were usually reserved for the very top brass. I recalled reading a report that there were only a couple of dozen in the whole country. The man with the cap opened the rear door and his bare-headed comrade pushed me onto a cold vinyl seat. He climbed in beside me, while his colleague walked around to the other side. Up front, a driver was seated with his hands on the wheel, and sitting next to him was Sasha. There was also someone sitting in the back seat next to me, and as I turned I saw that it was Sarah.

*

Sasha snapped at the driver to head off, and we passed through a barricade and turned onto a broad avenue. I caught the word 'Vladimir', and my heart sank: that was the prison east of Moscow where they had held both Greville Wynne and Gary Powers. But then he said it again and I realized that it was the name of the man with the cap and that he was asking why they had taken so long to fetch me. Vladimir replied that I'd been difficult, and Sasha grunted disapprovingly. They were in an almighty hurry, clearly, but there was something else to it – an edge of panic? I decided not to think about what it might mean: I'd find out soon enough.

I looked at Sarah. She sensed my gaze and turned to me. As our eyes met, a thousand thoughts went unspoken. She was wearing a shapeless grey dress. Although she seemed thinner and her blonde hair was cut brutally short, she looked much the same as when I'd last seen her, in the back seat of a limousine like this one about six months ago. I felt a hollowness in my stomach as I remembered it: we had come to a stop on a barricaded street, and I'd watched helplessly as she'd been swiftly bundled into another car and driven away. I'd vowed to myself that I would protect her come what may, but when the moment had arrived I'd offered no protest. But she had *survived*. I had long given up hope of that. I'd felt that they wouldn't risk giving her any freedom for fear she might reach the British embassy and tell them everything we had learned in Italy. As a junior member of the Service, she had very little information to give them. Once they had extracted it from her, I'd reasoned, they would have seen little point in keeping her alive.

But they had. I tried not to think about what they had put her through instead, but an image of the girl Yuri had kept in his rooms in the camp in Germany, and of the way he had flicked his tongue over his lips at his first sight of Sarah, flashed into my mind nevertheless. Repulsion and rage coursed through me.

It had soon become clear to me that Yuri, or Colonel Fedor Fedorovich Proshin as I now knew his real name to be, had been the mastermind behind my career as a Soviet agent, from my recruitment at the age of twenty onwards. He had greeted me in Moscow, but it was no hero's welcome. I was one of several British double agents who had ended up here: Kim Philby, Donald Maclean, Guy Burgess and George Blake. But, unlike them, I was no longer a Communist, and had been brought here against my will, whereas they had all defected by choice.

After I'd been put through a comprehensive – and extremely unpleasant – medical examination, Yuri had proceeded to interrogate me about every aspect of the twenty-four years since I had sought him out in a displaced persons camp in the British Zone of Germany. He hadn't presented it as an interrogation at first, even installing me in fairly comfortable quarters, but the armed guards had never left me with any doubt about the truth of the situation.

He had started every morning the same way: once I was seated, he would open up my dossier and read directly from the reports my handlers had sent to Moscow at whichever point in my career we had reached. After that, the questions would begin.

'Why did you cut off all contact for eighteen months after this meeting?'

'Why did you not mention that Burgess and Maclean had come under suspicion?'

'Why didn't you tell us about Penkovsky?'

And so on, ad infinitum. Part of me had been expecting it – the documents I'd discovered in Rome had revealed that for several years they had suspected me of being a plant by the Service, feeding them carefully selected secrets along with a healthy dose of disinformation: in effect, a triple agent.

That theory had eventually been discredited in '51 and I'd been cleared as 'highly valuable', but now Yuri revived it. The material I had taken so many risks to give them meant nothing to him. It was only the information I had *neglected* to hand over that he found telling. But while it was true that the higher I'd risen in the Service the greater my access to classified material had been, my seniority had often made it harder for me to hand material over, because so few others had such access. If it had ever come to light that the Soviets had this kind of information, I would have immediately come under suspicion.

Yuri had dismissed this argument with a wave of his hand. While my actions would have had me strung up in England, from his perspective I was now an erratic agent with perplexing gaps in his story, who for good measure had betrayed several Soviet agents and even killed two of them. It didn't help that I made no attempt to conceal that I was disgusted with myself for falling into their arms, and with him for the way in which he had recruited me.

He had finally lost patience with me in June, and it was then that I had been moved into Steklyashka, where one day I had been marched into a briefing room and been confronted by Sasha, whom I hadn't seen since we'd arrived in Moscow. He had been my handler since the early Fifties, but any hope that he might prove to be any more understanding as a result was rapidly dispelled. He had barely acknowledged our past relationship, and was even more hostile than Yuri had been. I'd always known that his friendliness towards me was contrived, of course, as real as the intimacy a prostitute shows a wealthy and potentially long-term client, but it had still come as a shock when it was switched off so swiftly, and so absolutely. The familiar 'My dear Paul' had no longer issued from his lips, and his benign condescension had been replaced by a cold and sometimes frightening implacability.

At first I'd thought his behaviour was a pose, a way to get me to talk more by making me want to recapture the old bonhomie, but I'd soon realized that there was nothing forced about it, and that this was in fact his real self – or, at least, his Soviet self.

I looked at him now, partly obscured by the back of his seat, staring at the road ahead of us. He was wearing a uniform and *ushanka*, neither of which I'd ever seen him wear before, and he didn't look right somehow. I knew every inch of his face, from the lines around the eyes to the bristles of his pointed beard, but I found it increasingly hard to associate him with the cheery fellow in the tweed coat and polka-dot tie I had met in an assortment of pubs, cinemas and dives in London, a collector's book of postage stamps under his arm. English Sasha had always seemed podgy and harmless, but Soviet Sasha was a burly bear of a man with an air of barely repressed violence emanating from him. Over the years he'd often told me that he loved London, and I wondered if that had simply been a lie to get me on his side, or if his recall to Moscow had hardened him, and he'd forgotten his appreciation of the good life he'd once led in the West.

Perhaps he was simply scared. My failures as an agent reflected badly on him, and possibly even placed him under suspicion of disloyalty. After Stalin's death, Khrushchev had been, relatively speaking, benign, but Brezhnev had started pushing things back in the other direction: arresting dissidents and sending them to labour camps or into 'internal exile'. Perhaps that was where we were all going now: to some *gulag* in Siberia where we would freeze our arses off until we died.

Whatever the reason, when Sasha had taken over my case any remaining pretence that I was simply an agent undergoing a debriefing had vanished. I was unequivocally a prisoner, placed in a small concrete cell and entitled to one bowl of thin soup and three cigarettes a day. Every morning and afternoon I had been made to write an account of my career, operation by operation, month by month. After that, I would be summoned into a small office, where he would question me at length on everything I'd written. We had reached June 1961.

The car took a sudden turn, throwing my shoulder against the door. The windows were covered by grey curtains, but there was a small gap near the edge and I peered through it at the streets speeding by. Giant portraits of Lenin lined the roads, but I saw very few other cars. It must still be quite early in the morning. Domes shone faintly in the distance, and there was a glint of copper in the sky, a refraction, I imagined, from the giant stars of the Kremlin. But then we took a turn — we didn't seem to be heading that way.

The car slowed to a halt in front of a nondescript building painted a faded orange, and I was dragged out by one of the men. The other stayed in the car with Sarah, and I wondered fleetingly if it would be the last time I saw her.

It had started to snow now and the wind was sharper, biting into my cheeks and stinging my eyelids. Sasha led the way to a sentry box manned by two lieutenants in light blue greatcoats, both armed with finely polished semiautomatic rifles. A pigeon pecking at the ground nearby suddenly came to a standstill and turned in the same direction, its chest puffed out, and for a moment it looked like it was imitating the sentries. All it needed was a few brass buttons and a miniature *ushanka* to complete the picture, but a moment later it returned to its pecking, and the illusion was broken.

Sasha handed some papers to one of the men, who looked through them, then turned and spoke into a small grate in the wall. There was a loud hissing noise, and I saw that the whole section of wall was, in fact, an air-locked door. With some effort, the sentry pulled it open and stepped inside. After a moment's hesitation, Sasha motioned to me, and we followed him in.

We were in a dimly lit space, smaller than the size of my cell. I could see the sentry just ahead, wrestling with the lock of another, much larger, door. Once he had opened it, we walked into a room with concrete walls and a large blanket of green netting in the middle. The sentry knelt down and pulled this to one side, revealing a small wire cage recessed several feet into the floor. He climbed down into it and Sasha and I followed. The sentry pulled a lever in a box on the side of the cage, and we started to descend with a loud cranking noise.

It was then that I recognized the mood I hadn't been able to identify in the car. It wasn't panic. It was fear. They were all terrified out of their wits, and I couldn't blame them. Those had been bomb-blast doors we had just come through.

We were entering a nuclear bunker.

II

As the machinery of the lift whirred, I tried to gather my thoughts. I knew very little about the Soviets' contingency plans in the event of a nuclear attack — few did — but years of surveillance by the West indicated that they had built a massive underground city in the area of Ramenki, a few miles outside Moscow. I didn't think we were there but still beneath the capital where it was thought there was a complex of command and control points and a bunker built by Stalin before the war, all of it connected by a secret second underground railway system.

I thought we must now be inside that labyrinth, but several things were puzzling me. First, why were we going into it at all? There couldn't have been an attack, because we had come here overground. Was it some sort of exercise, then, or simply a secret meeting? It seemed a little over the top for either, and didn't account for the level of fear I was sensing in Sasha and the others. And secondly, why on earth were they bringing *me* here? Since my arrival in May, their treatment of me had been overwhelmingly hostile, yet now I was apparently trusted enough to be taken to one of their most secret military locations.

The lift jolted to a sudden halt. The sentry gestured for us to step out, and when we had, he pulled the lever and the cage started ascending again, leaving me alone with Sasha. Another sentry stepped from the shadows and led us into a narrow passageway with curved steel walls. Lamps riveted to the walls were spaced every few feet, halos shimmering around them, but between them it was pitch dark. It was also unpleasantly clammy. I tried to catch my breath, but Sasha, directly behind me, pushed me forward.

We walked down the steel plankway of the passage, the echo of our footsteps flattened and tinny. After a few minutes, we reached a large door covered in a thick cushion of black leather. The sentry pushed a button on the wall and a few seconds later the door swung open. Sasha gestured to me to enter first, and I stepped through. He followed. The door immediately shut behind us, and a second later I heard the echo of the sentry's footsteps as he began the walk back up the corridor.

I took a breath and looked up. Lights shone down from sconces in the walls, and it took a moment for my vision to adjust. We were in a huge hall, the far end of which was taken up by a circular table with a segment cut out of its centre. This was encircled by thick marble pillars that held up an elaborate painted cupola that looked like it belonged in the Vatican. Seated around the table were around thirty elderly men, some of them wearing dark suits but most in uniform. A man was standing at the table. Unlike the others he was jacketless, his shirtsleeves rolled to his elbows. In one hand he clutched an amber cigarette holder, in the other a sheaf of papers he was brandishing at his audience. I didn't recognize him at first, because he was wearing spectacles and his hair was slightly in disarray, but then he looked up through dark eyes under thick eyebrows, and I realized with a start that it was Brezhnev.

*

He stared at Sasha and me for a moment, evidently caught in mid-sentence. Then he set down his papers.

'Who the hell is this?' he said, his voice a deep baritone.

There was a scraping noise and I followed it to about halfway down the table, where one of the men was pushing his chair back. It was Yuri. He was wearing the uniform of a Colonel-General: it was immaculate, perfectly pressed, with a line of glittering medals across the chest.

'Paul Dark, General Secretary,' he said. 'The British agent. You may remember I suggested fetching him earlier, in case he had any knowledge pertinent to the situation. His file is in the papers, Section Five.' He leaned over and picked up a folder from an attaché case on the table.

Brezhnev waved his hand as though swatting at a fly.

'Be seated.'

Yuri bowed extravagantly and then beckoned me with two fingers, like an emperor summoning a slave. I glared at him, but stepped forward. Yuri gestured towards a vacant chair next to him and I installed myself, the hard wood of the seat angling into my buttocks. Yuri recoiled from me a little, wrinkling his nose: it had been a few days since I'd had a shower. I repressed the urge to place my hands around his throat and crush his windpipe.

Sasha was still standing by the door, and Yuri nodded at him.

'Thank you, Alexander Stepanovich. That will be all.'

Sasha hesitated for a fraction of a second before saluting, but in that moment an odd expression came over his face. It wasn't quite disappointment, I thought — more like hurt. Perhaps he had been expecting to stay. He turned and marched back out of the door.

I looked around the rest of the room. It was in the grandiose style the Soviets reserved for their upper echelons. There were oil paintings on the walls, elaborate cornices, highly polished parquet floors and, arranged on the table, a dozen or more telephones, the Bakelite glistening under the glow of Art Deco lamps. One wall was taken up with a row of clocks giving the current time in Moscow, Washington, Peking, London and several other cities. It had just gone seven o'clock in the morning here. The wall behind Brezhnev was covered in red velvet curtains; I presumed to give the illusion that there were windows behind them. A large map of the world was spread out across the table, and around it were strewn pens, papers, bottles of Borzhom mineral water and glasses. It was much grander than the British bunkers I'd visited, which had been grim, skeletal places devoid of any luxuries — nothing but holes in the ground, as one minister had called them. But this place was just as lifeless in its way, and just as depressing. It wasn't real life, but a simulacrum of it. I wondered how long they'd been down here; I was already feeling claustrophobic, and I'd only just arrived.

One thing was abundantly clear. This wasn't an exercise, or a good spot for a meeting. Something had to be *seriously* wrong for Brezhnev to be in an underground bunker. Although he was in his early sixties, he looked much older. Everyone knew him to be stout, hearty and fond of a drink, as all good Russians were, but he looked a wreck. There were dark circles around his eyes, and I now saw that one hand was shaking. He looked like a bull that had been cornered: angry and ready to lash out.

I felt a momentary pang of pity for the men around the table, many of whom I recognized from Service dossiers. My eyes flicked around as though playing Pelmanism. Seated directly to Brezhnev's right was Kosygin, the Premier, a bulldog. Next to him was Suslov — he looked like a kindly old don, but his staunch Stalinism and behind-the-scenes machinations had earned him the nickname the 'Red Eminence'. Then there was Grechko, the Minister of Defence and head of the armed forces — the classic military type with hair cropped *en brosse*.

Next to him was Ivashutin, head of the GRU. Portly, around sixty, he was one of Brezhnev's old cronies, having known him since the war, when he had been a senior officer in SMERSH on the Ukrainian front. He had taken part in the arrest of Serov, and then been appointed head of the GRU in his place by Brezhnev. Opposite him sat Andropov, the new head of the KGB, inscrutable in horn-rimmed spectacles. He and Ivashutin were thought to detest each other, which was perhaps why they had been seated so far apart.

These grey, heavy men constituted the 'Supreme Command' or 'Defence Council', the core of the Politburo and decision-making power in a crisis — and they were mostly hardliners. As well as sending dissidents to work camps, Brezhnev was also cracking down on signs of reform in the satellite states, which had culminated in the ruthless intervention in Czechoslovakia the previous spring.

Several reports had reached the Service that Brezhnev had become significantly unpopular with the Soviet people as a result, and in January there had even been an attempt on his life. A soldier, apparently upset by the Prague invasion, had fled his base in Leningrad, taking with him two loaded Makarovs and four clips from his unit's safe. Arriving in Moscow, he had stolen a police uniform belonging to his father and, posing as an officer at one of the cordons leading into the Kremlin, had tried to shoot Brezhnev as he was being driven through for a homecoming celebration for several cosmonauts. But he got the wrong car and had hit one of the cosmonauts instead.

In the meantime, Brezhnev continued the roll-back to Stalinism. In his address to the Congress of the Polish Communist Party in November, he had stated that a threat to the security of any 'socialist' country was a threat to them all, and would be dealt with as such. The Brezhnev Doctrine, as it was soon known, overturned the idea of sovereign states that had been at the heart of the Warsaw Pact. I wondered if another state had decided to try to test his steel. This wasn't a group of men you would gather together on a whim.

Most alarming to me was Yuri's presence. He'd altered his appearance a little since I'd last seen him. His white hair was still shorn close to the skull, but he had cultivated a thin goatee to match it; I suspected because he wanted to appear more distinguished. He had unluckily conspicuous features for a spy — a strange snubbed nose and tiny eyes in a mass of leathery wrinkles — and the effect was of a mischievous schoolboy peering out of the face of an old man.

From his uniform and position at the table, it looked like he was Ivashutin's deputy. On my arrival in Moscow, he had given the impression of having long been sidelined from the *apparat*, an old hand who had been stepped over by younger men. And yet here he was, in the heart of the lion's den, deputy head of the GRU. Either he had been promoted in the last few months, or – more likely – he had only wanted me to believe he had been sidelined so that I would underestimate him, giving him an advantage in interrogation. Not for the first time he had pulled the wool over my eyes with infuriating ease.

Brezhnev had sat down, and was drinking water from a glass while he looked me over. His eyes were like bullet holes.

'Remind me, Colonel-General Proshin,' he said without adjusting his gaze. 'Why did you wish to bring this man here? Looking at his dossier, it seems we feel that he is not to be trusted.'

'That is not quite so, General Secretary,' Yuri replied evenly. 'We have been determining precisely what level of trust we can place in him at one of our secure facilities.'

Brezhnev sat back and folded his arms. 'For six months?'

Yuri's tiny eyes didn't flicker. 'We strive to be thorough, General Secretary. The dossier contains some provisional thoughts, but our plan was to make a more thorough assessment once we had gathered all the available information. However, considering the current situation, I requested permission to bring him before the Council because I felt that as a result of his former position as Deputy Chief of the British Service, he may be able to help us.'

'Or he may lie to us.'

Yuri nodded. 'That is naturally a possibility. But if so—'

'Could I just interject for a moment?' I said, and two dozen heads jerked in my direction. 'Would someone mind telling me what's going on?'

An hour previously, I would have thought I would be one of the last people the Soviet leadership would want to bring into their confidence, but they obviously wanted something from me and they would have to show their hand sooner or later. It was intimidating being in such company, but I had, after all, been in similar company in London, and I thought it was wise to try to establish that I was on the same level as they, rather than a circus act they could discuss and poke at will. If I could undermine Yuri at the same time, all the better. I hadn't seen the bastard in months, but I had good cause to loathe him. He had indeed placed me in a 'secure facility', and Christ knew what he'd done to Sarah.

Brezhnev lit another cigarette, and gestured to Yuri that he should answer my question. Yuri straightened his back and stared at me with unalloyed hatred radiating from his hobgoblin eyes.

'Very well,' he said. 'We would like you to tell us all you know about the West's plans for nuclear conflict.'

I took that in, eyeing Brezhnev's cigarette and wishing I had my own to puff. An image flashed into my mind: the toothless grin of the old man in the stand near Sloane Square Underground as he slid a pack of Players into my waiting fingers. I shook my head free of it.

'I don't know anything about that,' I said.

'Come,' said Yuri, and gave a slow, condescending smile. 'You were deputy head of the Service.'

'For about five minutes. I can tell you about the broad strategy, if you like, but the only people who know the details of the plans are those directly involved in them.'

'In the bunkers, you mean.'

He was trying to get me to give him something he could follow up on. I didn't react. I noted that this seemed to be his show, since none of the others were talking. That suggested the meeting had been called on account of information received by the GRU.

'You know where the bunkers are, of course?' he said.

'Not off by heart, no. I'm afraid I can't really tell you much about "the West" as a whole. I know a bit about the British strategy, a little about NATO's and next to nothing about the Americans'.'

Three seats down, I saw Andropov look away and purse his lips, and guessed it was the Americans they were interested in.

'Very well,' said Yuri, his tone a little more curt. 'Please tell us what you do know.'

JEREMY DUNS

I smiled sweetly at him, stalling for time so I could work out what was going on and how to react. I could simply refuse to cooperate, of course. I didn't much like being woken up, yelled at and *fetched* to an underground bunker without any explanation, and part of me was tempted to tell them where to stick it. But that would be foolish — if I didn't appear to be trying to answer their questions sincerely, they would simply put a bullet through the back of my head. They might do it anyway, but there was a chance they wouldn't. So swallow your pride, play nicely, sound convincing, and if you're very lucky they won't shoot you at the end of this and might even give you a slightly more comfortable cell.

The difficulty was in picking precisely which pieces of information I could safely tell them. Because I did, of course, know quite a lot about the West's plans for nuclear conflict, having been given a copy of the War Book on being appointed Head of Soviet Section in late '65. I had also taken part in dozens of meetings over the years on the intricacies of post-strike contingency plans, including with counterparts at NATO and CIA.

This time last year I had taken part in INVALUABLE, a top secret Whitehall exercise that had preceded NATO's wider scenario in Bonn. It was one of a series of seemingly interminable exercises carried out by a select handful of officials to test the War Book's contingency plans in case of an escalation to nuclear war with the Soviet Union. After a while they became a nuisance, and it was difficult to connect them with the idea of a real conflict. Was this a comparable Soviet exercise? It didn't seem like it — nobody had been sweating this much in London.

If so, it might be that other men in uniforms were scurrying into bunkers in other parts of the world. If the United States felt an attack was imminent, about a thousand people were to retreat to a complex of steel-protected buildings set inside Cheyenne Mountain in Colorado. Members of Congress would be evacuated to a bunker in White Sulphur Springs, Virginia, while the President would move to Camp David and the Pentagon to a facility nearby.

In the event that one of their nuclear command or ground launch centres were hit or their capability damaged, a round-the-clock airborne command post codenamed 'Looking Glass' would take over. They also had on patrol some forty submarines, loaded with Polaris nuclear-armed missiles.

In Britain, if ballistic missiles or some other form of explosive weapon were detected by the receivers at RAF Fylingdales or by the Royal Observer Corps, information about the objects' radar arrays, height, speed and inclination would immediately be fed into the Threat Report Panel in Fylingdales' operations room. If deemed a credible threat, the Home Office would be informed and could then issue the 'Four-Minute Warning' – so called because of the length of time between it being given and oncoming missiles reaching their targets, although it might in fact be as little as three and a half minutes.

The warning would be broadcast by the BBC on television and radio, and sirens would be sounded across the country. The warning would advise people to stay in their own homes, and to move to their fallout rooms. In reality, as I knew from discussions on the issue, very few people would survive a sustained nuclear strike. Even if they made it to shelter within four minutes, had stockpiled a fortnight's supply of provisions and were 'lucky' enough to survive the attack, after their food and water supplies had run out there would be nowhere to find more.

In the early days, the idea had been to try to protect the public as a whole from an attack, but the emphasis had shifted to protecting only those who would be needed to reconstruct the country. One early plan had been for the Prime Minister and a small group to stay in London and beat a retreat to a network of rooms under Whitehall, an extension of those built during the last war. But that had been scrapped after two secret reports in the mid-Fifties had painted a horrific picture of the consequences of an H-bomb attack on Britain.

Expert analysis of Whitehall's 'citadels', as the bunkers were known, had revealed that they might not withstand a direct strike, and that a single explosion could also block their exits, entombing the Prime Minister and his advisers below ground. The boffins had also estimated that an attack on Britain with ten hydrogen bombs would turn much of the country into a radioactive wasteland, and kill or seriously injure sixteen million people – around a third of the population. Another thirteen million people, many of them suffering from contamination, would be imprisoned in their shelters for at least a week. Reading the reports, it was hard to see how the country would ever be able to recover.

As a result, the plans had been changed so that if an attack seemed imminent, several days before the Four-Minute Warning led to ordinary members of the public uselessly shepherding their children into their feebly protected basements, the Cabinet, members of the royal family and senior members of the government, the military, the Service, Five and the scientific community would be evacuated to a 35-acre blast-proof bunker that had been built in the old limestone quarries in Corsham, Wiltshire, with a few hundred others retreating to underground operational headquarters around the country.

But in '63, Kim Philby defected to Moscow. He hadn't been indoctrinated into the Corsham plan, but some feared he might nevertheless have got wind of it. If so, the Russians could wipe Britain off the map simply by aiming missiles at London and the bunker in Wiltshire. And so, in May '68, a brand new plan had been put into place, known to only a handful of people.

If it looked like a nuclear attack was imminent, instead of the 'great and the good' being whisked to Corsham, they would instead be split into several groups. RAF helicopters based at Little Rissington in Gloucestershire would fly to Whitehall and wait at the Horse Guards Parade for the Prime Minister and a couple of dozen others – including a few from the Service – and each group would be flown to a different location. I was earmarked to be taken to Welbeck Abbey in Nottinghamshire, to the maze of rooms built beneath it in the nineteenth century by the agoraphobic fifth Duke of Portland. The idea that central government would evacuate to Corsham had been kept in place as a cover story, a decoy to protect the new plan and to stop anyone looking for the PYTHON sites, as they had been codenamed.

A thought crystallized in my mind. Despite the Service's fears that Philby had blown Corsham, it seemed clear from Yuri's questions that they did *not* know about it. If so, that meant that all the money and effort to create the PYTHON plan had been a waste. I had decided not to tell them when I learned about it last spring, and I certainly didn't want to tell them now. Apart from having lost any vestige of belief in their cause, I didn't want to be responsible for starting a nuclear war.

But I *could* tell them about Corsham, which was no longer in use, and make it seem very convincing – I had learned about it in '65, and had even been given a tour of the place. But before I answered, I needed to find out why were they asking. Were they planning to attack the West, and if so, why?

'The locations of the bunkers are not our primary concern,' said Yuri, smiling, and I wondered for an eerie moment whether he had managed to plant a bug in my mind. 'We're more interested in the procedures. How long would it take for a second strike to be launched following an order from the American President, for example?'

A cold, empty feeling crept through me. I didn't know the precise timing of the Americans' chain of command, but I knew that in Britain's case HMS *Resolution* and two other submarines were on constant patrol with American Polaris missiles aboard, and that they were primed to be launched within fifteen minutes of an order from the Prime Minister. But that was in the event of a decision to *retaliate*. Yuri had asked me about a second strike: in other words, if the Americans launched a first strike on the Soviet Union and then wanted to deliver a follow-up attack. I could only think of a few reasons to ask such a question, and I didn't like any of them.

'Why do you want to know this?' I said. 'Is the country under attack?'

Yuri glanced at Ivashutin, who in turn looked at Brezhnev. I kept silent, watching, waiting. They couldn't get anything detailed out of me if they didn't give me more information, and they'd gone to the trouble of bringing me here so presumably they wanted it. I suspected that protocol and habit made them reluctant to tell a foreigner what was going on, but it was absurd in this instance – it wasn't as if I could tell anyone. As the moments passed, I thought I sensed this understanding make its way around the table.

Finally, Brezhnev made a decision and nodded his head gently. Yuri took a deep breath and turned to me.

'Yes,' he said. 'The Soviet Union is under attack.'

I felt it like a blow to the stomach. Was it possible? It couldn't be nuclear, I realized at once. They wouldn't have spent the time bringing me here in that case, let alone doing so above ground. On the other hand, if it wasn't nuclear, what the hell were we doing in this bunker?

'What sort of attack?' I said, the words forming before my mind had even processed them.

Brezhnev tapped his cigarette against the nearest ashtray, and nodded again.

Yuri took another breath. 'The Americans launched a chemical attack on Paldiski and Hiiumaa yesterday,' he said. 'We are preparing our response.'

Paldiski and Hiiumaa were both in Estonia, facing the Gulf of Finland. The entire area was closed off to the public as it was home to dozens of military and naval installations: Hiiumaa and the surrounding islands were rumoured to be home to sizeable artillery batteries, while Paldiski was a major nuclear submarine base. I looked around the room, taking in the collection of grey faces, the ticking clocks, the portraits on the wall and the plume of smoke spiralling from Brezhnev's ghastly cigarette.

'What sort of chemical attack?' I said.

'A serious one. Over a dozen have been seriously injured – two men have already died. We have sent specialized troops to the area, as well as a team of experts to investigate. In addition,' – he glanced at the wall with the clocks – 'about ten hours ago our radars picked up eighteen B-52 Stratofortress bombers shortly after they had taken off from two American Air Force bases, Fairchild in Washington and March in California. We have analysed the take-off patterns and fuel consumption to calculate the weight of the aircraft, and have concluded that they are armed with thermonuclear weapons.'

I stared at him, and then took in the import of the large map on the table. There were lines running all over it: trajectories.

'Where are they now?'

He gave a grim smile, perhaps satisfied that I was catching up to the severity of the situation.

'They have been in a circling pattern for the past few hours, but now seem to be heading straight towards our eastern border. We also have reports that KC-135 aircraft have been deployed from Little Rock in Arkansas, and we believe they will meet up with the B-52s once they reach the coast of Canada.'

'For in-air refuelling.'

He nodded. 'The B-52s are travelling at around 800 kilometres an hour, and if they continue on their current path we expect them to cross into our airspace in just under five hours from now. That is, at noon our time.'

My first thought was that they must be part of a patrol. Back in the Fifties, the Americans had set up a system whereby they had a dozen nuclear-armed B-52s airborne around the clock, so that if the Soviets launched a surprise attack on their bases they would still be able to retaliate. But then I remembered that had changed. Early in '66, a USAF B-52 carrying four H-bombs had collided with a Stratotanker during mid-air refuelling over the Mediterranean. One of the H-bombs had fallen into the sea and it had taken several weeks to find it, while two of the remaining three that had fallen on land had spilled enriched uranium and plutonium over a Spanish fishing village, and had cost millions to clear up. Then last year one of the B-52s had crashed very close to their own airbase in Greenland, detonating the primary units of its thermonuclear weapons but, very luckily, not triggering a nuclear reaction. As a result of these incidents, Washington had, understandably, discontinued the airborne patrols.

So it couldn't be that. What the hell could it be, then, other than preparations for an attack? In-air refuelling was a bloody risky manoeuvre – one shift in the wind or mistake at the controls could lead to a crash, and this time they might not be as lucky as they had been in Greenland. I remembered a report on their Castle Bravo test on the Micronesian islands back in '54 saying that the explosion had been around 1,500 times more powerful than the atomic bombs used on Hiroshima and Nagasaki. No wonder we were underground.

'Have you used the hotline?' I said. This was the direct telex connection between Washington and Moscow that had been set up in '63 in the wake of the Cuban crisis so that the two superpowers could communicate about accidents or unexplained incidents and avert a potential disaster.

'No,' said Yuri. 'We do not need to ask our enemies if they have attacked us – we already know they have. Use of the hotline would alert them of this, and that we plan to retaliate. We don't plan to warn our enemies in advance – they did not warn us.'

I nodded, dazed. I'd attended several meetings about the setting up of that hotline. But the difference between a hypothetical situation and a real one couldn't be starker, and the logic of his reply was clear. The hotline only made sense if you suspected it was a mistake. If you had good reason to think you were under attack, it was counter-productive to use it. The hotline was a waste of time.

'You say you have evidence that the injuries in Paldiski and Hiiumaa are caused by chemical weapons. But couldn't this be a provocation from someone else – China, for example? Or an accident of some sort?'

He shook his head briskly. 'No doubt we were meant to conclude it was an accident, but there can no longer be any question of that. Several people have already been affected, and the toll is rising by the hour. As all the victims are crucial to our nuclear effort, and this has happened at precisely the same time that the United States has sent several nuclear-armed B-52s towards our border, it would seem foolish to see it as anything but deliberate, and that most likely it is part of preparations for a full-scale nuclear attack.

'As for the Chinese, we have finally started negotiations in Peking, so we don't think this is their doing. We already know that the Americans are using chemical agents in Vietnam, and this follows several other signals from them in the last couple of weeks that they are at an advanced state of readiness, and may be preparing to launch an attack against us. We have observed increased naval activity in the Gulf of Aden, and our ambassador in Washington was recently informed by Nixon himself that the United States is prepared to take "drastic action" as a result of our support of the North Vietnamese if the peace talks in Paris do not advance.'

'Have you talked to the North Vietnamese?'

'They are not under our control. They want our arms and training but don't listen to us if we try to interfere politically, as it is their war and they feel they know better. It seems Nixon has not taken this into account, and has decided he will attack us as a result.'

'But why has he not just launched a strike, then? Why attack your bases in Estonia and make it look like an accident?'

'Clearly, they have identified that many of our important military installations are located in this area and have decided to sabotage them in advance of a nuclear attack. The idea of making it look like an accident was presumably so that we would not be aware that it was a precursor to a nuclear strike. They must not have thought that we would rapidly be able to confirm the type of chemical used and therefore know it's an attack. And, of course, by making us doubt that the incident is an attack, they hope to delay our retaliation.'

'Yes, but even so—' I stopped. 'Hold on. You say you know what type of chemical is involved?'

'Yes, our researchers have examined several of the patients and have determined that it is one not found in the Soviet Union. It is mustard gas, but a form of it we have never encountered.'

I shivered, and a ripple of horror ran through me – a new form of mustard gas.

I looked at the map, and quickly located Paldiski on it.

Christ Almighty.

'It's not a chemical attack,' I said. 'It's a leak.'

III

Sunday, 11 March 1945, Hotel Torni, Helsinki, Finland

It was past midnight when there was a sharp knocking on my door. I opened it to see Templeton, dressed in a hat and topcoat, peering at me.

My first thought was that Father had been killed in action and he had come to inform me, immediately followed by a flash of shameful hope I might be right. As a boy, I had lain awake in my bed sickened and fascinated by fantasies of his death, and in recent months my mind had slipped back into this reflex of momentarily wishing for the worst news. At first it had disturbed me, but now I dismissed it for what it was: just a trick of the mind exacerbated by the tensions of the war.

'Meet me in the lobby in five minutes,' Templeton said, and there was a look in his eyes that spoke of conspiracies rather than condolences. 'In full uniform, please.'

I nodded and shut the door. Having dressed hurriedly, I raced down the carpeted staircase, wondering what would await me at the foot of it.

I had arrived in Helsinki a few months earlier, and was not enjoying it. I'd had a frustrating war. Shortly after leaving school I had been recruited into the Special Operations Executive, and had been put through rigorous training. After narrowly missing out on taking part in several operations, Father had arranged for me to be attached to the platoon guarding Churchill at Chequers. This sounded impressive, but the novelty of being close to the man as he chomped his cigar and chugged down brandy soon faded – the job mostly consisted of patrolling the house and grounds with a Tommy gun, and following him in a convoy of trucks and motor-cycles whenever he went for a stroll.

I had finally seen some real action in 1944, when I was dropped into France as part of a Jedburgh team, but the operation had been cut short after just a few weeks when it had become clear that the cell we had been sent to contact had been betrayed to the Germans.

After that, I'd been sent out here. I suspected Father had heard something about my time in France and had had a word in someone's ear to whisk me out of the line of fire. In 1941, before the Legation in Helsinki had been evacuated by the Finns and relocated to Lisbon, he had briefly served as the military attaché out here, and I'd visited him and helped out around the place during one Long Vac, delivering messages in between the endless cocktail parties.

Finland had by now surrendered to the Soviets for the second time but we had yet to restore diplomatic relations with them, so rather than returning to the Legation I had been posted on to the staff of the Allied Control Com mission, which was operating out of the Hotel Torni, a hideous watchtower-like building overlooking the centre of Helsinki. The Commission had been established to supervise the Finns' compliance with their armistice with Moscow and, although Allied in name, was almost completely dominated by the Russians. There were two hundred of them and just fifteen Brits, who were under firm instruction from London not to antag-onize the Russians. Finland was part of the Soviet sphere, at least until the end of the war.

None of the Brits spoke any Finnish, and it had been deemed a sound idea if someone could be found who did. My previous few weeks flitting about the Legation had presumably been on file, but nobody seemed to have realized that while my mother was a Finn, she was in fact a Swedish-speaker. As a result, I was fluent in Swedish but knew no Finnish at all.

On arrival, I had discovered that it made little odds anyway. The British contingent was led by Commodore Howie of the Royal Navy, but I reported to Colonel Colin Templeton, an old friend of Father's from Cairo whom I'd met a couple of times on school holidays. Officially the Army's representative, he was in reality an SOE officer and, despite being given the rank of lieutenant-colonel, I was his dogsbody. With every passing day, I resented the position all the more. My few weeks in France had nearly got me killed, but I had finally tasted action and was desperate for more. I was twenty years old, and the war was still raging elsewhere in Europe, while I spent my days in a hotel typing up the minutes of meetings about the minutiae of diplomatic protocol.

'Is it Japan, sir?' I asked Templeton as we stepped out of the hotel lobby and into the chill night air. The Americans had just fire-bombed Tokyo, destroying half the city, and I had spent the day collating reports on the situation. But Templeton shook his head.

'I'll explain in the Ghost,' he said, as we showed our passes to a sentry and crossed the courtyard.

The Ghost was a battered old Chevrolet, a former Finnish Army staff car that he had commandeered for his personal use. Every inch of its exterior had been whitewashed, including the windows, a legacy of its use at the front early in the war. Templeton had left it in this condition partly because he enjoyed the eccentricity of it, and partly because the camouflage suited his purposes. His instructions from London were for his presence here to be as invisible as possible: in a city often covered in snow, the Ghost allowed him to do just that.

It wasn't snowing now, but as many of the surrounding buildings were white the car still lived up to its name. Templeton's chauffeur opened the door and we were soon gliding through the city, cocooned behind the thickened frost of the glass. He wasted no time in getting to the point.

'When you were here in '41, I understand that you and Larry flew across to Stockholm by seaplane.'

I nodded, puzzled. My father and I had made the journey several times, in a couple of old single-seater Supermarines. Father had always been a racing fiend, and didn't much care if it was on land, air, water or a combination. I had relished the expeditions as opportunities to spend more time with him, but after a while had realized that he was using them to look at the possibility of moving Mother to an asylum in Stockholm. He did this a few months later, and there she had remained ever since. It didn't surprise me that our trips had ended up in my file, but I couldn't fathom why they were relevant now.

'Are you sending me to Sweden, sir?'

Templeton ignored the question. 'A few hours ago, our Russian friends here received a message from their consulate in Mariehamn, which is the capital of a group of demilitarized islands known as Ahvenanmaa in Finnish and Åland in Swedish. The place belongs to Finland, but is Swedish-speaking.'

I knew of it – an archipelago at the entrance of the Gulf of Bothnia. I had never been there, but some members of Mother's family had a summer residence on the western side. This was my immediate thought. It took me a few moments more to take in the other implication of what Templeton had just said: we had intercepted the Russians' message. If he was listening in to the Soviets' telephones in the hotel, I had severely underestimated him.

'The Russians' message was as follows,' Templeton said briskly. 'Yesterday evening, a body was discovered washed ashore on the Åland islands. The local police have identified it as being that of a German naval officer by the name of Wilhelm von Trotha.'

Corpses of naval officers being washed ashore? As the car jostled along, I examined Templeton's face to see if it was some sort of elaborate joke. But he was looking at me intently, apparently waiting for my thoughts on the matter.

'Could it be a provocation, sir?' I asked. Shortly before heading to France I'd heard talk of an operation in which we had secured a body from a morgue in London, dressed it in the uniform of a Royal Marine and landed it on the coast of Spain with a cache of false letters to fool the Germans into thinking we were planning to target Sardinia and Greece rather than Sicily. It had worked like a dream, but the Jerries would, of course, have realized that it had been a ruse, so perhaps someone had thought up a revenge plan.

'That was my first thought, too,' said Templeton. 'But it looks like this could be genuine.' He reached inside his coat and brought out a wodge of paper, which he unfolded and spread out on the upholstery between us. It was a large sea chart of Finland. After scanning it for a few moments, he pointed to a spot on the eastern archipelago labelled 'Degerby'.

'This is where they found the body. As you can see, it's very isolated: if someone deliberately placed a body there, the chances of it being discovered would have been exceptionally slim. More significantly, we know that this chap von Trotha was, in fact, the captain of a U-boat, U-745, which we have been tracking for some time. It left Danzig in December, and on January the eleventh it sank one of the Russians' minesweepers here.' He pointed to the map again, to a small island off the coast of Estonia. 'And it was last observed somewhere around' – he shifted his finger to a spot just west of the Gulf of Finland – 'here.'

'When you say "last observed", sir, do I understand that we believe the boat is out of action?'

'Yes. Its last signal was on the fourth of last month, and we suspect it was accidentally sunk by one of the Germans' own mines, either on that day or soon after. If so, the body may simply have floated ashore on the currents. As a matter of course, we would probably be interested in this chap, but we have also had information, from impeccable sources, that his U-boat was carrying a very special cargo: a new form of mustard gas. Mustard gas is a viscous liquid, of course, but this has apparently been mixed together in such a way as to make it even thicker, so it won't be affected by the temperatures in this part of the world. They call it "Winterlost", and if our sources are to be believed it's very strong stuff indeed – roughly twice as powerful as the usual variety.'

I didn't ask how he knew any of this, but guessed that the positions and dates were from the submarine tracking room at the Admiralty, and that the information on the mustard gas on von Trotha's U-boat had come from captured crewmen of other vessels.

'Despite all that,' Templeton said, 'it could still be some sort of deception operation mounted by the Germans. But we don't want to take any chances – and neither, it seems, do the Russians. The consulate in Mariehamn has been instructed to send someone to this island to secure von Trotha's personal effects before he is buried. We think they may also be sending one of their agents from Stockholm, perhaps under cover, but I've yet to receive confirmation of that. We don't know whether they are aware of the Uboat's special cargo – we haven't informed them – but we need to beat them to the corpse regardless.

'Our chemical warfare bods are of the opinion that this Winterlost would be an extremely dangerous weapon if turned on us – and also a very useful one for us to study. I've been in intensive signals with London for the last few hours, and they have instructed me that it should – indeed, must – be investigated. So I want you to get to this chap's body and see if he has any information on him that gives a more accurate indication of the location of U-745 than its last signal – and then bring back the mustard gas.'

I stared at him for a few moments. Through the whitewashed windows, I could just make out the Finnish countryside rushing by: dark impenetrable forests stretching into the distance.

'I thought you said the U-boat was believed to have been hit by a mine, sir.'

Templeton knitted his brows. 'Yes, but you've diving experience, haven't you?'

So that was what it was about. In early 1944, I had responded to a call for 'volunteers for hazardous service' sent out by the Royal Marines Office at the Admiralty. I had duly been summoned to report to HMS *Dolphin* in Portsmouth harbour, where I was informed that I would be trained as a diver for midget submarines.

After several weeks of training in a deep tank, I had been cleared for the next stage and sent with fifteen other men to Loch Cairnbawn in the far north of Scotland, where the details of the operation in question had finally been revealed to us: the Navy had managed to put the German battleship *Tirpitz* out of action in September, and were now training to attack the Laksevåg floating dock in Bergen.

As part of the provisional crew, I had been put in and out of the new 'X-Craft', wearing a claustrophobic diving suit nicknamed the 'Clammy Death' as I learned the art of oxygen-diving. But after just a few weeks in Scotland I was told that I hadn't been selected to take part in the operation. Bitterly disappointed, I'd been sent back into the arms of SOE, who had a training establishment in Arisaig. After a few weeks of lugging backpacks around the mountainside and being taught unarmed combat and other esoteric skills by a purple-nosed Scot, I had been sent to the Parachute Training School in Ringway, and shortly after that had finally been cleared to take part in an operation and dropped into France.

I gave an abridged version of this to Templeton and he listened intently, his eyes flickering in the shadows.

'But you have had diving training,' he said quietly, once I'd finished.

Very briefly, I wanted to say, and I'd hated every minute of it. But instead I mumbled a 'Yes, sir.'

He smiled softly. 'Good. I've got you all the requisite gear, anyway. And we know the Jerries often bring their boats in very close to the shore, so with any luck it should be relatively easy to get to.'

It was true that the German U-boats often hugged coastlines, and the Russians had captured one of them in shallow waters in these parts last summer. They had raised it and discovered a new type of acoustic torpedo on board, some details of which they had shared with us. But there was no guarantee that this particular U-boat had also sunk in shallow waters.

'You'll have a wireless set,' said Templeton. 'So once you have the location, signal back and I'll judge whether or not a dive is worth risking.'

Risking my neck, he meant.

'What about the Russians?' I asked. 'Presumably they'll already be on their way from Mariehamn, if they haven't already reached it.'

'We don't think they'll set out until dawn – they've no reason to suspect their message was intercepted. We also think it will take them a while. The archipelago is made up of thousands of tiny islets and is fearfully tricky to navigate by boat if you don't know it well, especially as quite a bit of the water is frozen over at the moment. All being well, you should be landing on the island' – he glanced at his wristwatch – 'in about three hours' time.'

Despite his confidence, I didn't like the sound of any of it. I'd wanted action, but I hadn't envisaged anything as hairy as this. Although Åland was, technically speaking, Allied territory, I was being sent to poach a weapon from right underneath the Russians' noses, and I didn't think they'd be overly understanding about it were they to catch me. The Russians weren't to be trusted. In the summer of '42, two Service agents armed with wireless sets had landed in Catalina flying boats at one of their bases in Lake Lakhta. The plan was for the Russians to insert them over the border into Norway, where they would monitor German naval movements along the coast. But the Russians had instead imprisoned both Service men for two months and then dropped them into Finland instead, where they had promptly been caught by the Germans, tortured and shot.

'What if the Russians do get there first, sir?' I said, trying to make my tone as unconcerned as possible. 'Or if I arrive at the same time?'

Templeton gave a small nod. He leaned forward and picked up something from between his feet that I hadn't noticed earlier: a leather briefcase. He pulled it onto his lap, unfastened the clasps, and brought out a fawn-coloured shoulder holster with a Browning 9mm pistol resting inside.

'I don't anticipate any trouble,' he said, 'but take this with you just in case.'

I wondered how to broach the next question, but he anticipated it.

'You must get to the submarine before anyone else,' he said, snapping the case shut and stowing it between his feet again. 'If anyone gets in your way, you have my permission to eliminate them.'

*

After about an hour's drive, we took a narrow road through a pine forest until we finally reached a small, secluded bay. We stepped out of the car and trudged towards a wooden hangar shielded by vegetation. Inside, a small seaplane sat silently under a mass of green and brown camouflage. It was a three-seater, one of the Norwegians' naval reconnaissance craft and, like the Ghost, had seen better days. Templeton said it had been used by the Norwegians against the Germans, then briefly by us and then by the Finns against the Russian subs along this stretch of the Baltic. According to the conditions of the armistice the Soviets had laid down, it should have been sent up to the north of the country to aid the Finns in their enforced mission to flush the Germans out, but Templeton had managed to keep it back from his Russian colleagues and arranged for it to be secreted here. 'Good craft are hard to come by,' he said with a sly smile.

We removed the scrim and he quickly showed me around it, but I'd flown seaplanes and time was of the essence. The plan was for me to land at the small jetty at Degerby, where the body had been reported. The local police there would no doubt be expecting a boatload of Russians from Mariehamn, but Templeton felt confident they would believe the Soviets had shared the information with their Allies, so I should be able to bluff my way through. I hoped to God he was right.

Templeton's chauffeur removed a suitcase from the car, and Templeton took me through the contents: 24-hour rations, Benzedrine tablets and a Siebe Gorman Sladen Suit – the 'Clammy Death' that had given me nightmares in Scotland. It had a breathing apparatus and twin aluminium cylinders that would provide enough oxygen for six hours, and I would be able to take it down to a depth of around thirty feet. Templeton seemed confident this would be the case – part of me hoped he was wrong and I would have to abort the operation.

But I kept such thoughts to myself, and climbed into the cockpit. Templeton showed me the wireless set, giving me the frequencies I would need to reach him. He didn't say where he would be, but presumably it wouldn't be too far away. Then he shook my hand solemnly and trudged back to the Ghost, a stoop-backed man in a topcoat and hat. His chauffeur opened the door for him and they set off down the road again. I watched as the car disappeared from view, then positioned the holster with the pistol under my left armpit. It felt heavy, and the leather of the holster cold even through my battledress.

I took a breath and examined the instruments and gauges around me, then strapped myself in. It was time to get going.

*

I was lost.

The Baltic lay beneath me, patches of ice glowing faintly in the moonlight, but I had no idea which part of Åland I was over, or even if I was over it at all. Templeton had marked Degerby on the chart, but the scale was too small and I had the growing sense that I was going around in circles. The wireless set wouldn't help: Templeton wouldn't have made it to his location yet and I didn't dare land.

A sudden gust of turbulence slammed me against the side of the cockpit and I desperately tried to keep my hands gripped on the control column, fighting down the panic as my mind was filled with the consequences of failure. Templeton would have to send a signal back to London: man down, operation unsuccessful, please send replacement agent, this time make sure it's someone with an ounce of bloody . . . And then, just as suddenly as it had hit, the wind subsided. I slumped back in the seat, my forehead soaked with sweat and my heart still racing, and managed to right the craft. Glancing down again, I realized I had dipped dangerously low. The ice was interrupted here and there by islets, and I glimpsed miniature coiled pine trees and pinkish rocks beneath the patches of ice. But there, over to the west, a lonely dot of orange light glowed like the tip of a cigarette. I consulted the chart, and did some quick calculations in my head.

Yes. It was Degerby.

I headed for it, lifting the nose but decreasing airspeed, and the shoreline began to take a sharper shape, until I could make out small wooden cabins dotted among the trees. A jetty came into view and I wheeled into a wind current and brought her down as gently as I could, the waves kicking up in a luminous curve of white spray. I lined up with the jetty and slowly brought her to a standstill, then climbed out.

I took in a lungful of air, savouring the freshness and the smell of the water, and then exhaled, my breath misting. I anchored, and took in my surroundings as the sweat finally started to cool on my skin. I was in a small bay, and it looked so peaceful in the moonlight, the water a perfect mirror reflecting the shoreline, that it was hard to imagine such a thing as war even existed. The wind had now vanished, as suddenly as it had appeared just minutes earlier.

The jetty led up to a rocky plateau, on which I could make out the outlines of some low buildings. I began walking towards them, but as I approached the shore I saw a silhouetted figure standing a few feet ahead of me. Before I had a chance to react, the figure had stepped forward, and the harbour lighting illuminated a stout man in a coat and cap with a deeply weathered face.

'Kjell Lundström,' he said in a deep baritone. 'Chief Constable of Degerby.'

I offered him my hand. 'Lieutenant-Colonel Paul Dark. I've come about the German.'

His grip was hard, even through my thick gloves. 'We have been expecting you. But I understood that Colonel Presnakov was to come by boat. We received no word of a seaplane.'

'Presnakov is on his way,' I said, replying in Swedish. 'I'm a British officer from the Allied Control Commission in Helsinki.'

He didn't answer for a moment, taking this in. Then he said: 'I didn't know Helsinki had been informed.'

'A last-minute change of plan,' I said. 'Someone higher up the chain of command decided it was important, and it wasn't my place to argue. I'm no happier about it than you are – I'd rather be asleep in my bed.'

He smiled at that, and I breathed an inward sigh of relief. My cover had, at least for the moment, been accepted.

'Your Swedish is excellent,' he said, as he helped me off the jetty and onto the rocks. 'Have you been here before?'

'No,' I said. 'But my mother's family has property in Eckerö.'

Lundström didn't reply, but I sensed he was satisfied with that answer. Russians were hated in this part of the world, so he no doubt felt more comfortable with a Swedish-speaking Brit with connections to the place, however tenuous they might be. He led me up a narrow pathway through the pines until we reached a small wooden shed, painted red with white window frames in the traditional style.

'Shall I show you the body, then?' he said, and now it was my turn to smile – it was a truism that Finns never wasted words, and even though these islands were Swedish-speaking it seemed that some of the Finnish spirit had rubbed off.

'Please,' I said.

Lundström removed some keys from his pocket and unlocked the door.

*

It was a waiting hall: freezing cold and lit by a single bulb, with two low benches against one wall. There was a long table in the middle of the room, and on it, half covered in a tarpaulin sheet, lay the corpse. I asked Lundström how many others had seen it, and he told me that so far only himself, his son, who acted as his assistant, and the coroner who had conducted the autopsy had done so.

'And the men who found him, of course. Two fishermen. They were out at Klåvskär when they saw something dark sticking up through the ice. One of them called me, so I took my son out to have a look.'

'So it's safe to walk on the ice at the moment?'

'Oh, yes — it's a few inches thick. We use picks to check it as we go along. That was what we used to get him out, in fact. Because what they'd seen was his head poking up through the ice, so we used a pick to cut him free. We put him on a sled and brought him back here for the autopsy. Drowning and exhaustion, the doctor said.'

I tried to imagine these grim tasks being conducted just a few hours earlier — the trek across the ice with the corpse on the sled.

'How far away is Klåvskär?' I asked.

'It's on the other side of this island.' He reached into a pocket and brought out a chart, which he unfolded and held up to the light. He bit his lip while he searched it and then, after a few moments, pointed a stubby finger triumphantly at a spot to the east and gestured for me to take a look. 'This was where they found him, in fact: Skepparskär.' I stared at the minuscule dot. Templeton had been right. It couldn't possibly be a provocation: there would have been no guarantee anyone would ever find the body in such a location.

Lundström folded the map back up and replaced it in his coat. 'He will be buried in the village church tomorrow,' he said. 'They have a special section for foreigners washed ashore.'

I looked up. 'Oh? Have there been many?'

'This is the seventh this winter. We had one coming from Riga in almost exactly the same spot in November. The currents move from the Estonian coast straight here.'

So it wasn't such an unusual spot to find a body. But still — two fishermen chancing by? I wouldn't base a deception operation on it. And seven bodies in one place was not all that many. There must be hundreds, if not thousands, scattered around the Baltic from sunken ships.

I nodded at Lundström, and he leaned forward and drew the tarpaulin to one side, revealing the body. I caught my breath and crossed myself. My country and his might be at war, but this had nevertheless been a fellow human being, and ideologies no longer counted for anything – at least, not for him.

He had been a tall man, perhaps six foot. His cap and boots were missing, but the rest of his uniform was intact, although it had been unbuttoned, presumably for the autopsy. The body looked to be in good condition, the hands and feet bare but unscathed, and not even frozen. The head was another matter. This was what had caught the fishermen's attention, and I understood why. It was a hideous shade of dark grey, and the left eye was badly disfigured, perhaps from having hit a rock or something similar. His throat, mouth and nose were covered in blood, some of which looked fresh. Lundström noticed my curiosity.

'He was wearing a life-jacket, but it was frozen to his back. When we turned him over to take it off, the blood came pouring out of him.'

I nodded, and bent a little closer. Beneath the frozen horror I could make out the remnants of an aristocratic face, a sweep of hair, a moustache and a small beard. Templeton had told me that the Admiralty listed von Trotha's date of birth as 1916 – could this man have been twenty-nine? It was hard to tell.

'Did the coroner estimate an age?'

Lundström nodded. 'Around thirty.'

I'd take his word for it.

There were no goggles or escape equipment. I tried to think what must have happened. Had he gone up to the conning tower to check something, and then they'd hit a mine? He could have been thrown into the air and then fallen into the sea, only for the currents to carry him up here.

I shuddered at the thought.

I lifted the identity disc from his neck and read: 'Wilhelm von Trotha. Seeoffizer 1936.' That must have been when he passed out. His effects had been placed in a wooden box next to him, and I sifted through them, feeling uncomfortably like a looter. There was a pocket watch and a wristwatch, both edged with rust.

'We wound the watch,' said Lundström. 'It still works.'

I saw he was right: the hand was sweeping slowly around the face. How long could he have been in the water, then, for the mechanism not to have frozen? Templeton had said his last signal had been over a month ago. Was it possible he had been in the water that long? I picked through the rest of the items: a folding knife, a pen, several *reichsmarks*, a nail file. I glanced at his hands. His nails had turned black, but his fingers were long and slender. For some reason, I suddenly saw him as a character in a Tolstoy story, the officer in his dazzling uniform visiting his country estate, playing the piano and then returning to his naval base and to the bowels of his craft.

I took a deep breath and returned to the pile of effects. There was a gold tooth – a relative's, perhaps? – a small mirror and, yes, there it was, just peeking out . . .

A booklet.

It was yellow, slim, with 'SOLDBUCH' printed on the cover in Gothic text. These, I knew from my training, were given to all German military, and contained the bearer's service record, vaccination and other medical details, as well as space for their own entries. Templeton was hoping von Trotha might have written down what cargo his boat was carrying, and left clues as to where it might have sunk. I picked up the book and waved it at Lundström.

'I'll take this,' I said. He nodded soberly.

I opened the booklet, and as I did, a loose sheaf fell out and fluttered to the floor. I bent to pick it up, and my heart started beating faster. It was an envelope.

Sealed orders.

There was a knock at the door, and I placed the envelope in my coat pocket. I nodded at Lundström, who went to open it. A boy with a pale bony face, perhaps a year or two younger than me, entered the room.

'Pappa . . .' He hesitated, as if unsure whether or not to interrupt.

'Yes? Well, spit it out, boy!'

'There is someone here to see you.'

He stood to one side, and another man walked into the room.

*

He was tall, fair-haired and wore a blue civilian suit and greatcoat, both of which looked like they had been made in Savile Row. He had a fleshy, sallow face and pale green eyes, which coolly took in the scene: two men hunched over a corpse. I felt myself shrink into my skin.

'Who are you?' said Lundström bluntly. 'Jan, please leave us.'

Lundström's son bowed briefly, and shut the door behind him. The wind whistling through a crack in one of the window frames suddenly sounded like a howling hurricane.

The man hadn't shown any sign of having heard Lundström's question. His eyes continued to scan the room, absorbing and processing all the available information, until finally he turned to Lundström, a fixed smile on his face, and extended a leather-gloved hand.

'Jasper Smythe, Second Secretary at the British Legation in Stockholm. Who does the seaplane belong to?'

I stepped forward.

'Me. Lieutenant-Colonel Paul Dark, from the Allied Control Commission in Helsinki. Would you mind if I see your papers? I wasn't told of anyone from Stockholm being sent here.'

He looked at me with undisguised surprise.

'Helsinki? I wasn't aware—'

'Please show me your papers,' I said firmly, 'and tell me who sent you here, and for what purpose.'

I moved my hand fractionally to my underarm. He registered the movement, and by a small inclination of his head showed he was not going to upset the precarious situation, and asked if he could remove his identification from his coat. I nodded in return, moving my hand to the barrel of my gun.

I shot him as soon as I saw the glint. The bullet hit him full in the chest, and a cloud of red mist rose from his coat, then dissolved, leaving his lapel splattered with blood. A moment later, his legs crumpled and he fell, landing on his knees. His eyes stared out, frozen in astonishment, and then he toppled forward, his head thudding dully against the floor.

The stench of cordite rose in my nostrils as I stared down at him, the sound of the shot still ringing in the air. My stomach was hollow, and my hands were shaking. With an effort I placed the Browning back in the holster. It had all gone terribly wrong, and I suddenly thought of how Templeton would react when I told him. He had said I must stop anyone who got in my way, but still I'd failed him.

I looked up at Lundström, whom I'd forgotten about, and saw fear in his eyes – he was worried he might be next. I quickly leaned down and pulled open Smythe's coat, doing my best to avoid the widening pool of blood and matter. His left hand was a mess of gristle and bone, but the forefinger was largely intact, and it was wrapped around the trigger of a Luger.

'He was going to shoot me,' I said, as calmly as I could. 'He was a Russian agent. You understand that, don't you?'

Lundström pursed his lips together and drew his breath sharply. I recognized the gesture as one Mother had sometimes used. It meant yes.

I moved to the door and opened it.

'Wait here,' I told Lundström. 'Don't touch a thing.'

*

I pulled the Browning back out of its holster and crept down the path leading to the jetty, my heart thudding fast. Lundström had said he was expecting a Presnakov – had there just been a change of personnel, or had the NKVD taken over because they knew about the Winterlost, and sent an agent disguised as a Brit? More importantly, had 'Smythe' come alone?

As I neared the jetty, I saw that there was a small motorboat tied up next to the seaplane. There was nobody in it, and I searched it quickly: it was empty. A bird circled above me, then swooped down and lit on one of the seaplane's pontoons, squawking some threat to the fish below. Then it lifted its wings and soared away, leaving just the sound of the waves lapping in the darkness.

I returned to the waiting hall, where Lundström was in the same position as I'd left him. He was in shock, but it passed as soon as I'd explained the situation to him: the Soviets would soon be wondering what had happened to 'Smythe', and would send someone else out to investigate. He immediately suggested that he arrange for Smythe's body to be buried along with von Trotha's in the nearby church. If the Russians sent someone else, he would deny all knowledge of having seen Smythe and they would have no choice but to take his word for it. They might suspect foul play, but there was always the possibility Smythe had suffered a mishap in the journey over here, and they wouldn't be able to prove otherwise or kick up any sort of a fight – after all, the dead man had supposedly been a Brit, not one of theirs. By the look on Lundström's face, he would enjoy stonewalling the Russians.

I agreed, and shook his hand, then returned to the seaplane. Von Trotha's sealed orders revealed what Templeton had suspected: U-745 had been carrying a new form of mustard gas, Winterlost, which was stored in a special compartment in the vessel's main storeroom. In the last entry in his notebook, dated 5 February, von Trotha had given his coordinates. I plotted them on the chart and found they were very close to a tiny island called Söderviken, just south of the Finnish port of Hanko. Presuming that the U-boat had been hit somewhere nearby, it might be in shallow enough waters for me to reach.

I took the wireless set out of its suitcase and crouched on the jetty with it, shivering as the wind snapped the rod aerial back and forth. I sent the signal to Templeton to say I had the coordinates and that they were close by, but didn't get any response. I checked the connections and sent the message again, and this time the 'dah-dit' came back in my earphones: proceed as planned.

I climbed back into the seaplane, stowed the set and strapped myself in, trying to steel my mind to the job ahead. It was coming up to six o'clock as I took off again, and a faint light was creeping into the sky. The ice stretched out for a few miles east of the archipelago, then broke up into open water. I flew as low as possible, looking for landmarks on von Trotha's chart, but apart from the occasional islet or rock the seascape seemed almost featureless, and I started to worry I would get lost again. I considered taking one of the Benzedrine tablets to wake myself up, but decided that fatigue wasn't the problem — if anything, I needed to calm down.

I finally spotted a small lighthouse and hovered above it as I searched for it on the chart. Having found it, I arrived about an hour later at the point von Trotha had marked, and landed in a squall of rain just as dawn was breaking. I climbed into the cumbersome diving suit and sealed it with the clamp, then went through all the checks with the breathing apparatus and the oxygen cylinders, fighting down my mounting sense of claustrophobia — Clammy Death, indeed. For one shaky moment, I fancied I saw a shape in the distance moving towards me over the water, but then it vanished; it was just a trick of the light. I remembered the lines of poetry one of the other lads at Loch Cairnbawn had always muttered to himself at this point:

> *Our plesance here is all vain glory,*
> *This fals world is but transitory,*
> *The flesh is bruckle, the Feynd is slee:*
> Timor mortis conturbat me.

I shuddered, then dismissed it from my mind. I had enough oxygen for six hours, I had used this type of equipment before, the Soviets were no longer a threat and the objective was at hand. I checked everything again one last time, then adjusted the mouthpiece and nose-clip, opened the cockpit door, clambered down to the pontoons and slipped into the dark water.

*

My eyes were stinging from the lack of sleep but all my senses bristled as I drifted through the silent world, staring out through the small window of the facepiece. Shoals of ghostly white fish flapped around me, their eyes and the tips of their fins glowing eerily, and I longed to reposition the mouthpiece, as one edge of it was cutting into my gums. It took me over two hours to find the boat, by which time my legs were exhausted from kicking and my arms felt numb. It was not quite on the shoreline, but in the stretch of islets leading into it. I remembered Templeton's words: 'It should be relatively easy to get to.' Yes, it had been – if you weren't the one doing the diving.

The U-boat looked vast, and as though it had been there for years rather than a month. Seaweed had already begun to wrap itself around the conning tower, and several inches were already buried in drifted sand. I approached it very slowly: Templeton had told me it could carry fourteen torpedoes and up to twenty-six mines. It looked to have been split roughly into two parts, with most of the damage in the middle section.

I swam past the gun deck and then floated down towards where I thought the main storeroom should be. The whole section was scrunched from the damage, but there was a narrow gap in the main hatch and, with some difficulty, I managed to haul it open and swim through.

It wasn't the storeroom, but the crew's quarters. The men were already starting to bloat, but I could see that some of their hands and chests looked like they were rotting away, and realized with a fright that they were burns, and that the mustard gas canisters must have leaked. Templeton had told me I had to obtain the canisters by any means, but we hadn't discussed what would happen if my only way of doing so would involve coming into contact with their contents, which could be fatal. I cursed myself for being so intimidated by his briefing that I hadn't asked such a basic question, but it was too late for that now.

I turned away from the sight of the men, and as I did I saw the canisters. There looked to be twenty or thirty of them: large steel drums with ridges around the centre. I could see where the lids of a few had come away and a yellowish-brown liquid had started to seep out. The operation was a bust. There was no rescuing any of this for Templeton — it was too bloody dangerous. But perhaps I could secure the place so that the Soviets wouldn't be able to get hold of the stuff either? I looked around and saw that several lengths of steel piping had fallen away from the walls. I leaned down carefully and picked one up. Could I block off the hatch? I looked towards it, and my stomach seized at the sight.

The hatch was closed.

I quickly swam towards it, willing myself to breathe normally and keep calm. The currents must have swung it shut after I'd swam through, and it now seemed to be completely jammed. I shoved my shoulder against it, and it buckled slightly — but stayed put. On the third shove, when it still didn't open, I realized I was going to die. I was shut at the bottom of the Baltic with these corpses, and before too long would become one myself. All I could think was how unfair it was that my life should end here. I hadn't experienced anything yet — I'd never even been in love. I kicked my legs at the hatch in a final frantic gesture, and the hinge moved forward and caught a current, and I rushed through the tiny space before it sealed behind me again, slamming shut finally on the occupants of U-745.

I didn't have the canisters, but I was free. Free — and alive.

IV

October 1969, Moscow

I shivered at the memory of the cold water and the dead eyes of the crewmen. I had tried to banish thoughts of the operation for years, although it had occasionally featured in my nightmares. My brief time in Finland had given me my first glimpse of a world in which we were as ruthless as our enemies and were already betraying our allies. It was also a source of personal shame: I had failed to complete the operation, and had killed a man to boot, although I had justified the latter to myself as being a matter of my life or his. I now wondered if some repressed feelings of guilt about Smythe had eased the Soviets' recruitment of me a few months later. Possibly – but I would probably have succumbed to Anna's charms anyway.

I had worried how to break the news to Templeton, but in the event he hadn't seemed overly concerned. He'd listened patiently to my debriefing, then asked a few questions, mainly about the precise position of the hatch when I'd left it. He wanted to know, of course, if it was firmly shut so that nobody else would be able to get in. I assured him this was the case, and persuaded myself it was, too, although a nagging doubt came to me in my dreams in the following weeks that it had not fully closed behind me.

He told me that Smythe was certainly an NKVD man, as there was nobody of that name at the Legation in Stockholm, and told me to put it out of my mind. 'They may still be our allies technically,' he said, 'but make no mistake – for all intents and purposes, they are our enemies now. He threatened to compromise your mission, and would certainly have tried to shoot you had the positions been reversed. Indeed, it sounds as though he was about to. You did the right thing – I would have done the same.' I handed over von Trotha's orders, and was dismissed. He never mentioned the operation to me again.

I had stayed on in Helsinki for a few more weeks, but then the Soviets entered Berlin and everything started happening very fast. I travelled to Stockholm to see Mother, this time taking an aeroplane, but it was a wasted journey, as she had simply stared through me with a blank gaze, drool spilling grotesquely from her mouth. On returning to Helsinki, Templeton pulled me in to his office and told me I was wanted back in London. I took the next flight from the airport, landing in a bank of fog. I spent a couple of weeks kicking my heels in Baker Street and wondering what I was supposed to be doing, before I was handed a coded cable from agent 2080 – Father – in which he requested I join him immediately at a farmhouse ten miles outside Lübeck, in the British Zone of Germany.

That operation had eventually brought me here, to this depressing conference room beneath Moscow. The men seated around me had listened in chilly silence as I had described my actions in 1945, but it didn't take long for them to respond. Suslov was the first to speak, and he addressed himself to Yuri.

'Is this your promised breakthrough?' he said with undisguised contempt. 'I am unimpressed. Why should we believe anything this man says? Of course he will argue that this is an accident, in order to stop us from attacking the West. In this situation, his loyalties aren't with us. He's useless – worse than Philby.'

That was interesting: they had already asked Philby. It made sense he hadn't been much help, as it had been years since he'd been involved in this sort of discussion in London, and by most accounts he was now a drunken wreck of a man – not that I was a shining example. But it put my presence here in a new, rather more unpleasant light: it seemed that it had been Yuri's brainwave to summon me, and it wasn't proving a popular decision.

'You're right,' I said to Suslov, and he swivelled to look at me. 'It would take a lot for me to argue that you should launch a nuclear attack on the West, but it's got nothing to do with patriotism. Nobody can win that war.'

'If I may, General Secretary,' broke in Yuri, 'it seems that this man's testimony may provide some of the answers we seek. He has told us that as a member of British intelligence he was sent to Finland to capture German chemical weapons at the end of the war, so that they could be used against us after it. As it seems that those very same chemical weapons *are* now being used against us, can it be plausible that the West is not involved? Surely the most likely scenario is that the British have returned to this sunken submarine and retrieved the mustard gas.'

I took a breath to calm myself. Had my recounting of my operation in Åland in 1945 just made Britain a target for a nuclear strike?

'Nobody knew the location of the U-boat apart from me and my immediate superior,' I said. 'And he is dead.'

'But he will have filed a report,' said Yuri, his forefingers pressed against his chin. 'As a result of your defection to us, your old colleagues in London will have investigated every document connected to your career, I think. Presumably they found a report on this from 1945, and decided to act on it.'

I stared at him. Could that have happened? He was right that they would have searched through everything. Could they have dug up reports Templeton had written for SOE in 1945? It was possible – they would certainly have been looking through his files. But most of SOE's files had been destroyed after the war, and it was hard enough even to find a Service file from those days. I thought of the canisters again, and of the liquid slowly seeping from them.

'The Service doesn't operate like that,' I said. 'If they had retrieved the mustard gas, they wouldn't have attacked your nearest submarine base with it. Nobody in the West has any interest in provoking a nuclear conflict.'

Ivashutin, the GRU head, gave a laugh as dry as a lizard's cough. 'Come, what sort of fools do you take us for?'

I turned to face him. 'I'm quite serious. The possibility of a surprise attack has been discussed, naturally — it's raised every few years, usually by one of the more belligerent generals, and usually when you lot have done something that annoys us. Then the call goes up: "Why don't we just hit the Russians, hard and fast?" But wiser heads always prevail. The relevant experts at NATO have calculated that a first strike would not be enough to disable you completely, and would simply result in you striking back. Until we come to a point where one side's forces seriously outweigh the other, the logic of deterrence still holds. But even if you don't subscribe to that view, this is clearly an accident — just look at the distances.'

I pulled the map on the table nearer to me and turned it to face Ivashutin. 'The U-boat sank here. Here are Paldiski and Hiiumaa. They're less than fifty miles away. It's obvious that the gas has leaked from the submarine and the currents have carried it to the shores of these bases, just as they carried Captain von Trotha's body.'

Ivashutin smiled. 'Or perhaps that was what we were meant to think. After all, your former colleagues in London know that you are in Moscow and are likely to tell us all this. Our bases are heavily fortified: leaking chemical weapons into the water nearby is an ingenious way of breaching the security.'

'What if he is right, though?' said a new voice, and I scanned the table to locate it — Andropov, the KGB chief. 'What if the Americans are simply conducting an exercise with the B-52s, and the incidents in Paldiski and Hiiumaa are accidental?'

'All of them occurring at the same time?' said Brezhnev. 'That seems very unlikely.'

Andropov switched on an obsequious smile. 'Indeed, General Secretary. But it may still be the case. Are we sure we want to risk the consequences if Comrades Ivashutin and Proshin are wrong in their assessment? If the West is really about to launch a surprise attack on us, what is their motive?'

Yuri's jaw muscles showed through his cheeks as he struggled to stay calm. 'Perhaps they feel sure they will be able to survive and win a protracted nuclear conflict,' he said carefully.

Ivashutin nodded. 'Yes, or perhaps they have underestimated our capability to retaliate. Perhaps putting a man on the moon has made them think they are invincible.'

Nobody laughed, and I understood it wasn't supposed to be a joke. So the Americans must have finally pulled it off since my arrival here, the great journey finally realized. I remembered last year's INVALUABLE exercise in Whitehall with a chill. Its imagined scenario to trigger a nuclear conflict had been that hawks in the Kremlin had been emboldened by placing a man on the moon. Now that event had apparently taken place, but it was the Americans who had done it. Could it be that hawks in Washington, newly elevated by the glory of beating the Soviets to the moon, had got hold of Nixon and persuaded him that a surprise strike was achievable? It was unthinkable, surely.

But there were nuclear-armed B-52s heading towards the Soviet border.

'My department takes the view that the West wants us to follow precisely your logic, Yuri Vladimirovich,' Ivashutin was saying. 'We think that this is a surprise attack that is designed to destroy us through our own uncertainty over whether or not we should retaliate. If we live to survive this, perhaps we should consider such a strategy ourselves.'

'Be quiet,' said Brezhnev. 'All of you.'

The room hushed immediately. The GRU and KGB hated each other's guts. They were wholly separate agencies, with competing structures in Moscow and embassies around the world. Both operated within and outside the Soviet Union, but the KGB spent most of its time wading in the weeds of individual espionage operations while the GRU was generally concerned with the big picture, including the biggest of all, the threat of an attack on the Soviet Union. This was the GRU's case, but from the way Andropov was speaking he appeared to have Brezhnev's ear more than Ivashutin.

This was peculiar, because Ivashutin was an old pal of Brezhnev's, and had been handpicked by him to head the GRU after Serov had been dismissed in '61 following the discovery that Penkovsky was working for the Service and CIA. Perhaps there was still some residual stain on the GRU's reputation as a result. Until that point, it had been almost invisible to the outside world, but Penkovsky had given the West a mass of information, some of which, I had discovered on becoming Head of Soviet Section, had helped avert nuclear war during the Cuban crisis.

There was no love lost between Andropov and Ivashutin. As I knew from personal experience, the KGB had recently sabotaged a major GRU operation in Nigeria – and presumably Andropov had been behind that.

'Is this possible?' Brezhnev said, addressing Yuri. 'Could it be that the events at these bases are the result of a chemical leak?'

'It is possible, General Secretary,' he conceded, glaring at me. 'But as you yourself pointed out, considering the Americans' actions it would seem too great a coincidence—'

'It is *not* a coincidence,' I said. 'It's an accident, and one that was bound to happen sooner or later. The Baltic is strewn with volatile chemical weapons, as you well know, because many of them were dumped there by you.'

'Is this true?' said Brezhnev.

'That was Zhukov's doing, General Secretary,' piped up Grechko. 'He ordered the practice when he was in command of the administration in Germany after the Great Patriotic War. But that was not until '47 or '48, and if I recall correctly it was not done anywhere in this area, but near the islands of Gotland and Bornholm.'

'It sounds like the sort of thing Zhukov would think up,' Brezhnev said. 'It's as well he retired when he did.'

'Indeed,' said Grechko, seizing the opportunity to take another kick at one of his predecessors. 'But he was not alone in the mistake: the British, French and Americans also dumped chemical weapons in the Baltic. Occasionally, some come to the surface, but I think I'm right in saying that this has never happened anywhere near these particular bases.'

Yuri nodded. 'That is correct, esteemed comrade. This is confirmed in the latest report by the investigating scientists, who have never even encountered this type of mustard gas before. I have also never heard of any attempt by either the British or ourselves to obtain such a weapon.'

'Someone notified your people in Helsinki about the U-boat captain in 1945,' I said, 'and they sent an agent out there to get to him. There will be a report on it in your files.'

'We don't have time to dig around in archives,' said Brezhnev. 'We must make a decision now.' He pushed his chair back and walked to the wall behind him, staring at the false window as though it were a real one looking out on the skyline of Moscow. Habit, I supposed. 'Comrade Grechko,' he said finally, addressing himself to the wall. 'What course of action do you advise?'

Grechko didn't hesitate. 'As you know, General Secretary, we have just completed the "Zapad" war game. One of our conclusions was that the West would be foolish to engage in any sort of preliminary war and would in reality be much more likely to defeat us with a surprise nuclear attack. It seems that they have come to the same conclusion. If they are indeed preparing to launch against us, I believe our best strategy is to launch our own attack before they do.'

He used the word *kontrapodgotovka*, a counter-preparation strike that would disrupt the enemy's first strike. But, of course, that assumed that the Americans were indeed planning a first strike.

Brezhnev nodded.

'If the Americans launch their weapons, how much notice will we have?'

Grechko grimaced. 'We estimate that our radars would detect

the missiles between fifteen and seventeen minutes of them hitting their target, General Secretary.'

'And how long will it take us to launch our missiles if I give the order to do so?'

'The 8K84s do not have their warheads attached, General Secretary, and once they have been armed they need to be warmed up for a few hours before they can be launched. But once they are primed and warmed up, the Strategic Rocket Forces can launch within seconds of receiving your signal.'

'Exactly how many hours does it take for the 8K84s to warm up once the warheads are attached?'

'Three hours, General Secretary.'

Brezhnev turned, and I saw that a pool of sweat had formed on his forehead. He drew a handkerchief from his trouser pocket and mopped at it unthinkingly.

'Attach the warheads,' he said.

Grechko's face flushed.

'Right away, General Secretary.'

He picked up the telephone nearest him, spoke into it for a few seconds and then replaced it.

I stared at the men around me, dumbfounded by the mounting madness. From memory, 8K84 was the Soviet name for the SS-11 intercontinental ballistic missile. Grechko had used the phrase *predvaritel'naya komanda* on the telephone: that was the preliminary alert command, given to combat crews as a trigger to prepare nuclear weapons for the next order, the *neposredstvennaya komanda*, or direct command to launch.

Brezhnev returned to his seat at the head of the table, and clasped his hands together.

'I would like some more detailed information on the B52s,' he said, his baritone now almost cracking. 'If they breach our no-go zone, I will give the order to launch a strike on our major targets in the West.'

I was also sweating now, and the room seemed to be closing in around me. In a few seconds, Brezhnev had placed the Soviet Union one step away from launching a nuclear attack. It sounded as if he were considering a tactical strike, rather than releasing the country's entire stockpile of missiles at once — what was referred to as 'R Hour' in Britain. But it made little difference. Even if he were to order a tactical strike, the West would retaliate at once and we would be facing full-scale nuclear war in a few hours' time, with Washington, London, Moscow and many other cities destroyed. Brezhnev didn't even need to order a strike at all for that to happen. If Washington got wind of the fact that part of the Soviets' nuclear arsenal had been moved to this position, they might themselves fear an imminent attack and choose to strike pre-emptively.

By believing the Americans were about to launch an attack, Brezhnev might have just pushed them into making one.

There must be some way to stop this.

'Call your consulate in Åland,' I said. 'I can't remember the precise coordinates, but the U-boat is south-east of an island called Söderviken. Get them to send one of their divers down, or if you don't have any find a local and pay them to do it. Once they've found the canisters, they can radio back the confirmation that they have leaked.'

Brezhnev tilted his head at Yuri. 'I think we have had quite enough of this man now. Is there anything else we wish to know from him?'

'Thank you for your patience, General Secretary,' said Yuri, and just the sound of his voice was now making me nauseated. 'I believe he may know the West's likely targets and the order in which they are likely to be attacked, but this may not be a fitting place to extract the information from him.'

'Give him to me,' said Andropov. 'My men will be able to break him in less than an hour.'

My stay in Steklyashka had been far from pleasant, but the KGB's headquarters, the Lubyanka, was notorious — it was known as

Moscow's tallest building, on account of the floors of cellars it was rumoured to have.

'Thank you for the offer of assistance, Yuri Vladimirovich,' said Yuri coolly. 'But I think we have a way to apply pressure in this case.'

'I think KGB and GRU should work together on this,' said Brezhnev. 'Yuri Vladimirovich, please have the prisoner taken into custody by your men. Fedor Fedorovich, I would like you to accompany him in order to exert your pressure, and to report back here with the results within the hour.'

Fedor Fedorovich, or Yuri as I still thought of him, looked a little paler, but nodded. 'Of course, General Secretary.' Andropov flicked the switch on his chair, while Yuri started packing his papers into his attaché case.

'This won't help,' I said, unable to keep the desperation from my voice. 'You're making a terrible mistake.'

Brezhnev ignored me, and helped himself to a glass of water. The door opened and two guards marched in, wearing brown coats with blue collar tabs: KGB. They were both armed, so I didn't resist as they escorted me out of the room, led by Yuri.

'I've told the truth, you fools!' I screamed as the door closed. But there was no reply, and they led me down the passageway and back to the lift.

V

The ZiL was still parked on the street, and I was pushed towards it, the barrel of a submachine-gun pushed hard against my spine. Snow was falling gently, and as a gust of it caught me in the face, I shivered in my thin suit, the sweat already cooling and sticking to my skin.

Sasha stepped out of the car and walked towards us. Yuri began speaking to him, but his voice was carried away by the wind and I didn't catch it: presumably he was explaining Brezhnev's Solomon-like decree that they were to cooperate with the KGB in torturing me. I wondered if any of them apart from Yuri had any inkling of what was being decided in the bunker, or that they would be left outside it to die with the rest of the population when the missiles hit. Perhaps Sasha did, which was why he had hesitated when Yuri had motioned for him to leave earlier.

As Yuri and Sasha talked, one of the KGB men spat on the ground. I followed the trajectory of the saliva through the air and it was in that moment, as I watched the globule freezing into ice, that I remembered the footage I had seen in a dark room in London one evening a decade or so earlier, of the hydrogen bomb tests we had conducted at Christmas Island in the Pacific. A flash of light had filled the entire screen, shocking even when experienced second-hand, and when it had eventually faded the image of a cloud had formed, growing and slowly expanding in new layers until it had finally plumed and billowed into the mushroom configuration, an almost obscenely beautiful formation hanging over the landscape it had just destroyed.

I closed my eyes to try to rid myself of the image, and a flake of snow came to rest on my eyelids, soft and wet, and I suddenly understood something I never really had before. I opened my eyes again and took in the tableau anew. This place, this moment, was unique in the universe. It was an ugly place, certainly, made up of concrete and saliva and ugly men in uniforms, but it was *our* place. And it was mine. All of it, from the grime in my teeth, the smell of the car's engine, the crispness in the air, the patterns of the shadows on the ground, the precise interplay of every living thing in every passing moment, even these thoughts rattling through my head . . . All of it was under threat. All of it could be just a few hours away from extinction – unless I acted.

And it wasn't just that if I didn't, nobody else would. This was something I *should* put right, as I was directly responsible: I hadn't destroyed the canisters, but had just left them in the U-boat. And, clearly, the hatch had not shut as firmly as I had thought it had.

But what the hell could I do?

Sasha turned and headed towards a Chaika parked across the road, while Yuri climbed into the front of the ZiL. The KGB men opened the rear door and I was again pushed into the back seat, next to Sarah.

Naturally, she was Yuri's 'pressure'. He had told Sasha to bring her along in case my appearance in front of the Supreme Command wasn't received well. Sarah might not know too much about the inner workings of the Service, but Yuri had, once again, played a long game, realizing that at some stage she might prove useful in extracting information from *me*. And so he had kept her alive for just that purpose.

I felt like retching, and as the car started up I shuddered at the thought of what lay in store for both of us at the end of the journey. No doubt they would attach electrodes to her or some such horror in an attempt to get me to reveal the locations of missile silos and command and control bunkers. But the problem was bigger than that: once we were inside the gates of the Lubyanka, I would never be able to warn anyone in the West about what was happening, and events would continue to spiral towards a nuclear conflict.

I looked at Yuri, who was staring straight ahead, his hands resting on the attaché case on his lap.

That case.

That case could be key. Presumably it contained all the papers that had been used for the meeting, and so would detail their concerns about the B-52s and the injuries at the Estonian bases; papers that would offer firm evidence that the Soviets mistakenly thought they were about to come under attack from the West and were preparing their own strike as a result. I realized I had to get out of this car before we reached the Lubyanka, and that case had to come with me. If I could get a message to the Service, the Americans might be able to defuse the situation by bringing the B-52s back to earth and explaining that they had nothing to do with the events in Estonia, and this madness could stop before it was too late.

All of which was easier said than done — I was in a moving car with armed men. In my first few weeks in Moscow I had thought of nothing but escape, and had drawn on old training patterns, obsessively keeping track of how many guards had been assigned to me, when they changed shifts and so on. I'd always been under cover of at least one submachine-gun on the daily walk I was allowed around the fenced pen on the roof, but I had persisted in following every move the guards made, just in case a sliver of an opportunity presented itself. It never had, and I had eventually resigned myself to the fact that I would never be free again. But now there was no choice: I *had* to find a way out.

But what about Sarah? I should, in normal operational circumstances, leave her behind. One man on the run had a small advantage against those seeking him — that of the needle in a haystack. But if we did manage to escape from this car, the two of us together would be a much easier target to describe, and hunt. But these weren't normal circumstances, and even if they were, I wasn't going to leave her to be taken back to a cell. If there were a nuclear attack it would make little odds, but if I managed to stop an attack from happening I couldn't bear the thought of her being in the Lubyanka. No, she had to come with me.

I scanned the interior of the car, searching for an idea. Armed men sat either side of us, the doors either side of them were locked and beyond the doors stretched Moscow and the vast expanse of the Soviet Union. A feeling of hopelessness rose up in me. I took a breath and smothered it. Now wasn't the time to give in; now was the time to sharpen all my senses.

Yuri motioned to the driver to take a shortcut and the car took a right turn. I caught a glimpse of a sentry box through the curtains, and realized we were crossing a bridge. We must be approaching the Kremlin. The Lubyanka was very close now.

I glanced across at Sarah. She was staring out of her window, apparently deep in thought. She looked tired, but otherwise in reasonable shape. I wasn't exactly on top form, but I had made sure to maintain a version of my regimen in my cell, partly to keep my strength up but primarily to occupy my mind. It had mostly consisted of press-ups and running on the spot and, naturally, had been on a much lighter scale than usual: the soup they'd been feeding me hadn't provided enough protein for anything more. But the result was that my body had become harder and leaner, and I was confident I could at least make a decent go of it.

But could she? Every couple of years, all Service officers had to take refresher training courses, usually at Fort Monckton, near Gosport, so she should know the basics. The courses admittedly tended to be a waste of time: as it was impossible to prepare for every eventuality in the field, most of the focus was on general preparedness, teaching how to remain vigilant and watch for lapses in the opposition's vigilance, and so on. But now we were in a situation similar to one that I'd been taught at Monckton − I hoped she'd been taught it, too. The objective had been to jump from a moving car while under close guard. To execute the manoeuvre, which was known as 'Duck and Dive', you needed at least one accomplice and could not be guarded by more than two people. We had two in the back and two in the front, but beggars can't be choosers.

With Duck and Dive, everything is in the timing. When the car slows, the first accomplice distracts one of the opposition. This has to be a distraction that won't get them shot, obviously, and it has to be believable. The simplest is a loud groan and a slump, imitating a fainting fit. While the first man reacts, the second agent attacks the other guard, shoves open the door and leaps out of the car. To make matters harder, I would have to grab the attaché case from Yuri as well, and hope that in the ensuing confusion Sarah and I would both be able to get out without getting shot. But anything was preferable to what they had in store for us at the Lubyanka. The moment to trigger it would be when the car was slowing but had not yet passed any checkpoints or sentries: after that we'd be trapped inside the walls of the Kremlin.

But how could I communicate all this to Sarah? The last time I'd seen her, she'd lost her hearing. I could check whether or not it had returned by making a noise and seeing if she reacted, but any diversion now would alert the men either side of us and make it harder to execute another one. She was staring down at her hands now. I looked at her, willing her to sense my gaze and look back at me. The car jolted, and in that moment she turned and our eyes met. 'Duck and dive,' I mouthed, then turned away.

She had nodded. She'd had the same thought.

With the course of action determined, I should have felt happy. But now I knew we would be risking our necks in a matter of moments, doubts returned. Well, there was no choice about it. Long ago, a cheerful Cockney instructor had told me that you never knew when you might have to call on your training, but when you did, you simply had to buckle down and get on with it.

Having fed myself this rather facile exhortation and swallowed it as best I could, I took a deep breath. The car had turned into Dzerzhinsky Square, and the imposing mustard-yellow block of the Lubyanka loomed in the headlights. At first glance it could have been mistaken for a French château, but for the barred windows on the lower floors. The tallest building in Moscow . . .

The car slowed on the turn and I braced myself. Not yet, not yet . . . *now*. I nodded at Sarah and smiled at her as I did, one last time perhaps, something to remember. She let out a groan and slumped into her seat. The guard next to her turned to see what had happened, as did my man, and I jerked my elbow up, catching him squarely on the jaw and sending him flying into the door.

Yuri turned to see what had happened and cursed, and I leapt forward, grabbing at the lapel of his jacket and pulling him closer. His hand flew up and I saw the case slipping from his lap. I yanked harder at his jacket, the top of my head bumping against the roof as I propelled myself between the gap in the two front seats and sprawled awkwardly between Yuri and the driver. In the driver's mirror I saw Sarah punching her man unceremoniously in his groin.

As his scream filled the small space, the car suddenly swerved, the driver no doubt jarred by the noise, and I took advantage of it and lunged back over to Yuri's side, my hand grabbing hold of the handle of the attaché case, which I swung up and into his face. The corner caught him under the neck and he screamed, and I wriggled the rest of my legs through the gap in the seats and slammed my free hand against Yuri's door until it gave way and fell open. Yuri tried to grab hold of my arm, but I punched down blindly and as he fell backwards onto the seat, I managed to scramble over him and shove the door wider, then hurled myself towards the opening, tumbling through it and out onto the street, keeping my head down and my arms wrapped tightly into my chest.

The impact shook my whole body as I hit the tarmac, but training took over and I went into a roll, resisting the temptation to touch the ground with my free hand, gripping the case as tightly as I could with the other, and then I was up and running, the sound of shouting behind me becoming subsumed by the noise of blaring horns in the traffic, letting the momentum carry my legs in their natural rhythm, my heart pounding so hard I thought my ribcage might burst, searching for cover.

VI

I surged on, keeping my body as low as possible, a rush of wind biting at my ears and cheeks. I desperately wanted to look back to check on Sarah, but I was still numb from the jolt of the landing and to turn now would lose vital moments. I was conscious of sunlight breaking through low clouds, and I squinted against the glare at the morning traffic swarming around the square. A Moskvitch beeped its horn angrily as it sped past, and then I reached the enormous statue of Dzerzhinsky and could see the other side of the pavement, just a few yards away. It was packed with pedestrians, many of them gathered outside a building with enormous arched windows on the corner, and my first thought was that some sort of protest was going on. But then something deep in my consciousness stirred, and I recognized the building from photographs. It was Detsky Mir, 'Children's World', Moscow's largest toy shop. It had been just after seven o'clock when I'd entered the bunker, and the larger shops in the city opened at eight, so either the place was about to open or it had already done so and people were queuing to enter. It didn't matter much which – it was a crowd, and that could only be good, so I headed for it.

I took momentary refuge behind a banner festooned with red ribbons and an enormous portrait of Lenin. Now, finally, I could see Sarah: she was in fact ahead of me, and making her way towards the same building. She was limping on one leg and wasn't going to beat any records, but she'd done it. Somehow, she'd done it. I took a breath and then leapt the last stretch to the pavement, my chest burning with the effort, and hurtled into the tail-end of the throng, pressing through a bank of woollen coats and getting swept along with the movement, looking to get closer to Sarah and fervently praying that the shop would be open and provide us with more options than the open air.

An elderly *bábushka* turned as I tried to squeeze past her, raising her arms in protest. I glared back with my most officious look, but she yelled something and grabbed hold of my sleeve. Others turned to see what the fuss was about, and as they did a gap appeared in the forest of bodies and I caught a glimpse of the KGB men emerging from the ZiL and running towards us, their guns raised. The Chaika wouldn't be far behind, and my mind flew to the moment when they would drag us to the building on the other side of the square. I yanked my arm away from the *bábushka* in desperation and pushed forward, moving deeper into the crowd and calling out 'Make way!' in Russian, holding the case above my head, until I had reached the entrance. The doors were open, and I forced my way through them.

Beneath a curved glass roof, hundreds of shoppers teemed through the vast central hall. Gaudy, cheap-looking toys lined the walls, vying for attention, while a loudspeaker in the ceiling told parents and children to meet near the entrance if they became separated. A queue of people made three loops around the hall and disappeared up a grand-looking stairwell leading to balcony floors above.

'Sarah!' I shouted out. 'Where are you?'

She had vanished. I headed for the foot of the stairs, and a young woman in the queue saw my frozen look and misinterpreted it. 'Don't worry,' she said. 'It moves quite fast.' But I'd already jostled past her, forcing people out of the way by making more official-sounding noises, not gaining any friends but climbing higher, higher, my feet flying, a few steps further away from the entrance below and hopefully out of sight.

As I neared the halfway point, I suddenly felt dizzy, and my vision filled with spots of dancing light. I steadied myself against the banister for a moment and looked down: in the blur below I saw several men in *ushankas* coming through the entrance, some wearing brown coats – KGB – and some grey ones – GRU. One of the latter suddenly caught sight of me, and our eyes locked. It was Yuri. He turned and shouted an order, his finger raised to point me out.

I shoved myself away from the banister just as the shot glanced off the latticed railings beneath it, sending a plume of metal fragments into the hall below. Everyone started screaming, and I began fighting against a tide of panicked shoppers, most of whom were now trying to flee upstairs. My head was still ringing from the sound of the shot as I pushed through the crush of flailing limbs and echoing cries, and scrambled up the remaining steps to the next floor.

That was when I saw Sarah, just a few feet ahead, her pace starting to flag a little. I ran towards her and she turned and stared at me, her face a mixture of elation and sheer terror.

She grabbed hold of my free hand, and I looked around in panic at the gallery stretching around the hall. It wouldn't be more than ten or twenty seconds before Yuri's men reached this floor. We needed to find a rear entrance, and fast. I looked around frantically but could see nothing, so I just picked one of the walkways and started running pell-mell down it, hoping to find another staircase as we went along. After about twenty yards it started to get crowded again, because the shot hadn't been heard this far in.

As Sarah and I plunged back into the crush of people crowding the counters, a deafening rattle suddenly filled my ears. I ducked instinctively, but then the noise faded and I looked up to see a scruffy-haired boy hurtling past us wielding a plastic machine gun over his head and screaming at the top of his lungs. He ran straight into his mother, who grabbed him by the arm and demanded he place the toy back on the shelves. After some protest, he did and

I watched, transfixed for a moment, before something jogged my brain. I raced over to the display and scanned the selection. It wasn't Hamleys – most of the items were crude East German plastic models. There was a black pistol that looked to have been modelled on the Tokarev TT, but I rejected it. The biggest box on the shelf showed a Vostok capsule deep in space, the blue seas of Earth far below it as it blasted into glory for the Motherland.

There was a rising commotion at the other end of the room and I guessed Yuri's men had now reached this floor and had started combing through it. I put the case down, then removed the Vostok from the shelf and ripped open the cardboard box. Sarah watched in confusion as I stamped the mould under my feet until it had broken into dozens of pieces. I leaned down and picked up a thin shard of crude plastic, and she nodded in mute understanding. I picked the case up again and we raced back into the crowd, looking around desperately for a till. I found it a few seconds later, in a section devoted to babies' clothes: a young salesgirl was clacking away at an abacus behind a large wooden desk.

I ran over to her, shouting at the top of my lungs: '*Empty the till! Now!*'

The girl looked up, her face frozen in horror, and shoppers started screaming and vacating the area. Through the crowd I glimpsed some of the GRU and KGB men by the staircase, and they were heading straight towards us. I jumped forward and grabbed the girl around the throat with one arm in a choke hold, then pressed the point of the shard against her collar-bone. She started whimpering and her arms flailed out, releasing the catch on the register.

Sarah leaned down and scooped out a handful of notes and coins, and I released my hold. The cashier placed her head in her hands, sobbing hysterically, but we were already on the move again, past singing mechanical birds and doll's houses and miniature tanks and parents shielding their children from the sight of the man and the woman fleeing from the secret police. At the other end of the gallery there was another stairwell, but as we made our way towards it I saw a man in a grey uniform emerging from the floor below. Panicking, I looked for another way out. There must be a service exit of some sort. Sarah had begun making her way along the wall, and I followed her, pressing one shoulder against the surface as we passed marble columns and ornate lamps. But there were no exits or stairwells, and the GRU man was rapidly gaining ground. I could hear his breathing behind us and feel movement in the air . . .

Door.

It was recessed into the wall, an oak monstrosity with brass Art Deco curlicues. I grabbed at the handle, but my hand was soaked with sweat and slipped clean. I transferred the attaché case to my other hand and tried again, desperate, but fared no better. I hefted my shoulder against it instead, and suddenly it flew open, revealing a small, spartan office containing a desk piled high with papers, a samovar, and a threadbare oriental rug. I called out to Sarah and she came running back to join me. There was another door diagonally opposite and we raced across to it, but I must have made a lot of noise shouting out because a woman suddenly came through it — thick spectacles, hair in a bun, brown serge suit — and I knocked into her elbow, righted myself and kept running, ignoring her as she shouted after us.

We were in a long corridor with bare concrete walls. There was a steel door at the end and I grabbed the handle, panicking that it would be locked. But it opened, and I was greeted with a blast of wind whipping into my face. Peering into it, I saw a metal fire escape leading to a tiny rectangular courtyard below. It looked deserted. I turned and started lowering myself down the ladder as fast as I could, one hand clutching the rungs and the other gripping the case. Slivers of wet snow from the platform above dropped onto my neck, but I ignored them and focused on navigating the ladder. When I reached the final rung, I leapt the last couple of yards to the ground, then caught my breath and looked around the courtyard as I waited for Sarah.

It was very quiet — almost peaceful. A couple of pigeons waddled around the space importantly, their eyes glossily taking in the intruder. The rear of Detsky Mir took up the whole of this side of the courtyard, with a few more fire escapes dangling down, and directly opposite was a similar-looking building, the paint peeling from the walls. To the left an alleyway cut between the two buildings, and I glimpsed a section of main road at the end of it with traffic streaming by.

Sarah landed and dusted herself off, and I pointed to the alley. She nodded and we headed towards it, but as we came through the arched entrance blue and red lights flashed ahead of us and I realized we would be spotted if we came straight out on the street. Sarah made to turn back, but my eye was caught by a shadow in the curved wall of the passage, a little darker than the rest of it.

'Wait,' I said. I ran over to take a closer look. Yes, there was a gap in the wall. A small flight of stone stairs led down to what looked like another passageway leading off horizontally from this one: it was much narrower, but dim light was visible at the far end. With any luck, it should bring us out somewhere that wasn't crawling with armed men. I beckoned to Sarah to come over and we headed down the stairs.

It was very dark, and as we reached the last step I realized the surface was softer beneath my feet, and that the passageway ahead was filled with several inches of stagnant water. No mind. I stepped down and began wading through it carefully, letting my eyes adjust and holding up the attaché case to make sure it didn't get wet. A few feet in, I saw a sheet of corrugated iron blocking the path. Cursing inwardly, I leaned down and grabbed a corner to pull it away, but it was too difficult to dislodge with one hand so I turned and motioned to Sarah to help me.

That was when I heard the noise. We both froze. It was a clanging sound — the fire escape in the courtyard? Perhaps the man I'd glimpsed coming up the staircase was on our tail.

We stood still, straining our ears. The clanging stopped, but was immediately replaced by the sound of rapid footsteps — boots, reverberating on stone. Was it just one pair or more? And would they head straight out of the courtyard into the adjoining alley, or would they search the courtyard first? I had the sudden fear that we might have left telltale footprints in the ground at the bottom of the ladder.

I lifted my feet very carefully – the dripping now seemed to echo thunderously around the small space – and moved to the wall to the left of me, flattening my back against the brickwork so I was in the deepest shadow available. Sarah saw what I'd done and moved to the same position by the opposite wall. The footsteps approached – it sounded like they had entered the alley. Would they run on, or stop to investigate?

They stopped.

I slowed my breathing, exhaling very gently through my nostrils, and turned the lapels of my jacket inward to hide the whiteness of my shirt.

The boots began to descend the stairs, but when they reached the final step there was silence. Could they see us? I tensed my muscles, and closed my eyes.

Legs splashed through the water. How many of them were there? I fixed on the breathing. It was one man. Alone. He could be no more than a couple of yards away from us now, and he was coming closer every second. I caught a sudden whiff of diesel-like cologne – yes, it was Vladimir, the little bastard who'd treated me like a dog in my cell this morning.

There's nothing in here. Turn around and leave.

He didn't take my extrasensory hint. I listened to him, his breathing shallow but drawing closer, and the air tightened behind my ears. I stood as still and as silent as I could, my fingers clamped around the handle of the briefcase, praying to God to stop this man from seeing us, please Lord, I'll do anything you ask, just make him turn around . . .

I jumped an inch as there was a very loud thud on the wall behind me, the sound of it vibrating in my eardrums. Peering into the darkness, I thought I saw the outline of a raised arm, and guessed that he had slapped his hand against the wall. Had it been just a gesture of frustration, or did he suspect something and was trying to bring us out? Had he heard my sharp intake of breath? I strained to catch a response.

He sniffed the air, and I wondered if he could smell my body odour, as Yuri had done and as I had smelled his cologne. Sarah and I would also both be emitting the smell of fear, the pheromone dogs can scent. The moments stretched out, as though on some sort of loop. Beads of sweat formed across my forehead, and my left hand started to cramp from gripping the case. I longed to move just a fraction, but knew I couldn't. I could try to kill him, of course, but it would have to be silent in case some of his colleagues were still in the vicinity. I tensed my other hand and the muscles in my forearm, ready.

A shadow suddenly moved and I saw to my horror that his hand was moving towards Sarah. He was reaching further and further in and there wasn't much more space – soon she would hit the corrugated sheet.

She let out a cry and I leapt on top of him, bringing my right hand down onto his neck with all the strength and speed I could muster. He staggered towards me but managed a half-turn and grabbed me by the neck with one very strong arm. Sputtering, my throat on fire, my eyes bulging, I watched him raise his other hand, a pistol clutched in it, and swung the attaché case at him. There was a flicker of light as the gun spun away and fell into the water with a clunking splash. While he was caught off balance, I leaned forward and smashed my knee up into his groin. He doubled over and started to cry out, but I couldn't risk any more noise so I jumped across and stamped my shoe on his head, pressing it down until the top of his scalp had disappeared into the water. The surface bubbled as he struggled to come up, but I kept my foot there, pushing his face to the bottom, and then the air was throbbing in my ears and his body went slack and I removed my foot and he slipped away, sinking into the water.

My muscles had also slackened, and I suddenly felt drained, but my heart was pulsing frantically. Flashes of light swam on my retina and I stood there, swaying a little and panting, my face slicked with sweat and the blood beating in my brain, conscious but detached, and for a moment I was suspended both from the world and from myself, swept up in a kind of oblivion, in the same state I had been on waking that morning of not knowing where I was, or even *who* I was.

I staggered back in the water, and as I steadied my breathing and the sweat cooled on my skin I tried to clear the mist in my mind, but the rage was still pulsing through my veins and as I looked down at the body one thought overrode all the others: *Not such an old man, am I? No, not such an old man* . . .

'Is he dead?'

I looked up to see Sarah watching me from the other wall, the whites of her eyes glowing in the surrounding darkness.

I nodded dumbly, staring back at her.

'You can talk,' I said, finally, my voice strangely muffled. 'When did you get your hearing back?'

She stepped forward. 'A few months ago.'

'Are you all right?' I said. 'I heard you cry out when he approached you.'

'I'm fine. He just gave me a fright, that's all.' She turned to the corrugated sheet and started trying to prise it away. 'Let's get out of here and find the embassy. I need to get home. My whole family must think I'm dead.'

I didn't answer for a moment, and she sensed the hesitation and stopped what she was doing.

'What's wrong?' she said.

I stepped away from the wall. 'Let's see if we can find this bastard's gun first, and I'll explain the rest on the way. We need to get moving.'

*

We spent several minutes searching for Vladimir's pistol, but with no luck: it had been lost somewhere in the water, perhaps finding a drain. We managed to move the iron sheet fairly easily, though, and waded through the rest of the passageway. After a couple of hundred yards, it widened and then emerged into another courtyard, which in turn led to a main street. A quick reconnaissance revealed no uniforms or sirens in the immediate area. I took Sarah by the arm and told her to keep her eyes fixed ahead as we walked through the throng of pedestrians hurrying past on their own paths to survival.

We were walking, not running, because we needed to be inconspicuous. The *militsiya* would probably have our descriptions by now, as might the *druzhinniki*, the force of citizen volunteers. A man walked towards us and for a moment I thought he had some sort of transmitters attached to his face, but it seemed they were miniature hot water bottles fitted to his ears and nose, presumably to ward off the cold. We passed an emaciated woman in a frayed black coat as she hustled along a group of children in bright red quilted jackets. Red was everywhere, here and there enlivened by splashes of gold in hammers and sickles, but the red stood out more against the largely monochrome landscape. The snow had stopped falling, but it was still freezing, and the bottom halves of our legs were soaked.

Sarah was shivering and coughed occasionally. My throat ached and the tips of my fingers throbbed in the wind, but the bigger problem was internal. My insides were in freefall – unsurprisingly so, as I'd just killed a man. I didn't see it as murder, though. Brezhnev had ordered ballistic missiles primed, and we were on the brink of a Third World War. Vladimir had been a GRU agent and his orders had been to capture us, and that would have led to our torture and, no doubt, death. That was justification enough, but in this case it hadn't simply been a case of him or the two of us; it had been him or, potentially, everyone.

Nevertheless, the adrenalin was still thrashing around my veins like a cat in a bag. After months in captivity I had escaped my cage, killed one of my pursuers and was now being hunted by the full strength of the Soviet apparatus. And I had brought Sarah with me again. Was this really preferable to leaving her behind, I wondered?

I turned to look at her, shivering in her tunic. 'How's your Russian?' I asked.

A group of young boys selling coat hangers approached, and she waited until they had passed before answering. 'Craddock marked me as fluent a couple of years ago.'

Craddock was a Cambridge don who had taught Service officers Russian since the war, and was notoriously hard to please.

'Good. We'll talk Russian together from now on. Let's get off the streets and find somewhere to warm up.'

We reached a turning and took it, then several more, until we were on a street called Neglinnaya. Along the opposite side of it from us was a row of buildings, most of them shops. But one was smaller than the rest, a squat brick-and-glass building, and people were milling around the entrance. On the awning above it said 'Victory'.

We headed towards it.

VII

The café was only marginally warmer than it had been outside: the mist of customers' breath mingled with cigarette smoke and steam from bowls of *shchi*. A transistor radio in the window blared out a folk song from Radio Moscow, the balalaikas keening like a troop of drunken bagpipers.

We walked through the tables looking for a free one. The furniture was in the same style as the architecture: a hideous hand-me-down modernism that, at a guess, was an attempt to look Scandinavian. They couldn't even get that right.

There were three tables with good views of the door, and after considering all three I indicated to Sarah that we should take the smallest of them. It was the farthest from any other occupied tables, and it was positioned in a small alcove of its own, meaning it was not in direct light and we could talk more easily.

We installed ourselves in the metal chairs, and looked around. There was a queue at the counter, but just as I was about to get back up again and join it a waitress passed by and I managed to attract her attention with an ingratiating smile. I ordered a couple of coffees and *sigarety* to secure our presence for a while, and as she sidled away I turned to Sarah. She was running her fingers through her crop of hair, her large blue eyes surveying the room, and for a moment she looked as she had done the first evening I'd met her: poised, elegant and without a care in the world. But then I saw that her jaw muscles were making tiny fluttering movements beneath her cheeks, and realized she was trying to stop her teeth chattering.

'It's good to see you again,' I said quietly, keeping my tone neutral for the benefit of anyone watching us. 'I'm sorry things turned out this way. I should never have let you come with me to the embassy in Rome.'

She looked across at me and gave a wan smile. 'You couldn't have stopped me.'

I looked into her eyes and saw fatigue and fear in them, but also pride. Well, she had outrun me at the start, surprising me. Then again, she was a good ten years younger than me, so perhaps she was the better field agent and I was teaching her to suck eggs. She had certainly proven herself in Italy. But I was getting ahead of myself. I'd known her barely a week, and most of that had been while we'd been confined together by her husband and his neo-fascist chums.

'So your hearing came back,' I said, 'just like that?'

She averted her gaze. 'Not quite. They gave me some treatment.'

'Yuri?'

She nodded fractionally, and my exhilaration that she had recovered was replaced by a surge of fury. I reached out to touch her hand, then thought better of it. The last thing she needed was people touching her. I didn't want to know what they had done to her, exactly, and I certainly wasn't going to ask her to recount it and live through it again here. But they would pay for it. Yuri would pay.

The waitress returned and placed two mugs of black coffee, a packet of twenty cigarettes and a box of matches on the table. I paid her with some of the coins I'd stolen, and she wandered off again.

I picked up the matchbox, which showed a picture of the Urals and proclaimed 'The best holiday is a motor tour'. I lit a cigarette for Sarah and then one for me, and inhaled it deeply into my lungs, luxuriating in the rich glow. After a few puffs, I took a sip of the coffee. It tasted pretty foul, but it was hot and strong, and this cheered me a little, because I knew that within half an hour the caffeine would be making its way through my bloodstream along with the nicotine, and would boost my energy and alertness. I had a feeling I was going to need it.

Yuri would have ordered his men to comb through the neighbourhoods surrounding Detsky Mir looking for us. He would be utterly furious that we had managed to get away. Had he told the Supreme Command yet, I wondered? Perhaps not, in the hope he could find us before anyone became too concerned. But every minute we were free was a problem for him, because eventually he would *have* to tell them, and Brezhnev would hit the roof.

At any rate, we were now the target of a manhunt, and it would only become more concerted as time went on and more resources were allocated to it. Once they found Vladimir, some of the men would be even hungrier to find us, because there was nothing like personal motive to get the blood pumping, as Vladimir had discovered to his cost. But perhaps there was a silver lining. If we managed to survive long enough, they might have to draw men from the nuclear strike preparations . . . No, that was probably too hopeful. The opposite might happen instead: Yuri and the others would realize I was planning to try to stop a strike from going ahead, and Brezhnev might start thinking about ordering it now to retain the chance of taking the West by surprise. By fleeing, I may have hastened the very event I was trying to stop.

'We're not going to the embassy,' said Sarah, 'are we? Or home.'

I put my mug down and looked up at her. 'I'm afraid not. We've got a crisis on our hands. Brezhnev and his generals believe the West is on the verge of launching a nuclear attack, and they're preparing to get their retaliation in first.'

She stared at me for a moment, then took a long drag of her cigarette as she considered it.

'And *is* the West about to launch a nuclear attack?' she said.

'I don't think so. But I can't be sure.'

I quickly told her about the meeting in the bunker, the B-52s, the mustard gas 'attack' and the U-boat. She took it all in, listening intently, her jaw tight but her expression giving nothing away.

'What about the hotline?' she asked when I'd finished.

'They haven't used it, and won't. They think it would warn the Americans they're on to them, and lose them a strategic advantage.'

'So how long do we have?'

'I don't know that, either,' I admitted. 'But it might not be long enough.'

'I see.' She stubbed out the remains of her cigarette in the ashtray and straightened her back in her chair. 'So what are we going to do? Do I take it that the case between your feet contains Yuri's documents from the meeting, and that you hope they offer firm enough evidence about what's going on to stop this?'

She was a pretty cool customer, I reckoned. I could see how she'd survived the last six months.

'Yes. But it depends on precisely what's in the case. Do you think you can hold the fort for a few minutes while I find a lavatory to look through it?'

'Yes,' she said. 'But please leave me the cigarettes.'

I nodded, giving her as encouraging a smile as I could muster, and then stood up and looked around for the toilets.

*

I found a room at the back of the establishment, and after waiting for it to be vacated, jumped in and locked myself in it. It was a tiny space, with a lavatory almost pressed against the basin and a grimy window looking out onto the street, protected by a thin grey cotton curtain.

I seated myself on the lavatory and looked at the case: to my horror, I saw there was a combination on it. I pressed the clasps down, hoping that Yuri had not thought to lock it for a ride to the Lubyanka, but it was fastened shut.

Shit.

I sat there for a moment, wondering how the hell I was going to break a six-digit combination, when I looked at the numbers again. The left-hand numbers read 446, and the right-hand ones read 683. But the 3 was not completely in the frame, the tip of the 2 below it just visible. Could it be that that frame was a little looser than the others, and that in all the movement since I'd grabbed the case in the car, that number had simply shifted? I looked at the numbers again, and saw a pattern: 44 66 8 . . . 8? I clicked the 3 several notches around until the 8 was in the window, then pressed the clasps again.

The case clicked open.

Thank Christ. Resting inside, snug as a bug, were several sheaves of documents, most of them stapled together. I took the lot out and started sifting through them. The first was a threat assessment, prepared by the GRU, on the supposed attacks on the bases in Estonia and the B-52 flights. It looked to have been written by Yuri, and reiterated a lot of information I'd heard in the meeting. There were maps of the affected bases and a report on the incidents there.

The index case was a 22-year-old lieutenant who had come back from one of the observation posts on the shoreline of the Paldiski base, having picked up an 'amber lump' that had washed ashore. Within a few hours he and some of his colleagues had experienced violent and repeated vomiting, and he and one other had lost their sight. A detailed chemical analysis concluded that the chemical involved was an unknown form of mustard gas that was much more viscous and powerful than had been seen previously.

The bloody fools. It fitted Winterlost precisely: these were classic mustard gas symptoms, and it had been contracted by touch to boot. It *had* to be a leak from the U-boat. I turned to the conclusion of the threat assessment:

```
There can be little doubt that the West has
launched a chemical attack on our bases in
Paldiski and Hiiumaa. The purpose seems to be
```

to put them out of action in advance of a surprise nuclear strike. As we have repeatedly advised – see the attached document, which we regard as still current – this is in keeping with our estimate of strategy among some of the hardline generals in the West. Our assessment at this time is that we must consider launching a nuclear strike, perhaps within the next twelve hours.

Within that timeframe, we will endeavour to bring to the Defence Council a clearer intelligence picture of the West's actions. Time is against us, but we have agents in place in the West who may have access to information about nuclear intentions and planning. Agents HOLA and ERIC have provided us with a very clear picture of the British development of nuclear research since the Great Patriotic War. We have issued secured instructions through our residency in London to initiate immediate contact with both.

Our colleagues in HVA also have an agent, MICHELLE, who is providing them with material from the British Director for Operations of NATO's General Secretariat. We also have several agents with experience of nuclear strategy in the West close at hand in Moscow, notably SONNY and INDEPENDENT, and it may be worth questioning them both for further insight into the strategies and actions we now face.

The document was undated, but must have been written within the last few hours. My codename was INDEPENDENT, and SONNY was Philby. But who the hell were HOLA, ERIC and MICHELLE?

Cairncross and Nunn May had both confessed, so none could be them. It seemed the GRU had at least two more doubles who remained unexposed in Britain and had been in operation since the war. The HVA was East German military intelligence, and if they had direct access to NATO's British Director for Operations, the Soviets should know pretty much everything Britain and NATO were planning in this field and be able to act accordingly.

But they didn't know everything. They hadn't seemed to know about Corsham, for instance, and they had brought me in to ask me very specific questions they didn't have the answers to. Some of this was doubtless down to the time factor. It could take an entire day to set up a meet with an agent – more if they couldn't get away from the office for a convincing reason. So even if ERIC, HOLA or MICHELLE knew about an impending attack, they might not be able to send any information about it in time. And while Brezhnev and his generals were waiting to hear from these agents, the pressure would be increasing. On top of which, even if reports came in from all three agents that they were *not* aware of any plan to attack, that wouldn't mean Brezhnev would discount the possibility altogether – very few people were informed of such things. Indeed, if you did know about an impending nuclear attack, you would probably be at a PYTHON site by now.

In all, this read more like a political statement, perhaps to position the GRU in Brezhnev's eyes as a better source of information than the KGB. And they certainly seemed like very impressive sources, but in this case, probably not highly placed enough to help.

The next file was the strategy document Yuri had referred to. It had been written by Ivashutin, the GRU head, and was dated 28 August 1964. It was five years old, but still seemed to represent their current thinking. I flicked through it, and my eyes lit on a paragraph towards the end:

The imperialist states are engaged in preparations for a war that is not at all defen-

sive. The substance of their military doctrine
is a surprise nuclear attack and offensive war
against the socialist countries.

My jaw clenched. I had *told* them this wasn't the case. In the winter of '63, Sasha and I had met at the cemetery in Southgate and I'd sat on a cold bench for hours while he'd questioned me about Britain's stance towards nuclear war. I'd been in Prague when the Cuban crisis had happened, and had been unable to leave the British embassy compound, so I'd spent most of the fortnight in the basement with Templeton and the rest of the staff, monitoring the radio and the cable traffic. But once the crisis was over, Moscow had wanted to know what the thinking was in Whitehall in the aftermath. I explained that from everything I'd heard, the Cuban crisis had scared the living shit out of everyone, even more than Berlin had back in '48, when Brooman-White had told me we were heading for atomic war. I had told Sasha in very clear terms that the last thing anyone in Whitehall or Washington wanted was to start a nuclear war. There might be a couple of cigar-chewing American generals who occasionally brought up the idea of a surprise attack, but there was no chance of such a thing ever happening and it was certainly not the West's military doctrine – far from it, in fact.

So either Sasha had failed to pass this information on to Moscow, or he had and it had been discounted. This was very worrying, because if this was the principle they were working from it meant they were much more likely to launch a strike. They had discovered what they thought were preparations for a surprise nuclear attack, confirming their mistaken view that the West was intent on making such a move. Brezhnev had already responded by priming missiles. He hadn't yet put them in the air, but if this was the way they viewed the West's intentions, how long would it be before he did? Glancing through the document, it seemed Ivashutin was ignoring the fact that retaliating before missiles landed in the Soviet Union wasn't going to stop them landing. Or was he? I turned back and started reading from the top. As I did, I realized that the Soviets had a completely different conception of nuclear war than had ever been imagined in the West:

> Strategic operations of nuclear forces will be characterized by unprecedented spatial expanse. They will instantaneously cover all continents of the earth, all main islands, straits, canals, i.e. the entire territory of the countries-participants of the aggressive coalition. However, the main events in all probability will take place in the Northern hemisphere – in Europe, North America and Asia. In this hemisphere, essentially all the countries, including the neutral countries, will suffer destructive consequences of massive nuclear strikes to some extent ...

After that cheerful preamble, Ivashutin veered into bizarre territory. While he admitted it would be impossible to defeat the West in a conventional war because of their greater military might on the ground, he then argued that nuclear weapons, far from being a deterrent, in fact provided the Soviet Union with the opportunity to reverse this situation:

> With the nuclear weapons currently available in the world, one can turn up the earth itself, move mountains and splash the oceans out of their shores. Therefore, the tasks that can be set for the strategic operations of nuclear forces in response to an aggression are realistic, even though they may seem to be based on fantasy.

The most aggressive forces of imperialism engaged in preparing a thermonuclear war against the socialist countries count on their ability to effectively paralyse socialist countries with an unexpected first strike, destroy their nuclear forces and thus achieve a victory while having saved their countries from a devastating retaliatory nuclear strike. However, there are very few people left – even among the most rabid imperialist military – who would believe in the feasibility of such plans. In the age of an unprecedented development of electronics, it is impossible to achieve a genuine surprise strike. The very first signs of the beginning of a nuclear attack by the imperialist aggressor will be discovered, which would give sufficient grounds for launching a retaliatory strike ...

It made no sense. On the one hand, Ivashutin claimed the West had a military doctrine of a surprise attack. On the other, he thought such an attack would always be detected early enough, and that very few in the West now believed it even possible. Either way, the situation he outlined was very close to the one they now faced, which I supposed was why they had included it in the papers for the Defence Council.

Let us suppose that the United States is actually capable of destroying the Soviet Union several times over. Does this mean any kind of military superiority? No, it does not, because the USSR possesses such strategic capabilities that ensure a complete destruction of the United States in the second strike. It does not matter how many times over the United States will be

```
destroyed. One does not kill a dead person
twice or three times.
```

He seemed to be arguing that a nuclear attack would destroy the
West, but have little impact on the Soviet Union. That was familiar
enough propaganda – the kind that could be read on a regular
basis in *Pravda* – but this was a top secret document by the head of
military intelligence about their strategy for nuclear war. If they
couldn't even be honest with themselves in such a document, there
was a serious problem. Was it that they couldn't admit the reality
of the situation to each other for political reasons – or were they
completely blinded to it? Worryingly, it seemed like the latter was
a real possibility. Discussing the West's military bases, Ivashutin
concluded that the major ones were in the US, Britain and West
Germany, and most could be destroyed by medium-range missiles
and bombers in a first launch.

But it was a section titled 'Ground Forces' Operations' that
stopped me in my tracks. It discussed ground troops overtaking
enemy territory and 'cleaning up the consequences' of nuclear
strikes.

```
Nuclear weapons will incur damage on troops
by shock wave, light emission and radioactive
emission. These are very dangerous factors, and
it is very difficult to protect oneself against
them. Still, we can soften the impact of nuclear
explosions. Tanks, trenches, dug outs, shelters,
natural hills - all give good protective cover
from the shock wave; they will substantially
reduce the damage. One has to protect the eyes
as well as face and open parts of the body
from light emission. Each soldier should have
dark eyeglasses, or a mask with dark glasses,
and gloves. A closed car, tank, gas mask or
```

```
an overcoat will help protect from the pene-
trating radiation . . .
```

'Zones of contamination' would be passed through by helicopters and 'protected vehicles' such as tanks, while 'clearing teams' would put out fires with explosions and cover radioactive ground with new soil. Roads would be cleaned with the help of 'street-sweeping vehicles operated from a distance'.

It seemed the Soviets believed that they could carry out an extensive ground war following a nuclear one. This was delusional. They wouldn't be able to send troops through the West after nuclear missiles had been launched, whatever precautions they took – there was no protection at all from that kind of contamination and I knew it, having read the Strath Report and several like it. As well as watching the footage, I'd also read the reports from Grapple X, our hydrogen bomb test on Christmas Island. At the flashpoint, the servicemen kneeling twenty miles from 'Ground Zero' facing in the other direction had been able to see the bones in their hands through their masks. The resulting fireball had been over a mile across, and the blast had scorched much of the island's earth. In a nuclear war, most of Europe would be a 'zone of contamination'.

I closed the folder and took a breath. I walked over to the tiny window and pulled the curtain back a fraction, but it didn't seem to look out onto anything, and the window was glued shut.

I had also pulled back the curtain on the world, I felt. The last few months had shown me more vividly than I could ever have imagined what a sham my life had been – now I saw that the whole of the Cold War was a hollow little sham. The document was amateurish, childish propaganda – and so misguided it was terrifying. The head of Soviet military intelligence thought they could send troops across Western Europe following a series of nuclear strikes, wearing dark glasses and with their coats wrapped tightly to avoid the contamination, the way ahead cleared by street-sweepers. Either he was lying to his superiors or, more likely, he was completely deluded. They could have recruited an army of double agents and they still wouldn't have a clue. Service, Five and JIC reports might get things wrong, but they were never worded in terms of outright propaganda. It was obvious that the Russians simply didn't have the mindset to understand the West. And that made the risk of war greater.

The fact that there could be no victors in nuclear conflict was the deterrent on which the whole fragile situation rested. But it seemed that some in the Soviet Supreme Command thought they could win such a war. If Ivashutin convinced Brezhnev of his view, he would be much more likely to order a strike.

Whitehall's INVALUABLE exercise had, in fact, been completely worthless. The scenario we had gone through had envisioned a gradual build-up of tensions, whereby a hawkish faction in Moscow had taken control of the Politburo and had begun flexing their muscles. But this was a much more frightening prospect: a war resulting from misunderstanding, acted on too rapidly.

Yuri had estimated the Soviets might have to consider launching a strike within twelve hours. But how many hours ago had he estimated that? In the meeting, he'd said that the B-52s would enter Soviet airspace at around noon if they continued on their current path. But would they continue on that path, or would they break off and circle again, as they had done earlier? How close would they have to get to Soviet airspace before Brezhnev acted? An hour away, perhaps two? Or would he hold off a little longer than that?

I stuffed the papers back into the case, locked it, and flushed the toilet. I walked over to the mirror and examined myself quickly. I didn't look too bad, considering. My suit was ragged and half-sodden, there were dark circles under my eyes and I was as pale as a monk, but none of these things were all that out of place in this part of the world.

I filled the basin with lukewarm water and splashed my face thoroughly, thinking through the take from the case. The documents proved what was happening – but they had to reach the right hands. I needed to find a way to show this material to the Service at once, because they could get into direct signals with London through their protected line, and from there someone could contact the Americans and get them to bring down their planes before it was too late.

But neither Sarah nor I could go anywhere near the embassy, because the moment we entered the gates we would be on British territory, and they would find a way to take us back to London and no doubt lock us both up. The embassy was also guarded, as all embassies were here, by Soviet sentries. I picked up the case and unlocked the door.

We couldn't go there — but they could come to us.

*

'Enough evidence?' asked Sarah once I'd sat down.

I nodded. 'More than enough. But I can't go to the embassy because they won't trust me, so I want to bring them here. I think we'll have more leverage.'

'I can call them,' she said. 'It might be better coming from me.'

'Yes, but I think I'll be able to get through quicker — nothing like the name of a traitor to prick up the ears. Do you mind?'

She didn't exactly smile, but her cheeks dimpled fractionally. 'Staying in the warm while you risk being picked up on the streets? I think I can manage.'

'Watch for any new arrivals, and get out fast if you see anything suspicious. If you're not here when I get back, I'll meet you at the main entrance to Detsky Mir in an hour from now.' I thought it unlikely that Yuri would think to send men back there. 'Agreed?'

She nodded. 'Agreed.'

Without thinking about it, I leaned down and kissed her lightly on the forehead. She didn't flinch, and I kept my lips there for a moment longer.

'I'll be back before you know it,' I said, and turned towards the door.

*

I walked quickly through the streets, scanning the corners and the reflections for signs of uniforms or anyone tailing me. At one point I saw a traffic policeman and crossed the road to avoid him, but otherwise the way was clear. The first public telephone I came across was broken, the guts of the box ripped out – so much for the crime-free Soviet Union. But there was another one farther down the same street, and it was in working order. Having read the instructions, I shoved a fifteen *kopek* coin in the slot and picked up the receiver, then dialled 09 for information: Moscow's only telephone directory is held at the Central Post Office and that was in Kirov Street, a long way away. I asked the operator for the number for the British embassy, presuming that the authorities couldn't be monitoring every call in the city immediately. After a few seconds I was given the number, and I dialled it. It rang for some time, but finally someone picked up.

'Good morning, this is the British embassy.'

Nasal quality to the voice. Didn't sound promising. One of those officious bastards.

'I would like to speak to Jonathan Fletcher-Peck.'

He got me to repeat the question as the line wasn't clear. There was a moment's hesitation, then: 'I'm sorry. Mr Fletcher-Peck is no longer with us.'

Shit.

Of course he bloody wasn't. The very fact that I knew he was the Head of Station meant they'd posted him back to London. Sasha hadn't got round to asking me the names of all known British agents, but no doubt he would have done soon enough. I'd effectively ruined Fletcher-Peck's career. Well, it wasn't the first, and now wasn't the time for a fit of remorse.

'Can I speak to his replacement, please? It's urgent.'

'I'm sorry, sir, he's not in the office at present. If you would like to leave a message, I'm sure——'

'This is an emergency,' I said. 'My name is Paul Dark.'

He paused, and I held my tongue. He would know my name, and I had to hope that he couldn't risk ignoring it.

'Can I take your number please, sir, and I'll call you back?'

'Yes, but do it from a telephone well outside the embassy, and please do it quickly. I'll wait here.'

I gave the number and replaced the receiver, then started pacing around the cubicle. There was no sign of any of Yuri's men. Yet. How long would it be before the message went out to every *militsiya* patrol in the city? All calls to and from the British embassy would be monitored as a matter of course, but the Station staff knew that and so rarely said anything of great interest on the internal lines. Under normal circumstances, the transcripts of the embassy's calls probably went to the KGB only once a week, if that, unless something notable was said. But if Yuri had thought on his feet, and if the bureaucratic wheels had turned fast enough, he would have given the order to report all calls to and from the British embassy at once. He could already have given that order, in fact, as they might be listening out for when the Service scrambled its staff to the cellars and senior officers said goodbye to their families.

And so I'd told them to call back from an outside telephone. In Prague, we'd always had at least one car on standby for situations such as this, and several call-boxes within a five-minute drive that we felt were not listened to with the same level of scrutiny as those inside the embassy. The calculation was that all telephones in the Soviet Union were likely to be bugged, but that it was impossible for the authorities to monitor every single conversation in the hope of catching discussions between foreign agents.

I couldn't remember precisely what Moscow Station's telephone set-up was, and wished I'd asked Sarah before leaving the café. I hoped the call-boxes they used weren't too far away, because I couldn't wait here long: every moment that passed gave Yuri more time to think of his next move. One of those would probably be to step up surveillance on the British embassy and follow anyone who left it, so if they didn't take the usual precautions they might find themselves tailed by a KGB or GRU car, which would then radio back which call-box to listen in on, and then the whole thing would be . . .

'Have you finished? Kindly make way.'

I looked up to see an elderly woman in a plastic coat glaring at me. She had already taken her money out of her purse and was trying to push past me. I told her I was still using the telephone, and she gave me a dirty look.

'I don't have all day to wait for you to receive calls, young man,' she said, and made to step into the cubicle. I stepped in front of her, barring her from reaching it.

'Get out of the way!' she shouted, raising a cane in my direction.

I had to do something, and fast. She was going to attract a patrol.

'I'm waiting for a call,' I said. 'Please wait, it won't take—'

The receiver rang and I swivelled and snatched at it.

'Yes?'

'This is the British embassy.'

Thank God. It was a new voice – a little lower in register, a little more authoritative. I nodded at the old woman, indicating that the call was the one I'd been expecting, and she stepped back, muttering curses before turning on her heel and stomping off down the street.

'Hello,' I said into the receiver. 'Thank you for calling back. Are you outside the embassy?'

'Yes.'

'Tailed?'

Hesitation, then a peevish: 'No.'

'Good. I need to meet with the Head of Station.'

He didn't say anything, but I could hear him breathing.

'I have information HMG needs to hear,' I said. 'It suggests Clasp.'

The breathing came to a sudden halt.

'Where?' said the voice, finally.

'Victory,' I said. 'It's a café on Neglinnaya. In half an hour's time. Tell him to come alone.'

I replaced the receiver.

*

I walked quickly back to the café, watching for tails again but also weighing up the response I'd received. I had taken a risk using the word 'Clasp'. It was the codeword to signify 'the beginning of a period of tension', usually meaning an impending nuclear strike. Or at least it *had* been the codeword – they might well have changed it now. It was risky, because I wanted the British to be aware that the Soviets were considering a strike so they could defuse the situation, not so they could panic and launch their own strike as a result.

But, I decided, that was rather unlikely. They would need a lot more than a phone call. During the Cuban crisis, when the Service had been running Penkovsky, Moscow Station had given him an emergency signal to use if the Soviets were about to launch a strike. He was to call a special number, breathe down the phone three times, hang up, and then do the same a minute later. The missile crisis passed, but a few weeks after it Cowell received just such a call. Protocol dictated he alert London at once, but he guessed that Penkovsky had been caught and had revealed the code under torture, so did not press the panic button.

This had comforted me in one way, but troubled me in another. The Service had done its best to avoid discussing Penkovsky's motives ever since, preferring to focus on the fact that he had helped avoid the Cuban crisis escalating to war. The possibility that the Soviets had genuinely wanted to provoke an attack from the West had been quickly discounted – it was suicidal. It seemed to me that what had most likely happened was that Penkovsky had told his interrogators that the code meant something much less dangerous. But *he* had known full well what it meant. In which case, he had decided that the world should end in nuclear war, and had tried to trigger it. If he had made the call a couple of weeks earlier, or made it to someone more jittery than Cowell, it might have happened.

I reached the Victory, but realized the moment I came through the door that something was wrong. The table where I'd left Sarah was vacant. She'd gone.

'Over here, darling!' said a lilting voice in Russian, and I turned towards it and saw her seated at a table on the other side of the room. I rushed over.

'What the hell's going on?' I said.

'Nothing. This table just came free and I realized it offered better protection from the windows.' I looked across and saw that she was right: it still had a view of the door, but we couldn't be seen from the street as easily. I slid into the seat next to her, my heart still thumping in my chest from the thought that she'd been captured.

I told her about the phone call, and asked her if anything had happened since I'd left. She gestured to a group of labourers who had come in and taken over a nearby table, and I looked them over. Their overalls were smeared with tar, their hands were deeply calloused and several had missing or rotten teeth. They were genuine. Apart from them, there were fifteen other people in the café: two were waitresses and the rest customers. There were probably a couple of people in the kitchen making the food, so that would make it seventeen. Of the remaining customers, five were grouped together and had the ragged jumpers, scarves and slightly febrile, furtive look of students. The remainder were either sitting alone or in pairs, including a couple of old men hunched over a chessboard. All had been here when I'd left, so were nothing to worry about. It was anyone new that we had to watch now: the Head of Station might think to send an advance party. They might want to try to use the occasion to kidnap us – especially me. The chance to capture a double didn't come along too often.

I looked around, searching for an alternative exit. I couldn't see one: no staircase or back door, and the window in the lavatory had been glued shut. There would probably be a way out to the street through the kitchen, but finding that in an emergency might prove difficult. I took a sip of coffee, my hand shaking a little as I lifted the mug. Had I just made a dreadful miscalculation in telling the Service where to find us? I wasn't sure if it would be much more preferable to being captured by Yuri's men.

A sound came from somewhere to the right, and I jerked my head towards it. It was laughter: one of the students had told a joke and it had gone down especially well. Several of the young men were throwing their heads back in hysterics, but on the other side of the table sat a slender girl smoking a cigarette, with just the hint of a smile on her lips. She was pretty: a brunette in a dark sweater and pleated woollen skirt. The young man who had told the joke kept glancing in her direction, but I could have told him he was wasting his time, because she didn't like him, she liked his friend with the beard. As if sensing my appraisal, the girl suddenly swept a coil of hair back with her fingers, turned her head and stared straight at me, exhaling smoke through her mouth. I turned away at once, and caught Sarah looking at me.

'Having fun?' she said, and I blushed.

The music that had been playing on the radio halted abruptly and a news bulletin began, discussing plans for the centenary of Lenin's birth the following year. I'd seen posters for it plastered along the street, proclaiming 'Lenin is more alive than the living'.

It was nine o'clock on the morning of Monday, 27 October, which made sense – my reckoning had been that it was the 25th, but I must have underestimated the time they'd held me under with drugs when I'd first arrived. It gave me a perverse pleasure that I'd been within two days of being right, despite them checking everything around me every evening to make sure I didn't make notches in the wall with my fingernails or any such thing. I'd counted in my head, and I'd kept it intact enough to count nearly six months to within two days.

I listened to the bulletin as I continued to survey the room, waiting for any mention of fugitive prisoners wanted for murder. None came, but I didn't think that would be the case with the next bulletin – if we were still alive by then. The programme wound up and another began, about a factory that was producing more than its quota purely because of its passionate devotion to Lenin.

'They didn't mention the attacks,' Sarah said. 'I suppose that's to be expected?'

I nodded. 'It's not like Cuba, when it was the Americans who accused them of mischief. This time it's they who have detected a threat, or think they have, and their reaction will be the utmost secrecy.'

'Presumably that means there won't be any warning, either. If they decide to strike, they'll just do it.'

'I'm afraid so. But let's not get grim.'

'What if he doesn't come?' she said. 'The Head of Station, I mean. What's our contingency, our "Plan B"?'

'He'll come,' I said, with more conviction than I felt. What if he decided it was a trap? I ran my hands across the surface of the table. Resting on top of it were salt and pepper pots, a dirty glass that looked like it still had a couple of inches of vodka left in it, presumably missed while clearing up the previous night, and a chipped ceramic ashtray. I picked up the latter and placed it on a free table nearby, because I knew the KGB installed microphones in such things. It was unlikely they'd done it here, because they were usually interested in restaurants frequented by foreigners, but I wasn't taking any chances. I tipped ash into my empty coffee cup instead.

'The Americans are out,' I said. 'They'd simply call the Service and ask for their take on it. The same goes for all the other Western embassies.'

'So it's this or bust? What about one of the Eastern embassies – China, for instance?'

'No, I think that's more likely to exacerbate the situation, don't you? The only thing I can think of is that we could try to get to the U-boat ourselves. If we could prove that the injuries at these bases are the result of a leak rather than an attack, it might be enough for them to draw back. If we got hold of the leaking canisters, we could get the Soviet embassy on the islands to signal Moscow that the mustard gas in them is of the same type that was found in the "attacks" on their bases fifty miles away.'

She looked unconvinced, as well she might. It wasn't just a matter of getting out of the country: we probably wouldn't even be able to get out of the city. We were being hunted by an army of dedicated professionals: I knew from reviewing the Penkovsky operation that Moscow was home to around 20,000 KGB agents.

'How would we reach the canisters? And what about the B-52s?'

'Not sure. But I think if we can show that at least one part of this is an accident, it will make them reconsider. I think it's the combination of the events in Estonia and the B-52 flights that has persuaded them they're about to be attacked. Take away the attacks on the bases and the B-52s aren't enough to wage a nuclear war over. The Americans may be playing silly buggers or trying to scare them, but by themselves the B-52s aren't conclusive.'

'That's not a contingency plan,' she said quietly. 'That's a prayer.'

I didn't reply. Behind the counter, one of the waitresses swore at a battered coffee-maker. My eyes flicked back and forth between the occupants of the room and the door, a dilapidated affair with paint sticking to the frame and a small bell that tinkled whenever anyone passed through it. It rang again now, and a girl emerged through the smoke and the steam. She was young, pretty and very Russian-looking, but that didn't mean much: you could find Russian-looking girls in England, and if you did you might decide to recruit one of them and post her here. But the girl immediately greeted the older woman behind the counter with a cheery wave and removed her quilted jacket, beneath which was a waitress's uniform.

It must now be at least twenty minutes since I'd made the call to the embassy. Twenty minutes more of Brezhnev and the others discussing warhead positions . . .

'Paul.'

I looked up at Sarah, and realized my knees were jerking under the table. I willed them to stop.

'Sorry.'

One of the waitresses, an older woman in a stained red smock with a kerchief wrapped around her head, waddled out from the kitchen with a tray of pastries and placed it in front of the chess-players, who set aside their game to tuck in. After months of eating nothing but thin soup and seeing nobody but my guards, there was something so normal about the scene that I suddenly wondered if I hadn't imagined the whole thing: the bunker, Brezhnev and all the rest. The normality was also depressing. This was daily life in Moscow, and it looked to be roughly akin to Britain during the Blitz. How could I have ever believed this was a society that could bring equality to all, to the extent that I'd chosen to betray my own country? Freedom, justice, peace for mankind . . . Why had I fallen for such a ludicrous fairy tale?

Anna, of course. She'd fed me with the romantic dash of Lermontov and Tolstoy and the rest of them – all perfect fodder for a twenty year old – before filling my head with Marx, presenting his nonsense in the same beguiling manner. I had a sudden memory of her leaning over my hospital bed, administering a poultice to the wound around my left kidney. I had winced as she'd pressed it, and she'd smiled down at me with those beautiful flashing eyes of hers.

'My poor boy,' she had said, her lips forming a pout of mocking, flirtatious concern.

I replayed the memory in my mind, as I had done many times before, narrowing it down to that one despicable gesture. Because my wound had been a real one, and it had been deliberately administered in order to have me hospitalized so that she could nurse me back to health and, while doing so, seduce me, after which she had been prepared to feign her own death – all of it part of Yuri's elaborate honey-trap operation to recruit me. And that moment, that gesture, showed a level of calculation and, I thought, pleasure in deceiving me that turned my insides out.

'*My poor boy.*' What a sick, twisted little bitch she had been. But what a sad, pathetic waste my life had been as a result of falling for her . . .

The bell above the door tinkled again, and I looked up to see a man in a long grey coat walk in, struggling with a large umbrella. I turned away, for one horrid moment thinking it might be Smale from London, but then my skin started prickling and I glanced back and the horror returned because, of course, it *was* him.

*

Christ, that was all we needed. I forced myself to keep my gaze on him. He'd managed to collapse the umbrella and was shaking excess rain from his coat as though trying to rid himself of fleas. He hadn't changed an iota since I'd last seen him, filling in forms for me to travel to Rome in that cramped corner office of his on the third floor of Century House.

He began making his way past tables towards the counter, and I almost expected someone to stop him, he looked so out of place. It was around freezing outside, but I knew from the amount of times the milk had curdled in my cell that it had been an Indian summer and nobody else in here was really dressed for winter – a few wore coats, but most were in jumpers and jackets. Smale, on the other hand, was wearing a fur-collared overcoat, scarf, gloves and an astrakhan *ushanka*, looking like an extra from *Doctor Zhivago*. Except that everything else about him said England: the bony little nose, the fish eyes, the pursed lips – even the way he was walking, his back a little hunched. He belonged in that building in London and nowhere else, and I was having trouble absorbing the information.

They had made *Smale* Head of Moscow Station.

He was now hovering near the counter like a constipated pheasant – he had seen us but was pretending he hadn't, and seemed to be deciding what to do next. After a few moments, he joined the queue and I ground my teeth as I watched him progress with it, his podgy pink face almost painfully conspicuous among the sallow complexions of the other customers. He reached the front of the line and ordered, and I held my breath, watching for a flicker of suspicion on the face of the waitress, but she didn't flinch, turning to the samovar without hesitating. She poured tea into a glass, and he took it, paid and then shuffled into the centre of the room with his tray, ostensibly looking for somewhere to sit. With studied carelessness, he stumbled into the back of the chair opposite mine, and asked loudly if it was free. His Russian was good: perhaps he'd gone for a top-up with Craddock.

I nodded. He thanked me and placed the tray on the table, then removed his coat and draped it over the back of the chair. I clenched my jaw at the sight of his beautifully starched white shirt, which looked like Jermyn Street, and which he had paired with a dark-green woollen tie. I suppose I should have been grateful it wasn't an Old Harrovian one and that he hadn't brought a bowler hat with him for good measure. He seated himself, crossing his legs. He had surprisingly small feet, which were squeezed into a pair of Lobb brogues. Most of the shoes worn by those around us didn't even have complete soles. I resolved to ignore all this, and just hope to God that anyone whose eyes rested on him would presume he was a Party official or one of the *nachalstvo* slumming it for breakfast. He'd managed to get past the waitress, at least. Oblivious to my concerns, he lifted the glass of tea by one of its filigreed handles and took a dainty sip of the hot liquid, staring sightlessly ahead.

He'd come and, it seemed, he'd come alone. It was possible he had people stationed outside, but nobody else had entered the place after him and I didn't think anyone who had come in earlier was a likely candidate. So I should have been pleased. But Smale presented greater problems than I'd anticipated, and it wasn't just his damn-fool getup. He'd always disliked me, even when I'd been the Service's boy wonder. Now he would hate me, and with good reason. It wasn't just that I was a traitor to my country: it was personal.

They had sent him out here under diplomatic cover even though I was in Moscow and knew he was with the Service. It wasn't overly dangerous, as the Russians were perfectly capable of working out for themselves who the spooks were in the embassies, just as the Service knew who the Soviets had under diplomatic cover in London. But, if asked, I would nevertheless have been able to run my finger down the list of embassy staff and pick him out as a Service officer. That was why London had sent Fletcher-Peck out earlier: he'd not been around in Blake or Philby's time. He had also been bloody useless, which was perhaps why they had decided not to use that tactic again. This time Smale had drawn the short straw, and if I knew Smale that was going to rankle, because quite apart from the unpleasant sensation of knowing his cover could be blown at any moment by a double agent, it meant he was never going to be Chief: he had already been marked down as disposable, and therefore a second-tier officer at best.

In short, he was probably one of the last people in the world who would be prepared to give me a fair hearing. But I *had* to get him to listen to me, and act on what I had to say, and I had to do it very fast.

'Thank you for coming,' I said. 'I know it can't have been an easy—'

'Was he worth it, then?' he broke in. He was talking to Sarah. 'Quite a price to pay for a quick roll in the hay, isn't it? Or were you betraying us earlier, as well?'

Christ. It was worse than I'd feared. He clearly had no idea what had happened.

'I've never betrayed anyone,' Sarah said quietly, but Smale wasn't listening, having turned back to me.

'And it's a bit early for vodka, isn't it?' He waved at the glass on the table and wrinkled his nose. 'You all seem to drink yourselves to death. Pity you can't take the honourable way out and just use a gun.'

'That's not my—' I stopped myself. There was no time to get into arguments. I had to placate him. His opening comments indicated a level of contempt that I recognized as not just personal but institutional. It looked like the initial shock had worn off and I had become a totemic name in the Service, along with Philby and the rest.

'Did you come alone?' I asked him, and he looked at me as though I had accused him of stealing the bishop's silverware.

'Of course. That was your stipulation.' He wanted to nail down that he was the honourable professional and I the dirty Commie traitor. If it made him feel better, fine. Anything was fine, as long as I could get him to listen.

'Thank you,' I said. 'I appreciate it. I would like your help, Hugh. I really need you to get a message to London.'

Smale leaned forward, his lips parting to show a row of yellowing fangs.

'So you're the new hotline,' he hissed, 'is that it?' He sat back again, pinching his nose. 'I must say, it's very poor form bandying emergency phrases around – even for you. Did you really expect us to take that at face value? In case you've forgotten, you no longer work for us – in fact, never did. And now we'll have to alter all our security procedures. Perhaps that was the idea. Very tedious. We've only just changed all the dead drops as a result of your coming over. The boys weren't too pleased with me for ordering it, as it wasn't so long ago they had to do the same on account of Blake.'

He was talking at rather than to me. His eyes were locked in a supercilious gaze, and I suddenly realized what was happening. He thought this was a showdown. I'd seen something similar in the aftermath of Philby's defection in '63: almost everyone in the Service who had crossed paths with him had developed the notion that they had played a crucial role in the saga. Sometimes this took the form that they had 'just known something wasn't right about him all along'; but a few had been deluded enough to think that they'd presented some sort of threat to Philby.

Smale had either forgotten or was ignorant of the fact that I had simply asked to meet the Head of Station here, and that until he'd walked through the door I hadn't known that was him. He had persuaded himself I'd asked him here because of our scant history together in the same office. And so he was listening to me with one ear, trying to figure out what angle I was playing, while in his mind's eye he was already drafting the chapter of his memoirs in which he related the curious incident in which he met the notorious double agent Paul Dark and his accomplice Sarah Severn in a seedy Moscow café.

I had to try another tack quickly. I had to find a way to make him see he wasn't going to live to write *My Life in Shadows: Three Decades as an Arse-Licking Creep in British Intelligence* if he didn't respond to what I was telling him.

'Please listen,' I said, as quietly and gently as I could – manners maketh man. 'This is a genuine emergency, and it's not about me. Yes, I made the dreadful mistake of working for the Soviets, and I wish I could turn back time and put it right. But, unfortunately, I can't. I'm very sorry for it, but I know that no apology or confession I make can change anything. Some mistakes can't be undone. But Sarah has never worked for the Russians, and I no longer am – in fact, they're chasing both our hides right now.' I saw the open disbelief on his face, and pressed on. 'But none of that matters. I'm talking about the possibility of very imminent nuclear war, so please can you try to set aside your understandable animosity towards me for a couple of minutes and hear me out?'

His face was very still apart from his eyes, which flickered all over me. Contemplating, weighing. The hubbub around us seemed to be in another room as I focused on him, and he on me. Finally, he cocked his head a little to one side.

'It's unfortunate for rather a lot of people that you can't turn back the clock,' he said, and gave his tea a ceremonial stir. 'Because quite a few of them are dead. But I'm listening.'

I leaned down and picked up the attaché case. 'The documents in here will provide all the evidence you need,' I said. I briefly explained about the mustard gas in the U-boat, the 'attacks' on the bases, the B-52 flights, the Soviets' interpretation of these events and Brezhnev's order to prime the missiles. Then I took out Yuri's threat assessment and placed it on the table.

He read it in silence, then pushed it back towards me and took another sip of tea.

'Very interesting,' he said grandly. 'Thank you for showing it to me. But you must understand, old chap, that I can't simply take all of this on trust. This document could be forged. We will have to analyse it, verify it against other sources and so on.'

'There's no time for any of that,' I said. 'And there's no earthly reason for me to be forging Soviet military documents. You need to get a message to London now so we can stop this going any further. Is Osborne still in charge?'

He didn't answer.

'Whoever is Chief needs to get the PM to call Brezhnev and tell him there's been a serious misunderstanding and there's no attack being planned. And the PM also needs to get hold of Nixon, sharpish, and get those B-52s back on the ground.'

He pinched at the knee of one of his trouser legs, realigning the crease so it was perfectly vertical, then looked up, his face expressionless. 'But you do see that I can't just take your word for all this, even if you have brought along a briefcase filled with official-looking documents. I couldn't take anyone's word for it, but especially not yours. You must see that?'

'This is no time for—'

'Paul.'

'What?'

Sarah nodded towards the window. A car had pulled up outside the café: a yellow Volga with a blue stripe along the side and a siren on its roof. *Militsiya*. A man in a blue coat and a peaked cap was at the wheel, and another was in the passenger seat.

Had someone in the café reported our presence? The waitress?

The old man by the door? They couldn't have *followed* either of us here – too much time had elapsed since Detsky Mir and my phone call if that had been the case. But had enough time elapsed for Yuri to have issued an alert to all available patrols with Sarah's and my descriptions? Despite its name the *militsiya* were simply the civilian police, subordinate to the Ministry of Internal Affairs. Could the wheels of Soviet bureaucracy be so well oiled that the GRU had reached every patrol car in the city since I'd killed Vladimir?

There was no way of knowing. I glanced at Smale.

'Did you keep radio silence about this meeting?'

'Of course,' he said sniffily. 'What do you take me for?'

It was my turn not to answer.

The car had parked, and the man on the passenger side had got out and begun walking towards the door of the café. Were they after us, or simply stopping for a bite to eat on their patrol?

I made a decision. I replaced Yuri's document in the case and closed it, then picked a fork off the table and held it stiff behind my back.

I handed the case to Sarah. 'Take this and follow me,' I said. I pushed my chair back, then lowered my head and walked smartly towards the counter, because that was the opposite of what he would expect and then I could get a blow in, surprise him, and double-back. The man pushed his way through the doors and strode confidently in to the café. As he approached the counter, our eyes met for a moment. My fingers tightened around the shaft of the fork as I prepared for the flicker of interest that would mean I would strike, but he ignored me and strode past, his eyes on the menu pinned up on a board behind the counter.

He wasn't here for us. I looked back at Smale, who was leaning forward but hadn't moved from the table. He didn't believe me about the threat, that much was clear, and I didn't know what it would take to budge him, if anything. It might take hours, but another *militsiya* man could walk in here in five minutes, and the next one might be looking for us, or be armed with our descriptions. And even if Smale did listen, there was no way to be certain he would get the message to the Americans fast enough to avert disaster.

The moments were slipping away. I had no idea how others might act, or how quickly. But the only other option was to try to get to Åland, to try to get back to the U-boat and prove that the leak originated from the canisters in it. That would mean finding a way past the roadblocks, and all the men hunting us . . . but it also meant we would have less interference. The only interference we would face would be from those trying to kill us.

Sarah was looking at me, waiting to see what I was up to. All my instincts were telling me we would be wasting time staying here trying to convince Smale any further. Sometimes all we have is our instincts. I motioned to Sarah and pushed open the door, stepping into the street and walking briskly, not looking back. The rain was coming down hard, and I stepped around a puddle in front of the Volga.

'What are we doing?' said Sarah from just behind me.

'Plan B,' I said. 'Get in the back of the car and be prepared.'

The man behind the wheel looked up in surprise as we reached him. As Sarah opened the rear door, I opened the one on the passenger side, leapt into the seat and placed the fork to his groin.

'Drive,' I said.

VIII

He was youngish, perhaps in his early thirties, with dark hair, blue eyes and a strong jawline: a model *militsiya* man. And so he hesitated. Perhaps he thought I was bluffing. I pressed the prongs of the fork into the cloth of his trousers and leaned in to his ear.

'If you haven't started this car by the time I've counted to three,' I whispered, 'I'll slice your balls off and drive myself. One . . .'

His jaw was clenched in fury, but he switched on the ignition and depressed the clutch. The starter coughed for a moment, then sputtered out. Christ. Looking around the car, I saw it wasn't in good shape: there was no mat beneath my feet, just the bare steel floor. I glanced back at the café and saw his colleague turn and spot us, alerted by the noise. He began running towards the entrance, his arms waving, shouting at us.

'Wave to him,' I hissed. 'And make it convincing.'

He glanced at me, then reluctantly lifted a hand from the wheel and half saluted his colleague, who peered at us, not understanding. I smiled at him and gestured with my hand to indicate that we were just taking a quick spin around the block. He would figure out what we were doing pretty soon, but it might just slow him down for a minute or two – and that minute might make all the difference.

Something moved in the rear-view mirror, and I saw another man already running across the street, his hands stuffed in his pockets. He had fair hair and a moustache, and I realized with a shock that it was Dawes – so much for Smale's gentlemanly regard for my stipulations.

I leaned into the fork again, and sweat broke out on the driver's face. But that wasn't helping him focus, so I relented a little. He tried the ignition again and this time the starter caught and we were off. The car jumped and tilted as we caught a wheel on a pothole, before righting as we came into the lane, directly behind a taxi.

'Put your foot down!' I shouted at him. I was looking at Dawes in the rear-view mirror: he'd reached the other side of the road and jumped into a light grey Pobeda containing one of his colleagues, and they were now only twenty yards or so behind, with just four cars between us. We had to lose them, because I didn't have time to be taken to the embassy and convince everyone I was telling the truth.

The driver accelerated, squinting through the windscreen. One of the wipers was broken, so it wasn't much use against the rain; it just kept getting stuck and drawing back early like a bird with an injured wing. Apart from the taxi there were no cars in front of us and I thought he was dramatizing to give his colleague a chance to catch up. I could also see that despite the fact I was holding something very sharp to his crotch, he was itching to make a move on me: perhaps because of the holster at his hip, which contained a Makarov; perhaps because I was having to keep the prongs a little at bay in case I skewered him by mistake. So I leaned across him very fast and snatched the gun with my other hand, then rammed it against his temple, removing the fork from his groin at the same time. Something about the sensation of cold steel pressed into his skull got through, and his squint disappeared.

I handed the fork to Sarah in the back seat, and told her to keep it handy in case he got any ideas. In the meantime, he pulled out to overtake the taxi. As we passed it, I told him to take a right, but he reacted too late and had to slow to swerve into it, the back wheels skidding on the tarmac. In the rear-view, I saw the Pobeda preparing to make the same turn. The *militsiya* man must have sensed my anger at his delayed reactions and feared I was going to pull the trigger, or perhaps I was pressing harder than I realized, because he accelerated again as the street widened. He swung a left, and then another right, bringing us onto a boulevard, Rozhdestvensky, its neo-classical buildings flashing by us, and I shouted at him to move into the Chaika Lane, the central one reserved for party officials, which was empty.

But the Pobeda had now made the corner as well and was gaining on us, so I told him to prepare to turn again, and this time he reacted faster, taking a side street on the right that, after a few bumpy yards, brought us out onto a small square. I glimpsed the entrance of an underground station and dozens of people queuing at a small market outside it, dead chickens hanging by their necks, and then the street narrowed again.

I told him to keep going, and to take as many turns as he could, while I kept an eye on the rear-view mirror for the Pobeda. I couldn't keep him in control like this for much longer, so I had to figure out a way to lose Dawes and friend first.

I turned back to the driver and asked him if he knew who we were. He didn't respond, but his eyes flicked over to me. 'I said do you know—'

'Yes! You're fugitives from justice.'

'Take the next left,' I told him, 'and keep your eyes on the road. Of course we're fugitives, but what else do you know about us?'

He took the turn well, and I grunted approval. The man could drive, and Dawes, or whoever he was in the car with, would have a job keeping up with us – for as long as I could keep this man under control.

'You are English,' he said. 'We were given instructions to look for you.'

There was a handset next to the radio, so presumably they were using a two- or three-way communications system.

'What were your instructions, exactly?'

'You are to be stopped by any means. Shoot on sight. Call back-up at once if needed.'

All of that was to be expected. The rain was intensifying, so I had to raise my voice against the sound of both it and the engine.

'Anything else?'

He registered a flicker of surprise. 'The whole Service has been put on the highest alert for civil disorder.'

An alert for impending unrest was another sign they were preparing for an attack. The Service's experts had predicted wide-spread riots and looting in Britain if it ever became clear a nuclear conflict was imminent.

'Was there any indication as to *why* we are fleeing justice?'

'That's not our concern. If State Security says you're fleeing from justice, you are.'

Give the order and the hounds will run.

'What measures are in place to stop us?'

'I can't speak for the other Services, but we had a full alert, with every available man scrambled and told to look for you intensively.'

'Roadblocks?'

'Yes, I believe—'

'Where?'

'I don't know. They are arranged by Central Control.'

A gust of wind smacked against my side of the car, and I tensed to stop myself from losing balance. The window on the passenger side would no longer close all the way, and a thin icy wind was whistling in through the gap. My hand was cramping from holding the pistol in such an awkward position, and I was getting worried that if there was another gust of wind or we went over another pothole I might accidentally pull the trigger. I locked my wrist and placed my other hand around my forearm to keep it in place, then stole another glance in the rear-view. The Pobeda was overtaking a red Moskvitch, coming into our lane, closing ground.

'The roadblocks,' I said to the driver. 'You must have favoured spots in the city.'

He nodded. 'We have sixteen points. Judging by the alert we were given, I expect most or even all of them will have been set up.'

I thought about this for a moment. That many meant there was no chance of our leaving the city without going through one. And there was no obvious way we could get through any of them, because they'd have several cars waiting and barricades blocking the way. I checked the rear-view again: the Pobeda was trying to make it past a small van, creeping ever closer.

'Keep making turns,' I said. 'Sarah, take hold of the gun, please.'

She leaned forward and I transferred the grip so that she was now holding the pistol in place at the driver's temple.

'Shoot him if he tries anything.' The man looked to be sneering, perhaps feeling he could overpower her. 'She was first in her class on the shooting range three years running,' I told him, 'so I wouldn't advise it.'

It was a reasonably good lie, because his sneer vanished. I leaned across and unhooked the latch of the glove compartment. Rummaging through, I saw two spare holsters and breast badges, a map and two small green booklets with gold stars pinned to the front. I took out the booklets and flicked one open. It was for his colleague. I quickly flicked open the other one, and the face of the man next to me stared up from the photograph. He was Sergeant Grigor Ivanovich Bessmertny of District C-12, and this was patrol car identification 1464. I could have got his name and rank out of him easily enough, but not the rest of it.

'What's the call sign of Central Control?' I asked. 'Lie, and I'll tell my companion here to shoot you in the head and I'll take over the wheel myself.'

He inhaled sharply through his nose.

'Big Bear.'

'And when you call in, how do you identify yourself? Fourteen Sixty-Four?'

'One Four Six Four.'

I dropped the booklet onto my lap and grabbed the handset from the radio, then pressed the transmit button and spoke into it. 'Big Bear, this is One Four Six Four reporting a possible sighting of the English fugitives, subject of earlier alert.'

There was a moment's silence, and then a crackle of static burst from the receiver.

'One Four Six Four, this is Big Bear. What is your current location, and that of the fugitives?'

I lifted the receiver again, looking out at the street signs. 'We are on Rozhdestvensky Boulevard, at the corner of Milyutinskiy. They are in a pale grey Pobeda' – I glanced in the rear-view mirror and read off Dawes's licence plate – 'which we saw them get into at a café on Neglinnaya a couple of minutes ago. Please send backup.'

Another crackle, and then: 'Thank you, One Four Six Four. Keep up the pursuit, and I will direct all cars in the area to help you out.'

They signed off, and I placed the receiver back in its hold. A few moments later Big Bear came on repeating my information, and moments after that there was the sound of a siren somewhere behind us. Dawes must have heard it too, because the Pobeda peeled away from behind us and took the next side street. I told Bessmertny to take a left, and that was when I spotted the other car.

It had appeared behind the Moskvitch as if from nowhere, presumably having cut in from one of the side streets. Was it in pursuit, though? Its bodywork was black, and I guessed it was a GAZ-23 – the special model created just for the KGB. From the outside, it looked exactly like a 21, which was what we were in, but it had a V8 engine under its bonnet, which meant it could reach 160 horsepower, as opposed to our 65: it was the most powerful car in the Soviet Union.

As it approached us, a man leaned out of the passenger window and opened up with a machine-pistol. A shot hit a rear tyre and we started to skid, losing control fast. A moment later the car was overtaking us and made to turn in the road to block us off. The man in the passenger seat was still shooting, and this time he hit the front windscreen. I started to scream at Bessmertny to yank the wheel around but my right hand was throbbing and when I looked down at it I realized why: it was covered in blood, and a spike of glass was sticking out of the flesh between my thumb and forefinger.

The image of it sent pain shooting through me, and I clenched my eyes shut as the roar of gunfire and engines around me increased, but then I thought of Brezhnev in the bunker and forced them open again. Half the windscreen had shattered, and chips of glass were strewn across the dashboard and wheel, but Bessmertny still had his hands gripped on the latter, his jaw clenched tight and his eyes staring wildly ahead. The 23 had made its turn and I screamed at him to steer us off the road, but the distance was too short. The driver in the 23 saw what was happening and tried to reverse, but he wasn't fast enough and our wheels locked as we began to slide towards him, the tyres squealing as they scraped across the road.

There was a massive jolt as we caught the front end of the 23 but I kept consciousness and even began to move my hands to the back of my head, until I remembered the glass and took them away again. I was being spun around, but my mind was in danger of detaching from the situation. Then panic rose to the surface as a car came from the other direction and I lunged towards the wheel, another surge of pain swelling through my hand as I did. There was a blast of the horn and then *whoosh*, the car had gone, but the road was still where I'd last seen it, which meant I was alive. Somehow we had righted on the road, and Bessmertny was still hunkered over, his hands in position. I leaned over and grabbed at the wheel to help him right us some more, looking in the mirror as I did and expecting to see the maniac with the gun leaning out of the window, but I saw nothing – just traffic streaming by, Moscow, life. The 23 had gone, either driven off the road or forced into a turning.

I turned to check on Sarah in the back.

'I'm fine,' she said. 'But we need to deal with your hand.'

'Get us somewhere quiet,' I told her, 'away from the centre.'

She nodded, and while she instructed Bessmertny to take turnings, I examined the wound. It looked worse than it was, I thought – there was just the one large shard and although it had produced a lot of blood, it looked to be relatively clear. There was always the risk contamination would spread, but we couldn't go to a hospital.

Soon the traffic started to thin out and we passed rows of concrete blocks of flats, squat and uniform. Sarah ordered a few more random turns until we had reached a small clearing that appeared to be an abandoned picnic area. Car tyres and pieces of rusting metal lay half-buried in a patch of overgrown grass, beyond which was a row of small wooden cabins. The stench of urine and faeces rose as we approached: public toilets. I told Bessmertny to pull up by some tree stumps, and once we had come to a standstill I took the key from the ignition and climbed out.

*

The area looked to be completely deserted, and the nearest road at least a mile away. The rain had stopped, but the clouds were still very low. I ripped away the sleeve of my jacket and balled it up and placed it in my mouth. Then, without looking at it, I yanked the spike of glass from my hand, my screams muffled as the pain seared through me in waves.

Once I'd steadied myself a little, I walked back to the car and tapped on Sarah's window. I gestured for her to hand me the gun, then opened the driver's door.

'Get out,' I said to Bessmertny. He did so, and I told him to walk towards the wooden cabins, focusing on keeping the Makarov on him steady despite using my left hand. Every muscle in my body was tensed, because if I were in his shoes I would be looking to turn suddenly and snatch the gun. So I kept a good distance from him, watching every move he made, waiting for any sign that he was about to try something. When we had gone a few yards, I told him to stop and undress. He didn't respond.

'Do it now!' I shouted.

He started removing his jacket. 'I wouldn't advise throwing it at me or anything like that,' I said as he reached the final button. 'You don't have anywhere to run. Just place it on the ground, understand?'

He nodded, sullen now or perhaps frightened, and he folded the jacket over his arm, then crouched and placed it on the ground. I told him to strip off the rest and he did, until finally it was all laid out and he was standing in front of me, shivering in billowing white underpants and a vest.

I told him to open the door of the cabin nearest him. Shivering, he did it, and I glimpsed a wooden shelf with a plastic lid.

'In,' I said.

He hesitated, considering whether to rush me. I kept my eyes level on his and tightened my grip on the butt of the gun.

'I'll shoot if you're not in there within five seconds,' I told him. 'Four.'

He walked in, and I stepped forward and turned the latch, locking it. He started thumping his fists on the door, and I told him that if he carried on I'd unlock it and finish the job. There was a thudding behind me and I turned to see Sarah running over from the car.

'What the hell are you doing?' she shouted as she reached me. 'You can't lock him in there! He'll freeze to death. It's not—'

'What?' I said, turning to her. 'Cricket? Would you rather I shot him, like you did Charles in Italy?'

I jerked my head back to avoid the slap and grabbed hold of her wrist, then twisted her round in a simple hold. She lashed out with her other arm and when that didn't work either, she tried to kick me in the groin, but my body was too far away, so she started thrashing about angrily, screaming at me to let her go. I dropped the hold, but made sure to keep the gun steady – not aimed at her, but present.

'You bastard,' she said, her eyes drilling into mine. 'You know what Charles did to me, and what he was planning to do to others. But you're worse than he was. You're no better than an animal.'

A thought flitted through my mind of a post-nuclear world: a few lost souls scurrying about in bunkers or foraging for food and water across contaminated ground until they finally succumbed to radiation poisoning.

'We're all animals,' I said, trying not to let my temper take over. 'We like to think we're civilized, but that's for peacetime. I'm sorry if this offends your sensibilities, but we are heading for nuclear war. If we take him with us, he'll try something. If we let him go, sooner or later he'll reach his colleagues.'

She flung her hands out in exasperation. 'And tell them what? We just ran a KGB car off the road! Half the radio transmissions in the city will be about us.'

'Yes, but we don't know precisely what they're saying. This man is a loose end. He'll get free, in time, or someone will find him. Just not immediately.'

'And how do you think they'll react when they find him? They'll probably double their efforts.'

'They'll have every man available after us already, and if any of them get the chance I promise you they'll shoot us on sight and won't hang about afterwards discussing the rights and wrongs of it. If we make it out the other side of this, we can go to the opera and pretend we're not animals again. But until then we've got to do whatever it takes to survive, even if it means abandoning fair play. Now get in the car, please. If you're not going to help me—'

'What?' she said, her nostrils flaring. 'You'll strip me to my knickers and lock me in with him?'

'No. I'll put you in the boot.'

She started to laugh, then caught my look. 'You would as well, wouldn't you?'

'Yes. We don't have *time* for this, Sarah. Now which is it to be?'

She didn't reply and the silence stretched out, but then there was the faint sound of a siren see-sawing in the distance. We both turned to it, cocking our heads to gauge whether it was getting any nearer. After a few seconds it faded away, but it seemed this had been enough to wake her up, because she turned to face me and gave the tiniest of nods.

'Good.' I took off my half-shredded jacket and walked across to Bessmertny's bundle of clothes. 'Because I need you to help me figure out what we're going to do next.'

Her eyes widened. 'You mean you don't know?'

I picked up Bessmertny's shirt and pulled it over the one I was already wearing. 'You heard what he said. They've got roadblocks set up across the city, and we won't be able to get past any of them as we are. They'll be checking their own cars just as thoroughly, and we don't have papers.'

I buttoned the jacket and reached for the trousers. Sarah watched me, her hands clamped under her armpits, and I picked up Bessmertny's coat and thrust it towards her. She hesitated for a moment, then took it and put it on. It was much too large for her, and with her boyish crop of hair it made her look like a Dickensian urchin.

I put on the trousers, boots and wristwatch, then drew the leather gloves over my hands, taking it slowly to avoid reopening the wound.

'What do you think?' I said.

'Convincing enough. But who are you going to say I am if we're stopped?'

'Climb in the back seat,' I said. 'I'll claim you're a suspect and I'm on the way to the station. But let's hope that doesn't happen. We need to find another form of transport fast if we're going to get out of Moscow.' I stopped myself from saying the next word on my lips – 'alive'.

We got in the car, me in the front and her in the back, and sat there, our brains churning, while we waited for the heater to take effect. I'd studied this country for most of my adult life, and knew the ranks and accompanying uniforms of all its forces, and the relationships between each force and the structure of the system as a whole. So I knew what to expect. This was the ultimate secret state, with armed police patrolling the streets to stop anyone who demonstrated the slightest sign of not following the regulations. Suspicion was the natural state of affairs here, and we would have to act accordingly.

But although I had a lot of facts and figures stored in my head, my knowledge of the Soviet way of life was woefully incomplete. Most of what I knew was second-hand, theoretical – and that could be the difference between life and death. Apart from a brief stint in Prague and several months in a prison cell, I'd never been to the Soviet Union. To make matters worse, we had no support: no sleepers, safe houses or people with hidden compartments in their trucks. And we had to find a way through the Soviets' security net *while they knew we were trying to do it*. It was close to impossible, and under normal circumstances I wouldn't even have been considering it.

We were stuck in the spider's web. But I did have some very specific knowledge that might help in this situation. I had studied the Soviets' border controls – both their strengths and weaknesses – in depth over the years, and at regular intervals. I had, admittedly, mostly been looking at them going the other way, as part of my contingency plans in the event that I'd suddenly need to defect. I hadn't had to put those plans into effect – as it turned out, I'd been forcibly defected after the operation in Italy, and Sarah along with me. Now I had to get from East to West, which was an entirely different prospect, and a hell of a lot more difficult.

I turned to Sarah. 'I said "we" a moment ago, but that's up to you. You can leave now and take your chances at the embassy or try to find your own way out of the country, or you can come along with me and help me get to the U-boat. The odds are I won't make it. I have no idea how much time we have, or if the Russians will even believe me if I find the canisters—'

'In which case, we'll die in a nuclear blast. I'm coming. What about the military airfields? Could we catch them by surprise and steal a plane?'

I nodded at her commitment, then considered her suggestion. I thought of the helicopters I'd seen that morning at Steklyashka. 'They'll be even more guarded than usual. And even if we got to one, they'd simply shoot us down.'

She was silent for a few moments. 'Can we get onto a fast train? Isn't there one that goes straight to Leningrad?'

'Yes, the Red Arrow. But they'll have men on the platforms of all the stations checking everyone, and even if we could find a way on board they'll be searching every nook and cranny of every carriage. The main problem is we don't have any papers, and in this country that means you effectively can't do anything.'

'What about dissidents – surely they have ways of forging documents?'

I turned to look at her. 'Do you know any dissidents?'

She shook her head. 'But surely we can find some. What about that group in the café – you know, the girl you couldn't tear your eyes away from and her friends? They might be able to help.'

'I was checking we weren't under surveillance,' I said, and her lip curled slightly. 'It's a good idea, but what about the practicalities? Say they were dissidents, or at least know how to get in contact with some. And say that they're also still sitting in that café, or that we can track them quickly by asking around. How would we convince them to help us?'

She nodded at the attaché case on the seat next to her. 'Show them the documents.'

'We can't just run around Moscow flashing the contents of that case to anyone we think looks sympathetic. If they turn out not to be, we'll be headed straight back to the Lubyanka. Even if we strike it lucky and do find some sympathizers, we'd be asking them to believe that the documents are genuine and risk their own freedom as a result. I think it's too much to expect from strangers. Do you know anyone in Moscow? Outside the embassy, I mean?'

'Sorry, not a soul. I mean, I once met Kim Philby at a party in Beirut, but obviously we can't approach him.'

There was an awkward silence, as my own treason suddenly hung in the air between us. Six months ago, this woman had stumbled upon a conspiracy to kill innocent civilians in Italy, orchestrated in part by her own husband. She had also discovered that I was a Soviet agent, but for that very reason I'd been the ideal person to turn to. Now we were confronted by a much graver crisis than the one we'd faced together in Italy, but half a year in a prison cell in Moscow was a lot of time, and I guessed that she'd spent some of it dwelling on the fact that my actions had also cost innocent lives over the years.

'Yes, Philby's out,' I said lightly, trying to break the tension. 'They summoned him to the bunker before me, and by all accounts he's still loyal to the cause. He'd hand us straight over to Yuri and Sasha, and probably take pleasure in doing it.'

I stopped, struck by a stray thought: Philby wasn't the only other double in Moscow.

'Maclean,' I said.

'*Donald* Maclean? Surely he's just as loyal to the Soviets as Philby?'

'I'm not so sure.'

I'd never met Maclean, but in many ways felt I knew him. The first I'd heard of him had been back in 1950, shortly after my arrival in Istanbul: an acquaintance at the Foreign Office had gleefully told me that the head of Chancery in Cairo and a few of his friends had got blind drunk and wrecked the flat of two girls who worked at the American embassy. That had been Maclean, the son of a distinguished Liberal MP, who had gone on to have a nervous breakdown before suddenly disappearing the following year with fellow diplomat Guy Burgess. The word had quickly travelled around the Station that both men were Soviet agents who, on the brink of being arrested by Five, had fled to Moscow.

Burgess and Maclean's vanishing act had been my first indication that I might not be the only Soviet agent within the British establishment. The idea had both terrified and comforted me. Terrified, because their exposure could mean mine was next: I hadn't known about them, but what if there were other doubles who knew about me? And if another double were caught by Five *before* fleeing the country, they might reveal what they knew under lights. But it was comforting in its way, too, because it meant I wasn't alone in the world, and that others were treading the same path.

As the years had gone by I'd felt the noose slowly tighten around my neck as it had become clear that, far from being alone, I was in fact one of several long-term agents the Soviets had succeeded in recruiting in Britain, all of whom either had access to or were part of the upper echelons of intelligence and policy-making. In '61, George Blake, a former SOE officer who had been the Service's Head of Station in Seoul, had confessed to being a Soviet agent. The following year, John Vassall, a private secretary to a Conservative minister, had admitted to passing secrets to the KGB ever since they had photographed him in compromising positions with other men. In '63, Kim Philby, at one point Head of Soviet Section and seen by many as a possible Chief, had defected to Moscow, which had been followed by the unmasking of Anthony Blunt, who had been a senior officer in Five. In '67, the Labour MP Bernard Floud had killed himself after being interrogated by Five – some in the Service thought he'd done so because he had been presented with evidence that he had been a Soviet agent. And finally, in March of 1969, a defector in Nigeria had put paid to my peaceful life in London, and here I was as a direct result.

'I always wondered if I would be able to defect,' I said to Sarah. 'Even when I thought I was working for the right side, something about heading to Moscow filled me with dread.'

'I can't imagine why!' she said, and looked purposefully out of the window at the wind whipping at the tree stumps.

I smiled, despite myself. 'Indeed. But before I had the pleasure of finding out for myself, I was very interested in what the defectors made of life out here. As Head of Soviet Section, I made sure I had access to all their letters back to England.'

Her forehead puckered. 'Didn't you realize that these men were hardly likely to paint a very accurate picture? The Russians would also have been monitoring what they wrote.'

'Yes, of course I knew that. I also felt they would probably put a positive angle on their experiences anyway. Nobody likes to contemplate the idea that all their work has been for nought.' I smiled grimly. 'It's not a pleasant realization. I thought they would try to convince themselves they were right all along, and fit the facts to their case. I knew all that, but I still paid close attention to their letters.'

In fact, it had been more like an obsession. Burgess had died of liver failure in '63, but Philby, Blake and Maclean were all alive and kicking, and continued correspondences with friends and family in Britain. I'd followed all their careers keenly, which hadn't been hard to do: the Station had spent an enormous amount of energy trying to determine what they were up to. The Americans had even concocted a plan to assassinate Maclean in the National restaurant in Moscow, but it had never materialized.

Of all the doubles, Maclean had always intrigued me the most. Blake, Burgess and Philby all seemed like adventurers in some way, turned on by the thrill of secrecy and deceit. But Maclean had always seemed to be at one remove: a traitor, yes, and according to many who'd known him, an arrogant prig and violent drunkard to boot. But I had studied his case in depth, and felt sure there was more to him.

Back in '58, *Time* had run an article on him and his American wife Melinda, in which they had been interviewed in their Moscow flat, where they lived under the names Mark and Natasha Frazer. Soviet Section had dissected every sentence of this article in a series of memoranda. Many of the memos had contained fanciful speculation as to what 'message' Maclean and the KGB had been trying to send in the interview, as well as a level of satisfaction that he appeared to be stuck in a dead-end job with marital difficulties and a drinking problem, having lost his wife to Philby and cut off relations with Burgess. But nobody could have given the piece the level of scrutiny I did.

The article made for depressing reading, and filled me with a resolve not to end up in the Soviet Union if I could help it. I'd missed my next meet with Sasha after reading it, and with the benefit of hindsight recognized that the article spelled the beginning of a secret inner realization that I was no longer the believer I'd claimed to be when I had sought out Yuri in 1945 and volunteered to serve the Soviet Union – and that perhaps I had never truly been one.

'And something in Maclean's letters makes you think we can approach him now?' said Sarah.

I nodded. 'Prague. After Moscow invaded last spring, I paid even closer attention to the defectors' letters. I wanted to see if it had weakened their resolve at all. Philby appeared completely unrepentant about it, and Blake's letters steered clear of politics. But there was something odd about Maclean's reaction. Back in '56, he sent letters to friends defending the actions in Hungary. I'd actually been comforted by his rhetoric. But his letters about Prague were different: reading between the lines, it seemed to me he thought the whole thing had been an outrage on the Soviets' part.'

'That's not enough to approach him,' she said. 'What if you read wrong? He'll just turn us straight over—'

'There's more. For the last few years, Maclean has worked as an editor at *International Affairs*, which is the Soviet Foreign Ministry's journal. That's really a seal of approval from the big boys in the KGB. Moscow Station sends the journal to London in the diplomatic bag every month, and I used to read the bloody thing from cover to cover. Maclean writes articles on foreign policy under a pseudonym, but in the last couple of years his veneer of Party dogma has slipped. Obviously, there's only so much you can say in such a journal, but my impression is that although he's still a firm Communist, he's bitterly opposed to Brezhnev's gang. On top of that, various reports have trickled in over the last couple of years claiming that, unknown to the KGB, he has been frequenting intellectual circles, and perhaps even visited the homes of suspected dissidents.'

I listened to the sound of the radiator humming beside me.

'Perhaps we should try Andropov's *dacha*,' she said. 'I hear he's also visited suspected dissidents.'

'Not the time for humour,' I said. 'I'm not saying he's another Sakharov, but faced with these documents, he might help us. Final point, and I hope this one will convince.'

'Me, or you?'

'Both. All the defectors keep very much to themselves, but occasionally they're allowed to see a journalist or an old acquaintance. Maclean has had very few visitors from the West since he arrived, but those who have met him have given an increasingly strange picture. A couple of years ago, an old friend of his from Cambridge was due to come out here as part of some delegation. I got wind of it and invited him out to dinner a couple of weeks before, and discreetly suggested he try to renew the acquaintance. As soon as he got back, I took him out again, and over pheasant and port he told me he'd managed to meet Maclean for about an hour between meetings – and that it had been very odd. Maclean had generally steered clear of controversial topics, but at one point he'd suddenly asked this chap if he was "a sleeper they had never got round to waking up".'

'"They", not "we".'

'Exactly. Maclean defected nearly twenty years ago, but still doesn't identify himself completely with the Soviets.'

Silence again. It was slender, I knew: the friend could have been exaggerating, or not recalled the wording correctly. But we had to find a way out of this city.

'Are you sure about this?' she said. 'If you're wrong—'

'Of course I'm not sure. But I think it's a better bet than approaching strangers.'

She breathed in. 'What about Yuri?' she said. 'He might suspect us of doing just this – Brits sticking together.'

'I'd be surprised. We only just came up with the idea ourselves, and it's hardly the most obvious move. And we know something about Maclean he doesn't.'

'All right. We need to find the journal's offices, I suppose?'

'Yes. There should be a map in the glove compartment.'

I turned the key in the ignition and began reversing towards the main road.

IX

9.54 a.m., 27 October 1969, Gorokhovsky Pereulok, Moscow

An office block loomed in front of us, immense and grey, a couple of cars parked on the street directly in front. I couldn't remember where Maclean lived, but I'd read the masthead of *International Affairs* a hundred times or more, and the address was always printed at the foot of the page: '14 Gorokhovsky Pereulok, Moscow'. Despite the anonymity of the building, this was a plush neighbourhood in one of the oldest parts of the city – we'd passed several eighteenth- and nineteenth-century palaces on the way.

We hadn't passed any *militsiya* patrols or GAZ-23s, but Yuri and his colleagues would be searching hard for this car, so logic dictated we lose it as soon as possible. Sarah was too young to pass for a senior female official in the fiercely male Soviet military environment, and if we went together that might confuse matters, so after a brief discussion we decided it was probably safer that she stayed in the car than risked being stopped on the street. I parked a few streets away outside a block of flats, and left her huddled under the blankets in the back, clutching the attaché case. We agreed that if I hadn't returned within twenty minutes she would try to make a break for the border alone.

There was a *militsiya* man on guard by the entrance: probably an undercover KGB officer assigned to the building in general, and Maclean in particular. I'd considered telephoning from a call-box, but had decided it was too risky. He might simply call his handler the moment he replaced the receiver, and I'd be picked up the moment I arrived at the arranged meeting point. No, if I wanted his cooperation, I would have to see him face to face. He might be under surveillance by the KGB, but after nearly two decades in the country I reckoned that the protection would be relatively light.

The *militsiya* man watched me as I approached, squinting, perhaps to see if I was someone he knew. He had a sergeant's shoulder-boards.

'Greetings, comrade!' I said, raising my hand, and hoping blood wasn't seeping through the glove.

'Good morning, comrade. What can I do for you?'

'I'm here to see the Englishman, Frazer. Is he in his office?'

He frowned at the mention of the name, and my stomach tensed as I waited to see if the gamble would pay off. Maclean might no longer work here, or be on holiday, or be using another name, or be in Minsk . . .

'Is there a problem?' he asked.

'No,' I said, 'I just need to ask him some questions. One of the other Englishmen has gone missing, and head office thinks this fool might know about it. I doubt it, but I've been sent to ask just in case.'

He considered this for a moment. 'That sounds like one of Vilshin's ideas.'

I smiled. 'No, this came directly from Andropov, would you believe?'

He whistled. Then his eyes narrowed. 'This is the first I've heard of it.'

'It's only just happened, and I was told to inform you about it. Everyone is in a panic, and it seems that when Andropov tells Vilshin to jump, he asks how high. Well, what would I know? It's my first week in this job – just came down from Leningrad.'

'Ah, I thought I didn't recognize you. Who were you working for up there?'

'Chap called Ledov. Even worse than Vilshin, I can tell you!'

'That would take some doing. But it sounds like you catch on fast – it's just as you say. Listen, can you wait here?'

'Gladly. But don't be too long, comrade – I don't want to freeze my balls off out here! Nobody told me it would be so cold down here.'

He smiled. 'Just wait until next week. I've heard it's going to get a lot worse. Hang on, I'll be back soon.'

He disappeared, and I wondered if he was going to make a quick telephone call to headquarters to check on my story. The uniform and a bit of blarney seemed to have done the trick, but the longer he took the worse it would be, because it might suddenly occur to him that he hadn't even asked me for my name or my papers. If this went wrong, we'd reached the end of the road. The *militsiya* man appeared at the door again. And looming behind him, looking rather anxious, was a very tall man in a shabby suit and a spotted bow tie.

Maclean.

*

I told the KGB man I would take Maclean for a walk for about an hour. He nodded and wished me well, and I gestured to Maclean to lead the way. We walked off down the street together, me and this giant whom I had read so much about but never met.

'What's this about?' he said suddenly, his voice surprisingly high-pitched. 'I have some important work I need to do this afternoon.'

'Paul Dark,' I said, indicating that he take the side street on the right.

He looked up at me, confused. 'Dark? But I never had anything to do with—'

He staggered back on his heels.

'I thought you were in custody.'

'I was.'

He reeled away from me, his hands outstretched.

'Get away!' he spat out in English. 'I don't want to get involved—'

I leaned over and grabbed at his bow tie, pulling him towards me and then turning him round and shoving him in the direction of the car. 'Get in,' I said quietly, showing him the Makarov.

*

They were both watching me: Sarah sitting upright in the back, and Maclean folded into the passenger seat as though he were an elaborate penknife. Looking at him close up, he seemed unbelievably old – the rakish cad from the wanted posters sent out by the FBI in 1951 was long gone. What was left of his hair was swept back in an almost Edwardian style, and there were enormous circles under his eyes. The eyes themselves were clear, though, so he just might have stopped the drinking. But when he opened his mouth, I was shocked to see that he had several teeth missing. All that remained that was familiar from the pictures I'd seen of him was the aristocratic sneer. He reminded me of an ancient butler in a Bela Lugosi film, answering the door of the haunted house to the innocent enquirer.

Well, I was no more innocent than he.

'I know we've never met,' I said, 'and you have no reason to trust me. But we do have something in common, I think. Please hear me out. Then, if you want to walk away, do.'

'We don't have anything in common,' he spat out. 'You were never one of us. You did it because you fell for a woman.'

I took a deep breath. 'This isn't about what we've done with our lives, or why. It's about the here and now.'

'I'm perfectly happy with what I'm doing here and now, thank you very much. I *worked* for the cause I believed in – you were too busy playing cloak-and-dagger games for kicks.'

'I was Deputy Chief of the Service,' I said, regretting it the moment the words came out of my mouth. Maclean turned his head away, no doubt delighted at having exposed my petty egoism. But I could have told him there were no kicks to be had in being tortured, imprisoned and shot at. I looked out of the window, and wondered how to explain the situation, and if I'd get any more of a hearing than I had done with Smale. I decided to dive in.

'Listen. Early this morning, I was taken to a bunker somewhere beneath this city. Brezhnev, Suslov, Andropov, Ivashutin and the rest of the gang were all there, chewing their cuticles off.' He was watching me now, silent, the hooded eyes very still. 'The lot of them are convinced the Americans are about to launch a nuclear strike from B-52s. As a result, Brezhnev is planning to launch a full-scale attack on the United States. Annihilation will ensue.'

Maclean shifted his bum and squinted at me to check I wasn't having him on.

'This isn't a prank,' I said. I turned to Sarah and she handed across the attaché case. I clicked it open and found the threat assessment, then held it out to Maclean. 'Take a look yourself.'

He hesitated for a moment, then took the papers. He sat reading them in silence for a few minutes, then looked up at me, his forehead wrinkled with lines.

'This isn't real,' he said, handing the papers back. 'It can't be.'

'Do we look like we've been in prison manufacturing forgeries?' said Sarah.

He went quiet. 'But it's just bluff, isn't it? Surely they can't seriously be contemplating a nuclear strike?'

I replaced the papers in the case, closed it, and placed it between my feet.

'What would you do if you were in their shoes?' I said. 'You have hard electronic and human intelligence showing the Americans are flying nuclear-armed B-52s straight towards your border, and at the same time there has apparently been a chemical attack on two of your heavily guarded naval bases, one of which is where you keep your nuclear submarines. Would you just sit tight and wait, hoping that the West isn't about to launch a surprise attack and wipe you out? Or would you get your retaliation in first?'

He thought about it for a few moments, then said: 'I hope I'd wait a little while, just in case.'

I nodded. 'And that's precisely what they're doing. But I'm afraid a little while is all we've got. Because if the planes continue their path towards the border, Brezhnev will decide an attack is imminent, and he'll launch a strike.'

'But why on earth would the Americans keep flying their planes towards the border?'

'I've no idea why they started doing it in the first place. The worst-case scenario is that they are in fact planning to launch an attack. If so, there's bugger all we can do and that's the end of it. But everything I know about military strategy in the West tells me that a surprise nuclear attack is not something we're interested in carrying out, for obvious reasons, and so it can't be that. Unfortunately, the Soviets don't believe me. I can't go into details because we don't have time, but the fact is that they're *wrong* about the chemical attack. The Americans may be playing silly buggers of one sort or another, but part of the puzzle simply doesn't fit and I'm damn sure they aren't planning to launch a nuclear strike.

'The Service's representatives here have shunned us and we're now being hunted by the KGB, GRU, *militsiya* and everyone else. If I'm wrong, and the Americans really are intending to attack, it doesn't matter a damn to you or anyone else that we've escaped, because this country and several others will be reduced to dust in a few hours. If I'm right, though, we might just be able to stop it happening. But we need to get to Finland to do that, and there are roadblocks all over this city to stop us from getting out. So you have to make a choice very quickly, I'm afraid. Either realize I'm telling the truth and try to help us get out of Moscow any way you can think of, and fast. Or guess that I'm lying, and tell us to go hang. But if you do that, you'd best be bloody sure of it, because you'll be risking nuclear Armageddon. You're our last hope, Donald. Please don't walk away.'

I stared at him. I hated begging, but now was no time for pride. We needed this man's help, and it had to come willingly or we'd get nowhere.

He had looked away again, and was tapping one foot against the side of the door. He bit a nail, then perhaps remembered my crack about cuticles and broke off. Finally, he looked up at me.

'Brezhnev was there, you say? Was he smoking?'

I nodded.

'What colour was his cigarette holder?'

That was easy. 'Amber.'

A look of awe came across his face. I thought it best not to mention that this fact was in all the Service's files and had even been reported in the world's press.

He stopped tapping his foot and looked back and forth between Sarah and me for a few moments, squinting. Then his mouth hardened.

'All right,' he said, finally. 'You're going to need papers, and I know the best forger in Moscow. But let's get out of this car.' He turned to me. 'And take off the jacket and cap, for God's sake – we'll never persuade him to help if you're in that get-up.'

X

We left the car where it was and walked. After about fifteen minutes we arrived at a block of flats, the concrete painted a pale green. It was lower than the one we'd been parked outside but in the same style, square and unadorned, with rows of tiny balconies jutting out onto the street. The front door had no one guarding it, and was unlocked. Maclean didn't break his stride; he just opened the door and walked in.

The hallway and stairwell were a shambles, the paint peeling from the walls and broken bottles and rubbish scattered around. We climbed a narrow flight of stairs and Maclean knocked on the door three times with his fist, waited a few seconds, then rapped twice. There was a shuffling noise, followed by the sound of a latch dropping, and then the door finally swung open. A man with a beard and thick spectacles peered out sceptically.

'Good morning, Anton,' said Maclean. 'I'm sorry to come unannounced like this, but we met a few months ago, at Zimshin's party. Do you remember? I need your help. I wouldn't usually think to impose on you, but it's of the utmost urgency.'

Anton looked us up and down for a moment, then peered over our shoulders to see if there were any more of us. Finally, he opened the door all the way and gestured us in.

*

We followed him through a tiny hallway and into the living room, which was dark, tiny and smelled strongly of alcohol and cigarettes.

It was also a tip: piles of books and papers took up most of the available space. A few stools were arranged around a table, along with a thin bed that had a blanket strewn across it: Anton had evidently been resting there when we rang the doorbell. Greying socks and underpants hung over a radiator, which had a saucepan tied to one of its corners with string – presumably to catch any drips – while a battered tape recorder emitted Bob Dylan at low volume from the top of a glass-fronted bookcase.

Anton gestured for us to sit in the stools while he propped himself on the edge of the bed. He was wearing a frayed shirt and baggy drawstring trousers held up with braces and his thick dark hair was swept back in majestic disarray. Judging by the titles of some of the books strewn about, he was a physicist of some sort. He was also clearly a dissident, because he was about my age and it was a Monday morning, so he should be in the same sort of office I'd just fished Maclean out of. Instead, he was at home, and for a scientist in this country that meant he must be in disgrace or at least under some form of suspicion. So my information about Maclean had been right: he did move in dissident circles. But would this one be willing to stick his neck out for a complete stranger? He was already rather angry, waving his arms accusingly at Maclean.

'Please explain yourself,' he said. 'And it had better be good, because I have no idea what precautions you took coming here.'

'We weren't tailed,' said Maclean. 'But these people really do need your help. They're British, and they need to get out of the country with some very important information that affects all of us.'

Anton looked at Maclean in astonishment, and then at me and Sarah.

'More British spies? Are you a madman?' He clenched his fists and stood up from the bed. 'Sorry, I thought this was serious. Get out, all of you. Now.'

Sarah tugged at my sleeve. 'Let's go,' she whispered. 'There must be another way.'

I shook my head and walked over to a pair of glass doors that led to a small balcony. I pulled the curtains aside slowly, almost expecting to see a mushroom cloud on the skyline. Silly of me. We wouldn't see it — it would just come. There probably wouldn't even be a Four-Minute Warning.

I glanced down at the street a few feet below. A handful of people were trudging by, coats wrapped tight against the chill, and I watched them for a few moments. But there didn't seem to be anything suspicious about them. I tugged the curtains back together and walked over to Anton, who looked like he was about to roll up his sleeves to fight me. I placed the attaché case on the table, opened it and took out Yuri's threat assessment.

'Is this a forgery?' I said, handing it to him.

He took it reluctantly, peering at it through his spectacles.

'No,' he said, after he'd read a few lines of it. 'This appears to be a genuine military intelligence document. How did you get hold of it?'

'Never mind that. Read the last sentence, please.'

He turned the page and read it aloud. '"Our assessment at this time is that we must consider launching a nuclear strike, perhaps within the next twelve hours."' He looked up at me, then at Maclean and Sarah. 'There must be some mistake,' he said. 'This cannot be right.'

I took a breath. *Stay calm.* 'If it weren't, we wouldn't be here. I listened to Brezhnev order ballistic missiles primed less than four hours ago. He and his generals are in a bunker as we speak, contemplating a full-scale nuclear attack on the West. If they do, the West will counter-attack. We, and millions of others, will die. We want to try to stop this happening, but we need your help.'

There was silence for a moment, except for Dylan, who was continuing his lament about the state of the world in the corner of the room. Then Anton started asking me a lot of questions, but I cut him off and explained that there wasn't any time. Maclean's colleagues might soon be wondering where he'd got to, and I couldn't afford to spend the day going over the intricacies of the B-52 flights and the mustard gas accident.

'Are you going to help us or not?'

Now he took a breath. He poked a finger at his glasses, then turned to Maclean.

'Do you trust these people? Are they telling the truth about this?'

Maclean tilted his head. 'I don't want to take the chance they're not, do you?'

Anton thought about that for a moment, then stretched out his hand to shake mine.

'Where do you need to go?'

We all breathed a sigh of relief. 'Finland,' I said.

'I see. Like Lenin! Well, you will need a lot of papers for that. I take it you don't have any at all?' I shook my head. 'Okay. Everyone needs to have a domestic passport, with *propiska*. An institutional work pass, a work book and of course *kharakteristika*. We will just have to hope that will be enough.'

'You mean they might ask for more than that?' I said.

'Yes. Some things require a *spravka*, a special permit.'

'What sort of things?'

He shrugged. 'Staying in a hotel, going to the hospital – even entering some libraries.'

'That's all right,' I said. 'We won't be doing any of those.'

I sounded more confident than I was.

'All right,' said Anton. 'Let's get started.'

*

Maclean left shortly afterwards – the last thing we wanted was for people to start wondering where he had got to. He agreed that if he heard anything about the situation from his colleagues he would try to return, using Anton's door knock code again.

Once he'd gone, Sarah and I helped Anton clear some space in the living room. The bed was a folding one, and it turned out that the bookcase opened on a hinge and the bed went in it, stored upright, along with the blanket and pillows.

'Now,' Anton said once everything had been packed away. 'I

think it might be best if you both clean yourselves up a bit first. And let's see if we can do something about your hand.' I'd taken off the gloves. 'Wait here.'

He pushed open a door to the right of the radiator and I caught a glimpse of a tiny bathroom housing a toilet and a washbasin. A few moments later he came back in with a first-aid kit. I winced as he applied antiseptic and a bandage, but thanked him for it. He motioned for Sarah to use the bathroom, and she nodded graciously and went in to wash herself. Then he turned back to me.

'We should also change your appearance. They will have a very detailed description of you by now, I think.'

He took off his spectacles and passed them over. I placed them over my nose, and blinked at the strength of them. I removed them at once, but agreed that they were a simple and effective prop.

'And some clothes,' said Anton. He squeezed past a pile of books and slid out a drawer in his magical bookcase. After some rummaging around, he removed a heavily wrinkled jacket and a gaudy cheese-cloth shirt. I unbuttoned Bessmertny's shirt and put both on. Anton passed me a hairbrush, and I arranged my hair so that it fell forward.

Sarah came out of the bathroom, her face looking a lot fresher, and muffled a laugh at my appearance. Anton smiled and did some more rummaging until he had located what looked like a black transistor radio. But I saw a lens sticking out of the front, and realized that it was, in fact, a camera.

'You have a darkroom here?' I asked.

He smiled, pleased at the question. 'It's an instant camera,' he said. 'A copy of the Polaroid — very new, and very rare. I can't tell you what I had to do to get hold of it. I've also had to make some very special modifications. It has completely changed the way I can make documents. Now, please stand over there.'

He pointed at an area of wall beside the bookcase. I moved towards it, and he fiddled about with the camera and positioned me as he wanted.

'Can you see?' Sarah asked him.

'I'm fine,' he said, but it seemed to take him quite a while to line up the shot. But once he had done it and taken the photo, he stripped off the backing sheet and we waited for the image to appear. It took about a minute. Bizarrely, instead of one image appearing, four did, precisely like passport photographs.

'Four lenses,' said Anton, beaming. 'It took me almost a month to figure out how to do it.'

'I'll take your word for it,' I said. 'What do we think, though? Will it pass muster?'

Sarah peered over and had a look. 'It's great,' she said. 'I doubt many people would recognize you from that.'

I grimaced. It wasn't most people I was worried about, but men at a roadblock examining every vehicle, armed with a description. But I smiled at her nevertheless. 'Let's see how you fare, then.'

Anton looked up at me with surprise. 'Oh, no!' he said. 'You misunderstand. I only have a set of papers that will fit you. I don't have any way of making papers for your friend.'

I stared at him. 'Well, that's wonderful to hear. But how the hell do you think we're going to get over the border if only one of us has papers?'

'It's all right, Paul,' said Sarah quietly. 'It's best you get away – you know where the U-boat is, after all. I'll find a way out somehow, don't worry.'

'Not a chance,' I said. 'I'm not leaving you here for the likes of Yuri to . . .' I pressed my nails into my palms. 'There has to be a way,' I said to Anton. 'You must have some documents you can adapt.'

He shook his head. 'You're lucky I have some that will suit you. All I can suggest is that the young lady might be able to fit in the boot of my car, if she is willing. It's a small space, but it should be possible.'

We glanced at each other, my earlier remark about putting her in the boot of Bessmertny's car hovering between us. But it was a good offer. It wasn't as good as papers, but a car was much safer than trying our luck with public transport.

'I'm willing,' Sarah said.

'Good.' I turned back to Anton. 'Where's your car and what does it look like?'

'It's parked on the other side of the street – a yellow Moskvitch. There are windscreen wipers in the glove compartment if you need them. And the radio has a special receiver installed. If you press the middle button, you should be able to hear what the *militsiya* are saying. That might come in useful.'

He took a set of keys out of his pocket and handed them over.

'Thank you,' I said, taking them.

'I wish I could do more. Now I have to get to work. My equipment is in the other room, and I would ask that you not observe. Please understand that this is not because I don't trust you . . .'

I nodded. He was worried that if we were caught, the authorities would torture us to discover the techniques he'd used to forge our papers. I was pretty sure they would have other things on their mind in that case but, after all, he was risking his freedom for the sake of two strangers and I didn't expect him to abandon his own self-interest entirely.

'How long will it take for you to prepare the documents?' I asked him.

He shrugged. 'Perhaps an hour?'

Christ. It seemed like an age, considering the situation I'd left behind in the bunker. But there was no way round it: without at least one set of papers, there was no way we were going to get out of the city, let alone the country.

Anton fetched a packet of stale-looking biscuits from the kitchen, poured us a couple of glasses of water and handed out two cigarettes, before retreating to the bedroom and closing the door behind him.

I lit the cigarette and gladly inhaled it. Sarah walked over to the tape recorder and found a cassette of Bach organ preludes, which she put on to replace Dylan. Something about the way she was standing, facing away from me, alerted me that something was wrong.

'Will you really be okay in the boot of a car?' I asked.

She nodded her head fractionally, but didn't turn. I thought about it for a moment, and realized she was frightened. I picked up the attaché case, opened it and took out the papers, fanning them across the table.

'I looked at some of these in the café, but there's much more of it, as you can see. A lot of it will be guff, I'm sure, but there might be something here that helps us know how they're thinking, and might help us stop this. Care to go through it with me?'

She turned and smiled, and I realized I'd guessed correctly: it was the inaction that was making her antsy, the waiting around. We seated ourselves as comfortably as we could and began reading through the papers. I started by tackling Ivashutin's strategy document again, reading it through from start to finish. I couldn't decide if he really believed that the warmongering imperialists could be overcome by the noble Soviets in their overcoats storming through a radioactive Western Europe, or whether the document was empty rhetoric that nobody in the Kremlin took seriously. I hoped for all our sakes that it was the latter.

'You might be interested in this,' said Sarah, and I looked up. She pushed across a thick bound dossier and I picked it up. There was a red star in a black circle on the front, and the word 'НЕЗАВИСИМЫЙ' in faded type.

'NEZAVISIMYJ', meaning 'independent' – this was my file. I'd discovered the same dossier in a flat in Rome six months ago, but that version had been a lot thinner. This, then, must be the GRU's master file, containing all the information they had on me.

I opened it up and was immediately confronted with several strips of film negatives. I held one up to the light and saw it was a photograph of me as a young man in SAS uniform, which must have been taken somewhere in the British Zone. It had been taken from some distance, and I was looking down at the ground, shielding my eyes from the sun with one arm raised. I started running through the rest of the strip. There was one of Anna, casually standing on the steps of the clinic, smoking a cigarette, and another with me and her in the ward, presumably taken with a camera she had hidden somewhere. There were dozens of the things. Presumably they had sent a few to Sasha in London for safekeeping, because he had shown me some in March to blackmail me into continuing to serve them.

I placed them to one side, exposing a document below. The cover page bore the title 'APPENDIX I: RECRUITMENT OF "INDEPENDENT"'. I turned it over and found a slim pamphlet; the edges of the pages were yellowing and torn, but the type was still legible. It was dated 12 June 1945, and was in the form of a letter from Yuri to Kuznetsov, who had then been the head of the GRU.

```
I met with agent LOTUS on the 6th to discuss
the progress of Operation JUSTICE, the latest
report on which I have enclosed with this
package (Operational Letter 16/H). At the same
meeting, we discussed the matter of LOTUS's
son, whom we have codenamed INDEPENDENT (see
Operational Letter 14/H).

    I hereby propose that we try to recruit
INDEPENDENT. The reason for doing so is simple:
in the coming years, he is very likely to rise
rapidly through the ranks of British Intelligence.
The fact that he is the son of one of our
agents gives us the means with which to recruit
him, and if we succeed he may prove more valu-
able than any of the others we have recruited
into the British network to date.
```

I already knew that I was 'Independent'; it seemed Father's code-name had been 'Lotus', and that their operation to find and execute war criminals in the British Zone of Germany had been JUSTICE. There was something disturbing about the phrase 'the British network to date' — how many had been in that, and who were they?

> INDEPENDENT is twenty years old and has already
> served with several British commando units. He
> is currently attached to the Allied Control
> Commission in Helsinki, where he is working
> under cover for the Special Operations Executive.
> He was placed there through the recommendation
> of LOTUS, and his performance so far has been
> exemplary — see my last report. LOTUS is opposed
> to the idea of recruiting his son, but is
> still afraid that we may use the compromising
> material we have regarding himself and BAIT.
> I feel confident he will be a completely willing
> participant in the operation.

'BAIT'? Who the hell was that, and what was the material about them that had compromised Father? My stomach roiled as I realized that my father had never been an ideological traitor, but had been blackmailed into serving the Russians. And that despite Yuri's claim that he was 'a completely willing participant', they had coerced him into trapping me, too.

> The relationship between LOTUS and the target
> offers us a great advantage, but will have to
> be handled with care. LOTUS's cover is that of
> a traditional right-wing member of the British
> upper classes and this, together with the intern-
> ment of his wife for German sympathies, has
> led to a distance between himself and
> INDEPENDENT, who naturally has no idea of his
> father's work for us. LOTUS has agreed that
> the best course would not be to try to mend

this distance, which would almost certainly prove too difficult, but instead to exploit it.

I propose a variation of the basic honey-trap operation we have used many times previously, including with LOTUS and BAIT, but with a few innovations resulting from the nature of the situation.

I took a breath and tried to clear my head. So Father had been the target of a honey trap — and presumably 'Bait' was his lover. And they had played this trick 'many times'. It looked like their recruitment plans had been a lot more systematic than I or anyone else had ever considered — almost routine.

And Father, behind that cold English mask of his, had apparently known all along that I resented him for his politics and for what he had done to Mother for hers. The stern handshake, the steely glare, the lack of any show of affection — had they all been part of his cover, then? Doubtless they were built in to his upbringing, but I was shocked that he had not only been aware of my feelings towards him but had also known how to exploit them; perhaps parents knew this sort of thing instinctively. But this was nevertheless a very different man to the one I thought I'd known. It showed a level of cynicism that made me resent him anew — but then I remembered the blackmail, and another picture emerged, of a man who was utterly desperate and trapped, and who was pressured into finding a way to recruit his son into the same situation.

I wasn't sure if I could read on. Did I need to know precisely how they'd gone about recruiting me? I didn't let myself answer the question: my fingers turned the page anyway.

PHASE ONE.
The operation should take place in the British Zone of Germany over the next six months, and run in conjunction with Operation JUSTICE. Agents

> LOTUS and KINDRED already have the list of Ukrainian traitors we suspect of hiding in the British Zone. LOTUS will contact INDEPENDENT and urgently request he come to Germany to support an operation of greatest secrecy. LOTUS has suggested invoking a direct order from Churchill, and I agree.
>
> PHASE TWO.
> LOTUS to introduce INDEPENDENT to KINDRED and inform him he is engaged in finding and liquidating war criminals. He will say they are Nazis who have killed British servicemen, rather than the scum who have killed our own agents.

I thought back to that first night in the safe house outside Lübeck, when Father had introduced me to Henry Pritchard and told me about the operation: the tiny sitting room lit by candles, Father talking about his meeting with Churchill, Pritchard standing to attention by the ramshackle wardrobe. Could I, in my wildest imaginings, have guessed that both were working for the Soviets? No, agents 'Lotus' and 'Kindred' had played their parts well – and I'd been an easy dupe.

The rest of Phase Two had taken place precisely as described: I'd helped Father trace his Nazi war criminals, unaware that they were Ukrainians who had killed Russian agents rather than British ones. And then had come the injury. Father had claimed that our final target was Gustav Meier, an SS officer who had raped and tortured members of the French Resistance, including children. All of this had been backed by forged documents he had briefly waved under my nose. Towards the end of September 1945, Father claimed to have discovered that Meier was working as a gardener near Hamburg, and we'd set off together to capture him. Naturally, it was a set-up.

'Meier' — even the name was included in Yuri's plan — was in fact a Soviet agent codenamed STILETTO for his expertise with knives, who had been brought in especially and instructed on how to cut me.

```
The wound we envision would be to one of the
kidneys and will be very painful, but shallow
and will heal within a relatively short time.
```

It had been *extremely* painful. Even now, I found it hard to believe it had only been a surface wound, and that I hadn't received genuine treatment for all those months. And then Phase Three: Father and Pritchard had taken me to the Red Cross hospital just outside Lübeck, where I was soon taken into the care of a nurse codenamed COMFORT — Anna.

```
You will recall COMFORT from earlier opera-
tions. She has now been at this hospital for
several months and her professionalism is
unparalleled. Once assigned to treating
INDEPENDENT, she will befriend and woo him,
playing on his youthful desires and ambitions
to rebel against his father and the establish-
ment he represents. Incidentally, LOTUS assures
us his son is sexually normal and will succumb
to her charms. If not, we will replace her
with IRINA.
```

So Anna was a veteran of honey traps — and they even had a back-up model, just in case I didn't fancy her! Well, Father had been right about my appetites. They'd found a beauty any red-blooded young male would have salivated over, especially if it were her job to make him do so. I wondered who her other victims had been: other Englishmen like myself? How many?

PHASE FOUR.

COMFORT will educate the target about our beliefs and aims, presenting them in a light he is most likely to appreciate. I have already briefed her extensively on how best to do this. If we are lucky, this alone may be enough, and she may be able to recruit him directly. But, judging from previous operations and the unusual biography of INDEPENDENT, it may prove a little more difficult. If that is the case, once she is certain that he has strong feelings for her, COMFORT will reveal to INDEPENDENT that she is one of our agents, under the guise of remorse and affection for him. She will also mention my cover name at the camp, and that I am her handler.

This strategy involves a certain amount of risk, but I am confident of INDEPENDENT's reaction – namely that he will angrily rebuff her and contact LOTUS to tell him that the British 'operation' has been exposed.

PHASE FIVE.

I would request a delivery of the new K4 nerve gas from Department 12 for the next part of the operation. Please send a package with the next courier from our Zone. I will administer the dose to COMFORT to induce catalepsy. Using our usual cosmetics techniques, we will then stage a death scene at the hospital, and ensure that INDEPENDENT sees with his own eyes that she has been 'killed'.

The next part of the operation involves the death of LOTUS. If all goes to plan, INDE-

PENDENT will seek an audience with his father, whom he will suspect is responsible for ordering the murder of COMFORT, due to the fact that he had recently informed him she was a foreign agent.

I have told LOTUS that the plan is for him to strenuously deny involvement to INDEPENDENT, while at the same time emphasizing that COMFORT was an enemy agent. But while I feel that plan would probably be enough to push INDEPENDENT to seek me out and offer to serve us, I do not think it would be psychologically damaging enough to sustain a long-term commitment from him. There is also the matter that LOTUS feels under substantial pressure, and is displaying predictable signs of neurosis as a result. His material has worsened lately, and in years to come he may be overlooked for promotion and have even less access to the sort of material we require.

In short, I think it is clear that INDE-PENDENT is the coming man, and so propose we sacrifice LOTUS in order to guarantee his replacement by his son. So, in place of the confrontation I have outlined and rehearsed with LOTUS, I suggest that he is instead liquidated and it be made to look as though he has taken his own life. INDEPENDENT will then, I am certain, believe that his father acted through guilt at having ordered the death of COMFORT. If my calculations are correct – and I would submit that they have not yet been wrong in such matters – INDEPENDENT will then seek me out here and offer his services as our agent, and

> the impact of the events surrounding his
> recruitment will drive him to be loyal to us
> in perpetuity.

Several more pages followed, but I'd got the picture. I shuffled the papers together and slid the pile back into the attaché case.

I knew a lot of it already, but hadn't run through all the ramifications. Some of it had been circling around the edges of my consciousness, where I'd let it linger, unwilling to poke the wound. And some of it had never occurred to me at all – the idea that Yuri had killed Father, for example. I had still believed it was suicide. But it was obvious, now that I thought about it: suicide wasn't really Father's style. And yes, the operation had been 'psychologically damaging', in just the way Yuri had foreseen: I had sought him out and nursed the dual wound of Anna's death and Father's ordering of it for years. Not in perpetuity, though. He'd got that bit wrong – not in perpetuity.

'Jesus!'

I looked up. The muscles in Sarah's cheek were visible as she clenched her jaw – she was reading Ivashutin's strategy document. She turned the paper over and stared at me. 'Isn't there someone else we can show this to? The Americans, or the French?'

I shook my head. 'Nobody in the West is going to believe us – we have to make the Russians understand they've made a mistake.'

'And we're sure they have, I take it? What if there has been a chemical attack on these bases?'

'It's possible,' I conceded. 'But I think it's just far too coincidental. There were thirty or more canisters of this precise chemical down there in 1945. If several have escaped to the surface and leaked towards the bases on the currents, I think you'd easily get this effect. Some novice sentry found a lump of the stuff that had washed ashore, picked it up and brought it into the base, after which others have touched it, too.'

'And the B-52 flights? How do you explain them?'

I couldn't. Although I'd told both Brezhnev and Maclean that I was certain the Americans weren't planning a strike, I was far from sure of that. I was hoping they were up to something else because I thought the mustard gas must have leaked from the U-boat. But I didn't *know* it.

And there was one other thing bothering me. When I'd come out of hospital in April, in the fortnight before Templeton's funeral, there had been a brief moment of panic when the North Koreans had shot down one of the Americans' reconnaissance planes over the Sea of Japan. For a few hours, the signals had been frantic, and Nixon had placed nuclear-armed fighters in South Korea on a fifteen-minute alert to attack the North. In the end he had changed his mind, and simply resumed the reconnaissance flights instead to signal that he wasn't going to back down. But he had nevertheless considered a nuclear strike. Could it be for some reason I didn't know of that he was considering it again, only this time against the Soviet Union?

'If the Americans are planning a strike, we can't stop them,' I said to Sarah. 'But if they aren't, we might be able to stop the Russians from reacting. So we have to act on the basis that they aren't. Does that make sense?'

She smiled, and placed her hand across the table. I took it in mine, savouring the warmth of her touch. I looked into her eyes, and remembered for a moment the sweat on her skin in the boat in Sardinia. We were a long way from there now.

There was the faint sound of typing coming from the other room.

'Let's hope he's ready soon,' I said. 'Did you find anything of interest in the papers so far?'

She shook her head. 'I don't think there was anything we didn't already know. How about you? Was that your file?'

'Yes.' There was little more to say about it, or little I wanted to, anyway.

'And what about the rest of it?' she said, pointing to some papers poking out under the dossier I had just read. 'Anything there?'

My stomach tightened and I pushed the other dossier aside. The document beneath was simply titled 'Report on INDEPENDENT'. I picked it up. It was dated 20 October 1969 – just a week ago.

'Are there any cigarettes left?' I said to Sarah, and she found the packet and lit one for me.

I stared down at the document, and breathed in the tar that might help me get through it. It looked to have been written by Sasha, and was addressed to Yuri.

⋆

Esteemed Comrade,

You asked me to give my reasons in writing for bringing INDEPENDENT to Moscow. It is my view, having been his handler for nearly twenty years, that when he was recruited in 1945, INDEPENDENT strongly believed himself to be setting out on a moral crusade. As we had hoped, he applied his adolescent sense of idealism to our cause, associating his service to us with vengeance for COMFORT's death at the hands (as he believed) of his father.

But although INDEPENDENT was able to convince himself that he was a Communist for the first few years of his work, this soon faded. He disagreed with our actions in Hungary in 1956, for instance, and on other occasions when I discussed such issues with him it was clear that he had become a believer only in the vaguest sense of the word, in a manner similar to many of our sympathizers in the West.

Due to his position and relationship with us, INDEPENDENT has long felt that he has a central role to play in the direction of political forces in the world. For him to be of use to us, it was necessary that we sustained his belief in this delusion. However, when he was threatened with exposure in March he discovered some limited information about the nature of his recruitment, namely that COMFORT was a honey trap.

As a result, he turned against both the British and us. This entire episode has been a disaster for us and for the KGB, who I hope I am not remiss in saying acted with great malice towards us in this affair, and at great cost to the Motherland. The results of this were discussed in my previous reports.

Following the fiasco in Nigeria, which resulted in the deaths of two of our agents by INDEPENDENT's hand, he was then targeted by a faction of neo-fascist hawks within British intelligence, whose links to covert groups in other NATO countries we have monitored for some time. Unfortunately, INDEPENDENT was not aware of our attitude towards these groups and their plans. This resulted in him nearly wrecking the hawks' actions in Italy, which would in turn have destroyed our own long-term strategy regarding this NATO action.

As these events took place at great speed across several countries, there was no possibility for me to communicate with Centre about every development, and I was forced to make several decisions without going through the usual channels or face the possibility of more disaster. I decided that it was in the best interest of the Motherland that INDEPENDENT not make public the NATO hawks' actions before we had deemed it politically expedient, and so I extracted him from Italy. As he was with another British agent, SARAH SEVERN, the wife of a hawk (now deceased), I decided she too must be extracted, or we would wake up to find the incidents in question across the front pages of newspapers across the world.

But I did not make this decision solely for wider strategic reasons. Since March, INDEPENDENT has effectively run amok, and I felt we needed to capture him before he could do yet more damage. A primary consideration was that he has been serving us for over two decades, and was at this time the deputy head of the British Service. In normal circumstances, this would have been a great victory for us. However, it had already become clear that INDEPENDENT had not just stopped serving us, but was working against us. By bringing him back to Centre, I felt we would be in a position to present his service to us without his interference, when and how we judged would cause the most propaganda damage to the West.

I confess that it has not worked out as easily as I had imagined. The British have so far managed to conceal the fact that he was one of our agents, reporting in the press simply that he died on assignment in Italy in May. My initial proposal was that we simply counter this with a press conference at which INDEPENDENT would appear and read a statement revealing that he has served us since 1945. I now feel that this would be unwise, mainly because INDEPENDENT is uncontrollable. Even with sedatives and the threat of the torture of SARAH SEVERN, for whom it is clear he has a sentimental attachment, I am not confident we would be able to control what he might say.

And there remains a wider problem: if we present his service to us to the international community, the propaganda benefit of revealing that such a senior figure in Western intelligence was an agent would be considerable in the short term, but in the longer term may cause us more damage than good. With previous British agents, the public revelation that they have served us has resulted in a pleasing level of anger from the Americans, and the British have yet to fully regain their trust as a result. In addition, the British cannot even trust themselves, and have spent much of their energy in recent years looking for more of our agents within their structures, to pleasingly unsuccessful effect.

In the case of INDEPENDENT, however, I feel that public exposure of such a senior figure in the Western intelligence structure would attract not only the attention of those within his own agency who have so far been concerned with trying to find members of our British network, but also others in Western intelligence. Some would no doubt conclude that INDEPENDENT must be one of several agents we have planted in their countries, and would investigate much more thoroughly than they have done to date. This would endanger many of our agents who are active or sleeping in the West.

As INDEPENDENT is no longer of use as an

> agent, and is rather a danger to us and a
> drain on resources, I suggest the time has
> come to liquidate him. It is probably advis-
> able to liquidate the girl, too.

I dropped the stub of the cigarette into my glass, and placed the document to one side. So they had wanted me dead, and Sarah, too. The report had been written only a week ago, so either Yuri had disagreed with Sasha's assessment or, more likely, he hadn't yet decided what to do about it and the current crisis had intervened.

Sasha had been right about one thing, though: I was uncontrollable. I wanted to break his fucking neck.

'Not good, then?' said Sarah.

'No,' I said. 'Not good.'

I walked to the doors leading to the balcony again. It had begun to hail, tiny hard pellets. My world and Sarah's had been reduced to this small flat, in its way no less a prison than the one from which we'd escaped. The cramped walls and ceiling made me want to run into the streets with her. But while the air would be crisp, the sky would be grey and men with steel-toed boots and loaded rifles were looking for us both with the intent to kill. And somewhere deep underground, surrounded by marble pillars and oil paintings, the walls were closing in on Brezhnev and the Supreme Command.

Soon, with any luck, we were going to try to cross a border. Which one, though? The maritime frontier was very tightly monitored by the Navy, with patrol craft along the whole stretch. They would also have stepped up their numbers and been given instructions to watch for us. But it is never possible to check all outgoing boats from a shoreline, however heavily you patrol it. Perhaps we could find a fisherman with an outboard motor willing to take us across the water. Perhaps.

We also had to decide where along the frontier to try to cross.

The 'attacks' were in a part of the country that was closed off to anyone without a special pass, and would now be under complete lockdown, with hundreds, if not thousands, of military personnel there. So we would have to give that whole area a wide berth. Our best bet might be to try to reach the U-boat from the other direction – from Åland. It was a longer way around, but it had some advantages. Yuri and his colleagues might soon realize we were planning to head for the U-boat, but probably wouldn't guess we would take such an indirect route. They would also be unable to coordinate the hunt for us, because if we managed to get into Finland they wouldn't easily be able to control their men there, or the Finns for that matter.

It was a very big if, though. There were twelve miles of protection either side of that frontier – the *pogranichnaya polosa*, or border strip – including sentries with dogs. And even if we found a way to get past the Soviet patrols in the area, we would still have the Finns to contend with on the other side, where it was almost as heavily guarded. Despite the difficult history between the two countries, the Finns regularly handed back anyone they caught coming over the border.

Another thought that had slowly been taking shape in my mind was the question of equipment. I needed to get back down into the U-boat to find the canisters, but to do that I would have to find a way to get hold of diving gear. I knew from the war that the Germans had made sure all their U-boats had self-contained diving suits on board, complete with oxygen flasks and air purifiers, but I had to get down there in the first place. Could I break into one of the Soviets' naval stations and steal one? It seemed a stretch. There was a naval base at Kronstadt, but that was fortified on its own island and I didn't fancy my chances there. Perhaps I could find equipment on Åland itself? I wondered what had happened in the intervening years to Kjell Lundström, the police constable from Degerby who had helped me in 1945 – perhaps he could help me again.

And then there was the problem of what to do if I did get down there. I was hoping it would be obvious that the canisters had leaked, and that I would be able to point this out to the Russians at their consulate in Mariehamn. But I had no idea if the Soviets still had a consulate on the archipelago – perhaps they had abandoned it in the intervening years. If so, I might have to try to reach Helsinki or Stockholm. But first I would have to find the canisters, and they might well have come loose from the U-boat and be many miles from it. I would either have to find them myself or bring the Russians close enough to them that I could take someone down there with me and force them to see the evidence for themselves . . .

The door to the bedroom opened and Anton emerged, his hair sticking out at even zanier angles than previously, his hands clutching a sheaf of booklets triumphantly. He was done. He spread them out on the table for our inspection – I had no way of telling, of course, but they certainly looked the part. He went through them carefully with me, explaining the purpose of each document and why I might be asked to show it, and after we had gone through it all once more I leaned over and gave him a bear hug.

'We may never be able to repay you, but thank you.'

There was an awkward silence as he shuffled his feet. Then there was a sound at the door: three muffled knocks. We stood still and waited. A couple of seconds passed and two more raps came. Sarah walked towards the door.

'Wait!' I said, but she had already opened it.

Maclean was standing in the doorway, a sombre expression on his face. It took me a moment to understand why. Directly behind him stood two men: one was Smale, and the other was William Osborne.

XI

'Move,' said Osborne, and Maclean jerked forward and staggered into the room, his eyes entreating me for forgiveness. The damn fool couldn't even check for tails properly.

Osborne stepped smartly into the room. He was clutching a Browning in one chubby little paw. With the other, he motioned for Smale to shut and lock the door, which he swiftly did. I saw that Smale wasn't empty-handed either, but instead of a gun he was carrying what looked like a black doctor's bag.

'Well, well,' said Osborne. 'Birds of a feather stick together. Sit down, all of you. Over there. Hands on your heads.' He gestured at the space by the wall where the bed had been, beside a tottering pile of books. Maclean, Anton, Sarah and I looked at each other, then did as he'd ordered. The flat, now occupied by six people, suddenly seemed very small indeed.

Osborne walked over and looked down at us with a sneer. There was something wrong with seeing him holding a silencer: he had always been the puppet-master, not the man who got his hands dirty. He looked much fatter than I remembered, almost grotesquely so, but perhaps that was because I'd spent six months in prison while he'd been eating jam buns. He was wearing thick tortoiseshell spectacles, a pinstripe suit and even had a handkerchief in his jacket pocket. Brandishing the gun, he looked like a Punch cartoon: the banker who had decided to rob the safe.

He ambled over to one of the stools and picked it up, then placed it directly in front of us and perched on it, his trousers riding up over his belly as he did so. From my vantage point, it was a most unattractive sight.

'Paul,' he said, peering down at me, 'I believe you are carrying a gun. Please remove it very carefully and place it on the floor like a good boy. I'll shoot if you try anything.'

'So you're Head of Station,' I said. 'And Smale's just your lackey.'

'You always were quick on the draw. Although not literally so in this case. The gun, please, now.'

I considered trying to shoot him, but thought better of it. He looked like he would fire without hesitation – and enjoy it. I removed the Makarov from my waistband.

'Careful now,' he said. 'We don't want anything to go off, do we?'

I placed it in front of me on the floor, and Smale scampered over and picked it up, then aimed it at my head.

'Who's Chief, then?' I said. 'Something must have gone awry for you to be out here.'

'I'll ask the questions,' he said. 'I must say, it is rare to find three traitors to their country in the same room.'

'Are you counting yourself in that?' said Sarah, and he swivelled to face her.

'No, my dear, I was counting you. I do like your hair – David Bailey's missing a cover shot. How disappointing that you've fallen for Paul's smooth words. But then, he always had a way with women. I should warn you, though, that they usually end up dead. I'm afraid you are very misguided if you think that anything I've done is in any way comparable to Donald and Paul's actions, or those of their masters. The Russians are much more unpleasant than I am – I would have thought you'd have realized that by now.'

'I should never have learned English,' Anton said suddenly, and we all turned to stare at him. 'You British will kill me.'

Despite ourselves, we all smiled – even Osbourne. But whatever companionship we felt in that moment evaporated quickly. Osborne's smile was that much more chilling.

'Be quiet, Anton,' said Maclean. 'This doesn't concern you.'

'No,' he said. 'I'm just being held at gunpoint in my own home.'

'Why did you send Smale to meet me?' I asked Osborne. 'Not to spare my feelings, I'm sure.'

He licked his lips, amused, or perhaps it was Anton's complaint that had entertained him. 'No,' he said. 'I wanted to surprise you at the embassy. Sadly, you skipped out rather early for us to bring you in. I must say it's been quite bothersome to find you again. But luckily we've been trailing Donald here for quite some time, and he doesn't have too many acquaintances who might help you escape the long arm of the Russian law.'

So that was it. They had probably paid visits to all the defectors, but when they'd gone to Maclean's office they found he'd left, and worked out from there where he might have taken me. Yes, quite some bother. I had to get away from them somehow, perhaps once we were outside the flat. I would have to make a move soon.

'Shall we head off, then?' I said. 'Presumably you have a car waiting?'

'Oh, we're not going anywhere just yet,' he smiled. 'You asked who had taken over as Chief. Innes has the title — at the moment, anyway. There was quite a storm after your little episode in Italy. Questions were even asked in the House. Innes is a busy little man, and he figured out what Hugh, I and others have been doing.'

'So you got shunted off here.'

'In a nutshell. But it's proved quite convenient, because now I can take my revenge, and at the same time use it to get myself back to London. The fact that Donald and Sarah are here as well makes it all that much more delicious.'

'Another frame-up? If Innes found out what you were up to in Italy—'

'Oh, I'll be much more careful this time. He hasn't discovered everything we were up to in Italy, anyway — we have a few surprises in store. But I suspect if I can deliver three dead traitors on a silver platter, nobody will ask too many questions.'

'Oh, really?' said Maclean, his voice strained but strident. 'Because I can assure you that the Russians will be very interested indeed.'

'Be quiet, Donald,' I said. 'Leave this to someone who knows about cloaks and daggers.'

Osborne smiled. 'Not such birds of a feather, after all. And I rather doubt your friends will care all that much — two burnt-out spooks and a dolly-bird, none of whom are of any use to anyone any longer. I suspect they'll be glad to be rid of the lot of you, in fact. Something to strike off the budget.'

'They might wonder who killed us, though,' I said. 'And ask awkward questions of the embassy.'

He let out a gleeful little chuckle. 'Who killed you? But don't you see, you're all going to kill each other: a suicide pact. Traitors, but also lovers.'

'That's absurd. Nobody would—'

'Oh, you'll be amazed what people will believe when told after the event,' Osborne said. 'It won't be too hard to whisper a few things in journalists' ears. They'll eat it up, I'm sure. "The traitors' love triangle" — I can see the headlines already.'

'I think you're all bluff, Osborne. You tried all that newspaper malarkey on me once before, remember. So how is Wilson these days? Still PM?'

He grimaced, and removed his glasses. He massaged the pink indentations on either side of the bridge of his nose with his fingers for a few seconds, and then replaced them.

'Wilson is still in power,' he said, 'for the moment, at any rate. And how kind of you to remind me about that failure of mine, and of your part in it. Well, this time I won't be satisfied with a hired thug pulling the trigger from afar. This time I want to see you suffer myself, and I want to be the one to administer that suffering.'

I thought back to the rubber room in London, and the bucket he had forced my head into. I didn't want to know what was in the doctor's bag. My stomach was churning just sitting in the same room with him.

'It sounds to me like you've gone soft in the head,' I said. 'I should have been on to you years ago — there was always something off about you.'

'And I, likewise, should have been on to you long ago. I had an inkling, though, back at that party of Templeton's in Istanbul when you raped Vanessa. Do you remember?'

I stared at him. He seemed to be serious.

'You're mad,' I said. 'Vanessa loved me, and did for years. It was your little jackboot Severn who tried to touch her up. You should have asked Colin Templeton; he'd have let you know.'

'But I did, Paul. And he told me very clearly that he had walked in on you fondling his daughter. Severn saved her from you, as you well know. Trying to save face in front of your new girlfriend?' He pursed his lips together as though chiding me.

'I've no idea where you're going with this fantasy, but it's not convincing me in the least. I left the party with Vanessa, and you must have seen that.'

'Yes, that was what upset Templeton so much.'

'He *asked* me to leave with her.'

'Not according to him.'

'Either you're lying or Templeton was. He told me quite clearly to take Vanessa home, so why he would want you to think I was . . . What else did he tell you about me?'

'Ah, I thought you might catch up. He told me he thought you were worth keeping an eye on. In case you were like Donald here, and his friends.'

I stared at him in horror. 'Templeton told you he suspected me of being a traitor?'

'Yes. Not quite in those words, of course. But he let it be known on several occasions, to me and a few others, that he had his doubts about your loyalty. I should have paid more attention to him.'

I blinked, trying to clear my head. Could Osborne be telling the truth? I thought back to the night Templeton had summoned me to his house in Swanwick. If he'd thought I was a traitor why the hell would he have invited me there, without Barnes to protect him, and with no weapon of his own? I went over it again in my mind – the moment I had raised the Luger and shot him. I'd thought at the time that he had realized then that I was the double. And then the thought came. Perhaps he had. Perhaps he'd had no idea before then that I was a double, but had merely told Osborne and others he suspected my loyalty to divert suspicion . . . from himself.

Burgess. Maclean. Philby. Vassall. Cairncross. Blake. Blunt. Pritchard. Father. Me.

And Templeton?

Was it possible? I hadn't been part of the Cambridge Ring, and had known nothing about any of them before they'd been discovered. Neither, by all accounts, had Blake or Vassall. I thought of a sentence in Sasha's report: 'This would endanger many of our agents who are active or sleeping in the West.' What if the Soviets had recruited not three, or four, or even ten men? What if they had recruited, say, twenty? Or more? And that only a handful of them had been exposed so far. At first blush the idea seemed absurd, but what if all the assumptions to date had been wrong and the level of Soviet penetration had been greater than anyone had even dared suspect – myself included?

Stay calm and think it through. I hadn't known about Pritchard or Father, but they had both known about me. So if Templeton had also been a double, he must have been recruited separately from them. In the aftermath of Burgess and Maclean's defections, both Five and the Service had twisted themselves in knots looking for further traitors. Pritchard had taken the role of an attack dog, accusing everyone in sight: at one point he had even claimed that the deputy of Five was a Soviet agent. Dossiers had been reopened; everyone had been questioned about their past. I had argued that these 'mole hunts' were divisive and that we were playing into the Soviets' hands by chasing our own tails and sowing suspicion everywhere.

And through it all, Templeton had played the middle ground

perfectly: the wise old sage, the kindly buffer, the voice of reason. But behind my back, to Osborne and others, he'd been softly voicing a private anguish: can we trust Paul, do you think? I mean, I love him almost as a son, but there's something not quite right . . . is there?

Simply because it had deflected attention from him.

And that evening in March at his house? Pritchard had presumed he was the Soviet agent codenamed RADNYA. Perhaps Templeton had, too. All three of us had been in the British Zone in 1945; perhaps all three of us had been Anna's honey traps.

I suddenly remembered Oliver Green. He had been a printer with Communist sympathies who had gone off to be an ambulance driver in Spain with the International Brigades. Then, in 1941, he had been arrested for possessing forged petrol coupons. When his house had been searched by the police, they had discovered a dark-room that had contained a Leica and dozens of secret military documents. This, in turn, had led to a soldier named Elliott, and eventually to a ring of fifteen British agents, all of whom were being run out of the Soviet Trade Legation.

The Green case had always bothered me a little, because nobody ever seemed in the least concerned by it. The implications seemed to have been completely missed by the Service. Here was a significant Soviet spy ring operating in Britain in the Thirties and Forties, with over a dozen agents. Had it been missed because Green and his colleagues had been working class? Because it was too uncomfortable to think about the implications?

Or had it been missed because many of the men looking at it had also been Soviet agents? My head reeled a little at that idea. It would involve a level of penetration that would change the whole picture of Britain's role in the Cold War. Indeed, it discounted it. If this were true, the Soviets had surely already won.

Or perhaps Osborne was just messing with my mind, and was trying to sow suspicions for reasons of his own. I couldn't think of any at this stage, but that meant little with him.

'You look confused,' he said. 'Thought you'd fooled Templeton, did you? He was never as daft as he looked, you know.'

No. No, perhaps he hadn't been. But this was all of little account. Osborne and Smale could be Andropov's long-lost brothers for all I cared, but it didn't help resolve the issue at hand.

'I'm not confused,' I said. 'I'm worried. Perhaps we could have this conversation and you can rip off my toenails after we've dealt with the impending nuclear crisis?'

He looked over at Smale, beaming. 'So you weren't lying! Well, well, my apologies. Lunch at the National it is.' He turned back to me. 'Come on, Paul, you can't seriously expect me to believe Brezhnev's about to launch nukes at us—'

There was a banging at the front door. Osborne turned, and in that moment I grabbed hold of the attaché case and held it up in front of my chest. Smale fired but it went wide anyway, and a fraction of a second later the front door swung down, splitting in two as it crashed to the floor, and men swarmed into the room waving guns and shouting. I flung the attaché case open, scattering documents like confetti over the room, and grabbed Sarah by the hand. Osborne was heading towards the door and I watched as one of the KGB men took aim and the shots hit him full in the chest and he fell to the floor, the inside of his jacket spreading out beneath him like a pair of black wings.

I launched myself into the balcony doors side-on, bracing myself for the impact. The glass smashed and crumbled over me, but I was through. Sarah came leaping through after me, and I careened into the balcony railings but used the momentum to grab hold of the ledge running along the top of them. It was shockingly cold, crusted with rime, and pain shot through my left hand as it came into contact with the wound, but I ignored it and hoisted my legs onto the ledge and climbed over, hooking my fingers around the outer edge of the shelf and letting my legs dangle below me.

Another shot rang out from inside the flat, and Sarah screamed. Without looking down, I let go and there was a rushing of wind in my ears and nose and then an almighty bone-crunching thud as I landed on the pavement. I looked up and caught a glimpse of Sarah's legs as her dress billowed around her and she landed next to me. It had all taken place in a matter of seconds – but we still had time on our side. A few yards away I could see a mustard-yellow Moskvitch.

'Come on!' I shouted at Sarah, and started running towards it.

XII

We reached the car and I scrambled with the key to unlock the boot. It was tiny. Sarah glanced at me for a moment, then climbed in, rolling herself up into the foetal position.

'Okay?'

She nodded, her chin against her knee.

'Hold tight,' I said.

I shut the door and ran around to the driver's seat. The temperature was around freezing, so I tried a brief burst of the starter without the accelerator, ready to catch it as soon as it took. It didn't. I waited a couple of seconds, drumming my hand against the wheel, and tried again. Nothing. A mushroom cloud forming, all because this country couldn't make cars that started. I gave it another go, craning my neck as I did to look up at the balcony. Gunfire was still coming from inside the flat, but God knew how long it would be before they came running for us. And . . . yes. *Bingo*.

I pulled out and roared down the street as fast as the thing would go, the treads of one of the front tyres squealing. I pressed the button on the radio and picked up the *militsiya* frequency, but the exchange was about a couple of drunkards who were causing trouble near the GUM store, not us. Presumably, the lieutenant at Maclean's building had finally wondered where we'd got to and called in, and the KGB also knew of his association with Anton. Maclean had grown complacent, careless or both, and had failed to realize he was under surveillance wherever he went, by both the British and the Russians.

The message might not have gone out yet, but this car would be compromised before too long because Yuri would soon figure out why we'd been at Anton's. The question was whether we could reach the first roadblock before he realized it and got a message to his men to look for anyone in a yellow Moskvitch with this registration. I hoped that the fact they'd stumbled in on two senior British diplomats holding one of their agents and a dissident at gunpoint would give them enough to disentangle for a while.

It had certainly given me a few things to disentangle: Colin Templeton a traitor? It couldn't be, surely. I told myself to leave it to one side for the time being, and think about it later . . . if there was a later.

A lifetime of training had taught me to keep my eye on an objective until the job was done, and to suppress feelings of panic, but this was different. We'd escaped Osborne and Yuri, but we were still a hell of a long way from the U-boat. In fact, we were around 700 miles from it in a shitty little Soviet car, with one of us in the boot and only one set of papers. Panic surged through me. The papers. I felt for the pocket of my jacket. Yes, they were still there.

I began heading west, keeping my speed at a reasonable limit so that I didn't attract any attention, and my eyes peeled for patrol cars and black Volgas. The rain had stopped, but mist was forming and visibility was poor. Dark clouds were pressing down on the city, but I noted them with satisfaction: it usually didn't get too cold when it was overcast, and the radiator in the car was bust. There was quite a lot of traffic around, and coupled with the mist it was making it heavy going. The street signs were all in Cyrillic, of course, and although my Russian was fluent, my brain was struggling to adjust to it, exacerbated by the shock of seeing Osborne and the pain still throbbing in my hand.

I had to figure out where to head now, and reduce the objective to a series of concrete moves and counter-moves. Counter-moves, because figuring out what the opposition was planning would be crucial if we were going to stay alive much longer. What would I do now in Yuri's shoes? From the brief flash of uniforms I'd seen in the flat, there had been both GRU and KGB officers there, so I suspected he and Andropov had had it out already, and had now agreed to join forces for both their sakes and to cooperate to their utmost to get us back. If they didn't recapture us, both their heads would be on the block. The Volgas and the men in the flat would be just the tip of the iceberg: I knew the *militsiya* had already been scrambled, and we could expect large numbers of GRU and KGB men to have been deployed, as well as the railway police, civilian police volunteers and customs and border guards. If I were stopped for speeding now, it would be the end of the line.

I wiped the sweat from my eyes and braced my shoulders, trying to suppress the fear. What if I couldn't locate the canisters, or find a way to show them to the Russians? What if I did and they simply didn't care, or didn't believe me regardless? What if I were too late? Brezhnev could have cracked under the pressure. The missiles could already be in the air.

There was something emerging in the mist by the side of the road and I peered through the window anxiously. A figure appeared, and I saw flashing lights and a red star on a white helmet.

Roadblock.

*

I removed Anton's spectacles from my jacket and put them on. It was a miracle he'd managed to take a photograph of me at all, because his lenses were so strong that within seconds my eyes began to throb and it became hard to see anything. I peered over my nose and saw that they had stretched several *militsiya* cars across the road in two rows to block it. The line of traffic was building up quickly as a result, because every time they let a car through they reversed one of the patrol cars in the first row a little way, let them through, closed the gap and then did the same in the second row. That meant they were taking a couple of minutes to clear each car. And it meant that they were being very thorough indeed.

The question was whether or not they knew about Anton. Bessmertny's wristwatch read ten past noon. It could be that Yuri and his men were still trying to sort out what had happened in the flat — or it could be that they had got on the radio and told these chaps to look for someone in Anton's car.

The car in front of me cleared through the set-up, and I was waved forward. One of the men knocked on my window and I rolled it down.

'Passport, comrade,' he said. They all looked the same — like schoolboys playing dress-up. This one had cut his chin shaving this morning, or perhaps it was a pimple he'd picked at. I handed him the passport and he took it and opened it.

'Move your head closer to me,' he said, and I did, feeling the heat of spotlights. He squinted at me, and then back down at the passport.

'What is your destination?' he asked. He had a pistol on his hip, one hand placed on it.

'Leningrad, officer.'

'A fine city. And what is the purpose of your visit there?'

There was a faint clunking sound from behind me, and I prayed he hadn't heard it in the surrounding din. I pushed Anton's spectacles up my nose — the frames were too large for me and kept slipping down — and tried not to look flustered.

'I'm visiting family,' I said.

He frowned. 'But it says here that you were born in Moscow. What family?'

The strength of the glasses was making me dizzy, and I could feel my pores opening and the sweat starting to bead.

'My second cousin,' I said. 'He moved there last year, and he wants to show me his new flat and introduce me to some of his colleagues.'

'What does he do?'

'The same as me — he's a physicist.'

He flicked through the pages, but I couldn't make out his expression through the lenses. I felt I might faint but I couldn't risk closing my eyes. If I looked over the glasses, he might think I was condescending to him so I stared straight ahead, not focusing, trying to shut off the message from my brain to my retinas so they weren't affected so much. Sirens were circling behind me, and then I heard a burst of static from one of the nearby cars, and a message being delivered through a transmitter. Was it Yuri or Sasha, telling them to stop a yellow Moskvitch with the following registration? I strained my ears but couldn't hear. Then one of the car doors slammed and I saw another officer approach and tap my man on the shoulder.

He turned, and the officer whispered something in his ear.

There was no way I could make it through two lines of cars. And at the first sign of any attempt, they would shoot.

The officers stepped back from the car. Oh, Christ. Were they about to try the boot?

The first officer stepped forward again, and leaned into my window.

'Please proceed,' he said, handing me my passport. 'My colleagues here will signal the way.'

XIII

The traffic from the roadblock began to thin out, and once I'd passed the fork for Kiev and was sure nobody was on my tail, I took some gravel lanes through a thicket of woods, then pulled over and helped Sarah climb out of the boot.

'How are you?' I said.

She grimaced, stretching her arms and legs. 'I've been better. I take it we're through, then?'

'For the time being.' She climbed into the passenger seat and I told her what had happened at the roadblock.

'So they got some sort of a message?' she said. 'I wonder what it was.'

'Good point.' I put the *militsiya* channel back on. There was some beeping and static, but then a message came on, which appeared to be on a loop. We listened to it in silence as I steered us back onto the motorway and headed towards Leningrad.

'Comrades, this is Colonel-General Shchelokov, and I have been asked by our General-Secretary, as Minister of Internal Affairs, to relay the following information to you on behalf of the Supreme Soviet. You were alerted earlier today that enemies of the state, two English spies, had escaped from our custody in Moscow, and were at large. They are, I regret to say, still at large, and must be apprehended at all costs. They are a menace to our society, and intend to cause the Soviet Union great harm. Be warned that they are also highly trained special forces operatives, and will stop at nothing, including murder.

'*Within the last few minutes, men within the Moscow* militsiya *discovered the body of one of their colleagues, Sergeant Grigor Ivanovich Bessmertny, who was left to die by these fugitives while on the run. His family has been informed, and a funeral is being arranged. It is now, I think, incumbent on all of us to honour the memory of Grigor Ivanovich Bessmertny, and bring his murderers to justice. After this message will follow a description of the fugitives, and other information that I hope will lead to their swift arrest, detention and trial. I offer my sincerest condolences to the family of Sergeant Bessmertny, and pay tribute to his gallantry and service. I call on you all, as my men and as his comrade, to hunt down his killers immediately.*'

'Christ,' said Sarah softly. I sensed there was also reproach in her voice, but I didn't regret what I'd done, even if it were true that he had died. He would have done the same – or shot me – had the situations been reversed.

'Listen,' I said, as the descriptions came on. They were mostly accurate, if perhaps a little unfair, except for one detail. 'Did you hear that? They think I'm wearing Bessmertny's uniform.'

'So? That's hardly going to bother them if they find us, is it? Your disguise isn't exactly foolproof.'

'That's not my point. Their wheels aren't turning fast enough. They've brought out a big gun, Shchelokov, to rile up the blood of the hounds. But that recording has to be at least an hour old. There was no mention of this car, or Anton, or what we're wearing now. That's why we made it through the roadblock. No doubt they'll record another message soon enough, but they're behind us for the time being. I don't think they know where we're headed yet.'

I turned to face her, and noticed that her smile was painted on.

'You need to get some sleep,' I said.

'I'd love to,' she smiled, 'but you keep talking.'

I shook off my jacket and handed it to her, and she tucked it under her chin and leaned against the window as I drove. When I looked over again a few minutes later, she was sleeping.

The traffic became sparser still, and I drove as hard as I could towards the border, my hands gripping the wheel until they turned numb. We passed cranes and television towers, restaurants and factories – the great dreary expanse of the Soviet Union. The road became rougher, and despite the low cloud cover, the temperature had dropped.

I started thinking about my life up to this point: what I had done, and what had brought me here. Or rather *who*, because it was mainly Anna who had brought me here: there was a straight line between our conversations in that Red Cross clinic in Germany in 1945 and this car in 1969. She hadn't dragged me here, though; I'd come along willingly. I had always chided her for being an idealist – but she had always known that I was one, too.

'You like to discuss specific events, Paul, but you avoid any discussion of principles. Don't you feel that society would be better if we were all equal – no more rich and poor?'

'And milk and honey flowing throughout the land? Of course. But it's a dream.'

'Everything is a dream if you do nothing about it. What have you been fighting for these last years? Wasn't it for a better world?'

'A world free of Nazism, yes.'

'Is that all you have learned? So now we simply return to what was before – the same old ways, the same old systems?'

'Yes. There was nothing wrong with them.'

'I don't think many people would agree with you, Paul. I think the last five years have brought everything into focus. Yes, Nazism was a great evil, and conveniently enough for your country many millions of my countrymen have died extinguishing it. But we cannot now be satisfied with simply living in a world that is not evil. Many of us want to live in a world that is fair, a world that has a chance of keeping peace between all men, instead of waging war on each other every few decades because one nation wants more of the cake than another. I never wanted to live in a country ruled by the Germans. But I don't want to be ruled by the Americans or the British, either . . .'

I had let myself be persuaded because, despite my token resistance, I'd been dissatisfied that the war had ended with no clear resolution. It did indeed seem as though we were about to return

to the old ways again, as though nothing had changed in the intervening bloodbath.

And, more simply, I'd fallen for her.

The music on the radio ended, and led into an international news
bulletin. I turned it up. I didn't think there would be anything of
any importance in it, but you could never tell. The first item was an
interview with a cosmonaut who had been part of the Soyuz 7 mission.
No mention was made of the fact that the Americans had put a man
on the moon. Perhaps they hadn't made that public either.

The next item was about a military coup that had just taken
place in Somalia, which was talked of in ecstatic terms by the
announcer – presumably there had been Soviet support for it. After
that, there was a report on the forthcoming talks on arms limitation with the Americans in Helsinki, which had apparently been
in dispute for some time. The tone was generally positive, but the
suggestion was that the Americans had already ceded to Soviet
demands for the talks to take place on their terms; I wondered if
the mention of it was deliberate. Well, everything was deliberate
with the Soviets when it came to the dissemination of news, but
was this a more precise message and, if so, who was its intended
audience and what reaction was it intended to spark? The delay in
the *militsiya* message suggested it wasn't directed at us, and it seemed
unlikely that such a report would make any difference to the
Americans if they truly were planning an attack.

An alternative was that it had been prepared earlier, say yesterday,
as part of a wider strategy to present the Americans in a bad light
over the talks, and it wasn't related to the current crisis. But no
wonder they were so bloody jittery: they'd lost the big prize in the
space race, were in a border dispute with the Chinese and just as
they were coming out of long negotiations with the Americans
over weapons reduction talks, Nixon had decided to fly some
nuclear-armed B-52s directly towards their border. Coupled with
a supposed chemical attack on two heavily fortified naval bases,
they'd snapped.

The bulletin came to an end. Once again, there had been no mention of a chemical attack, but I guessed they would reveal that only once they had retaliated, if then. There might not be a news service in place after a nuclear war, and there would probably be few people alive to listen to its broadcasts.

I suddenly wanted to forget the lot of it: the U-boat, the mustard gas, the men in the bunker in Moscow. Perhaps if we managed to escape over the border, we could head somewhere else instead, Sarah wearing my jacket in cars in other countries, smiling that soft smile.

I blinked the thought away and locked my wrists on the wheel. As I passed a restaurant by the side of the road, I remembered we hadn't eaten anything apart from a few stale biscuits at Anton's flat. I looked across at Sarah and realized that if we were going to get over the border it might be an idea to gather our strength. I pulled over a few miles later at a roadside restaurant with steam coming from the windows, and gently woke her.

We took a table facing the door and a surly, barrel-chested waitress walked over. I picked up the menu and ordered *kotlety* with black bread and coffee. The waitress curtly informed us that the food would take several minutes to prepare and sauntered off.

Sarah stifled a yawn, and I found myself aping her. I'd been driving for five hours without a break. I started going through my plan to cross the border, keeping my voice down to barely a murmur.

'Is it dark enough?' Sarah said. It was twilight now, the sky just a greying pink on the horizon.

'It'll have to do.' There was nothing to do now but head full pelt for the target, and hope. We would fill up fast with fuel and get going. I glanced through to the kitchen to see if there was any progress on the meal and saw that sitting on the shelf behind where the waitress was standing was a small transistor radio. And that she was talking to someone in the kitchen, and nodding towards us.

'I'll explain the rest in the car,' I said. 'We have to get out of here.'

I left a few token coins on the table, and we made for the door. The waitress came running out after us, but we were already at the car.

*

I headed back onto the road, putting my foot down. It had been a stupid, foolish, *stupid* bloody mistake. The *militsiya* would now be told precisely where we were, and they would hand the information over to Yuri and Sasha soon enough. I had just lost our advantage, and had painted a bull's-eye on our rear ends to boot, all because of my empty belly, which now felt even emptier.

I put my foot down, and a little less than two hours after leaving the restaurant we passed Leningrad, after which I cut around Vyborg and drove to its outskirts. As we approached the *pogranichnaya polosa*, the twelve-mile protected zone around the frontier, I took a detour into a gap in the undergrowth by the side of the road and pulled up. I took Anton's forgeries out of my jacket and placed them in the glove compartment – they would only help to identify us now. I told Sarah that if we were caught we would claim to be geologists.

One of the Russian playwrights, Denodovski, had defected at a literary fair in 1962, and in reviewing his debriefing documents I'd come across a curious mention he had made of the border conditions. He had said that on a trip to Karelia years earlier, when he'd been part of a group of geologists, the whole lot of them had been detained for three days by the border guard because they didn't have documents proving who they were. This, he claimed, was because the KGB had in fact banned geologists and certain other experts from carrying documents: they were afraid a foreign government might rob them and then use their specialized documents to justify a scientific presence near border areas and infiltrate the Soviet Union. But this meant that there was one valid reason not to have documents near the border.

Well, it wasn't the best cover in the world – they would probably only need to make a couple of telephone calls to establish from our descriptions alone that we were fugitives wanted for murder and various crimes against the state. But if we were caught, it would probably all be over anyway.

'Ready?' I asked, switching off the ignition.

She nodded, and we began to make our way through the bushes, treading very carefully. There were men with dogs patrolling this area, as well as three security fences, tripwires and watchtowers. But the entire length of this border was secured in this way, so this was as good a spot as any to attempt to cross.

Night had fallen now, but there was still some visibility. The mist had returned, though — swathes of it covered the ground and a foot or so above it — and I found that if I crept on my belly I could move for several yards at a time following bands of it between bushes and trees. I motioned to Sarah to do the same. I picked up a small stick and used it to feel in front of me for trip-wires. After I'd been doing this for fifteen minutes or so, I caught sight of the turret of a watch-tower poking out from a large clump of pines to my left: it wasn't quite a forest, but there was a lot of cover there. I pointed it out to Sarah, and we started making our way towards it, keeping as close to the ground as possible, watching for any sign of men or dogs.

I wanted to make a beeline directly for the watchtower for several reasons. Border control towers often lack heating in order to focus the minds of the guards, but even that doesn't always work and sentries in watchtowers tend to be less alert than their colleagues on the ground. One of my contingency plans for defection had involved making my way across from Finland, so I knew from studying the towers on the other side of the border that it was possible to avoid several lines of guard positions by crawling directly under the towers, where there were no additional sentries posted besides the men in them. I had no idea whether the Soviets used the same system on this side, because my plan had involved simply walking up to the nearest guard after crossing the frontier and surrendering, then waiting for the local KGB chief to be contacted and my bona fides to be established. We would simply have to hope.

Luckily, the mist was holding, and as we moved deeper into the woods I found I could cover ground a lot faster than before, when I'd had to stop every five seconds to find the next spot of cover. Unfortunately, I could see that Sarah's stamina was already flagging, and she was stopping not for cover but to catch her breath. I wasn't faring as well as I'd hoped I would, either. Earlier I had all but forgotten the ache in my hand, but now it came back as a stabbing pain and I found myself feeling disoriented.

I blinked to try to snap myself out of it. This was no time to start hallucinating. Well, at least I no longer had my Nigerian fever slowing me down. It was quite a year I'd had: I'd caught a deadly African disease, been shot at, tricked, exposed as a traitor, tortured by a madman in a dungeon in Sardinia and hunted to within an inch of my life. And now here I was, with the world on borrowed time, crouching by a pine tree in Russia with a woman I barely knew – and just a few miles away from the West again.

It was colder now, perhaps below freezing, and Anton's clothes didn't offer much protection. It was getting darker with every passing moment and the temptation to stand up in the ground mist was enormous, but we were safest here, creeping along side by side. Ahead of us, finally, I saw the criss-cross structure of the traditional wooden watchtower, and I tried to block out everything as I made the additional effort to keep as low as possible and move in fluid, unnoticeable movements, elbow over elbow, feeling the grass beneath me respond almost as though I were a snake, or a fish swimming through a current.

As the feet of the watchtower came into view, I felt something on my back. I turned, thinking someone had touched me, before I realized it was rain. My spirits sagged. Rain was good in one sense, in that it worsened the border guards' visibility. But in another sense it was terrible, because it released the body's natural scents, and dogs might pick up on those. But I couldn't see or hear any dogs around here. Perhaps they were taking it easy on a Monday on this part of the border. Perhaps this wouldn't be quite as difficult as we had . . .

The bark came suddenly, and made my shirt vibrate on my back.

I froze, and heard a rustle next to me as Sarah froze too.

It came again, and this time I located it — it was about twenty yards away, to our right. Two barks from two different dogs. They worked in pairs.

Do not panic. Now is not the time to panic.

Elbow over elbow. Move away, to cover. I could no longer see Sarah, but hoped she was doing the same.

There was a shout from somewhere above. The sentry in the tower wanted to know what was happening, talking either to the dogs or to a colleague on the ground.

'He's heard something!' It was his colleague replying, and he was close, perhaps twenty or thirty feet away.

Shit.

The rain was coming down in sheets now, and it was starting to hurt as it hit my spine and my calves. It was loud, as well, but that was good, because any senses it overrode for those hunting us helped. Elbow over elbow, elbow over elbow — just a few more yards to go. I couldn't see where the dogs' handler was, but border guards wore green uniforms precisely so they wouldn't be seen.

Finally, I made it under the watchtower. I was dry, at least, and hopefully that would mean my scent didn't get any stronger. But I had no real cover: no bushes, no trees; nothing but the wooden stilts holding up the tower. I squinted out into the darkness but couldn't see any sign of Sarah in the low mist. I grabbed hold of one of the stilts to lessen my own visibility, pressing myself into it, every muscle tensed. I clamped my eyes shut: children do it and think they cannot be seen, and we laugh at them. But I didn't dare open them, partly because the surface of my eyes might reflect light and give me away, partly through fear.

'Which way, boy?'

It was just one of the dogs that had picked up the scent, then. The voice was harder to locate now, but that was because the sound of the rain was drowning him out, rather than the distance. They might be even closer now – not yet close enough to see through the mist and rain, but close enough to smell or hear me.

There was a faint padding noise behind me, and I opened my eyes a fraction and saw the outline of Sarah's head emerging through the darkness. She had made it under, too. I reached out a hand and caught hold of her, and then pulled her in to the stilt. She was shaking very gently, and I covered her with my arms and pressed against her, urging her to control her fear, and thus her movements.

There was another vibration in the ground, and the front of my skull tingled as I realized it was the dog coming across the grass. It was heading straight for us. Gooseflesh formed on my arms and neck, as I waited for the animal to pounce on us. And then the vibrations stopped. It must be able to see us now, surely? I could hear it panting over the sound of our own breathing.

I stayed as still as I could, breathing through my mouth. Dogs see in monochrome and find it hard to focus over distance, so I hoped it saw four fuzzy grey wooden stilts holding up the tower through a screen of mist and rain. As a result of their vision, dogs mainly react to sources of movement, after which they investigate sound and scent. But in this case I thought the dog had been alerted by scent, the smell of our bodies brought out by the rain and exacerbated by our physical exertions over the last few hours. Now it was waiting to see if any of the stilts moved.

Judging by its reactions so far, this was a guard dog rather than a tracker. If so, it would be relying on air scent rather than following ground scent over a distance. That was an advantage, because air scent disperses more quickly. Now that we were under the tower and out of the rain, our scent would be harder to locate again. On the other hand, this type of dog would also have been trained to attack once it found its quarry.

It took a few steps closer to the tower, and barked again.

'Where are you, boy?'

I tried not to take too much hope from the question. It suggested the handler couldn't see through the rain either, and he would have much better eyesight than his dog. But it wasn't necessarily sight that would give us away. I could feel Sarah's heart hammering through her chest, as she could no doubt feel mine. The dog would be able to hear our heartbeats once it was within five feet of us.

If he found us, I'd have to kill him, because his training dictated he would try to kill us. Attack dogs are often overconfident – in training, they always win – and that might lead to mistakes. But it was a slim hope. I clasped my fist around the twig I'd been using to check for trip-wires. Could I use it? No, it would snap. I would have to use my hands. But then we would have to deal with the handler as well. And where was the other dog?

I had to calm down, because my heart was now thumping like a Salvation Army drum and I didn't want to add to the pheromones of fear and stress we would both be giving off. I tried to find a pleasant memory to latch onto, and the warmth of Sarah's skin reminded me of how she had looked that night in the embassy in Rome – her honey-blonde hair, eyes ringed with kohl, the white evening gown . . . But then I heard her catch her breath, and I thought instead of her in the Lubyanka, and saw a man attaching electrodes to the same arms that now held onto me in the darkness. She was here because of me and my actions. I'd promised myself I would keep her from harm in Moscow, and I'd failed. I had to get us through this. I couldn't fail her again.

Calm. Think of pleasant memories, pleasant memories . . . It was useless – all my memories ended badly. But I had to find one. And then it came to me: Miss Violet, the old tabby cat my parents had adopted off the street in Cairo; I'd played with her on school holidays. I thought of her great piles of fur, and running my hands through it to make her purr, and the way she had jumped on my lap, narrowing her eyes in pleasure . . .

Vibrations under my feet. I tensed, ready to leap up and strike.

But the vibrations were getting softer, fading.

The dog had turned around.

'Come on, boy. Let's get back into the hut, shall we, and stop playing games?'

*

I stood there, holding Sarah in my arms against the thin wooden strut. Above us, the sentry continued making his rounds. Sweat started pouring off me, as if in delayed reaction to the stress, and then it began to cool, sticking to my skin.

After a few minutes, Sarah very gently turned around. Her hands reached for my face, and then her lips grazed mine, and an electric current ran through me. I reached for her hands, and placed my fingers on her mouth. We weren't out of this yet. We were still in the Soviet Union.

Once the rain had subsided a little, I crouched down in the mist and indicated with my hand in hers which direction we were to go in. Once I was satisfied she understood, I set off, making sure I could hear the sound of her breathing. After we had inched forward like this for what seemed like hours, I finally made out the first fence, a wire one. After watching for some time, I concluded that there were two border guards patrolling this stretch, but neither had dogs and after they passed each other there was a three-minute gap before either of them reappeared again. If the mist held, we should be able to get across the stretch in that time.

While scouting the situation, I'd crept up to the fence where the shadow was deepest and had shovelled away some of the earth with my hands. As soon as the guards passed each other, I turned on my back and, using a stick to prop up the wires, shimmied my way under the lowest line of wires. I could see the whites of Sarah's eyes against the darkness, following my every move, and I watched as she carried out the same manoeuvre, a fraction of a second behind me. Once we were through, we began crawling to the other side, and carried out the same procedure. I'd lost count in my head and didn't want to waste any time looking at my wristwatch, but I reckoned we were already approaching the three-minute mark.

But we had made it through, and it seemed that the game was now more a test of our stamina. There were two other fences, and they were of the same type. The first only had one patrol guard, and was much easier to get through as a result, but the final fence had three guards. By now I was exhausted and could tell that Sarah was as well. But we had come this far.

She helped me dig the earth away and then we waited for the guards to pass and shimmied under as we had done before. But this time we'd been a little careless, because there was more of an incline here and we hadn't dug deep enough, so that just as we were coming free on the other side one of the coils of wire caught on my cheek and pulled at it. Without meaning to, I let out a cry, which I immediately muffled. But at once there was a bark. It was followed by the sound of footsteps and raised voices. The game was up.

'*Run!*' I whispered to Sarah, clambering to my feet. But I couldn't obey my own instruction, and was conscious of a searing pain and blood dripping down my face. There was a line of trees in the near distance and I watched as Sarah's silhouette stumbled towards it, but I was struggling to follow – my feet were slipping on the grass and my knees were shaking, and I fell before I'd gone even a few yards. Seconds later I was helped up by my arm, and I took in that the sleeve holding me was camouflaged. Somewhere to the left there was a dog on a leash, and the dog seemed interested in me. But I wasn't interested in the dog.

'I'm a geologist,' I said pathetically, placing the palm of my hand against my cheek to staunch the flow. 'I'm a geologist.'

There was no reply, and I looked up and saw that there were several men standing around me. My vision was starting to blur now, perhaps as a result of the fall, but a chill ran through me as I took in that they were all wearing gas masks. The masks were painted a sickly grey colour, and as a result it was like looking at a shoal of monstrous underwater creatures. It was all the more monstrous because the fact that they were wearing them could mean only one thing: a warning had been given.

This realization was confirmed by their behaviour. Without another word, they took hold of me, strapped me to a stretcher and carried me aboard a vehicle. As I came up the ramp, I saw another stretcher was already in there, and on it lay a beautiful woman in a grey dress with short hair, her eyes closed. My heart sank. Sarah hadn't made it more than a few yards farther than I had. There was no hope, then – none at all.

The engine started up and we set off at great speed. I closed my eyes and tried not to panic, focusing instead on the pain in my cheek, and when that wasn't enough I located the pain in my hand and thought about that as well.

Minutes later, my eyes opened again, my senses jarred by the squeal of metal: the doors of the jeep were opening, and I was being lifted out. It was still raining, and large drops splashed against my face. I could hear frantic but muffled orders being shouted around me, along with some sharp scraping sounds I couldn't identify. The angle of my body suddenly inclined steeply. Directly ahead I caught a glimpse of a bizarre structure, made of enormous blocks of stone covered in moss and camouflage – a bunker. I looked up at the sky, the water pouring from it, and the cloud directly above me seemed to redden and expand. As the stretcher entered a dark, cool space and began descending a flight of steps, I knew that I had failed, and that Brezhnev had finally done it.

XIV

I was being hunted by a pack of wolves through a ravaged countryside, but there was something wrong with my face. It was slowly
peeling away. Somewhere behind me, Colin Templeton shouted
orders at men wielding spears, laughing as they chased me. Anna
was there, too, caring for the dead on the battlefield, men without
eyes. I watched as she leaned down to kiss one on the mouth . . .

I woke, sweating, and when I tried to move realized instantly
that my hands and feet were manacled. It was dark, and it took a
few seconds for my eyes to adjust and work out what was directly
in front of them: the ceiling, made out of concrete, just a couple
of inches away, and an exposed wire jutting out of it. With my
nightmares still fresh in my head and no idea where I was, I cried
out in terror. I stopped immediately, because the proximity of the
ceiling meant that the sound bounced back, nearly deafening me.
And I was aware that there was someone in the room with me.

'Sarah?'

There was no reply for a few moments. Then: 'Yes.'

She was in the bunk beneath me.

'Are you all right?'

Silence.

'It's happened, hasn't it?'

She started sobbing and I looked up in despair, feeling as if I
might cry too, but finding I was unable to.

*

We lay there in the darkness for a time, trying not to think of what the future might hold, balanced between a nightmare and reality. Then, as if by magic, light crept into the room – someone had entered. A hand reached over and loosened the manacles on my ankles, and then released Sarah. After being pulled down a small stepladder, I found myself standing next to Sarah on a cement floor, facing two stocky men armed with machine-pistols.

They prodded us out of the room and along a narrow corridor, past rough concrete walls. One of them opened a thick steel door and we were pushed into a tiny room that contained nothing but a small wooden desk, a couple of plastic chairs and a naked bulb. I was pressed down into one of the chairs and Sarah into the other, and then the men took up position by the door, their hands on their weapons, their eyes expressionless. They hadn't said a word to either of us.

I stared at both of them with amazement. The country above us had just been destroyed, yet they were still gamely following orders as though nothing had happened. I hadn't thought the discipline went that deep, even here. Perhaps it was something to do with the training – or the bunker we were in. While the British ones had reserved space for cabinet ministers, royalty and civil servants, this one seemed to have been designed for the military, and infantry at that. Pack them in like sardines in a tin, with an inch's breathing space – I couldn't understand the logic of it. Perhaps they were intending to wait until the fallout had dissipated and then emerge and strike back, swelling over the border in their tanks and street-sweepers. Well, it wouldn't surprise me. All the British contingency plans had been riddled with holes, because nobody had had the balls to point out the truth: there was no possible way to survive a nuclear attack.

Not in the long term, anyway. Civil servants had wasted years writing documents and setting aside budgets for depots that would contain tons of flour, yeast and even sugary biscuits. But the brutal reality was that much of the world had been destroyed, and nobody was going to live long enough to rebuild it.

Most people would have been killed instantly in the first strikes. But the minority who had survived, like me and Sarah and whoever else was in this bunker, would suffer a much worse fate. We would struggle on for a couple of months down here and in other places like it, fighting among ourselves over the rapidly dwindling water and food supplies. At some point, someone would insist that the only option left was to go outside again and see if more water could be found, or search for those holes in the ground with the sacks of flour in them. A few souls would venture out, only to die slowly of radiation poisoning. The rest of us would sit down here waiting for them to return, gradually going mad. People would soon start to kill each other, and then themselves. But there would be little or no life on the surface for hundreds and hundreds of miles – and that meant that there was no way to survive in the long term. It didn't matter how many bunk beds you had.

The door opened and a man marched into the room. He was wearing a leather coat over his uniform so I couldn't make out his rank, but the sentries saluted him so he was obviously the bigwig. He was a tall man, completely bald, and with cheekbones so pronounced that his head resembled a skull. He somehow seemed precisely the sort of figure to meet in this situation: a god of the underworld. He pulled out a chair on the other side of the table, seated himself in it and leaned across the desk, staring at the two of us with bright blue eyes.

'We have little time,' he said, 'so I will dispense with the preliminaries.' He spoke in heavily accented English, which took me by surprise. 'I have the following information about you, which I wish you to confirm. You are British spies by the name of Paul Dark and Sarah Severn, and you have escaped from imprisonment in Moscow. My understanding is that you escaped from a moving car while being transported to the Lubyanka.'

'All right,' I said. 'We are. I couldn't give a damn any more. In fact, I want to die, and the sooner the better.'

Sarah turned to me, her eyes dulled with fear. I had brought her too far. Osborne had been right: all the women I ever cared about died – Mother, Anna, Vanessa. Now Sarah would die, too. I hadn't been able to save her, or anyone else. Better I go too, and fast.

The skull-faced man leaned back in his chair, and placed a couple of long, slender fingers to his lips. 'I don't understand.'

I shrugged. 'I would rather you did it than I do it myself. I don't intend to take up anyone's rations. It's my fault all this has happened, so let's get it over with quickly. A bullet to the back of the head, please.'

He took this in, and then leaned over the desk again.

'What madness is this?' he whispered. 'I have treated both of you remarkably well, Mister Dark. I arranged for your wounds to be fixed, and I even let you rest for a short time. I could have made life much worse for you, you know. You were caught crossing our border. And this is how you repay my kindness, by talking about rations like a crazy man? Yes, I will certainly have you shot if you don't start explaining yourself.'

I stared at him, and placed my hand against my cheek. There were stitches in it, brand new. I'd forgotten about cutting myself against the underside of the fence. There was something wrong with him. Not just with his words, but the whole manner in which he had said them: despite his demonic appearance, there was culture there, sophistication, altogether different from Sasha and the other thugs I'd encountered so far. His English was good, but his accent was peculiar.

Yes. The realization hit me. He wasn't a Russian at all, but a Finn. We'd reached Finland. We must have somehow made it across the line before the missiles had landed. That explained his comment about catching us crossing his border – in part, anyway. But what on earth did any of this matter *now*?

'When was the first strike?' I asked him. 'And how secure is this bunker?'

He pushed his chair back and stood, nostrils flared, and I wondered if he was about to hit me. And then something dawned on *him*, and he sat down again.

'Why did you try to cross the border?' he said.

I stared at him blankly. 'Do you really not know?'

He shook his head. 'There's a man called Proshin of military intelligence in Moscow. I received a signal from him a few hours ago: he asked that we step up the vigilance on our side of the border in case two British agents matching your descriptions tried to make it across. This was a highly unusual request, but it was also from an unusually senior source, so I listened. Especially because Proshin claimed that it was vital to the security of both of our countries that you be stopped at once.

'As a result, I immediately sent out your descriptions to my men and told them to keep watch for you. Shortly after doing so, you did try to cross our border, and we discovered you. Proshin has been informed of this, and I have granted permission for him and a small group of his men to cross our border to apprehend and interrogate you here, before they take you back to the Soviet Union. He asked me to keep you under armed guard until he arrives, which should be within the next' – he looked at his wristwatch – 'ten minutes or so. But I would like some answers from you before he gets here, because you have illegally crossed my border. So perhaps you can tell me why you did that, and indeed why you fled from Moscow in the first place?'

I looked at him, trying to take in all the new information and weigh it against the possible. He must be bluffing. I had seen the cloud redden above me, expanding – or had I somehow imagined it? I looked over at Sarah, but she seemed as confused as I was.

'Are you seriously trying to tell me that there *hasn't* been an attack yet?' I said.

He pressed his hands together, his forefingers sticking out like a gun and resting under his chin.

'What sort of attack?'

'Nuclear, of course!'

He shook his head. 'Are you trying to tell me that there has been one?'

'Have you looked outside lately?'

He clenched his jaw, and the hollows in his cheeks deepened further. 'I'm losing patience rapidly, Mister Dark. Yes, I have looked outside lately. I arrived here only a few minutes ago. I would advise that you explain yourself to me, and that you do so quickly. As I say, Proshin and his men will be here very soon. But I'm perfectly willing to tell them that, unfortunately, you were foolish enough to try to escape from confinement, and that as a result I had no alternative but to shoot both of you.'

'If there hasn't been an attack, what the hell are we doing in a nuclear bunker?'

'We're not. This place wasn't built to withstand a nuclear attack. We're in Miehikkälä, and this bunker is part of the Salpa defence line, built during the last war to protect us from the Russians. I had you brought here because I was flying directly from Åbo and there is a small area nearby in which a helicopter can land, and because I felt confident you wouldn't be likely to be able to escape from this place.'

'But why were your men wearing gas masks?' asked Sarah. 'They had them on when they found me, and . . .' She trailed off. 'They had gas masks.'

He took a deep breath. 'Some people farther down this coast have been affected by strange injuries in the last couple of days – we think some sort of hazardous chemical has drifted into the waters here, and a lot of fishermen and sailors have been badly afflicted, with their skin peeling away. Some of my patrols have been helping move people who have been affected, and are trying to investigate the source. All of them are wearing gas masks as a temporary precaution until we find out exactly what the cause of this is and how dangerous and contagious it is.'

My stomach had tightened, and I realized he wasn't bluffing. 'It's mustard gas,' I said. 'A particularly powerful form of it. It has leaked from a wrecked German U-boat on the seabed just off the coast of Söderviken. If there hasn't been an attack, you have to call Washington at once, or London.' I stopped. Neither would work. There was no reason why anyone would believe the head of the Finnish border guard, especially as *we* were the source of the information. We still had to get to the U-boat ourselves, find the canisters and show them to the Russians.

I tried another tack. 'You have to help get us there,' I said in Swedish, and he raised an eyebrow.

'You speak Swedish?'

He had said Åbo, rather than Turku, which was the Finnish name for it. 'My mother was from Åbo,' I said. 'Look, the Russians are convinced this chemical accident is part of a plot by the West to start a nuclear war. People at their bases in Paldiski and Hiiumaa have been showing injuries like the ones you mention. As you know that the symptoms are being experienced at several points along this coastline, and as it must be clear to you that until a few seconds ago both of us were utterly convinced that a nuclear attack had taken place, surely you can see I'm telling the truth about this. But the danger hasn't passed – a real nuclear strike could be ordered at any moment. You have to help us get to Åland, as soon as possible, so we can reach the U-boat and prove to the Russians that there has not been a chemical attack.'

He paused for a moment, then stood again, and walked briskly to the door.

'Thank you for the explanation, Mister Dark,' he said. I made to protest, but he hushed me. 'Please let me speak. You escaped from confinement in Moscow, and I have no doubt you will also try to escape from here. You are both clearly extremely resourceful and dangerous operatives.' He grabbed hold of the door handle. 'And I think,' he said, 'that you will succeed in escaping from here.'

I stared at him.

'You mean—'

He placed a finger to his lips. 'I lost several members of my family in the wars with the Russians. There is no, as I think you say in English, love lost between me and them. I don't believe someone could easily have invented the story you have just told me. I can, on the other hand, imagine that the Russians would react just as they have done if your story were true. So I will take a chance. Proshin and his colleagues will be furious with me, I'm sure, but they won't be able to prove I have done anything. In any case this country is not, I repeat *not*, a part of the Soviet Union. I would rather take the risk you are lying to me than that you are not, considering what you have said. But you have, if I understand you, very little time left. So let's not talk any more. It makes me uncomfortable – I've said more in this conversation than I have to my wife all this year. There is a helicopter upstairs. Shall we go?'

I looked at him, dumbfounded, and nodded. He smiled again, the most wonderful smile, and then opened the door.

*

Standing in the flattened grass outside the bunker was an Agusta Bell helicopter with orange and green livery. As we approached it, I turned to the Finn.

'I don't even know your name.'

He pulled off his coat and handed it to one of the sentries.

'General Jesper Raaitikainen.' He shouted at the pilot to come down from the cockpit, and then started to climb up himself. I looked on with alarm.

'What are you doing? We can fly this.' I pointed at Sarah. 'You have to stay here and meet Proshin, surely.'

He shook his head. 'Oh, no. I'm not sticking around for that bastard. Captain!' The pilot turned, and Raaitikainen spoke to him in rapid-fire Finnish. The pilot saluted smartly, then headed back to the entrance of the bunker. 'Nothing to worry about,' said Raaitikainen, smiling. 'My men will tell Proshin you kidnapped me with a pistol, and there was nothing they could do about it.'

'I would rather we went alone,' I said.

He ignored me, and clambered into the cockpit. 'Mister Dark, you're lucky you're going anywhere at all. I might also point out that you have no idea where we are, or how to get to Söderviken. But I do.' He looked down at us, and his face was again as stern as that underworld god I'd initially taken him for. 'I advise you to climb in here with me now — unless you wish to wait here for Proshin after all?'

Sarah looked at me, and I realized we had no choice. I helped her up, then climbed up myself, considering what his coming along might mean. He was right that we didn't know how to get to Söderviken, but what would happen once we got there? We needed to find a way to convince the Russians that the leak was an accident rather than an attack: taking along a general from a Western ally wouldn't help us do that, and they might believe it was another deception operation as a result. But it was better than no chance at all.

As Raaitikainen was busy checking the controls, one of the sentries began running towards us and shouted something up to him in Finnish. He listened, then turned to me and Sarah.

'The Russians have been sighted on the track leading here. Let's go!'

Raaitikainen shouted at his man on the ground, who saluted and stood back, and as he went through the checks and put the engine into warm-up we started to strap ourselves in.

XV

The world far below us was peaceful and still. As my eyes adjusted to the darkness, I dimly made out a landscape of ice and water, and at one point even thought I saw, clinging to the rocks of one of the small islands, a cluster of those curious miniature pines I'd seen in 1945. No doubt it was partly because I'd recently believed that nuclear Armageddon had already struck, but the serenity of it seemed almost unbearable.

If Brezhnev launched a strike, the Americans would retaliate with their Polaris missiles. The British plan was to target forty-eight Soviet cities, and the Americans would no doubt do the same. Leningrad, Paldiski and others were on that list, and while the blast wouldn't reach here, the fallout certainly would. I wondered if the B-52s were still in the air, circling as they waited for their instructions, and if so what the men in those cockpits were thinking as they looked down.

'You don't happen to have any diving equipment on board, do you?' I shouted over the noise of the engines.

'No!' Raaitikainen replied. 'But one of the coastguard stations in Åland will.' He caught my look and clapped me on the back. 'Don't worry. We'll find a way through this. We're nearly there now. Does it look like the world is about to end?'

I shook my head and began to reply, when the engine gave a shrill whine and we began to tilt.

'What's that?' Sarah called out.

'An engine?' I said, but realized almost at once that it wasn't that, but a shot.

I craned my neck, and saw the lights of a helicopter directly behind us. It looked like an Mi-8T, and it was firing its two PK machine guns directly at us.

'Oh, God,' moaned Sarah, rocking back into her seat. Raaitikainen was grappling with the stick, sweat pouring from his face, and I knew that we must have been hit somewhere. I unstrapped myself to help him take control, but we suddenly lurched again and I was thrown against the side of my seat, hitting my jaw and cutting open my cheek wound.

Dazed by the pain and dizzy from the motion, I tried to bring myself to a standing position, but I could see it was a losing battle. Raaitikainen had also been thrown, and was no longer holding the stick, and Sarah was now slumped back, her mouth in a rictus – we were in freefall. I crawled along the floor of the cockpit towards Raaitikainen's seat, but the sound of the engines suddenly rose in pitch and then there was an enormous crunching. I guessed that the rotors had hit something. I looked out of one of the perspex panels and saw a greyish-brown block of something, and then realized it was ice, and that we were underwater. I shouted across at Raaitikainen but he didn't reply. When I looked up, I saw why: the upper part of his head was covered in blood, and his eyes had rolled upwards. I fought my way towards Sarah and unfastened her seat belt. We were kicking at the forward section doors when the water started coming in.

*

Panicking, I gave another kick to the door, and this time it was enough to get it open. Freezing water gushed through in a torrent, nearly drowning me and pushing me back, but I kicked my legs harder until I was through the gap and out into the water. I couldn't see Sarah and tried to shout out to her, but it was useless.

The gush of water in the helicopter had shocked me, but now

it was chilling me through to my bones, and I knew I wouldn't be able to last long in it. My heart was seizing, and my core temperature had plummeted within the last few seconds. As I tried to swim to the surface, my body was suddenly wracked with a tremor. I swam desperately towards the chunks of ice, found one and grabbed hold of it, but then more tremors broke through me, and I focused all my mental energy on trying to stop them. But they kept coming, sharper and sharper. Here came another one. Clench, tighten, stop it, shut it down. I was losing control. Soon they would take me over completely. The effort was getting to me, and I realized my cognitive faculties were being affected. If this continued, my body would shut down, and death would soon follow.

This realization strengthened my mind and I kicked upwards with more force. Finally, I saw the surface of the water coming to meet me. I kicked and kicked again, until I reached the surface and was breathing, my teeth chattering as I caught my breath and took in great lungfuls of air.

We had crashed on the coastline of one of the islands, with the cockpit submerged in the water and the rest of the helicopter jutting out of it. I looked around for Sarah and saw her a few feet away, her head out of the water but her arms flailing. I looked up and immediately spotted the Russians above us. They were quite a long way up but had already begun descending, and they had seen us, too: machine-gun fire immediately split the water, and men were starting to climb out of the cockpit and down ropes.

With my arms still quaking, I grabbed hold of part of the skids and hoisted myself up onto the shoreline. Then I began making my way around the rocks to get closer to Sarah.

'Grab hold of me!' I shouted at her, stretching out my arm. I caught hold of her hand and pulled as hard as I could, hauling her onto the rocks.

She gasped and then coughed up water. Her eyes started to close. 'Don't give up now,' I whispered. 'Please don't give up now.'

Perhaps she heard me, because she placed the palms of her hands against the rocks and lifted herself to her knees.

I helped her to her feet and pointed to a line of woods behind us.

'Can you run?' I said.

She nodded dully, and we started making our way towards the woods. There were patches of snow and black ice, but adrenalin and the survival instinct had kicked in and we somehow managed to make our way across them. We had to get to cover. I couldn't have come this far to fail.

We reached the top of a slope and I looked out at a large field, lit by the moon. There were trees all around the perimeter, but the field itself was completely barren – just grass, broken up with patches of snow and ice. No cover. Behind us, the sound of the rotors was almost deafening. I resisted the urge to look, but clearly we couldn't go back down that way. Should we skirt the edge of the field and try to get around to the other side? That would be too obvious, and too time-consuming.

We had to find people, and warmth. There was a barn with white window frames at the far end of the field and, closer, an *utedass* – an outhouse. I turned to point it out to Sarah, but she wasn't there. I looked frantically back at where we had just come from, but she had disappeared. She must have fallen, and I couldn't see her in the snow over a ridge. I began to run back towards the water when a burst of machine-gun fire broke through the trees, cracking in my ears and making me drop to the ground instinctively.

Fuck.

I started running towards the *utedass*.

I had misjudged the situation horribly. Sarah was in worse shape than I had realized, and the Russians were much closer than I'd thought – gunfire clattered behind me before I was even halfway across the stretch, and the helicopter was now coming down to land in the field. I kept running, my arms starting to flail and my legs feeling like they might give way, heading for the door of the outhouse and praying it wouldn't be the last thing I saw before the bullets hit me in the back. I reached the door and opened it, then slammed it behind me.

It was pitch dark and, unsurprisingly, smelled foul. The gunfire had stopped for a moment, and I wondered if somehow I had fooled them and they'd lost sight of me. But then I heard a voice, and recognized it at once.

'Nobody move!' shouted Sasha. 'Hold your fire until I say.' His voice was controlled, confident. He was no stamp collector any more. I leaned forward a fraction of an inch and peered through a slat in the wood. There he was, his silhouette clear against the background of snow. He was packed up in a winter coat, *ushanka* still in place. And one gloved hand was gripping Sarah by the arm. She was hanging off him, crying, and I thought I could see the tears freezing on her cheeks. He looked triumphant, like a hunter with his prize.

'Come on, Paul!' he shouted, his voice echoing off the trees. 'Time to come out now.'

There was a small bench surrounding the toilet, and I climbed onto it. I prised the lid away, my thumbs shaking, and immediately recoiled at the stench. But the hole looked too small. I kicked at the side of it with the sole of my boot until the wood splintered and the hole widened. Then I held my shoulders tightly together, and lowered myself into it. The edges chafed against my skin through the wet clothes but I was in. I felt my legs sink into the frozen dried shit and piss and leaves, and vomit rose in my throat. I was in a small dugout under the outhouse — as I had hoped, it was open all around. And beyond me were trees. I ran blindly towards them. I must have gone fifty yards before I heard Sasha shouting again. But I was away from the Russians by then — for the moment.

XVI

I watched as Sasha and several men marched across the field towards the barn, dragging Sarah along with them. Having run far enough into the trees to be out of their line of sight, I'd picked up a piece of brush and swept away the tracks behind me. I hadn't spent as much time on it as I would usually have done, though, because everything I did now had to be a compromise. I had to take precautions if I wanted to stay alive, and if I wanted to get Sarah back. But the longer I took, the less likely it was that I would be able to reach the U-boat.

Once I was confident that I'd gone far enough in, I headed towards a ridge that overlooked the far corner of the field, and climbed onto the lower branches of a large pine. It was called the Fish Hook, a simple if unexpected manoeuvre, and it meant I could observe my hunters and get an idea of their strength and what equipment they'd brought with them.

Apart from Sarah, I could make out two others in the field: Sasha and another man. Both of them looked heavily armed, but Sasha's companion was also carrying a case, which even in the moonlight I recognized as being the type they had used in the war to carry long-range transceivers. Presumably the rest of the company had been dispersed to look for me.

Sasha knocked on the door of the cottage, and after a few seconds a man opened it. I couldn't see his face, but no doubt he was alarmed at the sight of Russian soldiers with a female prisoner. Sasha gestured with his arms, pointing back towards the helicopter. Perhaps the bastard was claiming that Sarah was an injured member of his party. The door opened more widely, and Sasha, his companion and Sarah stepped into the cottage.

I lowered myself from the branches and glanced through the thicket of trees at the small bay: I could make out the ripple of water under the sky, and some bulky shapes dotted in the trees: more cottages, or perhaps boathouses? It was so quiet one could hardly imagine that there were Soviet operatives hunting me out there, but Sasha would have sent a few and they would be searching for my tracks with torches.

It was equally hard to imagine that this place might soon be contaminated by fallout, but that too was real. The Soviets would want to stop me from reaching the West as a matter of course, but I had now made it across the border and they were still chasing me – and they were shooting to kill. The fact that Sasha was here confirmed that the situation hadn't changed since I'd left Moscow this morning. The fools thought I was trying to reach someone in authority in the West so I could warn them they were about to be attacked. Brezhnev had held his hand so far, but it looked like he was still poised to launch a strike against the West, and wanted to make sure that if he did he kept it a surprise.

It was also interesting that it had been Sasha in the helicopter, not Yuri. That suggested that *he* was the Proshin who had called Raaitikainen, not Yuri. So he was Yuri's son – why hadn't I realized it before? Well, they didn't look much alike. It made perfect sense, though. Yuri had been my first handler, and Sasha had been my last. It also explained why Sasha had been so surly towards me in Moscow: he had joined the GRU to follow in his old man's footsteps and had risen through the ranks, but had been taken off proper work by his father to deal with me, and he resented it. I knew the feeling.

It also seemed that Sasha had been given the task of finding and eliminating me, as well as a hunter-killer unit with which to do it.

I'd been part of a similar group once, but that was twenty-four years ago. These men were half my age, in peak physical condition and no doubt hungry for my blood on account of Bessmertny and whatever else they'd been told I'd done. Once they had found and killed me, Sasha would signal back to Moscow and Brezhnev would launch his strike on the West – provided he was prepared to wait even that long. There was always the possibility that Sasha would signal that they were still hunting me, and he felt the time was optimal.

I was alive for the time being, but what was my best course of action now? I was on an island in the middle of the Baltic, but I had no idea which one. It might not even be anywhere near Söderviken. I was soaked to the skin, my face was smeared with blood and faeces, and I was in the danger zone for hypothermia. The tremors hadn't returned, thankfully, but my heart rate had dramatically increased after we'd crashed into the water and my entire body had tensed up, so it was taking time for it to calm down again.

I hugged myself for warmth, and wondered if I should remove my clothes. They had stuck to my skin, and my shoes were starting to break apart. In 1945, I'd brought plastic bags to place over my socks, and then another pair of socks to place over the bags, in case I had been stranded and had needed to stop the onset of frostbite. There wasn't much chance of that happening now, but it was still below freezing: icicles were hanging from the lower fronds of the tree. I was losing heat because my clothes were wet, and my training dictated that I remove them and make a fire to dry them. But I didn't have time to do that, and being naked even for a short while in this environment would probably worsen my state. I might also need to approach one of the locals, and a man in wet clothes with shit all over his face would still be more welcome than a naked one. I decided to keep my clothes on for the time being.

My only advantage against Sasha and his men was that I was alone. Although that thought wasn't exactly comforting, because they had Sarah, it also meant that I could move much more easily than they could. There were thousands of islands here, and thousands of trees, outhouses and barns dotted among them: they couldn't begin to search them all. I also had a slim psychological advantage: the Russians had massively outnumbered the Finns in 1940, and had had a rude awakening. They would be keenly aware of this, and if any of them had fathers who had died in the war a part of them would be afraid to be in Finland. Angry and determined to find me, yes – but also a little afraid.

It was also an advantage that Sasha was here, and that he had brought that transceiver. If I could reach the canisters, get them out of the water and show them to him, I might still have a chance. If I could prove that the injuries at the bases were part of an accidental leak, he could then transmit a message to that effect back to Moscow. If he did, it would hold a lot more sway than if it came from an official in the Soviet consulate in Åland, which had been my plan to date.

But the new plan meant I would have to *let* them hunt me. I'd have to keep them just close enough that they would be on hand when I reached the mustard gas. But not so close that they could kill me before then. It was a tall order, but it was all I could think of. My first task was to find a diving suit.

I sat in the tree watching, and then Sasha and the other man came out of the barn and began walking towards the north-eastern edge of the field, where there was a dirt road. I waited a few more minutes for them to make their way down the path, then slowly lowered myself out of the branches.

As I picked up a piece of brush, I registered movement in my peripheral vision, but before I could turn I was pushed back by the force of a kick to my chest and lost my balance. I thudded into the trunk of the tree, and as I tried to regain my breath, I caught sight of my assailant: his face was streaked with mud and he was raising a gun at me. He brought his forearm down in a scything motion and I leapt to my right. As I did, I caught one of the branches with my hand and it sprang back and scratched the Russian's face. He cursed, and tried to aim again, so I dived for his feet and brought him down. He landed on the back of his head, his gun falling from his hand. I leaned over and punched him in the jaw, but my chest was tight with pain and the swing was slow as a result – it hardly made any impact. He kicked out again and his boot caught me in the shoulder. He started scrabbling towards his gun, which lay a few inches away from him on the ground. I knew he was going to make it, and turn and shoot me through the eyes. Desperate, I raised my arms for the branch above me and caught hold of something cold and wet. An icicle. I snapped it off and brought it down as hard as I could, and the point penetrated his throat before he had a chance to scream.

I retrieved the pistol, another Makarov, and placed it next to me. I started to strip off his trousers, which were nice and dry, but then a loud squelching sound burst from him and I froze. It was coming from beneath his jacket, which I removed to reveal a vest with several large pouches. Grenade, signal flare, knife, rations – and a small receiver.

The static cut off, and a voice broke through.

'*Medov, Zelenin, this is Rook – any sign of the target?*'

It was Sasha.

There was another burst of static, and then a new voice: '*This is Medov. No sign of him here.*'

Static, then Sasha came on again.

'*Zelenin, how about you?*'

I stared down at Zelenin's chest, panic sweeping through me. I couldn't reply – Sasha would recognize my voice at once. Even if I tried to disguise it, he would still know I wasn't Zelenin. But if I didn't answer, he would reason that I might have killed Zelenin and send men back this way to find me.

There was no time to waste. I put the pistol and transmitter in my pockets, then stumbled through the trees, my chest aching from the high kick, my body numb with cold. Fifteen agonizing minutes later I found a small cottage in a clearing, and I climbed the steps to the door and hammered on it. A woman opened it halfway, and peered out. She was old, with matted grey hair, and wore a faded blue dress and a white shawl. I pushed past her and staggered into the hallway, my eyes adjusting to the light and taking in the simple pine furniture, a fireplace, a kettle on a stove.

'I need your help,' I said in Swedish, my breathing coming hard. 'Please . . . Please call Degerby police station and ask for Constable Lundström.'

I took in her look of fear and astonishment, and then my legs buckled and I fell to the floor.

*

Someone was shaking me by the shoulder, and I opened my eyes. Looking up, I recognized the old woman, and asked her how long I had been out.

'Not long,' she said. 'Perhaps half an hour.'

I was still on the floor, and I rose to my feet. My chest felt constricted and I was aching all over, but my head was clear. Half an hour was a hell of a long time.

'The Russians. Have you seen any?'

She shook her head, and I realized she was frightened. I had a gun on my hip.

'I don't mean you any harm,' I said, and very slowly removed the pistol and placed it on a sideboard covered in lace, next to an antique clock. Her shoulders relaxed a little.

'Did you call Lundström in Degerby?' I asked.

She nodded. 'He said he would come at once – but Degerby is quite far away. I think you should clean up and get out of those clothes. I have some for you if you would like them.'

She led me to a small but spotless bathroom, where she had laid out a shirt, a pair of narrow twill trousers and calf-high boots. There was also a basin, which she had filled with water, and beside it a towel. I thanked her, and she bowed her head and closed the door.

I removed my shirt and dipped my head in the basin, rubbing off all the shit – no wonder she had looked frightened of me. There was a glass by the tap, and I poured water into it and gulped it down, then poured some more and gulped that too.

Sarah had been captured.

I removed the rest of my clothes and climbed into the ones the old woman had left for me. They were a reasonable fit, and they were dry. I would have liked to have washed properly and treated some of my aches and pains, but there was no time for that.

Sasha and his men would now be searching every inch of this area for me, and could get here before Lundström. As if to emphasize this point, there was a burst of noise from the pile of clothes on the floor, and I reached into the trouser pocket and took out the radio receiver.

'*Medov to Rook. Current location Map C, J11. Boathouse empty.*'

'*Rook to Medov. Any sign of disturbance?*'

'*None, Rook. There are several cottages along this section – I will move on to them now.*'

'*Understood. Report back in ten minutes. We have three hours to find him.*'

The device went silent.

Three hours to find me.

I had imagined I'd seen a nuclear attack when I'd been captured at the border, but part of me had refused to believe it was possible, despite hearing Brezhnev order the missiles primed myself. Sasha's presence here in Finland confirmed that the Russians wanted to stop me from warning anyone they were about to attack, but even that hadn't quite convinced me. The message on the receiver had. There was only one reason I could think of for them needing to finding me within the next three hours: it must be the deadline they had been given by Moscow. If they hadn't stopped me by then, Brezhnev was going to go ahead and launch a strike anyway. After that, it wouldn't be long before R-hour.

I poured some more water and sipped at it, but I'd lost my thirst. I stared at the glass in my hand, at the meniscus of the water curving up to meet the sides of it. From this angle the surface was like a silvery-grey ridge, and gave the illusion of being a separate object from the water. I replaced the glass on the basin, suddenly transfixed by the surface of the water. In my mind's eye, it was as though the water was the world, and the air above it what would happen to it after a nuclear attack. Those two separate realities were only held apart by that thin silvery line between them: me.

Focus, Paul.

I picked up the transmitter and returned to the living room, where the woman was placing logs on the fire.

'Thank you for the clothes,' I said. 'They're a good fit.'

She turned to look at me.

'They belonged to my husband,' she said, her eyes cavernous. 'He died last spring.'

Jesus. What had I walked into here?

There was a banging noise. The door. We both froze. I reached for the Makarov on the sideboard, and she shuffled to the door and unlocked it. A man in a police uniform, clutching a Lahti pistol, stepped into the room, his face weather-beaten and shaven, but nevertheless familiar.

'Kjell Lundström?' I said.

He lowered the pistol and furrowed his brow.

'No, I'm his son, Jan.'

He was slimmer than his father, but otherwise had come to resemble him in the intervening years.

'Thank God!' I said. 'I need to find a diving suit at once. Can you help?'

He stared at me for a few moments and then a look of recognition crossed his face.

'You are the British lieutenant-colonel who came here in 1945.'

'Yes!' I said, surprised that he'd even remembered my rank. 'But I'm afraid there's no time for catching up. I desperately need to find a diving suit – there's a German U-boat on the seabed a few miles south of Söderviken, and I need to get to it – fast.'

I led him into the hallway and quickly told him the story. His eyes widened, but he nodded his head rapidly. 'You're in luck,' he said. 'I know where the coastguards keep all their equipment, and I believe they have a few diving suits there.'

'Great. How do we get there?'

He stretched out a hand, and gave a slightly crooked smile. 'Come with me.'

*

We bid goodbye to the woman, and left her in her cottage in the woods, perhaps wondering if the world was about to end. I brought along the Makarov and the radio receiver. Lundström had a small speedboat tied up by the jetty, and as we walked down to it I asked him how his father was doing. His mouth tightened fractionally, and he told me he had died some years previously.

'I'm sorry to hear that,' I said. 'I didn't know him, but he seemed like a good man.'

Lundström nodded, his eyes focused straight ahead. 'He was,' he said quietly.

We climbed aboard. He took the wheel and I seated myself on a low bench, taking in the smells of diesel and grease. The water was wreathed in a low mist, the surface stippled with flecks of moonlight. The helicopter had crashed in a cluster of islands called Kumlinge, and now we were heading for an island called Storklubb, or Klobbo in local dialect. Lundström handed me a torch and I shone it ahead of us to light the way. As we left the bay through bobbing buoys, small islets started to hove into view, but Lundström didn't slow for them and we passed through smoothly. I noticed a small pile of greyish-white stones had been arranged on the tip of one of the islets, contrasting against the pink granite beneath, and guessed he was also using them to navigate.

He had explained that the coastguards had several stations on the island, but that this one had diving equipment stored in a cabin away from the barracks building, and that he was confident we could creep in. He knew where they kept the key. 'There are few secrets in this place,' he said. 'Especially if you're in law enforcement.'

We were going at about fifteen knots, I thought, and every few seconds we crested a wave and cold spray hit my face and froze my jaw.

'There should be some clothes under there,' he shouted over the noise of the motor, pointing to a line of low cupboards under the seating. 'I'd advise you to put on some more layers, because it will be even colder when we get out there.'

I bent down and slid one of the cupboards open and found an old rollneck sweater, which I pulled over my head, and a pair of canvas trousers, which I placed over the dead husband's. Lundström looked like a gun dog focused on a bird: with this man's help, I might be able to make it. I just had to hope that Sarah was still in one piece. I tried to focus on the task ahead. Once I got hold of the diving suit, I would have to try to locate the U-boat and dive for the canisters. But then I would have to get them out of the water, and find Sasha again . . .

I let my thoughts spin away as the smell of pines and seaweed carried on the air. We crested a large wave and spray covered the windscreen, obscuring the view for a second. Lundström had gone quiet, his face set. He took a large map from the dashboard and consulted it. Then he cut the motor.

'We'll be coming in soon,' he said.

He steered with a more intense concentration until, about five minutes later, we came to a pass between two small islands. Lundström slowed the boat and headed towards the one on the left. He climbed out and swiftly jumped onto the shore, tying the ropes to a metal ring attached to the remains of a small wooden quay, one half of which had fallen apart.

'Ryssbryggan,' he said, as I joined him on shore and tied the other rope. 'We used to be part of the Russian Empire, you know. They built this back in the First World War.' He finished tying up and looked across at me. 'I hate the fucking Russians,' he added. His jaw clenched for a moment, and then slackened again.

The jetty led onto a narrow dirt track through dense bushes and foliage, and we swiftly made our way along it, taking care to keep our heads down. 'That's their barracks,' Lundström whispered after a couple of minutes, pointing to a greyish-white building in a clearing ahead. 'But they keep the diving equipment in there.' He pointed to a tiny cabin with white window frames positioned a few dozen feet away from the main building, right on the water.

We ducked down and started crawling through a brush of long grass. Now I saw that there was a jetty here as well, but that it was occupied by several patrol boats – Sea-Hounds or something similar – which was presumably why we'd come via the broken quay instead.

Crack.

I sat, frozen still in the grass. It was just some twigs breaking under my feet, but had anyone inside the barracks heard the noise? The outline of Lundström's head was just visible against the deep blue of the sky a few feet ahead of me, and he was utterly still. The wind rustled near us, the water lapped softly against the side of the jetty, but there were no other sounds. Finally, Lundström ducked his head; he raised the palm of his hand and gestured for me to come forward.

Less than twenty seconds later we were at the edge of the cabin. Lundström crawled onto a small step leading to the door and I saw him feeling around with his hands until he lifted a key from a ledge beneath the step. Then he pawed his way up until he was in the doorway and stood. He beckoned me to join him again and I did. He looked at me for a moment, then inserted the key. He turned it. The click sounded terribly loud in the silence, and we waited to see if anything responded. When nothing did, he slowly eased the door open, and we stepped inside.

It was even darker than it had been outside, but after a few seconds my eyes began to adjust. We were in a small hallway with two wooden doors, similar to the one we had just come through. Lundström reached for the handle of the door to the right, then leaned his shoulder into it and opened it. I followed him into a room that felt a little larger than the hallway, but which was yet darker.

'In here,' Lundström whispered from the far corner, and I walked towards the sound of his voice. I heard him unhook a latch and he told me to go in ahead of him, which I did, but at the last moment something registered – heat – and I tried to pull back, but it was too late because I felt a rough shove at the base of my neck and I stumbled and fell to the floor. I heard the door slam shut and the latch hooking into place. It was lighter here, but incredibly hot, and I looked around the room with growing fear.

This wasn't a storage room for diving equipment. It was a sauna.

*

'Jan!' I shouted out, but there was no response. Understanding swept over me. Lundström had lured me here so he could lock me in. And he had left me here to burn to death.

The heat was unbelievably intense, and my clothes were already soaked in sweat. I tore at them frantically, struggling with the boots and then kicking them off. I grabbed the gun from my pocket, but realized at once that it was too light: he'd emptied it – presumably when I'd been putting on more clothes at his suggestion.

I looked around again and began to make out a few more items in the room. There was a rectangular window low in the wall on the right and through it I glimpsed reeds and rushes and a stretch of water. Most of the room was taken up with two benches in the shape of steps to sit on, and below them was a basket filled with small wooden logs, presumably firewood for the stove. Some metal crowbars rested against the wall – perhaps to open the window? I reached for them, but they burned my hands, so I went for the wood instead. Slightly cooler. I threw one of the logs at the window, but it just bounced back at me comically. I could hardly see straight now, because sweat was pouring into my eyes, making them sting. I wanted to wipe them but my hands were also soaked and I thought I'd probably just make them worse.

As I was trying to think what to do next, a loud hissing sound made me jump. After a couple of seconds I realized what it was, as my chest started to burn up as though someone had lit a blowtorch inside me. Lundström hadn't left; he had just poured water on the stove. Somewhere behind the pain I registered that this offered me some kind of leverage, but I struggled to grip the thought for long enough to follow it through, because the pain was so searing. I wanted to scream in agony, but if I did that I might bring the coastguards running, and with them ruin any chances I might have of stopping Brezhnev from going ahead with his strike. I grunted and groaned instead, biting my upper lip and tasting the hot sweat pouring off me. I crouched as close to the ground as I could but resisted the urge to lie down because I wasn't sure if I did that I'd have the strength to get back up.

And then the hissing came again. The thought came into my mind that I was experiencing pure fear. In London during the war, the V2s had panicked everyone because the sound of their falling had been heard only after they had done their damage. But this was how terror really worked: the sound came first, then a delay, and finally the inevitable. And here it came: the heat rising again, so fast I felt my skin was going to burn off and my internal organs catch fire.

I wanted to detach my mind so I wasn't as aware of the pain, but I knew it was crucial to hold on to my thoughts if I wanted to survive. A lucid thought broke in now: he must be opening the door to add water, and judging by the speed with which he was doing it the stove was probably very near the door. If I could muster the strength to reach it, perhaps I could get out, or at least stop him from pouring on any more water. I crawled in the direction of the heat, but it was agonizing and my skin started to sting as though it were about to bleed or peel off, and I recoiled instinctively. I had to fight my instincts, but it was getting harder to think straight.

'You murdered my father,' said a voice, startling me. It was Lundström, and the gentle tone he'd used before was now choked with rage. He hadn't left me here, but was standing outside the door making sure I couldn't escape. I turned to find the precise location of his voice – he was talking to me through the crack in the door.

'Jan!' I said. 'Please, for the love of God let me out of here so we can talk about this. I have no idea what you're talking about, but I can assure you I had nothing to do with your father's death—'

'You had everything to do with it!' He laughed bitterly. 'You have no idea how many times I thought of trying to find you. Once I even planned a trip to England, but I soon realized it was useless. I knew so little about you. But now here you are; you've fallen into my lap. It must be fate.'

I tried to move nearer to the door again, but the waves of heat were still too strong.

'For Christ's sake!' I said. 'Please open this fucking door before we all die!'

He laughed again. 'You think I believed your crazy story about the world being on the brink of a nuclear war? No. You are on a mission, naturally, but that is surely not what it's about. You claim to be the great hero who has come to rescue us all but I know who you really are, and what you're doing. You are using me, just as you used my father. But I will not make the same mistake he did, which was to believe you.'

Had he gone mad? He sounded it. He threw more water onto the stove and the heat came again, spreading through me even more rapidly. My eyes felt like they were bulging from my head, and that they might disconnect. I wondered how much more of this I could take, and whether or not I could find a way to end it. Just slip to the ground. Yes, how easy that would be. The world can hang. We'll all be dead anyway . . .

No, think, *think*. There must be some way out of here. Get to the door – he is pouring water on the stove through a gap in the door.

'The Russians came to see us the morning after you left,' he said. 'Pappa stonewalled them, and said he had never heard of any British agents visiting. But he was not a good liar, or they had other evidence. They went away but returned shortly after, with a very cruel man in charge – I think he had come from Moscow. He didn't believe Pappa's story, and so he had come out himself to question him. He brought several other men with him, and some . . . equipment. They took Pappa to a basement in their headquarters in Mariehamn and tortured him for three days. When that didn't work, they locked him inside a sauna much like this one and tried to boil him alive. By the end of it, he had told them everything – about you, the U-boat captain and the other agent. Now you are here, and I am going to make you suffer as they made Pappa suffer. I have a sauna nearly every day, and I know very well just how to make it hurt you: how much water to pour on, how long to wait. You'll see.'

I believed him.

'The man from Moscow,' I said, struggling to breathe. 'What was his name?'

'I don't remember.'

'Can you describe him?'

There was no answer.

'Please, Jan, I promise you I had no intention of any of that happening. But this is important. Do you remember what he looked like?'

'He was evil, that is all I can say. He looked like a . . . like a little boy, or a troll. He was pure evil.'

I fell back onto the bench.

Yuri.

Yuri had been here in 1945 – before he had recruited me in Germany.

I heard the hiss and knew what I had to do. I had about a second before the heat would hit me again. I leapt towards the door and slammed my shoulder into it, breaking it open. I lunged forward and grabbed Lundström by the collar as he stumbled backwards, his arms flailing. I brought my right hand down hard onto his wrist and gripped it, then swivelled into a half-turn and swung my other hand around to grab the barrel of the Lahti from below, jerking it back until it was parallel with the ground. He let out a scream as his trigger finger snapped, and the pistol dropped into my hand.

It was a heavy pistol. It reminded me of Father's Luger. I trained it on him.

'I'm sorry about your father,' I said. 'But there are more important things at the moment. Make another sound and I'll blow your head off. Understand?'

He nodded, his eyes darting wildly. He was still clutching a ladle in one hand and I took it from him and dropped it in a bucket of water on the floor. The steam was still blasting in the sauna behind me, and a thought came to me. 'How did you know it would be on?' I said. 'The sauna.'

'I know the coastguards. They have saunas every Monday night and it's someone's job to prepare it. So I knew it would already be hot.'

'What time do they have their sauna?'

'Midnight.'

I checked the watch on his wrist.

'That's in fifteen minutes. You meant to kill me before then? What if I hadn't died that fast and they had interrupted?'

He gave a cruel smile. 'They would understand. Half the people on this island know who you are, and what you did to my father.'

Enough. There was no time for this. I pressed the pistol against the back of his neck.

'Where can I find diving equipment?'

I had a couple of questions, but this was the most important one. I had to get to those canisters. But he didn't answer, and just glared at me.

'I don't know.'

I swivelled him round so he was facing me.

'Give me your best guess. You told me yourself there are few secrets here.'

He didn't respond, just jutted out his chin and glared. Generals in Moscow were debating launching a nuclear strike, and this man might be my only chance of stopping it.

'Tell me where I can find diving equipment or I'll shoot.'

Nothing – only a clench of his jaw, his eyes wild with fury. I couldn't get to the U-boat without a diving suit. If he knew enough to know the timetables of the coastguards' saunas, there had to be a good chance he would know where to find a suit. But he was stubborn. Perhaps he wanted me to kill him. Perhaps he was so mad he'd forgotten what fear was. No – he'd known how to scare me well enough. It gave me an idea. I grabbed him by the neck until he was standing, then motioned to the door of the sauna with the pistol.

'Get in,' I said.

He shook his head.

'Get in now!'

He opened the door and I pushed him into the space I'd been in just a few minutes earlier. A blast of heat hit me as I stepped in after him, and my skin prickled at the memory of the pain. Lundström had already started sweating. I grabbed one of his hands and placed the palm above the burning coals of the stove.

'Where can I find diving equipment?'

I thought I saw fear growing in his eyes then, but he didn't answer.

I slammed his hand down onto the coals, and he shrieked out. I removed it immediately – it had only been on for a fraction of a second. But it was enough.

'Next door,' he gasped, and pointed to the room adjacent.

I locked the sauna door then ran through and turned the light on. It was a dressing room: there was a line of towels and a poster illustrating the health benefits of the sauna. And laid out all along the benches and on the floor was diving equipment: suits, masks and air tanks. I found the suit that looked the newest, then picked up a mask and an attached hose and air tank, the mark Aga Divator.

Carrying my bounty over my arm, I returned to Lundström, who was whimpering and weeping with the pain.

'I'm sorry about your father,' I said. 'I never meant for that to happen. But I never said I was a hero.'

I locked the door behind me, then walked down the steps and headed through the bushes, back towards the jetty.

XVII

11.48 p.m., Monday, 27 October 1969, Storklubb, Åland

Lundström's map was just under the dashboard. I took it out and located Storklubb and Söderviken on it. It was thirty-six nautical miles away, but from memory the U-boat was easily found once at Söderviken. I started the boat up slowly, then once I'd reached open water took her as fast as she could go. The horizon was barely visible in the darkness, but my mind was cold and clear: now I was the gun dog.

I reached the area around Söderviken about an hour and a half later. In 1945, I'd been sure that the hatch leading to the crew's quarters had been sealed tightly. Clearly I'd been wrong, but had it just cracked open a little, allowing the liquid in the canisters to leak out through it, or had it opened entirely, in which case the canisters themselves might have floated out? If the latter had happened, I might get down to the U-boat only to find there were no canisters left, having floated off miles away. So I divided up the map into quadrants around the area to make it easier to search, then cut my speed and began drifting on the waves, looking for any telltale signs.

A wind was picking up, and I urged it to pass by — I could only dive if it remained calm, so a storm now would scupper everything. It was also playing tricks on my ears, and I kept imagining I heard the sound of an approaching helicopter. The thought of that filled me with dread. If Sasha and his men found me floating out here now, it was all over. But if I could get to the canisters first . . .

I took out the radio transmitter and looked it over. It had gone silent, but that might be because they had found Zelenin's body and realized I'd taken it, and didn't want to give me any more information by broadcasting anything I could pick up. But it had survived the heat of the sauna, and if I could transmit with it that might be the way through.

I drifted between islets, trying to locate the spot where I'd gone down in 1945. But it all looked the same. Then, finally, I saw something emerge in an area that was in the far north-eastern quadrant of my map – it looked a shade darker. I accelerated towards it and my heart started pounding. Yes, there was oil on the surface: a long thin coil of it stretching into the distance, growing thicker.

This was it. This was where U-745 had sunk.

I quickly dressed in the wetsuit, which was thick and heavy but a great improvement on the Clammy Death, and attached the mask and breathing tank. In one of the cupboards under the dashboard I found some waterproof sacking and took it out so I would have something to put the canisters in. I cut the engine, gave a last check that all the valves were secured, and recited the magic lines:

Our plesance here is all vain glory,
This fals world is but transitory,
The flesh is bruckle, the Feynd is slee:
Timor mortis conturbat me.

Then I climbed overboard and slipped down into the water.

*

It was much darker underwater but I saw the U-boat at once, lying like a giant wounded shark on the bed. I swam towards it, suddenly afraid I would be unable to carry the canisters up in the bag. How many would be enough to convince Sasha that this was the source of the 'attacks' in Estonia? Just one, or would I need more?

I hit a cold current and wondered if I were well enough protected in the diving suit. Was it thick enough? I thought of the tremors that had nearly killed me when I'd crashed in the helicopter with Raaitikainen. I dismissed it from my mind: there was no point in worrying about such things now.

I reached the boat and swam through the main deck, then down the flight of stairs and into the loading bay. The corpses of some of the crew were still there, sitting just as they had been when I was here twenty-four years earlier, and as I had seen them sporadically in my nightmares since. There was a rubber-soled shoe jammed against the furred-up pipes, and I remembered that crewmen had worn those during attacks so as not to alert the enemy. One of the men seemed to be looking at his wristwatch, but half his face had collapsed in on itself, and tiny fish were swimming through the crevices of his eyes.

I grimaced and turned away, then rounded the corner to the place I remembered the canisters had been. As I did, my forebrain began tingling before my eyes registered it. There was a hole where the steel hatch leading to the officers' quarters should be. Something was terribly wrong. I swam through in a daze, but I already knew what I would find.

The canisters were gone.

XVIII

I let the waterproof bag drop from my hands, and swam through, seeing if perhaps they had dislodged somewhere. But they hadn't – they were gone. There had been twenty or thirty of them here in 1945. If the hatch had burst open, they could all have tumbled out. But someone had been down here and *cut* the hatch open. It was a neat rectangular hole, and could only be man-made.

Who had done this, and when? And, more importantly, what had caused the leak to the bases? My stomach clenched, horrified I could have been so wrong.

It had been an attack all along.

Yuri had been right, back in the bunker in Moscow. Following the discovery that I was a double, the Service would have combed through every single document related to my career, both to assess the damage and to see if there was anyone else who had covered my tracks or turned a blind eye to my behaviour. And at some point someone must have come across Templeton's report on my operation here in 1945, and that had revealed an unexpected prize: a lovely little chemical weapon sitting at the bottom of the Baltic.

This discovery would have woven its way through the in- and out-trays until someone at Porton Down had confirmed that Winterlost was extremely effective and was still very much worth getting hold of, and so they had decided to come back to see if the canisters were still here and could be retrieved. In 1945 I had had to come in by seaplane under cover to reach this wreck, but nowadays they could simply fly a team of divers to Helsinki via BEA. Under cover of a diving expedition or something similarly innocuous, they could have cut open the hatch, hauled the canisters onto a boat, and then slipped into the Gulf of Finland and released them into the water along the coast near Paldiski. Then they could have simply sailed away again, and waited for the stuff to seep onto the shoreline and do its damage. Personnel at two of the Soviets' naval bases would then be incapacitated, and nobody could be blamed.

But it had gone wrong, because the Soviets hadn't seen it that way. When they had discovered that the chemical wasn't known to them, they had guessed the truth — that it was an attack by the West. And I had unwittingly confirmed it by telling them about my operation here in '45.

All that remained to be discovered was whether the attack on the bases was isolated and had come coincidentally at the same time as the Americans were conducting some sort of an exercise in the air, or whether the two events were linked, and the B-52 flights weren't part of an exercise at all, but the prelude to a nuclear strike. If that were so, Yuri and the others had read the situation correctly. The Service could have been called upon by the Americans to offer a diversion. The attack at Paldiski in particular would disrupt one of the Soviets' nuclear submarine bases just as they would need it, but would also confuse and distract them while the Americans prepared to launch their surprise attack.

But in either case the injuries at Paldiski and Hiiumaa were not accidental, and that meant that I now had no leverage whatsoever — nothing with which I could convince Sasha, Yuri or Brezhnev not to proceed with their plans to strike. There was no way of getting around it now. We were heading straight towards a nuclear conflict.

Dazed by the realization, I swam towards the hatch, looking to go round it one last time before heading back up. As I passed the door, I saw something flapping against the lower edge of it in the current. The cut hadn't been entirely clean, and something had caught on a tiny thorn in the metal. I leaned down and saw it was a small scrap of canvas, stringy and decaying. I recognized it as the same material that had been used to wrap the canisters – one must have torn when they'd taken them out, and this piece had been stuck here since. A fragment of text was still visible on it: 'NTERLOST'.

It was in a black Gothic typeface, instantly recognizable as the one used by the Nazis. I stared at it, still stunned by the fact that Osborne or Innes or whoever it had been had sent a team here to get these canisters, all to attack the Soviets' bases. It was madness – tantamount to provoking a nuclear war.

And then another thought struck me, and it sent an army of ants scuttling across my scalp. It hadn't been Osborne and the others who had planned the attacks: it had been Yuri.

He also had files on me. He had interrogated me about them on a daily basis, methodically going through my career week by week, month by month. I had never told him about my operation here, but he'd known about it already. Lundström had just told me Yuri had been here in 1945, and had been trying to find out what had happened.

It didn't matter precisely how he'd done it, but I knew he had. The Soviets had known about this secret all along. Perhaps they hadn't known the precise location of the boat; perhaps they'd been searching for it for a while. Yuri could have sent a small group of divers to retrieve the canisters, and then had them leaked to Estonia. I wasn't quite sure why yet, but it had to be something along those lines – because nobody in the West wanted to provoke a nuclear war.

I stared down at the scrap of material flapping from the door of the quarters for a moment. Then I leaned down and tried to prise it away with my fingers. It was caught fast. I tugged again, but realized that if I pulled too hard I might shred the surface even further and lose all remaining legibility of the fragment of text. Did I have enough oxygen in the tank to stay down here and unpick it? And what about Sasha's deadline of three hours? That must have nearly gone by now. I decided I would have to take it slowly despite both of these factors, because if I did pull too hard and that sliver of text vanished, all was lost anyway. I tried to set my panic aside and focus, but it was like weaving a thread through a needle and my fingers had started shaking. I placed my left hand around my right forearm to keep my grip in place like a clamp, and forced my fingers as far as they could go down the scrap. Then, as forcefully but with as much control as I could muster, I pulled at it. Slowly but surely, it spooled away from the thorn of metal, and into my hand. I turned it over. Yes, the letters were still legible.

I clenched it in my fist and swam back through the hatch. But as I came out of the boat, I saw a figure waiting for me in the water: a man in a diving suit. Sasha's dark beard sprouted from beneath the window of his helmet, and in one black-gloved hand he was clutching what looked like a pistol. He raised his hand and I jerked my body back without even thinking, only to see a plume of bubbles from the gun and hear a thudding boom behind me. I turned and watched as a thin dart bounced off the hull of the U-boat and spiralled down to the bed. A part of my brain registered that the Russians were rumoured to be developing a pistol that could fire darts underwater, but I couldn't remember anything about it. How many rounds could it fire? Was it four-barrelled? At this depth the aim would be compromised, as he'd just shown.

Sasha fired again, and this time the dart came very close to my feet, the force of the ripples spinning me away. I struggled to right myself but I'd lost orientation, and as I spun through the water I suddenly felt a blow to the back of my head. Had I hit the boat, or had it been Sasha? I flailed around, trying to lash out at him, but all I could see through my mask was a blur of movement and bubbles and then suddenly his eyes and mouth in the helmet. My oxygen was now getting close to running out, and I could feel my skull tightening under the pressure. I looked up and saw the surface of the water above me tilting with the waves, a separate reality from the world down here. I shut my eyes, feeling as though my head were about to explode, and swam upwards, praying I was moving away from Sasha.

I broke through the surface and gasped for air. I saw Lundström's boat immediately, floating on the waves, and began swimming towards it, but then I felt something slap me on the back. A hand gripped the inside of my diving suit and I was being hoisted onto land, patches of ice visible among the dark rocks, the wind howling around me. I looked up through water-clamped lashes and saw a man in camouflage, blond hair and blue eyes, his mouth snarling from the effort of lifting me. I tried to lash out but my strength had gone. He didn't seem to be trying to hurt me or shoot me so I let him pull me up. He dumped me onto a patch of ice as though I were a sack of coal, then moved away to some nearby rocks, and I saw that the case holding the transceiver was also there. He was the radio operator.

We were on a long, flat islet, and parked on it was the helicopter that had come for me earlier, squatting silently in the darkness. The radio operator shouted something and I looked over and saw that there was someone just a few yards away, standing by the water. He was wearing a leather coat. Yuri.

It took me another moment to register that there was a boy kneeling on the ice next to him and that he had the barrel of a gun pressed against his head, and a moment more to realize it wasn't a boy, it was Sarah, her short hair matted with sweat and her dress sticking to her skin. She was shivering and whimpering, and my stomach started contracting and I retched.

XIX

I clambered to my feet, my chest heaving and my head numb from being underwater, and screamed out at Yuri. He looked up at me and I thought I saw him smile.

'What do you have in your hand?' he shouted out at me. I looked down and realized that my fist was still clenched around the scrap of material I'd salvaged.

'Let her go!' I yelled again.

He held out his free hand. 'I would like you to bring me whatever you found down there. Or I will kill your girlfriend. Don't make me wait too long.'

I could hear Sarah sobbing, and saw a stream of saliva dripping from her mouth. Christ knew what he had put her through in the last few hours, and indeed in the last few months. I should never have brought her with me in the first place – I should have found a way of getting her to safety in Italy, and none of this would have happened. Her life now hung in the balance, and the tiny strip of canvas in my hand was all the leverage I had. But I couldn't give this to Yuri, because many more lives hung in the balance. Millions of lives, in London, Washington, Moscow . . .

'One last chance!' he called out. 'Come over here and give it to me.'

'I'm sorry, Sarah,' I said, and the tears came, finally – the tears for all the people I'd done this to.

Yuri fired, and I screamed as I saw the recoil and the impact.

Part of me felt that if I made a lot of noise myself I could cancel out the sound of the shot and it wouldn't have really happened.

Sarah fell forwards, her body splaying out and the blood spreading across the ice. Yuri lifted his gun and turned to me, preparing to shoot, but there was a burst of noise behind me and I turned to see Sasha breaking through the surface of the water.

Yuri's hand froze in mid-air.

'Are you all right, son?' he shouted, and he began to walk over the ice towards us. Sasha grabbed hold of the rocks and climbed ashore, gasping for air as I had done. I stumbled towards him and put out a hand to lift him up. He looked at me with shock, and as he came level with me I grabbed him with my other hand and passed him the fragment of the label.

He looked down at it, then peered at me, his eyes scanning my face. His expression turned from puzzlement to horror and then to slow realization. He looked up at his colleague, who was coming down to meet him. 'Get the radio!' he shouted. And then, to Yuri, who was now just a few feet away: 'Don't shoot him, Father – he was telling the truth. There was mustard gas down there. Look.' He opened his hand to show him the fragment. 'We must tell Moscow at once and make sure they cancel the command.'

Yuri stopped walking and stared down at his son. 'You fool!' he said. 'It makes no difference if there was mustard gas down there – the British have taken it and used it against us.'

'It's over, Yuri,' I said. 'You may be able to pull the wool over Sasha's eyes, but you can't pull it over mine. I'm no longer the boy you met in Germany in 1945.'

He turned to me and sneered, his face creasing so that his eyes nearly disappeared in the wrinkles. 'That wasn't the first time we met, comrade. For a while I was even afraid you might remember it. I've been told I have a memorable face. But you never made the connection. Then again, you have missed rather a lot of connections.'

'What the hell are you talking about?'

He looked out across the water, sniffing the sea air. 'I'm talking about New Year's Eve, 1939, in the Shepherd's Hotel, Cairo. You were fourteen. Your father introduced us, very briefly, and I asked you about school. And you were so pleased with yourself, because you were just about to enter a new one. Do you remember now?'

I remembered. It had been a wild party, one of the last before the war, and in some ways my induction into the adult world: I'd smoked my first cigarette and drunk my first cocktail that night, marvelling at the beautiful women in their evening gowns and the men chasing them around. I had danced in a heaving line to 'Auld Lang Syne' and nearly been crushed during the countdown as the crowd had roared in the new year, followed by the flags waving, the confetti and everyone embracing each other in the hot sticky Egyptian night. And yes, at one point in the evening Father had introduced me to a funny little Russian who had leaned over and asked me about school, and I had proudly told him I was going to Winchester next term.

The funny little Russian didn't seem so funny now.

'So you knew my father in Cairo,' I said.

'Yes. That was where we met, in fact, and where I recruited both him and Colin Templeton. It's a strange thing: I had hoped your father might become Chief of the Service one day, but in the end it was Templeton who did. But Colin was in the Army back then – how could I have guessed that things would turn out the way they did? Life has a strange way of working out sometimes, doesn't it?'

Templeton a traitor. 'Why?' I said, my mouth trying to catch up with all the thoughts swirling around my brain. 'Why?'

He tugged at his goatee as though I'd set him a mathematical puzzle. 'Why did they decide to serve us, you mean? Well, as you are no longer a boy and we are now so close to the endgame, perhaps it's time you learned the truth. Which is that they had no choice.'

'I don't understand,' I said. And I wasn't sure I wanted to.

'Oh,' he said, 'have you still not joined the dots? I photographed them, you see. I kept the negatives and persuaded both of them to serve as my agents, or their wives and superiors would receive copies of them, and they would be ruined. But I did it separately with each of them, you see. That was the genius of it! Neither knew I had recruited the other. Well, not at first. Your father eventually found out what I'd done, in Germany, shortly before I shot him.'

'You're saying he and Templeton . . .'

'Yes.'

I stared at him, anger rising from my stomach to my chest, making it hard for me to breathe. Father had always been a man's man: a record-breaking racing driver, a decorated commando. He had loathed 'queers', and that had been part of the reason I'd loathed him. But now I saw that this was precisely the cover he would have used if Yuri were telling the truth. Another thought struck me: Mother. Had he used her political views as a pretext to get her locked way, so that he could continue with his secret life?

No. It was unthinkable.

'You're lying,' I said. 'For some sick reason, you're lying.'

Yuri tilted his head to one side, amusement at my distress glinting in those evil little eyes. 'I'm afraid not, Paul. It's the truth, although they both did everything in their power to hide it from the rest of the world. You should know that many men suffer from this affliction, even those with families and children. Knowledge of this fact has served me well in my career, and that of several of my colleagues, for that matter. Burgess was always shameless about his disease, almost proud of it, but others have not been. I have found that men with secrets can be easily manipulated. Homosexuals also often make for excellent agents, because they have already spent years deceiving everyone they know – a lifetime of training, if you will. And your father and Templeton were not just casual lovers – they believed they were *in love with each other*, if you can imagine such a thing! Why do you think Templeton kept you so close to him after your father died, and nurtured your career as he did? You were his lover's son. No doubt you reminded him of your father. Perhaps he even imagined . . .'

I lunged at him, but he took a step back and I stumbled and fell onto the ice, exhausted and defeated. Yuri raised his arm and aimed the pistol at me.

'I think it is time to finish this.'

'Do it, then,' I said. 'It doesn't matter now, because we're all going to die anyway. But that's what you want, isn't it? Because you arranged the attacks on the bases. I wonder if you will be able to explain it to your son when the fallout appears and his skin starts peeling away.'

Sasha stared at me in disbelief and Yuri laughed.

'He's lying, my son,' he said calmly. 'He's just a sad little traitor trying to save his own skin. Why would I initiate an attack on our own country? It would be suicide. Do I strike you as suicidal?' He stretched out an arm at the absurdity of the idea.

'It's certainly suicide now,' I said, 'because the Americans will retaliate and the fallout will reach here. But it wasn't suicide when you thought of this plan, because you and all your cronies would be safe in the bunkers beneath Moscow. I think you're so deluded you believe nuclear war is worth it.'

'And I think your mind has gone . . .'

'No,' I said. 'You've told me some truths, and now it's time for your son to hear the truth about you. You planned this. I know it, because I worked in the West and nobody there is insane enough to try to start a nuclear war. But you are. I think you've calculated that even though both sides will be severely damaged, in the end the Soviet Union is so enormous that it will absorb the losses and continue, whereas the West will be destroyed for hundreds of years, a radioactive desert.'

He didn't say anything, and I watched as Sasha registered the hesitation, and in that moment saw the truth. I almost felt sorry for him.

'Father?' he said, and Yuri turned to him. He must have seen that he was disbelieved, because he gave a rueful smile.

'Yes, Sasha,' he said, 'this is true.' He lifted his chin. 'But I offer no apologies — we will rise again from this.' He turned back to me. 'You were the trigger for it,' he said. 'I sent you here in 1945 to find this U-boat, remember? It's something I have thought about for many years.'

He'd sent me here? Had he? I thought back to my dossier, and what Yuri had written about my time in Helsinki. *His performance so far has been exemplary . . .* Of course. I hadn't been trying to beat the Russians to the U-boat at all, but the British. Templeton had seen the signals from SOE in Stockholm about a U-boat captain being washed ashore in the Åland archipelago, and he had reported it to Moscow. Yuri had told him they wanted to get to the body before the British, and so Templeton had sent me out here armed with a Browning and warned about possible undercover Russian agents getting in my way. Jasper Smythe had been just who he had claimed to be, a British agent, and I'd killed him thinking he was a Russian.

'What was the idea of sending me here?' I asked 'Was it a trial run — something like that?'

He gave a shallow smile. 'Something like that. But I also very much wanted to get hold of the mustard gas, so I wasn't pleased at all that you failed in that part of the mission. I came here myself and questioned the local policeman at length to try to discover where exactly you had gone. He knew very little, unfortunately. But yes, I was interested in you because you were the son of an agent I had recruited five years earlier, and you seemed to have promise.'

Promise.

'So after my operation here, you decided to set up my recruitment in Germany, using Father and the honey trap with Anna.'

'Yes. But I had no idea at the time that it would work so well. You and your precious Anna! All these years later, and the woman is dead after trying to murder you, but you still can't stop talking about her. Isn't it amazing what we will do for love? Or what we think is love, anyway.'

I didn't reply to that. Not twenty yards away, Sarah was lying on the ice. But I had to stay calm with this bastard, for all our sakes.

'So what did you do next?' I asked, keeping my voice level with great effort. 'How did you find out where the U-boat was?'

'When Templeton told me you'd left the canisters behind, I was furious. But I decided there must still be a way of getting in.'

'So then you came back to get the canisters,' I said. I needed to know it all now.

'No, not then. Events overtook me, and I had other things to attend to. I set up the operation to recruit you in Germany, and that took a lot of time. But I knew that the mustard gas here wasn't going to go anywhere, and I kept it in the back of my mind to use at a later date. The existence of this weapon is just one of many secrets I have held in reserve over the years, to use when the time was right. The war came to a triumphant end and other things happened. I was decorated, and promoted, and moved departments. But I never forgot that there was a U-boat out here with a new form of mustard gas buried in it. And I thought of it again a few weeks ago, when Nixon made it clear to our ambassador in Washington that he was considering nuclear war against us. I thought he was playing games, and I knew that whatever he did, short of a nuclear strike itself, certain men close to Brezhnev would feel the same way.'

'So you decided to make the game seem more real by attacking two of your own naval bases.'

He nodded. 'In effect. When the Americans started moving ships in the Gulf of Aden, I realized they were planning something to try to scare us. I decided to play along. I sent a couple of my men out here to get the canisters, and then they released them towards the Estonian islands. I reported it as an attack, and made sure that this was taken seriously. We sent special troops to investigate. Then

Nixon sent his B-52s into the air, armed with nuclear weapons, and I realized the opportunity had finally come.'

'How did you know they weren't planning a real attack?'

'They had left several of their nuclear submarines in port, where they could be attacked easily – presumably because they wanted us to receive the signal that they were raising their nuclear alert, but couldn't risk doing it publicly because their citizens might panic and force a genuine crisis. The Americans' actions alone would never have been enough to persuade Brezhnev to initiate a strike. But I presented the evidence in a certain way. Nixon's threats to our ambassador, coupled with the activity of his navy, then this despicable chemical attack on our bases,' – he smiled gently – 'and now nuclear-armed bombers heading for our airspace . . . I persuaded Brezhnev to summon everyone to the bunker and informed them that as result of all this I thought we were about to be attacked by the West. Andropov and a few of the others were sceptical, as I'd suspected they would be. So I had you fetched from your cell. You performed beautifully, I must say, once again exceeding my expectations. You told us all about your operation here, confirming for everyone in the room that the chemical weapon originated from the West, just as I had argued. Brezhnev had no choice but to put us on a war footing. If he hasn't heard from me within the next ten minutes, he will launch a tactical strike against the United States and other countries, Britain, naturally, included.'

'And the Americans and the British will retaliate. Many Soviet citizens will die as a result, first in the blast, and then from the fallout.'

He didn't even flinch as I said it, just nodded his head. 'It is worth sacrificing the few for the many.'

'Yes,' I said. 'I'm familiar with that line of thinking.' I thought of Nigeria, where he had planned the assassination of one man in order to gain control of the country. And of Italy, where he had been content to watch many more killed in terrorist attacks. 'But this is different, isn't it?' I said. 'You're going to sacrifice millions of people today, not just a few. The British have forty-eight Soviet cities as their initial targets. I suspect the Americans have the same, or more.'

'Everything is relative,' he said. 'It is still a few compared to the many. The Soviet Union has two hundred and forty million citizens. A full-scale nuclear war may kill ten or even twenty million of them, but just think of the future after that. We will grow greater, and stronger. We will be in control, finally, not the West. We will never have another chance like this, not now that we have agreed to this insane idea to reduce our weapons. That will help the Americans, not us. The time for us to strike is now. Out of the horror will come a new dawn.'

His words echoed in the wind as it blasted around the island.

I turned to Sasha.

'So now you know,' I said. 'This isn't a choice between me and your father, or even between East and West. This is a choice between your father and the survival of our species for hundreds of years.'

Sasha slowly raised his pistol. He pointed it at my head, but then turned on his heels and aimed it towards his father.

Yuri's eyes darted towards him, but his face showed no other sign of distress.

'Put that away, Sasha,' he said, a little too casually. 'This man is a foreign agent, and he cannot be trusted. There are things you know nothing about, and cannot comprehend. Have faith in me – I am your father, but I am also your commanding officer. We will die here together, like men, for the greater glory of the Motherland.'

Sasha kept his gun hand steady. 'So this was your plan?' he said, his voice thick with suppressed rage. 'To cut off most of our limbs in the hope we will grow a few back faster than our enemy?'

'I told you to put the pistol down.' Yuri's voice had also turned colder. 'There is nothing you can do about this now, and there is nothing to fear.'

'But what about me, Father? How did I fit into your plan? Because it wasn't always for us to die out here together for the glory of the Motherland, was it? It was for you to be safely underground with the others. So what about me? You planned to leave me outside to die?'

As Sasha lifted the pistol, Yuri's eyes dulled for a moment as he realized he had lost, and then the bullet penetrated his forehead, the sound of the shot only reaching my ears after I'd seen its impact. Yuri stood there for a moment as though nothing had happened, and then his knees crumpled as if they were made of paper and he toppled onto the ice. In the same moment, Sasha swivelled and aimed his gun at me. I threw myself towards the ground, but I was too slow and the shot caught me somewhere in the stomach.

The back of my head hit the ice and I wondered why I couldn't feel any pain, and then it came, spreading through me like fire, and I felt the throb of the ice below me, or perhaps it was the throb of pain, they had merged, and I waited for the darkness. So this was where it ended – in the cold and the ice of this tiny island. My eyes were still open. Although my vision was blurring, I could see two figures in front of me – Sasha and the other one – and the case between them, open now, and inside a small black unit. After some time, I heard the familiar bursts of static and then Sasha's voice.

'*Moscow, this is Rook. Moscow, this is Rook. Do you read me?*'

'*Rook, this is Moscow. We read you. Four minutes to zero hour. Okay to proceed?*'

'*No, stand down from preliminary command, Moscow. I repeat, urgent, stand down from preliminary command. Event 12 is an accident, and I have the evidence for it. Do you read me?*'

'*Rook, we read you. Please give details.*'

'*Moscow, I am at the source of the accident. The Englishman was correct. I have evidence of the canisters in my hand and can see the chemical in the water. Raven has been killed in the line of duty, serving the Motherland with honour, but he confirmed this to me personally before he died. Event 12 is an accident. Please acknowledge this.*'

Seagulls shrieked in the distance, and time stretched out. How long had it been? A minute? Two? I didn't dare count the seconds.

And then it finally came: *'Rook, message received. Preliminary command has now been stood down.'*

I closed my eyes. I could hear the faint echo of my teeth chattering deep in my skull and the waves lapping against nearby rocks, again and again, as they had done for eons and would now do for eons more, all being well. Yes, but what was an eon, really? I twisted my head towards the sound and prised my eyes open a fraction. I was rewarded with the view of a wave churning into an eddy of water, swirling around and then releasing and starting again, the pattern of the sea in miniature, the pattern of life, perhaps, each time different, each wave lasting such a very short amount of time. I watched, fascinated, as the foam formed on the tip of the wave, and then broke and was subsumed into the darkness of the water, never to be seen again. I was like that foam, and so was everything else.

'Let's go,' said Sasha, somewhere far above me. 'It's over.'

'And the traitor?' asked the other man. I closed my eyes again, and held my breath. Fingers reached around my neck, and I braced myself for the final struggle. But he was checking my pulse.

'I can't feel anything, sir. Shall I dispose of the body?'

'No,' said Sasha, the man who had been my companion on so many occasions in the pubs and parks of London. 'The birds can feast on he and his girlfriend. But help me load my father into the helicopter. I will debrief you in the air.'

I had a sudden vision of a field, and palm trees, and then a glimpse of a driveway in the night and Templeton in slippers peering out from his door. The boots began to crunch away from me, and then there was the sound of the helicopter's engine and the rotors starting up and the wind howling as they took off, the noise cutting through the air until finally it had faded and there was no sound left but the lapping of the waves and a refrain running around and around in my mind.

Timor mortis conturbat me. Timor mortis conturbat me . . .

Author's Note

As in *Free Agent* and *Song of Treason*, I have made use of several historical facts in writing this novel. The Cold War saw several close calls regarding nuclear conflict, most notably the Cuban Missile Crisis in 1962; the incident in January 1968 when a nuclear-armed B-52 crashed seven miles from an American airbase in Thule, Greenland; and various incidents in late 1983, including misread signals creating fear within the Kremlin that the NATO exercise ABLE ARCHER 83 was being used as cover for an imminent nuclear attack, which led to the Soviet missile arsenal and military being put on high alert in preparation for a preemptive strike.

These are perhaps the best-known examples of the world coming to the brink of nuclear war, but there are others. In April 1969, after an American reconnaissance plane was shot down in the Sea of Japan, the United States placed tactical fighters armed with nuclear weapons on a 15-minute alert in the Republic of Korea to attack airfields in North Korea. In June of that year, the Americans' contingency plans for North Korea included the possibility of an attack with 70-kiloton nuclear weapons, codenamed FREEDOM DROP.

Another close call took place in October 1969, when President Nixon raised the United States' nuclear alert level by launching a series of secret manoeuvres that included implementing communications silence in several Polaris submarines and Strategic Air Commands and halting selected combat aircraft exercises. The most alarming manoeuvre was Operation GIANT LANCE. At 19.13 Coordinated Universal Time on 26 October, thermonuclear-armed B-52s took off from bases in the United States and headed towards the northern polar ice cap in the direction of the eastern border of the Soviet Union, where they flew in precisely the same pattern they would have done had they been launching a nuclear strike. Several more took off the next morning.

Officially referred to as the Joint Chiefs of Staff Readiness Test, these measures were part of Nixon's so-called 'Madman Theory': by posing as unpredictably volatile, he hoped to push the Soviet leaders into weaker positions for fear of provoking him. His objective in October 1969 was to stop the Vietnam War spiralling out of control by making it appear that the United States was considering a nuclear strike against the Soviet Union. The idea was that the generals in the Kremlin would be so shocked by the development that they would put pressure on the North Vietnamese to negotiate a peace settlement. Defense Secretary Melvin Laird and Colonel Robert Pursley both expressed opposition to the operation, fearing that the Soviets might interpret it as a real attack.

It is not yet known how the Kremlin interpreted Nixon's raising of the nuclear stakes in this dramatic manner. Melvin Laird has suggested that US intelligence intercepted Soviet communications expressing concern, and this has been supported by, among others, the Soviet ambassador to the United States, Anatoly Dobrynin, who has confirmed that the leadership in Moscow was informed of the American alert. On 20 October 1969, Dobrynin met Nixon and offered to start the long-delayed Strategic Arms Limitation Talks. Further discussions of this may have helped defuse the situation: the talks went ahead in Helsinki in November. But it seems Nixon and his staff may have underestimated how preoccupied the Soviets were with their border conflict with China. On 17 October, the Chinese government was preparing to be attacked by the Soviet Union: 940,000 soldiers were moved, and China's nuclear arsenal was readied. On 20 October, the same day Dobrynin met Nixon, authorities in Peking let it be known that they would open border negotiations with Moscow, as they were not prepared to let a 'handful of war maniacs' in the Kremlin launch a pre-emptive military strike over the issue. It may be that the Soviets successfully pursued their own 'Madman' strategy with China – it may also be that the Chinese went on alert in response to the Americans' manoeuvres, or the Soviets' response to them.

Nixon halted GIANT LANCE on 30 October. Thankfully, none of the B-52s entered Soviet airspace or crashed. This is especially lucky because an after-action report revealed that several of the B-52s had been orbiting in close contact with other planes in an air traffic situation that was deemed 'unsafe'. Had an accident taken place, the Kremlin would almost certainly have read it as an American attack, in which case global nuclear conflict would probably have ensued.

My main sources for information on GIANT LANCE were the declassified documents about the operation and several articles by William Burr, J. E. Rey Kimball, Scott D. Sagan and Jeremi Suri. I would like to express my gratitude to Professor Suri for taking the time to answer my questions about the incident.

For the purposes of my story, I have engineered it so that the Kremlin would consider retaliation more seriously than they may have done in reality. As well as the B-52s heading for Soviet airspace, I've invented a separate incident: the leaking of chemical weapons to the bases at Paldiski and Hiiumaa. Unlike GIANT LANCE, no such incident ever took place, but it is also inspired by historical fact. At the end of the Second World War, Britain, France, the United States and the Soviet Union formed the 'Continental Committee on Dumping' and disposed of some 296,103 tons of captured German chemical weapons, many of them in the Baltic Sea. Several countries continued to dump chemical weapons in the Baltic and elsewhere until around 1970. Most governments kept the extent of these programmes secret until the 1980s, when details began to emerge, but there are still notable gaps in the record.

At the time, it was argued that these chemical weapons would dissolve in water and therefore not harm anyone, but that has not proven to be the case. During the war, German scientists created Winterlost, a new formulation of mustard gas made with arsenic and phenyldichloroarsine that was more viscous and was capable of withstanding sub-zero temperatures. I have invented the idea that Winterlost was carried by U-745, but the substance itself is real, and a powerful chemical weapon. This type of mustard gas is insoluble, and leaks of it can still cause harm today. It is estimated that one fifth of the Nazis' production of toxic gases was dumped in the Baltic, including almost all of their Winterlost. Over the years, mustard bombs have been recovered on beaches in Poland, Germany and elsewhere, and many fishing nets have been contaminated and, in some cases, people harmed. In July and August 1969 four fishermen near Bornholm were seriously injured when mustard gas leaked from an object pulled onto deck. According to retired Soviet General Vello Vare, chemical weapons may have been dumped at two sites near Paldiski in the 1960s. I'm indebted to Dr Vadim Paka of the Shirshov Institute of Oceanography in Kaliningrad and John Hart of the Chemical and Biological Security Project in Stockholm for discussing these and related issues with me.

The Åland islands are a demilitarized Swedish-speaking part of Finland, and lie in a crucial strategic position in the Baltic. Hitler planned to invade the islands in 1944, but abandoned the idea after the Finnish armistice with the Soviet Union. Stalin also had plans to invade Åland, and also abandoned them. On 23 December 1944, U-745, a German type VIIC U-boat under the command of Kapitänleutnant Wilhelm von Trotha set out from Danzig into the Gulf of Finland. On 11 January 1945, it sank the Soviet minesweeper T-76 Korall off the Estonian island of Aegna. On 4 February, it sent its last radio signal, probably after being hit by a mine. On the evening of 10 March, von Trotha's body was discovered by fishermen frozen in the ice on the tiny island of Skepparskär in Föglö, in the south-east of the Åland archipelago. He was buried in the foreigners' section of Föglö church, at which members of his family placed a small plaque in 1999.

I have invented that U-745 had Winterlost as a cargo, and that the Soviets and British sent agents to Åland to investigate, but the description in Chapter III of the discovery of Wilhelm von Trotha's body, its recovery from Skepparskär, autopsy in Degerby, the appearance of the body and the details of the effects found on it are all taken from the police report written on 12 March 1945. I have imagined that the notebook mentioned in the police report was a *Soldbuch*. Several other details were provided to me by Eolf Nyborg, the son of the chief constable at the time, who saw the body, his wife Astrid, and Uno Fogelström, all of whom were living in Föglö at the time. I am very grateful to them for their help, as well as to Stefan Abrahamsson, Gunnar and Gunnel Lundberg, Karl-Johan Edlund, Kenneth Gustavsson and the staff of Föglö church, Mariehamn library, *Nya Åland* and *Ålandstidningen*. A special thanks to my parents-in-law, Karl-Johan and Anne-Louise Fogelström, for all their help and advice.

Some believe that the wreck of U-745 is near Hanko, but it has not yet been found. Neither has U-479, which went missing in the Gulf of Finland on 15 November 1944 with all fifty-one hands lost, nor U-676, which went missing somewhere between Åland and Osmussaar, with its last radio signal being received on 12 February 1945. U-679 was also sunk by depth charges from a Soviet anti-submarine vessel near Åland on 9 January 1945. In 2009, the Soviet submarine S-2, which sank in 1940, was discovered by a team of divers off the coast of Märket in the Åland archipelago.

I would also like to express my thanks to Gunnar Silander, Fredrik Blomqvist and Dan Lönnberg of the Åland coastguard for arranging the visit to their abandoned station in Storklubb — and for showing me the sauna there, built in 1961, which features in Chapter XVI.

The bunker described in Chapter II is the Reserve Command Post of the Supreme Commander-in-Chief of the Red Army, better known as Stalin's Bunker, near Partizanskaya Metro station. Now a part of the Central Museum of Armed Forces, it opened to the public in 1996. The decor I have described is inspired by the session hall in the museum, itself an estimate of how it looked when built. The bunker in Miehikkälä can also be visited, as can many others along the Salpa Line.

Despite the mass of material published about the Cold War, our perceptions of it are changing almost by the day. While I was writing this novel the first authorized account of MI6 operations was published, and several key documents about Britain's nuclear contingency plans were declassified. As a result, some of the information in the books in the bibliography that follows can now be seen as flawed or obsolete. The two reports mentioned in Chapter II are the Strath Report of 1955, declassified in 2002, and 'Machinery of Government in War', also from 1955 and declassified in 2008. Exercise INVALUABLE took place in September and October 1968, and FALLEX-68/GOLDEN ROD in October of that year.

All the details of the United States' and Britain's contingency plans for nuclear war mentioned in Chapter II are based on declassified files, with the exception of the locations earmarked for central government in Britain after 1968, which are informed speculation. Construction work on the bunker in Corsham began in 1957, but the plan to relocate the country's elite was exposed by an article by Chapman Pincher in the *Daily Express* in 1959, and a D-notice was hurriedly issued to stop more information leaking out. No further articles were written about it, and the plan was given a succession of codenames to protect it, including SUBTERFUGE, STOCKWELL, TURNSTILE and BURLINGTON.

In April 1963, a group of activists, 'Spies for Peace', discovered the existence of several bunkers that had been earmarked for regional government following a nuclear attack, and published pamphlets exposing some of their locations, to widespread media interest. As a result of this – and perhaps also, as Paul Dark speculates, the defection of Kim Philby – the plan to use the Corsham bunker as a post-strike shelter was abandoned. It seems it may have been kept as a cover story to discourage anyone from searching for the new sites, and many articles, documentaries and books have repeated disinformation about it since its existence was declassified by the Ministry of Defence and Cabinet Office in 2004. But documents declassified in 2010 show that a new plan, codenamed PYTHON, was put into place in May 1968. This involved senior officials being separated into groups and dispersed to several locations. While I was writing this novel, it was revealed that the royal yacht *Britannia* was a PYTHON site, but the number and location of the remaining sites is currently unknown. The fact that limited information about PYTHON is now being declassified may mean that this plan has also now been superseded or altered enough that it can be revealed without jeopardizing the security of the new arrangements. The idea that Welbeck Abbey is a PYTHON site is my speculation based on conversations with Mike Kenner, who has conducted an enormous amount of research on this topic. I'm grateful to him for taking the time to clarify many of the issues surrounding this and for sharing his research material with me, including many documents that were declassified as a result of his requests under the Freedom of Information Act.

That act has affected the way in which we understand our recent history, both for the better and for the worse. As a result of decades in which very little was revealed, a mountain of material is now being declassified. As an inevitable result, the National Archives gives more prominence to, and even issues press releases for, only a selection of the material it declassifies. It is the information in these files that is most often reported in newspapers and reproduced in books. However, an enormous amount of material is declassified by the National Archives, most of it with no fanfare, and much of this is not analysed or explored by journalists or historians.

It would be impossible for the National Archives to provide analysis for everything it declassifies, but the result is that information that may substantially change our view of history is hidden away in files that very few people are aware have even been released. Researchers keen to explore the ramifications of so much material must wade through it seeking to understand its context and, often, its secrets. After requesting that a government file be declassified, it goes through vetting to ensure it does not endanger national security. But once released, an eagle-eyed researcher might notice a passing mention to an appendix that has not been attached. A request is sent for the appendix to be declassified. After vetting, it is. The appendix mentions a codeword in passing – this leads to questions about the meaning of that codeword, and attempts to figure out which unclassified files might contain information about it. In other words, this is something of a maze, and there are still large gaps in our knowledge of what really happened in the Cold War.

Nevertheless, the British, American and other governments have declassified an enormous amount of material about the era in the last two decades. Much less has been declassified by the Russians. An exception is the report that Paul Dark reads in Chapter VII written by GRU chief Pyotr Ivashutin in 1964. The quoted excerpts are translations from the original document, carried out by and quoted courtesy of the Parallel History Project on NATO and the Warsaw Pact (www.php.isn.ethz.ch), the Center for Security Studies at ETH Zurich and the National Security Archive at the George Washington University on behalf of the PHP network. My thanks to the Parallel History Project and the Cold War International History Project for their work in analysing and making available so many documents, and in particular to Dr Vojtech Mastny for his helpful answers to my queries, and for his scholarship.

Also in Chapter VII, Dark reads a fictional document, but one in which several real Soviet agents are mentioned. Melita Norwood was exposed as HOLA in 1999, and ERIC was revealed to be Engelbert Broda in 2009. Both passed the Soviets documents about Britain's nuclear research programme. The East Germans' spy codenamed MICHELLE was Ursula Lorenzen, who was recruited by a honey trap in 1962. In 1967 she was appointed assistant to the British Director for Operations in NATO's General Secretariat in Brussels.

During the Cold War, the British press became obsessed with the identity of 'the Fifth Man', but the known double agents now number many more than five – and even those may only represent the tip of an iceberg. In Chapter XI, Paul Dark names several British agents who served the Soviet Union, but does not mention Melita Norwood, Ivor Montagu, J. B. S. Haldane, Goronwy Rees, Raymond Fletcher, Geoffrey Prime, Arthur Wynn, Leo Long, Tom Driberg, Bob Stewart, Edith Tudor Hart or others who passed information to Soviet intelligence before 1969 but had not yet been exposed. I believe the Soviet Union may have recruited many more agents in Britain and elsewhere than have been revealed to date, as part of a wide-ranging plan to plant long-term sleepers in the West.

Donald Maclean *was* discreetly involved with dissidents in Moscow after his defection, and was a friend of Roy Medvedev. The old acquaintance from Cambridge who was asked if he might be a sleeper 'they' had never got around to waking up was Kenneth Sinclair-Loutit – this incident is discussed in Robert Cecil's biography of Maclean, *A Divided Life*.

The instant camera used by Anton is a Foton, which was produced in very limited numbers in the Soviet Union in 1969. Paul and Sarah's method of crossing the Soviet–Finnish border is inspired by a successful attempt made by defector Georgi Ivanov, described by Nigel Hamilton in the 1990 book *Frontiers*. The pistol fired underwater in Chapter XVIII is a prototype of a *Spetsialnyj Podvodnyj Pistolet* ('Special Underwater Pistol'), or SPP-1. Vladimir Simonov began work on the design in 1960, and it was finally accepted for use by the Soviet Navy in 1971.

The thinking behind Yuri's attempt to provoke a nuclear war in the novel was inspired by an aspect of Cold War nuclear strategy mentioned by Nigel Calder in his 1979 book *Nuclear Nightmares*:

> Many people, including experts in weapons and strategy, comfort themselves by imagining that the superpowers will

consider a 'counterforce first strike' only if it can be over-whelmingly disabling. But 'damage limitation' in American parlance and the 'counter-battery' operations of Soviet doctrine remain desirable goals for the military men on both sides. If there is going to be a nuclear war, it is better to be hit by 5,000 warheads than by 10,000. Such reasoning leads to pitiless arithmetic: 'If I can kill a hundred million on his side with a loss of only fifty million on my side, and smash his industry more thoroughly than he smashes mine, I have not lost, because we can restore the damage faster and our ideology will prevail in the world.' The Soviet military leaders have reasoned in that sort of fashion at least since the fall of Khrushchev . . .

Finally, I would like to thank Helmut Schierer, John Dishon, Emma Lowth, Arianne Burnette, my agent Antony Topping and my editors Mike Jones in the UK and Kathryn Court in the US for their wealth of helpful insights and suggestions on the novel, and my wife and daughters for their unending patience as I wrote it.

Select Bibliography

Declassified documents

Cable from Strategic Air Command Headquarters to 12 Air Division et al., Increased Readiness Posture, 23 October 1969, Top Secret (Air Force, FOIA Release)

'Government War Book Exercises Held During 1968: INVALUABLE' (The National Archives, PRO, CAB 164/375)

'Machinery of government in war: Report of working party and related papers' (The National Archives, DEFE 13/46, 1955)

Memorandum, Secretary of Defense Laird to National Security Adviser Kissinger, 25 June 1969, Subject: Review of US Contingency Plans for Washington Special Actions Group (FOIA release)

Plan of Actions of the Czechoslovak People's Army for War Time, 14 October 1964 (Central Military Archives, Prague, Collection Ministry of National Defense, Operations Department, 008074/ ZD-OS 64, pp. 1–18. Translated by Svetlana Savranskaya of the National Security Archive, Washington DC, and Anna Locher of the Center for Security Studies and Conflict Research, Zurich)

Soviet Study of the Conduct of War in Nuclear Conditions: Memorandum from Ivashutin to Zakharov, 28 August 1964 (Central Archives of the RF Ministry of Defense (TsAMO), Podolsk. Translated by Svetlana Savranskaya of the National Security Archive)

'Soviet Wartime Management: The Role of Civil Defense in Leadership Continuity', Vol. II – Analysis, Interagency Intelligence Memorandum NI IIM 83-10005JX (Washington DC: Director of

Central Intelligence, December 1983, Top Secret; partially declassified in 1997)

Speech by Marshal Grechko at the 'Zapad' Exercise, 16 October 1969 (VS. OS-OL, krab. 2915, 999-154, cj 18004, VUA. Translated by Sergey Radchenko for the National Security Archive)

'Thermonuclear weapons fallout: Report by a group of senior officials under chairmanship of W. Strath' (The National Archives, CAB 134/940. Records of the Cabinet Office: Minutes and Papers, 1955)

Articles and books

'An Observer', *Message from Moscow* (Jonathan Cape, 1969)

'At Home with the Frazers' (in *Time*, 3 February 1958)

Charles Arnold-Baker, *For He is an Englishman: Memoirs of a Prussian Nobleman* (Jeremy Mills Publishing, 2007)

J. Beddington and A. J. Kinloch, 'Munitions Dumped at Sea: A Literature Review' (Imperial College London, 2005)

Bruce G. Blair, *The Logic of Accidental Nuclear War* (The Brookings Institution, 1993)

George Blake, *No Other Choice* (Jonathan Cape, 1990)

Genrikh Borovik, ed. Phillip Knightley, *The Philby Files: The Secret Life of the Master-Spy* – KGB Archives Revealed (Little, Brown and Company, 1994)

Vladimir Bukovsky, *To Build a Castle* (André Deutsch, 1978)

S. Ye. Bulenkov, et al., *Soviet Manual of Scuba Diving* (translation of April 1969 Soviet Ministry of Defence document, University Press of the Pacific, Hawaii, 2004)

William Burr and J. E. Rey Kimball, 'Nixon's Secret Nuclear Alert: Vietnam War Diplomacy and the Joint Chiefs of Staff Readiness Test, October 1969' (in *Cold War History*, 2003)

Nigel Calder, *Nuclear Nightmares: An Investigation into Possible Wars* (BBC, 1980)

Robert Cecil, *A Divided Life: A Biography of Donald Maclean* (Coronet, 1990)

Ron Chepesiuk, 'A sea of trouble?' (in *The Bulletin of the Atomic Scientists*, September 1997)

Bob Clarke, *The Illustrated Guide to Armageddon: Britain's Cold War* (Amberley, 2009)

Dick Combs, *Inside the Soviet Alternate Universe* (Pennsylvania State University Press, 2008)

Patrick Dalzel-Job, *Arctic Snow to Dust of Normandy* (Pen & Sword, 2005)

Michael Dobbs, *One Minute to Midnight* (Arrow, 2009)

Stephen Dorril, *MI6: Inside the Covert World of Her Majesty's Secret Intelligence Service* (Touchstone, 2000)

Ronald Eyre, et al., *Frontiers* (BBC, 1990)

George Feifer, *Moscow Farewell* (Viking, 1976)

Benjamin B. Fischer, 'A Cold War Conundrum: The 1983 Soviet War Scare' (Center for Study of Intelligence, Central Intelligence Agency, September 1997)

Fodor's Guide to Europe (Hodder and Stoughton, 1969)

M. R. D. Foot, *SOE: The Special Operations Executive, 1940–1946* (BBC, 1984)

Kenneth Gustavsson, *80 År på Havet: Sjöbevakningen på Åland, 1930–2010* (PQR, 2010)

Peter Hennessy, *The Secret State: Preparing for the Worst, 1945–2010* (Penguin, 2010)

Bjarne Henriksson, *1939 – Ett Ödeesmättay År För Åland* (Landskapsarkivet, Mariehamn, 1989)

Keith Jeffery, *MI6: The History of the Secret Intelligence Service, 1909–1949* (Bloomsbury, 2010)

Kalevi Keskinen and Jorma Mäntykoski, *Suomen Laivasto Sodassa 1939–1945/The Finnish Navy at War in 1939–1945* (Tietoteos, 1991)

Fredrik Laurin, 'Scandinavia's Underwater Time Bomb' (in *The Bulletin of the Atomic Scientists*, March 1991)

Jak P. Mallmann Showell (ed.), *What Britain Knew and Wanted to Know About U-Boats*, Volume 1 (International Submarine Archive, 2001)

Vojtech Mastny, 'How Able Was "Able Archer"?: Nuclear Trigger and Intelligence in Perspective' (in *Journal of Cold War Studies*, Vol. 11, No. 1, Winter 2009, pp. 108–123, MIT)

Vojtech Mastny and Malcolm Byrne (eds), *A Cardboard Castle? An Inside History of the Warsaw Pact, 1955–1991* (Central European University Press, 2005)

Zhores Medvedev, *The Medvedev Papers* (Macmillan, 1971)

Louis Mountbatten (foreword), *Combined Operations: The Official Story of the Commandos* (Macmillan, 1943)

Nagel's Encyclopedia Guide: Leningrad and Its Environs (Nagel, 1969)

Bruce Page, David Leitch and Phillip Knightley, *Philby: The Spy Who Betrayed A Generation* (Sphere, 1977)

Eleanor Philby, *The Spy I Loved* (Hamish Hamilton, 1968)

Kim Philby, *My Silent War* (Grafton, 1989)

Rufina Philby with Hayden Peake and Mikhail Lyubimov, *The Private Life of Kim Philby: The Moscow Years* (St Ermin's Press, 2003)

Scott D. Sagan and Jeremi Suri, 'The Madman Nuclear Alert: Secrecy, Signaling, and Safety in October 1969' (in *International Security*, Spring 2003)

Marlise Simons, 'Discarded War Munitions Leach Poisons Into the Baltic', *New York Times*, 20 June 2003

Göran Stenlid, *Ålands väder under 1900-talet* (Ålands Museum, 2001)

Jeremi Suri, 'The Nukes of October: Richard Nixon's Secret Plan to Bring Peace to Vietnam' (in *Wired*, 16.03, 25 February 2008)

Viktor Suvorov, *Aquarium: The Career and Defection of a Soviet Military Spy* (Hamish Hamilton, 1985)

Olli Vehviläinen, *Finland and the Second World War: Between Germany and Russia* (Palgrave, 2002)

Leonid Vladimirov, *The Russians* (Pall Mall Press, 1968)

Nigel West and Oleg Tsarev, *The Crown Jewels* (HarperCollins, 1999)

Greville Wynne, *The Man From Moscow* (Hutchinson, 1967)

Greville Wynne, *The Man From Odessa* (Granada, 1983)